The Complete
Dr Nikola—
Man of Mystery

The Complete
Dr Nikola—
Man of Mystery

Volume 2

The Lust of Hate ~~hero~~ *not a good*
hero — wimpy
Predictable
*

Dr Nikola's Experiment *Book #2*
*

Farewell, Nikola *Book #3*
Finale

Guy Boothby

LEONAUR

The Complete Dr Nikola—Man of Mystery: Volume 2
The Lust of Hate, Dr Nikola's Experiment & Farewell, Nikola
by Guy Boothby

Leonaur is an imprint of Oakpast Ltd

Material original to this edition and this editorial selection
copyright © 2009 Oakpast Ltd

ISBN: 978-1-84677-620-5 (hardcover)
ISBN: 978-1-84677-619-9 (softcover)

http://www.leonaur.com

Publisher's Notes

Contents

Skip this one —

The Lust of Hate

wimpy hero —
(cries + faints)
+ totally predictable.

My Chance in Life

Let me begin by explaining that I have set myself the task of telling this story for two sufficient reasons. The first, because I consider that it presents as good a warning to a young fellow as he could anywhere find, against allowing himself to be deluded by a false hatred into committing a sin that at any other time he would consider in every way contemptible and cowardly; and the second, because I think it just possible that it may serve to set others on their guard against one of the most unscrupulous men, if man he is—of which I begin to have my doubts—who ever wore shoe leather. If the first should prove of no avail, I can console myself with the reflection that I have at least done my best, and, at any rate, can have wrought no harm; if the second is not required, well, in that case, I think I shall have satisfactorily proved to my reader, whoever he may be, what a truly lucky man he may consider himself never to have fallen into Dr. Nikola's clutches. What stroke of ill fortune brought me into this fiend's power I suppose I shall never be able to discover. One thing, however, is very certain, that is that I have no sort of desire ever to see or hear of him again. Sometimes when I lie in bed at night, and my dear wife—the truest and noblest woman, I verily believe, who ever came into this world for a man's comfort and consolation—is sleeping by my side, I think of all the curious adventures I have passed through in the last two years, and then fall to wondering how on earth I managed to come out of them alive, to say nothing of doing so with so much happiness as is now my portion. This sort of moralising, however, is not telling my tale; so if you will excuse me, kind reader, I will bring myself to my bearings and plunge into my narrative forthwith.

By way of commencement I must tell you something of myself and my antecedents. My name is Gilbert Pennethorne; my mother was a

Tregenna. and if you remember the old adage—"By Tre—, Pol— and Pen—You may know the Cornishmen," you will see that I may claim to be Cornish to the backbone.

My father, as far back as I can recollect him, was a highly respectable, but decidedly choleric, gentleman of the old school, who clung to his black silk stock and high-rolled collar long after both had ceased to be the fashion, and for a like reason had for modern innovations much the same hatred as the stagecoach man was supposed to entertain for railway engines. Many were the absurd situations this animosity led him into. Of his six children—two boys and four girls—I was perhaps the least fortunate in his favour. For some reason or another—perhaps because I was the youngest, and my advent into the world had cost my mother her life—he could scarcely bring himself at any time to treat me with ordinary civility. In consequence I never ventured near him unless I was absolutely compelled to do so. I went my way, he went his—and as a result we knew but little of each other, and liked what we saw still less. Looking back upon it now, I can see that mine must have been an extraordinary childhood.

To outsiders my disposition was friendly almost to the borders of demonstrativeness; in my own home, where an equivalent temperament might surely have been looked for, I was morose, quick to take offence, and at times sullen even to brutishness. This my father, to whom opposition of any kind was as hateful as the Reform Bill, met with an equal spirit. Ridicule and carping criticism, for which he had an extraordinary aptitude, became my daily portion, and when these failed to effect their purpose, corporal punishment followed sure and sharp. As a result I detested my home as cordially as I loathed my parent, and was never so happy as when at school—an unnatural feeling, as you will admit, in one so young. From Eton I went up to Oxford, where my former ill luck pursued me. Owing to a misunderstanding I had the misfortune to incur the enmity of my college authorities during my first term, and, in company with two others, was ignominiously "sent down" at the outset of my second year. This was the opportunity my family had been looking for from the moment I was breeched, and they were quick to take advantage of it. My debts were heavy, for I had never felt the obligation to stint myself, and in consequence my father's anger rose in proportion to the swiftness with which the bills arrived. As the result of half an hour's one-sided conversation in the library, with a thunder-shower pattering a melancholy accompaniment upon the window panes, I received a cheque for five thousand pounds with which to meet my University liabilities, an uncomplimentary review of my life, past and present, and a curt announcement that I need never trouble the parental roof with my society in the future. I took him at his word, pocketed the cheque, expressed a hypocritical regret that I had caused him so much anxiety; went up to my room and collected my belongings; then, having bidden my sisters farewell in icy state in the drawing-room, took my seat in the dog-cart, and was driven to the station to catch the express to town. A month later I was on my way to Australia with a draft for two thousand pounds in my pocket, and the smallest possible notion of what I was going to do with myself when I reached the Antipodes.

In its customary fashion ill luck pursued me from the very moment I set foot on Australian soil. I landed in Melbourne at a particularly unfortunate time, and within a month had lost half my capital in a plausible, but ultimately unprofitable, mining venture. The balance I took with me into the bush, only to lose it there as easily as I had done the first in town. The aspect of affairs then changed completely. The so-called friends I had hitherto made deserted me with but one exception. That one, however, curiously enough the least respectable of the lot, exerted himself on my behalf to such good purpose that he obtained for me the position of storekeeper on a Murrumbidgee sheep station. I embraced the opportunity with alacrity, and for eighteen months continued in the same employment, working with a certain amount of pleasure to myself, and, I believe, some satisfaction to my employers. How long I should have remained there I cannot say, but when the Banyah Creek gold-field was proclaimed, I caught the fever, abandoned my employment, and started off, with my swag upon my back, to try my fortune. This turned out so poorly that less than seven weeks found me desperate, my savings departed, and my claim,—which I must in honesty confess showed but small prospects of success—seized for a debt by a rascally Jew storekeeper upon the Field. A month later a new rush swept away the inhabitants, and Banyah Creek was deserted. Not wishing to be left behind I followed the general inclination, and in something under a fortnight was prostrated at death's door by an attack of fever, to which I should probably have succumbed had it not been for the kindness of a misanthrope of the field, an old miner, Ben Garman by name. This extraordinary individual, who had tried his luck on every gold-field of importance in the five colonies and was as yet as far off making his fortune as when he had first taken a shovel in his hand, found me lying unconscious alongside the creek. He carried me to his tent, and, neglecting his claim, set to work to nurse me back to life again. It was not until I had turned the corner and was convalescent that I discovered the curiosity my benefactor really was. His personal appearance was as peculiar as his mode of life. He was very short, very broad, very red faced, wore a long grey beard, had bristling, white eye-brows, enormous ears, and the largest hands and feet I have ever seen on a human being. Where he had hailed from originally he was unable himself to say. His earliest recollection was playing with another small boy upon the beach of one of the innumerable bays of Sydney harbour; but how he had got there, whether his parents had just emigrated, or whether they had been out long enough for him to have been born in the colony were points of which he pronounced himself entirely ignorant. He detested women, though he could not explain the reason of his antipathy, and there were not two other men upon the field with whom he was on even the barest speaking terms. How it came about that he took such a fancy to me puzzled me then and has continued to do so ever since, for, as far as I could see, save a certain leaning towards the solitary in life, we had not a single bond in common. As it was, however, we were friends without being intimate, and companions by day and night without knowing more than the merest outside rind of each other's lives.

As soon as I was able to get about again I began to wonder what on earth I should do with myself next. I had not a halfpenny in the world, and even on a gold-field it is necessary to eat if one desires to live, and to have the wherewithal to pay if one desires to eat. I therefore placed the matter before my companion and ask his advice. He gave it with his usual candour, and in doing so solved my difficulty for me once and for all.

"Stay with me, lad," he said, "and help me to work the claim. What with the rheumatism and the lumbago I'm none so spry as I used to be, and there's gold enough in the old shaft yonder to make the fortunes of both of us when once we can get at it."

Naturally I lost no time in closing with his offer, and the following morning found me in the bowels of the earth as hard at work with pick and shovel as my weakness would permit. Unfortunately, however, for our dream of wealth, the mine did not prove as brilliant an investment as its owner had predicted for it, and six week's labour showed us the futility of proceeding further. Accordingly we abandoned it, packed our swags, and set off for a mountain range away to the southward, on prospecting thoughts intent. Finding nothing to suit us there, we migrated into the west, where we tried our hands at a variety of employments for another eighteen months or thereabouts. At length, on the Diamintina River, in Western Queensland, we parted company, myself to take a position of storekeeper on Markapurlie station in the same neighbourhood, and Ben to try his luck on a new field that had just come into existence near the New South Wales border.

For something like three years we neither saw nor heard anything of each other. Whether Ben had succeeded on the field to which he had proceeded when he had said "goodbye" to me, or whether, as usual, he had been left stranded, I could only guess. My own life, on the other hand, was uneventful in the extreme.

From morning till night I kept the station books, served out rations to boundary riders and other station hands, and, in the intervals, thought of my old life, and wondered whether it would ever be my lot to set foot in England again. So far I had been one of Fate's failures, but though I did not know it, I was nearer fortune's money bag then than I had ever been in my life before.

The manager of Markapurlie was a man named Bartrand, an upstart and a bully of the first water. He had never taken kindly to me nor I to him. Every possible means that fell in his way of annoying me he employed; and, if the truth must be told, I paid his tyranny back with interest. He seldom spoke save to find fault; I never addressed him except in a tone of contempt which must have been infinitely galling to a man of his suspicious antecedents. That he was only waiting his chance to rid himself of me was as plain as the nose upon his face, and for this very reason I took especial care so to arrange my work that it should always fail to give him the opportunity he desired. The crash, however, was not to be averted, and it came even sooner than I expected.

One hot day, towards the end of summer, I had been out to one of the boundary rider's huts with the month's supply of rations, and, for the reason that I had a long distance to travel, did not reach the station till late in the afternoon. As I drove up to the little cluster of buildings beside the lagoon I noticed a small crowd collected round the store door. Among those present I could distinguish the manager, one of the overseers (a man of Bartrand's own kidney, and therefore his especial crony), two or three of the hands, and as the reason of their presence there, what looked like the body of a man lying upon the ground at their feet. Having handed my horses over to the black boy at the stockyard, I strode across to see what might be going forward. Something in my heart told me I was vitally concerned in it, and bade me be prepared for any emergency.

Reaching the group I glanced at the man upon the ground, and then almost shouted my surprise aloud. He was none other then Ben

13

Garman, but oh, how changed! His once stalwart frame shrunk to half its former size, his face was pinched and haggard to a degree that frightened me, and, as I looked, I knew there could be no doubt about one thing, the man was as ill as a man could well be and yet be called alive.

Pushing the crowd unceremoniously aside, I knelt down and spoke to him. He was mumbling something to himself and evidently did not recognise me.

"Ben," I cried, "Ben, old man, don't you remember Gilbert Pennethorne? Tell me what's wrong with you, old fellow."

But he only rolled his head and muttered something about "five hundred paces north-west from the creek and just in a line with the blasted gum."

Realizing that it was quite useless talking to him, and that if I wished to prolong his life I must get him to bed as soon as possible, I requested one of the men standing by to lend a hand and help me to carry him into my hut. This was evidently the chance Bartrand wanted.

"To the devil with such foolery," he cried. "You, Johnstone, stand back and let the man alone. I'll not have him malingering here, I tell you. I know his little game, and yours too, Pennethorne, and I warn you, if you take him into your hut I'll give you the sack that instant, and so you remember what I say."

"But you surely don't want the man to die?" I cried, astonished almost beyond the reach of words at his barbarity. "Can't you see how ill he is? Examine him for yourself. He is delirious now, and if he's not looked to he'll be dead in a few hours."

"And a good job too," said the manager brutally. "For my part, I believe he's only shamming. Any way I'm not going to have him doctored here. If he's as ill as you say I'll send him up to the Mail Change, and they can doctor him there. He looks as if he had enough money about him to pay Gibbs his footing."

As Garman was in rags and his condition evidenced the keenest poverty, this sally was treated as a fine joke by the overseer and the understrappers, who roared with laughter, and swore that they had never heard anything better in their lives. It roused my blood, however, to boiling pitch, and I resolved that, come what might, I would not desert my friend.

"If you send him away to the Mail Change," I cried, looking Bartrand square in the eye, "where you hope they won't take him in—and, even if they do, you know they'll not take the trouble to nurse him—you'll be as much a murderer as the man who stabs another to the heart, and so I tell you to your face."

14

Bartrand came a step closer to me, with his fists clenched and his face showing as white with passion as his tanned skin would permit.

"You call me a murderer, you dog?" he hissed. "Then, by God, I'll act up to what I've been threatening to do these months past and clear you off the place at once. Pack up your traps and make yourself scarce within an hour, or, by the Lord Harry, I'll forget myself and take my boot to you. I've had enough of your fine gentleman airs, my dandy, and I tell you the place will smell sweeter when you're out of it."

I saw his dodge, and understood why he had behaved towards Ben in such a scurvy fashion. But not wanting to let him see that I was upset by his behaviour, I looked him straight in the face as coolly as I knew how and said—

"So you're going to get rid of me because I'm man enough to want to save the life of an old friend, Mr. Bartrand, are you? Well, then, let me tell you that you're a meaner hound than even I took you for, and that is saying a great deal. However, since you wish me to be off I'll go."

"If you don't want to be pitched into the creek yonder you'll go without giving me any more of your lip," he answered. "I tell you I'm standing just about all I can carry now. If we weren't in Australia, but across the water in some countries I've known, you'd have been dangling from that gum tree over yonder by this time."

I paid no attention to this threat, but, still keeping as calm as I possibly could, requested him to inform me if I was to consider myself discharged.

"You bet you are," said he, "and I'll not be happy till I've seen your back on the sand ridge yonder."

"Then," said I, "I'll go without more words. But I'll trouble you for my cheque before I do so. Also for a month's wages in lieu of notice."

Without answering he stepped over Ben's prostrate form and proceeded into the store. I went to my hut and rolled up my swag. This done, I returned to the office, to find them hoisting Ben into the tray buggy which was to take him to the Mail Change, twenty miles distant. The manager stood in the veranda with a cheque in his hand. When I approached he handed it to me with an ill-concealed grin of satisfaction on his face.

"There is your money, and I'll have your receipt," he said. Then, pointing to a heap of harness beyond the veranda rails, he continued, "Your riding saddle is yonder, and also your pack saddles and bridles. I've sent a black boy down for your horses. When they come up you can clear out as fast as you please. If I catch you on the run again look out, that's all."

"I'll not trouble you, never fear," I answered. "I have no desire to see you or Markapurlie again as long as I live. But before I go I've got something to say to you, and I want these men to hear it. I want them to know that I consider you a mean, lying, contemptible murderer. And, what's more, I'm going to let them see me cowhide you within an inch of your rascally life."

I held a long green-hide quirt in my hand, and as I spoke I advanced upon him, making it whistle in the air. But surprised as he was at my audacity he was sufficiently quick to frustrate my intention. Rushing in at me he attempted to seize the hand that held the whip, but he did not affect his purpose until I had given him a smart cut with it across the face. Then, seeing that he meant fighting, for I will do him the justice to say that he was no coward, I threw the thong away and gave him battle with my fists. He was not the sort of foe to be taken lightly. The man had a peculiar knack of his own, and, what was more, he was as hard as whalebone and almost as pliable. However he had not the advantage of the training I had had, nor was he as powerful a man. I let him have it straight from the shoulder as often and as hard as he would take it, and three times he measured his full length in the dust. Each time he came up with a fresh mark upon his face, and I can tell you the sight did me good. My blood was thoroughly afire by this time, and the only thing that could cool it was the touch of his face against my fist. At last I caught him on the point of the jaw and he went down all of a heap and lay like a log, just as he had fallen, breathing heavily. The overseer went across to him, and kneeling by his side, lifted his head.

"I believe you've killed him," said he, turning to me with an evil look upon his face.

"Don't you believe it," I answered. "It would have saved the hangman a job if I had, for, you take my word for it, he'll live to be hung yet."

I was right in my first assertion, for in a few moments the manager opened his eyes and looked about him in a dazed fashion. Seeing this I went off to the stock yard and saddled my horses, then, with a last look at the station and my late antagonist, who at that moment was being escorted by the overseer to his own residence, I climbed into my saddle, and, taking the leading rein of the pack horse from the black boy's hand, set off over the sand hills in the direction taken by the cart containing poor Ben.

Reaching the Mail Change—a miserable iron building of four rooms, standing in the centre of a stretch of the dreariest plain a man could well imagine—I interviewed the proprietor and engaged a

16

room in which to nurse my sick friend back to life. Having done this I put Ben to bed and endeavoured to discover what on earth was the matter with him. At that moment I verily believe I would have given anything I possessed, or should have been likely to possess, for five minutes' conversation with a doctor. I had never seen a case of the kind before, and was hopelessly fogged as to what course I should pursue in treating it. To my thinking it looked like typhoid, and having heard that in such cases milk should be the only diet, I bespoke a goat from the landlord's herd and relegated her to Ben's exclusive use.

My chief prayer for the next month was that it might never be necessary for me to pass through such an awful time again. For three weeks I fought with the disease night and day, one moment cheered by a gleam of hope, the next despairing entirely of success. All the time I was quite aware that I was being spied upon, and that all my sayings and doings were reported to the manager by my landlord when he took over the weekly mail bag. But as I had no desire to hide anything, and nothing, save Ben's progress, to tell, this gave me but the smallest concern. Being no longer in his employ, Bartrand could do me no further mischief, and so long as I paid the extortionate charge demanded by the proprietor of the shanty for board and residence, I knew he would have no fault to find with my presence there.

Somewhere or another I remembered to have read that, in the malady from which I believed my old friend was suffering, on or about the twenty-first day the crisis is reached, and afterwards a change should be observable. My suspicions proved correct, for on that very day Ben became conscious, and after that his condition began perceptibly to improve. For nearly a week, though still as feeble as a month-old child, he mended rapidly. Then, for some mysterious reason he suffered a relapse, lost ground as fast as he had gained it, and on the twelfth day, counting from the one mentioned above, I saw that his case was hopeless, and realised that all my endeavours had been in vain.

How well I remember that miserable afternoon! It had been scorchingly hot ever since sunrise, and the little room in which I watched beside the sick man's bed was like a furnace. From my window I could see the stretch of sun baked plain rising and falling away towards the horizon in endless monotony. In the adjoining bar I could hear the voices of the landlord and three bushmen who, according to custom, had come over to drink themselves into delirium on their hard-earned savings, and were facilitating the business with all possible despatch. On the bed poor Ben tumbled and tossed, talking wildly to himself and repeating over and over again the same words I had heard him utter that afternoon at Markapurlie—"five hundred paces north-west from the creek, and just in a line with the blasted gum." What he meant by it was more than I could tell, but I was soon to discover, and that discovery was destined to bring me as near the pit of damnation as it is possible for a man to get without actually falling into it.

A little before sundown I left the bedroom and went out into the veranda. The heat and the closeness of the sick room had not had a good effect upon me, and I felt wretchedly sick and ill. I sat down on a bench and took in the hopeless view. A quarter of a mile away across the plain a couple of wild turkeys were feeding, at the same time keeping a sharp look-out about them, and on the very edge of the north-eastern horizon a small cloud of dust proclaimed the coming of the mail coach, which I knew had been expected since sunrise that morning. I watched it as it loomed larger and larger, and did not return to my patient until the clumsy, lumbering concern, drawn by five panting horses, had pulled up before the hostelry. It was the driver's custom to pass the night at the Change, and to go on again at daylight the following morning.

When I had seen the horses unharnessed and had spoken to the driver, who was an old friend, I made my way back to Ben's room. To my delight I found him conscious once more. I sat down beside the bed and told him how glad I was to see that his senses had returned to him.

"Ay, old lad," he answered feebly, "I know ye. But I shan't do so for long. I'm done for now, and I know it. This time tomorrow old Ben will know for hisself what truth there is in the yarns the sky-pilots spin us about heaven and hell."

"Don't you believe it, Ben," I answered, feeling that although I agreed with him it was my duty to endeavour to cheer him up. "You're worth a good many dead men yet. You're not going out this trip by a great deal. We shall have you packing your swag for a new rush before you can look round. I'll be helping sink a good shaft inside a month."

"Never again," he answered; "the only shaft I shall ever have anything to do with now will be six by two, and when I'm once down in it I'll never see daylight again."

"Well you're not going to talk any more now. Try and have a nap if you can. Sleep's what you want to bring your strength back."

"I shall have enough and to spare of that directly," he answered. "No, lad, I want to talk to you. I've got something on my mind that I must say while I've the strength to do it."

But I wouldn't hear him.

18

"If you don't try to get to sleep," I said, "I shall clear out and leave you. I'll hear what you've got to say later on. There will be plenty of time for that by and bye."

"As you please," he replied resignedly. "It's for you to choose. If you'd only listen, I could tell you what will make you the richest man on earth. If I die without telling you, you'll only have yourself to thank for it. Now do you want me to go to sleep?"

"Yes, I do!" I said, thinking the poor fellow was growing delirious again. "I want you to try more than ever. When you wake up again I'll promise to listen as long as you like."

He did not argue the point any further, but laid his head down on his pillow again, and in a few moments was dozing quietly.

When he woke again the lamp on the rickety deal table near the bed had been lit some time. I had been reading a Sydney paper which I had picked up in the bar, and was quite unprepared for the choking cry with which he attracted my attention. Throwing down the paper I went across to the bed and asked him how he felt.

"Mortal bad," was his answer. "It won't be long now afore I'm gone. Laddie, I must say what I've got to say quickly, and you must listen with all your ears."

"I'll listen, never fear," I replied, hoping that my acquiescence might soothe him. "What is it you have upon your mind? You know I'll do anything I can to help you."

"I know that, laddie. You've been a good friend to me, an' now, please God, I'm going to do a good stroke for you. Help me to sit up a bit."

I lifted him up by placing my arm under his shoulders, and, when I had propped the pillows behind him, took my seat again.

"You remember the time I left you to go and try my luck on that new field down south, don't you?"

I nodded.

"Well, I went down there and worked like a galley slave for three months, only to come off the field a poorer man than I went on to it. It was never any good, and the whole rush was a fraud. Having found this out I set off by myself from Kalaman Township into the west, thinking I would prospect round a bit before I tackled another place. Leaving the Darling behind me I struck out for the Boolga Ranges, always having had a sort of notion that there was gold in that part of the country if only folk could get at it."

He panted, and for a few moments I thought he would be unable to finish his story. Large beads of perspiration stood upon his forehead, and he gasped for breath, as a fish does when first taken from the water. Then he pulled himself together and continued:

"Well, for three months I lived among those lonely hills, for all the world like a black fellow, never seeing a soul for the whole of that time. You must remember that for what's to come. Gully after gully, and hill after hill I tried, but all in vain. In some places there were prospects, but when I worked at them they never came to anything. But one day, just as I was thinking of turning back, just by chance I struck the right spot. When I sampled it I could hardly believe my eyes. I tell you this, laddie," here his voice sunk to a whisper as he said impressively, "there's gold enough there to set us both up as millionaires a dozen times over."

I looked at him in amazement. Was this delirium? or had he really found what he had averred? I was going to question him, but he held up his hand to me to be silent.

"Don't talk," he said; "I haven't much time left. See that there's nobody at the door."

I crossed and opened the door leading into the main passage of the dwelling. Was it only fancy, or did I really hear someone tip-toeing away? At any rate whether anybody had been eavesdropping or not, the passage was empty enough when I looked into it. Having taken my seat at the bedside again, Ben placed his clammy hand upon my arm and said—

"As soon as I found what I'd got, I covered up all traces of my work and cut across country to find you. I sent you a letter from Thargomindah telling you to chuck up your billet and meet me on the road, but I suppose you never received it?"

I shook my head. If only I had done so what a vast difference it might have made in both our lives.

"Well," continued Ben, with increased difficulty, "as no letter came I made my way west as best I could, to find you. On Cooper's Creek I was taken ill, and a precious hard time I had of it. Every day I was getting worse, and by the time I reached Markapurlie I was done for, as you know."

"But what did you want with me?" I asked, surprised that he should have taken so much trouble to find me when Fortune was staring him in the face.

"I wanted you to stand in with me, lad. I wanted a little capital to start work on, and I reckoned as you'd been so long in one place, you'd probably have saved a bit. Now it's all done for as far as I'm concerned. It seems a bit rough, don't it, that after hunting for the right spot

20

all my life long, I should have found it just when it's no use to me? Howsoever, it's there for you, laddie, and I don't know but what you'll make better use of it than I should have done. Now listen here."

He drew me still closer to him and whispered in my ear—

"As soon as I'm gone make tracks for the Booiga Ranges. Don't waste a minute. You ought to do it in three weeks, travelling across country with good horses. Find the head of the creek, and follow it down till you reach the point where it branches off to the east and leaves the hills. There are three big rocks at the bend, and half a mile or so due south from them there's a big dead gum, struck by lightning, maybe. Step five hundred paces from the rocks up the hillside fair north-west, and that should bring you level with the blasted gum. Here's a bit of paper with it all planned out so that you can't make a mistake."

He pulled out half a sheet of greasy note-paper from his bosom and gave it to me.

"It don't look much there; but you mark my words, it will prove to be the biggest gold mine on earth, and that's saying a deal! Peg out your claim as soon as you get there, and then apply to Government in the usual way for the Discoverer's Eight. And may you make your fortune out of it for your kindness to a poor old man."

He laid his head back, exhausted with so much talking, and closed his eyes. Nearly half-an-hour went by before he spoke again. Then he said wearily,—

"Laddie, I won't be sorry when it's all over. But still I can't help thinking I would like to have seen that mine."

He died almost on the stroke of midnight, and we buried him next day on the little sandhill at the back of the grog shanty. That I was much affected by the poor old man's decease it would be idle to deny, even if I desired to do so. The old fellow had been a good mate to me, and, as far as I knew, I was the only friend he had in the world. In leaving me his secret, I inherited all he died possessed of. But if that turned out as he had led me to expect it would do, I should, indeed, be a made man. In order, however, to prevent a disappointment that would be too crushing, I determined to place no faith in it. My luck had hitherto been so bad that it seemed impossible it could ever change. To tell the truth, I was feeling far too ill by this time to think much about anything outside myself. During the last few days my appetite had completely vanished, my head ached almost to distraction, and my condition generally betokened the approach of a high fever.

As we left the grave and prepared to return to the house, I reeled. Gibbs, the landlord, put his arm round me to steady me.

21

"Come, hold up," he said, not unkindly. "Bite on the bullet, my lad. We shall have to doctor you next if this is the way you are going on."

I felt too ill to reply, so I held my tongue and concentrated all my energies on the difficult task of walking home. When I reached the house I was put to bed, and Gibbs and his slatternly wife took it in turns to wait upon me. That night I lost consciousness, and remember nothing further of what happened until I came to my senses, in the same room and bed which had been occupied by Ben, some three weeks later. I was so weak then that I felt more of a desire to die and be done with it, than to continue the fight for existence. But my constitution was an extraordinary one, I suppose, for little by little I regained my strength, until, at the end of six weeks, I was able to leave my bed and hobble into the veranda. All this time the story of Ben's mine had been simmering in my brain. The chart he had given me lay where I had placed it before I was taken ill, namely, in my shirt pocket, and one morning I took it out and studied it carefully. What was it worth? Millions or nothing? But that was a question for the future to decide.

Before putting it back into its hiding place I turned it over and glanced at the back. To my surprise there was a large blot there that I felt prepared to swear had not been upon it when Ben had given it to me. The idea disquieted me exceedingly. I cudgelled my brains to find some explanation for it, but in vain. One thought made me gasp with fright. Had it been abstracted from my pocket during my illness? If this were so I might be forestalled. I consoled myself, however, with the reflection that, even if it had been examined by strangers, no harm would be done, for beyond the bare points of the compass it contained no description of the place, or where it was situated; only the plan of a creek, a dotted line running five hundred paces north-west and a black spot indicating a blasted gum tree. As Ben had given me my directions in a whisper, I was convinced in my own mind that it was quite impossible for anyone else to share my secret.

A week later I settled my account with Gibbs, and having purchased sufficient stores from him to carry me on my way, saddled my horses and set off across country for the Boolga Ranges. I was still weak, but my strength was daily coming back to me. By the time I reached my destination I felt I should be fit for anything. It was a long and wearisome journey, and it was not until I had been a month on the road that I sighted the range some fifty miles or so ahead of me. The day following I camped about ten miles due north of it, and had the satisfaction of knowing that next morning, all being well, I should be at my destination. By this time the idea of the mine, and the possibility of the riches that awaited me, had grown upon me to such an extent that I could think of nothing else. It occupied my waking thoughts, and was the continual subject of my dreams by night. A thousand times or more, as I made my way south, I planned what I would do with my vast wealth when I should have obtained it, and to such a pitch did this notion at last bring me that the vaguest thought that my journey might after all be fruitless hurt me like positive pain.

That night's camp, so short a distance from my Eldorado, was an extraordinary one. My anxiety was so great that I could not sleep, but spent the greater part of the night tramping about near my fire, watching the eastern heavens and wishing for day. As soon as the first sign of light was in the sky I ran up my horses, saddled them, and without waiting to cook a breakfast, set off for the hills which I could see rising like a faint blue cloud above the tree tops to the south. Little more than half-an-hour's ride from my camp brought me to the creek, which I followed to the spot indicated on the chart. My horses would not travel fast enough to keep pace with my impatience. My heart beat so furiously that I felt as if I should choke, and when I found the course of the stream trending off in a south-easterly direction, I felt as if another hour's suspense must inevitably terminate my existence.

Ahead of me I could see the top of the range rising quite distinctly above the timber, and every moment I expected to burst upon the plain which Ben had described to me. When I did, I almost fell from my saddle in sheer terror. The plain was certainly there, the trend of the river, the rocks and the hillside were just as they had been described to me, but there was one vital difference—the whole place was covered with tents, and alive with men. The field had been discovered, and now, in all human probability, my claim was gone. The very thought shook me like the ague. Like a madman I pressed my heels into my horse's sides, crossed the creek and began to climb the hill. Pegged-out claims and a thousand miners, busy as ants in an ant heap, surrounded me on every side. I estimated my five hundred paces from the rocks on the creek bank, and pushed on until I had the blasted gum, mentioned on the chart, bearing due south. Hereabouts, to my despair, the claims were even thicker than before—not an inch of ground was left unoccupied.

Suddenly, straight before me, from a shaft head on the exact spot described by Ben, appeared the face of a man I should have known anywhere in the world—it was the face of my old enemy Bartrand. Directly I saw it the whole miserable truth dawned upon me, and I understood as clearly as daylight how I had been duped.

Springing from my saddle and leaving my animals to stray where they would, I dashed across the intervening space and caught him just as he emerged from the shaft. He recognised me instantly, and turned as pale as death. In my rage I could have strangled him where he stood, as easily as I would have done a chicken.

"Thief and murderer," I cried, beside myself with rage and not heeding who might be standing by. "Give up the mine you have stolen from me. Give up the mine, or, as I live, I'll kill you."

He could not answer, for the reason that my grip upon his throat was throttling him. But the noise he made brought his men to his assistance. By main force they dragged me off, almost foaming at the mouth. For the time being I was a maniac, unconscious of everything save that I wanted to kill the man who had stolen from me the one great chance of my life.

"Come, come, young fellow, easy does it," cried an old miner, who had come up with, the crowd to enquire the reason of the excitement. "What's all this about? What has he done to you?"

Without a second's thought I sprang upon a barrel and addressed them. Speaking with all the eloquence at my command, I first asked them if there was anyone present who remembered me. There was a dead silence for nearly a minute, then a burly miner standing at the back of the crowd shouted that he did. He had worked a claim next door to mine at Banyan Creek, he said, and was prepared to swear to my identity whenever I might wish him to do so. I asked him if he could tell me the name of my partner on that field, and he instantly answered "Old Ben Garman." My identity and my friendship with Ben having been thus established, I described Ben's arrival at Markapurlie, and Bartrand's treatment of us both. I went on to tell them how I had nursed the old man until he died, and how on his deathbed he had told me of the rich find he had made in the Boolga Ranges. I gave the exact distances, and flourished the chart before their faces so that all might see it. I next described Gibbs as one of Bartrand's tools, and commented upon the ink-stain, on the back of the plan which had aroused my curiosity after my illness. This done, I openly taxed Bartrand with having stolen my secret, and dared him to deny it. As if in confirmation of my accusation, it was then remembered by those present that he had been the first man upon the field, and, moreover, that he had settled on the exact spot marked upon my plan. After this, the crowd began to imagine that there might really be something in the charge I had brought against the fellow. Bartrand, I discovered later, had followed his old Queensland

tactics, and by his bullying had made himself objectionable upon the field. For this reason the miners were not prejudiced in his favour.

In the middle of our dispute, and just at the moment when ominous cries of "Lynch him" were beginning to go up, there was a commotion behind us, and presently the Commissioner, accompanied by an escort of troopers, put in an appearance, and enquired the reason of the crowd. Having been informed, the great man beckoned me to him and led me down the hill to the tent, which at that time was used as a Court House. Here I was confronted with Bartrand, and ordered to tell my tale. I did so, making the most I could of the facts at my disposal. The Commissioner listened attentively, and when I had finished turned to Bartrand.

"Where did you receive the information which led you to make your way to this particular spot?" he asked.

"From the same person who gave this man his," coolly replied Bartrand. "If Mr. Pennethorne had given me an opportunity, I would willingly have made this explanation earlier. But on the hill yonder he did all the talking, and I was permitted no chance to get in a word."

"You mean to say then," said the Commissioner in his grave, matter-of-fact way, "that this Ben Garman supplied you with the information that led you to this spot—prior to seeing Mr. Pennethorne."

"That is exactly what I do mean," replied Bartrand quickly. "Mr. Pennethorne, who at that time was in my employment as storekeeper upon Markapurlie Station, was out at one of the boundary riders' huts distributing rations when Garman arrived. The latter was feeling very ill, and not knowing how long he might be able to get about, was most anxious to find sufficient capital to test this mine without delay. After enquiry I agreed to invest the money he required, and we had just settled the matter in amicable fashion when he fell upon the ground in a dead faint. Almost at the same instant Mr. Pennethorne put in an appearance and behaved in a most unseemly manner. Unless his motives are revenge, I cannot conceive, your worship, why I should have been set upon in this fashion."

The Commissioner turned to me.

"What have you to say to this?" he asked.

"Only that he lies," I answered furiously. "He lies in every particular. He has been my enemy from the very first moment I set eyes upon him, and I feel as certain as that I am standing before you now, that Ben Garman did not reveal to him his secret. I nursed the old man on his deathbed, and if he had confided his secret to any one he would have been certain to tell me. But he impressed upon me the fact that he had not done so. When he was dead I became seriously ill in my turn, and the information that led to this man's taking up the claim was stolen from me, I feel convinced, while I was in my delirium. The man is a bully and a liar, and not satisfied with that record, he has made himself a thief."

"Hush, hush, my man," said the Commissioner, soothingly. "You must not talk in that way here. Now be off, both of you, let me hear of no quarrelling, and tomorrow I will give my decision."

We bowed and left him, each hating the other like poison, as you may be sure.

Next morning a trooper discovered me camped by the creek, and conducted me to the Commissioner's presence. I found him alone, and when I was ushered in he asked me to sit down.

"Mr. Pennethorne," said he, when the trooper had departed, "I have sent for you to talk to you about the charge you have brought against the proprietor of the 'Wheel of Fortune' mine on the hillside yonder. After mature consideration, I'm afraid I cannot further consider your case. You must see for yourself that you have nothing at all to substantiate the charge you make beyond your own bald assertion. If, as you say, you have been swindled, yours is indeed a stroke of bad luck, for the mine is a magnificent property; but if, on the other hand—as I must perforce believe, since he was first upon the field—Bartrand's statement is a true one, then I can only think you have acted most unwisely in behaving as you have done. If you will be guided by me, you will let the matter drop. Personally I do not see that you can do anything else. Bartrand evidently received the news before you did, and, as I said just now, in proof of that we have the fact that he was first on the field. There is no gainsaying that."

"But I was ill and could not come," I burst out. "I tell you he stole from me the information that enabled him to get here at all."

"Pardon me, I do not know that. And now it only remains for me to ask you to remember that we can have no disturbance here."

"I will make no disturbance," I answered. "You need have no fear of that. If I cannot get possession of my property by fair means I shall try elsewhere."

"That does not concern me," he replied. "Only, I think on the evidence you have at present in your possession you'll be wasting your time and your money. By the way, your name is Gilbert Pennethorne, is it not?"

"Yes," I said, without much interest, "and much good it has ever done me."

"I ask the question because there's an advertisement in the *Sydney Morning Herald* which seems to be addressed to you. Here it is!"

He took up a paper and pointed to a few lines in the "agony" column. When he handed it to me I read the following:

If Gilbert Pennethorne, third son of the late Sir Anthony William Pennethorne, Bart., of Polton-Penna, in the County of Cornwall, England, at present believed to be resident in Australia, will apply at the office of Messrs. Grey and Dawkett, solicitors, Maoquarie Street, Sydney, he will hear of something to his advantage.

I looked at the paper in a dazed sort of fashion, and then, having thanked the Commissioner for his kindness, withdrew. In less than two hours I was on my way to Sydney to interview Messrs. Grey and Dawkett. On arriving I discovered their office, and when I had established my identity, learned from them that my father had died suddenly while out hunting, six months before, and that by his will I had benefited to the extent of five thousand pounds sterling.

Three days later the excitement and bitter disappointment through which I had lately passed brought on a relapse of my old illness, and for nearly a fortnight I hovered between life and death in the Sydney Hospital. When I left that charitable institution it was to learn that Bartrand was the sole possessor of what was considered the richest gold mine in the world, and that he, after putting it into the hands of reliable officers, had left Australia for London.

As soon as I was quite strong again I packed up my traps, and, with the lust of murder in my heart, booked a passage in a P. and O. liner, and followed him.

27

CHAPTER 1

England Once More

When I reached England, the icy hand of winter was upon the land. The streets were banked feet high with snow, and the Thames at London Bridge was nothing but a mass of floating ice upon which an active man could have passed from shore to shore. Poor homeless wretches were to be seen sheltering themselves in every nook and cranny, and the morning papers teemed with gruesome descriptions of dead bodies found in drifts, of damage done to property, and of trains delayed and snowed up in every conceivable part of the country. Such a winter had not been experienced for years, and when I arrived and realised what it meant for myself, I could not but comment on my madness in having left an Australian summer to participate in such a direful state of things.

Immediately on arrival I made my way to Blankerton's Hotel, off the Strand, and installed myself there. It was a nice, quiet place, and suited me admirably. The voyage home from Australia had done me a world of good—that is to say as far as my bodily health was concerned—but it was doubtful whether it had relieved my brain of any of the pressure recent events in Australia had placed upon it. Though nearly three months had elapsed since my terrible disappointment in the Boolga Ranges, I had not been able to reconcile myself to it; and as the monotonous existence on board ship allowed me more leisure, it probably induced me to brood upon it more than I should otherwise have done. At any rate, my first thought on reaching London was that I was in the same city with my enemy, and my second to wonder how I could best get even with him. All day and all night this idea held possession of my brain. I could think of nothing but my hatred of the man, and as often as I saw his name mentioned in the columns of the Press, the more vehement my desire to punish him became. Looking back on it now it seems to me that I could not have been quite right in my head at that time, though to all intents and purposes I was as rational a being as ever stepped in shoe leather. In proof of what I mean, I can remember, times out of number, talking sensibly and calmly enough in the smoking room, and then going upstairs to my bedroom and leaning out of my window, from which a glimpse of the Strand was obtainable, to watch the constant stream of passers by and to wonder if Bartrand were among the number. I would imagine myself meeting him and enticing him into one of those dark passages leading from the gas-lit thoroughfare, and then, when I had revealed my identity, drawing a knife from my sleeve and stabbing him to his treacherous heart. On another occasion I spent hours concocting a most ingenious plan for luring him on to the Embankment late at night, and arranging that my steps to my hotel, feeling about as miserable as it would be possible for a man to be. What did life contain for me now? I asked myself this question for the hundredth time, as I walked up the sombre street; and the answer was, Nothing—absolutely nothing. By judiciously investing the amount I had inherited under my father's will I had secured to myself an income approaching two hundred pounds a year, but beyond that I had not a penny in the world. I had been sick to death of Australia for some years before I had thought of leaving it, and my last great disappointment had not furnished me with any desire to return to it. On the other hand I had seen too much of the world to be able to settle down to an office life in England, and my enfeebled constitution, even had I desired to do so, would have effectively debarred me from enlisting in the Army. What, therefore, was to become of me—for I could not entertain the prospect of settling down to a sort of vegetable existence on my small income—I could not see. "Oh, if only I had not been taken ill after Ben's death," I said to myself again and again; "what might I not then have done?" As it was, that scoundrel Bartrand had made millions out of what was really my property, and as a result I was a genteel pauper without a hope of any sort in the world. As the recollection of my disappointment came into my mind, I ground my teeth and cursed him; and for the rest of my walk occupied myself thinking of the different ways in which I might compass his destruction, and at the same time hating myself for lacking the necessary pluck to put any one of them into execution.

As I reached the entrance to my hotel a paper boy came round the corner crying his wares.

"'Ere yer are, sir; 'orrible murder in the West End," he said, running to meet me; and, wanting something to occupy me until breakfast

should be ready, I bought a copy and went in and seated myself by the hall fire to read it. On the second page was a column with the following headline, in large type:

Shocking Tragedy in the West End

Feeling in the humour for this sort of literature, I began to read. The details were as follows:

It is our unfortunate duty to convey to the world this morning the details of a ghastly tragedy which occurred last night in the West End. The victim was Major-General Charles Brackington, the well-known M.P. for Pollingworth, whose speech on the Short Service Extension Bill only last week created such a sensation among military men. So far the whole affair is shrouded in mystery, but, it is believed, the police are in possession of a clue which will ultimately assist them in their identification of the assassin. From inquiries made we learn that Major-General Brackington last night visited the Royal Shakespeare Theatre in company with his wife and daughter, and having escorted them to Chester Square, where his residence is situated, drove back to the Veteran Club, of which he is one of the oldest and most distinguished members. There he remained in conversation with some brother officers until a quarter past twelve o'clock, when he hailed a passing hansom and bade the man drive him home. This order was given in the hearing of one of the Club servants, whose evidence should prove of importance later on. From the time he left the Club until half-past one o'clock nothing more was seen of the unfortunate gentleman. Then Police-Sergeant Maccinochie, while passing along Piccadilly, discovered a man lying in the centre of the road almost opposite the gates of the Royal Academy. Calling the constable on the beat to his assistance, he carried the body to the nearest gas lamp and examined it. To his horror he recognised Major-General Brackington, with whose features he was well acquainted. Life, however, was extinct. Though convinced of this fact, he nevertheless obtained a cab and drove straightway to Charing Cross Hospital, where his suspicions were confirmed. One singular circumstance was then discovered—with the exception of the left eyebrow, which had been cut completely away, evidently with some exceedingly sharp instrument, there was not a wound of any sort or description upon the body. Death, so the medical authorities

31

asserted, had been caused by an overdose of some anaesthetic, though how administered it was impossible to say. The police are now engaged endeavouring to discover the cabman, whom it is stated, the Club servant feels sure he can identify.

With a feeling of interest, for which I could not at all account, seeing that both the victim and the cabman, whom the police seemed determined to associate with the crime, were quite unknown to me, I re-read the paragraph, and then went in to breakfast. While I was eating I turned the page of the paper, and propping it against the cruet stand, scanned the fashionable intelligence. Sandwiched in between the news of the betrothal of the eldest son of a duke, and the demise of a well-known actress, was a paragraph which stirred me to the depths of my being. It ran as follows:

It is stated on reliable authority that Mr. Richard Bartrand, the well-known Australian millionaire, has purchased from the executors of the late Earl of Mount Chennington the magnificent property known as Chennington Castle in Shropshire, including several farms, with excellent fishing and shooting.

* * * * * * * *

I crushed the paper up and threw it angrily away from me. So he was going to pose as a county magnate, was he—this swindler and liar!—and upon the wealth he has filched from me? If he had been before me then, I think I could have found it in my heart to kill him where he stood, regardless of the consequences.

After breakfast I went for another walk, this time in a westerly direction. As I passed along the crowded pavements I thought of the bad luck which had attended me all my life. From the moment I entered the world nothing seemed to have prospered that I had taken in hand. As a boy I was notorious for my ill-luck at games; as a man good fortune was always conspicuously absent from my business ventures; and when at last a chance for making up for it did come in my way, success was stolen from me just as I was about to grasp it.

Turning into Pall Mall, I made my way in the direction of St. James's Street, intending to turn thence into Piccadilly. As I passed the Minerva Club the door swung open, and to my astonishment my eldest brother, who had succeeded to the baronetcy and estates on my father's death, came down the steps. That he recognised me there could be no doubt. He could not have helped seeing me even if he had wished to do so, and for a moment, I felt certain, he did not know what to do. He and I had never been on good terms, and when I realised that, in spite of my many years' absence from home, he was not inclined to offer me a welcome, I made as if I would pass on. He, however, hastened after me, and caught me before I could turn the corner.

"Gilbert," he said, holding out his hand, but speaking without either emotion or surprise, "this is very unexpected. I had no notion you were in England. How long is it since you arrived?"

"I reached London yesterday," I answered, with a corresponding coolness, as I took his hand. For, as I have said, there was that in his face which betrayed no pleasure at seeing me.

He was silent for half a minute or so, and I could see that he was wondering how he could best get rid of me.

"You have heard of our father's death, I suppose?" he said at last.

"I learnt the news in Sydney," I replied. "I have also received the five thousand pounds he left me."

He made no comment upon the smallness of the amount in proportion to the large sums received by himself and the rest of the family, nor did he refer in any other way to our parent's decease. Any one watching us might have been excused had they taken us for casual acquaintances, so cool and distant were we with one another. Presently I enquired, for politeness sake, after his wife, who was the daughter of the Marquis of Belgravia, and whom I had, so far, never seen.

"Ethelberta unfortunately is not very well at present," he answered. "Sir James Peckleton has ordered her complete rest and quiet, and I regret, for that reason, I shall not be able to see as much of you as I otherwise should have hoped to do. Is it your intention to remain very long in England?"

"I have no notion," I replied, truthfully. "I maybe here a week—a year—or for the rest of my life. But you need not be afraid, I shall not force my society upon you. From your cordial welcome home, I gather that the less you see of me the more you will appreciate the relationship we bear to one another. Good morning."

Without more words I turned upon my heel and strolled on down the street, leaving him looking very uncomfortable upon the pavement. There and then I registered a vow that, come what might, I would have no more to do with my own family.

Leaving Pall Mall behind me, I turned up St. James's Street and made my way into Piccadilly. In spite of the slippery roads, the streets were well filled with carriages, and almost opposite Burlington House I noticed a stylish brougham drawn up beside the footpath. Just as I reached it the owner left the shop before which it was standing, and crossed the pavement towards it. Notwithstanding the expensive fur coat he wore, the highly polished top hat, and his stylish appearance generally, I knew him at once for Bartrand, my greatest enemy on earth. He did not see me, for which I could not help feeling thankful; but I had seen him, and the remembrance of his face haunted me for the rest of my walk. The brougham, the horses, even the obsequious servants, should have been mine. I was the just, lawful owner of them all.

After dinner that evening I was sitting in the smoking room looking into the fire and, as usual, brooding over my unfortunate career, when an elderly gentleman, seated in an armchair opposite me, laid his paper on his knee and addressed me.

"It's a very strange thing about these murders," he said, shaking his head. "I don't understand it at all. Major-General Brackington last night, and now Lord Beryworth this morning."

"Do you mean to say there has been another murder of the same kind today?" I enquired, with a little shudder as I thought how nearly his subject coincided with the idea in my own head.

"I do," he answered. "The facts of the case are as follows:—At eleven o'clock this morning the peer in question, who, you must remember, was for many years Governor of one of our Australian capitals, walked down the Strand in company with the Duke of Garth and Sir Charles Mandervan. Reaching Norfolk Street he bade his friends 'goodbye,' and left them. From that time until a quarter past one o'clock, when some children went in to play in Dahlia Court, Camden Town, and found the body of an elderly gentleman lying upon the ground in a peculiar position, he was not seen again. Frightened at their discovery, the youngsters ran out and informed the policeman on the beat, who returned with them to the spot indicated. When he got there he discovered that life had been extinct for some time."

"But what reason have the authorities for connecting this case with that of Major-General Brackington?"

"Well, in the first place, on account of the similarity in the victims' ranks; and in the second, because the same extraordinary anaesthetic seems to have been the agent in both cases; and thirdly, for the reason that the same peculiar mutilation was practised. When Lord Beryworth was found, his left eyebrow had been cut completely away. Strange, is it not?"

"Horrible, I call it," I answered with a shudder. "It is to be hoped the police will soon run the murderer to earth."

If I had only known what I do now I wonder if I should have uttered that sentiment with so much fervour? I very much doubt it.

The following evening, for some reason or another, certainly not any desire for enjoyment, I visited a theatre. The name or nature of the piece performed I cannot now remember. I only know that I sat in the pit, in the front row, somewhere about the middle, and that I was so hemmed in by the time the curtain went up, that I could not move hand or foot. After the little introductory piece was finished the more expensive parts of the house began to fill, and I watched with a bitter sort of envy the gaiety and enjoyment of those before me. My own life seemed one perpetually unpleasant dream, in which I had to watch the happiness of the world and yet take no share in it myself. But unhappy as I thought myself then, my cup of sorrow was as yet far from being full. Fate had arranged that it should be filled to overflowing, and that I should drink it to the very dregs.

Five minutes before the curtain rose on the play of the evening, there was a stir in one of the principal boxes on the prompt side of the side of the house, and a moment later two ladies and three gentlemen entered. Who the ladies, and two of the gentlemen were I had no notion; the third man, however, I had no difficulty in recognising, he was Bartrand. As I saw him a tremor ran through me, and every inch of my body quivered under the intensity of my emotion. For the rest of the evening I paid no attention to the play, but sat watching my enemy, and writhing with fury every time he stooped to speak to those with whom he sat, or to glance superciliously round the house. On his shirt front he wore an enormous diamond, which sparkled and glittered like an evil eye. So much did it fascinate me that I could not withdraw my eyes from it, and as I watched I felt my hands twitching to be about its owner's throat.

When the play came to an end, and the audience began to file out of the theatre into the street, I hastened to the front to see my enemy emerge. He was standing on the steps, with his friends, putting on his gloves, while he waited for his carriage to come up. I remained in the crowd, and watched him as a cat watches a bird. Presently a magnificent landau, drawn by the same beautiful pair of thoroughbred horses I had seen in the morning, drew up before the portico. The footman opened the door, and the man I hated with such a deadly fervour escorted his friends across the pavement and, having placed them inside, got in himself. As the vehicle rolled away the bitterest curse my brain could frame followed it. Oh, if only I could have found some way of revenging myself upon him, how gladly I would have seized upon it.

Leaving the theatre I strolled down the street, not caring very much where I went. A little snow was falling, and the air was bitterly cold. I passed along the Strand, and not feeling at all like bed, turned off to my left hand, and made my way towards Oxford Street. I was still thinking of Bartrand, and it seemed to me that, as I thought, my hatred became more and more intense. The very idea of living in the same city with him, of breathing the same air, of seeing the same sights and meeting the same people was hideously repulsive to me. I wanted him out of the world, but I wanted to do the deed myself, to punish him with my own hand; I wanted to see him lying before me with his sightless eyes turned up to the skies, and his blood crimsoning the snow, and to be able to assure myself that at last he was dead, and that I, the man he had wronged, had killed him. What would it matter? Supposing I were hung for his murder! To have punished him would surely have been worth that. At any rate I should have been content.

When I reached Oxford Street I again turned to my left hand, and walked along the pavement as far as the Tottenham Court Road, thence down the Charing Cross Road into Shaftesbury Avenue. By this time the snow was falling thick and fast. Poor homeless wretches were crouched in every sheltered corner, and once a tall man, thin and ragged as a scarecrow, rose from a doorway, where he had been huddled up beside a woman, and hurried after me.

"Kind gentleman," he said in a voice that at any other time could not have failed to touch my heart, "for the love of God, I implore you to help me. I am starving, and so is my wife in the doorway yonder. We are dying of cold and hunger. We have not touched bite or sup for nearly forty-eight hours, and unless you can spare us the price of a night's lodging and a little food I assure you she will not see morning."

I stopped and faced him.

"What will you do for it?" I asked, with a note in my voice that frightened even myself. "I must have a bargain. If I give you money, what will you do for it?"

"Anything," the poor wretch replied. "Give me money, and I swear I will do anything you may like to ask me."

"Anything?" I cried. "That is a large word. Will you commit murder?"

I looked fixedly at him, and under the intensity of my gaze he half shrunk away from me.

"Murder?" he echoed faintly.

"Murder? Yes, murder," I cried, hysterically. "I want murder done. Nothing else will satisfy me. Kill me the man I'll show you, and you shall have all you want. Are you prepared to do so much to save your life?"

He wrung his hands and moaned. Then he pulled himself together. "Yes, I'll do anything," he answered hoarsely. "Give me the money; let me have food first."

As he spoke his wife rose from the doorstep, and came swiftly across the snow towards us. She must have been a fine-looking woman in her day; now her face, with its ghastly, lead-coloured complexion and dark, staring eyes was indescribably horrible. On her head she wore the ruins of a fashionable bonnet.

"Come away!" she cried, seizing the man fiercely by the arm. "Can't you see that you are talking to the Devil, and that he's luring your soul to hell? Come away, my husband, I say, and leave him! If we are to die, let us do it here in the clean snow like honest folk, not on the scaffold with ropes round our necks. There is your answer, Devil!"

As she said this she raised her right hand and struck me a blow full and fair upon the mouth. I felt the blood trickle down my lip.

"Take that, Devil," she shouted; "and now take your temptations elsewhere, for you've met your match here."

As if I were really the person she alluded to, I picked up my heels and ran down the street as hard as I could go, not heeding where I went, but only conscious that at last I had spoken my evil thoughts aloud. Was I awake, or was I dreaming? It all seemed like some horrible nightmare, and yet I could feel the hard pavement under my feet, and my face was cold as ice under the cutting wind.

Just as I reached Piccadilly Circus a clock somewhere in the neighbourhood struck one. Then it dawned upon me that I had been walking for two hours. I stood for a moment by the big fountain, and then crossed the road, and was about to make my way down the continuation of Regent Street into Waterloo Place, when I heard the shrill sound of a policeman's whistle. Almost immediately I saw an officer on the other side of the road dash down the pavement. I followed him, intent upon finding out what had occasioned the call for assistance. Bound into Jermyn Street sped the man ahead of me, and close at his heels I followed. For something like three minutes we continued our headlong career, and it was not until we had reached Bury Street that we sounded a halt. Here we discovered a group of men standing on the pavement watching another man, who was kneeling beside a body upon the ground. He was examining it with the assistance of his lantern.

"What's the matter, mate?" inquired the officer whom I had followed from Piccadilly. "What have you got there?"

"A chap I found lying in the road yonder," replied the policeman upon his knees. "Have a look at him, and then be off for a stretcher. I fancy he's dead; but, anyway, we'd best get him to the hospital as soon as maybe."

My guide knelt down, and turned his light full upon the victim's face. I peered over his shoulder in company with the other bystanders. The face we saw before us was the countenance of a gentleman, and also of a well-to-do member of society. He was clothed in evening dress, over which he wore a heavy and expensive fur coat. An opera hat lay in the gutter, where it had probably been blown by the wind, and an umbrella marked the spot where the body had been found in the centre of the street. As far as could be gathered without examining it, there was no sign of blood about the corpse; one thing, however, was painfully evident—the left eyebrow had been severed from the face *in toto*. From the cleanness of the cut the operation must have been performed with an exceedingly sharp instrument.

A more weird and ghastly sight than that snow-covered pavement, with the flakes falling thick and fast upon it, the greasy road, the oil-skinned policemen, the curious bystanders, and the silent figure on the ground, could scarcely be imagined. I watched until the man I had followed returned with an ambulance stretcher, and then accompanied the mournful cortege a hundred yards or so on its way to the hospital. Then, being tired of the matter, I branched off the track, and prepared to make my way back to my hotel as fast as my legs would take me.

My thoughts were oppressed with what I had seen. There was a grim fascination about the recollection of the incident that haunted me continually, and which I could not dispel, try how I would. I pictured Bartrand lying in the snow exactly as I had seen the other, and fancied myself coming up and finding him. At that moment I was passing Charing Cross Railway Station. With the exception of a policeman sauntering slowly along on the other side of the street, a drunken man staggering in the road, and a hansom cab approaching us from Trafalgar Square, I had the street to myself. London slept while the snow fell, and murder was being done in her public thoroughfares. The hansom came closer, and for some inscrutable reason I found myself beginning to take a personal interest in it. This interest became even greater when, with a spluttering and sliding of feet, the horse came to a sudden standstill alongside the footpath where I stood. Next moment a man attired in a thick cloak threw open the apron and sprang out.

"Mr. Pennethorne, I believe?" he said, stopping me, and at the same time raising his hat.

"That is my name," I answered shortly, wondering how he knew me and what on earth he wanted. "What can I do for you?"

He signed to his driver to go, and then, turning to me, said, at the same time placing his gloved hand upon my arm in a confidential way:

"I am charmed to make your acquaintance. May I have the pleasure of walking a little way with you? I should be glad of your society, and I can then tell you my business."

His voice was soft and musical, and he spoke with a peculiar languor that was not without its charm. But as I could not understand what he wanted with me, I put the question to him as plainly as I could without being absolutely rude, and awaited his answer. He gave utterance to a queer little laugh before he replied:

"I want the pleasure of your company at supper for one thing," he said. "And I want to be allowed to help you in a certain matter in which you are vitally interested, for another. The two taken together should, I think, induce you to give me your attention."

"But I don't know you," I blurted out. "To the best of my belief I have never set eyes on you before. What business, therefore, can you have with me?"

"You shall know all in good time," he answered. "In the meantime let me introduce myself. My name is Nikola. I am a doctor by profession, a scientist by choice. I have few friends in London, but those I have are the best that a man could desire. I spend my life in the way that pleases me most; that is to say, in the study of human nature. I have been watching you since you arrived in England, and have come to the conclusion that you are a man after my own heart. If you will sup with me as I propose, I don't doubt but that we shall agree admirably, and what is more to the point, perhaps, we shall be able to do each other services of inestimable value. I may say candidly that it lies in your power to furnish me with something I am in search of. I, on my part, will, in all probability, be able to put in your way what you most desire in the world."

I stopped in my walk and faced him. Owing to the broad brim of his hat, and the high collar of his cape, I could scarcely see his face. But his eyes riveted my attention at once.

"And that is?" I said.

"Revenge," he answered, simply. "Believe me, my dear Mr. Pennethorne, I am perfectly acquainted with your story. You have been wronged; you desire to avenge yourself upon your enemy. It is a very natural wish, and if you will sup with me as I propose, I don't doubt but that I can put the power you seek into your hands. Do you agree?"

All my scruples vanished before that magic word revenge, and, strange as it my seem, without more ado I consented to his proposal. He walked into the road and, taking a whistle from his pocket, blew three staccato notes upon it. A moment later the hansom from which he had jumped to accost me appeared round a corner and came rapidly towards us. When it pulled up at the kerb, and the apron had been opened, this peculiar individual invited me to take my place in it, which I immediately did. He followed my example, and sat down beside me, and then, without any direction to the driver, we set off up the street.

For upwards of half-an-hour we drove on without stopping, but in which direction we were proceeding I could not for the life of me discover. The wheels were rubber-tyred and made no noise upon the snow-strewn road; my companion scarcely spoke, and the only sound to be heard was the peculiar bumping noise made by the springs, the soft pad-pad of the horse's hoofs, and an occasional grunt of encouragement from the driver. At last it became evident that we were approaching our destination. The horse's pace slackened; I detected the sharp ring of his shoes on a paved crossing, and presently we passed under an archway and came to a standstill.

"Here we are at last, Mr. Pennethorne," said my mysterious conductor. "Allow me to lift the glass and open the apron."

He did so, and then we alighted. To my surprise we stood in a square courtyard, surrounded on all sides by lofty buildings. Behind the cab was a large archway, and at the further end of it the gate through which we had evidently entered. The houses were in total darkness, but the light of the cab lamps was sufficient to show me a door standing open on my left hand.

"I'm afraid you must be very cold, Mr. Pennethorne," said Nikola, for by that name I shall henceforth call him, as he alighted, "but if you will follow me I think I can promise that you shall soon be as warm as toast."

As he spoke he led the way across the courtyard towards the door I have just mentioned. When he reached it he struck a match and advanced into the building. The passage was a narrow one, and from its appearance, and that of the place generally, I surmised that the building had once been used as a factory of some kind. Half-way down the passage a narrow wooden staircase led up to the second floor, and in Indian file we ascended it. On reaching the first landing my guide opened a door which stood opposite him, and immediately a bright light illumined the passage.

"Enter, Mr. Pennethorne, and let me make you welcome to my poor abode," said Nikola, placing his hand upon my shoulder and gently pushing me before him.

I complied with his request, half expecting to find the room poorly furnished. To my surprise, however, it was as luxuriously appointed as any I had ever seen. At least a dozen valuable pictures—I presume they must have been valuable, though personally I know but little about such things—decorated the walls; a large and quaintly-carved cabinet stood in one corner and held a multitude of china vases, bowls, plates, and other knick-knacks; a massive oak sideboard occupied a space along one wall and supported a quantity of silver plate; while the corresponding space upon the opposite wall was filled by a bookcase reaching to within a few inches of the ceiling, and crammed with works of every sort and description. A heavy pile carpet, so soft that our movements made no sound upon it, covered the floor; luxurious chairs and couches were scattered about here and there, while in an alcove at the farther end was an ingenious apparatus for conducting chemical researches. Supper was laid on the table in the centre, and when we had warmed ourselves at the fire that glowed in the grate, we sat down to it. As if to add still further to my surprise, when the silver covers of the dishes were lifted, everything was found to be smoking hot. How this had been managed I could not tell, for our arrival at that particular moment could not have been foretold with any chance of certainty, and I had seen no servant enter the room. But I was very hungry, and as the supper before me was the best I had sat down to for years, you may suppose I was but little inclined to waste time on a matter of such trivial importance.

When we had finished and I had imbibed the better part of two bottles of Heidseck, which my host had assiduously pressed upon me, we left the table and ensconced ourselves in chairs on either side of the hearth. Then, for the first time, I was able to take thorough stock of my companion. He was a man of perhaps a little above middle height, broad shouldered, but slimly built. His elegant proportions, however, gave but a small idea of the enormous strength I afterwards discovered him to possess. His hair and eyes were black as night, his complexion was a dark olive hue, confirming that suspicion of foreign extraction which his name suggested, but of which his speech afforded no trace. He was attired in faultless evening dress, the dark colour of which heightened the extraordinary pallor of his complexion.

"You have a queer home here, Dr. Nikola!" I said, as I accepted the cheroot he offered me.

"Perhaps it is a little out of the common," he answered, with one of his queer smiles; "but then that is easily accounted for. Unlike the general run of human beings, I am not gregarious. In other words, I am very much averse to what is called the society of my fellow man; I prefer, under most circumstances, to live alone. At times, of course, that is not possible. But the idea of living in a flat, shall we say, with perhaps a couple of families above me, as many on either side, and the same number below; or in an hotel or a boarding-house, in which I am compelled to eat my meals in company with half-a-hundred total strangers, is absolutely repulsive to me. I cannot bear it, and therefore I choose my abode elsewhere. A private dwelling-house I might, of course, take, but that would necessitate servants and other encumbrances; this building suits my purposes admirably. As you may have noticed, it was once a boot and shoe factory; but after the proprietor committed suicide by cutting his throat—which, by the way, he did in this very room—the business failed; and until I fell across it, it was supposed to be haunted, and, in consequence, has remained untenanted."

"But do you mean to say you live here alone?" I enquired, surprised at the queerness of the idea.

"In a certain sense, yes—in another, no. That is, I have a deaf and dumb Chinese servant who attends to my simple wants, and a cat who for years has never left me."

"You surprise me more and more!"

"And why? Considering that I know China better than you know that part of London situated, shall we say, between Blackfriars Bridge and Charing Cross, and have spent many years of my life here, the first should not astonish you. And as I am warmly attached to my cat, who has accompanied me in all my wanderings about the globe, I cannot see that you should be surprised at the other. Perhaps you would like to see both?"

As may be supposed, I jumped eagerly at the opportunity; and upon my saying so, Nikola pressed a knob in the wall at his side. He had hardly taken his finger away before my ear detected the shuffling of feet in the passage outside. Next moment the door opened, and in walked the most hideous man I have ever yet beheld in my life. In Australia I had met many queer specimens of the Chinese race, but never one whose countenance approached in repulsiveness that of the man Nikola employed as his servant. In stature he was taller than his master, possibly a couple or three inches above six feet, and broad in proportion. His eyes squinted inwardly, his face was wrinkled and seamed in every direction, his nose had plainly been slit at some time or another, and I noticed that his left ear was missing from his head. He was dressed in his native costume, but when he turned round I noticed that his pigtail had been shorn off at the roots.

"You are evidently puzzled about something," said Nikola, who had been watching my face.

"I must confess I am," I answered. "It is this. If he is deaf and dumb, as you say, how did he hear the bell you rang, and also how do you communicate your orders to him?"

"This knob," replied Nikola, placing his finger on the bell-push, "releases a smaller shutter and reveals a disc that signifies that I desire his services. When I wish to give him instructions I speak to him in his own language, and he answers it. It is very simple."

"But you said just now that he is deaf and dumb," I cried, thinking I had caught him in an equivocation. "If so, how can he hear or speak?"

"So he is," replied my host, looking at me as he spoke, with an amused smile upon his face. "Quite deaf and dumb."

"Then how can you make him hear. And how does he reply?"

"As I say, by word of mouth. Allow me to explain. You argue that because the poor fellow has no tongue wherewith to speak, and his ears are incapable of hearing what you say to him, that it is impossible for him to carry on a conversation. So far as your meaning goes, you are right. But you must remember that, while no sound can come from his lips, it is still possible for the words to be framed. In that case our eyes take the place of our ears, and thus the difficulty is solved. The principle is a simple one, and a visit to any modern deaf and dumb school in London will show you its efficacy. Surely you are not going to ask me to believe you have not heard of the system before?"

"Of course I have heard of it," I answered, "but in this case the circumstances are so different."

"Simply because the man is a Chinaman—that is all. If his skin were white instead of yellow, and he wore English dress and parted his hair in the middle, you would find nothing extraordinary in it. At any rate, perpetual silence on the part of a servant and physical inability to tittle-tattle of the affairs one would wish kept a secret, is a luxury few men can boast."

"I agree with you; but how did the poor fellow come to lose his faculties?"

"To let you into that secret would necessitate the narration of a long and, I fear to you, uninteresting story. Suffice that he was the confidential servant of the Viceroy of Kweichow until he was detected in an amiable plot to assassinate his master with poisoned rice. He was at once condemned to die by *ling-chi* or the death of a thousand cuts, but by the exercise of a little influence which, fortunately for him, I was able to bring to bear, I managed to get him off."

"I wonder you care to have a man capable of concocting such a plot about you," I said.

"And why? Because the poor devil desired to kill the man he hated, is it certain that he should wish to terminate the existence of his benefactor, for whom he has a great affection? Moreover, he is a really good cook, understands my likes and dislikes, never grumbles, and is quite conscious that if he left me he would never get another situation in the world. In the nineteenth century, when good servants are so difficult to procure, the man is worth a gold mine—a Wheel of Fortune, if you like."

"You would argue, then," I said, disregarding the latter part of his speech, "that if a man hates another he is justified in endeavouring to rid the world of him?"

"Necessarily it must depend entirely on the circumstances of the case," replied Nikola, leaning back in his chair and steadfastly regarding me. "When a man attempts to do, or succeeds in doing, me an injury, I invariably repay him in his own coin. Presume, for instance, that a man were to rob you of what you loved best, and considered most worth having, in the world—the affection of your wife, shall we say?—in that case, if you were a man of spirit you would feel justified in meting out to him the punishment he deserved, either in the shape of a duel, or severe personal chastisement. If he shot at you in any country but England, you would shoot at him. Eye for eye, and tooth for tooth, was the old Hebrew law, and whatever may be said against it, fundamentally it was a just one."

I thought of Bartrand, and wished I could apply the principle to him.

"I fear, however," continued Nikola, after a moment's pause, "that in personal matters the men of the present day are not so brave as they once were. They shelter themselves too much behind the law of the land. A man slanders you; instead of thrashing him you bring an action against him for libel, and claim damages in money. A man runs away with your wife; you proclaim your shame in open court, and take gold from your enemy for the affront he has put upon your honour. If a man thrashes you in a public place, you don't strike him back; on the contrary, you consult your solicitor, and take your case before a magistrate, who binds him over to keep the peace. If, after all is said and done, you look closely into the matter, what is crime? A very pliable term, I fancy. For instance, a duke may commit an offence, and escape scot free, when, for the same thing, only under a different name, a costermonger would be sent to gaol for five years. And *vice versa*. A subaltern in a crack regiment may run up tailors' bills—or any others, for that matter—for several thousands of pounds and decamp without paying a halfpenny of the money, never having intended to do so from the very beginning, while if a chimney sweep were to purloin a bunch of radishes from a tray outside a greengrocer's window, he would probably be sent to gaol for three months. And yet both are stealing, though I must confess society regards them with very different eyes. Let clergymen and other righteous men say what they will, the world in its heart rather admires the man who has the pluck to swindle, but he must do so on a big scale, and he must do so successfully, or he must pay the penalty of failure. Your own case, with which, as I said earlier, I am quite familiar, is one in point. Everyone who has heard of it, and who knows anything of the man, feels certain that Bartrand stole from you the information which has made him the millionaire he is. But does it make any difference in the world's treatment of him? None whatever. And why? Because he swindled successfully. In the same way they regard you as a very poor sort of fellow for submitting to his injustice."

"Curse him!"

"Exactly. But, you see, the fact remains. Bartrand has a house in Park Lane and a castle in Shropshire. The Duke of Glendower dined with him the night before last, and one of the members of the Cabinet will do so on Saturday next. Yesterday he purchased a racing stable and a stud, for which he paid twenty thousand pounds cash; while I am told that next year he intends building a yacht that shall be the finest craft of her class in British waters. It is settled that he is to be presented at the next levee, and already he is in the first swim of the fashionable world. If he can only win the Derby this year, there is nothing he might not aspire to. In ten years, if his money lasts and he is still alive, he will be a peer of the realm and founding a new family."

"He must not live as long. Oh, if I could only meet him face to face and repay him for his treachery!"

"And why not? What is there to prevent you? You can walk to his house any morning and ask to see him. If you give the butler a fictitious name and a tip he will admit you. Then, when you get into the library, you can state your grievance and, having done so, shoot him dead."

I uttered a little involuntary cry of anger. Deeply as I hated the man, it was not possible for me seriously to contemplate murdering him in cold blood. Besides—no, no; such a scheme could not be thought of for a moment.

"You don't like the idea?" said Nikola, with that easy nonchalance which characterised him. "Well, I don't wonder at it; it's bizarre, to say the least of it. You would probably be caught and hanged, and hanging is an inartistic termination to the career of even an unsuccessful man. Besides, in that case, you would have lost your money and your life; he only his life, so that the balance would still be in his favour. No; what you want is something a little more subtle, a little more artistic. You want a scheme that will enable you to put him out of the way, and, at the same time, one that will place you in possession of the money that is really yours. Therefore it must be done without any *esclandre*. Now I don't doubt you would be surprised if I were to tell you that in the event of his death you would find yourself his sole heir."

"His sole heir?" I cried. "You must be mad to say such a thing."

"With due respect, no more mad than you are," said this extraordinary man. "I have seen the will for myself—never mind how I managed it—and I know that what I say is correct. After all, it is very feasible. The man, for the reason that he has wronged you, hates you like poison, and while he lives you may be sure you will never see a penny of his fortune. But he is also superstitious, and believing, as he does, that he stands a chance of eternal punishment for swindling you as he did, he is going to endeavour to obtain a mitigation of his sentence by leaving you at his death what he has not been able to spend during his lifetime. If you die first, so much the worse for him; but I imagine he is willing to risk that."

I rose from my chair, this time thoroughly angered.

"Dr. Nikola," I said, "this is a subject upon which I feel very deeply. I have no desire to jest about it."

"I am not jesting, my friend, I assure you," returned Nikola, and, as he said so, he went to an escritoire in the corner. "In proof that what I say is the truth, here is a rough draft of his will, made yesterday. You are at liberty to peruse it if you care to do so, and as you are familiar with his writing, you can judge for yourself of its worth."

I took the paper from his hand and sat down with it in my chair again. It certainly was what he had described, and in it I was named as sole and undivided heir to all his vast wealth. As I read, my anger rose higher and higher. From this paper it was evident that the man knew he had swindled me, and it was also apparent that he was resolved to enjoy the fruits of his villainy throughout his life, and to leave me what he could not use when he died, and when I would, in all human probability, be too old to enjoy it. I glanced at the paper again, and then handed it back to Nikola, and waited for him to speak. He watched me attentively for a few seconds, and then said in a voice so soft and low that I could scarcely hear it—

"You see, if Bartrand were to be removed after he had signed that you would benefit at once."

I did not answer. Nikola waited for a few moments and then continued in the same low tone—

"You hate the man. He has wronged you deeply. He stole your secret while you were not in a position to defend yourself, and I think he would have killed you had he dared to do so. Now he is enjoying the fortune which should be yours. He is one of the richest men in the world—with your money. He has made himself a name in England, even in this short space of time—with your money. He is already a patron of sport, of the drama, and of art of every sort—with your money. If you attempt to dispute his possession, he will crush you like a worm. Now the question for your consideration is: Do you hate him sufficiently to take advantage of an opportunity to kill him if one should come in your way?"

He had roused my hate to such a pitch that before I could control myself I had hissed out "Yes!" He heard it, and when I was about to protest that I did not mean it, held up his hand to me to be silent.

"Listen to me," he said. "I tell you candidly that it is in my power to help you. If you really wish to rid yourself of this man, I can arrange it for you in such a way that it will be impossible for any one to suspect you. The chance of detection is absolutely nil. You will be as safe from the law as you are at this minute. And remember this, when you have rid yourself of him, his wealth will be yours to enjoy just as you please. Think of his money—think of the power it gives, think of the delight of knowing that you have punished the man who has wronged you so shamefully. Are you prepared to risk so much?"

My God! I can remember the horror of that moment even now. As I write these words I seem to feel again the throbbing of the pulses in my temples, the wild turmoil in my brain, the whirling mist before my eyes. In extenuation, I can only hope that I was, for the time being, insane. Shameful as it may be to say so, I know that while Nikola was speaking, I hungered for that man's death as a starving cur craves for food.

"I don't want his money," I cried, as if in some small extenuation of the unutterable shame of my decision. "I only want to punish him—to be revenged upon him."

"You consent, then?" he said quietly, pulling his chair a little closer, and looking at me in a strange fashion.

As his eyes met mine all my own will seemed to leave me. I was powerless to say anything but "Yes, I consent."

Nikola rose to his feet instantly, and with an alertness that surprised me after his previous languor.

"Very good," he said; "now that that is settled, we can get to business. If you will listen attentively, I will explain exactly how it is to be done."

CHAPTER 2

A Gruesome Tale

"There are three things to be borne in mind," said Nikola, when I had recovered myself a little: "the first is the dependent point, namely, that the man has to be, well, shall we call it, relieved of the responsibility of his existence! Secondly, the deed must be done at once; and, thirdly, it must be accomplished in such a manner that no suspicion is aroused against you. Now, to you who know the world, and England in particular, I need scarcely explain that there are very few ways in which this can be done. If you desire to follow the melodramatic course, you will decoy your enemy to an empty house and stab him there; in that case, however, there will, in all probability, be a tramp taking refuge in the coal cellar who will overhear you, the marks of blood on the floor will give evidence against you, and—what will be worse than all—there will be the body to dispose of. It that procedure does not meet with your approval, you might follow him about night after night until you find an opportunity of effecting your purpose in some deserted thoroughfare; but then you must take into consideration the fact that there will always be the chance of his calling out, or in other ways attracting the attention of the neighbourhood, or of someone coming round the corner before you have quite finished. A railway train has been tried repeatedly, but never with success; for there is an increased difficulty in getting rid of the body, while porters and ticket collectors have a peculiar memory for faces, and history shows that whatever care you may take you are bound to be discovered sooner or later. In his own house the man is as secure, or more so, than he would be in the Tower of London; and even if you did manage to reach him there, the betting would be something like a million to one that you would be detected. No; none of these things are worthy of our consideration. I came to this conclusion in another and similar case in which my assistance was invoked three months ago. If one wants to succeed in murder, as in anything else, one must endeavour to be original."

"For heaven's sake, man, choose your words less carefully!" I cried, with a sudden fierceness for which I could not afterwards account. "You talk as if we were discussing an ordinary business transaction."

"And are we not?" he replied calmly, paying no attention to my outburst of temper. "I am inclined to think we are. You desire to revenge yourself upon a man who has wronged you. For a consideration I find you the means of doing it. You want—I supply. Surely supply and demand constitute the component parts of an ordinary business transaction?"

"You said nothing just now about a consideration. What is it to be?"

"We will discuss that directly."

"No, not directly. Now! I must know everything before I hear more of your plans."

"By all means let us discuss it then. Properly speaking, I suppose I should demand your soul as my price, and write the bond with a pen dipped in your blood. But, though you may doubt it, I am not Mephistopheles. My terms are fifty thousand pounds, to be paid down within six months of your coming in to your money. I think you will admit that that is a small enough sum to charge for helping a man to obtain possession of nearly two millions. I don't doubt our friend Bartrand would pay three times as much to be allowed to remain on in Park Lane. What do you think?"

The mere mention of Bartrand's name roused me again to fury.

"You shall have the money," I cried. "And much good may it do you. Come what may, I will not touch a penny of it myself. I want to punish him, not to get his fortune. Now what is your scheme?"

"Pardon me, one thing at a time if you please."

He crossed to the escritoire standing in the corner of the room, and from a drawer took a sheet of paper. Having glanced at it he brought it to me with a pen and ink.

"Read it, and when you have done so, sign. We will then proceed to business."

I glanced at it, and discovered that it was a legally drawn up promise to pay Dr. Antonio Nikola fifty thousand pounds within six months of my succeeding to the property of Richard Bartrand, of Park Lane, London, and Chennington Castle, Shropshire, should such an event ever occur. Dipping the pen into the ink I signed what he had written, and then waited for him to continue. He folded up the paper with great deliberation, returned it to its place in the escritoire, and then seated himself opposite me again.

"Now I am with you hand and glove," he said with a faint smile upon his sallow face. "Listen to my arrangement. In considering the question of murder I have thought of houses, trains, street stabbings, poisonings, burnings, drowning, shipwreck, dynamite, and even electricity; and from practical experience I have arrived at the conclusion that the only sure way in which you can rid yourself of an enemy is to do the deed in a hansom cab."

"A hansom cab?" I cried. "You must be mad. How can that be safe at all?"

"Believe me, it is not only the safest, but has been proved to be the most successful. I will explain more fully, then you will be able to judge of the beautiful simplicity of my plan for yourself. The cab I have constructed myself after weeks of labour, in this very house; it is downstairs now; if you will accompany me we will go and see it."

He rose from his chair, took up the lamp that stood upon the table, and signed to me to follow him. I did so, down the stairs by which he had ascended, and along the passage to a large room at the rear of the building. Folding doors opened from it into the yard, and, standing in the centre of this barn-like apartment, its shafts resting on an iron trestle, was, a hansom cab of the latest pattern, fitted with all the most up-to-date improvements.

"Examine it," said Nikola, "and I think you will be compelled to admit that it is as beautiful a vehicle as any man could wish to ride in; get inside and try it for yourself."

While he held the lamp aloft I climbed in and seated myself upon the soft cushions. The inside was lined with Russia leather, and was in every way exquisitely fitted. A curious electric lamp of rather a cumbersome pattern, I thought, was fixed on the back in such a position as to be well above the rider's head. A match-box furnished the bottom of one window, and a cigar-cutter the other; the panels on either side of the apron were decorated with mirrors; the wheels were rubber tyred, and each of the windows had small blinds of heavy stamped leather. Altogether it was most comfortable and complete.

"What do you think of it?" said Nikola, when I had finished my scrutiny.

"It's exactly like any other hansom," I answered. "Except that it is finished in a more expensive style than the average cab, I don't see any difference at all."

"There you refer to its chief charm," replied Nikola, with a grim chuckle. "If it were different in any way to the ordinary hansom, detection would be easy. As it is I am prepared to defy even an expert to discover the mechanism without pulling it to pieces."

"What is the mechanism, then, and what purpose does it serve?"

"I will explain."

He placed the lamp he held in his hand upon a bracket on the wall, and then approached the vehicle.

"In the first place examine these cushions," he said, pointing to the interior. "You have doubtless remarked their softness. If you study them closely you will observe that they are pneumatic. The only difference is that the air used is the strongest anaesthetic known to science. The glass in front, as you will observe now that I have lowered it, fits into a slot in the apron when the latter is closed, and thus, by a simple process, the interior becomes air-tight. When this has been done the driver has but to press this knob, which at first sight would appear to be part of the nickel rein-support, and a valve opens on either side of the interior—in the match-box in the right window, in the cigar-cutter in the left; the gas escapes, fills the cab, and the result is—well, I will leave you to imagine the result for yourself."

"And then?" I muttered hoarsely, scarcely able to speak distinctly, so overcome was I by the horrible exactness and ingenuity of this murderous affair.

"Then the driver places his foot upon this treadle, which, you see, is made to look as if it works the iron support that upholds the vehicle when resting, the seat immediately revolves and the bottom turns over, thus allowing the body to drop through on to the road. Its very simplicity is its charm. Having carried out your plan you have but to find a deserted street, drive along it, depress the lever, and be rid of your fare when and where you please. By that time he will be far past calling out, and you can drive quietly home, conscious that your work is accomplished. Now what do you think of my invention?"

For a few moments I did not answer, but sat upon an upturned box close by, my head buried in my hands.

The agony of that minute no man will ever understand. Shame for myself for listening, loathing of my demoniacal companion for tempting me, hatred of Bartrand, and desire for revenge, all struggled within me for the mastery. I could scarcely breathe; the air of that hateful room seemed to suffocate me. At last I rose to my feet, and as I did so another burst of fury seized me.

"Monster! Murderer!" I cried, turning like a madman on Nikola, who was testing the appliances of his awful invention with a smile of quiet satisfaction on his face. "Let me go, I will not succumb to your temptations. Show me the way out of this house, or I will kill you."

Sobs shook my being to its very core. A violent fit of hysteria had seized me, and under its influence I was not responsible for what I said or did.

Nikola turned from the cab as calmly as if it had been an ordinary hansom which he was examining with a view to purchase, and, concentrating his gaze upon me as he spoke, said quietly:

"My dear Pennethorne, you are exciting yourself. Pray endeavour to be calm. Believe me, there is nothing to be gained by talking in that eccentric fashion. Sit down again and pull yourself together."

As I looked into his face all my strength seemed to go from me. Without a second's hesitation I sat down as he commanded me, and stared in a stupid, dazed fashion at the floor. I no longer had any will of my own. Of course I can see now that he had hypnotised me; but his methods must have been more deadly than I have ever seen exercised before, for he did not insist upon my looking into his eyes for any length of time, nor did he make any passes before my face as I had seen professional mesmerists do. He simply glanced at me—perhaps a little more fixedly than usual—and all my will was immediately taken from me. When I was calm he spoke again.

"You are better now," he said, "so we can talk. You must pay particular attention to what I am going to say, and what I tell you to do you will do to the letter. To begin with, you will now go back to your hotel, and, as soon as you reach it, go to bed. You will sleep without waking till four o'clock this afternoon; then you will dress and go for a walk. During that walk you will think of the man who has wronged you, and the more you think of him the fiercer your hatred for him will become. At six o'clock you will return to your hotel and dine, going to sleep again in the smoking-room till ten. When the clock has struck you will wake, take a hansom, and drive to 23, Great Gunter Street, Soho. Arriving at the house, you will ask for Levi Solomon, to whom you will be at once conducted. He will look after you until I can communicate with you again. That is your programme for the day. I order you not to fail in any single particular of it. Now you had better be off. It is nearly six o'clock."

I rose from my seat and followed him out into the passage like a dog; thence we made our way into the yard. To my surprise a cab was standing waiting for us, the lamps glaring like fierce eyes into the dark archway which led into the street.

"Get in," said Nikola, opening the apron. "My man will drive you to your hotel. On no account give him a gratuity, for I do not countenance it, and he knows my principle. Good night."

I obeyed him mechanically, still without emotion, and when I was seated the cab drove out into the street.

Throughout the journey back to the hotel I sat in the corner trying to think, and not succeeding. I was only conscious that, whatever happened, I must obey Nikola in all he had told me to do. Nothing else seemed of any importance.

On approaching my residence, I wondered how I should obtain admittance; but, as it turned out, that proved an easy matter, for when I arrived the servants were already up and about, and the front door stood open. Disregarding the stare of astonishment with which I was greeted, I went upstairs to my room, and in less than ten minutes was in bed and fast asleep.

Strangely enough, considering the excitement of the previous twenty-four hours, my sleep was dreamless. It seemed only a few minutes from the time I closed my eyes till I was awake again, yet the hands of my watch had stood at half-past six a.m. when I went to bed, and when I opened my eyes again they chronicled four o'clock exactly. So far I had fulfilled Nikola's instructions to the letter. Without hesitation I rose from my bed, dressed myself carefully, and when I was ready, donned my overcoat and went out for a walk.

The evening was bitterly cold, and heavy snow was falling. To keep myself warm I hurried along, and as I went I found my thoughts reverting continually to Bartrand. I remembered my life at Markapurlie, and the cat-and-dog existence I had passed there with him. Then the memory of poor old Ben's arrival at the station came back to me as distinctly as if it had been but yesterday, and with its coming the manager's brutality roused me afresh. I thought of the fight we had had, and then of the long weeks of nursing at the wretched Mail Change on the plains. In my mind's eye I seemed to see poor old Ben sitting up in bed telling me his secret, and when I was once more convalescent, went over, day by day, my journey to the Boolga Ranges, and dreamt again the dreams of wealth that had occupied my brain then, only to find myself robbed of my fortune at the end. Now the man who had stolen my chance in life was one of the richest men in England. He had in his possession all that is popularly supposed to make life worth the living, and while he entertained royalty, bought racehorses and yachts, and enjoyed every advantage in life at my expense, left me to get along as best I might. I might die of starvation in the gutter for all he would care. At that moment I was passing a newsagent's stall.

On a board before the door, setting forth the contents of an evening newspaper, was a line that brought me up all standing with surprise, as the sailors say. "Bartrand's Generosity.—A Gift to the People," it ran. I went inside, bought a copy of the paper, and stood in the light of the doorway to read the paragraph. It was as follows:

> Mr. Richard Bartrand, the well-known Australian millionaire, has, so we are informed, written to the London County Council offering to make a free gift to the city of that large area of ground recently occupied by Montgomery House, of which he has lately become the possessor. The donor makes but one stipulation, and that is that it shall be converted into public gardens, and shall be known in the future as Bartrand Park. As the ground in question was purchased at auction by the millionaire last week for the large sum of fifty thousand pounds, the generosity of this gift cannot be overestimated.

To the surprise of the newsagent I crushed the paper up, threw it on the ground, and rushed from the shop in a blind rage. What right had he to pose as a public benefactor, who was only a swindler and a robber? What right had he to make gifts of fifty thousand pounds to the people, when it was only by his villainy he had obtained the money? But ah! I chuckled to myself, before many hours were over I should be even with him, and then we would see what would happen. A hatred more intense, more bitter, than I could ever have believed one man could entertain for another, filled my breast. Under its influence all my scruples vanished, and I wanted nothing but to cry quits with my enemy.

For more than half an hour I hurried along, scarcely heeding where I went, thinking only of my hatred, and gloating over the hideous revenge I was about to take. That I was doing all this under Nikola's hypnotic influence I now feel certain; but at the time I seemed to be acting on my own initiative, and Nikola to be only playing the part of the *deus ex machina*.

At last I began to weary of my walk, so, hailing a hansom, I directed the driver to convey me back to my hotel. As I passed through the hall the clock over the billiard-room door struck six, and on hearing it I became aware that in one other particular I had fulfilled Nikola's orders. After dinner I went into the smoking-room, and, seating myself in an easy chair before the fire, lit a cigar. Before I had half smoked it I was fast asleep, dreaming that I was once more in Australia and tossing on a bed of sickness in the Mail Change at Markapurlie. A more vivid dream it would be impossible to imagine. I saw myself, pale and haggard, lying upon the bed, unconscious of what was passing around me. I saw Bartrand and Gibbs standing looking down at me. Then the former came closer, and bent over me. Next moment he had taken a paper from the pocket of my shirt, and carried it with him into the adjoining bar. A few minutes Later he returned with it and replaced it in the pocket. As he did so he turned to the landlord, who stood watching him from the doorway, and said—"You're sure he's delirious, that he's not shamming?"

"Shamming? Poor beggar," answered Gibbs, who after all was not such a bad fellow at heart. "Take a good look at him and see for your-self. I hope I may never be as near gone as he is now."

"So much the better," said Bartrand with a sneer, as he stepped away from the bed. "We'll save him the trouble of making us his legatees."

"You don't mean to steal the poor beggar's secret, surely?" replied Gibbs. "I wouldn't have told you if I'd thought that."

"More fool you then," said Bartrand. "Of course I'm not going to steal it, only to borrow it. Such chances don't come twice in a life-time. But are you sure of your facts? Are you certain the old fellow said there was gold enough there to make both of them millionaires half-a-dozen times over?"

"As certain as I'm sitting here," answered Gibbs.

"Very good; then I'm off tonight for the Boolga Ranges. In ten days I'll have the matter settled, and by the time that dog there gets on to his feet again we'll both be on the high road to fortune."

"And I'm only to have a quarter of what you get? It's not fair, Bartrand."

Bartrand stepped up to him with that nasty, bullying look on his face that I knew so well of old.

"Look here, my friend," he said, "You know Richard Bartrand, don't you? And you also know what I can tell about you. I offer you a fourth of the mine for your information, but I don't give it to you for the reason that I'm afraid of you, for I'm not. Remember I know enough of your doings in this grog shanty to hang you a dozen times over; and, by the Lord Harry, if you make yourself a nuisance to me I'll put those on your track who'll set you swinging. Stand fast by me and I'll treat you fair and square, but get up to any hanky-panky and I'll put such a stopper on your mouth that you'll never be able to open it again."

Gibbs leaned against the door with a face like lead. It was evident that however much he hated Bartrand he feared him a good deal more. A prettier pair of rogues it would have been difficult to find in a long day's march.

"You needn't be afraid, Mr. Bartrand," he said at last, but this time in no certain voice. "I'll not split on yon as long as you treat me fairly. You've been a good friend to me in the past, and I know you mean me well though you speak so plain."

"I know the sort of man with whom I have to deal, you see," returned Bartrand with another nasty sneer. "Now I must get my horse and be off. I've a lot to do if I want to get away tonight."

He went out into the veranda and unhitched his reins from the nails on which they were hanging.

"Let me have word directly that carrion in there comes to himself again," he said, as he got into the saddle. "And be sure you never breathe a word to him that I've been over. I'll let you know all that goes on as soon as we've got our claim fixed up. In the meantime, mum's the word. Goodbye."

Gibbs bade him goodbye, and when he had watched him canter off across the plain returned to the room where I lay. Evidently his conscience was reproving him, for he stood by my bed for some minutes looking down at me in silence. Then he heaved a little sigh and said under his breath, "You miserable beggar, how little you know what is happening, but I'm bothered if I don't think after all that you're a dashed sight happier than I am. I'm beginning to wish I'd not given you away to that devil. The remembrance of it will haunt me all my life long."

I woke up with his last speech ringing in my ears, and for a moment could scarcely believe my own eyes. I had imagined myself back in the bush, and to wake up in the smoking room of a London hotel was a surprise for which I was not prepared. The clock over the door was just striking eleven as I rose to my feet and went out into the hall. Taking my coat down from a peg I put it on, and then, donning my hat and turning up my collar, went out into the street. Snow was still falling, and the night was bitterly cold. As I walked I thought again of the dream from which I had just wakened. It seemed more like a vision intended for my guidance than the mere imagining of an over-excited brain. How much would I not have given to know if it was only imagination, or whether I had been permitted to see a representation of what had really happened? This question, however, I could not of course answer.

On reaching the Strand I hailed a hansom and bade the driver convey me with all speed to 23, Great Gunter Street, Soho.

"Twenty-three, Great Gunter Street?" repeated the man, staring at me in surprise. "You don't surely mean that, sir?"

"I do," I answered. "If you don't like the job I can easily find another man."

"Oh, I'll take you there, never fear, sir," replied the man; "but I didn't know perhaps whether you was aware what sort of a crib it is. It's not the shop gentlemen goes to as a general rule at night time, except maybe they're after a dog as has been stole, or the like."

"So it's that sort of place is it?" I answered. "Well, I don't know that it matters. I'm able to take care of myself."

As I said this I got into the vehicle, and in half a minute we were driving down the Strand in the direction of Soho. In something under a quarter of an hour we had left Leicester Square behind us, crossed Shaftesbury Avenue, and turned into Great Gunter Street. It proved to be exactly what the driver had insinuated, neither a respectable nor a savoury neighbourhood; and when I saw it and its inhabitants I ceased to wonder at his hesitation. When he had proceeded half-way down the street he pulled his horse up before the entrance to what looked like a dark alley leading into a court. Realising that this must be my destination I opened the apron and sprang out.

"Number 23 is somewhere hereabouts, sir," said the driver, who seemed to derive a certain amount of satisfaction from his ignorance of the locality. "I don't doubt but what one of these boys will be able to tell you exactly."

I paid him his fare and sixpence over for his civility, and then turned to question a filthy little gutter urchin, who, with bare feet and chattering teeth, was standing beside me.

"Where is 23, my lad?" I inquired. "Can you take me to it?"

"Twenty-three, sir?" said the boy. "That's where Crooked Billy lives, sir. You come along with me and I'll show you the way."

"Go ahead then," I answered, and the boy thereupon bolted into the darkness of the alley before which we had been standing. I followed him as quickly as I could, but it was a matter of some difficulty, for the court was as black as the Pit of Tophet, and seemed to twist and turn in every conceivable direction. A more unprepossessing place it would have been difficult to find. Half-way down I heard the boy cry out 'Hold up, mother!' and before I could stop I found myself in collision with a woman who, besides being unsteady on her legs, reeked abominably of gin. Disengaging myself, to the accompaniment of her curses, I sped after my leader, and a moment later emerged into the open court itself. The snow had ceased, and the three-quarter moon, sailing along through swift flying clouds, showed me the surrounding houses. In one or two windows, lights were burning, revealing sights which almost made my flesh creep with loathing. In one I could see a woman sewing as if for her very life by the light of a solitary candle stuck in a bottle, while two little children lay asleep, half-clad, on a heap of straw and rags in the corner. On my right I had a glimpse of another room, where the dead body of a man was stretched upon a mattress on the floor, with two old hags seated at a table beside it, drinking gin from a black bottle, turn and turn about. The wind whistled mournfully among the roof tops; the snow had been trodden into a disgusting slush everywhere, save close against the walls, where it still showed white as silver; while the reflection of the moon gleamed in the icy puddles golden as a spade guinea.

"This is number 23," said my conductor, pointing to the door before which he stood.

I rewarded him, and then turned my attention to the door indicated.

Having rapped with my knuckles upon the panel, I waited for it to be opened to me. But those inside were in no hurry, and for this reason some minutes elapsed before I heard anyone moving about; then there came the sound of shuffling feet, and next moment the door was opened an inch or two, and a female voice inquired with an oath— which I will omit—what was wanted and who was wanting it.

To the first query I replied by asking if Levi Solomon lived there, and, if he did, whether I could see him. The second I shirked altogether. In answer I was informed that Levi Solomon did reside there, and that if I was the gentleman who had called to see him about a hansom cab I was to come in at once.

The door was opened to me, and I immediately stepped into the grimiest, most evil-smelling passage it has ever been my ill luck to set foot in. The walls were soiled and stained almost beyond recognition; the floor was littered with orange peel, paper, cabbage leaves, and garbage of all sorts and descriptions, while the stench that greeted me baffles description. I have never smelled anything like it before, and I hope I may never do so again.

The most I can say for the old lady who admitted me is that she matched her surroundings. She was short almost to dwarfishness, well-nigh bald, and had lost her left eye. Her dress consisted of a ragged skirt, and in place of a body—I believe that is the technical expression—she wore a man's coat, which gave a finishing touch of comicality to the peculiar outline of her figure. As soon as she saw that I had entered, she bade me shut the door behind me and follow her. This I did by means of a dilapidated staircase, in which almost every step was taken at the risk of one's life, to the second floor. Having arrived there, she knocked upon a door facing her; and I noticed that it was not until she had been ordered to enter that she ventured to turn the handle.

"The gentleman what has come about the 'ansom keb," she said, as she ushered me into the room.

The apartment was lit by two candles stuck in their own wax upon a little deal table, and by their rays I could distinguish the man I had come in search of standing by the fireplace awaiting me. He did not greet me until he had made certain, by listening at the keyhole, that the old woman had gone downstairs. He was a quaint little fellow, Jewish from the soles of his feet to the top of his head. He had the nose of his race, little beady eyes as sharp as gimlets, and a long beard which a little washing might have made white. He was dressed in a black frock coat two sizes too large for him, black trousers that would have fitted a man three times his size, and boots that had been patched and otherwise repaired till their original maker would not have known them again.

"Mr. Pennethorne, I presume," he began, rubbing his hands together and speaking as if he had a bad cold in his head. "I am delighted to see you. I am sorry that I cannot ask you to sit down, but I have no chair to give you. For the same reason I cannot offer you refreshment. Have you had a good look at me?"

My surprise at this abrupt question prevented my replying for a moment; then I insinuated that I thought I should know him again, after which, with a muttered "That's all right," he blew out one of the candles, remarking that, as we now knew each other, we could conduct our business quite as well with half the light.

"I received word from our mutual acquaintance Dr. Nikola this morning," he began, when the illumination had been thus curtailed, "that you would be coming to see me. Of course I did not ask the business, for Dr. Nikola is my friend, and I obey and trust him to the letter. By his instructions I am to fit you with a disguise, and then to take you to the place where you will discover a certain hansom cab awaiting you."

I nodded. At the very mention of the cab my old hatred of Bartrand sprang up again, and I began to question the Jew as to where we were to find it and what I was to do when I had got it. But this impetuosity did not meet with his approval.

"My young friend, you must not be in such a hurry," he said, wagging his head deprecatingly at me.

"We shall have to be sure we make no mistake, otherwise the doctor would not be pleased, and I should not like to risk that. Have you known Dr. Nikola very long?"

"I met him this morning for the first time in my life," I answered, realising on what intimate terms we now stood, considering the length of our acquaintance.

"If that is so you have much to learn regarding him," the Jew replied. "Let us be very careful that we do not risk his displeasure. Now we will get to work, for it is nearly time for us to be going."

As he spoke he crossed to a cupboard in the corner of the room, and took from it some garments which he placed upon the table in the centre.

"Here we have the very identical things," he said, "and when you've got them on, you'll be as smart a cabby as any that mounts his box in the streets of London. Try this and see how it suits you."

He handed me a bushy black beard, which worked on springs, and assisted me to fasten it to my face. When it was made secure he stepped back and examined it critically; then with a muttered "that will do," turned to the garments on the table, and selected from the heap a tarpaulin cape, such as cabmen wear in wet weather. This I fixed round my shoulders. A sou'wester was next placed upon my head, and when this was done, as far as I was concerned, we were ready to be off. My curious acquaintance was not long in making his toilet, and five minutes later found us passing out of the filthy alley into Great Gunter Street once more.

"I'll go first," said the Jew. "You follow two or three paces behind me. It's just as well we should not be seen together."

I accordingly took up my position a few steps in the rear, and in this fashion dodged along behind him, until we reached the corner of Wardour and Pultney Streets. Here my guide stopped and looked about him. Evidently what he wanted was not forthcoming, for he began to grow uneasy, and stamped up and down the pavement, looking eagerly in each direction. All the time I did not venture to approach him. I was considering what I was about to do. I thought of my father, and my brother and sisters, and wondered what they would have thought if they could have known to what a pass I had fallen. What would my poor mother have said if she had lived? But she, as far as I could learn from those who had known her, had been a gentle Christian woman, and if she had lived I should in all probability never have left England. In that case I should not have known Bartrand, and this revenge would then not have been necessary. By what small chances are our destinies shaped out for us!

At last the rattle of wheels sounded, and a moment later a smart hansom cab, which I recognised as that shown me by Nikola at his house that morning, drove down the street and pulled up at the corner where we stood. The lamps glowed brightly in the frosty air, and it was evident the horse was one of spirit, for he tossed his head and pawed the ground with impatience to be off again.

The driver descended from his perch, while the Jew went to the horse's head. The other was a tall fellow, and until he came into the light of the lamps I could not see his face. To my surprise, he did not speak, but stood fumbling in the pocket of his oilskin for something, which proved to be a letter. This he handed to me.

I opened it and scanned its contents. It was, of course, from Nikola.

Dear—
Everything is arranged, and I send you this, with the cab, by my servant, who, as you know, will not reveal anything. As soon as you receive it, mount and drive to Pall Mall. Be opposite the Monolith Club punctually at 11.30 and once there, keep your eyes open for the man we want. I will arrange that he shall leave exactly as the clock chimes, and will also see that he takes your cab. When you have dropped your fare in a quiet street, drive as fast as you can go to Hogarth Square, and wait at, or near, the second lamppost on the left-hand side. I will pick you up there, and will arrange the rest. The man in question has been entertaining a distinguished company, including two dukes and a Cabinet Minister, at dinner this evening, but I have arranged to meet and amuse him at twelve. May good luck attend you.
Yours, *N*

I stuffed the note into my pocket and then glanced at my watch. It was exactly a quarter-past eleven, so if I wanted to be at the rendezvous at the time stated it was necessary that I should start at once. Without more ado, I climbed on to the seat at the back, wound the rug I found there round my legs, put on the badge the Chinaman handed up to me, and, whipping up the horse, much to the Jew's consternation, drove off down the street at a rapid pace. As I turned into Great Windmill Street snow began to fall again, and I gave an evil chuckle as I reflected that even the forces of Nature were assisting me in my murderous intentions. In my heart I had no pity for the man whom I was about to kill. He had robbed me as cruelly as one man could rob another, and now I was going to repay him for his treachery.

CHAPTER 3

The Lust of Hate

The cab horse was a fine animal, and spun along to such good purpose that when I turned from Waterloo Place into Pall Mall I had, contrary to my expectations, still some few minutes to spare. Now that the actual moment for putting into effect the threats I had so often uttered against the man who had wronged me so cruelly, had arrived, strange to say I was seized with a sudden and inexplicable feeling of compassion for him. Badly as he had injured me, and desirous as I was of repaying him for his treachery, I discovered I could not bring myself to do what I had arranged without reluctance. If it had been a matter of fair fighting, with the certainty of no one interfering between us, it would have been a totally different matter, and I could have gone into it with a light heart; but now to decoy him to his death by the aid of Nikola's science was an act of cowardice at which my whole nature revolted.

Feeling half inclined to put off—if not for ever, at least for that evening the dastardly deed I had had arranged for me—I drove slowly down the street, quite unable to resist the temptation of seeing the man whom, if I wished to do so, I could kill so easily. In the event of his hailing me as had been arranged, I would reply that I was engaged, and leave him to find another vehicle, unconscious of the narrowness of his escape. At any cost I would not let him set foot in my conveyance. While I was thus arguing with myself I was drawing closer and closer to the Monolith Club. Already I could discern the stalwart form of the commissionaire standing upon the steps under the great lamp. At the moment that I approached, two men left the building arm in arm, but neither of them was the man I wanted. Little by little their steps died away in the distance, and so nicely had I timed my arrival that the clock at the Palace ahead chimed the half-hour exactly as I came opposite the steps. At the same instant the doors of the Club opened, and Bartrand

63

and another man, whom I recognised instantly as Nikola, came out. The mere sight of the man I hated shattered all my plans in an instant. In the presence of the extraordinary individual accompanying him I had not sufficient pluck to cry "engaged"; so, when the commissionaire hailed me, there was nothing for it but to drive across the road and pull up alongside the pavement, as we had previously arranged.

"You're in luck's way, Bartrand," cried Nikola, glancing at my horse, which was tossing his head and pawing the ground as if eager to be off again; "that's a rare good nag of yours, cabby. He's worth an extra fare."

I grunted something in reply, I cannot remember what. The mere sight of Bartrand standing there on the pavement scanning the horse, had roused all my old antipathy; and, as I have said, my good resolves were cast to the winds like so much chaff.

"Well, for the present, *au revoir*, my dear fellow," said Nikola, shaking hands with his victim. "I will meet you at the house in half-an-hour, and if you care about it you can have your revenge then; now you had better be going. Twenty-eight, Saxeburgh Street, cabby, and don't be long about it."

I touched my hat and opened the apron for Bartrand to step inside. When he had done so he ordered me to lower the glass, and not be long in getting him to his destination or I'd hear of it at the other end. He little thought how literally I might interpret the command.

Leaving Nikola standing on the pavement looking after us, I shook up my horse and drove rapidly down the street. My whole body was tingling with exultation; but that it would have attracted attention and spoiled my revenge, I felt I could have shouted my joy aloud. Here I was with my enemy in my power; by lifting the shutter in the roof of the cab I could see him lolling inside—thinking, doubtless, of his wealth, and little dreaming how close he was to the poor fellow he had wronged so cruelly. The knowledge that by simply pressing the spring under my hand I could destroy him in five seconds, and then choosing a quiet street could tip him out and be done with him for ever, intoxicated me like the finest wine. No one would suspect, and Nikola, for his own sake, would never betray me. While I was thinking in this fashion, and gloating over what I was about to do, I allowed my horse to dawdle a little. Instantly an umbrella was thrust up through the shutter and I was ordered, in the devil's name, to drive faster.

"Ah! my fine fellow," I said to myself, "you little know how near you are to the master by whom you swear. Wait a few moments until I've had a little more pleasure out of your company, and then we'll see what I can do for you."

On reaching Piccadilly I turned west, and for some distance followed the proper route for Saxeburgh Street. All the time I was thinking, thinking, and thinking of what I was about to do. He was at my mercy; any instant I could make him a dead man, and the cream of the jest was that he did not know it. My fingers played with the fatal knob, and once I almost pressed it. The touch of the cold steel sent a thrill through me, and at the same instant one of the most extraordinary events of my life occurred. I am almost chary of relating it, lest my readers may feel inclined to believe that I am endeavouring to gull them with the impossible. But, even at the risk of that happening, I must tell my story as it occurred to me. As I put my hand for the last time upon the knob there rose before my eyes, out of the half dark, a woman's face, and looked at me. At first I could scarcely believe my own eyes. I rubbed them and looked again. It was still there, apparently hanging in mid-air above the horse I was driving. It was not, if one may judge by the photographs of famous beauties, a perfect face, but there was that in it that made it to me the most captivating I had ever seen in my life—I refer to the expression of gentleness and womanly goodness that animated it. The contour of the face was oval, the mouth small and well-shaped, and the eyes large, true, and unflinching. Though it only appeared before me for a few seconds, I had time to take thorough stock of it, and to remember every feature. It seemed to be looking straight at me, and the mouth to be saying as plainly as any words could speak—"Think of what you are doing, Gilbert Pennethorne; remember the shame of it, and be true to yourself." Then she faded away; and, as she went, a veil that had been covering my eyes for months seemed now to drop from them, and I saw myself for what I really was—a coward and a would-be murderer.

We were then passing down a side street, in which—fortunately for what I was about to do—there was not a single person of any sort to be seen. Happen what might, I would now stop the cab and tell the man inside who I was and with what purpose I had picked him up. Then he should go free, and in letting him understand that I had spared his life I would have my revenge. With this intention I pulled my horse up, and, unwrapping my rug from my knees, descended from my perch. I had drawn up the glass before dismounting, the better to be able to talk to him.

"Mr. Bartrand," I said, when I had reached the pavement, at the same time pulling off my false beard and my sou'wester, "this business has gone far enough, and I am now going to tell you who I am and what I wanted with you. Do you know me?"

65

Either he was asleep or he was too surprised at seeing me before him to speak, at any rate he offered no reply to my question.

"Mr. Bartrand," I began again, "I ask you if you are aware who I am?"

Still no answer was vouchsafed to me, and immediately an overwhelming fear took possession of me. I sprang upon the step and tore open the apron. What I saw inside made me recoil with terror. In the corner, his head thrown back and his whole body rigid, lay the unfortunate man I had first determined to kill, but had since decided to spare. I ran my hands, all trembling with terror, over his body. The man was dead—and I had killed him. By some mischance I must have pressed the spring which opened the valve, and thus the awful result had been achieved. Though years have elapsed since it happened, I can feel the agony of that moment as plainly now as if it was but yesterday.

When I understood that the man was really dead, and that I was his murderer—branded henceforth with the mark of Cain—I sat down on the pavement in a cold sweat of terror, trembling in every limb. The face of the whole world had changed within the past few minutes—now I knew I could never be like other men again. Already the fatal noose was tightening round my neck.

While these thoughts were racing through my brain, my ears, now preternaturally sharp, had detected the ring of a footstep on the pavement a hundred yards or so away. Instantly I sprang to my feet, my mind alert and nimble, my whole body instinct with the thought of self-preservation. Whatever happened I must not be caught, redhanded, with the body of the murdered man in my possession. At any risk I must rid myself of that, and speedily, too.

Climbing to my perch again I started my horse off at a rapid pace in the same direction in which I had been proceeding when I had made my awful discovery. On reaching the first cross-roads I branched off to the right, and, discovering that to be a busy thoroughfare, turned to the left again. Never before had my fellow-man inspired me with such terror. At last I found a deserted street, and was in the act of pressing the lever with my foot when a door in a house just ahead of me opened, and a party of ladies and gentlemen issued from it. Some went in one direction, others in a contrary, and I was between both. To drop the body where they could see it would be worse than madness, so, almost cursing them for interrupting me, I lashed my horse and darted round the first available corner. Once more I found a quiet place, but this time I was interrupted by a cab turning into the street and coming along behind me. The third time, however, was more successful. I looked carefully about me. The street was empty in front and behind. On either side were rows of respectable middle-class houses, with never a light in a window or a policeman to be seen.

Trembling like a leaf, I stopped the cab, and when I had made sure that there was no one looking, placed my foot upon the lever. So perfect was the mechanism that it acted instantly, and, what was better still, without noise. Next moment Bartrand was lying upon his back in the centre of the road. As soon as his weight released it the bottom of the vehicle rose, and I heard the spring click as it took its place again. Before I drove on I turned and looked at him where he lay so still and cold on the pure white snow, and thought of the day at Markapurlie, when he had turned me off the station for wanting to doctor poor Ben Garman, and also of the morning when I had denounced him to the miners on the Boolga Ranges, after I had discovered that he had stolen my secret and appropriated my wealth. How little either of us thought then what the end of our hatred was to be! If I had been told on the first day we had met that I should murder him, and that he would ultimately be found lying dead in the centre of a London street, I very much doubt if either of us would have believed it possible. But how horribly true it was!

As to what I was now, there could be no question. The ghastly verdict was self-evident, and the word rang in my brain with a significance I had never imagined it to possess before. It seemed to be written upon the houses, to be printed upon the snow-curdled sky. Even the roll of the wheels beneath me proclaimed me a murderer. Until that time I had had no real conception of what that grisly word meant. Now I knew it for the most awful in the whole range of our English language.

All this time I had been driving aimlessly on and on, having no care where I went, conscious only that I must put as great a distance as possible between myself and the damning evidence of my crime. Then a reaction set in, and I became aware that to continue driving in this half-coherent fashion was neither politic nor sensible, so I pulled myself together and tried to think what I had better do. The question for my consideration was whether I should hasten to Hogarth Square as arranged and hand the cab over to Nikola, or whether I should endeavour to dispose of it in some other way, and not go near that dreadful man again. One thing was indisputable: whatever I did, I must do quickly. It was nearly one o'clock by this time, and if I wanted to see him at the rendezvous I must hurry, or he would have gone before I reached it. In that case, what should I do with the cab?

After anxious thought I came to the conclusion that I had better find him and hand him his terrible property. Then, if I wished to give him the slip, I could lead him to suppose I intended returning to my hotel, and afterwards act as I might deem best for my own safety. This once decided, I turned the vehicle round, whipped up the horse, and set off for Hogarth Square as fast as I could go. It was a long journey, for several times I missed my way and had to retrace my steps; but at last I accomplished it and drove into the Square. Sure enough at the second lamp-post on the left hand side, where he had appointed to meet me, three men were standing beside a hansom cab, and from the way they peered about, it was evident they were anxiously awaiting the arrival of someone. One I could see at first glance was Nikola, the other was probably his Chinese servant, the man who had brought me the cab earlier in the evening, but the third's identity I could not guess. Nor did I waste time trying.

As I approached them Nikola held up his hand as a signal to me to stop, and I immediately pulled up and got down. Not a question did he ask about my success or otherwise, but took from the second cab a bowler hat and a top coat, which I recognised as the garments I had left at Levi Solomon's that evening.

"Put these on," he said, "and then come with me as quickly as you can. I have a lot to say to you."

I did as he ordered me, and when my sou'wester and cape had been tossed into the empty cab, he beckoned me to follow him down the square. His servant had meanwhile driven that awful cab away.

"Now, what have you to tell me?" he asked, when we had walked a little distance along the pavement.

I stopped and faced him with a face, I'll be bound, as ashen as that of a corpse.

"I have done your fiendish bidding," I hissed. "I am—God help me—unintentionally what you have made me—a murderer."

"Then the man is dead, is he?" replied Nikola, with icy calmness. "That is satisfactory. Now we have to divert suspicion from yourself. All things considered, I think you had better go straight back to your hotel, and keep quiet there until I communicate with you. You need have no fear as to your safety. No one will suspect you. Hitherto we have been most successful in eluding detection."

As he spoke, the memory of the other murders which had shocked all London flashed through my brain, and instantly I realised everything. The victims, so the medical men stated, had in each case been killed by some anaesthetic: they had been found in the centre of the road, as if dropped from a vehicle, while their faces had all been mutilated in the same uncanny fashion. I turned and looked at the man by my side, and then, in an unaccountable fit of rage, threw myself upon him. The men who actually did the deeds were innocent—here was the real murderer—the man who had instigated and egged them on to crime. He had led my soul into hell, but he should not escape scot free.

The suddenness of my passion took him completely by surprise, but only for an instant. Then, with a quick movement of his hands, he caught my wrists, and held me in a grip of iron. I was disarmed and powerless, and he knew it, and laughed mockingly.

"So you would try and add me to your list, would you, Mr. Gilbert Pennethorne? Be thankful that I am mercifully inclined, and do not punish you as you deserve."

Without another word he threw me from him, with the ease of a practised wrestler, and I fell upon the pavement as if I had been shot. The shock brought me to my senses, and I rose an altogether different man, though still hating him with a tenfold loathing as the cause of all my misery. Having once rid himself of me however, he seemed to think no more of the matter.

"Now be off to your hotel," he said sharply, "and don't stir from it until I communicate with you. By making this fuss you might have hung yourself, to say nothing of implicating me. Tomorrow morning I will let you know what is best to be done. In the meantime, remain indoors, feign ill health, and don't see any strangers on any pretext whatever."

He stood at the corner of the Square, and watched me till I had turned the corner, as cool and diabolical a figure as the Author of all Evil himself. I only looked back once, and then walked briskly on until I reached Piccadilly Circus, where I halted and gazed about me in a sort of dim confused wonderment at my position. What a variety of events had occurred since the previous night, when I had stood in the same place, and had heard the policeman's whistle sound from Jermyn Street, in proclamation of the second mysterious murder! How little I had then thought that within twenty-four hours I should be in the same peril as the murderer of the man I had seen lying under the light of the policeman's lantern! Perhaps even at this moment Bartrand's body had been discovered, and a hue and cry was on foot for the man who had done the deed. With this thought in my mind, a greater terror than I had yet felt came over me, and I set off as hard as I could go down a bye-street into Trafalgar Square, thence by way of Northumberland Avenue on to the Embankment. Once there I leant upon the coping and looked down at the dark water slipping along so silently on its way to the sea. Here was my chance if only I had the pluck to avail myself of it. Life had now no hope left for me. Why should I not throw myself over, and so escape the fate that must inevitably await me if I lived? One moment's courage, a little struggling in the icy water, a last choking cry, and then it would all be over and done with, and those who had the misfortune to call themselves my kinsmen would be spared the mortification of seeing me standing in a felon's dock. I craned my neck still further over the side, and looked at the blocks of ice as they went by, knocking against each other with a faint musical sound that sounded like the tinkling of tiny bells. I remembered the depth of the river, and pictured my sodden body stranded on to the mud by the ebbing tide somewhere near the sea. I could fancy the conjectures that would be made concerning it. Would anyone connect me with—but there, I could not go on. Nor could I do what I had proposed. Desperate as was my case, I found I still clung to life with a tenacity that even crime itself could not lessen. No; by hook or crook I must get out of England to some place where nobody would know me, and where I could begin a new life. By cunning it could surely be managed. But in that case I knew I must not go back to my hotel, and run the risk of seeing Nikola again. I distrusted his powers of saving me; and, if I fell once more under his influence, goodness alone knew what I might not be made to do. No; I would make some excuse to the landlord to account for my absence, and then creep quietly out of England in such a way that no one would suspect me. But how was it to be managed? To remain in London would be to run endless risks. Anyone might recognise me, and then capture would be inevitable. I turned out my pockets and counted my money. Fortunately, I had cashed a cheque only the day before, and now had nearly forty pounds in notes and gold in my purse; not very much, it is true, but amply sufficient for my present needs. The question was: Where should I go? Australia, the United States, South America, South Africa? Which of these places would be safest? The first and second I rejected without consideration. The first I had tried, the second I had no desire to visit. Chile, the Argentine, or Bechuanaland? It all depended on the boats. To whichever place a vessel sailed first, to that place I would go.

Casting one last glance at the ice-bound water below me, and with a shudder at the thought of what I had contemplated doing when I first arrived upon the Embankment, I made my way back into the Strand. It was now close upon three o'clock, and already a few people were abroad. If I were not out of London within a few hours, I might be caught. I would go directly I had decided what it was imperative I should know. Up one street and down another I toiled until at last I came upon what I wanted, a small restaurant in a back street, devoted to the interests of the early arrivals at Covent Garden Market. It was only a tiny place, shabby in the extreme, but as it just suited my purpose, I walked boldly in, and ordered a cup of cocoa and a plate of sausages. While they were being prepared I seated myself in one of the small compartments along the opposite wall, and with my head upon my hands tried to think coherently. When the proprietor brought me the food, I asked him if he could oblige me with the loan of writing materials. He glanced at me rather queerly, I thought, but did not hesitate to do what I asked. When he had gone again I dipped the pen into the ink and wrote a note to the proprietor of my hotel, telling him that I had been suddenly taken out of town by important business, and asking him to forward my boxes, within a week, to the cloak room, Aberdeen railway station, labelled "to be called for." I chose Aberdeen for the reason that it was a long distance from London, and also because it struck me that if enquiries were made by the police it would draw attention off my real route, which would certainly not be in that direction. I then wrote a cheque for the amount of my account, enclosed it, and having done so sealed up the letter and put it in my pocket. On an adjoining table I espied a newspaper, which I made haste to secure. Turning to the column where the shipping advertisements were displayed, I searched the list for a vessel outward bound to one of the ports I had chosen. I discovered that to Chile or any of the South American Republics there would not be a boat sailing for at least a week to come. When I turned to South Africa I was more fortunate; a craft named the *Fiji Princess* was advertised to sail from Southampton for Cape Town at 11 a.m. on this self-same day. She was of 4,000 tons burden, but had only accommodation for ten first-class passengers and fifty in the steerage. What pleased me better still, she would only call at Tenerife on the way. The steerage fare was fifteen pounds, and it was by this class I determined to travel. My mind once made up, the next thing to decide was how to reach Southampton without incurring suspicion. To catch the boat this could only be done by rail, and to further increase my store of knowledge I had again to borrow from the proprietor of the restaurant. From the time table he lent me I found that a train left Waterloo every morning at six o'clock, which would get me to the docks before nine o'clock, thus allowing me two full hours in which to make my preparations and to get on board in comfortable time; that is, supposing she sailed at the hour stated. But I had still three hours to put in in London before the train would start, and how to occupy them without running any risk

71

I could not tell. It was quite impossible for me to remain where I was, and yet to go out and walk about the streets would be dangerous in the extreme. In that time Nikola might get hold of me again, and I believe I dreaded that more than even falling into the clutches of the law. Suddenly I was struck by what seemed a splendid idea. What if I walked out of London to some station along the line where the train would pick me up? In that case no one would be able to remember seeing me start from Waterloo, and I should be believed to be still in London. The thought was no sooner born in my brain than I picked up my hat and prepared to be off.

When I paid at the counter for my meal, and also for the note paper with which the proprietor had obliged me, I strode out of the restaurant and down the street into the Strand again. Surbiton, I reflected, was twelve miles from Waterloo, and, besides being quiet, it was also one of the places at which I had noticed that the train was advertised to call. I had almost three hours before me in which to do the distance, and if I walked at the rate of five miles an hour it was evident I should accomplish it with ease. To Surbiton, therefore, I would go.

Having made my way back to Charing Cross, I passed down Whitehall and over Westminster Bridge to the Lambeth Palace Road. Under the influence of my new excitement I felt easier in my mind than I had been since I made my awful discovery three hours before, but still not easy enough to be able to pass a policeman without a shudder. Strangely enough, considering that I had had no sleep at all, and had been moving about all night, I was not conscious of the least fatigue, but strode along the pavement at a swinging pace, probably doing more than I had intended when I had first set out. The snow had ceased, but a nasty fog was rising from the river to take its place. I pictured the state of London when day should break, and devoutly thanked Heaven that I should be well out of it by that time. I could imagine the newsboys running about the streets with cries of "Another 'orrible murder! A millionaire the victim." I seemed to see the boards stuck before shop doors with the same ghastly headline, and I could realise the consternation of the town, when it awoke to find the mysterious assassin still at work in its midst. Then would follow the inquest. The porter at the Monolith Club would be called upon to give evidence, and would affirm that he had seen the deceased gentleman step into a smart hansom, driven by a cabman dressed in an oilskin cape and a sou'wester, and would probably remember having noticed that the cabby was a gruff fellow with a bushy, black beard. The next witnesses would be the finders of the body, and after that the same verdict would be returned—"Wilful murder against some person or persons unknown"—as had been given in the previous cases.

If only Nikola remained faithful to me I should probably have time to get out of England before the police could stop me, and, once among the miners of the Rand, I should be able to arrange matters in such a way that recognition would be almost an impossibility. With a sigh of relief at this comfortable thought, I pushed on a little faster along the Wandsworth Road until I reached Clapham Junction Station. As I did so I looked at my watch. It was just a quarter to four, and already the footpaths were becoming dotted with pedestrians.

Leaving Clapham Junction behind me, I passed along the Lavender Hill Road, through Wandsworth, and struck out along the road to West Hill, then across Putney Heath, through Kingston Vale, and so into Kingston. From that quaint old riverside town to Surbiton is but a step, and exactly as the church clocks in the latter place were chiming a quarter to six, I stood on the platform of the railway station prepared to board my train when it should come in sight. The last four miles had been done at a fast pace, and by the time I had taken my ticket I was completely worn out. My anxiety was so keen that I could not sit down, but waited until I should be safely on board the train. The cries of the newsboys seemed still to be ringing in my ears—"Another 'orrible murder! Discovery of the body of a famous millionaire!"

To while away the time I went out of the station again and explored the deserted streets, passing houses in which the owners still lay fast asleep, little dreaming of the miserable man who was tramping along in the cold outside. A biting north wind blew over the snow, and chilled me to the marrow. The leaden hand of despair was pressing hard upon my heart, and when I looked at the rows of trim, matter-of-fact residences on either side of me, and thought of the gulf that separated their inmates from myself, I groaned aloud in abject misery.

At five minutes to the hour I returned to the station, and, just as I reached it, punctual almost to the tick of the clock, the train made its appearance round the bend of the line. With the solitary exception of an old man I was the only passenger from this station; and, as soon as I had discovered an empty third-class compartment, I got in and stowed myself away in a corner. Almost before the train was out of the station I was fast asleep, dreaming of Nikola and of the horrible events of the night just past. Once more I drove the cab along the snow-covered streets; once more that strange woman's face rose before me in warning; and once more I descended from my seat to make the horrible discovery that my enemy was dead. In my agony I must have shrieked aloud, for the noise I made woke me up. An elderly man, possibly a successful country butcher from his appearance, who must have got in at some station we had stopped at while I slept, was sitting in the corner opposite, watching me.

"You have been having a pretty bad nightmare these last few minutes, I should say, mister," he observed, with a smile. "I was just going to give you a shake up when you woke yourself by screaming out like that."

An awful fear came over me. Was it possible that in my sleep I had revealed my secret?

"I am sorry I disturbed you," I said, faintly, "but I am subject to bad dreams. Have I been talking very much?"

"Not so far as I've heard," he answered; "but you've been moaning and groaning as if you'd got something on your mind that you wanted to tell pretty bad."

"I've just got over a severe illness," I replied, relieved beyond measure to hear that I had kept my dreadful secret to myself, "and I suppose that accounts for the uneasy way in which I sleep."

My companion looked at me rather searchingly for a few seconds, and then began to fumble in his greatcoat pocket for something. Presently he produced a large spirit flask.

"Let me give you a drop of whiskey," he said, kindly. "It will cheer you up, and you look as if you want it right down bad."

He poured about half a wineglassful into the little nickel-plated cup that fitted the bottom of the flask, and handed it to me. I thanked him sincerely, and tossed it off at one gulp. It was neat spirit, and ran through my veins like so much fire. Though it burnt my throat pretty severely, it did me a world of good, and in a few moments I was sufficiently recovered to talk reasonably enough.

At nine o'clock almost to the minute we drew up at Southampton Docks, and then, bidding my fellow passenger good morning, I quickly quitted the station. Before I left London I had carefully noted the address of the steamship company's agents, and, having ascertained the direction of their office, I made my way towards it. Early as was the hour I found it open, and upon being interrogated by the clerk behind the counter, stated my desire to book as steerage passenger for Cape Town by the steamer *Fiji Princess*, which they advertised as leaving the docks that day. The clerk looked at me with some surprise when I said "steerage," but, whatever he may have thought, he offered no comment upon it.

"What is your name?" he inquired, dipping his pen in the ink.

I had anticipated this question, and replied "George Wrexford" as promptly as if it had really been my patronymic.

Having paid the amount demanded, and received my ticket in exchange, I asked what time it would be necessary for me to be on board.

"Half-past ten without fail," he answered. "She will cast off punctually at eleven; and I give you fair warning Captain Hawkins does not wait for anything or anybody."

I thanked him for his courtesy and left the office, buttoning up my ticket in my pocket as I went down the steps. In four hours at most, all being well, I should be safely out of England; and, for a little while, a free man. By half-past nine I had purchased a small outfit, and also the few odds and ends—such as bedding and mess utensils—that I should require on the voyage. This done I hunted about till I found a small restaurant, again in a back street, which I entered and ordered breakfast. As soon as I smelt the cooking I found that I was ravenous, and twice I had to call for more before my hunger was satisfied."

Towards the end of my meal a paper boy put in an appearance, and my heart well-nigh stopped when I heard the girl beyond the counter enquire if there was "any startling news this morning."

"'Nother terrible murder in London," answered the lad with fiendish glibness; and as he spoke my over-taxed strength gave way, and I fell back in my chair in a dead faint.

I suppose for a few moments I must have quite lost consciousness, for I can recollect nothing until I opened my eyes and found a small crowd collected round me, somebody sponging my forehead, and two people chafing my hands.

"How do you feel now?" enquired the nervous little man who had first come to my assistance.

"Better, thank you," I replied, at the same time endeavouring to sit up. "Very much better. What has been the matter with me?"

"A bit of a faint, that's all," another answered. "Are you subject to them?"

"I've been very ill lately," I said, giving them the same reply as I had done to the man in the train, "and I suppose I overtaxed my strength a little this morning. But, thanks to your kindness, I feel ever so much better now."

As soon as I had recovered sufficiently, I paid my bill, and, having again sincerely thanked those who had assisted me, left the shop and hurried off to the docks as fast as I could go. It was now some few minutes after ten o'clock.

The *Fiji Princess* was a fair-sized vessel of an old-fashioned type, and very heavily laden; indeed, so heavy was she that she looked almost unsafe beside the great American liner near which she was berthed.

Having clambered on board I enquired my way to the steerage quarters, which were forward, then stowed away my things and endeavoured to make myself as comfortable as circumstances would permit in the place which was to be my home for the next five weeks or so. For prudence sake I remained below until I heard the whistle sound and could tell by the shaking that the steamship was moving. Then, when I had satisfied myself that we were really under way, I climbed the gangway that led to the deck and looked about me. Slowly as we were moving, we were already a hundred yards from the wharf side, and in a few minutes would be well out in Southampton Water. Eight aft a small crowd of passengers were grouped at the stern railings, waving their handkerchiefs and hats to a similar group ashore. Forward we were less demonstrative, for, as I soon discovered, the steerage passengers consisted only of myself, a circumstance which you may be very sure I did not by any means regret.

By mid-day we were in the Solent, and by lunch time the Isle of Wight lay over our taffrail. Now, unless I was stopped at Tenerife, I was certain of a month's respite from the law. And when I realised this I went to my berth and, sinner as I was, knelt down and offered up the heartiest prayer of gratitude I have ever in my life given utterance to.

CHAPTER 4

A Strange Coincidence

If any man is desirous of properly understanding the feelings of gratitude and relief which filled my breast as the *Fiji Princess* steamed down channel that first afternoon out from Southampton, he must begin by endeavouring to imagine himself placed in the same unenviable position. For all I knew to the contrary, even while I stood leaning on the bulwarks watching the coast line away to starboard, some unlucky chance might be giving the police a clue to my identity, and the hue-and-cry already have begun. When I came to consider my actions during the past twenty-four hours, I seemed to be giving my enemies innumerable opportunities of discovering my whereabouts. My letter to the manager of the hotel, which I had posted in the Strand after leaving the Covent Garden restaurant, would furnish proof that I was in town before five o'clock—the time at which the box was cleared on the morning of the murder. Then, having ascertained that much, they would in all probability call at the hotel, and in instituting enquiries there, be permitted a perusal of the letter I had written to the manager that morning. Whether they would believe that I had gone north, as I desired they should suppose, was difficult to say; but in either case they would be almost certain to have all the southern seaports watched. I fancied, however, that my quickness in getting out of England would puzzle them a little, even if it did not baffle them altogether.

Unfortunately, the *Fiji Princess* had been the only vessel of importance sailing from Southampton on that particular day, and owing to the paucity of steerage passengers, I felt sure the clerk who gave me my ticket would remember me sufficiently well to be able to assist in the work of identification. Other witnesses against me would be the porters at Surbiton railway station, who had seen me arrive, tired and dispirited, after my long walk; the old man who had given me whiskey on the journey down; and the people in the restaurant where I had been taken ill would probably recognise me from the description. However, it was in my favour that I was here on the deck of the steamer, if not devoid of anxiety, at least free from the clutches of the law for the present.

The afternoon was perfectly fine, though bitterly cold; overhead stretched a blue sky, with scarcely a cloud from horizon to horizon; the sea was green as grass, and almost as smooth as a millpond. Since luncheon I had seen nothing of the passengers, nor had I troubled to inquire if the vessel carried her full complement. The saloon was situated right aft in the poop, the skipper had his cabin next to the chart room on the hurricane deck, and the officers theirs on either side of the engine-room, in the alley ways below. My quarters—I had them all to myself, as I said in the last chapter—were as roomy and comfortable as a man could expect for the passage-money I paid, and when I had made friends with the cook and his mate, I knew I should get through the voyage in comparative comfort.

At this point I am brought to the narration of the most uncanny portion of my story: a coincidence so strange that it seems almost impossible it can be true, and one for which I have never been able, in any way, to account. Yet, strange as it may appear, it must be told; and that it is true, have I not the best and sweetest evidence any man could desire in the world? It came about in this way. In the middle of the first afternoon, as already described, I was sitting smoking on the fore hatch, and at the same time talking to the chief steward. He had been to sea, so he told me, since he was quite a lad; and, as I soon discovered, had seen some strange adventures in almost every part of the globe. It soon turned out, as is generally the way, that I knew several men with whom he was acquainted, and in a few minutes we were upon the most friendly terms. From the sea our conversation changed to China, and in illustration of the character of the waterside people of that peculiar country, my companion narrated a story about a shipmate who had put off in a sampan to board his boat lying in Hong Kong harbour, and had never been seen or heard of again.

"It was a queer thing," he said impressively, as he shook the ashes out of his pipe and re-charged it, "as queer a thing as ever a man heard of. I spent the evening with the chap myself, and before we said 'goodbye' we arranged to go up to Happy Valley the Sunday morning following. But he never turned up, nor have I ever set eyes on him from that time to this. Whether he was murdered by the sampan's crew or whether he fell overboard and was drowned in the harbour, I don't suppose will ever be known."

"A very strange thing," I said, as bravely as I could, and instantly thought of the bond I had in common with that sampan's crew.

"Aye, strange; very strange," replied the steward, shaking his head solemnly; "but there's many strange things done now-a-days. Look at these here murders that have been going on in London lately. I reckon it would be a wise man as could put an explanation on them."

All my blood seemed to rush to my head, and my heart for a second stood still. I suffered agonies of apprehension lest he should notice my state and have his suspicions aroused, but he was evidently too much engrossed with his subject to pay any attention to my appearance. I knew I must say something, but my tongue was cleaving to the roof of my mouth. It was some moments before I found my voice, and then I said as innocently as possible—

"They are certainly peculiar, are they not? Have you any theory to account for them?"

This was plainly a question to his taste, and it soon became evident that he had discussed the subject in all its bearings on several occasions before.

"Do you want to know what I think?" he began slowly, fixing me with an eye that he seemed to imagine bored through me like an augur. "Well, what I think is that the Anarchists are at the bottom of it all, and I'll tell you for why. Look at the class of men who were killed. Who was the first? A Major-General in the army, wasn't he? Who was the second? A member of the House of Lords. Who was the third?"

He looked so searchingly at me that I felt myself quailing before his glance as if he had detected me in my guilt. Who could tell him better than I who the last victim was?

"And the third—well, he was one of these rich men as fattens on Society and the workin' man, was he not?"

He pounded his open hand with his fist in the true fashion, and his eyes constantly challenged me to refute his statements if I were in a position to do so. But—heaven help me!—thankful as I would have been to do it, I was not able to gainsay him. Instead, I sat before him like a criminal in the dock, conscious of the danger I was running, yet unable for the life of me to avert it. Still, however, my tormentor did not notice my condition, but returned to the charge with renewed vigour. What he lacked in argument he made up in vehemence. And for nearly an hour I had to sit and bear the brunt of both.

"Now, I'll ask you a question," he said for the twentieth time, after he had paused to watch the effect of his last point. "Who do the Anarchists mostly go for? Why for what we may call, for the sake of argument, the leaders of Society—generals, peers, and millionaires. Those are the people, therefore, that they want to be rid of."

"You think then," I said, "that these—these crimes were the work of a party instead of an individual?"

He half closed his eyes and looked at me with an expression upon his face that seemed to implore me to contradict him.

"You know what I think," he said; then with fine conceit, "If only other folk had as much savee as we have, the fellows who did the work would have been laid by the heels by this time. As it is they'll never catch them—no, not till the moon's made of cream cheese."

With this avowal of his settled opinion he took himself off, and left me sitting on the hatch, hoping with all my heart and soul that, if in this lay my chance of safety, the world might long retain its present opinion. While I was ruminating on what he had said, and feeling that I would give five years of my life to know exactly how matters stood ashore, I chanced to look up at the little covered way on the hurricane deck below the bridge. My heart seemed to stand still. For the moment I thought I must be asleep and dreaming, for there, gazing across the sea, was the same woman's face I had seen suspended in mid-air above my cab on the previous night. Astonishing as it may seem, there could be no possible doubt about it—I recognised the expressive eyes, the sweet mouth, and the soft, wavy hair as plainly as if I had known her all my life long.

Thinking it was still only a creation of my own fancy, and that in a moment it would fade away as before, I stared hard at it, resolved, while I had the chance, to still further impress every feature upon my memory. But it did not vanish as I expected. I rubbed my eyes in an endeavour to find out if I were awake or asleep, but that made no difference. She still remained. I was quite convinced by this time, however, that she was flesh and blood. But who could she be, and where had I really seen her face before? For something like five minutes I watched her, and then for the first time she looked down at the deck where I sat. Suddenly she caught sight of me, and almost at the same instant I saw her give a little start of astonishment. Evidently she had also seen me in some other place, but could no more recall it than myself.

As soon as she had recovered from her astonishment she glanced round the waste of water again and then moved away. But even when she had left me I could not for the life of me rid myself of my feeling of astonishment. I reviewed my past life in an attempt to remember where I had met her, but still without success. While I was wondering, my friend the chief steward came along the deck again. I accosted him, and asked if he could tell me the name of the lady with the wavy brown hair whom I could see talking to the captain at the door of the chart house. He looked in the direction indicated, and then said:

"Her name is Maybourne—Miss Agnes Maybourne. Her father is a big mine owner at the Cape, so I'm told. Her mother died about a year ago, I heard the skipper telling a lady aft this morning, and it seems the poor young thing felt the loss terribly. She's been home for a trip with an old uncle to try and cheer her up a bit, and now they are on their way back home again."

"Thank you very much," I said. "I have been puzzling over her face for some time. She's exactly like someone I've met some time or other, but where, I can't remember."

On this introduction the steward favoured me with a long account of a cousin of his—a steward on board an Atlantic liner—who, it would appear, was always being mistaken for other people; to such a length did this misfortune carry him that he was once arrested in Liverpool on suspicion of being a famous forger who was then at large. Whether he was sentenced and served a term of penal servitude, or whether the mistake was discovered and he was acquitted, I cannot now remember; but I have a faint recollection that my friend described it as a case that baffled the ingenuity of Scotland Yard, and raised more than one new point of law, which he, of course, was alone able to set right in a satisfactory manner.

Needless to say, Miss Maybourne's face continued to excite my wonder and curiosity for the remainder of the afternoon; and when I saw her the following morning promenading the hurricane deck in the company of a dignified grey-haired gentleman, with a clean-shaven, shrewd face, who I set down to be her uncle, I discovered that my interest had in no way abated. This wonderment and mystification kept me company for longer than I liked, and it was not until we were bidding "goodbye" to the Channel that I determined to give up brooding over it and think about something else.

Once Old England was properly behind us, and we were out on the open ocean, experiencing the beauties of a true Atlantic swell, and wondering what our portion was to be in the Bay of Biscay, my old nervousness returned upon me. This will be scarcely a matter for wonder when you reflect that every day we were drawing nearer our first port of call, and at Tenerife I should know whether or not the police had discovered the route I had taken. If they had, I should certainly be arrested as soon as the vessel came to anchor, and be detained in the Portuguese prison until an officer should arrive from England to take charge of me and conduct me home for trial. Again and again I pictured that return, the mortification of my relatives, and the excitement of the Press; and several times I calmly deliberated with myself as to whether the best course for me to pursue would not be to drop quietly overboard some dark night, and thus prevent the degradation that would be my portion if I were taken home and placed upon my trial. However, had I but known it, I might have spared myself all this anxiety, for the future had something in store for me which I had never taken into consideration, and which was destined to upset all my calculations in a most unexpected fashion.

How strange a thing is Fate, and by what small circumstances are the currents of our lives diverted! If I had not had my match-box in my pocket on the occasion I am about to describe, what a very different tale I should have had to tell. You must bear with me if I dwell upon it, for it is the one little bit of that portion of my life that I love to remember. It all came about in this way: On the evening in question I was standing smoking against the port bulwarks between the fore rigging and the steps leading to the hurricane deck. What the exact time was I cannot remember. It may have been eight, and it might possibly have been half-past; one thing, at any rate, is certain: dinner was over in the saloon, for some of the passengers were promenading the hurricane deck. My pipe was very nearly done, and, having nothing better to do, I was beginning to think of turning in, when the second officer came out of the alley way and asked me for a match. He was a civil young fellow of two or three-and-twenty, and when I had furnished him with what he wanted, we fell into conversation. In the course of our yarning he mentioned the name of the ship upon which he had served his apprenticeship. Then, for the first time for many years, I remembered that I had a cousin who had also spent some years aboard her. I mentioned his name, and to my surprise he remembered him perfectly.

"Blakeley," he cried; "Charley Blakeley, do you mean? Why, I knew him as well as I knew any man! As fine a fellow as ever stepped. We made three voyages to China and back together. I've got a photograph of him in my berth now. Come along and see it."

On this invitation I followed him from my own part of the vessel, down the alley way, past the engine-room, to his quarters, which were situated at the end, and looked over the after spar deck that separated the poop from the hurricane deck. When I had seen the picture I stood at the door talking to him for some minutes, and while thus engaged saw two ladies and a gentleman come out of the saloon and go up the ladder to the deck above our heads. From where I stood I could hear their voices distinctly, and could not help envying them their happiness. How different was it to my miserable lot!

Suddenly there rang out a woman's scream, followed by another, and then a man's voice shouting frantically, "Help, help! Miss Maybourne has fallen overboard."

The words were scarcely out of his mouth before I had left the alley way, crossed the well, and was climbing the ladder that led to the poop. A second or two later I was at the taffrail, had thrown off my coat, mounted the rail, and, catching sight of a figure struggling among the cream of the wake astern, had plunged in after her. The whole thing, from the time the first shriek was uttered until I had risen to the surface, and was blowing the water from my mouth and looking about me for the girl, could not have taken more than twenty seconds, and yet in it I seemed to live a lifetime. Ahead of me the great ship towered up to the heavens; all round me was the black bosom of the ocean, with the stars looking down at it in their winking grandeur.

For some moments after I had come to the surface I could see nothing of the girl I had jumped overboard to rescue. She seemed to have quite disappeared. Then, while on the summit of a wave, I caught a glimpse of her, and, putting forth all my strength, swam towards her. Eternities elapsed before I reached her. When I did I came carefully up alongside, and put my left arm under her shoulders to sustain her. She was quite sensible, and, strangely enough, not in the least frightened.

"Can you swim?" I asked, anxiously, as I began to tread water.

"A little, but not very well," she answered. "I'm afraid I am getting rather tired."

"Lean upon me," I answered. "Try not to be afraid; they will lower a boat in a few moments, and pick us up."

She said no more, but fought hard to keep herself afloat. The weight upon my arm was almost more than I could bear, and I began to fear that if the rescue boat did not soon pick us up they might have their row for nothing. Then my ears caught the chirp of oars, and the voice of the second officer encouraging his men in their search for us.

"If you can hold on for another three or four minutes," I said in gasps to my companion, "all will be well."

"I will try," she answered, bravely; "but I fear I shall not be able to. My strength is quite gone."

Her clothes were sodden with water, and added greatly to the weight I had to support. Not once, but half-a-dozen times, seas, cold as ice, broke over us; and once I was compelled to let go my hold of her. When I rose to the surface again some seconds elapsed before I could find her. She had sunk, and by the time I had dived and got my arm round her again she was quite unconscious. The boat was now about thirty yards distant from us, and already the men in her had sighted us and were pulling with all their strength to our assistance. In another minute or so they would be alongside, but the question was whether I could hold out so long. A minute contained sixty seconds, and each second was an eternity of waiting.

When they were near enough to hear my voice I called to them with all my strength to make haste. I saw the bows of the boat come closer and closer, and could distinctly distinguish the hissing of the water under her bows.

"If you can hold on for a few seconds longer," shouted the officer in command, "we'll get you aboard."

I heard the men on the starboard side throw in their oars. I saw the man in the bows lean forward to catch hold of us, and I remember saying, "Lift the lady; I can hold on," and then the boat seemed to fade away, the icy cold water rose higher and higher, and I felt myself sinking down, down, down, calmly and quietly into the black sea, just fading out of life as happily as a little child falls asleep.

When I came to my senses again I found myself lying in a bunk in a cabin which was certainly not my own. The appointments were decidedly comfortable, if not luxurious; a neat white-and-gold wash-stand stood against the bulkhead, with a large mirror suspended above it. Under the porthole, which was shaded with a small red curtain, was a cushioned locker, and at one end of this locker a handy contrivance for hanging clothes. Two men—one a young fellow about my own age, and the other the elderly gentlemen with whom I had often seen Miss Maybourne walking—were standing beside me watching me eagerly. When they saw that I had recovered consciousness they seemed to consider it a matter for congratulation.

"So you know us again, do you?" said the younger man, whom I now recognised as the ship's doctor. "How do you feel in yourself?"

"Not very bright just at present," I answered truthfully. "But I've no doubt I shall be all right in an hour or two." Then, when a recollection of what had occasioned my illness came over me, I said, "How is Miss Maybourne? I hope they got her on board safely?"

"Thanks to you, my dear sir, they did," said the old gentleman, who I discovered later was her uncle, as I had suspected. "I am glad to be able to tell you that she is now making rapid progress towards recovery. You must get well too, and hear what the entire ship has to say about your bravery."

"I hope they'll say nothing," I answered. "Anybody could have done it. And now, how long have I been lying here?"

"Since they brought you on board last night—about twelve hours. You were unconscious for such a long time that we were beginning to grow uneasy about you. But, thank goodness, our clever doctor here has brought you round at last."

The young medico resolved to stop this flow of flattery and small talk, so he bade me sit up and try to swallow some beef tea he had had prepared for me. With his assistance I raised myself, and when I had polished off as much of the food as I was able to manage, he made me lie down once more and try to get to sleep again. I did exactly as I was ordered, and, in less time than it takes to tell, was in the land of Nod. It was not until I was up and about again that I learnt the history of the rescue. Immediately Miss Maybourne's shriek had roused the ship, and I had sprung overboard to her assistance, the chief officer, who was on the bridge, ran to the engine-room telegraph and gave the signal to stop the vessel; the second officer by this time, with commendable activity, had accompanied the carpenter, who among others had heard the alarm, to one of the quarter boats, and had her ready for lowering by the time a crew was collected. At first they had some difficulty in discovering us, but once they did so they lost no time in picking us up. Miss Maybourne was quite unconscious when they took her from my arms, and I believe as soon as I felt myself relieved of her weight I too lost my senses and began to sink. A boat-hook, however, soon brought me to the surface. Directly we reached the ship's deck the captain gave orders that I should be conveyed to an empty cabin at the end of the saloon, and it was here that I found myself when I returned to consciousness.

For what length of time I slept after the doctor and Miss Maybourne's uncle left the cabin I cannot say. I only know that when I woke the former would not hear of my getting up as I desired to do, but bade me make the best of a bad job and remain where I was until he examined me the following morning. It must have been after breakfast that he came to see me, for I heard the bell go, and half an hour later the voices of the passengers die away as they left the table and went on deck.

"Good morning, Mr. Wrexford," he said, as he shut the door behind him and came over to the bunk. "How are you feeling today? Pretty well, I hope?"

"I feel quite myself again," I answered. "I want to get up. This lying in bed is dreary work."

"I daresay you find it so. Anyway, I'll not stop you from getting up now, if you're so minded; that is provided you eat a good breakfast first."

"I think I can meet you on that ground," I said with a laugh. "I'm as hungry as a hunter. I hope they're going to give me something pretty soon."

"I can satisfy you up on that point," he replied. "I saw the steward preparing the tray as I came through the saloon. Yes, you must hurry up and get on deck, for the ladies are dying to shake you by the hand. I suppose you're not aware that you are the hero of the hour?"

"I'm sorry to hear it," I said in all sincerity. "There has been a terrible lot of fuss made over a very simple action."

"Nonsense, my dear fellow, there hasn't been anything said yet. You wait till old Manstone gets hold of you. He would have said his say yesterday but for my preventing him, and ever since then he has been bottling it up for you when you're well enough to receive it."

"Who is this Mr. Manstone of whom you speak? I don't think I know him."

"Why you must remember, he's Miss Maybourne's uncle—the old gentleman who was in here with me yesterday when you came to your senses again. You must have seen him walking with her on deck—a fine, military-looking old chap, with a big grey moustache."

"Now that you describe him, I remember him perfectly," I said; "but I had never heard his name before. I wish you'd tell him from me that I don't want anything more said about the matter. If they want to reward me, let them do it by forgetting all about it. They couldn't do anything that would please me more."

"Why, what a modest chap you are, to be sure," said the doctor. "Most men would want the Royal Humane Society's medal, and some would even aspire to purses of sovereigns."

"Very probably. But down on my luck, as I am, I don't want either. The less notoriety I derive, the happier man I shall be. To change the subject, I hope Miss Maybourne is better?"

"Oh, she's almost herself again now. I expect to have her up and about again today. Surely you will not mind receiving her thanks?"

"I should not be so churlish, I hope," I remarked; "but all the same, I would rather she said nothing about the matter. That is the worst part of doing anything a little out of the ordinary: one must always be thanked, and praised, and made a fuss of till one begins to regret ever having committed an action that could produce such disastrous results."

"Come, come, you're looking at the matter in a very dismal light, I must say," he cried. "Nine out of every ten men, I'm certain, would have given their ears for the chance you had of rescuing Agnes May-bourne. That it should have come to a man who can't appreciate his good fortune seems like the irony of Fate."

I was about to reply to his jesting speech in a similar strain when there was a tap at the door, and a steward entered bearing a tray. The smell of the food was as good as a tonic to me, and when the doctor had propped me up so that I could get at it in comfort, I set to work. He then left me to myself while he went to see his other patient—the lady of whom we had just been speaking—promising to return in a quarter of an hour to help me dress.

I had just finished my meal, and was placing the tray upon the floor in such a way that the things upon it could not be spilt if the vessel should roll, when there came another tap at the door, and in response to my cry "come in," the captain of the ship appeared, and behind him the elderly gentleman whom the doctor had described to me as Miss Maybourne's uncle, under whose care she was travelling to South Africa.

"Good morning, Mr. Wrexford," said the captain, politely, as he advanced towards me and held out his hand. "I hope you are feeling better?"

"I am perfectly well again now, thank you," I replied. "The doctor is going to let me get up in a few minutes, and then I shall be ready to return to my old quarters forward."

"And that is the very matter I have come in to see you about," said the skipper. "First, however, I must tell you what the entire ship's company, both passengers and crew, think of your bravery the night before last. It was as nobly done, sir, as anything I have ever seen, and I heartily congratulate you upon it."

"Thank you very much," I answered; "but I must really ask you to say no more about it. I have already been thanked ever so much more than I deserve."

"That could not be," impetuously broke in Mr. Manstone, who had not spoken hitherto. "On my own behalf and that of my niece I, too, thank you most heartily; and you may rest assured I shall take care that a full and proper account of it is given my brother when I reach South Africa."

"Until we do so, I hope, Mr. Wrexford," said the skipper, "that you will take up your quarters in this cabin, and consider yourself a saloon passenger. I'm sure the owners would wish it, and for my part I shall be proud to have you among us."

"And I say 'Hear, hear!' to that," added Mr. Manstone.

For a moment I hardly knew what to say. I was touched by his kindness in making the offer, but in my position I could not dream of accepting it. This notoriety was likely to do me quite enough harm as it was.

"I thank you," I said at last, "and I hope you will fully understand how grateful I am to you for the kindness which prompts the offer. But I think I will remain in my old quarters forward, if you have no objection. I am quite comfortable there; and as I made my choice on principle at the beginning, I think, with your permission, I would rather not change it now."

"But my dear sir," began the captain, "you must let us show our appreciation in some practical form. We could never let you off quietly, as you seem to wish."

"You have already done more than enough," I answered. "You have told me what you thought of my action, and you have also made me this offer, the value of which, you may be quite sure, I fully appreciate. I have felt compelled to decline it, and under those circumstances I think it would be best to let the subject drop.

"You are too modest by half, Mr. Wrexford," said Miss Maybourne's uncle. "Far too modest."

For some time the two gentlemen did their best to persuade me to forego my decision, but, hard as they tried, they did not succeed. There were so many reasons why I should not take up my residence among the first saloon passengers aft, and as I reviewed them in my mind, I became more than ever convinced that it would be madness for me to forego my resolution.

When they discovered that I was not to be moved they shook hands again, and then left me. Five minutes later the doctor came in to help me dress. He carried a bundle of clothes in his arms, and when he had shut the door behind him he threw them on the locker under the porthole.

"Your own clothes, I'm sorry to say, Wrexford," he began, "are completely spoiled; so if you'll allow me, I'm going to lend you these till you can see about some more. We are men of pretty much the same build, so what fits me should fit you, and *vice versa*. Now, if you're ready, let me give you a hand to dress, for I want to get you on deck into the fresh air as soon as possible."

Half an hour later I was ready to leave my cabin. The doctor's clothes fitted me admirably, and after I had given a look round to see that I had not left anything behind me, I followed the medico out into the saloon. Fortunately, there were very few people about, but, to my horror, those who were there would insist upon shaking hands with me, and telling me what they thought of my action before they would let me escape. To add to my discomfort, when I left the saloon and passed along the spar deck towards my own quarters I had to run the gauntlet of the rest of the passengers, who clustered round me, and overwhelmed me with a chorus of congratulations on my recovery. I doubt very much if ever there was more fuss made over an act of common humanity than that made by the passengers of the *Fiji Princess* over mine. If I had saved the lives of the whole ship's company, captain and stokers included, there could not have been more said about it.

Reaching my own quarters forward I went down to my berth, in search of a pipe and a pouch of tobacco, and when I had found them, sat myself down on the fore-hatch and began to smoke. It was a lovely morning, a merry breeze hummed in the shrouds, and the great steamer was ploughing her way along with an exhilarating motion that brought my strength back quicker than any doctor's physic. On the bridge my old friend the second officer was pacing up and down, and when he saw me he came to the rail, and waved his hand in welcome.

The chief steward also found me out, and embraced the opportunity for telling me that my conduct reminded him of a cousin's exploits in the Hooghly, which said narrative I felt constrained to swallow with a few grains of salt. When he left me I sat where I was and thought how pleasant it was, after all, to find that there were still people in the world with sufficiently generous natures to appreciate a fellow creature's actions. One question, however, haunted me continually: What would the folk aboard this ship say when they knew my secret? And, above all, what would Miss Agnes Maybourne think when she should come to hear it?

Chapter 5

The Wreck of the Fiji Princess

That afternoon I was sitting in my usual place on the fore-hatch, smoking and thinking about our next port of call, and what a miserable figure I should cut before the ship's company if by any chance I should be arrested there, when I became conscious that someone had come along the hurricane deck and was leaning on the rails gazing down at me. I looked up, to discover that it was none other than Miss Maybourne. Directly she saw that I was aware of her presence she moved towards the ladder on the port side and came down it towards where I sat. Her dress was of some dark-blue material, probably serge, and was cut in such a fashion that it showed her beautiful figure to the very best advantage. A sweeter picture of an English maiden of gentle birth than she presented as she came down the steps it would have been difficult to find. Kindness and sincerity were the chief characteristics of her face, and I felt a thrill of pride run through me as I reflected that she owed her life to me.

When she came up to where I stood, for I had risen on seeing her approaching me, she held out her hand with a frank gesture, and said, as she looked me in the eyes:

"Mr. Wrexford, you saved my life the night before last, and this is the first opportunity I have had of expressing my gratitude to you. I cannot tell you how grateful I am, but I ask you to believe that so long as I live I shall never cease to bless you for your heroism."

To return an answer to such a speech would not seem a difficult matter at first thought, and yet I found it harder than I would at any other time have imagined. To let her see that I did not want to be thanked, and at the same time not to appear churlish, was a very difficult matter. However, I stumbled out some sort of a reply, and then asked her how she had managed to fall overboard in that extraordinary fashion.

"I really cannot tell you," she answered, without hesitation. "I was leaning against the rails of the hurricane deck talking to Miss Dursley and Mr. Spicer, when something behind me gave way, and then over I went backwards into the water. Oh, you can't imagine the feeling of utter helplessness that came over me as I rose to the surface and saw the great ship steaming away. Then you nobly sprang in to my assistance, and once more hope came into my heart. But for you I might now be dead, floating about in the depths of that great sea. Oh! it is an awful thought."

She trembled like a leaf at the notion, and swept her pretty hands across her face as if to brush away the thought of such a thing.

"It was a very narrow escape," I said. "I must confess myself that I thought the boat would never reach us. And yet how cool and collected you were!"

"It would have meant certain death to have been anything else," she answered. "My father will be indeed grateful to you when he hears of your bravery. I am his only child, and if anything were to happen to me I don't think he would survive the shock."

"I am very grateful to Providence for having given me such an opportunity of averting so terrible a sorrow," I said. "But I fear, like everyone else, you attach too much importance to what I did. I simply acted as any other decent man would have done had he been placed in a similar position."

"You do not do yourself justice," she said. "But, at any rate, you have the satisfaction of knowing, if it is any satisfaction to you, that Agnes Maybourne owes her life to you, and that she will never forget the service you have rendered her."

The conversation was growing embarrassing, so I turned it into another channel as soon as possible. At the same time I wanted to find out something which had been puzzling me ever since I had first seen her face, and that was where I had met her before. When I put the question she looked at me in surprise.

"Do you know, Mr. Wrexford," she said, "that I was going to ask you that self-same question? And for rather a strange reason. On the night before we sailed, you must understand, I was sleeping at the house of an aunt who lives a few miles outside Southampton. I went to bed at ten o'clock, after a rather exciting day, feeling very tired. Almost as soon as my head was upon the pillow I fell asleep, and did not wake again until about half-past twelve o'clock, when I suddenly found myself wide awake sitting up in bed, with a man's pale and agonised face staring at me from the opposite wall. For a few moments I thought I must be still asleep and dreaming, or else seeing a phantom. Almost before I could have counted five it faded away, and I saw no more of it. From that time forward, like yourself, I was haunted with the desire to remember if I had ever seen the man's face before, and, if so, where. You may imagine my surprise, therefore, when I found the owner of it sitting before me on the hatch of the very steamer that was to take me to South Africa. Can you account for it?"

"Not in the least," I answered. "Mine was very much the same sort of experience, only that I was wide awake and driving down a prosaic London street when it happened. I, too, was endeavouring to puzzle it out the other day when I looked up and found you standing on the deck above me. It seems most uncanny."

"It may have been a warning from Providence to us which we have not the wit to understand."

"A warning it certainly was," I said truthfully, but hardly in the fashion she meant. "And one of the most extraordinary ever vouchsafed to mortal man."

"A fortunate one for me," she answered with a smile, and then offering me her dainty little hand, she bade me "goodbye," and went up the steps again to the hurricane deck.

From that time forward I saw a good deal of Miss Maybourne; so much so that we soon found ourselves upon comparatively intimate terms. Though I believe to others she was inclined to be a little haughty, to me she was invariably kindness and courtesy itself. Nothing could have been more pleasant than her manner when we were together; and you may be very sure, after all that I had lately passed through, I could properly appreciate her treatment of me. To be taken out of my miserable state of depression, and, after so many years of ill fortune, to be treated with consideration and respect, made me feel towards her as I had never done towards a woman in my life before. I could have fallen at her feet and kissed her shoes in gratitude for the luxury of my conversation with her. It was the luckiest chance for both of us when I went aft that night to see that photograph in the second officer's cabin. Had I not been there I should in all probability never have heard Miss Maybourne's shriek as she went over the side, and in that case she would most certainly have been drowned; for I knew that, unaided and weighed down by her wet clothes as she was, she could never have kept afloat till the boat reached her. Strange as it may seem, I could not help deriving a sort of satisfaction from this thought. It was evident that my refusal to accept the captain's kind offer to take possession, for the rest of the voyage, of the vacant berth aft, had created a little surprise among the passengers. Still, I believe it prejudiced the majority in my favour. At any rate, I soon discovered that my humble position forward was to make no sort of difference in their treatment of me; and many an enjoyable pipe I smoked, and twice as many talks I had with one and another, sitting on the cable range, or leaning over the bows watching the vessel's nose cutting its way through the clear green water.

One morning, after breakfast, I was forward watching the effect just mentioned, and, as usual, thinking what my sensations would be if I should be arrested at Tenerife, when I heard footsteps behind me. On looking round I discovered Miss Maybourne and the skipper coming towards me.

"Good morning, Mr. Wrexford," said the former, holding out her hand. "What a constant student of nature you are, to be sure. Every morning lately I have seen you standing where you are now, looking across the sea. My curiosity could hold out no longer, so this morning I asked Captain Hawkins to escort me up here in order that I might ask you what you see."

"I'm afraid you will hardly be repaid for your trouble, Miss Maybourne," I answered with a smile, as the captain, after shaking hands with me and wishing me good morning, left us to speak to one of the officers who had come forward in search of him.

"But surely you must see something—King Neptune, or at least a mermaid," she persisted. "You are always watching the water."

"Perhaps I do see something," I answered bitterly. "Yes; I think you are right. When I look over the sea like that I am watching a man's wasted life. I see him starting on his race with everything in his favour that the world can give. I see a school career of mediocrity, and a university life devoid of any sort of success; I can see a continuity of profitless wanderings about the world in the past, and I am beginning to believe that I can make out another just commencing. Disgrace behind, and disgrace ahead; I think that is the picture I have before me when I look across the sea, Miss Maybourne. It is an engrossing, but hardly a pretty one, is it?"

"You are referring to your own life, I suppose?" she said, quietly. "Well, all I can say is that, from what I have seen of you, I should consider that you are hardly the man to do yourself justice."

"God forbid," I answered. "If I were to do that it would be impossible for me to live. No; I endeavour, as far as I am able, to forget what my past has been."

She approached a step closer to me, and placed her little white hand on my arm as it lay on the bulwark before her.

"Mr. Wrexford," she said, with an earnestness I had not hitherto noticed in her, "I hope you will not consider me impertinent if I say that I should like to know your history. Believe me, I do not say this out of any idle curiosity, but because I hope and believe that it may be in my power to help you. Remember what a debt of gratitude I owe you for your bravery the other night. I cannot believe that a man who would risk his life, as you did then, can be the sort of man you have just depicted. Do you feel that you can trust me sufficiently to tell me about yourself?"

"What there is to tell, with certain reservations, of course, you shall hear. There is no one to whom I would confess so readily as to yourself. I will not insult you by asking you to let what I tell you remain a, secret between us, but I will ask you to try not to judge me too harshly."

"You may be sure I shall not do that," she replied; and then realising what her words implied, she hung her head with a pretty show of confusion. I saw what was passing in her mind, and to help her out of her difficulty plunged into the story of my miserable career. I told her of my old home in Cornwall, of my mother's death, and my father's antipathy to me on that account. On my Eton and Oxford life I dwelt but lightly, winding up with the reason of my being "sent down," and the troubles at home that followed close upon it. I described my bush life in Australia, and told her of the great disappointment to which I had been subjected over the gold mine, suppressing Bartrand's name, and saying nothing of the hatred I had entertained for him.

"After that," I said in conclusion, "I decided that I was tired of Australia, and, having inherited a little money from my father, came home, intending to get something to do and settle down in London. But I very soon tired of England, as I tired of every other place and hence my reason for going out to seek my fortune in South Africa. Now I think I have given you a pretty good idea of my past. It's not an edifying history, is it? It seems to me a parson might moralise very satisfactorily upon it."

"It is very, very sad," she answered. "Oh, Mr. Wrexford, how bitterly you must regret your wasted opportunities."

"Regret!" I said. "The saddest word in the English language. Yes, I think I do regret."

"You only 'think?' Are you not sure? From your tale one would suppose you were very sorry."

"Yes, I think I regret. But how can I be certain? The probabilities are that if I had my chance over again I should do exactly the same. As Gordon, the Australian poet, sings:—

"'For good undone, and gifts misspent and resolutions vain,

94

"'Tis somewhat late to trouble. This I know—

"I should live the same life, if I had to live again;

"And the chances are I go where most men go.'

"It's not a pretty thought, perhaps, to think that one's bad actions are the outcome of a bad nature, but one is compelled to own that it is true."

"You mustn't talk like that, Mr. Wrexford," she cried; "indeed, you mustn't. In all probability you have a long life before you; and who knows what the future may have in store for you? All this trouble that you have suffered may be but to fit you for some great success in after life."

"There can never be any success for me, Miss Maybourne," I said, more bitterly than I believe I had spoken yet. "There is no chance at all of that. Success and I parted company long since, and can never be reconciled to each other again. To the end of my days I shall be a lonely, homeless man, without ambition, without hope, and without faith in any single thing. God knows I am paying dearly for all I have done and all that I have failed to do."

"But there is still time for you to retrieve everything. Surely that must be the happiest thought in this frail world of ours. God, in His mercy, gives us a chance to atone for whatever we have done amiss. Believe me, I can quite realize what you feel about yourself. But at the same time, from what I have seen of you, I expect you make more of it than it really deserves."

"No, no; I can never paint what I have done in black enough colours. I am a man eternally disgraced. You try to comfort me in your infinite compassion, but you can never take away from me, try how you will, the awful skeleton that keeps me company night and day—I mean the recollection of the past."

She looked at me with tears of compassion in her lovely eyes. I glanced at her face and then turned away and stared across the sea. Never in my life before had hope seemed so dead in my heart. Now, for the first time, I realized in all its naked horror the effect of the dastardly deed I had committed. Henceforward I was a social leper, condemned to walk the world, crying, "Unclean! unclean!"

"I am so sorry—so very sorry for you," Miss Maybourne said, after the little pause that followed my last speech. "You cannot guess how much your story has affected me. It is so very terrible to see a man so richly endowed as yourself cast down with such despair. You must fight against it, Mr. Wrexford. It cannot be as bad as you think."

"I am afraid I am past all fighting now, Miss Maybourne," I answered. "But I will try, if you bid me do so."

As I spoke I looked at her again. This time her eyes met mine fearlessly, but as they did so a faint blush suffused her face.

"I bid you try," she said very softly. "God give you grace, and grant you may succeed."

"If anything can make me succeed," I replied, "it will be your good wishes. I will do my best, and man cannot do more. You have cheered me up wonderfully, and I thank you from the bottom of my heart."

"You must not do that. I hope now I shall not see you looking any more across the sea in the same way that you were this morning. You are to cheer up, and I shall insist that you report progress to me every day. If I discover any relapse, remember, I shall not spare you, and my anger will be terrible. Now goodbye; I see my uncle signalling to me from the hurricane deck. It is time for me to read to him."

"Goodbye," I said, "and may God bless you for your kindness to one who really stood in want of it."

After that conversation I set myself to take a more hopeful view of my situation. I told myself that, provided I managed to reach my destination undetected, I would work as never man ever worked before to make an honourable place for myself among those with whom my lot should be cast. The whole of the remainder of my life I vowed, God helping me, should be devoted to the service of my fellow creatures, and then on the strength of their respect and esteem I would be able to face whatever punishment Providence should decree as the result of my sin. In the strength of this firm resolve I found myself becoming a happier man than I had been for years past.

By this time we had left Madeira behind us, and were fast approaching Tenerife. In another day and a half, at the longest calculation, I should know my fate.

That night I had been smoking for some time on the fo'c'sle, but after supper, feeling tired, had gone to my bunk at an earlier hour than usual. For some reason my dreams were the reverse of good, and more than once I woke in a fright, imagining myself in danger. To such a state of nervousness did this fright at last bring me that, unable to sleep any longer, I got out of bed and dressed myself. When I was fully attired I sought the deck, to discover a fine starlight night with a nice breeze blowing. I made my way to my usual spot forward, and, leaning on the bulwark, looked down at the sea. We were now in the region of phosphorescent water, and the liquid round the boat's cutwater sparkled and glimmered as if decked with a million diamonds. In the apex of the bows the look-out stood, while black and silent behind him the great ship showed twice its real size in the darkness.

The lamps shone brilliantly from the port and starboard lighthouses, and I could just manage to distinguish the officer of the watch pacing up and down the bridge with the regularity of an automaton. There was something about the silence, and that swift rushing through the water—for we must have been doing a good sixteen knots—that was most exhilarating. For something like an hour I stood and enjoyed it. My nervousness soon left me, and to my delight I found that I was beginning to feel sleepy again. At the end of the time stated I made my way towards the ladder leading from the topgallant fo'c'sle to the spar deck, intending to go below, but just as I reached it a man appeared from the shadow of the alley way, approached the bell, and struck three strokes—half-past one—upon it. At the same instant the look-out called "All's well!" The words were scarcely out of his mouth before there was a shuddering and grinding crash forward, then a sudden stoppage and heeling over of the great craft, and after that a dead, ghastly silence, in which the beating of one's heart could be distinctly heard.

The confusion of the next few minutes can be better imagined than described. The vessel had slipped off and cleared herself from the obstruction whatever it was that had caught her, and was now going on her way again, but at reduced speed. I heard the skipper open his cabin door and run up the ladder to the bridge shouting, "What has happened?" The officer of the watch replied, but at the same instant the sailors and firemen off duty came pouring out of the fo'c'sle shouting, "She's sinking! She's sinking!" The engine-room telegraph had meanwhile been rung, and the ship was perceptibly stopping. I stood where I was, wondering all the time what I had better do.

"Every man to his station," bellowed the skipper, coming to the rails of the bridge, and tunnelling his mouth with his hands so that his voice might be heard above the din. "Be steady, men, and remember that the first man who gives any trouble I shall shoot without warning." Then, turning to the chief officer, he signed to him to take the carpenter and hasten forward in an endeavour to ascertain the nature of the injuries the vessel had received.

By this time all the passengers were on deck, the women pale and trembling, and the men endeavouring to calm and reassure them as well as they were able. I made my way up the ladder to the hurricane deck, and as I did so felt the vessel give a heavy lurch, and then sink a little deeper in the water. A moment later the chief officer and carpenter crossed the well and hurried up the ladder to the bridge. We all waited in silence for the verdict that meant life or death to everybody.

"Ladies and gentleman," said the skipper, coming down from the bridge, after a short conversation with them, and approaching the. anxious group by the chart room door, "I am sorry to have to tell you that the ship has struck a rock, and in a short time will be no longer habitable for us. I want, however, to reassure you. There is ample boat accommodation for twice the number of our ship's company, so that you need have no possible fear about leaving her. How long it will be before we must go I cannot say. There is a strong bulkhead between us and the water which may stand long enough for us to reach Tenerife, which is only about a hundred miles distant. I think, however, it would be better for us to be prepared for any emergency. The ladies will therefore remain on deck, while the gentlemen go down to their cabins and bring them such warm clothing as they can find. The night is cold, and in case we may have to take to the boats before morning it will be well for everybody to make themselves as warm as possible."

Without more ado the male portion of the passengers ran down the stairway to the saloon like so many rabbits, I following at their heels to see if I could be of assistance. Into the cabins we rushed at random, collecting such articles of apparel as we could find, and carrying them on deck with all possible haste. The necessity for speed was so great that we did not pause to make selection or to inquire as to ownership, but took what we could lay our hands on and were thankful for the find. In the cabin I entered I noticed a pair of cork jackets pushed under a bunk. I dragged them out, and heaped them on the top of the other things I had collected. Then a sudden inspiration seized me. On the rack in the saloon I had noticed a large flask. I took possession of it, and then, collecting the other things I had found, ran on deck again. I could not have been gone half a minute, but even in that short space of time a change had come over the ship. Her bows were lower in the water, and I trembled when I thought of the result of the strain on the bulkhead. I found Miss Maybourne standing just where I had first seen her, at a little distance from the others, aft of the chart-room and beside the engine-room skylight. She was fully dressed, and had a little girl of eight with her, the only daughter of a widow named Bailey, of whom she was very fond.

"Miss Maybourne," I cried, throwing down the things I had brought on the deck as I spoke, and selecting a thick jacket from the heap, "I found these clothes in a cabin. I don't know who they belong to, but you must put on as much as you can wear."

She obeyed me willingly enough, and when I had buttoned the

last garment up I insisted on her putting on one of the cork lifebelts. As soon as she was clothed I put another garment on the child, and then attached the second lifebelt to her body. It was too big for her to wear, but fastened round her shoulders I knew it would answer the same purpose.

"But yourself, Mr. Wrexford?" cried Miss Maybourne, who saw my condition. "You must find a cork jacket for yourself, or you will be drowned."

At the very instant that I was going to answer her the vessel gave a sudden pitch, and before the boats could be lowered or anything be done for the preservation of the passengers, she began to sink rapidly. Seeing that it was hopeless to wait for the boats, I dragged my two companions to the ladder leading to the after spar deck. When I reached it, I tore down the rail just at the spot where Miss Maybourne had fallen overboard on the Spanish coast a few nights before, and, this done, bade them jump into the sea without losing time. Miss Maybourne did so without a second thought; the child, however, hung back, and cried piteously for mercy. But, with the ship sinking so rapidly under us, to hesitate I knew was to be lost, so I caught her by the waist, and, regardless of her screams, threw her over the side. Then, without waiting to see her rise again, I dived in myself. The whole business, from the moment of the first crash to the tune of our springing overboard, had not lasted five minutes. One thing was self-evident—the bulkhead could not have possessed the strength with which it had been credited.

On coming to the surface again I shook myself and looked about me. Behind me was the great vessel, with her decks by this time almost on a level with the water. In another instant she would be gone. True enough, before I had time to take half a dozen strokes there was a terrific explosion, and next instant I was being sucked down and down by the sinking ship. How far I went, or how long I was beneath the waves, I have no possible idea. I only know that if it had lasted much longer I should never have lived to reach the surface again or to tell this tale. But after a little while I found myself rising to the surface, surrounded by wreckage of all sorts and descriptions.

On reaching the top, I looked about me for the boats, which I felt sure I should discover; but, to my surprise, I could not distinguish one. Was it possible that the entire company of the vessel could have gone down with her? The thought was a terrible one, and almost unnerved me. I raised myself in the water as well as I was able, and as I did so I caught sight of two people within a few yards of me. I swam towards them, and to my joy discovered that they were Miss Maybourne and the child upon whom I had fastened the cork life-preservers a few minutes before.

"Oh, Mr. Wrexford," cried Miss Maybourne, in an agonised voice. "What are we to do? This poor child is either dead, or nearly so, and I can see no signs of any boat at all."

"We must continue swimming for a little while," I answered, "and then we may perhaps be picked up. Surely we cannot be the only survivors?"

"My poor, poor uncle!" she cried. "Can he have perished! Oh, it is too awful!"

The cork lifebelts were keeping them up famously, and on that score I felt no anxiety at all. But still the situation was about as desperate as it well could be. I had not the least notion of where we were, and I knew that unless we were picked up we should be better drowned at once than continue to float until we died of starvation. However, I was not going to frighten my only conscious companion by such gloomy anticipations, so I passed my arm round the child's waist and bade Miss Maybourne strike out for the spot where the ill-fated *Fiji Princess* had gone down. At the same time I asked her to keep her eyes open for a boat, or at least a spar of some sort, upon which we could support ourselves until we could find some safer refuge. On the horrors of that ghastly swim it will not be necessary for me to dilate. I must leave my readers to imagine them for themselves. Suffice it that for nearly a quarter of an hour we paddled aimlessly about here and there. But look as we might, not a sign of any other living soul from aboard that ship could we discover, nor anything large enough upon which three people could rest. At last, just as I was beginning to despair of saving the lives of those whom Providence had so plainly entrusted to my care, I saw ahead of us a large white object, which, upon nearer approach, proved to be one of the overturned lifeboats. I conveyed the good news to Miss Maybourne, and then, with a new burst of energy, swam towards it and caught hold of the keel. She was a big craft, and, to my delight, rode high enough out of the water to afford us a resting-place. To pull myself and the child I carried on to her, and to drag Miss Maybourne up after me, was the work of a very few moments. Once there, we knew we were safe for the present.

CHAPTER 6

The Salvages

For some minutes we lay upon the bottom of the up-turned boat too exhausted to speak. I still held the unconscious form of little Esther Bailey in my arms, and protected her, as well as I was able, from the marauding seas. Though the waves about us upheld many evidences of the terrible catastrophe, such as gratings, broken spars, portions of boat gear, still, to my astonishment, I could discover no signs of any bodies. Once, however, I was successful in obtaining possession of something which I knew would be worth its weight in gold to us: it was an oar, part of the equipment of one of the quarter boats I imagined; half the blade was missing, but with what remained it would still be possible for us to propel the boat on which we had taken refuge.

What a terrible position was ours, lodged on the bottom of that overturned lifeboat, icy seas breaking upon us every few seconds, the knowledge of our gallant ship, with all our friends aboard, lying fathoms deep below the surface of the waves, and the remembrance that the same fate might be ours at any moment; no possible notion of where we were, no provisions or means of sustaining life, and but small chance of being picked up by any passing boat!

It was Miss Maybourne who spoke first, and, as usual, her conversation was not about herself.

"Mr. Wrexford," she said, and her teeth chattered as she spoke, "at any risk something must be done for that poor child you hold in your arms, she will die else. Do you think we could manage to get her up further on to the boat and then try to chafe her back to consciousness?"

"By all means let us try," I answered, "though I fear it will prove a difficult matter. She seems very far gone, poor little mite."

With the utmost care I clambered further up the boat till I sat with my burden astride the keel. In the darkness we could scarcely see each other, but once the child was placed between us we set to work rubbing her face and hands and trying by every means in our power to restore consciousness. Suddenly a great thought occurred to me. I remembered the flask I had taken from the cabin where I had found the clothes. In an instant I had dived my hand into my pocket in search of it, almost trembling with fear lest by any chance it should have slipped out when I had dived overboard, but to my delight it was still there. I had pulled it out and unscrewed the stopper before anyone could have counted a dozen, taking the precaution to taste it in order to see that it was all right before I handed it to Miss Maybourne. It was filled with the finest French brandy, and, having discovered this, I bade her take a good drink at it. When she had done so I put it to the child's mouth and forced a small quantity between her lips.

"Surely you are going to drink some yourself," said my companion, as she saw me screw on the top and replace it in my pocket.

But I was not going to do anything of the sort. I did not need it so vitally as my charges, and I knew that there was not enough in the bottle to justify me in wasting even a drop. I explained this and then asked her if she felt any warmer.

"Much warmer," she answered, "and I think Esther here feels better too. Let us chafe her hands again."

We did so, and in a few minutes had the satisfaction of hearing the poor mite utter a little moan. In less than an hour she was conscious once more, but so weak that it seemed as if the first breath of wind that came our way would blow the life out of her tiny body. Poor little soul, if it was such a terrible experience for us, what must it have been for her?

What length of time elapsed from the time of our heading the boat before daylight came to cheer us I cannot say, but, cramped up as we were, the darkness seemed to last for centuries. For periods of something like half an hour at a time we sat without speaking, thinking of all that had happened since darkness had fallen the night before, and remembering the rush and agony of those last few dreadful minutes on board, and the awful fact that all those whom we had seen so well and strong only a few hours before were now cold and lifeless for ever. Twice I took out my flask and insisted on Miss Maybourne and the child swallowing a portion of the spirit. Had I not brought that with me, I really believe neither of them would have seen another sunrise.

Suddenly Miss Maybourne turned to me.

"Listen, Mr Wrexford," she cried. "What is that booming noise? Is it thunder?"

I did as she commanded, but for some moments could hear nothing save the splashing of the waves upon the boat's planks. Then a dull, sullen noise reached my ears that might very well have been mistaken for the booming of thunder at a great distance. Thunder it certainly was, but not of the kind my companion imagined. It was the thunder of surf, and that being so, I knew there must be land at no great distance from us. I told her my conjecture, and then we set ourselves to wait, with what patience we could command, for daylight.

What a strange and, I might almost say, weird dawn that was! It was like the beginning of a new life under strangely altered conditions. The first shafts of light found us still clinging to the keel of the overturned boat, gazing hopelessly about us. When it was light enough to discern our features, we two elder ones looked at each other, and were horrified to observe the change which the terrible sufferings of the night had wrought in our countenances. Miss Maybourne's face was white and drawn, and she looked years older than her real age. I could see by the way she glanced at me that I also was changed. The poor little girl Esther hardly noticed either of us, but lay curled up as close as possible to her sister in misfortune.

As the light widened, the breeze, which had been just perceptible all night, died away, and the sea became as calm as a mill pond. I looked about me for something to explain the noise of breakers we had heard, but at first could see nothing. When, however, I turned my head to the west I almost shouted in my surprise, for, scarcely a mile distant from us, was a comparatively large island, surrounded by three or four reef-like smaller ones. On the larger island a peak rose ragged and rough to a height of something like five hundred feet, and upon the shore, on all sides, I could plainly discern the surf breaking upon the rocks. As soon as I saw it I turned excitedly to Miss Maybourne.

"We're saved!" I cried, pointing in the direction of the island; "look there—look there!"

She turned round on the boat as well as she was able and when she saw the land, stared at it for some moments in silence. Then with a cry, "Thank God!" she dropped her head on to her hands and I could see her shoulders shaken by convulsive sobs. I did my best to console her, but she soon recovered of her own accord, and addressed herself to me again.

"These must be the Salvage Islands of which the captain was speaking at dinner last night," she said. "How can we reach the shore? Whatever happens, we must not drift past them."

"Have no fear," I answered; "I will not let that happen, come what may."

So saying, I shifted my position to get a better purchase of the water, and then using the broken oar began to paddle in the direction of the biggest island. It was terribly hard work, and a very few moments showed me that after all the horrors of the night I was as weak as a kitten. But by patience and perseverance I at last got the boat's head round and began to lessen the distance that separated us. At the end of nearly half an hour we were within an hundred yards of the shore. By this time I had decided on a landing-place. It was a little bit of open sandy beach, perhaps sixty yards long, without rocks, and boasting less surf than any other part of the island I could see. In addition to these advantages it was nearer, and I noted that that particular side of the island looked more sheltered than the others.

Towards this haven of refuge I accordingly made my way, hoping that I should not find any unexpected danger lurking there when I should be too close in to be able to get out again. It was most necessary for every reason that we should save the boat from damage, for by her aid alone could we hope to make our way out to passing ships, or, if the worst came, to strike out on our own account for the Canary Islands. That the rocks we were now making were the Salvage Group, as Miss Maybourne had said, I had no doubt in my own mind, though how the skipper came to be steering such a course was more than I could tell.

At last we were so close that I could see the sandy bottom quite distinctly only a fathom or so below us. A better landing-place no man could have wished for. When we were near enough to make it safe I slid off the boat into the water, which was just up to my hips, and began to push her in before me. Having grounded her I took Miss Maybourne in my arms and carried her out of the water up on to the beach and then went back for the child. My heart was so full of gratitude at being on dry land again and having saved the two lives entrusted to my care that I could have burst into tears on the least encouragement.

Having got my charges safely ashore, I waded into the water again to have a look at the boat and, if possible, to discover what had made her capsize. She was so precious to us that I dared not leave her for an instant. To my delight she looked as sound as the day she had been turned out of the shipwright's yard, and I felt if once I could turn her over she would carry us as well as any boat ever built. But how to do that, full of water as she was, was a problem I could not for the life of me solve. Miss Maybourne's wits, however, were sharper than mine and helped me out of the difficulty.

"There is a rope in her bows, Mr. Wrexford," she cried; "why not drive the oar into the sand and fasten her to that? then when the tide goes out—you see it is nearly full now—she will be left high and dry, the water will have run out of her, and then you will be able to do whatever you please to her."

"You've solved the difficulty for me in a very simple fashion," I answered. "What a duffer I was not to have thought of that."

"The mouse can help the lion sometimes, you see," she replied, with a wan little smile that went to my heart.

Having got my party safely ashore, and made my boat fast to the oar, as proposed by Miss Maybourne, the next thing to be done was to discover a suitable spot where we might fix our camp, and then to endeavour to find some sort of food upon which we might sustain our lives until we should be rescued. I explained my intentions to my elder companion, and then, leaving them on the beach together, climbed the hillside to explore. On the other sides of the island the peak rose almost precipitously from the beach, and upon the side on which we stood it was, in many places, pretty stiff climbing. At last, however, to my great delight, on a small plateau some thirty yards long by twenty deep, I discovered a cave that looked as if it would suit my purpose to perfection. It was not a large affair, but quite big enough to hold the woman and the child even when lying at full length. To add to my satisfaction, the little strip of land outside was covered with a coarse grass, a quantity of which I gathered and spread about in the cave to serve as a bed. This, with a few armfuls of dry seaweed, which I knew I should be able to obtain on the beach, made an excellent couch.

What, however, troubled me more than anything else, was the fear that the island might contain no fresh water. But my doubts on that head were soon set at rest, for on the hillside, a little below the plateau on which I had discovered the cave, was a fair-sized pool, formed by a hollow in a rock, which, when I tasted it, I found to contain water, a little brackish it is true, but still quite drinkable. There was an abundance of fuel everywhere, and if only I could manage to find some shell fish on the rocks, or hit upon some way of catching the fish swimming in the bay, I thought we might manage to keep ourselves alive until we were picked up by some passing boat.

Descending to the beach again, I told Miss Maybourne of my discoveries, and then taking poor little Esther in my arms we set off up the hill towards the cave. On reaching it I made them as comfortable as I could and then descended to the shore again in search of food.

Leaving the little sandy bay where we had landed, I tramped along as far as some large rocks I could see a couple of hundred yards or so to my left hand. As I went I thought of the strangeness of my position. How inscrutable are the ways of Providence! However much I might have hated Bartrand, had I not met Nikola I should in all probability never have attempted to revenge myself on him. In that case I should not have been compelled to fly from England at a moment's notice, and should certainly not have sailed aboard the *Fiji Princess*. Presuming, therefore, that all would have gone on without me as it had done with me, Miss Maybourne would have been drowned off the coast of Spain, and the *Fiji Princess* would have gone to the bottom and nobody have been left to tell the tale. It was a curious thought, and one that sent a strange thrill through me to think what good had indirectly resulted from my misfortune.

Reaching the rocks mentioned above, I clambered on to them and began my search for limpets. Once more Fate was kind to me. The stones abounded with the molluscs, the majority of which were of larger sizes than I had met with in my life before. In considerably less than five minutes I had detached a larger supply than our little party would be able to consume all day.

My harvest gathered, I filled my handkerchief and set off for the plateau again. About half-way I looked up, to find Miss Maybourne standing at the cave mouth watching me. Directly she saw me approaching, she waved her hand to encourage me, and that little gesture set my heart beating like a wheat-flail. It was the first dawning of a knowledge that was soon to give me the greatest pain I had ever yet known in my life.

On reaching the plateau, I hastened towards her and placed my spoils at her feet.

"Fortune is indeed kind to us," I said. "See what splendid limpets I have obtained from the rocks down yonder. I was beginning to be afraid lest there should be nothing edible on the island."

"But how are we to cook them?" she answered, with a little shudder, for I must confess the things did not look appetising. "I could not eat them raw."

"I have no intention that you shall," I cried, reassuringly. "I am going to light a fire and cook them for you."

"But how can you light a fire? Have you any matches dry enough?"

I took from my waistcoat pocket a little Japanese match-box, the lid of which closed with a strong spring, and opened it in some trepidation. So much depended on the discovery I was about to make. With a trembling hand I pressed back the lid, and tipped the contents into my palm. Fortunately, the strength of the spring and the tight fit of the cover rendered the box almost water-tight, and for this reason the dozen or so matches it contained were only a little damp. In their present state, however, they were quite useless.

"I think," I said, turning them over and examining them closely, "that if I place them in a dry spot they will soon be fit for use."

"Let me do it for you," she said, holding out her hand. "You have done everything so far. Why should I not be allowed to help you?"

"I shall be only too glad to let you," I answered. "I want to cut the fish out of their shells and prepare them for the fire."

So saying, I handed over the precious matches to her care; and then, taking my clasp knife from my pocket, set about my work. When it was finished, and I had prepared an ample meal for three people, I placed it in a safe place in the cave, and then set about collecting a supply of fuel for the fire.

When this work was done I determined to climb to a point of vantage and search the offing for a sail. Just as I was starting, however, Miss Maybourne called to me to know where I was going. I informed her of my errand, and she immediately asked permission to accompany me. I told her that I should be very glad of her company, and when she had looked into the cave at the little child, who was still fast asleep, we set off together.

From the encampment we climbed the hillside for a hundred feet or so, and then, reaching another small plateau, turned our attention to the sea. Side by side we looked across the expanse of blue water for the sail that was to bring deliverance to us. But no sign of any vessel could be seen—only a flock of seagulls screeching round the rocks below us, and another wheeling roundabout in the blue sky above our heads.

"Nothing there," I said bitterly. "Not a single sail of any kind."

A fit of anger, as sudden as the squall that ruffles the surface of a mountain lake, rose in my breast against Fate. I shook my fist fiercely at the plane of water softly heaving in the sunlight, and but for my companion's presence could have cursed our fate aloud. I suppose Miss Maybourne must have understood, for she came a little closer to me and laid her hand soothingly upon my arm.

"Mr. Wrexford," she said, "surely you who have hitherto been so brave are not going to give way now, just because we cannot see a ship the first time we look for one. No! No! I know you too well, and I cannot believe that."

"You shame me, Miss Maybourne," I replied, recovering myself directly. "Upon my word, you do. I don't know what made me give way like that. I am worse than a baby."

"I won't have you call yourself names either. It was because you are tired and a little run down," she answered. "You have done too much. Oh, Mr. Wrexford, I want you to grant me a favour. I want you to kneel with me while I thank God for His great mercy in sparing our lives. We owe everything to Him. Without His help where should we be now?"

"I will kneel with you with pleasure," I said, "if you wish it, but I am not worthy. I have been too great a sinner for God to listen to me."

"Hush! I cannot let you say that," she went on. "Whatever your past may have been, God will hear you and forgive you if you pray aright. Remember, too, that in my eyes you have atoned for all your past by your care of us last night. Come, let us kneel down here."

So saying, she dropped on to her knees on that little plateau, and without a second's hesitation I followed her example. It must have been a strange sight for the gulls, that lovely girl and myself kneeling, side by side, on that windy hillside. Overhead rose the rugged peak of the mountain, below us was the surf-bound beach, and on all sides the treacherous sea from which we had so lately been delivered. What were the exact words of the prayer Miss Maybourne sent up to the Throne of Grace I cannot now remember; I only know it seemed to me the most beautiful expression of thankfulness for the past, and supplication for guidance and help in the future that it would be possible for a human being to give utterance to. When she had finished we rose, and having given a final glance round, went down the hill again. On reaching our camping-place she went to the cave to ascertain how little Esther was, while I sought the spot where she had set the matches to dry. To my delight they were now ready for use. So placing them back in my box as if they were the greatest treasures I possessed on earth—as they really were just then—I went across to the fire I had built up. Then striking one of the matches upon a stone I lit the grass beneath the sticks, and in less time than it takes to tell had the satisfaction of seeing a fine bonfire blazing before me. This done, I crossed to the cave to obtain the fish I had placed there. On entering, I discovered Miss Maybourne kneeling beside the child.

"How is she now?" I enquired, surprised at discovering the poor little mite still asleep upon the bed of grass.

"She is unconscious again," answered Miss Maybourne, large tears standing in her beautiful eyes as she spoke. "Oh, Mr. Wrexford, what can we do to save her life?"

"Alas! I cannot tell," I replied. "Shall we give her some more brandy? I have still a little left in the flask."

"We might try it," she said. "But I fear it will not be much use. What the poor little thing needs most is a doctor's science and proper nursing. Oh! if I only knew what is really the matter, I might be able to do something for her. But, as it is, I feel powerless to help her at all."

"At any rate, let us try the effect of a few sips of this," I said, as I took the flask from my pocket. "Even if it does no good, it cannot possibly do any harm."

I knelt beside her, and having opened the little child's mouth, poured into it a few drops of the precious spirit. We then set to work and chafed her hands as briskly as possible, and in a few minutes were rewarded by seeing the mite open her eyes and look about her.

"Thank God," said Miss Maybourne, devoutly. "Oh, Esther darling, do you know me? Do you remember Aggie?"

To show that she understood what was said to her, the little one extended her hand and placed it in that of her friend. The action was so full of trust and confidence that it brought the tears to my eyes.

"How do you feel now, darling?" asked her friend, as she lifted the little sufferer into a more comfortable position.

"A pain here," faltered Esther, placing her hand on the side of her head. Then looking round the cave as if in search of someone, she said, "Miss Maybourne, where is mother?"

At this point my pluck forsook me altogether, and seizing the fish for which I had come, I dashed from the cave without waiting to hear what answer the brave girl would give her. When she joined me, ten minutes later, large tears were running down her cheeks. She made no attempt to hide them from me, but came across to where I knelt by the fire, and said, in a choking voice:

"I have been preparing that poor child for the sad news she must soon hear, and I cannot tell you how miserable it has made me. Do you really think in your own heart that we are the only people who escaped from that ill-fated vessel? Isn't it just possible that some other boat may have been lowered, and that the child's mother may be among those who got away in her? Tell me exactly what you think, without hiding anything from me, I implore you."

"Of course it may be just possible, as you say, that a boat did get away; but I must confess that I think it is most, unlikely. Had such a thing occurred, we should have been almost certain to have seen her, and in that case we should have been able to attract her attention, and she would have picked us up. No, Miss Maybourne. I wish I could comfort you with such an assurance; but I fear it would be cruel to buoy you up with any false hopes, only to have them more cruelly shattered later on. I'm afraid we must accustom ourselves to the awful thought that the *Fiji Princess* and all her company, with the exception of ourselves, have met a watery grave. Why I should have been saved when so many worthier people perished I cannot imagine."

"To save us, Mr. Wrexford," she answered. "Think what you are saying, and remember that but for you we should not be here now."

"I thank God, then, for the opportunity He gave me," I answered; and what I said I meant from the very bottom of my heart.

Whatever she may have thought of my speech, she vouchsafed no reply to it; but on looking up a moment later, I discovered that her face was suffused with a beautiful blush that was more eloquent than any words. After that I turned my attention to the meal which I was preparing, and gave her time to recover herself a little.

Having no pot in which to cook the fish, I had to use the largest of the shells I had discovered. These did not prove altogether a good substitute, but as they were all I had got, I had to make the best of them or go without.

When the mussels were sufficiently done, I lifted them off the fire and invited my companion to taste the dish. She did so, and the grimace which followed told me that she was not over pleased at the result. I followed her example, and felt obliged to confess that they made but poor fare to support life upon.

"If we cannot get something better, I don't know what we shall do," she cried. "These things are too horrible."

"Perhaps I may be able to hit upon a way of catching some fish," I said; "or it is just possible I may be able to get a trap and catch some birds. There is no knowing what I may not be able to do with a little practice. In the meantime, you must endeavour to swallow as much of this mess as possible, and try to get the little one in the cave there to do the same."

Putting some of the fish into another shell, I gave it to her, and she carried it off to her sick friend. After I had scraped and washed it carefully, I filled a larger shell with pure water from the pool and gave it to them to drink. When they had finished their meal—and it was not much that they ate—I called Miss Maybourne outside and informed her that I was going to build up a large fire, after which I should set off on a tramp round the island to see if I could discover anything better to eat. While I was away, I advised her to dry her own and the child's things by the blaze, for though we had been some time under the influence of the hot sun, still our garments could not be said to be anything like dry. She promised to do as I wished, and when I had piled what remained of my heap of fuel upon the fire I made my way down to the shore, and then set off for a tramp round the island.

My first call was at the group of rocks from which I had gathered the shellfish of which my companion had so strongly disapproved. I wanted to see if I could discover a place where it would be possible for me to construct some sort of a trap for fish. But though I searched diligently, nothing suitable could I find. At last I had to give it up in despair, and set my brain to work on another plan for stocking my larder. That fish were plentiful I could see by looking over the edges of the rocks, but how I was to capture them was by no means so plain. I think at that moment I would have given a year of my life for the worst hook and line I had used as a boy among the sticklebacks of Polton Penna.

Leaving the rocks behind me, I turned the point and made for the brow of a low hill that overlooked the sea on the further side. I had noticed that the sea birds gathered here in greater numbers than elsewhere, and when I reached the cliff, to my surprise and delight, I found the ground literally covered with nests. Indeed, it was a matter of some difficulty to move without treading upon the eggs. My delight can scarcely be overestimated, for here was a new food supply, and one that, while it would be unlikely to give out for some weeks to come, would be infinitely preferable to the wretched limpets upon which we had almost made up our minds we should have to subsist. I hastened to fill my handkerchief and pockets with the spoil, and when I could stuff in no more, continued my walk in a much easier, and consequently more thankful, frame of mind.

As I tramped along, glancing ever and anon at the sea, the sordid details of my past life rose before me. When I considered it, I felt almost staggered by the change that had come over me. It seemed scarcely possible that so short a time could have passed since I had plotted against Bartrand and had been so miserable in London. In my present state of usefulness, I felt as if centuries had elapsed since then, instead of barely a couple of weeks, as was really the case. I wondered what would be said in England when the news got into the papers, as I supposed it inevitably must, that I had found a watery grave in the ill-fated *Fiji Princess*. Would there be anyone to regret me? I very much doubted it. One hope occurred to me. Perhaps, under cover of the supposition that I was dead, I might manage to outwit the law after all, and then an opportunity would be afforded me of beginning a new life in a strange land—the land that was the home of Agnes Maybourne.

From a consideration of this important chance I fell to thinking of the girl herself. Could it have been for the reason that I was ultimately to save her life that Fate had raised her face before my eyes to warn me that miserable night in London? It looked very much like it. If, however, that was the beginning, what was the sequel to be? for surely it could not be intended that Fate, having brought me so far, should suddenly abandon me at the end. "Oh! if I were only clean handed like my fellow-men," I cried, in miserable self-abasement, "how happy might I not be!" For I must mention here that in my own mind I had quite come to the conclusion that Agnes Maybourne entertained a liking for me. And, God knows, I on my side had discovered that I loved her better than my own soul. What was to be the end of it all? That the future alone could decide.

The other side of the island—that is to say, the side exactly opposite that upon which we had landed—was almost precipitous, and at the foot of the cliffs, extending for some distance out into the sea, were a number of small islets, upon which the seas broke with never-easing violence. I searched that offing, as I had done the other, for a sail, but was no better rewarded. As soon as I had made certain that there was nothing in sight, I turned upon my tracks and hastened back to the plateau as fast as I could go. For some reason or another, I experienced a great dread lest by any chance something ill might have befallen my charges. But when I reached the beach below the plateau and looked up, to see the fire still burning brightly and Miss Maybourne moving about between it and the cave, I was reassured.

The tide by this time had gone out, and the lifeboat lay high and dry upon the beach. Before rejoining my companions I made my way towards her.

To roll her over into her proper position was only a matter of small difficulty now that the water was out of her, and once this was accomplished I was able to satisfy myself as to her condition. As far as I could gather, there was nothing amiss with her, even her oars lay fastened to the thwarts as usual. How she could have got into the water was a mystery I could not solve for the life of me. I examined her most carefully, and having done so, found some pieces of wood to act as rollers, and dragged her up the beach till I had got her well above high water mark. After that I picked up my parcel of eggs and climbed the hill to the plateau. It was now well on into the afternoon, and I had still much to do before nightfall.'

When I showed Miss Maybourne the eggs I had found, she expressed her great satisfaction, and we immediately cooked a couple to be ready against the little sufferer's waking.

The rest of the afternoon was spent in carrying drift wood from the beach to the plateau; for I had determined to keep a good flare burning all night, in case any ships might happen to pass, and think it worth their while to stand off and on till daylight should show them the reason of it. When I had stacked it ready to my hand there was yet another supply of grass to be cut, with which to improve the bed-places in the cave. Then my own couch had to be prepared somewhere within call. After which there was the evening meal to cook. By the time this was done, darkness had fallen, and our first night on the island had commenced.

When I bade Miss Maybourne "good night" she was kind enough to express her thanks a second time for the trouble I had taken. As if the better to give point to her gratitude, she held out her hand to me. I took it and raised it to my lips. She did not attempt to stop me, and then, with another "good night," she passed into the cave, and I was left alone.

For hours I sat watching my blaze and listening to the rumbling of the surf upon the shore. The night was as still as a night could well be. Not even a breath of wind was stirring. When I laid myself down in my corner between the rocks near the cave's mouth, and fell asleep, it was to dream of Agnes Maybourne and the happiness that might have been mine but for the one dread thing which had made it quite impossible.

CHAPTER 7

A Bitter Disappointment

Long before daylight I was awake, thinking of our unenviable position, and wishing for the ladies' sakes that I could do something to improve it. But, as far as I could see, I had done everything that was possible by mortal man. Somehow, though I valued their eggs above gold, I had no fancy for the sea birds themselves. What I wanted most was a contrivance with which to capture some of the fish in the bay. A line I could easily make by unravelling the painter of the lifeboat; the hook, however, beat me. A hair-pin would have done admirably; but, unfortunately, Miss Maybourne's hair covered her shoulders just as she had run up from her cabin on hearing the first alarm. An ordinary pin would have been invaluable; but among the three of us we could not muster even one. Just as daylight broke, however, I solved my difficulty in the simplest fashion possible, and could have kicked myself round the island, if it had been possible, for my stupidity in not having thought of it sooner. In my tie I wore a long gold pin, with an escutcheon top, which had been given me in Australia years before. The remembrance of it no sooner came into my mind than I had whipped it out of the tie, and had bent the point into a fair-sized hook. This done, I rose from my couch between the rocks, and having replenished the fire, which still showed a red glow, hastened down the hillside to where the boat lay upon the sands. From the painter I extracted sufficient strands to make a line some thirty feet long, and to this I attached my hook. I very much doubt if a fish were ever honoured before with so grand a hook.

Just as the sun's first rays were shooting up beyond the placid sea line, and the sea and heavens were fast changing from a pure pearl grey to every known colour of the rainbow, I pushed the boat into the water, and rowed out for half a mile or so. Then, having baited my hook with mussel, I threw it overboard, and seating myself, line in hand, in the stern, awaited results. I looked at the island, showing so clear and rugged in the bright morning light, and thought of Miss Maybourne and the sick child. If the truth must be confessed, I believe I was happier then, even in such straits and upon so inhospitable a shore, than I had ever been before. When I thought of Bartrand, as I had last seen him, lying stretched out in the snow in that quiet street, and remembered my struggle with Nikola in Golden Square, my walk through sleeping London to Surbiton, and my journey to Southampton, it all seemed like some horrible dream, the effects of which I was at last beginning to rid myself. It was hard to believe that I had really gone through it all; that I, the man now fishing so quietly in this boat, in whom Miss Maybourne believed so much, was in reality Gilbert Pennethorne, the perpetrator of one of the mysterious murders which had entirely baffled the ingenuity of the London police. I could not help wondering what she would say if anyone should tell her the true history of the man in whom she placed such implicit confidence. Would she credit it or not?

While I was thinking of this, I felt a sharp tug upon my line, and when I drew it in, I found, to my delight, a nice fish impaled upon the hook. Having released him and placed him securely at the bottom of the boat, I did not lose a moment in throwing the line overboard again. Within a quarter of an hour I had landed five splendid fellows, and was as pleased with my success as if I had just been created Lord Chancellor of England. Today, at any rate, I told myself, Miss Maybourne and the little girl should have a nice breakfast.

Arriving at the beach I sprang out, and, using the same means as before, drew my boat up out of reach of the tide. Then, taking my prizes with me, I made my way up the hillside to the plateau. Just as I reached it, Miss Maybourne made her appearance from the cave and came towards me.

"Look!" I cried, holding up the fish as I spoke. "Are these not beauties?"

"They are indeed splendid," she answered. "But how did you manage to obtain them? I thought you said last night that you could think of no way of making a hook?"

"So I did. But since then I have remembered the gold pin I wore in my tie. I found that it made a most excellent hook, and with its assistance I managed to get hold of these gentlemen. But, in my triumph, I am forgetting to enquire how you and your little friend are this morning. You were fairly comfortable in the cave, I hope?"

"Quite comfortable, thank you," she answered, gravely. "But poor little Esther is no better this morning. In fact, if anything, I fancy she is worse. She was delirious for some time in the night, and now she is in a comatose condition that frightens me more than her former restlessness. It goes to my heart to see her in this state."

"Is there nothing we can do for her, I wonder?" I said, as I prepared my fish for the fire.

"I fear we are powerless," replied Miss Maybourne. "The only thing I can imagine to be the matter with her is that she must have been struck by something when we were sucked under by the sinking ship. She complains continually of pains in her head."

"In that case, I fear there is nothing for it but to wait patiently for some ship, with a doctor on board, to come in sight and take us off."

"In the meantime, she may die. Oh, poor little Esther! Mr. Wrexford, this helplessness is too terrible."

What could I say to comfort her? In my own mind I saw no hope. Unless a vessel hove in sight, and she chanced to carry a doctor, the child must inevitably die. As soon as the breakfast was cooked, I went into the cave and looked at her. I found the little thing stretched upon the grass I had thrown down for a bed. She was unconscious, as Miss Maybourne had said, and was breathing heavily. Her pulse was almost unnoticeable, and occasionally she moaned a little, as if in pain. It was a sight that would have touched the most callous of men, and in spite of that one sinister episode in my career, I was far from being such a hero.

At midday there was no change perceptible in her condition. By the middle of the afternoon she was worse. Miss Maybourne and myself took it in turns to watch by her side; in the intervals, we climbed the hill and scanned the offing for a sail. Our vigilance, however, was never rewarded—the sea was as devoid of ships as our future seemed of hope.

After a day which had seemed an eternity, the second night of our captivity on the island came round. A more exquisite evening could scarcely be imagined. I had been watching by the sick child's side the greater part of the afternoon, and feeling that, if I remained on shore, Miss Maybourne would discover how low-spirited I was, I took the boat and rowed out into the bay, to try and obtain some fish for our supper. This was not a matter of much difficulty, and in less than a quarter of an hour I had hauled on board more than we could possibly have eaten in three meals. When I had finished, I sat in my boat watching the sunset effects upon the island. It was indeed a scene to remember, and the picture of it, as I saw it then, rises before me now as clearly as if it were but yesterday.

To right and left of the points which sheltered the bay, the deep green of the sea was changed to creaming froth, where the surf caught the rocks; but in the little indentation which we had made our home the wavelets rippled on the sand with the softest rhythm possible. The sky was cloudless, the air warmer than it had been for days past. The glow of sunset imparted to the western cliffs a peculiar shade of pink, the beauty of which was accentuated by the deep shadows cast by the beetling crags. On the hillside, directly opposite where my boat was anchored, I could see the plateau, and on it my fire burning brightly. I thought of the brave woman nursing the sick child in the cave, and of the difference she had made in my lonely life.

"Oh, God!" I cried, "if only You had let me see the chance that was to be mine some day, how easy it would have been for me to have ordered Nikola and his temptation to stand behind me. Now I see my happiness too late, and am consequently undone for ever."

As I thought of that sinister man and the influence he had exercised upon my life, I felt a thrill of horror pass over me. It seemed dreadful to think that he was still at large, unsuspected, and in all probability working some sort of evil on another unfortunate individual.

In my mind's eye I could see again that cold, impassive face, with its snake-like eyes, and hear that insinuating voice uttering once more that terrible temptation. Surely, I thought, the dread enemy of mankind must be just such another as Dr. Nikola.

When the sun had disappeared below the sea line, the colour of the ocean had changed from all the dazzling tints of the king-opal to a sombre coal-black hue, and myriads of stars were beginning to make their appearance in the sky, I turned my boat's head, and pulled towards the shore again. A great melancholy had settled upon me, a vague sense of some impending catastrophe, of which, try how I would, I found I could not rid myself.

On reaching the plateau, I made my way to the cave, and looked in. I discovered Miss Maybourne kneeling beside the child on the grass. As soon as she saw me she rose and led me out into the open.

"Mr. Wrexford," she said, "the end is quite close now, I feel sure. The poor little thing is growing weaker every moment. Oh, it is too terrible to think that she must die because we have not the means to save her."

I did my best to comfort her, but it was some time before I achieved any sort of success. When she had in a measure recovered her composure, I accompanied her back to the cave and examined the little sufferer for myself. Alas! one glance showed me how very close the end was. Already the child's face and hands were cold and clammy, her respiration was gradually becoming more and more difficult. She was still unconscious, and once I almost thought she was dead.

All through that dreadful night she lingered on. Miss Maybourne remained with her until close upon midnight, when I relieved her. Shortly before sunrise I went to the mouth of the cave and looked out. The stars were almost gone from the sky, and the world was very still. When I returned, I thought the child had suddenly grown strangely quiet, and knelt down to examine her. The first grey shafts of dawn showed me that at last the end had come. Death had claimed his victim. Henceforth we need feel no more concern for poor little Esther—her sufferings were over. She had gone to join her mother and the little ones who had lost their lives two days before. Having convinced myself that what I imagined was correct, I reverently closed the little eyes and crossed the frail hands upon her breast, and then went out into the fresh air. The sun was in the act of making his appearance above the peak, and all our little world was bathed in his glory. I looked across to the place between the rocks where I usually slept, and saw Miss Maybourne rising from her rest. My presence outside the cave must have told her my news, for she came swiftly across to where I stood.

"It is all over," she said, very quietly. "I can see by your face that the end has come."

I nodded. For the life of me, I could not have spoken just then. The sight of that agonised face before me and the thought of the dead child lying in the cave behind me deprived me of speech entirely. Miss Maybourne noticed my condition, and simply said, "Take me to her." I did as she commanded, and together we went back to the chamber of death. When we reached it, my companion stood for a few moments looking at the peaceful little figure on the couch of grass, and then knelt down beside it. I followed her example. Then, holding my hand in hers, she prayed for the child from whose body the soul had just departed; then for ourselves still left upon the island. When she had finished, we rose, and, after a final glance at our dead companion, went out into the open air again.

By this time I had got so much into the habit of searching the sea for ships that I did it almost unconsciously. As I passed the cave I glanced out across the waste of water. Then I stood stock still, hardly able to believe the evidence of my eyes. There, fast rising above the horizon, were the sails of a full-rigged ship. Miss Maybourne saw them as soon as I did, and together we stood staring at the vessel with all our eyes. My companion was the first to speak."

"Do you think she will come near enough to see us," she cried, in a voice I hardly recognized, so agitated was it.

"She must be made to see us," I answered, fiercely. "Come what may, she must not pass us."

"What are you going to do? How are you going to prevent it? Tell me, and let me help you if I can."

A notion had seized me, and I determined to put it into practice without an instant's delay.

"Let us collect all the wood we can find and then make a large bonfire. When that has been done, we must launch the boat and pull out to intercept her. If she sees the flare she will make her way here, and if she does not, we may be able to catch her before she gets out of our reach. Thus in either case we shall be saved."

Without another word we set to work collecting wood. By the time the hull of the vessel was above the horizon we had accumulated a sufficient quantity to make a large beacon. We did not set fire to it at once, however, for the reason that I had no desire to waste my smoke before those on board the ship would be able to distinguish it from the light clouds hovering about the peaks above. But before we could dream of leaving the island there were two other matters to be attended to. The first was to fill up the mouth of the cave with stones, for there was no time to dig a grave, and so convert it into a rough sepulchre; the second was to cook and eat our breakfast. It was certain we should require all our strength for the undertaking, and to attempt such a long row on an empty stomach would, I knew, be worse than madness. These things I explained to Miss Maybourne, who willingly volunteered to officiate as cook while I set about the work first mentioned. In something less than a quarter of an hour I had rolled several large rocks into the mouth of the cave, and upon these had placed others until the entrance was effectually barricaded. By the time this work was completed it was necessary to light the bonfire. This I did, setting fire to the dry grass at the bottom with a log from the blaze at which Miss Maybourne had just been cooking. In a few minutes we had a flare the flames of which could not have been less than twenty feet in height.

We ate our breakfast with our eyes fixed continually upon the advancing ship. So far she seemed to be heading directly for the island, but my fear was that she might change her course without discovering our beacon, and in that case be out of range before we could attract her attention. Our meal finished therefore, I led Miss Maybourne down the hill to the beach, and then between us we pushed the lifeboat into the water. My intention was to row out a few miles and endeavour to get into such a position that whatever course the vessel steered she could not help but see us.

As soon as we had pushed off from the shore I turned the boat's head, and, taking up the oars, set to work to pull out to sea. It was not altogether an easy task, for the boat was a heavy one and the morning was strangely warm. The sky overhead was innocent of cloud, but away to the west it presented a hazy appearance; the look of which I did not altogether like. However, I stuck to my work, all the time keeping my eyes fixed on the rapidly advancing ship. She presented a fine appearance, and it was evident she was a vessel of about three thousand tons. I hoped she would turn out to belong to our own nationality, though under the circumstances any other would prove equally acceptable. At present she was distant from us about six miles, and as she was still heading directly for the island I began to feel certain she had observed our signal. For this reason I pointed my boat's head straight for her and continued to pull with all the strength I possessed. Suddenly Miss Maybourne uttered a little cry, and seeing her staring in a new direction I turned in my seat to discover what had occasioned it.

"She is leaving us," cried my companion, in agonized tones, pointing to the vessel we had been attempting to intercept. "Look, look, Mr. Wrexford, she is leaving us!"

There was no need for her to bid me look, I was watching the ship with all my eyes. Heaven alone knows how supreme was the agony of that moment. She had gone about, and for this reason it was plain that those on board had not seen our signal. Now, unless I could manage to attract her attention it would be most unlikely that she would see us. In that case we might die upon the island without a chance of escape. At any cost we must intercept her. I accordingly resumed my seat again and began to pull wildly after her. Fortunately the breeze was light and the sea smooth, otherwise I should have made no headway at all. But when all was said and done, with both wind and tide in my favour, it was but little that I could accomplish. The boat, as I have already said, was a large and heavy one, and my strength was perhaps a little undermined by all I had gone through in the last two or three days. But, knowing what depended on it, I toiled at the oars like a galley slave, while Miss Maybourne kept her eyes fixed upon the retreating ship. At the end of an hour I was obliged to give up the race as hopeless. My strength was quite exhausted, and our hoped-for saviour was just showing hull down upon the horizon. Realizing this I dropped my head on to my hands like the coward I was and resigned myself to my despair. For the moment I think I must have forgotten that I was a man, I remembered only the fact that a chance had been given us of escaping from our prison, and that just as we were about to grasp it, it was snatched away again. Our fate seemed too cruel to be endured by mortal man.

"Courage, friend, courage," said Miss Maybourne, as she noticed my condition. "Bitter as our disappointment has been we have not done with hope yet. Because that vessel did not chance to rescue us it does not follow that another may not do so. Had we not better be getting back to the island? It is no use our remaining here now that the ship is out of sight."

I saw the wisdom contained in her remark, and accordingly pulled myself together and set to work to turn the boat's head in the direction we had come. But when we had gone about, my dismay may be imagined at discovering that a thick fog had obscured the island, and was fast bearing down upon us. Those on board the vessel we had been chasing must have seen it approaching, and have thought it advisable to give the island and its treacherous surroundings as wide a berth as possible.

"Can you see the land at all, Mr. Wrexford?" asked Miss Maybourne, who had herself been staring in the direction in which our bows were pointing.

"I must confess I can see nothing of it," I answered. "But if we continue in this direction and keep our ears open for the sound of the surf, there can be no doubt as to our being able to make our way back to the bay."

"How thick the fog is," she continued, "and how quickly it has come up! It makes me feel more nervous than even the thought of that ship forsaking us."

I stared at her in complete surprise. To think of Miss Maybourne, whom I had always found so cool and collected in moments of danger, talking of feeling nervous! I rallied her on the subject as I pulled along, and in a few moments she had forgotten her fear.

While I pulled along I tried to figure out what distance we could be from the island. When we discovered that the vessel had turned her back on us I had been rowing for something like half an hour.

At the rate we had been travelling that would have carried us about a couple of miles from the shore. After we had noticed the change in her course we had probably pulled another four at most. That being so, we should now be between five and six miles from land—two hours' hard work in my present condition. To add to the unpleasantness of our position, the fog by this time had completely enveloped us, and to enable you to judge how dense it was I may say that I could only just distinguish my companion sitting in the stern of the boat. Still, however, I pulled on, pausing every now and again to listen for the noise of the surf breaking on the shore.

The silence was intense; the only sound we could hear was the tinkling of the water as it dripped off the ends of the oars. There was something indescribably awful about the utter absence of noise. It was like the peace which precedes some great calamity. It stretched the nerves to breaking pitch. Indeed, once when I allowed myself to think what our fate would be if by any chance we should miss the island, I had such a shock as almost deprived me of my power of thinking for some minutes.

For at least an hour and a half I pulled on, keeping her head as nearly as possible in the same direction, and expecting every moment to hear the roar of the breakers ahead. The fog still remained as thick as ever, and each time I paused in my work to listen the same dead silence greeted me as before. Once more I turned to my work, and pulled on without stopping for another quarter of an hour. Still no sound of the kind we hoped to hear came to us. The island seemed as difficult to find in that fog as the proverbial needle in the bundle of hay.

The agony of mind I suffered was enough to turn a man's brain. If only the fog would lift and let us have a glimpse of where we were, it would have been a different matter, but no such luck. It continued as thick as ever, wreathing and circling about us like the smoke from the infernal regions. At last I drew in my oars and arranged them by my side. Under the circumstances it was no use wasting what remained of my strength by useless exertion.

From that time forward—that is to say for at least six hours—we drifted on and on, the fog remaining as dense as when we had first encountered it. Throughout that time we kept our ears continually strained for a sound that might guide us, but always without success. By this time it must have been considerably past three in the afternoon, and for all we knew to the contrary we might still be miles and miles out of our reckoning. All through this agonizing period, however, Miss Maybourne did not once complain, but bore herself with a quiet bravery that would have shamed the veriest coward into at least an affectation of courage. How bitterly I now reproached myself for having left the island to pursue that vessel I must leave you to imagine. But for that suicidal act of folly we might now be on dry land, if not perhaps as luxuriously housed as we should have liked, at least safer than we were now. The responsibility for that act of madness rested entirely upon my shoulders, and the burden of that knowledge was my continual punishment.

At last I was roused from my bitter thoughts by my companion exclaiming that she thought the fog was lifting a little in one particular quarter. I looked in the direction indicated and had to admit that the atmosphere certainly seemed to be clearer there than elsewhere. Still, however, there was no noise of breakers to be heard.

The light in the quarter pointed out by my companion was destined to be the signal for the fog's departure, and in less than a quarter of an hour, starting from the time of our first observing it, the whole expanse of sea, from horizon to horizon, stood revealed to us. We sprang to our feet almost simultaneously, and searched the ocean for the island. But to our horror it was not to be seen. We were alone on the open sea without either water or food, any real knowledge of where we were, or without being able to tell from which quarter we might expect assistance to come. A more dreadful situation could scarcely be imagined, and when I considered the sex and weakness of my companion, and reflected what such a fate would mean for her, I could have cursed myself for the stupidity which had brought it all about.

For some moments after we had made our terrible discovery, neither of us spoke. Then our glances met and we read our terror in each other's eyes.

"What are we to do? What can we do?" cried Miss Maybourne, running her eyes round the horizon and then meeting my gaze again.

I shook my head and tried to think before I answered her.

"For the moment I am as powerless as yourself to say," I replied. "Even if we could fix the direction, goodness only knows how far we are from the island. We may be only distant ten miles or so, or we may be twenty. It must be nearly four o'clock by this time, and in another four hours at most darkness will be falling; under cover of the night we may miss it again. On the other hand we cannot exist here without food or water. Oh, Miss Maybourne, to what straits have I brought you through my stupidity. If we had stayed on the island instead of putting off on this fool's chase you would be safe now."

"You must not blame yourself, Mr. Wrexford," she answered. "Indeed you must not! It is not just, for I was quite as anxious as yourself to try and intercept the vessel. That we did not succeed is not our fault, and in any case I will not let you reproach yourself."

"Alas! I cannot help it," I replied. "And your generosity only makes me do so the more."

"In that case I shall cease to be generous," she said. "We will see how that plan works. Come, come, my friend, let us look our situation in the face and see what is best to be done. Believe me, I have no fear. God will protect us in the future as He has done in the past."

I looked at the noble girl as she said this, and took heart from the smile upon her face. If she could be so brave, surely I, who called myself a man, must not prove myself a coward. I pulled myself together and prepared to discuss the question as she desired. But it was the knowledge of our utter helplessness that discounted every hope. We had no food, we had no water. True, we might pull on; but if we did, in which direction should we proceed? To go east would be to find ourselves, if we lived so long—the chances against which were a thousand to one—on the most unhealthy part of the long coast line of Africa. To pull west would only be to get further out into mid-ocean, where, if we were not picked up within forty-eight hours, assistance would no longer be of any use to us. The Canary Islands, I knew, lay somewhere, say a hundred miles, to the southward, but we could not pull that distance without food or water, and even if we had a favourable breeze, we had no sail to take advantage of it. To make matters worse, the fishing line and hook I had manufactured for myself out of my scarf-pin, had been left on the island. Surely any man or woman might be excused for feeling melancholy under the pressure of such overwhelming misfortunes.

While we were thus considering our position the sun was sinking lower and lower to his rest, and would soon be below the horizon altogether. The sea was still as calm as a mill-pond, not a breath of air disturbed its placid surface. We sat just as we had done all day: Miss Maybourne in the stern, myself amidships. The oars lay on either side of me, useless as the rudder, the yoke lines had scarcely been touched since the ship had turned her back on us. When I look back on that awful time now, every detail of the boat, from the rowlocks to the grating on the bottom, seems impressed on my memory with a faithfulness that is almost a pain. I can see Miss Maybourne sitting motionless in the stern, her elbows on her knees and her face buried in her hands.

At last to rouse her and take her out of herself, I began to talk. What I said I cannot recollect, nor can I even recall the subject of my conversation. I know, however, that I continued to talk and insisted upon her answering me. In this way we passed the time until darkness fell and the stars came out. For the past hour I had been suffering agonies of thirst, and I knew, instinctively, that my companion must be doing the same. I followed her example and dabbled my hands in the water alongside. The coolness, however, while proving infinitely refreshing to my parched skin, only helped to intensify my desire for something to drink. I searched the heavens in the hope of discovering a cloud that might bring us rain, but without success.

"Courage," said Miss Maybourne again, as she noticed me drop my head on to my hands in my despair. "As I said just now, we are in God's hands; and I feel certain we shall be saved at last."

As if in mockery of her faith I noticed that her voice had lost its usually clear ring, and that it was lower than I had ever hitherto heard it. But there was a note of conviction in it that showed me how firm her belief was. For my own part I must confess that I had long since given up all hope. In the face of so many calamitous circumstances it seemed impossible that we could be saved. My obvious duty there was to endeavour by every means in my power to make death as easy as possible for the woman I loved.

In the same tedious fashion hour after hour went by and still we remained as we were, floating idly upon the bosom of the deep. Twice I tried to persuade Miss Maybourne to lie down at the bottom of the boat and attempt to obtain some sleep, but she would not hear of such a thing. For myself I could not have closed my eyes for five minutes, even if by doing so I could have saved my life. Every faculty was strained to breaking pitch, and I was continually watching and listening for something, though what I expected to see or hear I could not have told if I had been asked. I pray to God that I may never again be called upon to spend such another absolutely despairing night.

CHAPTER 8

We Are Saved!

The calm with which we had so far been favoured was not, however, destined to be as permanent as we imagined, for towards the middle of the night the wind got up, and the sea, from being as smooth as glass, became more boisterous than I altogether liked. Miss Maybourne, who now seemed to be sunk into the lethargy from which she had roused me, lifted her head from her hands, and at intervals glanced over her shoulder apprehensively at the advancing waves. One thing was very evident: it would never do to let our boat drift broadside on to the seas, so I got out the oars again, and to distract my companion's thoughts, invited her to take the helm. She did as I requested, but without any sign of the eagerness she had hitherto displayed. Then, for something like an hour, we struggled on in this crab-like fashion. It was Herculean labour, and every minute found my strength becoming more and more exhausted. The power of the wind was momentarily increasing, and with it the waves were assuming more threatening proportions. To say that I did not like the look of affairs would be to put my feelings very mildly. To tell the truth, I was too worn out to think of anything, save what our fate would be if by any chance we should be on the edge of an hurricane. However, I knew it would not do to meet trouble half-way, so by sheer force of will I riveted my attention upon the boat, and in thus endeavouring to avert the evil of the present, found sufficient occupation to prevent me from cross-questioning the future.

Suddenly Miss Maybourne, who, as I have said, had for some time been sitting in a constrained attitude in the stern, sprang to her feet with a choking cry.

"Mr. Wrexford," she said, in a voice that at any other time I should not have recognised as hers, "I must have something to drink or I shall go mad."

Fearing she might fall overboard in her excitement, I leapt up, seized her in my arms, and dragged her down to her seat again. Had I not done so, I cannot say what might not have happened.

"Let me go," she moaned. "Oh, for Heaven's sake, let me go! You don't know what agony I am suffering."

I could very well guess, for I had my own feelings to guide me. But it was my duty to try and cheer her at any cost, and upon this work I concentrated all my energies, at the same time keeping the boat's head in such a position that the racing seas should not overwhelm her—no light work, I can assure you. When at last I did succeed in calming her, she sat staring straight ahead of her like a woman turned to stone. It was pitiful to see a woman, who had hitherto been so brave, brought so low. I put my arm round her waist the better to hold her, and, as I did so, watched the black seas, with their tips of snowy foam, come hissing towards us. Overhead the stars shone brightly, and still not a vestige of a cloud was to be seen. It seemed like doubting Providence to believe that, after all the dangers from which we had been preserved since we had left England, we were destined to die of starvation in an open boat in mid-Atlantic. And yet how like it it looked.

After that one outburst of despair Miss Maybourne gave no more trouble, and when she had been sitting motionless beside me for an hour or thereabouts fell fast asleep, her head resting on my arm. Weak and suffering as I was, I was not so far gone as to be unable to feel a thrill of delight at this close contact with the woman I loved. What would I not have given to have been able to take her in my arms and have comforted her properly!—to have told her of my love, and, in the event of her returning it, to have faced King Death side by side as lovers. With her hand in mine Death would not surely be so very terrible. However, such a thing could not be thought of. I was a criminal, a murderer flying from justice; and it would have been an act of the basest sacrilege on my part to have spoken a word to her of the affection which by this time had come to be part and parcel of my life. For this reason I had to crush it and keep it down; and, if by any chance we should be rescued, I would have to leave her and go out to hide myself in the world without allowing her ever to suspect the thoughts I had had in my mind concerning her. God knows, in this alone I had suffered punishment enough for the sin I had unintentionally committed.

At last the eastern stars began to lose something of their brilliance, and within a short period of my noticing this change, the wind, which had been sensibly moderating for some time past, dropped to a mere zephyr, and then died away completely. With its departure the violence of the waves subsided, and the ocean was soon, if not so smooth as on the previous day, at least sufficiently so to prevent our feeling any further anxiety on the score of the boat's safety.

One by one the stars died out of the sky, and a faint grey light, almost dove-coloured in its softness, took their place. In this light our boat looked double her real size, but such a lonely speck upon that waste of water that it would have made the heart of the boldest man sink into his shoes with fear. From the above-mentioned hue the colour quickly turned to the palest turquoise, and again to the softest pink. From pink it grew into a kaleidoscope of changing tints until the sun rose like a ball of gold above the sea-line—and day was born to us. In the whole course of my experience I never remember to have seen a more glorious sunrise. How different was it in its joyous lightness and freshness to the figures presented by the two miserable occupants of that lonely boat!

At last Miss Maybourne opened her eyes, and, having glanced round her, sat up. My arm, when she did so, was so cramped and stiff that for a moment I could scarcely bear to move it. She noticed this, and tried to express her regret, but her tongue refused to obey her commands. Seeing this, with an inarticulate sound she dropped her head on to her hands once more. To restore some animation into my cramped limbs, I rose and endeavoured to make my way to the bows of the boat. But, to my dismay, I discovered that I was as weak as a month-old child. My legs refused to support the weight of my body, and with a groan I sank down on the thwart where I had previously been rowing.

For upwards of half an hour we remained as we were, without speaking. Then I suddenly chanced to look along the sea-line to the westward. The atmosphere was so clear that the horizon stood out like a pencilled line. I looked, rubbed my eyes, and looked again. Could I be dreaming, or was it a delusion conjured up by an overtaxed brain. I shut my eyes for a moment, then opened them, and looked again. No, there could be no mistake about it this time. A ship was in sight, and heading directly for us! Oh, the excitement of that moment, the delirious joy, the wild, almost cruel, hope that seized me! But, mad with longing though I was, I had still sufficient presence of mind left to say nothing about my discovery to Miss Maybourne until I was sure of my facts. She was sitting with her back towards it, and therefore could not see it. So, while there was any chance of the vessel leaving us, I was not going to excite her hopes, only to have them blighted again. There would be plenty of time to tell her when she was close enough to see us.

For what seemed an eternity I kept my eyes fixed upon the advancing vessel, watching her rise higher and higher above the waves. She was a large steamer, almost twice the size of the ill-fated *Fiji Princess*. A long trail of smoke issued from her funnels; and at last, so close did she come, I could distinguish the water frothing at her bows with the naked eye. When she was not more than three miles distant, I sprang to my feet.

"We're saved, Miss Maybourne!" I cried frantically, finding my voice and strength as suddenly as I had lost them. "We're saved! Oh, thank God, thank God!"

She turned her head as I spoke, and looked steadily in the direction I pointed for nearly a minute. Then, with a little sigh, she fell upon the gunwale in a dead faint. I sprang to her assistance, and, kneeling at her feet, chafed her hands and called her by name, and implored her to speak to me. But in spite of my exertions, she did not open her eyes. When a quarter of an hour had elapsed, and she was still insensible, I began to wonder what I should do. To remain attending to her might mean that we should miss our deliverer. In that case we should both die. At any cost, and now more than ever, I knew I must attract the steamer's attention. She was not more than a mile behind us by this time, and, if I could only make her see us, she would be alongside in a few minutes. For this reason I tore off my coat, and, attaching it to an oar, began to wave it frantically above my head. Next moment a long whistle came across the waves to me. It was a signal that our boat had been observed, and never did a sound seem more musical to a human ear. On hearing it, I stood up again, and, shading my eyes with my hands, watched her approach, my heart beating like a piston-rod. Closer and closer she came, until I could easily read the name, *King of Carthage*, upon her bows. When she was less than a hundred yards distant, an officer on the bridge came to the railings, and hailed us.

"Boat, ahoy!" he cried. "Do you think you can manage to pull alongside? or shall we send assistance to you?"

In reply—for I could not trust my voice to speak—I got out my oars, and began to row towards her. Short as was the distance, it took me some time to accomplish it. Seeing this, the same officer again hailed me, and bade me make fast the line that was about to be thrown to me. The words were hardly out of his mouth before the line in question came whistling about my ears. I seized it as a drowning man is said to clutch at a straw, and, clambering forward, secured it to the ring in the bows. When that was done, I heard an order given, and willing hands pulled us quickly alongside.

By the time we reached it the gangway had been lowered, and a couple of men were standing at the foot of it ready to receive us. I remember leaning over to fend her off, and I also have a good recollection of seeing one of the men—the ship's doctor I afterwards discovered him to be—step into the boat.

"Can you walk up the steps yourself, or would you like to be carried?" he asked, as I sank down on the thwart again.

"Carry the lady," I answered huskily; "I can manage to get up myself. Take her quickly, or she will die."

I saw him pick Miss Maybourne up, and, assisted by the quartermaster who had accompanied him, carry her up the ladder. I attempted to follow, only to discover how weak I really was. By the exercise of sheer will, however, I managed to scramble up, holding on to the rail, and so gained the deck. Even after all this lapse of time I can distinctly see the crowd of eager faces pressed round the top of the ladder to catch a glimpse of us, and I can hear again the murmurs of sympathy that went up as we made our appearance. After that all seems a blank, and I can only believe what I am told—namely, that I looked round me in a dazed sort of fashion, and then fell in a dead faint upon the deck.

When I recovered consciousness again, I had to think for a moment before I could understand what had happened. I found myself in a handsomely-furnished cabin that I had never seen before. For an instant I imagined myself back again on the ill-fated *Fiji Princess*. Then a tall, red-bearded man—the same who had carried Miss Maybourne up from the boat—entered, and came towards me. Through the door, which he had left open, I could see the awning-covered promenade-deck outside. As soon as I saw him I tried to sit up on the velvet-cushioned locker upon which I had been placed, but he bade me be content to lie still for a little while.

"You will be far better where you are," he said. "What you want is rest and quiet. Take a few sips of this, and then lie down again and try to get to sleep. You have some arrears to make up in that line, or I'm mistaken."

He handed me a glass from the tray above my couch, and held it for me while I drank. When I had finished I laid myself down again, and, instead of obeying him, began to question him as to where I was. But once more I was forestalled, this time by the entrance of a steward carrying a bowl of broth on a tray.

"You see we're determined, one way or another, to close your mouth," he said, with a laugh. "But this stuff is too hot for you at present.

130

We'll put it down here to cool, and in the meantime I'll answer not more than half-a-dozen questions. Fire away, if you feel inclined."

I took him at his word, and put the one question of all others I was longing to have answered.

"How is the lady who was rescued with me?"

"Doing as well as can be expected, poor soul," he replied. "She's being well looked after, so you need not be anxious about her. You must have had a terrible time in that boat, to judge from the effects produced. Now, what is the next question?"

"I want to know what ship this is, and how far we were from the Salvages when you picked us up?"

"This vessel is the *King of Carthage*—Captain Blockman in command. I'm afraid I can't answer your last question offhand, for the reason that, being the doctor, I have nothing to do with the navigation of the ship; but I'll soon find out for you."

He left the cabin, and went to the foot of the ladder that led to the bridge. I heard him call the officer of the watch, and say something to him. Presently he returned.

"The Salvages lie about seventy miles due nor'-nor'-east of our present position," he said.

"Nor'-nor'-east?" I cried. "Then I was even further out in my calculations than I expected."

"Why do you ask about the Salvages?"

"Because it was on a rock off those islands that our ship, the *Fiji Princess*, was lost. We put off from the island to try and catch a sailing vessel that came in sight yesterday morning. A dense fog came on, however, and during the time it lasted we lost both the ship we went out to stop and also our island. Ever since then we have been drifting without food or water."

"You have indeed had a terrible experience. But you've a splendid constitution, and you'll soon get over the effects of it. And now tell me, were no others saved from the wreck?"

"As far as we could tell, with the exception of our three selves, not a single soul."

"You say 'three selves,' but we only rescued the lady and yourself. What, then, became of the third?"

"The third was a child about eight years old. The poor little thing must have been hurt internally when we were sucked under by the sinking ship, and her condition was probably not improved by the long exposure we had to endure on the bottom of the boat from which you rescued us. She scarcely recovered consciousness, and died on the island a short time before we left it in our attempt to catch the vessel I spoke of just now."

"I never heard a sadder case," said the doctor. "You are indeed to be pitied. I wonder the lady, your companion, came through it alive. By the way, the skipper was asking me just now if I knew your names."

"The lady is Miss Maybourne, whose father is a well-known man at the Cape, I believe."

"Surely not Cornelius Maybourne, the mining man?"

"Yes, she is his daughter. He will be in a terrible state when the *Fiji Princess* is reported missing."

"I expect he will; but, fortunately, we shall be in Cape Town almost as soon as she would have been, and he will find that his daughter, thanks to your care, is safe and sound. Now I am not going to let you talk any more. First, take as much of this broth as you can manage, and then lie down and try to get to sleep again. As I said just now, I prophesy that in a few days you'll be up and about, feeling no ill-effects from your terrible adventure."

I obeyed him, and drank the broth. When I had done so I lay down again, and in a very short time was once more in the Land of Nod. When I opened my eyes again the cabin was almost dark. The doctor was still in attendance, and, as soon as he saw that I was awake, asked me if I would like to get up for a little while. I answered that I should be only too glad to do so; and when he had helped me to dress, I took possession of a chair on the promenade-deck outside. It was just dinner-time in the saloon, and by the orders of the captain, who came personally to enquire how I was, I was served with a meal on deck. Nothing could have exceeded the kindness and thoughtfulness of the officers and passengers. The latter, though anxious to hear our story from my own lips, refrained from bothering me with questions; and thinking quiet would conduce to my recovery, allowed me to have the use of that end of the deck unmolested. As soon as I could do so, I enquired once more after Miss Maybourne, and was relieved to hear that she was making most satisfactory progress towards recovery. After dinner the captain came up, and seating himself in a chair beside me, asked a few questions concerning the foundering of the *Fiji Princess*, which information, I presumed, he required for his log.

"You have placed Mr. Maybourne very deeply in your debt," he said, after a little further conversation; "and I don't doubt but there will be many who will envy your good fortune in having conferred so signal a service upon his daughter. By the way, you have not told us your own name."

My heart gave a great jump, and for the moment I seemed to feel myself blushing to the roots of my hair. After the great kindness I had already received from everyone on board the vessel, it seemed worse than ungrateful to deceive them. But I dared not tell the truth. For all I knew to the contrary, my name might have been proclaimed everywhere in England before they left.

"My name is Wrexford," I said, feeling about as guilty as a man could well do.

"Any relation to the Wrexfords of Shrewsbury?" asked the captain with mild curiosity.

"Not that I'm aware of," I answered. "I have been living out of England for many years, and have no knowledge of my relations."

"It's not a common name," continued the skipper; "that is why I ask. Sir George Wrexford is one of our directors, and a splendid fellow. I thought it was just possible that you might be some connection of his. Now, if you will excuse me, I'll be off. Take my advice and turn in early. I'm sorry to say we're carrying our full complement of passengers, so that I cannot give you a proper berth; but I've ordered a bed to be made up for you in my chart-room, where you have been all day today. If you can manage to make yourself comfortable there it is quite at your service."

"It is very kind of you to put yourself to so much inconvenience," I answered. "I fear by the time we reach Cape Town I shall have caused you a considerable amount of trouble."

"Not at all! Not at all!" the hospitable skipper replied, as he rose to go. "I'm only too glad to have picked you up. It's our duty to do what we can for each other, for we none of us know when we may be placed in a similar plight ourselves."

After he left me, I was not long in following the good advice he had given me; and when I had once reached my couch, fell into a dreamless sleep, from which I did not wake until after eight o'clock next morning. Indeed, I don't know that I should have waked even then, had I not been disturbed by the noise made by someone entering the cabin. It proved to be the doctor.

"How are you feeling this morning?" he asked, when he had felt my pulse.

"Ever so much better," I replied. "In fact, I think I'm quite myself again. How is Miss Maybourne?"

"Still progressing satisfactorily," he answered. "She bids me give you her kind regards. She has been most constant in her enquiries after your welfare."

I don't know whether my face had revealed my secret, or whether it was only supposition on his part, but he looked at me pretty hard for a moment, and then laughed outright.

"You may not know it," he said, "but when all's said and done, you're a jolly lucky fellow."

I sighed, and hesitated a moment before I replied.

"I'm afraid you're mistaken," I said. "Luck and I have never been companions. I doubt if there is a man in this world whose career has been more devoid of good fortune than mine. As a boy, I was unlucky in everything I undertook. If I played cricket, I was always either bowled for a duck's egg, or run out just as I was beginning to score. If there was an accident in the football field, when I was playing, I was invariably the sufferer. I left Oxford under a cloud, because I could not explain something that I knew to be a mistake on the part of the authorities. I quarrelled with my family on the same misunderstanding. I was once on the verge of becoming a millionaire, but illness prevented my taking advantage of my opportunity; and while I was thus delayed another man stepped in and forestalled me. I had a legacy, but it brought me nothing but ill-luck, and has finally driver me out of England!"

"And since then the tide of ill-fortune has turned," he said. "A beautiful and wealthy girl falls overheard—you dive in, and rescue her. I have heard about that, you see. The ship you are travelling by goes to the bottom—you save your own and the same girl's life. Then, as if that is not enough, you try your luck a third time; and, just as a terrible fate seems to be going to settle you for good and all, we heave in sight and rescue you. Now you have Miss Maybourne's gratitude, which would strike most men as a more than desirable possession, and at the same time you will have her father's."

"And, by the peculiar irony of fate, both come to me when I am quite powerless to take advantage of them."

"Come, come, you mustn't let yourself down like this. You know very well what the end of it all will be, if you spend your life believing yourself to be a marked man."

"You mean that I shall lose my reason? No, no! you needn't be afraid of that. I come of a hard-headed race that has not been in the habit of stocking asylums."

"I am glad of that. Now what do you say to getting up? I'll have your breakfast sent to you in here, and after you've eaten it, I'll introduce you to some of the passengers. On the whole, they are a nice lot, and very much interested in my two patients."

I thanked him, and, to show how very much better I felt, sprang out of bed and began to dress. True to his promise, my breakfast was brought to me by a steward, and I partook of it on the chart-room table. Just as I finished the doctor reappeared, and, after a little conversation, we left the cabin and proceeded out on to the deck together. Here we found the majority of the passengers promenading, or seated in their chairs. Among them I noticed two clergymen, two or three elderly gentlemen of the colonial merchant type, a couple of dapper young fellows whom I set down in my own mind as belonging to the military profession, the usual number of elderly ladies, half a dozen younger ones, of more or less fascinating appearances, and the same number of children. As soon as they saw me several of those seated rose and came to meet us. The doctor performed the necessary introductions, and in a few minutes I found myself seated in a comfortable deck-chair receiving innumerable congratulations on my recovery. Strange to say, I did not dislike their sympathy as much as I had imagined I should do. There was something so spontaneous and unaffected about it that I would have defied even the most sensitive to take offence. To my astonishment, I discovered that no less than three were personal friends of Miss Maybourne's, though all confessed to having failed in recognising her when the boat came alongside. For the greater part of the morning I remained chatting in my chair, and by mid-day felt so much stronger that, on the doctor's suggestion, I ventured to accompany him down to the saloon for lunch. The *King of Carthage* was a finer vessel in every way than the ill-fated *Fiji Princess*. Her saloon was situated amidships, and could have contained the other twice over comfortably. The appointments generally were on a scale of great magnificence; and, from what I saw at lunch, the living was on a scale to correspond. I sat at a small table presided over by the doctor, and situated near the foot of the companion ladder. In the pauses of the meal I looked round at the fine paintings let into the panels between the ports, at the thick carpet upon the floor, the glass dome overhead, and then at the alley-ways leading to the cabins at either end. In which direction did Miss Maybourne's cabin lie, I wondered. The doctor must have guessed what was passing in my mind, for he nodded his head towards the after-alley on the starboard side, and from that time forward I found my eyes continually reverting to it.

Luncheon over, I returned to the promenade-deck, and, after a smoke—the first in which I had indulged since we left the island—acted on the doctor's advice, and went to my cabin to lie down for an hour or so.

When I returned to the deck, afternoon tea was going forward, and a chair having been found for me, I was invited to take a cup. While I was drinking it, the skipper put in an appearance. He waited until I had finished, and then said he would like to show me something if I would accompany him along the deck to his private cabin. When we reached it, he opened the door and invited me to enter. I did so, and, as I crossed the threshold, gave a little start of surprise, for Miss Maybourne was there, lying upon the locker.

"Why, Miss Maybourne!" I cried, in complete astonishment, "this is a pleasant surprise. I had no idea you were about again. I hope you are feeling stronger."

"Much stronger," she answered. "I expect I shall soon be quite myself again, now that I have once made a start. Mr. Wrexford, I asked Captain Blockman to let me see you in here for the first time, in order that I might have an opportunity of expressing my gratitude to you before we face the passengers. You cannot imagine how grateful I am to you for all you have done for me since that awful night when the *Fiji Princess* went down. How can I ever repay you for it?"

"By becoming yourself again as quickly as possible," I answered; "I ask no better payment."

I thought she looked at me in rather a strange way as I said this; but it was not until some time later that I knew the reason of it. At the time I would have given worlds to have spoken the thoughts that were in my mind; but that being impossible, I had to hold my tongue, though my heart should break under the strain. We were both silent for a little while, and then Miss Maybourne took my hand, and I could see that she was steeling herself to ask me some question, and was not quite certain what answer she would receive to it.

"Mr. Wrexford," she began, and there was a little falter in her voice as she spoke, "you told me on board the *Fiji Princess* that you were going to South Africa to try and obtain employment. You must forgive my saying anything about it, but I also gathered from what you told me that you would arrive there without influence of any sort. Now, I want you to promise me that you will let papa help you. I'm sure he will be only too grateful for the chance. It would be a kindness to him, for he will remember that, but for you, he would never have seen me again."

"I did not do it for the sake of reward, Miss Maybourne," I answered, with an outburst of foolish pride that was not very becoming to me.

"Who knows that better than I?" she replied, her face flushing at the thought that she had offended me. "But you must not be angry with me. It would be kind of you to let me show my gratitude in some way. Papa would be so glad to give you letters of introduction, or to introduce you personally to people of influence, and then there is nothing you might not be able to do. You will let him help you, won't you?"

If she could only have known what she was asking of me! To be introduced to the prominent people of the colony was the very last thing in the world I wanted. My desire was to not only attract as little attention as might be, but also to get up country and beyond the reach of civilization as quickly as possible.

However, I was not going to make Miss Maybourne unhappy on the first day of her convalescence, so I promised to consider the matter, and to let her know my decision before we reached Cape Town. By this compromise I hoped to be able to hit upon some way out of the difficulty before then.

From that day forward the voyage was as pleasant as it would be possible for one to be. Delicate as was our position on board, we were not allowed for one moment to feel that we were not upon the same footing as those who had paid heavily for their accommodation. The officers and passengers vied with each other in showing us kindnesses, and, as may be imagined, we were not slow to express our gratitude.

Day after day slipped quickly by, and each one brought us nearer and nearer to our destination. As the distance lessened my old fears returned upon me. After all the attention I had received from our fellow-travellers, after Miss Maybourne's gracious behaviour towards me, it will be readily imagined how much I dreaded the chance of exposure. How much better, I asked myself, would it not be to drop quietly overboard while my secret was still undiscovered, than to stay on board and be proclaimed a murderer before them all?

On the evening prior to our reaching Cape Town I was leaning on the rails of the promenade deck, just below the bridge, when Miss Maybourne left a lady with whom she had been conversing, and came and stood beside me. The evening was cool, and for this reason she had thrown a lace mantilla, lent her by one of the passengers, over her head, and had draped it round her shapely neck. It gave her an infinitely charming appearance; indeed, in my eyes, she appeared the most beautiful of all God's creatures—a being to be loved and longed for beyond all her sex.

"And so tomorrow, after all our adventures, we shall be in Cape Town," she said. "Have you thought of the promise you gave me a fortnight ago?"

"What promise was that?" I asked, though I knew full well to what she alluded.

"To let papa find you some employment. I do hope you will allow him to do so."

I looked at her as she stood beside me, one little hand resting on the rail and her beautiful eyes gazing across the starlit sea, and thought how hard it was to resist her. But at any cost I could not remain in Cape Town. Every hour I spent there would bring me into greater danger.

"I have been thinking it over as I promised," I said, "and I have come to the conclusion that it would not be wise for me to accept your offer. I have told you repeatedly, Miss Maybourne, that I am not like other men. God knows how heartily I repent my foolish past. But repentance, however sincere, will not take away the stain. I want to get away from civilization as far and as quickly as possible. For this reason immediately we arrive I shall start for the Transvaal, and once there shall endeavour to carve out a new name and a new life for myself. This time, Providence helping me, it shall be a life of honour."

"God grant you may succeed!" she said, but so softly that I could scarcely hear it.

"May I tell myself that I have your good wishes, Miss Maybourne?" I asked, with, I believe, a little tremor in my voice.

"Every good wish I have is yours," she replied. "I should be worse than ungrateful, after all you have done for me, if I did not take an interest in your future."

Then I did a thing for which it was long before I could forgive myself. Heaven alone knows what induced me to do it; but if my life had depended on it I could not have acted otherwise. I took her hand in mine and drew her a little closer to me.

"Agnes," I said, very softly, as she turned her beautiful face towards me, "tomorrow we shall be separated, perhaps never to meet again. After tonight it is possible, if not probable, that we shall not have another opportunity of being alone together. You don't know what your companionship has been to me. Before I met you, I was desperate. My life was not worth living; but you have changed it all—you have made me a better man. You have taught me to love you, and in that love I have found my belief in all that is good—even, I believe, a faith in God. Oh, Agnes, Agnes! I am not worthy to touch the ground you have walked on, but I love you as I shall never love woman again!"

She was trembling violently, but she did not speak. Her silence had the effect, however, of bringing me to myself, and it showed me my conduct in all its naked baseness.

"Forgive me," I whispered; "it was vile of me to have insulted you with this avowal. Forget—and forgive, if you can—that I ever spoke the words. Remember me only as a man, the most miserable in the whole world, who would count it heaven to be allowed to lay down his life for you or those you love. Oh, Agnes! is it possible that you can forgive me?"

This time she answered without hesitation.

"I have nothing to forgive," she said, looking up into my face with those proud, fearless eyes that seemed to hold all the truth in the world; "I am proud beyond measure to think you love me."

When I heard these precious words, I could have fallen at her feet and kissed the hem of her dress; but I dared not speak, lest I should forget myself in my joy, and say something for which I should never be able to atone. Agnes, however, was braver than I.

"Mr. Wrexford," she said, "you have told me that you love me, and now you are reproaching yourself for having done so. Is it because, as you say, you are poor? Do you think so badly of me as to imagine that that could make any difference to me?"

"I could not think so badly of you if I tried," I answered.

"You have said that you love me?"

"And I mean it. I love you as I believe man never loved woman before—certainly as I shall never love again."

Then, lowering her head so that I could not see her face, she whispered—

"Will it make you happier if I say that I love you?"

Her voice was soft as the breath of the evening rustling some tiny leaf, but it made my heart leap with a delight I had never known before, and then sink deeper and deeper down with a greater shame.

"God forbid!" I cried, almost fiercely. "You must not love me. You shall not do so. I am not worthy even that you should think of me."

"You are worthy of a great deal more," she answered. "Oh, why will you so continually reproach yourself?"

"Because, Agnes, my conscience will not let me be silent," I cried. "Because, Agnes, you do not know the shame of my life."

"I will not let you say 'shame,'" she replied. "Have I not grown to know you better than you know yourself?"

How little she knew of me! How little she guessed what I was! We were both silent again, and for nearly five minutes. I was the first to speak. And it took all the pluck of which I was master to say what was in my mind.

"Agnes," I began, "this must be the end of such talk between us. God knows, if I were able in honour to do so, I would take your love, and hold you against the world. But, as things are, to do that would be to proclaim myself the most despicable villain in existence. You must not ask me why. I could not tell you. But some day, if by chance you should hear the world's verdict, try to remember that, whatever I may have been, I did my best to behave like a man of honour to you."

She did not answer, but dropped her head on to her hands and sobbed as if her heart would break. Then, regaining her composure a little, she stood up again and faced me. Holding out her hand, she said:

"You have told me that you love me. I have said that I love you. You say that we must part. Let it be so. You know best. May God have mercy on us both!"

I tried to say "Amen," but my voice refused to serve me, and as I turned and looked across the sea I felt the hot salt tears rolling down my cheeks. By the time I recovered my self-possession she had left me and had gone below.

CHAPTER 9

South Africa

Even o'clock next morning found us entering Table Bay, our eventful journey accomplished. Overhead towered the famous mountain from which the Bay derives its name, its top shrouded in its cloth. At its foot reposed the town with which my destiny seemed so vitally connected, and which I was approaching with so much trepidation. As I stood on the promenade deck and watched the land open out before me, my sensations would have formed a good problem for a student of character. With a perception rendered abnormally acute by my fear, I could discern the boat of the port authorities putting off to us long before I should, at any other time, have been able to see it. It had yet to be discovered whether or not it contained a police official in search of me. As I watched her dipping her nose into the seas, and then tossing the spray off from either bow, in her haste to get to us, she seemed to me to be like a bloodhound on my track. The closer she came the more violently my heart began to beat, until it was as much as I could do to breathe. If only I could be certain that she was conveying an officer to arrest me, I felt I might find pluck enough to drop overboard and so end the pursuit for good and all. But I did not know, and the doubt upon the point decided me to remain where I was and brave the upshot.

As I watched her, I heard a footstep upon the deck behind me. I turned my head to find that it was Miss Maybourne. She came up beside me, and having glanced ashore at the city nestling at the foot of the great mountain, and then at the launch coming out to meet us, turned to address me.

"Mr. Wrexford," she began, "I am going to ask you to do me a great favour, and I want you to promise me to grant it before I tell you what it is."

"I'm afraid I can hardly do that," I answered. "But if you will tell me what it is, I will promise to do it for you if it is in any way possible."

"It is this," she said: "I want you, in the event of my father not meeting me, to take me home. Oh don't say no, Mr. Wrexford, I want you so much to do it. Surely you will not deny me the last request I make to you?"

She looked so pleadingly into my face that, as usual, it required all my courage not to give way to her. But the risk was too great for me even to contemplate such a thing for a moment. My rescue of the daughter of Cornelius Maybourne, and my presence in Cape Town, would soon leak out, and then it would be only a matter of hours before I should be arrested. Whatever my own inclinations may have been, I felt there was nothing for it but for me to refuse.

"I am not my own master in this matter," I replied, with a bitterness which must have shown her how much in earnest I was. "It is impossible that I can remain so long in the place. There are the most vital reasons in the world against it. I can only ask you to believe that."

I saw large tears rise in her eyes, though she turned hurriedly away in the hope that I should not see them. To see her weep, however, was more than I could bear, and under the influence of her trouble my resolutions began to give way. After all, if I was destined to be arrested, I might just as well be taken at Mr. Maybourne's house as elsewhere—perhaps better. Besides, it was more than likely, in the event of no warrant having been issued, Mr. Maybourne, whose influence, I had been told, was enormous in the colony, might prove just the very friend of all others I wanted. At any rate, if I were not taken before the time came for going ashore, I would do as she wished. I told her this, and she immediately thanked me and went down below again.

Just as I announced my decision the launch came alongside, and a moment later her passengers were ascending the accommodation ladder, which had been lowered to receive them. They were three in number, and included—so I was told by a gentleman who stood beside me—the harbour master, the officer of health, and another individual, about whose identity my informant was not quite assured. I looked at the last-named with no little apprehension; my nervousness endowed him with all the attributes of a police official, and my mind's eye could almost discover the manacles reposing in his coat pocket. I trust I may never pass through such another agonizing few minutes as I experienced then. I saw the party step on to the spar deck, where they shook hands with the purser and the chief officer, and watched them as they ascended to the promenade deck and made their way towards the bridge. Here they were received by the skipper. I leaned against the rails, sick with fear and trembling in every limb, expecting every moment to feel a heavy hand upon my shoulder, and to hear a stern voice saying in my ear—"Gilbert Pennethorne, I arrest you on a charge of murder."

But minute after minute went by, and still no one came to speak the fatal words. The ship, which had been brought to a standstill to pick up the boat, had now got under weigh again, and we were approaching closer and closer to the docks. In less than half an hour I should know my fate.

As soon as we were safely installed in dock, and everyone was looking after his or her luggage, saying "goodbye" and preparing to go ashore, I began to look about me for Miss Maybourne. Having found her we went to the chart-room together to bid the captain "goodbye," and to thank him for the hospitality and kindness he had shown us. The doctor had next to be discovered, and when he had been assured of our gratitude, we made enquiries for Mr. Maybourne. It soon became evident that he was not on board, so, taking his daughter under my protection, we said our final farewells and went down the gangway. For the first time in my life I set foot on South African soil.

The Custom House once passed, and the authorities convinced that we had nothing to declare, I hailed a cab and invited Miss Maybourne to instruct the driver in which direction he was to proceed. Half an hour later we had left the city behind us, and were driving through the suburbs in the direction of Mr. Maybourne's residence. After following a pretty road for something like a mile, on either side of which I noticed a number of stately residences, we found ourselves confronted with a pair of large iron gates, behind which was a neat lodge. But for the difference in the vegetation, it might very well have been the entrance to an English park. Through the trees ahead I could distinguish, as we rolled along the well-kept drive, the chimneys of a noble residence; but I was quite unprepared for the picture which burst upon my view when we turned a corner and had the whole house before us. Unlike most South African dwellings, it was a building of three stories, surmounted by a tower. Broad verandas ran round each floor, and the importance of the building was enhanced by the fact that it stood on a fine terrace, which again led down by a broad flight of steps to the flower gardens and orangery. A more delightful home could scarcely be imagined; and when I saw it, I ceased to wonder that Miss Maybourne had so often expressed a preference for South Africa as compared with England.

When the cab drew up at the front door I jumped out, and was about to help my companion to alight when I heard the front door open, and next moment a tall, fine-looking man, about sixty years of age, crossed the veranda and came down the steps. At first he regarded me with a stare of surprise, but before he could ask me my business, Miss Maybourne had descended from the vehicle and was in his arms. Not desiring to interrupt them in their greetings I strolled down the path. But I was not permitted to go far before I heard my name called. I turned, and went back to have my hand nearly shaken off by Mr. Maybourne.

"My daughter says you have saved her life," he cried. "I'll not ask questions now, but I thank you, sir—from the bottom of my heart I thank you. God knows you have done me a service the value of which no man can estimate."

The warmth of his manner was so much above what I had expected that it left me without power to reply.

"Come in, come in," he continued in a voice that fairly shook with emotion. "Oh, let us thank God for this happy day!"

He placed his arm round his daughter's waist, and drew her to him as if he would not let her move from his side again. I followed a few steps behind, and should have entered the house had I not been recalled by the cabman, who ventured to remind me that he had not yet been paid.

I instantly put my hand into my pocket, only to have the fact recalled to me that I possessed no money at all. All my capital had gone to the bottom in the *Fiji Princess*, and I was absolutely penniless. The position was an embarrassing one, and I was just reflecting what I had better do, when I heard Mr. Maybourne come out into the veranda again. He must have divined my difficulty, for without hesitation he discharged the debt, and, apologizing for not having thought of it, led me into the house.

Passing through an elegantly-furnished hall we entered the dining-room. Here breakfast was laid, and it was evidently from that meal that Mr. Maybourne had jumped up to receive us.

"Now, Mr. Wrexford," he cried, pointing to a chair, "sit yourself down yonder, and let me hear everything from the beginning to the end. Heaven knows I can hardly believe my good fortune. Half an hour ago I was the most miserable man under the sun; now that I have got my darling back safe and sound, I believe I am the happiest."

"Had you then heard of the wreck of the *Fiji Princess*?" I enquired.

"Here is a telegram I received last night," he said, handing me a paper he had taken from his pocket. "You see it is from Tenerife, and says that nothing has yet been heard of the vessel which was then more than a fortnight overdue. Agnes tells me that you were rescued by the King of Carthage. I understood she was expected about mid-day today, and I had resolved to visit her as soon as she got into dock, in order to enquire if they had any tidings to report regarding the lost vessel. How little I expected to find that you were safe on board her, Aggie! Mr. Wrexford, you can have no idea of the agony I have suffered this week past."

"On the contrary," I answered, "I think I can very well imagine it."

"And now tell me your story. I must not be cheated of a single detail."

I saw from the way he looked at me that he expected me to do the narrating, so I did so, commencing with the striking of the vessel on the rock, and winding up with an account of our rescue by the *King of Carthage*. He listened with rapt attention until I had finished, and then turned to his daughter.

"Has Mr. Wrexford told me everything?" he asked with a smile.

"No," she answered. "He has not told you half enough. He has not told you that when I fell overboard one night, when we were off the Spanish coast, he sprang over after me and held me up until a boat came to our assistance. He has not told you that when the vessel sank he gave his own life-belt up to me, nor has he given you any idea of his constant kindness and self-sacrifice all through that dreadful time."

Mr. Maybourne rose from his chair as she finished speaking, and came round to where I sat. Holding out his hand to me, he said, with tears standing in his eyes:

"Mr. Wrexford, you are a brave man, and from the bottom of my heart I thank you. You have saved my girl, and brought her home safe to me; as long as I live I shall not be able to repay the debt I owe you. Remember, however, that henceforth I am your truest friend."

But I must draw a curtain over this scene. If I go into any further details I shall break down again as I did then. Suffice it that Mr. May-bourne refused to hear of my leaving his house as I proposed, but insisted that I should remain as his guest until I had decided what I intended to do with myself.

"For the future you must look upon this as your home in South Africa," he said. "I seem powerless to express my gratitude to you as I should like. But a time may come when I may even be able to do that."

"You have more than repaid me, I'm sure," I replied. "I have every reason to be deeply grateful to you for the way you have received me."

He replied in his former strain, and when he had done so, the conversation turned upon those who had been lost in the ill-fated *Fiji Princess*. It was easy to see that his brother-in-law's death cut him to the quick.

After luncheon that day I found myself alone with Mr. Maybourne. I was not sorry for this, as I wanted to sound him as to my future movements. As I have so often said, I had no sort of desire to remain in Cape Town, and judged that the sooner I was up country, and out of civilization, the better it would be for me.

"You must forgive my being frank with you, Mr. Wrexford," said my host, as we lit cigars preparatory to drawing our chairs into the veranda; "but I have gathered from what you yourself have said and from what my daughter has told me, that you are visiting South Africa on the chance of obtaining some sort of employment. Is this so?"

"That is exactly why I am here," I said. "I am most anxious to find something to do as soon as possible."

"In what direction will you seek it?" he asked. "What is your inclination? Remember, I may be able to help you."

"I am not at all particular," I answered. "I have knocked about the world a good deal, and I can turn my hand to most things. But if a choice were permitted me, I fancy I should prefer mining of some sort to anything else."

"Indeed! I had no idea you understood that sort of work."

"I have done a good deal of it," I replied, with a little touch of pride, for which next moment I found it difficult to account, considering the result to which it had brought me.

He asked one or two practical questions, which I was fortunately able to answer to his satisfaction, and then was silent for a couple of minutes or so. At last he consulted his pocket-book, and then turned to me.

"I fancy, Mr. Wrexford," he said, "that you have come in the nick of time for both of us. We may be able to do each other mutual services."

"I am very glad to hear that," I answered. "But in what possible way can I help you?"

"Well, the matter stands like this," he said. "As you are doubtless aware, my business is mostly in connection with mining, both in this colony and its neighbours. Well, information has lately reached me concerning what promises to prove a first-class property in Mashonaland, eighty-five miles from Bulawayo. The mine has been excellently reported on, and is now being got into good going order. It only needs a capable manager at its head to do really well. Of course such a man is easily procured in a country where every man seems to be engaged in mining, more or less; and yet for that very self-same reason I am unable to make a selection. The available men all know too much, and I have private reasons for wishing this mine to be well looked after. Now the question is, would you care for the post?"

Needless to say, I embraced the opportunity in much the same manner as a hungry trout jumps at a fly. If I could only manage to get up there without being caught the appointment would suit me in every way. Mr. Maybourne seemed as pleased at my acceptance of it as I was at his offer; and when, after a little further conversation—in which I received many useful hints and no small amount of advice—it was revealed to his daughter, she struck me as being even more delighted than either her father or myself. I noticed that Mr. Maybourne looked at her rather anxiously for a moment as if he suspected there might be some sort of understanding between us, but whatever he may have thought he kept it to himself. He need, however, have had no fear on that score. Circumstances had placed an insurmountable barrier between myself and any thought of marriage with his daughter.

As the result of our conversation, and at my special desire, it was arranged that I should start for my post on the following day. Nobody could have been more eager than I was to be out in the wilds. But, with it all, my heart felt sad when I thought that after tomorrow I might never see the woman I so ardently loved again. Since the previous night, when on the promenade-deck of the steamer I had told her of my love, neither of us had referred in any way to the subject. So remote was the chance that I should ever be able to make her my wife that I determined, so far as possible, to prevent myself from giving any thought to the idea. But I was not destined after all to leave without referring to the matter.

That evening after dinner we were sitting in the veranda outside the drawing-room, when the butler came to inform Mr. Maybourne that a neighbour had called to see him. Asking us to excuse him for a few moments he left us and went into the house. When we were alone together I spoke to my companion of her father's kindness, and told her how much I appreciated it. She uttered a little sigh, and as this seemed such an extraordinary answer to my speech, I enquired the reason of it.

"You say you are going away tomorrow," she answered, "and yet you ask me why I sigh! Cannot you guess?"

"Agnes," I said, "you know I have no option but to go. Do not let us go over the ground we covered last night. It would be best not for both our sakes; you must see that yourself."

"You know that I love you, and I know that you love me—and yet you can go away so calmly. What can your love be worth?"

"You know what it is worth," I answered vehemently, roused out of myself by this accusation. "And if ever the chance occurs again of proving it you will be afforded another example. I cannot say more."

"And is it always to be like this, Gilbert," she asked, for the first time calling me by my Christian name. "Are we to be separated all our lives?"

"God knows—I fear so," I murmured, though it cut me to the heart to have to say the words.

She bowed her head on her hands with a little moan, while I, feeling that I should not be able to control myself much longer, sprang to my feet and went across to the veranda rails. For something like five minutes I stood looking into the dark garden, then I pulled myself together as well as I was able and went back to my chair.

"Agnes," I said, as I took possession of her little hand, "you cannot guess what it costs me to tell you how impossible it is for me ever to link my lot with yours. The reason why I cannot tell you. My secret is the bitterest one a man can have to keep, and it must remain locked in my own breast for all time. Had I met you earlier it might have been very different—but now our ways must be separate for ever. Don't think more hardly of me than you can help, dear. Remember only that as long as I live I shall call no other woman wife. Henceforward I will try to be worthy of the interest you have felt in me. No one shall ever have the right to say ought against me; and, if by any chance you hear good of me in the dark days to come, you will know that it is for love of you I rule my life. May God bless and keep you always."

She held up her sweet face to me, and I kissed her on the lips. Then Mr. Maybourne returned to the veranda; and, half-an-hour later, feeling that father and daughter would like a little time alone together before they retired to rest, I begged them to excuse me, and on a pretence of feeling tired went to my room.

Next morning after breakfast I drove with Mr. Maybourne into Cape Town, where I made the few purchases necessary for my journey. In extension of the kindness he had so far shown me, he insisted on advancing me half my first year's salary—a piece of generosity for which you may be sure I was not ungrateful, seeing that I had not a halfpenny in the world to call my own. Out of this sum I paid the steamship company for my passage—much against their wish—obtained a ready-made rig out suitable for the rough life I should henceforth live, also a revolver, a rifle, and among other things a small gold locket which I wished to give to Agnes as a keepsake and remembrance of myself.

At twelve o'clock I returned to the house, and, after lunch, prepared to bid the woman I loved "goodbye." Of that scene I cannot attempt to give you any description—the pain is too keen even now. Suffice it that when I left the house I carried with me, in addition to a sorrow that I thought would last me all my life, a little square parcel which, on opening, I found to contain a photo of herself in a Russia leather case. How I prized that little present I will leave you to guess.

Two hours later I was in the train bound for Johannesburg.

CHAPTER 10

I Tell My Story

Six months had elapsed since I had left Cape Town, and on looking back on them now I have to confess that they constituted the happiest period of my life up to that time. I had an excellent appointment, an interesting, if not all-absorbing, occupation, comfortable quarters, and the most agreeable of companions any man could desire to be associated with. I was as far removed from civilization as the most misanthropic of men, living by civilized employment, could hope to get. Our nearest town, if by such a name a few scattered huts could be dignified, was nearly fifty miles distant, our mails only reached us once a week, and our stores once every three months. As I had never left the mine for half a day during the whole of the time I had been on it, I had seen no strange faces, and by reason of the distance and the unsettled nature of the country, scarcely half-a-dozen had seen mine.

"The Pride of the South," as the mine had been somewhat grandiloquently christened by its discoverer, was proving a better property than had even been expected, and to my astonishment, for I had made haste to purchase shares in it, my luck had turned, and I found myself standing an excellent chance of becoming a rich man.

One thing surprised me more and more every day, and that was my freedom from arrest; how it had come about that I was permitted to remain at large so long I could not understand. When I had first come up to Rhodesia I had found a danger in everything about me. In the rustling of the coarse veldt grass at night, the sighing of the wind through the trees, and even the shadows of the mine buildings and machinery. But when week after week and month after month went by and still no notice was taken of me by the police, my fears began to abate until, at the time of which I am about to speak, I hardly thought of the matter at all. When I did I hastened to put it away from me in much the same way as I would have done the remembrance of some unpleasant dream of the previous week. One consolation, almost cruel in its uncertainty, was always with me. If suspicion had not so far fallen on me in England, it would be unlikely, I argued, ever to do so; and in the joy of this thought I began to dream dreams of the happiness that might possibly be mine in the future. Was it to be wondered at therefore that my work was pleasant to me and that the wording of Mr. Maybourne's letters of praise seemed sweeter in my ears than the strains of the loveliest music could have been. It was evident that my star was in the ascendant, but, though I could not guess it then, my troubles were by no means over; and, as I was soon to find out, I was on the edge of the bitterest period of all my life.

Almost on the day that celebrated my seventh mouth in Mr. May-bourne's employ, I received a letter from him announcing his intention of starting for Rhodesia in a week's time, and stating that while in our neighbourhood he would embrace the opportunity of visiting "The Pride of the South." In the postscript he informed me that his daughter had decided to accompany him, and for this reason he would be glad if I would do my best to make my quarters as comfortable as possible in preparation for her. He, himself, he continued, was far too old a traveller to be worth considering.

I was standing at the engine-room door, talking to one of the men, when the store-keeper brought me my mail. After I had read my chief's letter, I felt a thrill go through me that I could hardly have diagnosed for pleasure or pain. I felt it difficult to believe that in a few weeks' time I should see Agnes again, be able to look into her face, and hear the gentle accents of her voice. The portrait she had given me of herself I carried continually about with me; and, as a proof of the inspection it received, I may say that it was already beginning to show decided signs of wear. Mr. Maybourne had done well in asking me to see to her comfort. I told myself I would begin my preparations at once, and it should go hard with me if she were not pleased with my arrangements when she arrived.

While I was mentally running my eye over what I should do, Mackinnon, my big Scotch overseer, came up from the shaft's mouth to where I stood, and reported that some timbering which I had been hurrying forward was ready for inspection. After we had visited it and I had signified my approval, I informed him of our employer's contemplated visit, and wound up by saying that his daughter would accompany him. He shook his head solemnly when he heard this.

"A foolish thing," he said, in his slow, matter-of fact way, "a very foolish thing. This country's nae fit for a lady at present, as Mr. Maybourne kens well eno'. An' what's more, there'll be trouble among the boys (natives) before vera long. He'd best be out of it."

"My dear fellow," I said, a little testily I fear, for I did not care to hear him throw cold water on Mr. Maybourne's visit in this fashion, "you're always thinking the natives are going to give trouble, but you must confess that what you prophesy never comes off."

He shook his head more sagely than before.

"Ye can say what ye please," he said, "I'm nae settin' up for a proph-et, but I canna help but see what's put plain before my eyes. As the proverb says 'Forewarned is forearmed.' There's been trouble an' dis-content all through this country-side for months past, an' if Mr. May-bourne brings his daughter up here—well, he'll have to run the risk of mischief happenin' to the lass. It's no business o' mine, however. As the proverb says—'Let the wilful gang their own gait.'"

Accustomed as he was to look on the gloomy side of things, I could not but remember that he had been in the country a longer time than I had, and that he had also had a better experience of the treacherous Matabele than I could boast.

"In your opinion, then," I said, "I had better endeavour to dissuade Mr. Maybourne from coming up?"

"Nae! Nae! I'm na' sayin' that at all. Let him come by all means since he's set on it. But I'm not going to say I think he's wise in bring-ing the girl."

With this ambiguous answer I had to be content. I must confess, however, that I went back to the house feeling a little uneasy in my mind. Ought I to write and warn Mr. Maybourne, or should I leave the matter to chance? As I did not intend to send off my mail until the following day, I determined to sleep on it.

In the morning I discovered that my fears had entirely vanished. The boys we employed were going about their duties in much the same manner as usual, and the half-dozen natives who had come in during the course of the day in the hope of obtaining employment, seemed so peaceably inclined that I felt compelled to dismiss Mackin-non's suspicions from my mind as groundless, and determined on no account to alarm my friends in such needlessly silly fashion.

How well I remember Mr. and Miss Maybourne's arrival! It was on a Wednesday, exactly three weeks after my conversation with Mackin-non just recorded, that a boy appeared with a note from the old gen-tleman to me. It was written from the township, and stated that they had got so far and would be with me during the afternoon. From that time forward I was in a fever of impatience. Over and over again I examined my preparations with a critical eye, discussed the meals with the cook to make sure that he had not forgotten a single particular, drilled my servants in their duties until I had brought them as near perfection as it was possible for me to get them, and in one way and another fussed about generally until it was time for my guests to arrive. I had fitted up my own bedroom for Miss Maybourne, and made it as comfortable as the limited means at my disposal would allow. Her father would occupy the overseer's room, that individual sharing a tent with me at the back.

The sun was just sinking to his rest below the horizon when I espied a cloud of dust on the western veldt. Little by little it grew larger until we could distinctly make out a buggy drawn by a pair of horses. It was travelling at a high rate of speed, and before many minutes were over would be with us. As I watched it my heart began to beat so tumultuously that it seemed as if those around me could not fail to hear it. In the vehicle now approaching was the woman I loved, the woman whom I had made up my mind I should never see again.

Five minutes later the horses had pulled up opposite my veranda and I had shaken hands with my guests and was assisting Agnes to alight. Never before had I seen her look so lovely. She seemed quite to have recovered from the horrors of the shipwreck, and looked even stronger than when I had first seen her on the deck of the *Fiji Princess*, the day we had left Southampton. She greeted me with a fine show of cordiality, but under it it was easy to see that she was as nervous as myself. Having handed the horses and buggy over to a couple of my boys, I led my guests into the house I had prepared for them.

Evidently they had come with the intention of being pleased, for they expressed themselves as surprised and delighted with every arrangement I had made for their comfort. It was a merry party, I can assure you, that sat down to the evening meal that night—so merry, indeed, that under the influence of Agnes' manner even Mackinnon forgot himself and ceased to prophesy ruin and desolation.

When the meal was finished we adjourned to the veranda and lit our pipes. The evening was delightfully cool after the heat of the day, and overhead the stars twinkled in the firmament of heaven like countless lamps, lighting up the sombre veldt till we could see the shadowy outline of trees miles away. The evening breeze rustled the long grass, and across the square the figure of our cook could just be seen, outlined against the ruddy glow of the fire in the hut behind him. How happy I was I must leave you to guess. From where I sat I could catch a glimpse of my darling's face, and see the gleam of her rings as her hand rested on the arm of her chair. The memory of the awful time we had spent together on the island, and in the open boat, came back to me with a feeling that was half pleasure, half pain. When I realized that I was entertaining them in my abode in Rhodesia, it seemed scarcely possible that we could be the same people.

Towards the end of the evening, Mr. Maybourne made an excuse and went into the house, leaving us together. Mackinnon had long since departed. When we were alone, Agnes leant a little forward in her chair, and said:

"Are you pleased to see me, Gilbert?"

"More pleased than I can tell you," I answered, truthfully. "But you must not ask me if I think you were wise to come."

"I can see that you think I was not," she continued. "But how little you understand my motives. I could not——"

Thinking that perhaps she had said too much, she checked herself suddenly, and for a little while did not speak again. When she did, it was only about the loneliness of my life on the mine, and such like trivial matters. Illogical as men are, though I had hoped, for both our sakes, that she would not venture again on such delicate ground as we had traversed before we said goodbye, I could not help a little sensation of disappointment when she acted up to my advice. I was still more piqued when, a little later, she stated that she felt tired, and holding out her hand, bade me "good-night," and went to her room.

Here I can only give utterance to a remark which, I am told, is as old as the hills—and that is, how little we men understand the opposite sex. From that night forward, for the first three or four days of her visit, Agnes' manner towards me was as friendly as of old, but I noticed that she made but small difference between her treatment of Mackinnon and the way in which she behaved towards myself. This was more than I could bear, and in consequence my own behaviour towards her changed. I found myself bringing every bit of ingenuity I possessed to bear on an attempt to win her back to the old state. But it was in vain! Whenever I found an opportunity, and hinted at my love for her, she invariably changed the conversation into such a channel that all my intentions were frustrated. In consequence, I exerted myself the more to please until my passion must have been plain to everyone about the place. Prudence, honour, everything that separated me from her was likely to be thrown to the winds. My infatuation for Agnes Maybourne had grown to such a pitch that without her I felt that I could not go on living.

One day, a little more than a week after their arrival, it was my good fortune to accompany her on a riding excursion to a waterfall in the hills, distant some seven or eight miles from the mine. On the way she rallied me playfully on what she called "my unusual quietness." This was more than I could stand, and I determined, as soon as I could find a convenient opportunity, to test my fate and have it settled for good and all.

On reaching our destination, we tied our horses, by their reins, to a tree at the foot of the hill, and climbed up to the falls we had ridden over to explore. After the first impression, created by the wild grandeur of the scene, had passed, I endeavoured to make the opportunity I wanted.

"How strangely little circumstances recall the past. What place does that remind you of?" I asked, pointing to the rocky hill on the other side of the fall.

"Of a good many," she answered, a little artfully, I'm afraid. "I cannot say that it reminds me of one more than another. All things considered, there is a great sameness in South African scenery."

Cleverly as she attempted to turn my question off, I was not to be baulked so easily.

"Though the likeness has evidently not impressed you, it reminds me very much of Salvage Island," I said, drawing a step closer to her side. "Half-way up that hill one might well expect to find the plateau and the cave."

"Oh, why do you speak to me of that awful cave," she said, with a shudder; "though I try to forget it, it always gives me a nightmare."

"I am sorry I recalled it to your memory, then," I answered. "I think in spite of the way you have behaved towards me lately, Agnes, you are aware that I would not give you pain for anything. Do you know that?"

As I put this question to her, I looked into her face. She dropped her eyes and whispered "Yes."

Emboldened by my success I resolved to push my fate still further.

"Agnes," I said, "I have been thinking over what I am going to say to you now for some days past, and I believe I am doing right. I want to tell you the story of my life, and then to ask you a question that will decide the happiness of the rest of it. I want you to listen and, when I have done, answer me from the bottom of your heart. Whatever you say I will abide by."

She looked up at me with a startled expression on her face.

"I will listen," she said, "and whatever question you ask I will answer. But think first, Gilbert; do you really wish me to know your secret?"

"God knows I have as good reasons for wishing you to know as any man could have," I answered. "I can trust you as I can trust no one else in the world. I wish you to hear and judge me. Whatever you say, I will do and abide by it."

She put her little hand in mine, and having done so, seated herself on a boulder. Then, after a little pause, she bade me tell her all.

"In the first place," I said, "I must make a confession that may surprise you. My name is not Wrexford, as I have so long led you to suppose. It is Pennethorne. My father was Sir Anthony Pennethorne, of Polton-Penna, in Cornwall. I was educated at Eton and Oxford; and, as you will now see, I got no good from either. After a college scrape, the blame for which was thrown upon me, my father turned me out of England with a portion of my inheritance. I went to Australia, where I tried my hand at all sorts of employment, gold mining among the number. Details of my life out there, with one exception, would not interest you; so I will get on to the great catastrophe, the results of which were taking me out of England when I first met you. Up to this time ill-luck had constantly pursued me, and I had even known the direst poverty. You may imagine, therefore, what my feelings were when an old friend, a man with whom I had been partner on many gold-fields, told me of a place which he had discovered where, he said, there were prospects of sufficient gold to make us both millionaires half a dozen times over. He, poor fellow, was dying at the time, but he left his secret to me, bidding me take immediate advantage of it. True to my promise, I intended to set off to the place he had found as soon as he was buried, and having discovered it, to apply to Government for right to mine there, but fate was against me, and I was taken seriously ill. For weeks I hovered between life and death. When I recovered I saddled my horse, and, dreaming of all I was going to accomplish with my wealth, when I had obtained it, made my way across country by the chart he had given me. When I arrived at the spot it was only to learn that my greatest enemy in the world, a man who hated me as much as I did him, had filched my secret from me in my delirium, and had appropriated the mine. You cannot imagine my disappointment. I wanted money so badly, and I had counted so much on obtaining this, that I had almost come to believe myself possessed of it. What need to tell the rest? He became enormously rich, and returned to England. In the meantime my father had died, leaving me a sufficient sum, when carefully invested, to just keep me alive. With this to help me I followed my enemy home, resolved, if ever a chance arose, to revenge myself upon him. When I arrived I saw his name everywhere.

156

I found his wealth, his generosity, his success in life, extolled in every paper I picked up; while I, from whom he had stolen that which gave him his power, had barely sufficient to keep me out of the workhouse. You must understand that I had been seriously ill, for the second time, just before I left Australia, and perhaps for this reason—but more so, I believe, on account of the great disappointment to which I had been subjected—I began to brood over my wrongs by day and night, and pine for revenge. I could not eat or sleep for it. Remember, I do not say this in any way to excuse myself, but simply to show you that my mind was undoubtedly not quite itself at the time. At any rate, to such a pitch of hatred did I at length work myself that it was as much as I could do to prevent myself from laying violent hands upon my enemy when I saw him in the public streets. After I had been entertaining the devil in this fashion for longer than was good for me, he in return sent one of his satellites to complete my ruin. That man—such a man as you could not picture to yourself—put before me a scheme for getting even with my enemy, so devilish that at first I could hardly believe he was in earnest. So insidiously did he tempt me, playing upon my hatred and increasing my desire for revenge, that at last I fell into his net as completely as he could wish. The means were immediately found for getting my victim into my clutches, and then nothing remained but to work out the hideous crime that had been planned for me."

I stopped for a moment and looked at Agnes, who was cowering with her face in her hands. She did not speak, so I continued my gruesome tale.

"I need not tell you how I got the man in my power, nor in what manner it was arranged that I should kill him. I will content myself with telling you that when I had got him, and could have killed him by lifting my little finger, difficult as you may find it to believe it, I saw your face before me imploring me to repent. There and then I determined to throw off my disguise, to let him know who I was, and what I intended to do to him; after that I would have bidden him go, and have left him to his own conscience. But, to my horror, when I got down from my box—for I was driving him in a cab—I found that in some devilish fashion my work had been anticipated for me—the man was dead, killed by the same fatal agency that had been given to me to do the deed. Try for one moment to imagine my position. In one instant I stood in that quiet London street, stamped with the brand of Cain. Never again could I be like my fellow men. Henceforth I must know myself for what I was—a murderer, whose proper end should be the gallows. In an agony of terror I got rid of the body—left it in the street in fact—and fled for my very life. While the town was still abed and asleep I tramped away into the country, and at a suburban station caught the earliest train to Southampton. On arrival there I booked my passage in the *Fiji Princess* for South Africa, and went on board. The rest you know. Now, Agnes, that you have heard my wretched story, you can see for yourself why I was so desirous of getting out of civilization as quickly as possible. You can judge for yourself whether I was right or wrong in refusing to allow you to say you loved me. God knows you cannot judge me more harshly than I judge myself."

She looked up at me with terror-stricken eyes.

"But you did not mean to kill the man," she cried. "You repented—you said so just now yourself.

"If it had not been for me the man would not have died," I answered. "No, no! Agnes, you cannot make me out innocent of his death, however hard you try."

A look of fresh life darted into her face. It was as if she had been struck by a brilliant idea that might mean my salvation.

"But how do you know that you killed the man?" she asked. "Are you quite certain that he was dead when you looked at him?"

"Quite certain," I answered. "I examined him most carefully. Besides, I have made enquiries since and elicited the fact that he has never been seen or heard of since that awful night. There have been advertisements in the papers offering rewards for any information concerning him."

She did not reply to this, only sat and rocked herself to and fro, her face once more covered in her hands. I knelt beside her, but did not dare, for very shame, to attempt to comfort her.

"Agnes," I said, "speak to me. If it only be to say how much you loathe me. Your silence cuts me to the heart. Speak to me, tell me my fate, advise me as to what I shall do. I swear by God that whatever you tell me, that I will do without questioning or comment."

Still she did not answer. When I saw this I rose to my feet, and in my agony must have turned a little from her. This action evidently decided her, for she sprang up from the boulder on which she had hitherto been sitting, and, with a choking cry, fell into my arms and sobbed upon my shoulder.

"Gilbert," she moaned, "come what may, I believe in you. Nothing shall ever convince me that you would have killed the man who so cruelly wronged you. You hated him; you longed to be revenged on him; but you never would have murdered him when it came to the point."

In answer I drew her closer to me.

"Agnes, my good angel," I said; "what can I say to you for the comfort you give me? You have put fresh life into me. If only you believe in me, what do I care for the world? Heaven knows I did not mean to kill the man—but still the fact remains that he is dead, and through my agency. Though morally I am innocent, the law would certainly hold me guilty."

"You do not mean to say that the police will take you?" she cried, starting away from me with a gesture of horror.

"If I am suspected, there can be no doubt that they will do so. How it happens that I have not been arrested ere this I cannot imagine."

"But, Gilbert, you must not let them find you. You must go away—you must hide yourself."

"It would be no use, they would find me sooner or later, wherever I went."

"Oh, what can you do then? Come what may I shall not let you be taken. Oh God, I could not bear that."

She glanced wildly round, as if she fancied the minions of the law might already be on my track. I endeavoured to soothe her, but in vain. She was thoroughly frightened, and nothing I could say or do would convince her that I was not in immediate danger. At last, to try and bring her to a reasonable frame of mind, I adopted other tactics.

"But, Agnes, we are missing one point that is of vital importance," I said. "Knowing what I am, henceforward everything must be over between us."

"No, no!" she cried, with a sudden change of front. "On the other hand, you have shown me that there is more reason than ever that I should love you. If you are in danger, this is the time for me to prove what my affection is worth. Do you value my love so lightly that you deem it only fit for fair weather? When the world is against you, you can see who are your friends."

"God bless you, darling," I said, kissing her sweet upturned face. "You know that there is no one in this world so much to me as you; and for that very reason I cannot consent to link your fate with such a terrible one as mine."

"Gilbert," she said, "if you repulse me now you will make me miserable for life. Oh, why must I plead so hard with you? Cannot you see that I am in earnest when I say I wish to share your danger with you?"

I was silent for a few moments. In what way could I make her see how base a thing it would be on my part to pull her down into the maelstrom of misery that might any day draw me to my doom? At last an idea occurred to me.

"Agnes," I said, "will you agree to a compromise? Will you promise me to take a year to think it over? If at the end of that time I am still at liberty I will go to your father, tell him my story as I have today told it to you, and, if he will still have anything to do with me, ask him for your hand. By that time I shall probably know my fate, you will be able to see things more clearly, and I shall not feel that I have taken advantage of your love and sympathy."

"But I want to be with you and to help you now."

"Believe me, you can help me best by agreeing to my proposal. Will you make me happy by consenting to what I wish?"

"If it will please you I will do so," she said, softly.

"God bless you, dear," I answered.

And thus the matter was concluded.

CHAPTER 11

A Terrible Surprise

Nearly a week had elapsed since I had made my confession to Agnes at the falls, and in three days it was Mr. Maybourne's intention to set out on his return journey to the South. During the whole of that period not one word had been said by Miss Maybourne regarding my story. But if she did not refer to it in speech it was easy to see that the subject was never absent from her mind. On two occasions I heard her father question her as to the reason of her quietness, and I saw that each time she found it a more difficult task to invent a satisfactory reply. What this meant to me you will readily understand. I could not sleep at night for thinking of it, and not once but a thousand times I bitterly regretted having burdened her mind with my unhappy secret.

Two afternoons prior to our guests' departure I was sitting in my veranda reading the letters which had been brought to the mine by the mailman at midday. Mr. Maybourne was sitting near me, also deep in his correspondence, while his daughter had gone to her own room for the same purpose. When I came to the end of my last epistle I eat with it in my hand, looking out across the veldt, and thinking of all that had happened since I had said goodbye to old England.

From one thing my thoughts turned to another; I thought of my wandering life in Australia, of poor old Ben Garman, of Markapurlie, and last of all of Bartrand. The memory of my hatred for him brought me home again to London, and I saw myself meeting Nikola in the Strand, and then accompanying him home to his extraordinary abode. As I pictured him seated in his armchair in that oddly-furnished room, all my old horror of him flashed back upon me. I seemed to feel the fascination of his eyes just as I had done that night when we visited that murderous cab in the room below.

While I was thinking of him, I heard a footstep on the path that led round the house, and presently Mackinnon appeared before me. He beckoned with his hand, and understanding that he desired to speak to me, I rose from my chair and went out to him.

"What is it?" I enquired, as I approached him, for at that hour he was generally in the depths of the mine. "Has anything gone wrong."

"That's as ye care to take my words or no," he answered, wheeling about and leading me out of earshot of the house. There was something in his manner that frightened me, though I could not for the life of me have said why. When we reached the fence that separated my garden from the open veldt I stopped, and leaning on the rails, once more asked him why he had called me out.

"I told ye a fortnight ago that there was trouble brewing for us with the natives," he said impressively. "I warned ye a week ago that 'twas no better. Now I tell ye its close upon us, and if we're not prepared, God help us all."

"What do you mean? Don't speak in enigmas, man. Tell me straight out what you are driving at."

"Isn't that what I'm trying to do?" he said. "I tell ye the whole country's in a ferment. The Matabele are out, and in a few hours, if not before, we shall have proof of it."

"Good God, man!" I cried, "how do you know this? And why did you not make me see the importance of it before?"

"'Ye can lead a horse to the water but ye canna make him drink,' says the proverb," he answered. "Ye can tell a man of danger, but ye canna make him see it. An' so 'twas with ye. I told ye my suspicions a fortnight past, but 'twas only this minute I came to know how bad it really was."

"And how have you come to hear of it now?"

"Step this way an' I'll show ye."

He led me to a small hut near the kitchen. On reaching it, he opened it and showed me a man stretched out upon a bed of sacks and grass. He was a white man, and seemed utterly exhausted.

"This man's name," said Mackinnon, as if he were exhibiting some human curiosity, "is Andrews. He's a prospector, and we've been acquent for years. Now tell your yarn, Andrews, and let Mr. Wrexford here see how bad the matter is."

"I've not much to tell, sir," said the man addressed, sitting up as he spoke. "It came about like this: I am a prospector, and I was out away back on the river there, never dreaming there was mischief in the wind. Then my boys began to drop hints that there was likely to be trouble, and I'd best keep my weather eye open. At first I didn't believe them, but when I got back to camp at mid-day today and found both my servants murdered, my bullocks killed, and my rifles and everything else of value stolen, I guessed who had done it. Fortunately, they had passed on without waiting for me, so I got into the saddle again and came here post haste to warn you. I tell you this, the Matabele are rising. The *impi* that murdered my men is under one of the king's sons, and by this time they are not twenty miles distant from this spot. There can be no doubt that they are travelling this way. From what my boys told me, Bulawayo is surrounded, while three more *impis* are travelling night and day with the same object as the one I now warn you of, namely, to cut off the advance of the troops being pushed forward to oppose them from the south."

"Do you mean this? On your oath, are you telling me the truth?"

"God strike me dead if I'm not," he answered, solemnly. "Look at me, sir, I've made my way in here as hard as a man could come, riding for his life. That should be proof enough; but if it isn't, Mr. Mackinnon here will speak for me, I'm sure."

"That I will," said Mackinnon. "I've known you long enough, and always found you a straightforward man."

I stood for a few moments deep in thought.

"How far do you think they are away from us at the present moment?"

"Not more than twenty miles at most, sir. I left my camp on the river about mid-day, and I've been here about a quarter of an hour. I came in as hard as I could ride; say five hours riding at twelve miles an hour, making a big detour of about twenty miles, to avoid them. That should make between fifteen and twenty miles away now if they did five miles an hour straight across country."

"And you're sure they mean war?"

"There's not a doubt of it, sir. I know the vermin too well by this time not to be certain of that."

"Then I must tell Mr. Maybourne at once. Come with me Mackinnon, and you too, Andrews, if you can manage it. We must hold a council of war and see what's best to be done."

I led them across the small paddock to my office, and then went on to the house in search of my employer. I found him pacing up and down the veranda, looking rather disturbed.

"Wrexford, my dear fellow," he began, on seeing me, "I have been looking for you. I want a few moments' earnest conversation with you."

"And I with you, sir," I answered.

He led me beyond the veranda before he spoke again.

"You must hear me first. What I want to see you about is as important as life and death to us all. I have received a number of letters by the mail, and one and all warn me that there is likely to be trouble with the Matabele—The Chartered Company have seen it coming, I am told, and are taking all the necessary steps to secure life and property, but there is no knowing when the brutes may not be on us, and what they may not do if they start with the upper hand. Now, you see, if I were alone I should have no hesitation in remaining to see it out—but there is Agnes to consider; and, with a woman in the question, one has to think twice before one ventures upon such a course."

"That is the very thing I came over to see you about, sir. Serious news has just reached me, and—well, to tell you the truth, we are in danger now, this very minute. If you will step over to my office, I have a man there who has seen the enemy within forty miles of this place, and he tells me they are advancing in our direction even now."

His face, for an instant, became deadly pale, and I noticed that he glanced anxiously at the sitting-room door.

"Steady, Wrexford, for heaven's sake," he said. "Not too loud, or Agnes will hear. We musn't frighten her before we are absolutely obliged. Come to the office and let me see this man for myself."

Together we walked over to my den where Mackinnon and Andrews were awaiting us.

Mr. Maybourne nodded to the former and then looked searchingly at the latter.

"I am told that you have seen the Matabele under arms today," he began, coming straight to the point, as was characteristic of him.

"My servants were killed by them, and my camp was looted about forty miles from this office," replied Andrews, meeting Mr. Maybourne's glance without flinching.

"At what number should you estimate them?"

"Roughly speaking, from what I saw of them from a hill nearly a mile distant, I should say they were probably two thousand strong. They were in full war dress, and from what my servants had hinted to me that morning, I gathered that they are led by one of the king's sons."

"You have no doubt in your mind that they are coming this way?"

"I don't think there's a shadow of a doubt about it, sir. They're probably trying to effect a junction with another *impi*, and then they'll be ready to receive any troops that may come up against them from the South."

"There's something in that," said Mr. Maybourne, reflectively. "And now I am going to ask you the most important question of all, gentlemen. That is, what's to be done? If we abandon this place, the mine and

164

the buildings will be wrecked for certain. At the best we can only reach the township, where we can certainly go into laager, but in my opinion we shall be even worse off there than we are here. What do you say?"

There could not be any doubt about the matter in my opinion. In the township we should certainly be able to make up a larger force, but our defences could not be made so perfect, while to abandon the mine was an act for which none of us were prepared.

"Very well then," continued Mr. Maybourne, when he had heard that we agreed with him, "in that case the best thing we can do is to form a laager here, and prepare to hold out until the troops that I have been told are on their way up can rescue us. How are we off for arms and ammunition, Wrexford?"

"I will show you," I said, and forthwith led the way through the office into a smaller room at the back. Here I pointed to an arm-rack in which twenty-two Winchester repeating rifles, a couple of Martini-Henris, and about thirty cutlasses were arranged.

"How may men capable of firing a decent shot can we muster?" asked Mr. Maybourne, when he had overhauled the weapons.

"Nineteen white men, including ourselves, and about half-a-dozen natives."

"And how much ammunition have we?"

"I can tell you in a moment," I answered, taking up a book from the table and consulting it. "Here it is. Two thousand cartridges for the repeating rifles, two hundred for the Martinis, and a thousand for the six revolvers I have in this drawer."

"A good supply, and I congratulate you on it. Now let us get to work. Ring the bell, Mr. Mackinnon, and call all the hands up to the house. I'll talk to them, and when I've explained our position, we'll get to work on the *laager*."

Ten minutes later every man had been informed of his danger, and was taking his share of work upon the barricades. Wagons, cases, sacks of flour, sheets of iron—everything, in fact, which would be likely to give shelter to ourselves and resistance to the enemy was pressed into our service, while all that would be likely to afford cover to the enemy for a hundred yards or so round the house was destroyed. Every tank that could be utilized was carried to the house and filled with water. The cattle were driven in, and when small earthworks had been thrown up and the stores had been stacked in a safe place, we felt we might consider ourselves prepared for a siege. By nightfall we were ready and waiting for the appearance of our foe. Sentries were posted, and in order that the township might be apprised of its danger and also that the troops who were hourly expected, as Mr. Maybourne had informed us, might know of our peril, a man was despatched on a fast horse with a letter to the inhabitants.

Having accompanied Mr. Maybourne round the square, and assured myself that our defences were as perfect as the limited means at our disposal would permit, our store of arms was brought from the office and the distribution commenced. A Winchester repeating rifle and a hundred cartridges, a cutlass, and a revolver, were issued to each white man, and after they were supplied the native boys were called up. To our astonishment and momentary dismay only one put in an appearance. The rest had decamped, doubtless considering discretion the better part of valour. When, however, we saw the stuff of which they were made this did not trouble us very much.

As soon as every man had received his weapons, and had had his post and his duties pointed out to him, Mr. Maybourne and I left them to their own devices, and went up to the house. The former had told his daughter of our danger, and for this reason I was prepared to find her, if not terrified, at least showing some alarm. But to my amazement I discovered her hard at work preparing a meal for the garrison, just as calmly and quietly as if nothing out of the common were occurring. She greeted me with a smile, showed me her puddings boiling on the fire, and pointed to a number of buckets which stood about the veranda. These were filled with some peculiar-looking fluid; and I enquired what it might be. In answer I was told that it was oatmeal and water.

"If we are to fight," said this daughter of war, "you will find it thirsty work. I shall put these buckets, with mugs, at convenient places, so that you may assuage your thirst if occasion serves."

I noticed also that she had prepared a large quantity of lint in case it should be required, and had arranged a number of mattresses in the veranda. Her courage put fresh heart into me, as without doubt it did into everyone else who saw her. I told her that she was braver than the boldest man amongst us, and she thereupon showed that she still had sufficient of the woman left in her to blush with pleasure at the compliment.

"If the enemy were only forty miles away at midday," said Mr. Maybourne as we carried the men's tea out into the open to them, "they ought to be close at hand now. When we've done our meal we'll post extra sentries; for though I do not for a moment expect they'll attack us in the dark, it would never do to allow ourselves to be surprised."

I agreed with him; and, accordingly, as soon as our tea was finished, men were placed not only at the four corners of the *laager*, but at equal distances between them. The remainder lay down to rest wherever they could make themselves most comfortable. I found myself about the only exception to the rule; and, do what I would, I could not sleep. Having tried for an hour and a half, and found it still impossible, I went across to the veranda and sat down in one of the cane chairs there. I had not been there many moments before I was joined by Agnes, who seated herself beside me. I reproved her for not resting after her labours of the day.

"I could not sleep," she answered. "Brave as you call me, I am far too nervous to rest. Do you really think the enemy will attack us in the morning?"

"Not knowing their plans, I cannot say," I replied, "but I must confess it looks terribly like it."

"In that case I want you to promise me something, Gilbert."

"What is it?" I asked. "You know there is nothing I would not do for you, Agnes. What am I to promise?"

"That if we are overpowered you will not let me fall into their hands alive. You may think me a coward, but I dread that more than any thought of death."

"Hush! You must not talk like that. Have no fear, we will not let you fall into their hands. You know that there is not a man upon the mine who would not give his life for you."

She leaned a little forward and looked into my face. "I know you would protect me, would you not?"

"Wait and see. The man who touches you, Agnes, will have to do it over my dead body. Do you know that tonight, for some reason or other, I feel more superstitious than I have ever done before. I can't rid myself of the thought that I am near the one vital crisis of my life."

"What do you mean, Gilbert? You frighten me."

"I cannot tell you what I mean, for I don't know myself. I think I'm what the Scotch call 'fey'"

"I have prayed to God for you," she said. "He who has protected us before will do so again. Let us do our duty and leave the rest to Hun."

"Amen to that," I answered solemnly; and then with a whispered "good-night" she got up and went into the house again.

Hour after hour I sat on in the veranda, as much unable to sleep as I had been at the beginning. At intervals I made a circuit of the sentries, and convinced myself that no man was sleeping at his post, but for the greater part of the time I sat staring at the winking stars.

Though I searched the open space outside the *laager* over and over again, not a sign of the enemy could I discover. If they were there, they must have been keeping wonderfully quiet. The sighing of the breeze in the long veldt grass was the only sound that I could distinguish.

I heard the clock in the house behind me strike one, two, and then three. By the time the last hour sounded, it was beginning to grow light. From where I sat in the veranda, I could just discern the shadowy outline of the wagons, and distinguish the figures of the sentries as they paced to and fro at their posts.

Thinking it was time to be astir, I rose from my chair and went into the house to help Agnes by lighting the fire for her, and putting the kettles on to boil.

I had just laid the sticks, and was about to set a match to them, when a shot rang out on the northern side of the *laager*. It was immediately followed by another from the south. I waited to hear no more, but snatched up my rifle from the table and ran out into the open. Before I had crossed the veranda, shots were being fired in all directions, and on reaching my post, I discovered a black crowd advancing at a run towards us.

"Steady men, steady," I heard Mr. Maybourne shout as he took up his station. "Don't lose your heads whatever you do. Keep under cover, and don't fire till you're certain your shot will tell."

The words were hardly out of his mouth before the enemy were upon us, brandishing their *assegais* and shields, and yelling in a manner that would have chilled the blood of the oldest veteran. It was the first time I had ever fired a shot at my fellow man, and for the moment I will confess to feeling afraid. However, that soon passed, and I found myself taking aim, and firing as coolly as the best of them. Though I was hardly conscious that I had pulled the trigger, I saw the man directly in front of me—a fine, tall fellow with a nodding head-dress of feathers—suddenly throw up his arms and fall forward on his face, tearing at the ground with his hands in his death agony. But I was not able to do more than glance at him before two others were upon me. This time I fired with more deliberation than before, with the result that both went down, one after the other, like ninepins. Then for what seemed a year, but must in reality have been about three minutes, I continued to fire, depressing the finger lever between each shot and tipping out the empty cartridge with automatic regularity. In front of my defences a ghastly pile of bodies was fast accumulating, and by craning my neck to right and left, I could discern similar heaps before the shelters of my next-door neighbours.

This desire to ascertain how my friends were getting on was, however, nearly my undoing; for if I had been more intent upon my own concerns, I should have seen a man wriggling along on the ground towards me. Just, however, as he was about to hurl his *assegai* I caught sight of him, and brought my rifle to the shoulder. Seeing this, he rose to his feet with a jump, and hurled his spear. I dodged with the quickness of lightning, and heard it strike the tyre of the wheel behind me. At the same instant I covered him and pulled the trigger. To my horror the rifle did not go off. I had fired my nine shots, and the magazine was empty. But my wits did not desert me for long. Before the savage had time to clamber on to the wheel and raise his *knobkerrie*, I was within striking distance, and, swinging my rifle by the barrel high into the air, brought the butt down upon his head with a crash that might have been heard yards away. It crushed in his skull like an egg-shell, and he fell like a log and never moved again.

As he went down a sudden peace descended upon the field, and for a moment or two every man wondered what had happened. The smoke quickly cleared away, and when it did we saw that the foe had retired. I accordingly clambered back to my old position, and looked about me. My throat was like a lime kiln, and my eyes were dry as dust. But I was not going to take any refreshment, though a bucket stood quite close to me, until I had refilled my rifle. This done, I crossed to the bucket, filled the mug and drank its contents with a relish such as I had never known in my life before. When I had handed it to another man, I turned about and endeavoured to take stock of our company. From where I stood I could see two men stretched out upon the ground. The one nearest me I knew instantly. It was Mackinnon, and a single glance was sufficient to tell me that he was dead. The other I could not for the moment identify. Mr. Maybourne, I was relieved to see, was unhurt save for a wound on his left hand, which he explained he had received in a hand-to-hand encounter in his corner.

"We've taught the brutes a lesson in all conscience," he said. "I don't fancy they'll be as eager next time. How many men have we lost?"

In order to find out, we walked quickly round our defences, encouraging the garrison as we went, and bidding them replenish the magazines of their rifles while they had the chance.

On the other side of the house we discovered Agnes, busily engaged binding up the wounds of those who had been hurt. She was deadly pale, but her bravery was not a bit diminished. When we got back to our own quarters we had counted three dead men, two placed hors de combat by their wounds, and five more or less cut and scratched. Of the enemy we estimated that at least a hundred had fallen before our rifles, never to rise again.

For something like half-an-hour we stood at our posts, waiting to be attacked, but the foe showed no sign of moving. I was just wondering what the next move would be when I heard a shout from the right. I gripped my rifle and peered ahead of me, but there was nothing to be seen save the foe crouching behind their shelters in the distance.

"What is it?" I cried to my right-hand neighbour. "What do they see?"

"A horseman," he replied, "and coming in our direction."

"Is he mad?" I cried, "or doesn't he see his danger?"

My informant did not reply, and a moment later I saw for myself the person referred to. He was mounted on a grey horse, and was riding as fast as his animal could travel in our direction. I turned my eyes away from him for a moment. When I looked again I saw a man rise from behind a bush and hurl a spear at him. The cruel weapon was thrown with unerring aim and struck the horse just behind the saddle. He leapt into the air, and then with a scream of agony that could be heard quite plainly where we all stood watching, dashed frantically towards us. He had not, however, gone a hundred yards before he put his foot into a hole, and fell with a crash to the ground, to lie there motionless. His neck was broken, so we discovered later.

From where I stood, to the place where the man and beast lay, was scarcely eighty yards; thence, on to the spot where the enemy were in ambush, not more than a hundred. For some reason—why, I shall never be able to explain—an irresistible desire to save the injured man came over me. I could not have resisted it, even had I wished to do so. Accordingly, I placed my rifle against the axle, sprang upon the box of the wagon wheel, vaulted over, and ran as hard as I could go towards the victim of the accident. Ahead of me I could distinctly see the nodding plumes of the foe as they crouched behind their enormous shields. They did not, however, move, and I was thus enabled to reach the man's side, and to take him in my arms unmolested. I had not gone ten yards on my return journey, however, before I heard their yells, and knew that they were after me. Fortunately, I had nearly a hundred and twenty yards start; but I had a heavy man to carry, and was quite out of breath. However, I was not going to be beaten, so putting out every ounce of strength I boasted in my body, I raced on. By the time I reached the wagons again, the foe were not fifty yards behind me. A couple of *assegais* whistled passed my ears as I climbed over the wheel and dropped my burden on the ground, but fortunately neither hit me. So exhausted was I that for a moment I leant against the wagon, unable to move. But the instinct of self-preservation gave me strength, and picking up my rifle I let drive blindly at the nearest of the foe who was already on the wheel before me. I saw the man's forehead open out like a cracked walnut as my shot caught it, and a moment later he fell forward on the tyre—dead. I threw him off in time to shoot the next man as he took his place. Of the following five minutes my only recollection is a sense of overpowering heat; a throat and mouth parched like the sands of the Great Sahara; a rifle growing every moment hotter in my hand, and dominating all the necessity of stemming, at any cost, the crowd of black humanity that seemed to be overwhelming me. How long the fight lasted I cannot say. But at last a cheer from the other side of the *laager* reached me, and almost at the same instant the enemy turned tail and fled for their lives. Then, with an empty rifle at my feet, a dripping cutlass in one hand, and a still smoking revolver in the other, I leant against the wagon and laughed hysterically till I fell fainting to the ground.

CHAPTER 12

The End

When I recovered consciousness I found a stranger dressed in uniform kneeling beside me. What was more singular still I was not under the wagon as before, but was lying surrounded by a dozen or so of my comrades in the veranda of my own house. Agnes was kneeling beside me, and her father was holding a basin of water at my feet.

"There is nothing at all to be alarmed about, my dear young lady," the man in uniform was saying as he felt my pulse. "Your friend here will live to fight another day, or a hundred other days for that matter. By this time tomorrow he'll be as well as ever." Then, turning to me, he asked: "how do you feel now?"

I replied that I felt much stronger; and then, looking up at Mr. Maybourne, enquired if we had beaten off the enemy.

"They have been utterly routed," replied the gentleman I addressed. "The credit, however, is due to Captain Haviland and his men; but for their timely arrival I fear we should have been done for. Flesh and blood could not have stood the strain another half hour."

"Stuff and nonsense," said the doctor, "for such I afterwards discovered he was, all the credit is due to yourselves; and, by George, you deserve it. A finer stand was never made in this country, or for that matter in any other."

After a few minutes' rest and another sip of brandy, I managed to get on to my feet. It was a sad sight I had before me. Stretched out in rows beyond the veranda rails were the bodies of the gallant fellows who had been killed—twelve in number. On rough beds placed in the veranda itself and also in the house were the wounded; while on the plain all round beyond the laager might have been seen the bodies of the Matabele dead. On the left of the house the regiment of mounted infantry, who had so opportunely come to our assistance, were unsaddling after chasing the enemy, and preparing to camp.

After I had had a few moments' conversation with the doctor, Mr. Maybourne and Agnes came up to me again, and congratulated me on having saved the stranger's life. The praise they gave me was altogether undeserved, for, as I have already explained, I had done the thing on the spur of the moment without for an instant considering the danger to which I had exposed myself. When they had finished I enquired where the man was, and in reply they led me into the house.

"The doctor says it is quite a hopeless case," said Agnes, turning to me in the doorway; "the poor fellow must have injured his spine when his horse fell with him."

I followed her into the room which had once been my own sleeping apartment. It was now filled with wounded. The man I had brought in lay upon a mattress in the corner by the window, and, with Agnes beside me, I went across to him. Once there I looked down at his face, and then, with a cry that even on pain of death I could not have kept back, I fell against the wall, as Agnes afterwards told me, pallid to the very lips. I don't know how to tell you who I saw there; I don't know how to make you believe it, or how to enable you to appreciate my feelings. One thing was certain, lying on the bed before me, his head bandaged up, and a bushy beard clothing the lower half of his face, was no less a person than Richard Bartrand—my old enemy and the man I believed myself to have murdered in London so many months before. I could hardly believe my eyes; I stared at him and then looked away— only to look back again half expecting to find him gone. Could this be any mistake? I asked myself. Could it be only a deceiving likeness, or an hallucination of an overtaxed brain? Hardly knowing what I did I dragged Agnes by the wrist out of the house to a quiet corner, where I leant against the wall feeling as if I were going to faint again.

"What is the matter, Gilbert?" she cried. "Oh, what is the matter with you?"

"Matter!" I almost shouted in my joy. "This is the matter. I am free—free—free! Free to marry you—free to do as I please, and live as I please, and go where I please!!! For there in that bed is my old enemy, the man I told you I had killed."

For a second she must have thought me mad, for I noticed she shrank a step away from me, and looked at me with an apprehensive glance. But she soon recovered her composure, and asked if I were certain of what I said.

"As certain as I am that you are standing before me now," I answered. "I should know him anywhere. Where is the doctor?"

A moment later I had found the doctor.

"Doctor," I said, "there is a man in that room yonder whom, I am told, you say has a broken back. He is unconscious. Will he remain so until he dies?"

"Most probably," was the other's matter-of-fact reply as he began to bind up the arm of the man he had been operating on. "Why do you ask?"

"Because it is a matter of the most vital importance that I should speak with him before he dies. All the happiness of my life and another's depends upon it."

"Very well. Don't worry yourself. I'll see what I can do for you. Now go away and be quiet. I'm busy."

I went away as he ordered me, and leant against the veranda rails at the back of the house. My head was swimming, and I could hardly think coherently. Now that Bartrand was alive, every obstacle was cleared away—I was free to marry Agnes as soon as her father would let me; free to do whatever I pleased in the world. The reaction was almost more than I could bear. No words could over-estimate my relief and joy.

Half an hour later the doctor came to me.

"Your man is conscious now," he said. "But you'd better look sharp if you want to ask him anything. He won't last long."

I followed him into the house to the corner where the sick man lay. As soon as he saw me, Bartrand showed with his eyes that he recognized me.

"Pennethorne," he whispered, as I knelt by the bed, "this is a strange meeting. Do you know I've been hunting for you these nine months past?"

"Hunting for me?" I said. "Why, I thought you dead!"

"I allowed it to be supposed that I was," he answered. "I can tell you, Pennethorne, that money I swindled you out of never brought me an ounce of luck—nor Gibbs either. He turned cocktail and sent his share back to me almost at once. He was drinking himself to death on it, I heard. Now look at me, I'm here—dying in South Africa. They tell me you saved me today at the risk of your life."

"Never mind that now," I said. "We've got other things to talk about."

"But I must mind," he answered. "Listen to what I have to tell you, and don't interrupt me. Three nights before I disappeared last winter, I made my will, leaving you everything. It's more than the value of the mine, for I brought off some big speculations with the money, and almost doubled my capital. You may not believe it, but I always felt

174

sorry for you, even when I stole your secret. I'm a pretty bad lot, but I couldn't steal your money and not be a bit sorry. But, funny as it may seem to say so, I hated you all the time too—hated you more than any other man on God's earth. Now you've risked your life for me, and I'm dying in your house. How strangely things turn out, don't they?"

Here the doctor gave him something to drink, and bade me let him be quiet for a few moments. Presently Bartrand recovered his strength, and began again.

"One day, soon after I arrived in London from Australia, I fell in tow with a man named Nikola. I tell you, Pennethorne, if ever you see that man beware of him, for he's the Devil, and nobody else. I tell you he proposed the most fiendish things to me and showed me such a side of human nature that, if I hadn't quarrelled with him and not seen so much of him I should have been driven into a lunatic asylum. I can tell you it's not altogether a life of roses to be a millionaire. About this time I began to get threatening letters from men all over Europe trying to extort money from me for one purpose or another. Eventually Nikola found out that I was the victim of a secret society. How he managed it, the deuce only knows. They wanted money badly, and finally Nikola told me that for half a million he could get me clear. If I did not pay up I'd be dead, he said, in a month. But I wasn't to be frightened like that, so I told him I wouldn't give it. From that time forward attempts were made on my life until my nerve gave way—and in a blue funk I determined to forego the bulk of my wealth and clear out of England in the hopes of beginning a new life elsewhere."

He paused once more for a few moments; his strength was nearly exhausted, and I could see with half an eye that the end was not far distant now. When he spoke again his voice was much weaker, and he seemed to find it difficult to concentrate his ideas.

"Nikola wanted sixty thousand for himself, I suppose for one of his devilments," he said, huskily. "He used every means in his power to induce me to give it to him, but I refused time after time. He showed me his power, tried to hypnotize me even, and finally told me I should be a dead man in a week if I did not let him have the money. I wasn't going to be bluffed, so I declined again. By this time I distrusted my servants, my friends, and everybody with whom I came in contact. I could not sleep, and I could not eat. All my arrangements were made, and I was going to leave England on the Saturday. On the Wednesday Nikola and I were to meet at a house on special business. We saw each other at a club, and I called a hansom, intending to go on and wait for him. I had a dreadful cold, and carried some cough drops in a little silver box in my pocket. He must have got possession of it, and substituted some preparations of his own. Feeling my cough returning, I took one in the cab as I drove along. After that I remember no more till I came round and found myself lying in the middle of the road, half covered with snow, and with a bruise the size of a tea-cup on the back of my head. For some reason of his own Nikola had tried to do for me; and the cabman, frightened at my state, had pitched me out and left me. As soon as I could walk, and it was daylight, I determined to find you at your hotel, in order to hand over to you the money I had stolen from you, and then I was going to bolt from England for my life. But when I reached Blankerton's I was told that you had left. I traced your luggage to Aberdeen; but, though I wasted a week looking, I couldn't find you there. Three months ago I chanced upon a snapshot photograph taken in Cape Town, and reproduced in an American illustrated paper. It represented one of the only two survivors of the *Fiji Princess*, and I recognised you immediately, and followed you, first to Cape Town and then, bit by bit, out here. Now listen to me, for I've not much time left. My will is in my coat-pocket; when I'm dead, you can take it out and do as you like with it. You'll find yourself one of the richest men in the world, or I'm mistaken. I can only say I hope you'll have better luck with the money than I have had. I'm glad you've got it again; for, somehow, I'd fixed the idea in my head that I shouldn't rest quietly in my grave unless I restored it to you. One caution! Don't let Nikola get hold of it, that's all—for he's after you, I'm certain. He's been tracking you down these months past; and I've heard he's on his way here. I'm told he thinks I'm dead. He'll be right in his conjecture soon."

"Bartrand," I said, as solemnly as I knew how, "I will not take one halfpenny of the money. I am firmly resolved upon that. Nothing shall ever make me."

"Not take it? But it's your own. I never had any right to it from the beginning. I stole your secret while you were ill."

"That may be; but I'll not touch the money, come what may."

"But I must leave it to somebody."

"Then leave it to the London hospitals. I will not have a penny of it. Good heavens, man, you little know how basely I behaved towards you!"

"I've not time to hear it now, then," he answered. "Quick! let me make anew will while I've strength to sign it."

Pens, paper, and ink were soon forthcoming; and at his instruction Mr. Maybourne and the doctor between them drafted the will. When it was finished the dying man signed it, and then those present witnessed it, and the man lay back and closed his eyes. For a moment I thought he was gone, but I was mistaken. After a silence of about ten minutes he opened his eyes and looked at me.

"Do you remember Markapurlie?" he said. That was all. Then, with a grim smile upon his lips, he died, just as the clock on the wall above his head struck twelve. His last speech, for some reason or other, haunted me for weeks.

Towards sundown that afternoon I was standing in the veranda of my house, watching a fatigue party digging a grave under a tree in the paddock beyond the mine buildings, when a shout from Mr. Maybourne, who was on his way to the office, attracted my attention. "When I reached his side, he pointed to a small speck of dust about a mile to the northward.

"It's a horseman," he cried; "but who can it be?"

"I have no possible notion," I answered; "but we shall very soon see."

The rider, whoever he was, was in no hurry. When he came nearer, we could see that he was cantering along as coolly as if he were riding in Rotten Row. By the time he was only a hundred yards or so distant, I was trembling with excitement. Though I had never seen the man on horseback before, I should have known his figure anywhere. It was Dr. Nikola. There could be no possible doubt about that. Bartrand was quite right when he told me that he was in the neighbourhood.

I heard Mr. Maybourne say something about news from the township, but the real import of his words I did not catch. I seemed to be watching the advancing figure with my whole being. When he reached the *laager* he sprang from his horse, and then it was that I noticed Mr. Maybourne had left my side and was giving instructions to let him in. I followed to receive him.

On reaching the inside of our defences, Nikola raised his hat politely to Mr. Maybourne, while he handed his reins to a trooper standing by.

"Mr. Maybourne, I believe," he said. "My name is Nikola. I am afraid I am thrusting myself upon you in a very unseemly fashion, and at a time when you have no desire to be burdened with outsiders. My friendship for our friend Wrexford here must be my excuse. I left Bulawayo at daylight this morning in order to see him."

He held out his hand to me and I found myself unable to do anything but take it. As usual it was as cold as ice. For the moment I was so fascinated by the evil glitter in his eyes that I forgot to wonder how he knew my assumed name. However, I managed to stammer out something by way of a welcome, and then asked how long he had been in South Africa.

"I arrived two months ago," he answered, "and after a week in Cape Town, where I had some business to transact, made my way up here to see you. It appears I have arrived at an awkward moment, but if I can help you in any way I hope you will command my services. I am a tolerable surgeon, and I have the advantage of considerable experience of assegai wounds."

While he was speaking the bell rang for tea, and at Mr. Maybourne's invitation Dr. Nikola accompanied us to where the meal was spread—picnic fashion—on the ground by the kitchen door. Agnes was waiting for us, and I saw her start with surprise when her father introduced the newcomer as Dr. Nikola, a friend of Mr. Wrexford's. She bowed gravely to him, but said nothing. I could see that she knew him for the man Bartrand had warned me against, and for this reason she was by no means prepossessed in his favour.

During the meal Nikola exerted all his talents to please. And such was his devilish—I can only call it by that name—cleverness, that by the time we rose from the meal he had put himself on the best of terms with everyone. Even Agnes seemed to have, for the moment, lost much of her distrust of him. Once out in the open again I drew Nikola away from the others, and having walked him out of earshot of the house, asked the meaning of his visit.

"Is it so hard to guess?" he said, as he seated himself on the pole of a wagon, and favoured me with one of his peculiar smiles. "I should have thought not."

"I have not tried to guess," I answered, having by this time resolved upon my line of action; "and I do not intend to do so. I wish you to tell me."

"My dear Pennethorne-Wrexford, or Wrexford-Pennethorne," he said quietly, "I should advise you not to adopt that tone with me. You know very well why I have put myself to the trouble of running you to earth."

"I have not the least notion," I replied, "and that is the truth. I thought I had done with you when I said goodbye to you in Golden Square that awful night."

"Nobody can hope to have done with me," he answered, "when they do not act fairly by me."

"Act fairly by you? What do you mean? How have I not acted fairly by you?"

"By running away in that mysterious fashion, when it was agreed between us that I should arrange everything. You might have ruined me."

"Still I do not understand you! How might I have ruined you?"

This time I took him unawares. He looked at me for a moment in sheer surprise.

"I should advise you to give up this sort of thing," he said, licking his lips in that peculiar cat-like fashion I had noticed in London. "Remember I know everything, and one word in our friend Maybourne's ear, and—well—you know what the result will be. Perhaps he does not know what an illustrious criminal he is purposing to take for a son-in-law."

"One insinuation like that again, Nikola," I cried, "and I'll have you put off this place before you know where you are. You dare to call me a criminal—you, who plotted and planned the murders that shocked and terrified all England!"

"That I do not admit. I only remember that I assisted you to obtain your revenge on a man who had wronged you. On summing up so judiciously, pray do not forget that point."

Nikola evidently thought he had obtained an advantage, and was quick to improve on it.

"Come, come," he said, "what is the use of our quarrelling like a pair of children? All I want of you is an answer to two simple questions."

"What are your questions?"

"I want to know, first, what you did with Bartrand's body when you got rid of it out of the cab."

"You really wish to know that?"

He nodded.

"Then come with me," I said, "and I'll tell you." I led him into the house, and, having reached the bed in the corner, pulled down the sheet.

He bent over the figure lying there so still, and then started back with a cry of surprise. For a moment I could see that he was nonplussed as he had probably not been in his life before, but by the time one could have counted twenty, this singular being was himself again.

"I congratulate you," he said, turning to me and holding out his hand. "The king has come into his own again. You are now one of the richest men in the world, and I can ask my second question."

"Be certain first," I said. "I inherit nothing from Mr. Bartrand."

"What do you mean by that? I happen to know that his will was made in your favour."

"You are quite mistaken. He made a later will this afternoon, leaving all his money and estates to four London hospitals."

Nikola's face went paler than I had ever seen it yet. His thin lips trembled perceptibly. The man was visibly anxious.

"You will excuse my appearing to doubt you, I hope," he said, "but may I see that will?"

I called Mr. Maybourne into the room and asked him if he had any objection to allowing Dr. Nikola to see the paper in question. He handed it to him without hesitation, keeping close to his elbow while he perused it. The Doctor read it slowly from beginning to end, examined the signature, noted the names of the executors, and also of the witnesses, and when he had done so, returned it to Mr. Maybourne with a bow.

"Thank you," he said, politely. "It is excellently drawn up, and, with your evidence against me, I fear it would be foolish for me to dispute it. In that case, I don't think I need trouble your hospitality any further."

Then, turning to me, he led me from the house across to where his horse was standing.

"Goodbye, Pennethorne," he said. "All I can say of you is that your luck is greater than your cleverness. I am not so *blasé* but I can admire a man who can surrender three millions without a sigh. I must confess I am vulgar enough to find that it costs me a pang to lose even my sixty thousand. I wanted it badly. Had my coup only come off, and the dead man in there not been such an inveterate ass, I should have had the whole amount of his fortune in my hands by this time, and in six months I would have worked out a scheme that would have paralyzed Europe. As it is, I must look elsewhere for the amount. When you wish to be proud of yourself, try to remember that you have baulked Dr. Nikola in one of his best-planned schemes, and saved probably half-a-million lives by doing so. Believe me, there are far cleverer men than you who have tried to outwit me and failed. I suppose you will marry Miss Maybourne now. Well, I wish you luck with her. If I am a judge of character, she will make you an able wife. In ten years' time you will be a commonplace rich man, with scarcely any idea outside your own domestic circle, while I—well the devil himself knows where or what I shall be then. I wonder which will be the happier? Now I must be off. Though you may not think it, I always liked you, and if you had thrown in your lot with me, I might have made something of you. Goodbye."

He held out his hand, and as he did so he looked me full in the face. For the last time I felt the influence of those extraordinary eyes. I took the hand he offered and bade him goodbye with almost a feeling of regret, mad as it may seem to say so, at the thought that in all probability I should never see him again. Next moment he was on his horse's back and out on the veldt making for the westward. I stood and watched him till he was lost in the gathering gloom, and then went slowly back to the house thinking of the change that had come into my life, thanking God for my freedom.

* * * * * * * *

Three months have passed since the events just narrated took place, and I am back in Cape Town again, finishing the writing of this story of the most adventurous period of my life, in Mr. Maybourne's study. Tomorrow my wife (for I have been married a week today) and I leave South Africa on a trip round the world. What a honeymoon it will be!

"The Pride of the South," you will be glad to hear, has made gallant strides since the late trouble in Rhodesia, and as my shares have quadrupled in value, to say nothing of the other ventures in which I have been associated with my father-in-law, I am making rapid progress towards becoming a rich man. And now it only remains for me to bring my story to a close. By way of an epilogue let me say that no better, sweeter, or more loyal wife than I possess could possibly be desired by any mortal man. I love her with my whole heart and soul, as she loves me, and I can only hope that every masculine reader who may have the patience to wade through these, to me, interminable pages, may prove as fortunate in his choice as I have been. More fortunate, it is certain, he could not be.

Dr Nikola's Experiment

CHAPTER 1

Tired of Life

It is sad enough at any time for a man to be compelled to confess himself a failure, but I think it will be admitted that it is doubly so at that period of his career when he is still young enough to have some flickering sparks of ambition left, while he is old enough to be able to appreciate at their proper value the overwhelming odds against which he has been battling so long and unsuccessfully.

This was unfortunately my condition. I had entered the medical profession with everything in my favour. My father had built up a considerable reputation for himself, and, what he prized still more, a competency as a country practitioner of the old-fashioned sort in the west of England. I was his only child, and, as he was in the habit of saying, he looked to me to carry the family name up to those dizzy heights at which he had often gazed, but upon which he had never quite been able to set his foot. A surgeon I was to be, willy-nilly, and it may have been a throw-back to the parental instinct alluded to above, that led me at once to picture myself flying at express speed across Europe in obedience to the summons of some potentate whose life and throne depended upon my dexterity and knowledge.

In due course I entered a hospital, and followed the curriculum in the orthodox fashion. It was not, however, until I was approaching the end of my student days that I was burnt with that fire of enthusiasm which was destined in future days to come perilously near consuming me altogether. Among the students of my year was a man by whose side I had often worked—with whom I had occasionally exchanged a few words, but whose intimate I could not in any way have been said to be. In appearance he was a narrow-shouldered, cadaverous, lantern-jawed fellow, with dark, restless eyes, who boasted the name of Kelleran, and was popularly supposed to be an Irishman. As I discovered later, however, he was not an Irishman at all, but hailed from the Black

Country—Wolverhampton, if I remember rightly, having the right to claim the honour of his birth. His father had been the senior partner in an exceedingly wealthy firm of hardware manufacturers, and while we had been in the habit of pitying and, in some instances I am afraid, of looking down upon the son on account of his supposed poverty, he was, in all probability, in a position to buy up every other man in the hospital twice over.

The average medical student is a being with whom the world in general has by this time been made fairly familiar. His frolics and capacity—or incapacity, as you may choose to term it—for work have been the subject of innumerable jests. If this be a true picture, then Kelleran was certainly different to the usual run of us. In his case the order was reversed: with him, work was play, and play was work; a jest was a thing unknown, and a practical joke a thing for which he allowed it to be seen that he had not the slightest tolerance.

I have already said that my father had amassed a competency. I must now add that up to a certain point he was a generous man, and for this reason my allowance, under different circumstances, would have been ample for my requirements. As ill luck would have it, however, I had got into the wrong set, and before I had been two years in the hospital was over head and ears in such a quagmire of debt and difficulties that it looked as if nothing but an absolute miracle could serve to extricate me. To my father I dared not apply: easy-going as he was on most matters, I had good reason to know that on the subject of debt he was inexorable. And yet to remain in my present condition was impossible. On every side tradesmen threatened me; my landlady's account had not been paid for weeks; while among the men of the hospital not one, but several, held my paper for sums lost at cards, the mere remembrance of which was sufficient to send a cold shiver coursing down my back every time I thought of them. From all this it will be surmised that my position was not only one of considerable difficulty but that it was also one of no little danger. Unless I could find a sum either to free myself, or at least to stave off my creditors, my career, as far as the world of medicine was concerned, might be considered at an end. Even now I can recall the horror of that period as vividly as if it were but yesterday.

It was on a Thursday, I remember, that the thunder-clap came. On returning to my rooms in the evening I discovered a letter awaiting me. With trembling fingers I tore open the envelope and drew out the contents. As I feared, it proved to be a demand from my most implacable creditor, a money-lender to whom I had been introduced by a fellow-student. The sum I had borrowed from him, with the assistance of a friend, was only a trifling one, but helped out by fines and other impositions it had increased to an amount which I was aware it was hopelessly impossible for me to pay. What was I to do? What could I do? Unless I settled the claim (to hope for mercy from the man himself was, to say the least of it, absurd), my friend, who, I happened to know, was himself none too well off at the moment, would be called upon to make it good. After that how should I be able to face him or any one else again? I had not a single acquaintance in the world from whom I could borrow a sum that would be half sufficient to meet it, while I dared not go down to the country and tell my father of my folly and disgrace. In vain I ransacked my brains for a loophole of escape. Then the whistle of a steamer on the river attracted my attention, filling my brain with such thoughts as it had never entertained before, and I pray, by God's mercy, may never know again. Here was a way out of my difficulty, if only I had the pluck to try it. Strangely enough, the effect it had upon me was to brace me like a draught of rare wine. This was succeeded by a coldness so intense that both mind and body were rendered callous by it. How long it lasted I cannot say; it may have been only a few seconds—it may have been an hour before consciousness returned and I found myself still standing beside the table, holding the fatal letter in my hand. Like a drunken man I fumbled my way from the room into the hot night outside. What I was going to do I had no notion. I wanted to be alone, in some place away from the crowded pavements, if possible, where I could have time to think and to determine upon my course of action.

With a tempest of rage, against I knew not what or whom, in my heart, I hurried along, up one street and down another, until I found myself panting, but unappeased, upon the Embankment opposite the Temple Gardens. All round me was the bustle and life of the great city: cabs, containing men and women in evening dress, dashed along; girls and their lovers, talking in hushed voices, went by me arm in arm; even the loafers, leaning against the stone parapet, seemed happy in comparison with my wretched self. I looked down at the dark water gliding so pleasantly along below me, and remembered that all I had to do, as soon as I was alone, was to drop over the side, and be done with my difficulties for ever. Then in a flash the real meaning of what I proposed to do occurred to me.

"You coward," I hissed, with as much vehemence and horror as if I had been addressing a real enemy instead of myself, "to think of taking this way out of your difficulty! If you kill yourself, what will become of the other man? Go to him at once and tell him everything. He has the right to know."

The argument was irresistible, and I accordingly turned upon my heel and was about to start off in quest of the individual I wanted, when I found myself confronted with no less a person than Kelleran. He was walking quickly, and swung his cane as he did so. On seeing me he stopped.

"Douglas Ingleby!" he said: "well, this is fortunate! You are just the man I wanted."

* * * * * * * *

I murmured something in reply, I forget what, and was about to pass on. I had bargained without my host, however. He had been watching me with his keen dark eyes, and when he made as if he would walk with me I was not altogether surprised.

"You do not object to my accompanying you I hope?" he inquired, by way of introducing what he had to say. "I've been wanting to have a talk with you for some days past."

"I'm afraid I'm in rather a hurry just now," I answered, quickening my pace a little as I did so.

"That makes no difference at all to me," he returned. "As I think you are aware, I am a fast walker. Since you are in a hurry, let us step out."

We did so, and for something like fifty yards proceeded at a brisk pace in perfect silence. His companionship was more than I could stand, and at last I stopped and faced him.

"What is it you want with me?" I asked angrily. "Cannot you see that I am not well tonight, and would rather be alone?"

"I can see you are not quite yourself," he answered quietly, still watching me with his grave eyes. "That is exactly why I want to walk with you. A little cheerful conversation will do you good. You don't know how clever I am at adapting my manner to other people's requirements. That is the secret of our profession, my dear Ingleby, as you will some day find out."

"I shall never find it out," I replied bitterly. "I have done with medicine. I shall clear out of England, I think—go abroad, try Australia or Canada—anywhere, I don't care where, to get out of this!"

"The very thing!" he returned cheerily, but without a trace of surprise. "You couldn't do better, I'm sure. You are strong, active, full of life and ambition; just the sort of fellow to make a good colonist. It must be a grand life, that hewing and hacking a place for oneself in a

188

new country, watching and fostering the growth of a people that may some day take its place among the powers of the earth. Ah! I like the idea. It is grand! It makes one tingle to think of it."

He threw out his arms and squared his shoulders as if he were preparing for the struggle he had so graphically described. After that we did not walk quite so fast. The man had suddenly developed a strange fascination for me, and, as he talked, I hung upon his words with a feverish interest I can scarcely account for now. By the time we reached my lodgings, I had put my trouble aside for the time being, but when I entered my sitting-room and found the envelope which had contained the fatal letter still lying upon the table, it all rushed back upon me, and with such force that I was well-nigh overwhelmed. Kelleran meanwhile had taken up his position on the hearthrug, whence he watched me with the same expression of contemplative interest upon his face to which I have before alluded.

"Hullo!" he said at last, after he had been some minutes in the house, and had had time to overhaul my meagre library, "what are these? Where did you pick them up?"

He had taken a book from the shelf, and was holding it tenderly in his hand. I recognised it as one of several volumes of a sixteenth-century work on Surgery that I had chanced upon on a bookstall in Holywell Street some months before. Its age and date had interested me, and I had bought it more out of curiosity than for any other reason. Kelleran, however, could scarcely withdraw his eyes from it.

"It's the very thing I've been wanting to make my set complete," he cried, when I had described my discovery of it. "Perhaps you don't know it, but I'm a perfect lunatic on the subject of old books. My own rooms, where, by the by, you have never been, are crammed from floor to ceiling, and still I go on buying. Let me see what else you have."

So saying, he continued his survey of the shelves, humming softly to himself as he did so, and pulling out such books as interested him, and heaping them upon the floor.

"You've the beginning of a by no means bad collection," he was kind enough to say, when he had finished. "Judging from what I see here, you must read a good deal more than most of our men."

"I'm afraid not," I answered. "The majority of these books were sent up to me from the country by my father, who thought they might be of service to me. A mistaken notion, for they take up a lot of room, and I've often wished them at Hanover."

"You have, have you? What a Goth you are!" he continued. "Well, then, I'll tell you what I'll do. If you want to get rid of them, I'll buy the lot, these old beauties included. They are really worth more than I can afford, but if you care about it, I'll make you a sporting offer of a hundred and fifty pounds for such as I've put upon the floor. What do you say?"

I could scarcely believe I heard aright. His offer was so preposterous, that I could have laughed in his face.

"My dear fellow," I cried, thinking for a moment that he must be joking with me, and feeling inclined to resent it, "what nonsense you talk! A hundred and fifty for the lot: why, they're not worth a ten-pound note, all told. The old fellows are certainly curious, but it is only fair that I should tell you that I gave five and sixpence for the set of seven volumes, complete."

"Then you got a bargain such as you'll never find again," he answered quietly. "I wish I could make as good an one every day. However, there's my offer. Take it or leave it as you please. I will give you one hundred and fifty pounds for those books, and take my chance of their value. If you are prepared to accept, I'll get a cab and take them away tonight. I've got my chequebook in my pocket, and can settle up for them on the spot."

"But, my dear Kelleran, how can you afford to give such—" Here I stopped abruptly. "I beg your pardon—I know I had no right to say such a thing."

"Don't mention it," he answered quietly. "I am not in the least offended, I assure you. I have always felt certain you fellows supposed me to be poor. As a matter of fact, however, I have the good fortune, or the ill, as I sometimes think, since it prevents my working as I should otherwise be forced to do, to be able to indulge myself to the top of my bent without fear of the consequences. But that has nothing to do with the subject at present under discussion. Will you take my price, and let me have the books, or not? I assure you I am all anxiety to get my nose inside one of those old covers before I sleep tonight."

Heaven knows I was eager enough to accept, and if you think for one moment you will see what his offer meant to me. With such a sum I could not only pay off the money-lender, but well-nigh put myself straight with the rest of my creditors. Yet all the time I had the uneasy feeling that the books were by no means worth the amount he had declared to be their value, and that he was only making me the offer out of kindness.

"If you are sure you mean it, I will accept," I said. "I am awfully hard up, and the money will be a godsend to me."

"I am rejoiced to hear it," he replied, "for in that case we shall be doing each other a mutual good turn. Now let's get them tied up. If you wouldn't mind seeing to that part of the business, I'll write the cheque and call the cab."

Ten minutes later he and his new possessions had taken their departure, and I was back once more in my room standing beside the table, just as I had done a few hours before, but with what a difference! Then I had seen no light ahead, nothing but complete darkness and dishonour; now I was a new man, and in a position to meet the majority of calls upon me. The change from the one condition to the other was more than I could bear, and when I remembered that less than sixty minutes before I was standing on that antechamber of death, the Embankment, contemplating suicide, I broke down completely, and sinking into a chair buried my face in my hands and cried like a child.

Next morning, as soon as the bank doors were open, I entered and cashed the cheque Kelleran had given me. Then, calling a cab, I made my way with a light heart, as you may suppose, to the office of the money-lender in question. His surprise at seeing me, and on learning the nature of my errand, may be better imagined than described. Having transacted my business with him, I was preparing to make my way back to the hospital, when an idea entered my head upon which I immediately acted. In something under ten minutes I stood in the bookseller's shop in Holy-well Street where I had purchased the volumes Kelleran had appeared to prize so much.

"Some weeks ago," I said to the man who came forward to serve me, "I purchased from you an old work on medicine entitled 'The Perfect Chi-surgeon, or The Art of Healing as practised in divers Ancient Countries.'"

"Seven volumes very much soiled—five and sixpence," returned the man immediately. "I remember the books."

"I'm glad of that," I answered. "Now, I want you to tell me what you would consider the real value of the work."

"If it were wanted to make up a collection it might possibly be worth a sovereign," the man replied promptly. "Otherwise, not more than we asked you for it."

"Then you don't think any one would be likely to offer a hundred pounds for it?" I inquired.

The man laughed outright.

"Not a man in the possession of his wits," he answered. "No, sir, I think I have stated the price very fairly, though of course it might fetch a few shillings more or less, according to circumstances."

"I am very much obliged to you," I said; "I simply wanted to know as a matter of curiosity."

With that I left the shop and made my way to the hospital, where I found Kelleran hard at work. He looked up at me as I entered, and nodded, but it was lunch time before I got an opportunity of speaking to him.

"Kelleran," I said, as we passed oat through the great gates, "you deceived me about those books last night. They were not worth anything like the value you put upon them."

He looked me full and fair in the face, and I saw a faint smile flicker round the corners of his mouth.

"My dear Ingleby," he said, "what a funny fellow you are, to be sure! Surely if I choose to give you what I consider the worth of the books I am at perfect liberty to do so. If you are willing to accept it, no more need be said upon the subject. The value of a thing to a man is exactly what he cares to give for it, so I have always been led to believe."

"But I am convinced you did not give it because you wanted the books. You knew I was in straits and you took that form of helping me. It was generous of you indeed, Kelleran, and I'll never forget it as long as I live. You saved me from—but there, I cannot tell you. I dare not think of it myself. There is one thing I must ask of you. I want you to keep the books and to let the amount you gave me for them be a loan, which I will repay as soon as I possibly can."

I was aware that he was a passionate man: for I had once or twice seen him fly into a rage, but never into a greater one than now.

"Let it be what you please," he cried, turning from me. "Only for pity's sake drop the subject: I've had enough of it."

With this explosion he stalked away, leaving me standing looking after him, divided between gratitude and amazement.

I have narrated this incident for two reasons: firstly because it will furnish you with a notion of my own character, which I am prepared to admit exhibits but few good points; and in the second because it will serve to introduce to you a queer individual, now a very great person, whom I shall always regard as the Good Angel of my life, and, indirectly it is true, the bringer about of the one and only real happiness I have ever known.

From the time of the episode I have just described at such length to the present day, I can safely say I have never touched a card nor owed a man a penny-piece that I was not fully prepared to pay at a moment's notice. And with this assertion I must revert to the statement made at the commencement of this chapter—the saddest a man can make. As I said then, there could be no doubt about it that I was a failure. For though I had improved in the particulars just stated, Fate was plainly against me. I worked hard and passed my examinations with comparative ease; yet it seemed to do me no good with those above me. The sacred fire of enthusiasm, which had at first been so conspicuously absent, had now taken complete hold of me; I studied night and day, grudging myself no labour, yet by some mischance everything I touched recoiled upon me, and, like the serpent of the fable, stung the hand that fostered it. Certainly I was not popular, and, since it was due almost directly to Kelleran's influence that I took to my work with such assiduity, it seems strange that I should also have to attribute my non-success to his agency. As a matter of fact, he was not a good leader to follow. From the very first he had shown himself to be a man of strange ideas. He was no follower or stickler for the orthodox; to sum him up in plainer words, he was what might be described as an experimentalist. In return, the authorities of the hospital looked somewhat askance upon him. Finally he passed out into the world, and the same term saw me appointed to the position of House Surgeon. Almost simultaneously my father died; and, to the horror of the family, an examination of his affairs proved that instead of being the wealthy man we had supposed him there was barely sufficient, when his liabilities were paid, to meet the expenses of his funeral. The shock of his death and the knowledge of the poverty to which she had been so suddenly reduced proved too much for my mother, and she followed him a few weeks later. Thus I was left, so far as I knew, without kith or kin in the world, with but few friends, no money, and the poorest possible prospects of ever making any.

To the circumstances under which I lost the position of House Surgeon I will not allude. Let it suffice that I did lose it, and that, although the authorities seemed to think otherwise, I am in a position to prove, whenever I desire to do so, that I was not the real culprit The effect, however, was the same. I was disgraced beyond hope of redemption, and the proud career I had mapped out for myself was now beyond my reach for good and all.

Over the next twelve months it would perhaps be better that I should draw a veil. Even now I scarcely like to think of them. It is enough for me to say that for upwards of a month I remained in London, searching high and low for employment. This, however, was easier looked for than discovered. Try how I would, I could hear of nothing. Then, wearying of the struggle, I accepted an offer made me, and left England as surgeon on board an outward-bound passenger steamer for Australia.

Ill luck, however, still pursued me, for at the end of my second voyage the Company went into liquidation, and its vessels were sold. I shipped on board another boat in a similar capacity, made two voyages in her to the Cape, where on a friend's advice I bade her goodbye, and started for Ashanti as surgeon to an Inland Trading Company. While there I was wounded in the neck by a spear, was compelled to leave the Company's service, and eventually found myself back once more in London tramping the streets in search of employment. Fortunately, however, I had managed to save a small sum from my pay, so that I was not altogether destitute; but it was not long before this was exhausted, and then things looked blacker than they had ever done before. What to do I knew not. I had long since cast my pride to the winds, and was now prepared to take anything, no matter what. Then an idea struck me, and on it I acted.

Leaving my lodgings on the Surrey side of the river, I crossed Blackfriars Bridge, and made my way along the Embankment in a westerly direction. As I went I could not help contrasting my present appearance with that I had shown on the last occasion I had walked that way. Then I had been as spruce and neat as a man could well be; boasted a good coat to my back and a new hat upon my head. Now, however, the coat and hat, instead of speaking for my prosperity, as at one time they might have done, bore unmistakable evidence of the disastrous change which had taken place in my fortunes. Indeed, if the truth must be confessed, I was about as sorry a specimen of the professional man as could be found in the length and breadth of the Metropolis.

* * * * * * * *

Reaching the thoroughfare in which I had heard that Kelleran had taken up his abode, I cast about me for a means of ascertaining his number. Compared with that in which I myself resided, this was a street of palaces, but it seemed to me I could read the characters of the various tenants in the appearance of each house-front. The particular one before which I was standing at the moment was frivolous in the extreme: the front door was artistically painted, an elaborate knocker ornamented the centre panel, while the windows were without exception curtained with dainty expensive stuffs. Everything pointed to the mistress being a lady of fashion; and having put one thing and another together, I felt convinced I should not find my friend there. The next I came to was a residence of more substantial type. Here everything was solid and plain, even to the borders of severity.

If I could sum up the owner, he was a successful man, a lawyer for choice, a bachelor, and possibly, and even probably, a bigot on matters of religion. He would have two or three friends—not more—all of whom would be advanced in years, and, like himself, successful men of business. He would be able to appreciate a glass of dry sherry, and would have nothing to do with anything that did not bear the impress of a gilt-edged security. As neither of these houses seemed to suggest that they would be likely to know anything of the man I wanted, I made my way further down the street, looking about me as I proceeded. At last I came to a standstill before one that I was prepared to swear was inhabited by my old friend. His character was stamped unmistakably upon every inch of it: the untidy windows, the pile of books upon a table in the bow, the marks upon the front door where his impatient foot had often pressed while he turned his latchkey: all these spoke of Kelleran, and I was certain my instinct was not misleading me. Ascending the steps, I rang the bell. It was answered by a tall and somewhat austere woman of between forty and fifty years of age, upon whom a coquettish frilled apron and cap sat with incongruous effect. As I afterwards learnt, she had been Kelleran's nurse in bygone years, and since he had become a householder had taken charge of his domestic arrangements, and ruled both himself and his maidservants with a rod of iron.

"Would you be kind enough to inform me if Mr. Kelleran is at home?" I asked, after we had taken stock of each other.

"He has been abroad for more than three months," the woman answered abruptly. Then, seeing the disappointment upon my face, she added, "I don't know when we may expect him home. He may be here on Saturday, and it's just possible we may not see him for two or three weeks to come. But perhaps you'll not mind telling me what your business with him may be?"

"It is not very important," I answered humbly, feeling that my position was, to say the least of it, an invidious one. "I am an old friend, and I wanted to see him for a few minutes. Since, however, he is not at home, it does not matter, I assure you. I shall have other opportunities of communicating with him. At the same time, you might be kind enough to tell him I called."

"You'd better let me know your name first," she replied, with a look that suggested as plainly as any words could speak that she did not for an instant believe my assertion that I was a friend of her master's.

"My name is Ingleby," I said. "Mr. Kelleran will be sure to remember me. We were at the same hospital."

She gave a scornful sniff as if such a thing would be very unlikely, and then made as if she would shut the door in my face. I was not, however, to be put off in this fashion. Taking a card from my pocket, one of the last I possessed, I scrawled my name and present address upon it and handed it to her.

"Perhaps if you will show that to Mr. Kelleran he would not mind writing to me when he comes home," I said. "That is where I am living just now."

* * * * * * * *

She glanced at the card, and, noting the locality, sniffed even more scornfully than before. It was evident that this was the only thing wanting to confirm the bad impression I had already created in her mind. For some seconds there was an ominous silence.

"Very well," she answered, at length, "I'll give it to him. But—why, Heaven save us! what's the matter? You're as white as a sheet. Why didn't you say you were feeling ill?"

I had been running it rather close for more than a week past, and the news that Kelleran, my last hope, was absent from England had unnerved me altogether. A sudden giddiness seized me, and I believe I should have fallen to the ground had I not clutched at the railings by my side. It was then that the real nature of the woman became apparent. Like a ministering angel she half led, half supported me into the house, and seated me on a chair in the somewhat sparsely furnished hall.

"Friend of the master, or no friend," I heard her say to herself, "I'll take the risk of it."

I heard no more, for my senses had left me. When they returned I found myself lying upon a sofa in Kelleran's study, the housekeeper standing by my side, and a maidservant casting sympathetic glances at me from the doorway.

"I'm afraid I have put you to a lot of trouble," I said, as soon as I had recovered myself sufficiently to speak. "I cannot think what made me go off like that. I have never done such a thing in my life before."

"You can't think?" queried the woman, with a curious intonation that was not lost upon me. "Then it's very plain you've not much wit about you. I think, young man, I could make a very good guess at the truth if I wanted to. How–somever, let that be as it may, I'll put a bit of it right before you leave this house, or my name's not what it is." Then turning to the maid, who was still watching me, she continued sharply, "Be off about your business, miss, and do as I told you. Are you going to waste all the afternoon standing there staring about you like a baby?"

196

The girl tossed her head and disappeared, only to return a few minutes later with a tray, upon which was set out a substantial meal of cold meat.

On the old woman's ordering me to do so I sat down to it, and dined as I had not done for months past.

"There," she said, with an air of triumph as I finished, "that will make a new man of you." Then, having done all she could for me, and repenting, perhaps, of the leniency she had shown me, she returned to her former abrupt demeanour, and informed me, in terms there was no mistaking, that her time was valuable, and it behoved me to be off about my business as soon as possible. While she had been speaking, my eyes had travelled round the room until they lighted upon the mantelpiece (it was covered with pipes, books, photographs, and all the innumerable odds and ends that accumulate in a bachelor's apartment), where I discovered my own portrait with several others. I remembered having given it to Kelleran two years before. It was not a very good one, but with its assistance I proposed to establish my identity and prove to my stern benefactress that I was not altogether the impostor she believed me to be.

"I cannot tell you how grateful I am to you for all you have done," I said, as I rose and prepared to take my departure from the house. "At the same time I am very much afraid you do not altogether believe that I am the friend of your master's that I pretend to be."

"Tut, tut!" she answered. "If I were in your place I'd say no more about that. Least said soonest mended, is my motto. I trust, however, I'm a Christian woman, and do my best to help folk in distress. But I've warned ye already that I've eyes in my head and wit enough to tell what's o'clock just as well as my neighbours. Why, bless my soul, you don't think I've been all my years in the world without knowing what's what, or who's who?"

She paused as if for breath; and, embracing the opportunity, I crossed the room and took from the chimneypiece the photograph to which I have just alluded.

"Possibly this may help to reassure you," I said, as I placed it before her. "I do not think I have changed so much, since it was taken, that you should fail to recognise me."

She picked up the photo and looked at it, reading the signature at the bottom with a puzzled face.

"Heaven save us, so it is!" she cried, when the meaning of it dawned upon her. "You are Mr. Ingleby, after all? Well, I am a softy, to be sure. I thought you were trying to take me in. So many people come here asking to see him, saying they were at the hospital with him that you've got to be more than careful. If I'd have thought it really was you, I'd have bitten my tongue out before I'd have said what I did. Why, sir, the master talks of you to this day: it's Ingleby this, and Ingleby that, from morning till night. Many's the time he's made inquiries from gentlemen who've been here, in the hopes of finding out what has become of ye."

* * * * * * * *

"God bless him!" I said, my heart warming at the news that he had not forgotten me. "We were the best of friends once."

"But, Mr. Ingleby," continued the old woman after a pause, "if you'll allow me to say so, I don't like to see you like this. You must have seen a lot of trouble, sir, to have got in such a state."

"The world has not treated me very kindly," I answered, with an attempt at a smile, "but I'll tell Kelleran all about it when I see him. You think it is possible he may be home on Saturday?"

"I hope so, sir, I'm sure," she replied. "You may be certain I'll give him your address, and tell him you've called, the moment I see him."

I thanked her again for her trouble, and took my departure, feeling a very different man as I went down the steps and turned my face citywards. In my own heart I felt certain Kelleran would do something to help me. Had I known, however, what that something was destined to be, I wonder whether I should have awaited his coming with such eagerness.

As it transpired, it was on the Friday following my call at his house that, on returning to my lodgings after another day's fruitless search for employment, I found the following letter awaiting me. The handwriting was as familiar to me as my own, and it may be imagined with what eagerness I tore open the envelope and scanned the contents. It ran:

My Dear Ingleby,

It was a pleasant welcome home to find that you are in England once more. I am sorry, however, to learn from my housekeeper that affairs have not been prospering with you. This must be remedied, and at once. I flatter myself I am just the man to do it. It is possible you may consider me unfeeling when I say that there never was such luck as your being in want of employment at this particular moment. I've a billet standing ready and waiting for you; one of the very sort you are fitted for, and one that you will enjoy, unless you have lost your former tastes and inclinations. You have never met Dr. Nikola, but you must do so without delay. I tell you, Ingleby, he is the most wonderful man with whom I have ever been brought in contact. We chanced upon each other in St. Petersburg three months ago, and since then he's fascinated me as no other man has ever done. I have spoken of you to him, and in consequence he dines with me tonight in the hope of meeting you. Whatever else you do, therefore, do not fail to put in an appearance. You cannot guess the magnitude of the experiment upon which he is at work. At first glance, and in any other man, it would seem incredible, impossible, I might almost say absurd. When, however, you have seen him, I venture to think you will not doubt that he will carry it through. Let me count upon you tonight, then, at seven.

Always your friend,

Andrew Fairfax Kelleran

I read the letter again. What did it mean? At any rate, it contained a ray of hope. It would have to be a very curious billet, I told myself, under present circumstances, that I would refuse. But who was this extraordinary individual, Dr Nikola, who seemed to have exercised such a fascination over my enthusiastic friend? Well, that I had to find out for myself.

CHAPTER 2

A New Impetus

The clocks in the neighbourhood had scarcely ceased striking as I ascended the steps of Kelleran's house and rang the bell. Even had he not been so impressive in his invitation there was small likelihood of my forgetting the appointment I had been waiting for it, hour by hour, with an impatience that can only be understood when I say that each one was bringing me nearer the only satisfying meal I had had since I last visited his abode.

The door was opened to me by the same faithful housekeeper who had proved herself such a ministering angel on the previous occasion. She greeted me as an old friend, but with a greater respect than she had shown when we had last talked together. This did not prevent her, however, from casting a scrutinising eye over me, as much as to say, "You look a bit more respectable, my lad, but your coat is very faded at the seams, your collar is frayed at the edge, and you sniff the smell of dinner as if you have not had a decent meal for longer than you care to think about"; all of which, had she put it into so many words, would have been perfectly true.

"Step inside," she said; "Mr. Kelleran's waiting for you in the study, I know." Then sinking her voice to a whisper she added: "There's duck and green peas for dinner, and as soon as the other gentleman arrives I shall tell cook to dish. He'll not be long now."

What answer I should have returned I cannot say, but as she finished speaking a door farther down the passage opened, and my old friend made his appearance, with the same impetuosity that always characterised him.

"Ingleby, my dear fellow," he cried, as he ran with outstretched hand to greet me, "I cannot tell you how pleased I am to see you again. It seems years since I last set eyes on you. Come in here; I want to have a good look at you. We've hundreds of things to say to each other, and heaps of questions to ask, haven't we? And, by Jove, we must look sharp about it too, for in a few minutes Nikola will be here. I asked him to come at a quarter past seven, in order that we might have a little time alone together first."

So saying, he led me into his study, the same in which I had returned to my senses after my fainting fit a few days before, and when he had done so he bade me seat myself in an easy chair.

"You can't think how good it is to see you again, Kelleran," I said, as soon as I could get in a word. "I had begun to think myself forgotten by all my friends."

"Bosh!" was his uncompromising reply. "Talk about your friends—why, you never know who they are till you're in trouble! At least, that's what I think. And, by the way, let me tell you that you do look a bit pulled down. I wonder what idiocy you've been up to since I saw you last. Tell me about it. You won't smoke a cigarette before dinner? Very good! now fire away!"

Thus encouraged, I told him in a few words all that had befallen me since we had last met. While I was talking he stood before me, his face lit up with interest, and to all intents and purposes as absorbed in my story as if it had been his own.

"Well, well, thank goodness it is all over now," he said, when I had brought my tale to a conclusion. "I think I've found you a billet that will suit you admirably, and if you play your cards well there's no saying to what it may not lead. Nikola is the most marvellous man in the world, as you will admit when you have seen him. I, for one, have never met anybody like him; and as for this new scheme of his, why, if he brings it off, I give you my word it will revolutionise Science."

I was too well acquainted with my friend's enthusiastic way of talking to be surprised at it; at the same time I was thoroughly conversant with his cleverness, and for this reason I was prepared to believe that, if he thought well of any scheme, there must be something out of the common in it.

"But what is this wonderful idea?" I asked, scarcely able to contain my longing, as the fumes of dinner penetrated to us from the regions below. "And how am I affected by it?"

"That I must leave for Dr. Nikola to tell you himself," Kelleran replied. "Let it suffice for the moment that I envy you your opportunity. I believe if I had been able to avail myself of the chance he offered me of going into it with him, I should have been compelled to sacrifice you. But there, you will hear all about it in good time, for if I am not mistaken that is his cab drawing up outside now. It is one of his peculiarities to be always punctual to the moment What do you make the right time by your watch?"

I was obliged to confess that I possessed no watch. It had been turned into the necessaries of existence long since. Kelleran must have realised what was passing in my mind, though he pretended not to have noticed it; at any rate he said, "I make it a quarter past seven to the minute, and I am prepared to wager that's our man."

A bell rang, and almost before the sound of it had died away the study door opened, and the housekeeper, with a look of awe upon her face which had not been there when she addressed me, announced "Dr. Nikola."

Looking back on it now, I find that, in spite of all that has happened since, my impressions of that moment are as fresh and clear as if it were but yesterday. I can see the tall, lithe figure of this extraordinary man, his sallow face, and his piercing black eyes steadfastly regarding me, as if he were trying to determine whether or not I was capable of assisting him in the work upon which he was so exhaustively engaged. Never before had I seen such eyes; they seemed to look me through and through, and to read my inmost thoughts.

"This gentleman, my dear Kelleran," he began, after they had shaken hands, and without waiting for me to be introduced to him, "should be your friend Ingleby, of whom you have so often spoken to me. How do you do, Mr. Ingleby? I don't think there is much doubt but that we shall work admirably together. You have lately been in Ashanti, I perceive."

I admitted that I had, and went on to inquire how he had become aware of it; for as Kelleran had not known it until a few minutes before, I did not see how he could be acquainted with the fact.

"It is not a very difficult thing to tell," he answered, with a smile at my astonishment, "seeing that you carry about with you the mark of a Gwato spear. If it were necessary I could tell you some more things that would surprise you: for instance, I could tell you that the man who cut the said spear out for you was an amateur at his work, that he was left-handed, that he was short-sighted, and that he was recovering from malaria at the time. All this is plain to the eye; but I see our friend Kelleran fancies his dinner is getting cold, so we had better postpone our investigations for a more convenient opportunity."

We accordingly left the study and proceeded to the dining-room. All day long I had been looking forward to that moment with the eagerness of a starving man, yet when it arrived I scarcely touched anything. If the truth must be confessed, there was something about

202

this man that made me forget such mundane matters as mere eating and drinking. And I noticed that Nikola himself was even more abstemious. For this reason, save for the fact that he himself enjoyed it, the bountiful spread Kelleran had arranged for us was completely wasted.

During the progress of the meal no mention was made of the great experiment upon which our host had informed me Nikola was engaged. Our conversation was mainly devoted to travel. Nikola, I soon discovered, had been everywhere, and had seen everything. There appeared to be no place on the face of the habitable globe with which he was not acquainted, and of which he could not speak with the authority of an old resident. China, India, Australia, South America, North, South, East, and West Africa, were as familiar to him as Piccadilly, and it was in connection with one of the last-named Continents that a curious incident occurred.

We had been discussing various cases of catalepsy; and to illustrate an argument he was adducing, Kelleran narrated a curious instance of lethargy with which he had become acquainted in Southern Russia. While he was speaking I noticed that Nikola's face wore an expression that was partly one of derision and partly of amusement.

"I think I can furnish you with an instance that is even more extraordinary," I said, when our host had finished; and as I did so, Nikola leaned a little towards me. "In fairness to your argument, however, Kelleran, I must admit that while it comes under the same category, the malady in question confines itself almost exclusively to the black races on the West Coast of Africa."

"You refer to the Sleeping Sickness, I presume?" said Nikola, whose eyes were fixed upon me, and who was paying the greatest attention to all I said.

"Exactly—the Sleeping Sickness," I answered. "I was fortunate enough to see several instances of it when I was on the West Coast, though the one to which I am referring did not come before me personally, but was described to me by a man, a rather curious character, who happened to be in the district at the time. The negro in question, a fine healthy fellow of about twenty years of age, was servant to a Portuguese trader at Cape Coast Castle. He had been up country on some trading expedition or other, and during the whole time had enjoyed the very best of health. For the first few days after his return to the coast, however, he was unusually depressed. Slight swelling of the cervical glands set in, accompanied by a tendency to fall asleep at any time. This somnolency gradually increased; cutaneous stimulation was tried, at first with comparative success; the symptoms, however, soon recurred, the periods of sleep became longer and more frequent, until at last the patient could scarcely have been said to be ever awake. The case, so my informant said, was an extremely interesting one."

"But what was the result?" inquired Kelleran, a little impatiently. "You have not told us to what all this is leading."

"Well, the result was that in due course the patient became extremely emaciated—a perfect skeleton, in fact. He would take no food, answered no questions, and did not open his eyes from morning till night. To make a long story short, just as my informant was beginning to think that the end was approaching, there appeared in Cape Coast Castle a mysterious stranger who put forward claims to a knowledge of medicine. He forgathered with my man, and after a while obtained permission to try his hand upon the negro."

"And killed him at once, of course?" "Nothing of the sort. The result was one that you will scarcely credit. The whole business was most irregular, I believe, but my friend was not likely to worry himself much about that. This new man had his own pharmacopoeia—a collection of essences in small bottles, more like what they used in the Middle Ages than anything else, I should imagine. Having obtained possession of the patient, he carried him away to a hut outside the town and took him in hand there and then.

"The man who told me about it, and who, I should have said, had had a good experience of the disease, assured me that he was as certain as any one possibly could be that the chap could not live out the week; and yet when the new-comer, ten days later, invited him to visit the hut, there was the man acting as his servant, waiting at table, if you please, and to all intents and purposes, though very thin, as well as ever he had been in his life."

"But, my dear fellow," protested Kelleran, "Guerin says that out of the 148 cases that came under his notice 148 died."

"I can't help what Guerin says," I answered, a little warmly I am afraid. "I am only telling you what my friend told me. He gave me his word of honour that the result was as he described. The strangest part of the whole business, however, has yet to be told. It appears that the man had not only cured the fellow, but that he had the power of returning him to the condition in which he found him, at will. It wasn't hypnotism, but what it was is more that I can say. My informant described it to me as being about the uncanniest performance he had ever witnessed."

"In what way?" asked Kelleran. "Furnish us with a more detailed account. There was a time when you were a famous hand at a diagnosis."

"I would willingly do so," I answered; "unfortunately, however, I can't remember it all. It appears that he was always saying the most mysterious things and putting the strangest questions. On one occasion he asked my friend, as they were standing by the negro's bedside, if there was any one whose image he would care to see? Merton at first thought he was making fun of him, but seeing that he was in earnest he considered for a moment, and eventually answered that he would very much like to see the portrait of an old shipmate who had perished at sea some six or seven years prior to his arrival on the West Coast. As soon as he had said this the man stooped over the bed and opened the sleeping nigger's eyes. 'Examine the retina, he said, and I think you will see what you want.' My friend looked."

"With what result?" inquired Kelleran. Nikola said nothing, but smiled, as I thought, a trifle sceptically.

"It seems an absurd thing to say, I know," I continued, "but he swore to me that he had before him the exact picture of the man he had referred to; and what is more, standing on the deck of the steamer just as he had last seen him. It was as clear and distinct as if it had been a photograph."

"And all the time the negro was asleep?"

"Fast asleep!" I answered.

"I should very much like to meet your friend," said Kelleran emphatically. "A man with an imagination like that must be an exceedingly interesting companion. But seriously, my dear Ingleby, you don't mean to say you wish us to believe that all this really happened?"

"I am telling you what he told me," I answered. "I cannot swear to the truth of it, of course, but I will go so far as to say that I do not think he was intentionally deceiving me."

Kelleran shrugged his shoulders incredulously, and for some moments an uncomfortable silence ensued. This was broken by Nikola.

"My dear Kelleran," he said, "I don't think you are altogether fair to our friend Ingleby. As he admits, he was only speaking on hearsay, and under these circumstances he might very easily have been deceived. Fortunately, however, for the sake of his reputation I am in a position to corroborate all he has said."

"The deuce you are!" cried Kelleran; while I was too much astonished to speak, and could only stare at him in complete surprise. "What on earth do you mean? Pray explain."

"I can only do so by saying that I was the man who did this apparently wonderful thing."

Kelleran and I continued to stare at him in amazement. It was too absurd. Could he be laughing at us? And yet his face was serious enough.

"You do not seem to credit my assertion," said Nikola, quietly. "And yet I assure you it is correct. I was the mysterious individual who appeared in Cape Coast Castle, who brought with him his own pharmacopoeia, and who wrought the miracle which your friend appears to have considered so wonderful."

"The coincidence is too extraordinary," I answered, as if in protest.

"Coincidences are necessarily extraordinary," Nikola replied. "I do not see that this one is more so than usual."

"And the miracle?"

"Was in reality no miracle at all," he answered; "it was merely the logical outcome of a perfectly natural process. Pray do not look so incredulous. I am aware that my statement is difficult to believe, but I assure you, my dear Ingleby, that it is quite true. However, proof is always better than mere assertion, so, since you are still sceptical, let me make my position right with you. For reasons that will be self-evident I cannot produce the effect in a negro's eye, but I can do so in a way that will strike you as being scarcely less extraordinary. If you will draw up your chairs I will endeavour to explain."

Needless to remark, we did as he desired; and when we were seated on either side of him waited for the manifestation he had promised us.

Taking a small silver box, but little larger than a card-case, from his pocket, he opened it and tipped what might have been a teaspoonful of black powder into the centre of a dessert plate. I watched it closely, in the hope of being able to discover of what it was composed. My efforts, however, were unavailing. It was black, as I have already said, and from a distance resembled powdered charcoal. This, however, it could not have been, by reason of its strange liquidity, which was as great as that of quicksilver, and which only came into operation when it had been exposed to the air for some minutes. Hither and thither the stuff ran about the dish, and I noticed that as it did so it gradually lost its original sombre hue and took to itself a variety of colours that were as brilliant as the component tints of the spectrum. These scintillated and quivered till the eyes were almost blinded by their radiance, and yet they riveted the attention in such a manner that it was well-nigh, if not quite, impossible to look away or to think of anything else. In vain I tried to calm myself, in order that I might be a cool and collected observer of what was taking place. Whether there was any perfume thrown off by the stuff upon the plate I cannot say, but as I watched it my head began to swim and my eyelids felt as heavy as lead. That this was not fancy upon my part is borne out by the fact that Kelleran afterwards confessed to me that he experienced exactly the same sensations. Nikola, however, was still manipulating the dish, turning it this way and that, as if he were anxious to produce as many varieties of colour as possible in a given time. It must have been upwards of five minutes before he spoke. As he did so he gave the plate an extra tilt, so that the mixture ran down to one side. It was now a deep purple in colour.

"I think if you will look into the centre of the fluid you will see something that will go a long way towards convincing you of the truth of the assertion I made just now," he said quietly, but without turning his head to look at me.

I looked as he desired, but at first could see nothing save the mixture itself, which was fast turning from purple to blue. This blue grew gradually paler; and as I watched, to my astonishment, a picture formed itself before my eyes. I saw a long wooden house, surrounded on all sides by a deep veranda. The latter was covered with a beautiful flowering creeper. On either side of the dwelling was a grove of palms, and to the right, showing like a pool of dazzling quicksilver between the trees, was the sea. And pervading everything was the sensation of intense heat. At first glance I could not recall the house, but it was not long before I recognised the residence of the man who had told me the story which had occasioned this looked at it again, and could even see the window of the room in which I had recovered from my first severe attack of fever, and from which I never thought to have emerged alive. With the sight of it the recollection of that miserable time came back to me, and Kelleran and even his friend Nikola were, for the moment, forgotten.

"From the expression upon your face I gather that you know the place," said Nikola, after I had been watching it for a few moments. "Now look into the veranda, and tell me if you recognise the two men you see seated there."

I looked again, and saw that one was myself, while the other, the man who was leaning against the veranda rail smoking a cigar, was the owner of the house itself. There could be no mistake about it. The whole scene was as plain before my eyes as if it had been a photograph taken on the spot.

"There," said Nikola, with a little note of triumph in his voice, "I hope that will convince you that when I say I can do a thing, I mean it"

So saying he tilted the saucer, and the picture vanished in a whirl of colour. I tried to protest, but before I had time to say anything the liquid had in some strange fashion resolved itself once more into a powder, Nikola had tipped it back into the silver box, and Kelleran and I were left to put the best explanation we could upon it. We looked at each other, and, feeling that I could not make head or tail of what I had seen, I waited for him to speak.

"I never saw such a thing in my life," he cried, when he had found sufficient voice. "If any one had told me that such a thing was possible I would not have believed him. I can scarcely credit the evidence of my senses now."

"In fact, you feel towards the little exhibition I have just given you very much as you did to Ingleby's story a quarter of an hour ago," said Nikola. "What a doubting world it is, to be sure! The same world which ridiculed the notion that there could be anything in vaccination, in the steam engine, in chloroform, the telegraph, the telephone, or the phonograph. For how many years has it scoffed at the power of hypnotism! How many of our cleverest scientists fifty years ago could have foretold the discovery of argon, or the possibility of being able to telegraph without the aid of wires? And because the little world of today knows these things and has survived the wonder of them, it is convinced it has attained the end of wisdom. The folly of it! Tonight I have shown you something for which less than a hundred years ago I should have been stoned as a wizard. At my death the secret will be given to the world, and the world, when it has recovered from its astonishment, will say, 'How very simple! why did no one discover it before?' I tell you, gentlemen," Nikola continued, rising and standing before the fireplace, "that we three, tonight, are standing on the threshold of a discovery which will shake the world to its foundations."

When he had moved, Kelleran and I had also pushed back our chairs from the table, and were now watching him as if turned to stone. The sacred fire of enthusiasm, which I thought had left me for ever, was once more kindling in my breast, and I hung upon his words as if I were afraid I might lose even a breath that escaped his lips. As for Nikola himself, his usually pallid face was aglow with excitement.

"The story is as old as the hills," he began. "Ever since the days when our first parents trod the earth there have been men who have aimed at discovering a means of lengthening the span of life. From the very infancy of science, the wisest and cleverest have devoted their lives to the study of the human body, in the hope of mastering its secret. Assisting in the search for that particular something which was to revolutionise the world, we find Zosimus the Theban, the Jewess Maria, the Arabian Geber, Hermes Trismegistus, Linnaeus, Berzelius, Cuvier, Raymond Lully, Paracelsus, Roger Bacon, De Lisle, Albertus Magnus, and even Dr. Price. Each in his turn quarried in the mountain of Wisdom, and died having failed to discover the hidden treasure for which he sought. And why? Because, egotistical as it may seem on my part to say so, they did not seek in the right place. They commenced at the wrong point, and worked from it in the wrong direction. But if they failed to find what they wanted, they at least rendered good service to those who were to follow after, for from every failure something new was learned. For my part I have studied the subject in every form, in every detail. For more years than I can tell you, I have lived for it, dreamed of it, fought for it, and overcome obstacles of the very existence of which no man could dream. The work of my predecessors is known to me; I have studied their writings, and tested their experiments to the last particular. All the knowledge that modern science has accumulated I have acquired. The magic of the East I have explored and tested to the uttermost. Three years ago I visited Tibet under extraordinary circumstances. There, in a certain place, inaccessible to the ordinary man, and at the risk of my own life and that of the brave man who accompanied me, I obtained the information which was destined to prove the coping-stone of the great discovery I have since made. Only two things were wanting then to . . complete the whole and to enable me to get to work. One of these I had just found in St. Petersburg when I first met you, Kelleran; the other I discovered three weeks ago. It has been a long and tedious search, but such labour only makes success the sweeter. The machinery is now prepared; all that remains is to fit the various parts together. In six months' time, if all goes well, I will have a man walking upon this earth who, under certain conditions, shall live a thousand years."

I could scarcely believe that I heard aright. Was the man deliberately asking us to believe that he had really found the way to prolong human life indefinitely? It sounded very much like it, and yet this was the Nineteenth Century and . . . But at this point I ceased my speculations. Had I not, only that evening, witnessed an exhibition of his marvellous powers? If he had penetrated so far into the Unknowable—at least what we considered the unknowable—as to be able to work such a miracle, why should we doubt that he could carry out what he was now professing to be able to do?

"And when shall we be permitted to hear the result of your labours?" asked Kelleran with a humility that was surprising in a man usually so self-assertive.

"Who can say?" asked Nikola. "These things are more or less dependent on Time. It may be only a short period before I am ready; on the other hand a lifetime may elapse. The process is above all a gradual one, and to hurry it might be to spoil everything. And now, my dear Kelleran, with your permission I will bid you good-night. I leave for the North at daybreak, and I have much to do before I go. If I am not taking you away too soon, Ingleby, perhaps you would not mind walking a short distance with me. I have a good deal to say to you."

"I shall be very pleased," I answered; and the look that Kelleran gave me showed me that he considered my decision a wise one.

"In that case come along," said Nikola. "Good-night, Kelleran, and many thanks for the introduction you have given me. I feel quite sure Ingleby and I will get on admirably together."

He shook hands with Kelleran, and passed into the hall, leaving me alone with the man who had proved my benefactor for the second time in my life.

"Good-night, old fellow," I said, as I shook him by the hand. "I cannot thank you sufficiently for your goodness in putting me in the way of this billet. It has given me another chance, and I shan't forget your kindness as long as I live." "Don't be absurd," Kelleran answered. "You take things too seriously. I feel sure the advantage is as much Nikola's as yours. He's a wonderful man, and you're the very fellow he requires: between you, you ought to be able to bring about something that will upset the calculations of certain pompous old fossils of our acquaintance. Good-night, and good luck to you!"

So saying, he let us out by the front door, and stood upon the doorstep watching us as we walked down the street. It was an exquisite night. The moon was almost at the full, and her mellow rays made the street almost as light as day. My companion and I walked for some distance in silence. He did not speak, and I already entertained too much respect for him to interrupt his reverie. More than once I glanced at his tall, graceful figure, and the admirably shaped head, which seemed such a fitting case for the extraordinary brain within.

"As I said just now," he began at length, as if he were continuing a conversation which had been suddenly interrupted, "I leave at daybreak for the North of England. For the purposes of the experiment I am about to make, it is vitally necessary that I should possess a residence far removed from other people, where I should not run any risk of being disturbed. For this reason I have purchased Allerdeyne Castle, in Northumberland, a fine old place overlooking the North Sea. It is by no means an easy spot to get at, and should suit my purposes admirably. I shall not see you before I go, so that whatever I have to say had better be said at once. To begin with, I presume you have made up your mind to assist me in the work I am about to undertake?"

"If you consider me competent," I answered, "I shall be only too glad to do so."

"Kelleran has assured me that I could not have a better assistant," he replied, "and I am willing to take you upon his recommendation. If you have no objection to bring forward, we may as well consider the matter settled. Have you any idea as to the remuneration you will require?"

I answered that I had not, and that I would leave it to him to give me whatever he considered fair. In reply he named a sum that almost took my breath away. I remarked that I should be satisfied with half the amount, whereupon he laughed good-humouredly.

"I'm afraid we're neither of us good business men," he said. "By all the laws of trade, on finding that I offered you more than you expected, you should have stood out for twice as much. Still, I like you all the better for your modesty. Now my road turns off here, and I will bid you good-night. In an hour I will send my servant to you with a letter containing full instructions. I need scarcely say that I am sure you will carry them out to the letter."

"I will do so, come what may," I answered seriously.

"Then good-night," he said, and held out his hand to me. "All being well, we shall meet again in two or three days."

"Good-night," I replied.

Then, with a wave of his hand to me, he sprang into a hansom which he had called up to the pavement, gave the direction to the driver, and a moment later was round the corner and out of sight. After he had gone, I continued my homeward journey.

I had not been in the house an hour before I was informed that some one was at the door desiring to see me. I accordingly hurried downstairs, to find myself face to face with the most extraordinary individual I have ever seen in my life. At first glance I scarcely knew what to make of him, but when the light from the hall lamp fell upon his face, I saw that he was a Chinaman, and the ugliest I have ever seen in all my experience of the Mongolian race. His eyes squinted terribly, and a portion of his nose was missing. It was the sort of face one sees in a nightmare, and, accustomed as I was by my profession to horrible sights, I must admit my gorge rose at him. At first it did not occur to me to connect him with Nikola.

"Do you want to see me?" I inquired, in some astonishment.

211

He nodded his head, but did not speak. "What is it about?" I continued. He uttered a peculiar grunt, and produced a letter and a small box from his pocket, both of which he handed to me. I understood immediately from whom he came. Signing to him to remain where he was until I could tell him whether there was an answer, I turned into the house and opened the letter. Having read it, I returned to the front door.

"You can tell Dr. Nikola that I will be sure to attend to it," I said. "You savee?"

He nodded his head, and next moment was on his way down the street. When he was out of sight I returned to my bedroom, and, lighting the gas, once more perused the communication I had received. As I did so a piece of paper fell from between the leaves. I picked it up, to discover that it was a cheque for one hundred pounds payable to myself. The letter ran:

My dear Ingleby,

According to the promise I made you this evening, I am sending you herewith by my Chinese servant, your instructions, as clearly worked out as I can make them. To begin with, I want you to remain in town until Monday next. On the morning of that day, if all goes well, you will be advised by the agent of the Company in London of the arrival in the river of the steamship *Dona Mercedes*, bound from Cadiz to Newcastle. On receipt of that information you will be good enough to board her and to inquire for Don Miguel de Moreno and his great-granddaughter, who are passengers by the boat to England. I have already arranged with the Company for your passage, so you need have no anxiety upon that score.

You will find the Don a very old man, and I beg that you will take the greatest possible care of him. For this reason I have sent you the accompanying drugs, each of which is labelled with the fullest instructions. They should not be made use of unless occasion absolutely requires.

(Here followed a list of the various symptoms for which I was to watch, and an exhaustive resume of the treatment I was to employ in the event of certain contingencies arising.)

On the arrival of the vessel in Newcastle I will communicate with you again. In the meantime I send you what I think will serve to pay your expenses until we meet.

Believe me,
Your sincere friend,
Nikola

P.S.—One last word of warning. Should you by any chance be brought into contact with a certain Mongolian of very sinister appearance, with half an ear missing, have nothing whatsoever to do with him. Keep out of his way, and above all let him know nothing of your connection with myself. This, I beg you to believe, is no idle warning, for all our lives depend upon it.

Having thoroughly mastered the contents of this curious epistle, I turned my attention to the parcel which accompanied it. This I discovered was made up of a number of small packets evidently containing powders, and two-ounce phials of some tasteless and scentless liquid, to which I was quite unable to assign a name.

Once more I glanced at the letter, in order to make sure of the name of the man whose guardian I was destined for the future to be. De Moreno was the name, and it was his granddaughter who was accompanying him. In an idle, dreamy way, I wondered what the latter would prove to be like. For some reason or another I found myself thinking a good deal of her, and when I fell asleep that night it was to dream that she was standing before me with outstretched hands, imploring me to save her not only from a certain one-eared Chinaman, but also from Nikola himself.

CHAPTER 3

The Mysterious Chinaman

After my meeting with Nikola at Kelleran's house, it was a new prospect that life opened up for me. I confronted the future with a smiling face, and no longer told myself, as I had done so often of late, that Failure and I were inseparable companions, and for any success I might hope to achieve in the world I had better be out of it. On the contrary, when I retired to rest after the receipt of Nikola's letter, as narrated in the preceding chapter, it was with a happier heart than I had known for more than two years past, and a fixed determination that, happen what might, even if his wonderful experiment came to naught, my new employer should not find me lacking in desire to serve him. As for that experiment itself, I scarcely knew what to think of it. To a man who had studied the human frame, its wonderful mechanism combined with its many deficiencies and limitations, it seemed impossible it could succeed. And yet, strange as it may appear to say so, there was something about Nikola that made one feel sure he would not embark upon such an undertaking if he were not quite certain, or at least had not a well-grounded hope, of being able to bring it to a favourable issue. However, successful or unsuccessful, the fact remained that I was to be associated with him, and the very thought of such co-operation was sufficient to send the blood tingling through my veins with new life and strength.

* * * * * * * *

During the two days that elapsed between my meeting with Nikola and the arrival of the vessel for which he had told me to be on the look-out, I saw nothing of Kelleran. I was not idle, however. In the first place it was necessary for me to replenish my wardrobe, which, as I have already observed, stood in need of considerable additions, and in the second I was anxious to consult some books of reference to which Nikola had directed my attention. By the time I had done these things, I had not, as may be supposed, very much leisure left, either for paying visits or for receiving them. I was careful, however, to write thanking him for the good turn he had done me, and wishing him goodbye in case I did not see him before I left.

It was between eight and nine o'clock on the Monday morning following that I received a note from the Steamship Company, to which Nikola had referred, advising me that their vessel the *Dona Mercedes* had arrived from Cadiz and was now lying in the river, and would sail for the North at eleven o'clock precisely. Accordingly I gathered my luggage together, what there was of it, and made my way down to her. As Nikola had predicted, I found her lying in the Pool.

On boarding her I was confronted by a big, burly man with a long brown beard, which blew over either shoulder and met behind his head as if it were some new kind of comforter. I inquired for the skipper.

"I am the captain," he answered. "And I suppose you are Dr. Ingleby. I had a letter from the owners saying you were going North with us. You may be sure we'll do our best to make you comfortable. In the meantime the steward will show you your berth and look after your luggage."

As he said this he beckoned a hand aft and sent him below in search of the official in question.

"I think you have a lady and gentleman on board who are expecting me?" I remarked, after the momentary pause which followed the man's departure.

"That I have, sir," he answered with emphasis; "and a nice responsibility they've been for me. I wouldn't undertake another like it if I were paid a hundred pounds extra for my trouble. But perhaps you know the old gentleman?"

"I have never seen him in my life," I replied, "but I have to take charge of him until we get to the North."

"Then I wish you joy of your work," he continued. "You'll have your time pretty fully occupied, I can tell you."

"In what way?" I inquired. "I shall consider it a favour if you will tell me all you can about him. Is the old gentleman eccentric, or what is the matter with him?"

"Eccentric?" replied the skipper, rolling his tongue round the word as if he liked its flavour, "Well, he may be that for all I know, but it's not his eccentricity that gives the trouble. It's his age! Why, I'll be bound he's a hundred, if he's a day. He's not a man at all, only a bag of bones; can't move out of his berth, can't walk, can't talk, and can't do a single hand's turn to help himself. His bones are almost through his skin, his eyes are sunk so far into his head that you can only guess what they're like, and when he wants a meal, or when he's got to have one, I should say, for he's past wanting anything, why, I'm blest if he hasn't to be fed with pap like a baby. It's a pitiful sort of a plight for a man to come to. What do you think? He'd far better be dead and buried."

I thought I understood. Putting one thing and another together, the reason of the old man's journey North could easily be guessed. At that moment the seaman, whom the skipper had sent in search of the steward, made his appearance from the companion, followed by the functionary in question. To the latter's charge I was consigned, and at his suggestion I followed him to the cabin which had been set aside for my accommodation. It proved to be situated at the after end of the saloon, and was as small and poorly furnished a place as I have ever slept in. To make use of the old nautical expression, there was scarcely room in it to swing a cat. Tiny as it was, however, it was at least better than the back street lodgings I had so lately left; and when I reflected that I had paid all I owed, had fitted myself out with a new wardrobe, and was still upwards of fifty pounds in pocket, to say nothing of being engaged on deeply interesting work, I could have gone down on my knees and kissed the grimy planks in thankfulness.

"I'm afraid, sir, it's not as large as some you've been accustomed to," said the talkative steward apologetically, as he stowed my bags away in a corner.

"How do you know what I've been accustomed to?" I asked, with a smile, as I noticed his desire for conversation.

"I could tell it directly I saw you look round this berth," he answered. "People can say what they please, but to my thinking there's no mistaking a man who's spent any time aboard ship. What line might you have been in, sir?"

I told him, and had the good fortune to discover that he possessed a brother who had served the same employ. Having thus established a bond in common, I proceeded to question him about my future charges; only to find that this was a subject upon which he was very willing to enlarge.

"Well, sir," he began, seating himself familiarly on the edge of my berth and looking up at me, "I don't know as how I ought to speak about the old gentleman at all, seeing he's a passenger and you're, so to speak, in charge of him; but this I do say without fear or favour, that who ever brought him away from his home and took him to sea at his time of life did a wrong and cruel action. Why, sir, I make so bold as to

216

tell you that from the moment he was brought aboard this ship until this very second, he has not spoke as much as five words to me or to anybody else. He just lays there in his bunk, hour after hour, with his eyes open, looking at the deck above him, and as likely as not holding his great-granddaughter's hand, not seeming to see or hear anything, and never letting one single word pass his lips. I've known what it is to wait upon sick folk myself, having spent close upon eight months in a hospital ashore, but never in my life, sir, and I give you my word it's gospel truth I'm telling you, have I seen anything like the way that young girl waits upon him. You'll find her a-sitting by him after breakfast, and if you go in at eight bells she'll be still the same. She has her meals brought to her and eats 'em there, and at night she gets me to make her up a bed on the deck alongside of him."

"She must indeed be devoted," I answered, considerably touched at the picture he drew.

"Devoted is no name for it," replied the man with conviction. "And it's by no means pleasant work for her, sir, I can assure you. Why, more than once when I've gone in there I've found her leaning over the bunk, her face just as white as the sheet there, holding a little looking-glass to his lips to see if he was breathing. Then she'd heave a big sigh of relief to find that there was still life in him, put the glass back in its place, and sit down beside him again, and go on holding his hand, for all the world as if she was determined to cling on to him until the Judgment Day. It would bring the tears into your eyes, I'm sure, sir, to see it."

"You have a tender heart, I can see," I said, "and I think the better of you for it. Do you happen to know anything of their history— where they hail from or who they are?"

"There is one thing I do know," he answered, "and that is that they're English and not Spaniards, as the cook said, and as you might very well think yourself from the name. I believe the old gentleman was a merchant of some sort in Cadiz, but that must have been fifty years ago. The young lady is his great-granddaughter, and I was given to understand that her father and mother have been dead for many years. From one thing and another I don't fancy they've got a penny to bless themselves with, but it's plain there's somebody paying the piper, because the skipper got orders from the office, just before we sailed, that everything that could be done for their comfort was to be done, and money was to be no object. But there, here I am running on in this way to you, sir, who probably know all about them better than I do."

"I assure you I know nothing at all, or at least very little," I answered. "I have simply received instructions to meet them here, and to look after the old gentleman until he reaches Newcastle. What will become of them then I can only guess. I presume, however, I may rely on you for assistance during the voyage, should I require it?"

"I'll do anything I can, sir, and you may be very sure of that," he replied. "I've taken such a liking to that young lady that there's nothing I wouldn't do in reason to make her feel a bit happier. For it's my belief she's far from easy in her mind just now. I remember once hearing an Orient steward tell of a man what was tied up with a sword hanging over his head by a single hair; he never knew from one minute to another when it would fall and do for him. Well, that's the way, I fancy, Miss Moreno is feeling. There's a sword hanging over her head or her great-grandfather's, and she doesn't know when it'll drop."

"What did you say her name was?" I inquired, for I had for the moment forgotten it.

"Moreno, sir," he replied. "The old gentleman is Don Miguel, and she is the Dona Consuelo de Moreno."

"Thank you," I said. "And now, if you will tell me where their cabin is, I think I will pay the old gentleman a visit."

"Their cabin is the one facing yours, sir, on the starboard side. If it will be any convenience to you, sir, I'll tell the young lady you're aboard. I know she expects you, because she said so only this morning."

"Perhaps it would be better that you should tell her," I replied. "If you will give her my compliments and say that I will do myself the pleasure of waiting upon her as soon as it is convenient for her to see me, I shall be obliged. I will remain here until I receive her answer."

The man departed on his errand, and during his absence I spent the time making myself as comfortable as my limited quarters would permit. It was not very long, however, before he returned to inform me that the young lady would be pleased to see me as soon as I cared to visit their cabin.

Placing my stethoscope in my pocket, and having thrown a hasty glance into the small looking-glass over the washstand, in order to make sure that I presented a fairly respectable appearance, I left my quarters and made my way across the saloon. Since then I have often tried to recall my feelings at that moment, but the effort has always been in vain. One thing is certain, I had no idea of the importance the incident was destined to occupy in the history of my life.

I knocked upon the door, and as I did so heard some one rise from a chair inside the cabin. The handle was softly turned, and a moment later the most beautiful girl I have ever seen in my life stood before me. I have said "the most beautiful girl," but this does not at all express what I mean, nor do I think it is in my power to do so. Let me, however, endeavour to give you some idea of what Dona Consuelo de Moreno was like.

Try to picture a tall and stately girl, in reality scarcely twenty years of age, but looking several years older. Imagine a pale, oval face, lighted by dark lustrous eyes with long lashes and delicately pencilled brows, a tiny mouth, and hair as black as the raven's wing. Taken altogether, it was not only a very beautiful face, but a strong one, and as I looked at her I wondered what the circumstances could have been that had brought her into the power of my extraordinary employer. That she was in his power I did not for a moment doubt.

Closing the cabin door softly behind her, she stepped into the saloon.

"The steward tells me that you are Dr. Ingleby," she began, speaking excellent English, but with a slight foreign accent. Then, holding out her tiny hand to me with charming frankness, she continued: "I was informed by Dr. Nikola, in a letter I received this morning, that you would join the vessel here. It is a great relief to me to know you are on board."

I said something, I forget what, in answer to the compliment she paid me, and then inquired how her aged relative was.

"He seems fairly well at present," she answered. "As well, perhaps, as he will ever be. But, as you may suppose, he has given me a great deal of anxiety since we left Cadiz. This vessel is not a good sea boat, and in the Bay of Biscay we had some very rough weather—so rough, indeed, that more than once I thought she must inevitably founder. However, we are safely here now, so that our troubles are nearly over. I don't want you to think I am a grumbler. But I am keeping you here when perhaps you would like to see grandpapa for yourself?"

I answered in the affirmative, whereupon she softly opened the door again, and, beckoning me to follow, led the way into the cabin.

If my own quarters on the other side of the saloon had seemed small, this one seemed even smaller. There was only one bunk, and it ran below the port-hole. In this an old man was lying with his hands clasped upon his breast.

"You need not fear that you will wake him," said the girl beside me. "He sleeps like this the greater part of the day. Sometimes he frightens me, for he lies so still that I become afraid lest he may have passed away without my noticing it."

I did not at all wonder at her words. The old man's pallor was of that peculiar ivory-white which is never seen save in the very old, and

219

then, strangely enough, in men oftener than women. His eyes were deeply sunken, as were his cheeks. At one time—forty years or so before—it must have been a powerful face; now it was beautiful only in its soft, harmonious whiteness. A long beard, white as the purest snow, fell upon, and covered his breast, and on it lay his fleshless hands, with their bony joints and long yellow nails. The better to examine him, I knelt down beside the bunk and took his right wrist between my finger and thumb. As I expected, the pulse was barely perceptible. For a moment I inclined to the belief that the end, of which his great-granddaughter had spoken only a few moments before, had come, but a second examination proved that such was not the case. I gently replaced his hand, and then rose to my feet.

"I can easily understand your anxiety," I said. "I think you are wonderfully brave to have undertaken such a voyage. However, for the future—that is to say, until we reach Newcastle—you must let me share your watch with you."

"It is very kind of you to offer to do so," she replied, "but I could not remain away from him. I have had charge of him for such a long time now that it has become like second nature to me. Besides, if he were to wake and not find me by his side, there is no saying what might happen. I am everything to him, and I know so well what he requires."

As she said this, she gave me a look that I could not help thinking was almost one of defiance, as if she were afraid that by attending to the old man's wants I might deprive her of his affection. I accordingly postponed consideration of the matter for the moment, and, having asked a few questions as to the patient's diet, retired, leaving them once more alone together. From the saloon I made my way up to the poop. The tide was serving, and preparations were being made for getting under way.

* * * * * * * *

Ten minutes later our anchor was at the cathead, and we were steaming slowly down the river, and I had begun one of the most extraordinary voyages it has ever fallen to the lot of man to undertake. During the afternoon I paid several visits to my patient's cabin; but on no occasion could I discover any change in his condition. He lay in his bunk just as I had first seen him; his sunken eyes stared at the woodwork above his head, and his left hand clasped that of his great-granddaughter. To my surprise, the motion of the vessel seemed to cause him little or no inconvenience, and, fortunately for him, his nurse was an excellent sailor. It was in vain I tried to induce her to let me take her place while she went up to the deck for a little change.

220

Her grandfather might want her, she said, and that excuse seemed to her sufficient to justify such trifling with her health. Later on, however, after dinner, I was fortunate enough to be able to induce her to accompany me to the deck for a few moments, the steward being left in charge of the patient, with instructions to call us should the least change occur. By this time we were clear of the river, and our bows were pointed in a northerly direction. Leaving the miserable companion, which ascended to the poop directly from the cuddy, we began to pace the deck. The night was cold, and, with a little shiver, my companion drew her coquettish mantilla more closely about her shoulders. There was something in her action which touched me in a manner I cannot describe. In some vague fashion it seemed to appeal to me not only for sympathy but for help. I saw the beautiful face looking up at me, and as we walked I noted the proud way in which she carried herself, and the sailor-like fashion in which she adapted herself to the rolling of the ship. It was a beautiful moonlight night, and had the vessel remained upon an even keel, it would have been very pleasant on deck. To be steady, however, was a feat the crazy old tub seemed incapable of accomplishing.

We had paced the poop perhaps half a dozen times when my companion suddenly stopped, and placing her hand upon my arm, said:

"Dr. Ingleby, you are in Dr. Nikola's confidence, I believe. Will you tell me why we are going to the North of England?"

Her question placed me in an awkward predicament. As I have said above, her loneliness, not to mention the devotion she showed to her aged relative, had touched me more than a little. On the other hand, I was Nikola's servant, employed by him for a special work, and I did not know whether he would wish me to discuss his plans with her.

"You do not answer," she continued, as she noticed my hesitation. "And yet I feel sure you must know. It all seems so strange. Only a few weeks ago we were in our own quiet home in Spain, without a thought of leaving it. Then Dr. Nikola came upon the scene, and now we are on board this ship going up to the North of England: and for what purpose?"

* * * * * * * *

"Did Nikola furnish you with no reason?" I inquired.

"Oh yes," she replied. "He told me that if I would bring my grandfather to England to see him he would make him quite a strong man again. For some reason or another, however, I feel certain there is something behind it that is being kept from me. Is this so?"

"I am not in a position to give you any answer that would be at all likely to satisfy you," I replied, I am afraid, a little ambiguously, "for I really know nothing. It is only fair I should tell you that I only met Dr. Nikola, myself, for the first time a few days ago."

"But he sent you here to be with my grandfather," she continued authoritatively. "Surely, Dr. Ingleby, you must be able to throw some light upon the mystery which surrounds this voyage?"

I shook my head, and with a little sigh of regret she ceased to question me. A few minutes later she gave me a stately bow, and, bidding me goodnight, prepared to go below. Knowing that I had deceived her, and hoping to find some opportunity of putting myself right with her, I followed her down the companion-ladder and along the saloon to her cabin.

"Perhaps I had better see my patient before I retire to rest," I said, as we stood together at the door, holding on to the handrail and balancing ourselves against the rolling of the ship.

She threw a quick glance at me, as if for some reason she were surprised at my decision; the expression, however, passed from her face as quickly as it had come, and opening the door she entered the cabin, and I followed her. She could scarcely have advanced a step towards the bunk before she uttered an exclamation of surprise and horror. The steward, who was supposed to have been watching the invalid, was fast asleep, while the latter's head had slipped from its pillow and was now lying in a most unnatural position, his chin in the air, his eyes open, but still fixed upon the ceiling in the same glassy stare I have described before. In her dismay the girl said something in Spanish which I am unable to interpret, and leaning over the bunk, gazed into her great-grandfather's face as if she were afraid of what she might find there. The steward meanwhile had recovered his senses, and was staring stupidly from one to the other of us, hardly able to realise the consequences of his inattention. Though all this has taken some time to describe it was in reality the action of a moment; then signing to the steward to stand back, and gently pushing the young girl to one side, I knelt down and commenced my examination of my patient. There could be no doubt about one thing, the old man's condition was eminently serious. If he lived at all, there was but little more than a flicker of life left in him. How to preserve that flicker was a question that at first glance appeared impossible to answer. It would have been better, and certainly kinder, to have let him go in peace. This, however, I was in honour bound not to do. He was Nikola's property, whose servant I also was, and if it were possible to keep him alive I knew I must do it.

"Oh, Dr. Ingleby, surely he cannot be dead?" cried the girl behind me, in a voice that had grown hoarse with fear. "Tell me the worst, I implore you."

"Hush!" I answered, but without looking round. "You must be brave. He is not dead. Nor will he die if I can save him."

Then turning to the steward, who was still with us, I bade him hasten to my cabin and bring me the small bag he would find hanging upon the peg behind the door. When he returned with it I took from it one of the small bottles it contained, the contents of which I had been directed by Nikola to use only in the event of the case seeming absolutely hopeless. The mixture was tasteless, odourless, and quite colourless, and of a liquidity equal to water. I poured the stipulated quantity into a spoon and forced it between the old man's lips. Somewhat to my surprise—for I must confess, after what I had seen of Nikola's power a few nights before, I had expected an instantaneous cure—the effect was scarcely perceptible. The eyelids flickered a little, and then slowly closed; a few seconds later a respiratory movement of the thorax was just observable, accompanied by a heavy sigh. For upwards of an hour I remained in close attendance upon him, noting every symptom, and watching with amazement the return of life into that aged frame from which I had begun to think it had departed for good and all. Once more I measured the quantity of medicine and gave it to him. This time the effect was more marked. At the end of ten minutes a slight flush spread over the sunken cheeks, and his breathing could be plainly distinguished. When, after the third dose, he was sleeping peacefully as a little child, I turned to the girl and held out my hand.

"He will recover," I said. "You need have no further fear. The crisis is past."

She was silent for a moment, and I noticed that her eyes had filled with tears. "You have done a most wonderful thing," she answered, "and have punished me for my rudeness to you on deck. How can I ever thank you?"

"By ceasing to give me credit to which I am not entitled," I replied, I fear a little brusquely. "This medicine comes from Dr. Nikola, and I think should be as good a proof as you can desire of the genuineness of his offer and of his ability to make your grandfather a strong and hearty man again."

"I will not doubt him any more," she said: and after that, having made her promise to call me should she need my services, I bade her good' night and left the cabin, meaning to retire to rest at once. The stuffiness of my berth, however, changed my intention. After all that had transpired, it can scarcely be wondered at that I was in a state of fever-ish excitement. In love with my profession as I was, it will be readily understood that I had sufficient matter before me to afford plenty of food for reflection. I accordingly filled my pipe and made my way to the deck. Once there, I found that the appearance of the night had changed; the moonlight had given place to heavy clouds, and rain was falling. The steamer was still rolling heavily, and every timber groaned as if in protest against the barbarous handling to which it was being subjected. Stowing myself away in a sheltered place near the alley-way leading to the engine-room, I fell to considering my position. That it was a curi-ous one, I do not think any one who has read the preceding pages will doubt. A more extraordinary could scarcely be imagined, and what the upshot of it all was to be was a thing I could not at all foresee.

Having finished my pipe, I refilled it and continued my meditations. At a rough guess, I should say I had been an hour on deck when a cir-cumstance occurred which was destined to furnish me with even more food for reflection than I already possessed. I was in the act of knocking the ashes out of my pipe before going below, when I became aware that something, I could not quite see what, was making its way along the deck in my direction under the shadow of the starboard bulwark. At first I felt inclined to believe that it was only a trick of my imagination, but when I rubbed my eyes and saw that it was a human figure, and that it was steadily approaching me, I drew back into the shadow and awaited developments. From the stealthy way in which he advanced, and the trouble he took to prevent himself being seen, I argued that, whoever the man was, and whatever his mission might be, it was not a very reputable one. Closer and closer he came, was lost to view for an instant behind the mainmast, and then reappeared scarcely a dozen feet from where I stood. For a moment I hardly knew what course to adopt. I had no desire to rouse the ship unnecessarily, and yet, for the reasons just stated, I felt morally certain that the man was there for no lawful purpose. However, if I was going to act at all, it was plain I must do so without loss of time. Fortune favoured me, for I had scarcely arrived at this decision before the chief engineer, whose cabin looked out over the deck, turned on his electric light. A broad beam of light shot out and showed me the man standing beside the main hatch steadfastly regard-ing me. Before he could move I was able to take full stock of him, and what I saw filled me with amazement. The individual was a Chinaman, and his head presented this peculiarity, that half his left ear was missing.

As I noted the significant fact to which I have just alluded, the rec-ollection of Nikola's letter flashed across my mind, in which he had warned me to keep my eyes open for just such another man. Could this be the individual for whom I was to be on the look-out? It seemed extremely unlikely that there could be two Mongolians with the same peculiar deformity, and yet I could scarcely believe, even if it were the same and he had any knowledge of my connection with Nikola, that he would have the audacity to travel in the same ship with me. It must not be supposed, however, that I stayed to think these things out then. The light had no sooner flashed out upon him and revealed his sinister personality, than the switch was turned off and all was darkness once more. So blinding was the glare while it did last, however, that fully ten seconds must have elapsed before my eyes became accustomed to the darkness. When I could see, the man had vanished, and though I crossed the hatch and searched, not a sign of him could I discover.

****

"Whoever he is," I said to myself, "he has at least the faculty of being able to get out of the way pretty quickly. I wonder what . . . but there, what's the use of worrying myself about him? He's probably a fireman who has been sent aft on a message to the steward, and when I see him in the daylight I shall find him like anybody else."

But while I tried to reassure myself in this fashion I was in reality far from being convinced. In my own mind I was as certain that he was the man against whom Nikola had warned me as I could well be of anything. The chief engineer at that moment stepped from his cabin into the alley-way. Here, I thought to myself, was an opportunity of settling the matter once and for all. I accordingly accosted him. I had been introduced to him earlier in the day by the captain, so that he knew who I was.

"That is not a very pretty fireman of yours," I began, "that China-man with half an ear missing. I saw him a moment ago coming along the deck here. Where does he hail from?"

The chief engineer, who, I may remark en passant, was an Ab-erdonian, and consequently slow of speech, hesitated for a moment before he replied.

"That's mighty queer," he said at length. "Ye're the second mon who's seen him the night. D'ye tell me ye saw him this meenit? And if I may make so bold, where might that have been?"

"Only a few paces from where we are standing now," I answered. "I was smoking my pipe in the shelter there, when suddenly I detected a figure creeping along in the shadow of the bulwarks. Then you turned on your electric, and the light fell full and fair upon his face. I saw him perfectly. There could be no doubt about it. He was a Chinaman, and half his left ear was missing."

The chief engineer sucked at his pipe for upwards of half a minute.

"Queer, queer," he said, more to himself than to me, "'tis vera queer. 'Twas my second in yonder was saying he met him at eight bells in this alley-way. And yet I've been officially acquented there's no such person aboard the ship."

"But there must be," I cried. "Don't I tell you I saw the man myself, not five minutes ago? I would be willing to go into a court of law and swear to the fact."

"Dinna swear," he answered. "I'll nae misdoubt yer word."

With this assurance I was conducted forthwith to the chart room, where we discovered the skipper stretched upon his settee, snoring voluminously.

"Do you mean to tell me that you really saw the man?" he inquired, when my business had been explained to him.

I assured him that I did mean it. I had seen him distinctly.

"Well, all I can say is that it's the most extraordinary business I ever had to do with," he answered. "The second engineer also says he saw him. Directly he told me I had the ship searched, but not a trace of the fellow could I discover. We'll try again."

Leaving the chart room, he called the bos'un to him, and, accompanied by the chief engineer and myself, commenced an exhaustive examination of the vessel. We explored the quarters of the crew and firemen forrard, the galley, stores, and officers' cabins in both alleyways, and finally the saloon aft, but without success. Not a trace of the mysterious Mongolian could we find. The skipper shook his head.

"I don't know what to think about it," he said.

I knew that meant that he had his doubts as to whether I had not dreamt the whole affair. The inference was galling, and when I bade him goodnight and went along to my cabin, I wished I had said nothing at all about the matter. Nevertheless, I was as firmly convinced that I had seen the man as I was at the beginning. In this frame of mind I prepared myself for bed. Before turning into my bunk, however, I took down the small bag in which I kept the drugs Nikola had given me and of which he had told me to take such care. I was anxious to have them close at hand in case I should be sent for by Dona Consuelo during the night. To assure myself that they had not been broken by the rolling of the ship I opened the bag and looked inside. My astonishment may be imagined on discovering that it was empty. The drugs were gone.

CHAPTER 4

The Chinaman's Escape

The night on which I discovered that Nikola's drugs had been stolen was destined to prove unpleasant in more senses than one. The sweetest-tempered of men could scarcely have failed to take offence had they been treated as the captain had treated me. I had told him in so many words, and with as much emphasis as I was master of, that I had distinctly seen the Chinaman standing upon the main deck of his steamer. The second engineer had also entered the same report; his evidence, however, while serving to corroborate my assertion, was of little further use to me, inasmuch as I had still better proof that what I said was correct—namely, that the medicines were missing. Under the circumstances it was small wonder that I slept badly. Even had the cabin been as large as a hotel bedroom, and the bunk the latest invention in the way of comfortable couches, it is scarcely possible I should have had better rest. As it was, the knowledge that I had been outwitted was sufficient to keep me tumbling and tossing to and fro, from the moment I laid my head upon the pillow until the sun was streaming in through my porthole next morning. Again and again I went over the events of the previous day, recalling every incident with photographic distinctness; but always returning to the same point. How the man could have obtained admittance to the saloon at all was more than I could understand, and, having got there, why he should have stolen the bottles of medicine when there were so many other articles which would have seemed to be of infinitely more value to him, scattered about, was, to say the least of it, incomprehensible. Hour after hour I puzzled over it, and at the end was no nearer a solution of the enigma than at the beginning. At first I felt inclined to believe that I must have taken them from the bag myself and for security's sake have placed them elsewhere. A few moments' search, however, was sufficient to knock the bottom out of that theory. Hunt high and low, where I would, I could discover no traces of the queer little bottles. Then I remembered that when I had sent the steward for them to the Don's cabin the previous afternoon, I had taken them from the bag and placed them upon the deck beside the old man's bunk. Could I have left them there? On reconsidering the matter more carefully, however, I remembered that before leaving the cabin I had replaced them in my bag, and that as I carried them back to my berth I had bumped the satchel against the corner of the saloon table and was afraid I might have broken them. This effectually disposed of that theory also. At last the suspense of irritation, by whichever name you may describe it, became unbearable, and unable to remain in bed any longer, I rose, dressed myself, and prepared to go on deck. Entering the saloon, I found the steward busied over a number of coffee-cups.

"Good morning, sir," he said, looking up from his work. "If you'll excuse my saying so, sir, you're about early."

"I was late in bed," I answered, with peculiar significance. "How is it, my friend, that you allow people, who have no right here, to enter the saloon and to thieve from the passengers' cabins?"

"To thieve, sir!" the man replied in a startled tone; "I'm sure I don't understand you, sir. I allow no one to enter the saloon who has no right to be there."

I glanced at him sharply, wondering whether the fellow was as innocent as he pretended to be.

"At any rate," I said, "the fact remains that some one entered my cabin last night, while I was on deck, and stole the medicines with which I am treating the old gentleman in the cabin yonder."

The man looked inexpressibly shocked. "God bless my soul alive, sir—you don't mean that!" he said, with a falter in his voice. "Surely you don't mean it?"

"But I do mean it," I answered. "There can be no sort of doubt about it. When I left the old gentleman's cabin yesterday I carried the bag containing the medicines back with me to my own berth, locked it, and hung it upon the peg beside the looking-glass with my own hands. After that I went on deck, returned to my cabin an hour or so later, opened the bag, and the bottles were gone."

"But, sir, have you any idea who could have taken them?" the man replied. "I hope you don't think, sir, as how I should have allowed such a thing to take place in this saloon with my knowledge?"

"I hope you would not," I answered, "but that does not alter the fact that the things are missing."

"But don't you think, sir, the young lady herself might have come in search of you, and when she found you were not there did the next best thing and took away the medicines to use herself?"

"At present I do not know what to think," I replied with some hesitation, for that view of the case had not presented itself to me. "But if there has been anything underhand going on, I think I can promise the culprit that it will be made exceedingly hot for him when we reach our destination."

Having fired this parting shot, I left him to the contemplation of his coffee-cups and made my way up the companion-ladder to the deck above. It was a lovely morning, a brisk breeze was blowing, and the steamer was running fairly steady under a staysail and a foresail. It was not the sort of morning to feel depressed, and yet the incidents of the previous night were sufficient to render me more than a little uncomfortable. Nikola had trusted me, and in the matter of the medicines at least I had been found wanting. I believe at the moment I would have given all I possessed—which was certainly not much, but still a good deal to me—to have been able to solve the mystery that surrounded the disappearance of those drugs. Shortly before eight bells the skipper emerged from the chart room and came along the hurricane deck towards the poop. Seeing me he waved his hand, and, after he had ascended the ladder from the main deck, bade me good morning. "I'm afraid our accommodation is not very good," he said, "but I trust you have passed a fairly comfortable night. No more dreams of one-eared Chinamen, I hope?"

From the tone in which he spoke it was plain that he imagined I must have been dreaming on the previous evening. Had it not been for the seriousness of my position with Nikola, I could have laughed aloud when I thought of the shell I was about to drop into the skipper's camp.

"Dreams or no dreams, Captain Windover," I replied, "I have to make a very serious complaint to you. It will remain then for you to say whether you consider that the assertion I made to you last night was, or was not, founded upon fact. As I believe you are aware, I was instructed by my principal, Dr. Nikola, to join this vessel in the Thames and to take charge of Don Miguel de Moreno until his arrival in Newcastle-on-Tyne. Dr. Nikola was fully aware of the difficulty and responsibility of the task he had assigned to me, and for this reason he furnished me with a number of very rare drugs which I was to administer to the patient as occasion demanded. In the letter of instructions which I received prior to embarking, I was particularly warned to beware of a certain Chinaman whose peculiar characteristic was that he had lost half an ear. In due course I joined your vessel, and attended the Don, used the drugs to which I have referred, and afterwards returned them to my cabin. A quarter of an hour or so later I made my way to the deck, where I found myself suddenly brought face to face with the Asiatic of whom I had been warned. On the recommendation of the chief engineer I reported the matter to you; you searched the ship, found no one at all like the man I described, and from that time forward set down the story I had told you either as a fabrication on my part, or the creation of a dream."

"Pardon me, my dear sir, not a fabrication," the skipper began: "only a—"

"Pardon me in your turn," I replied: "I have not quite finished. As I have inferred, you treat the matter with contempt. What is the result? I return to my cabin, and, before retiring to rest, in order to make sure that they are ready at hand in case I should require them during the night, open the bag in which the medicines until that moment had been stored. To my consternation they are not there. Some one had entered my cabin during my absence and stolen them. I leave you to put what construction on it you please, and to say what that some one was."

The captain's face was a study. "But—but—" he began.

"Buts will not mend the matter," I answered, I am afraid rather sharply. "There can be no getting away from the fact that they are gone, and that some one must have taken them. They could scarcely walk away by themselves."

"But supposing your suspicions to be correct, what possible use could a few small bottles of unknown medicine be to a man like that, a Chinaman? Had he taken your watch and chain, or your money, I could understand it; but from what you say, I gather that nothing else is missing."

"Nothing else," I replied, in the tone of a man who is making an admission that is scarcely likely to add to the weight of the argument he is endeavouring to adduce.

"Besides," continued the skipper, "there are half a hundred other ways in which the things might have been lost or mislaid. Last night the ship was rolling heavily: why might they not have tumbled out and have slipped under your bunk or behind your bags? I have known things like that occur."

"And would the ship have closed the bag again, may I ask?" I answered scornfully. "No, no! Captain, I am afraid that won't do. The man I reported to you last night, the one-eared Chinaman, is aboard your ship, and for some reason best known to himself he has stolen some of my property, thereby not only inconveniencing me but placing in absolute danger the life of the old man whom I was sent on board to take care of. As the thief is scarcely likely to have jumped overboard, he must be on board now; and as he would not be likely to have stolen the bottles only to smash them, it stands to reason that he must have them in his keeping at the present moment."

"And suppose he has, what do you want me to do?"

"I want you to find him for me," I answered, "or, if you don't care to take the trouble, to put sufficient men at my disposal and allow me to do so."

On hearing this the captain became very red and shifted uneasily on his feet.

"My dear sir," he said a little testily, "much as I would like to put myself out to serve you, I must confess that what you ask seems a little unreasonable. Don't I tell you I have already searched the ship twice in an attempt to find this man, and each time without success? Upon my word I don't think it is fair to ask me to do so again."

"In that case I am very much afraid I have no alternative but to make a complaint to you in writing and to hold you responsible, should Don Miguel de Moreno lose his life through this robbery which has been committed, and which you will not help me to set right."

What the captain would have answered in reply to this I cannot say; it is quite certain, however, that it would have been something sharp had not the Dofia Consuelo made her appearance from the companion hatch that moment. She struck me as looking very pale, as if she had passed a bad night. The skipper and I went forward together to meet her.

"Good morning," I said, as I took the little hand she held out to me. "I hope your great-grandfather is better this morning?"

"He has passed a fairly good-night, and is sleeping quietly at present," she answered. "The steward is sitting with him now while I come up for a few moments to get a little fresh air on deck."

The skipper made some remark about the beauty of the morning, and while he was speaking I watched the girl's face. There was an expression upon it I did not quite understand.

"I am afraid you have not passed a very good-night," I said, after the other had finished. "Yesterday's anxiety must have upset you more than you allowed me to suppose."

"I will confess that it did upset me," she answered, with her pretty foreign accent and the expressive gesticulation which was so becoming to her. "I have had a wretched night. I had such a terrible dream that I have scarcely recovered from it yet."

"I am sorry to hear that," the skipper and I answered almost together, while I added, "Pray tell us about it."

"It does not seem very much to tell," she answered, "and yet the effect it produced upon me is just as vivid now as it was then. After you left the cabin last night, Dr. Ingleby, I sat for a little while by my grandfather's side, trying to read; but finding that impossible, I retired to rest, lying upon the bed the steward is kind enough to make up for me upon the floor. I was utterly worn out, and almost as soon as I closed my eyes I fell asleep. How long I had been sleeping I cannot say, but suddenly I felt there was some one in the room who was watching me: who it was I could not tell, but that it was some one, or something, utterly repulsive to me I felt certain. In vain I endeavoured to open my eyes, but, as in most nightmares, I found it impossible to do so; and all the time I could feel this loathsome thing, whatever it was, drawing closer and closer to me. Then, putting forth a great effort, I managed to wake, or perhaps to dream that I did so. I had much better have kept my eyes closed, for leaning over me was the most horrible face I have ever seen or imagined. It was flatter than that of a European, with small, narrow eyes, and such cruel eyes."

"Good heavens!" I cried, unable to keep silence any longer, "can it be possible that you saw him too?"

Meanwhile the skipper, who had been leaning against the bulwarks, his hands thrust deep in his pockets and his cap upon the back of his head, suddenly sprang to attention.

"Can you remember anything else about the man?" he inquired.

The girl considered for a moment.

"I do not know that I can," she answered. "I can only repeat what I said before, that it was the most awful face I have ever seen in my life.—Stay, there is one other thing that I remember. I noticed that half his left ear was missing."

"It is the Chinaman!" I cried, with an air of triumph that I could no longer suppress. And as I said it I took from my pocket the letter of instruction Nikola had sent me the week before, and read aloud the passage in which he referred to the one-eared Chinaman of whom I was to beware. The effect was exactly what I imagined it would be.

"Do you mean to tell me I was not dreaming after all?" the Dona inquired, with a frightened expression on her face.

"That is exactly what I do mean," I answered. "And I am glad to have your evidence that you saw the man, for the reason that it bears out what I have been saying to our friend the captain here."

Then turning to that individual, I continued: "I hope, sir, you will now see the advisability of instituting another search for this man. If I were in your place I would turn the ship inside out, from truck to keelson. It seems to me outrageous that a rascal like this can hide himself on board, and you, the captain, be ignorant of his whereabouts."

"There is no necessity to instruct me in my duty," he answered stiffly, and then going to the companion called down it for the steward, who presently made his appearance on deck.

"Williams," said the skipper, "Dr. Ingleby informs me that a theft was committed in his cabin last night. He declares that a man made his way into the saloon, visiting not only his berth, but that of Don Miguel de Moreno. How do you account for this?"

"Dr. Ingleby did say something to me about it this morning, sir," the steward replied: "but to tell you the plain truth, sir, I don't know what to think of it. It's the first time I've ever known such a thing happen. Of course I shouldn't like to say as how Dr. Ingleby was mistaken."

"You had better not," I replied, so sharply that the man jumped with surprise.

"Anyway, sir," the steward continued, "I feel certain that if the man had come aft I should have heard him. I am a light sleeper, as the saying is, and I believe that a cat coming down the companion-ladder would be enough to wake me, much less a man."

"On this occasion you must have slept sounder than usual," I said. "At any rate the fact remains that the man did come; and I have to ask you once more, Captain, what you intend to do to find my stolen property?"

"I must take time to consider the matter," the captain replied. "If the man is aboard the ship, as you assert, I will find him, and if I do find him he had better look out for squalls—that's all I can say."

"And at the same time," I added, "I hope you will severely punish any member of your crew who may have been instrumental in secreting him on board."

As I said this I glanced at the steward, and it seemed to me his always sallow face became even paler than usual.

"You need not bother yourself about that," said the skipper: "you may be sure I shall do so."

Then, lifting his cap to the Dona Consuelo, he went forward along the deck; while the steward, having informed us that breakfast was upon the table, returned to the companion-ladder and disappeared below.

"What does all this mystery mean, Dr. Ingleby?" inquired my companion, as we turned and walked aft together.

"It means that there is more at the back of it than meets the eye," I replied. "Before I left London I was warned by Dr. Nikola, as you heard me say just now, to beware of a certain Asiatic with only half an ear. What Nikola feared he would do I have no notion, but there seems to be no doubt that this is the man."

"But he has done us no harm," she replied, "beyond frightening me; so if the captain takes care that he does not come as far as the saloon again, it does not seem to me we need think any more about him."

"But he has done us harm," I asserted—"grievous harm. He has stolen the medicine with which I treated your great-grandfather so successfully yesterday."

On hearing this she gave a little start.

"Do you mean that if he should become ill again in the same way that he did yesterday, you would be unable to save him?" she inquired, almost breathlessly.

"I cannot say anything about that," I answered. "I should of course do my best, but I must confess the loss of those drugs is a very serious matter for me. They are exceedingly valuable, and were specially entrusted to my care."

"And you think that Dr. Nikola will be angry with you for having lost them?" she said.

"I am very much afraid he will," I answered. "But if he is, I must put up with it. Now let us come below to breakfast." With that I led her along the deck and down the companion-ladder to the saloon.

"Before we sit down to our meal I think it would perhaps be as well if I saw your great-grandfather," I said. "I should like to convince myself that he is none the worse for his attack yesterday."

Upon this we entered the cabin together, and I bent over the recumbent figure of the old man. He lay just as he had done on the previous day; his long thin hands were clasped upon his breast, and his eyes looked upward just as I remembered seeing them. For all the difference that was to be seen, he might never have moved since I had left him so many hours before.

"He is awake," whispered his great-granddaughter, who had looked at him over my shoulder. Then, raising her voice a little, she continued, still in English, "This is Dr. Ingleby, grandfather, whom your friend Dr. Nikola has sent to take care of you."

"I thank you, sir, for your kindness," replied the old man, in a voice that was little louder than a whisper. "You must forgive me if my reception of you appears somewhat discourteous, but I am very feeble. A month ago I celebrated my ninety-eighth birthday, and at such an age, I venture to assert, much may be forgiven a man."

"Pray do not apologise," I replied. "I am indeed glad to find you looking so much better this morning."

"If to be still alive is to be better, then I suppose I must be," he answered, in a tone that was almost one of regret; and then continued, "The days of our age are threescore years and ten; and though men be so strong that they come to fourscore years, yet is their strength but labour and sorrow; labour and sorrow—aye, labour and sorrow."

"Come, come, sir," I said, "you must not talk like this. You are not very comfortable here, but we are nearly at our journey's end. Once there, you will be able to rest more quietly and in greater comfort than it is possible for you to do in this tiny cabin."

"You speak well," he answered, "when you say that I am nearly at my journey's end." [section missing?] God knows at least a dozen small boats; and thinking Nikola might be in one of them, I went forward to the gangway in search of him, but though I scanned the faces below me, his was not among them. For the reason that we were so late getting into the river, and knowing that the vessel would be likely to remain for some time to come, I argued that in all probability he had put off boarding her until the morning. I accordingly turned away, and was about to walk aft when a hand was placed on my shoulder.

"Well, friend Ingleby," said a voice that there was no mistaking, and which I should have known anywhere, "what sort of a voyage have you had, and how is your patient progressing?"

"Dr. Nikola!" I cried in astonishment, as I turned and found him standing before me. "I was just looking for you in the boats alongside. I had no idea you were on board."

"I came up by the other gangway," Nikola replied. "But you have not answered my question. How is your patient?"

"He is still alive," I answered, "and I fancy, if possible, a little better than when we left London. But he is so feeble that to speak of his being well seems almost a sarcasm. Yesterday for a few moments I thought he was gone, but with the help of the drugs you gave me I managed to bring him round again. This morning he was strong enough to converse with me."

"I am pleased to hear it," he replied. "You have done admirably, and I congratulate you. Now we must think about their trans-shipment."

"Trans-shipment?" I replied. "Is it possible they have to make another journey?"

"It is more than possible—it is quite certain," he answered. "Allerdeyne Castle is a matter of some fifty miles up the coast, and a steam yacht will take us there. A bed has been prepared for the old gentleman in the saloon, and all we have to do is to get him off this boat and on board her. You had better let me have those drugs and I'll mix him up a slight stimulus. He'll need it."

This was the question I had been dreading all along, but the die was cast and willy-nilly the position had to be faced.

"I should like to speak to you upon that matter," I said. "I very much fear that you will consider me to blame for not having exercised greater care over them, but I had no idea they would be of any value to any one who did not know the use of them."

"Pray what do you mean?" he asked, with a look of astonishment that I believe was more than half assumed. "To what are you alluding? Have you had an accident with the drugs?"

While we had been talking we had walked along the main deck, and were approaching the entrance leading therefrom to the cuddy, the light from which fell upon his face. There was a look upon it that I did not like. When he was in an affable mood Nikola's countenance was singularly prepossessing: when, however, he was put out by anything it was the face of a devil rather than a man.

"I exceedingly regret having to inform you that last night the drugs in question were stolen from my cabin."

In a moment he was all excitement.

"By the man of whom I bade you beware, of course—the one-eared Chinaman?"

* * * * * * * *

"The same," I answered; and went on to inform him of all that had transpired since my arrival on board, including my trouble with the captain and the suspicions I entertained, without much foundation I'm afraid, against the steward. He heard me out without speaking, and when I had finished bade me wait on deck while he went below to the Morenos' cabin. While he was gone I strolled to the side, and once more stood watching the lights reflected in the water below. On an old tramp steamer a short distance astern of us a man was singing. It was one of Chevalier's coster songs, and I could recognise the words quite distinctly. The last time I had heard that song was in Cape Coast Castle, just after I had recovered from my attack of fever; and I was still pursuing the train of thought it conjured up, when I noticed a boat drawing into the circle of light to which I have just alluded. It contained two men, one of whom was standing up while the other rowed. A second or two later they had come close enough for me to see the face of the man in the bows. To my amazement he was a Chinaman! So overwhelming was my astonishment that I uttered an involuntary cry, and, running to the skylight, called to Nikola to come on deck. Then, bounding to the bulwarks again, I looked for the boat. But I was too late. Either they had achieved their object, or my prompt action had given them a fright. At any rate, they were gone.

"What do you want?" cried Nikola, who by this time had reached the deck.

"The Chinamen!" I cried. "I saw one of them a moment ago in a boat alongside."

"Where are they now?" he inquired.

"I cannot see them. They have disappeared into the darkness again; but when I called to you they were scarcely twenty yards away. What does their presence here signify, do you think?"

"It signifies that they know that I am on board," answered Nikola, with a queer sort of smile upon his face. "It means also that, although this is the nineteenth century and the law-abiding land of England, if we were to venture a little out of the beaten track ashore tonight, you and I would stand a very fair chance of having our throats cut before morning. It has one other meaning, and that is that you and I must play the old game of the partridge and its nest, and lure them away from this boat while the skipper transfers Don Miguel and his great-granddaughter to the yacht I have in waiting down the river."

"That is all very well," I interrupted, "but I am not at all sure the skipper would be willing. To put it bluntly, he and I have already had a few words together over this matter."

"That will make no difference," Nikola answered. "I assure you you need have no fear that he will play us false: he knows me far too well to attempt that. I will confer with him at once, and while I am doing so you had better get your traps together. We will then go ashore and do our best to draw these rascals off the scent."

So saying, Nikola made his way forward towards the chart room, while I went through the cuddy to my own berth. The steward carried my bags out on to the main deck, and, after I had spoken a word or two with Dona Consuelo, I followed him. Five minutes later Nikola joined me, accompanied by the captain. I had bidden the latter goodbye earlier in the evening, and Nikola was giving him one last word of advice, when I happened to glance towards the alley-way on the port side. Imagine my surprise—nay, I might almost say my consternation—on beholding, standing in the dark by the corner of the main hatch, the same mysterious Chinaman who I felt certain had committed the robbery of the drugs the previous night.

"Look, look," I cried to my companions; "see, there is the man again!"

They wheeled round and looked in the direction to which I pointed. At the same moment the man's right arm went up, and from where I stood I could see something glittering in the palm. An inspiration, how or by what occasioned I shall never be able to understand, induced me to seize Nikola by the arm and to swing him behind me. It was well that I did so, for almost before we could realise what was happening, a knife was thrown, and stood imbedded a good three inches in the bulwark, exactly behind where Nikola had been standing an instant before. Then, springing on to the ladder which leads from the main to the hurricane deck, he raced up it, jumped on to the rail, and dived headlong into the water alongside. By the time we reached the deck whence he had taken his departure, all we could see was a boat pulling swiftly in the direction of the shore.

"That settles it, friend Ingleby," said Nikola.

"We have no alternative now but to make our way ashore and do as I proposed. If you are ready, come along. I think I can safely promise you an adventure."

CHAPTER 5

Allerdeyne Castle

When, nowadays, I look back upon the period I spent in Nikola's company, one significant fact always strikes me, and that is the enormous number of risks we managed to cram into such a comparatively short space of time. During my somewhat chequered career I have perhaps seen as much of what is vaguely termed life as most men: I have lived in countries the very reverse of civilised; I have served aboard ships where there has been a good deal more sandbagging and hazing than would be considered good for the average man's Christian temperament; and as for actual fighting, well, I have seen enough of that to have learnt one lesson—one which will probably cause a smile to rise on the face of the inexperienced—and that is to keep out of it as far as possible, and on all occasions to be afraid of firearms.

I concluded my last chapter with an account of our arrival in New-castle, and explained how we were preparing to go ashore, when the one-eared Chinaman, who I felt convinced had committed the robbery of the previous night, made his appearance before us and came within an ace of taking Nikola's life. Had it not been for my presence of mind, or instinct, by whichever term you please to call it, I verily believe it would have been the end of all things for the Doctor. As it was, however, the knife missed its mark, and a moment later the man had sprung up the ladder to the hurricane deck and leaped the rail and plunged into the river. Being desirous of preventing the China-man from following us and by that means becoming aware that we were leaving for the north in Nikola's yacht, we determined to make our way ashore and permit them to suppose that we were remaining in Newcastle for some length of time. Accordingly we descended into the wherry alongside, and ordered the boatman to pull us to the nearest landing-stage.

"Keep your eyes open and your wits about you," whispered Nikola, when we had left the boat and were making our way up to the street. "They are certain to be on the look-out for us."

As you may be sure, I did not neglect his warning. I had had one exhibition of that diabolical Celestial's skill in knife throwing, and when I reflected that in a big town like Newcastle there were many dark corners and alley-ways, and also that a knife makes but little or no noise when thrown, I was more determined than ever to neglect no opportunity of looking after my own safety. When we reached the street at the rear of the docks Nikola cast about him for a cab, but for some minutes not one was to be seen. At last a small boy obtained one for us, and when the luggage had been placed on the roof we took our seats in it. Nikola gave the driver his instructions, and in a short time we were bowling along in the direction of our hotel. Throughout the drive I could see no signs of the enemy. I was in the act of wondering how such a game as we were then playing could possibly help us if the Celestials had failed to see us come ashore, when Nikola turned to me, and in his usual quiet voice said:

"I wonder if you have noticed that we are being followed?"

I replied that I certainly had not, nor could I see how he could tell such a thing.

"Very easily," he said: "I will prove that what I say is correct. Do you remember the small boy who went in search of a cab?"

I answered that I did, whereupon he bade me examine our reflection as we passed the next shop window. I did so, and could plainly distinguish a small figure seated on the rail at the back. Save this atom, ourselves, and a solitary policeman, the street was deserted.

"I do see a small boy," I answered; "but may he not be coming with us to try and obtain the job of carrying our luggage?"

"He is engaged upon another now. When he came up from the river he was on the look-out for us, although, as you may have noticed, he pretended to be asleep in a doorway. He obtained the cab for us, and as you stepped into it he ranged up alongside and handed something to the driver. When we alight he will wait to see that our luggage is carried in, after which he will decamp and carry the information to his employers, who will endeavour to cut our throats as soon as the opportunity occurs."

"You look at the matter in an eminently cheerful light," I said. "For my own part I have no desire to give them the chance just yet. Is there no way in which we can prevent such a possibility occurring?"

"It is for that reason that we are here," Nikola replied. "I can assure you I am no more anxious to die than you are. There would be a good deal of irony in having perfected a scheme for prolonging life, only to meet one's death at the hand of a Chinese ruffian in a civilised English tower."

"Then what is your plan?" I inquired.

"I will tell you. But do not let us speak so loud: little pitchers have long ears. My notion is that we make for the hotel, the name of which I was careful to give the driver in the hearing of the boy. We will engage a couple of rooms there, order breakfast for tomorrow morning, still in the hearing of the boy, and afterwards get out of the way as quietly as possible."

"It sounds feasible enough," I replied, "if only we can do it. But do you think the men will be so easily fooled?"

"Well, that remains to be proved. However, we shall very soon find out."

"A pretty sort of thing you've let yourself in for, Master Ingleby!" I thought to myself as Nikola lapsed into silence once more. "A week ago you were starving in a back street in London, and now it looks very much as if you are going to be murdered in affluence in Newcastle. However, you've let yourself in for it, and have only yourself to blame for the result."

Consoling myself in this philosophic way, I held my peace until the cab drew up before the hostelry to which my companion had alluded. As soon as we were at a standstill, Nikola alighted and went into the hotel to inquire about rooms. As we had agreed, I remained in the cab until he returned.

"It's all right, Ingleby," he cried, as he crossed the pavement again. "They're very full, but we can have the rooms until the day after tomorrow. After that we must look elsewhere. Now let us get the traps inside."

The porter emerged and took our luggage, and we accompanied him into the building. As we did so I saw the ragged urchin who had ridden behind the cab draw near the portico.

The manager received us in the hall. "Numbers 59 and 60," he said to the porter. "Would you care for any supper, gentlemen?" We thanked him, but declined, and then followed the porter upstairs to the rooms in question. Having seen my luggage safely installed and the man on his way downstairs, Nikola showed himself ready for business.

"When you get into these sort of scrapes," he said, "it is just as well to have a good memory. I know these rooms of old, and directly I saw the position we were in I thought they might prove of use to us. I once did the manager a good turn, and when I explain matters to him

241

I fancy he will understand why we have taken up our abode with him only to leave again so suddenly. Have you a sheet of notepaper and an envelope in your bag?"

I produced them for him, whereupon he wrote a note, and having placed a bank-note inside, addressed it to his friend.

"I'll leave it on the chimneypiece, where the chambermaid will be certain to see it," he said. "I have told the manager that we are obliged to leave in this unceremonious fashion in order to rid ourselves of some unpleasant fellow-travellers, who have been following us about with what I can only think must be hostile intent. Until we return I have asked him to take charge of your baggage, so that you need have no fear on that score. I am sorry you should have to lose it, but I can lend you anything you may require until you get possession of it again. Now, if only we can get out of this window and down to the Tyneside once more, without being seen, I think we may safely say we have given Quong Ma the slip for good and all."

So saying he crossed the room and threw open the window.

"We are both active men," Nikola continued, "and should experience small difficulty in dropping on to the roof of the outhouse below; thence we can make our way along the wall to the back. Are you ready?"

"Quite ready," I answered; whereupon he crawled out of the window and, holding on by both hands, lowered himself until his feet were only a yard or so above the roof of the outhouse to which he had referred. Then he let go and dropped. I followed his example, after which we made our way in Indian file along the wall, passed the stables, and dropped without adventure into the dark lane at the rear of the hotel. It was the first time in my life I had left a building of that description in such an unceremonious fashion, yet, strangely enough, I remember, it caused me no surprise. In Nikola's company the most extraordinary performances seemed commonplace, and in the natural order of things.

"From now forward we must proceed with the greatest caution," said my companion, as we regained our feet and paused before making our way down the dark lane towards a small street at the farther end. "They are scarcely likely to watch the back of the hotel, but it will be safer for us to suppose them to be doing so."

Acting up to this decision, we proceeded with as much caution as if every shadow were an enemy and every doorway contained a villainous Celestial. We saw nothing of the men we feared, however, and eventually reached the thoroughfare leading to the docks, without further adventure. But, fortunate as we had been, we were not destined to get away as successfully as we had hoped to do. We were within sight of the river when something, I cannot now remember what, induced me to look back. I did so just in time to catch a glimpse of a figure emerging from the shadow of a tall building. At any other time such a circumstance would have given rise to no suspicion in my mind; but, worked up to such a pitch as I was then, I seemed gifted with an unerring instinct that told me as plainly as any words that the man in question was following us, and that he was the Chinaman we were so anxious to avoid. I pointed him out to Nikola, and asked whether he agreed with me as to the man's identity.

"We will soon decide that point," was his reply. "Slacken your pace for a moment, and when I give the word wheel sharply round and walk towards him."

We executed this manoeuvre, and began to walk quickly back in the direction we had come. The mysterious figure was still making his way along the darker side of the street; and our suspicions were soon confirmed, for on seeing us turn he turned also, and a few seconds later disappeared down a side street.

"He is spying on us, sure enough," said Nikola, "and I do not see how we are going to baffle him. Let us hasten on to the river and trust to luck to get on board the yacht without his finding out where we have gone."

Once more we turned ourselves about, and in something less than five minutes had reached the landing-place for which we were steering. Then pulling a whistle from his pocket, Nikola blew three sharp notes upon it. An answer came from the deck of the yacht out in the stream. It had scarcely died away before a boat put off from alongside the craft and came swiftly towards us.

"It is only a question of minutes now," said Nikola, throwing a hasty glance round him. "Time versus the Chinaman, and if I am not mistaken "—here the boat drew up at the steps—"time has the best of it. Come along, my friend; let us get on board."

I followed him down the steps and took my place in the dinghy. The men pulling bent to their oars, and we shot out into the stream.

"Look," said Nikola, pointing to the place we had just left: "I thought our friend would not be very far behind us."

I followed with my eyes the direction in which he pointed, and, sure enough, I could just distinguish a dark figure standing upon the steps.

"They would like to catch me if they could," observed the Doctor, with a shrug of his shoulders and one of his peculiar laughs. "If they have tried once they have done so a hundred times. I will do them the credit of saying that their plans have been admirably laid, but Fate has stood by me, and on each occasion they have miscarried. They tried it first at Ya-Chow-Fu, then at I-chang, afterwards in Shanghai, Rangoon, Bombay, London, Paris, and St. Petersburg, and I can't tell you how many other places; but as you see, they have not succeeded so far."

"But why should they do it?" I asked. "What is the reason of it all?"

"That is too long a story for me to tell you now," he replied, as the boat drew up at the accommodation-ladder. "You shall hear it another day. Our object now must be to get away from Newcastle without further loss of time."

I followed him along the deck to where a short stout man stood waiting to receive us.

"Are you ready, Stevens?" asked Nikola.

"All ready, sir," the other replied, with the brevity of a man who is not accustomed to waste his words.

"In that case let us start as quickly as possible."

"At once," the man replied, and immediately went forward; while Nikola conducted me down a prettily arranged and constructed companion-ladder to the saloon below. As we reached it I heard the tinkle of the telegraph from the bridge to the engine room, and almost simultaneously the screw began to revolve and we were under way. After the darkness outside, the brilliant light of the saloon in which we now stood was so dazzling that I failed to notice the fact that a bed-place had been made up behind the butt of the mizzen mast. Upon this lay the old Don, and seated by his side, and holding his hand, was the Dona Consuelo.

"My dear young lady," said Nikola in his kindest manner, as he advanced towards her, "I fear you must be worn out. However, we are under way again now, and I have instructed my servant to prepare a cabin for you, in which I trust you will be fairly comfortable."

Dona Consuelo had risen, and was standing looking into his face as if she were frightened of something he was about to say.

"I am not at all tired," she said, "and if you don't mind, I would far rather remain here with my great-grandfather."

"As you wish," answered Nikola abstractedly. Then, stooping, he raised the old man's left hand and felt his pulse. The long, thin fingers of the Doctor, indicative of his extraordinary skill as a surgeon, seemed to twine round the other's emaciated wrist, while his face wore a look I had never seen upon it before—it was that of the born enthusiast, the man who loves his profession more than aught else in the world. While, however, I was observing Nikola, you must not suppose I was regardless of the Dona Consuelo. To a student of character, the expression upon her face could scarcely have been anything but interesting. While Nikola was conducting his examination, she watched him as if she dreaded what he might do next. Fear there was in abundance, but of admiration for the man I could discover no trace. The examination concluded, Nikola addressed two or three pertinent questions to her concerning her great-grandfather's health during the voyage, which she answered with corresponding clearness and conciseness. The old man himself, however, though conscious, did not utter a word, but lay staring up at the skylight above his head, just as I had seen him do on board the *Dona Mercedes*.

Fully five hours must have elapsed before we reached our destination; indeed, day had broken, and the sun was in the act of rising, when a gentle tapping upon the skylight overhead warned Nikola that our voyage was nearly at an end. Leaving the old man in his great-granddaughter's care, Nikola signed to me to follow him to the deck.

"It may interest you to see your future home," he said, as we stepped out of the companion into the cool morning air, and looked out over the sea, which the rim of the newly risen sun was burnishing until it shone like polished silver. At the moment the yacht was entering a small bay, surrounded by giant cliffs, against which the great rollers of the North Sea broke continuously. The bay itself was in deep shadow, and was as dreary a place as any I have seen. I looked about me for a dwelling of any sort, but not a sign of such a thing could I discover: only a long stretch of frowning cliff and desolate, wind-swept tableland.

"At first glance it does not look inviting," said Nikola, with a smile upon his face, as he noticed the expression upon mine. "I confess I have seen a more hospitable coast-line, but never one better fitted for the work we have in hand."

"But I do not see the castle," I replied. "I have looked in every direction, but can discover no trace of it."

"One of its charms," he continued triumphantly. "You cannot see it because at present it is hidden by yonder headland. When we are safely in the bay, however, you will have a good view of it. It is a fine old building, and in bygone days must have been a place of considerable importance. Ships innumerable have gone to pieces in sight of its turrets; while deep down in its own foundations I am told there are dungeons enough to imprison half the county. See, we are opening up the bay now, and in five minutes shall be at anchor. I wonder what result we shall have achieved when we next steam between these heads."

While he was speaking we had passed from the open sea into the still water of the bay, and the yacht was slowing down perceptibly. Gradually the picture unfolded itself, until, standing out in bold relief upon the cliffs like some grim sentinel of the past, the castle which, for some time to come at least, was destined to be my home came into view. Who its architect had been I was never able to discover, but he must have been impregnated with the desolation and solemn grandeur of the coast, and in his building have tried to equal it. As Nikola had said, a place better fitted for the work we had come to do could not have been discovered in the length and breadth of England. The nearest village was upwards of twelve miles distant; farms or dwelling-houses there were none within view of its towers. Tourists seldom ventured near it, for the reason that it was not only a place difficult of approach, but, what was perhaps of more importance, because there was nothing of interest to be seen when you reached it. As I gazed at it, I thought of the girl in the saloon below, and wondered what her feelings would be, and what her life would be like, in such a dismal place. I glanced at Nikola, who was gazing up at the grim walls with such rapt attention that it was easily seen his thoughts were far away. Then the telegraph sounded, and the screw ceased to revolve, The spell was broken, and we were recalled to the realities of the moment.

"I was miles away," said Nikola, looking round at me.

"I could see you were," I answered.

"You would be very surprised if you knew of what I was thinking," he continued. "I was recalling a place not unlike this, but ten thousand miles or more away. It is a monastery, similarly situated, on the top of enormous cliffs. It was there I obtained the secret which is the backbone of the discovery we are about to test. I have been in some queer places in my time, but never such a one as that. But we haven't time to talk of that now. What we have to do is to get the old man ashore and up to yonder building. If anything were to happen to him now, I think it would break my heart."

"And his great-granddaughter's also," I put in; "for you must admit she is devoted to him."

He threw a quick glance at me, as if he were trying to discern how far I was interested in the beautiful girl in the saloon below. Whatever conclusion he may have come to, however, he said nothing to me upon the subject. Having ordered the captain to see the boat—which had been specially prepared for the work of carrying the old gentleman ashore—brought alongside, he made his way to the saloon, and I accompanied him.

"We have reached our destination, Dona Consuelo," he said, as he approached the bed, beside which she was sitting.

As he spoke, there leapt into her eyes the same look of terror I had noticed before. It reminded me more than anything else of the expression one sees in the eyes of a rabbit when the snare has closed upon it. As I noticed it, for the first time since I had known him, a feeling of hatred for Nikola came over me. It was not until we were in the boat and were making our way ashore that I found an opportunity of speaking to her without Nikola overhearing us.

"Courage, my dear young lady, courage!" I said. "Believe me, there is nothing to fear. I will pledge my life for your safety."

She gave me a look of gratitude, and stooped as if to arrange the heavy travelling-rug covering her aged relative. In reality I believe it was to hide the tears with which her eyes were filled. From that moment there existed an indefinable, real bond between us; and though I did not realise it at the moment, the first mark had been made upon the chain with which Nikola imagined he had bound me to him.

On reaching that side of the bay on which there was a short strip of beach, the boat was grounded. The four sailors immediately took up the litter upon which the old man lay, and carried it ashore. The path up to the castle was a steep and narrow one, and the work of conveying him to the top was by no means easy. Eventually, however, it was accomplished, and we stood before the entrance to the castle. Moat there was none, but in place of it, and spanned by the drawbridge—a ponderous affair, something like fifty feet long by ten wide—was an enormous chasm going sheer down in one drop fully two hundred feet. At the bottom water could be seen; and at night, when the tide came in, the gurgling and moaning that rose from it was sufficient to appal the stoutest heart.

"Welcome to Allerdeyne Castle!" said Nikola, as we crossed the bridge and entered the archway of the ancient keep. Then, bending over the old man on the litter, he added: "When you cross this threshold again, my old friend, I hope that you will be fully restored to health and strength—a young man again in every sense of the word. Dona Consuelo, I am all anxiety to hear your opinion of the apartments I have caused to be prepared for you."

Moving in procession as before, we crossed the great courtyard, which echoed to the sound of our footsteps, and, reaching a door on the farther side, entered and found ourselves standing in a well-proportioned hall, from which a staircase of solid stone, up which a dozen soldiers might have marched abreast, led to the floors above.

With Nikola still in advance, we made the ascent, turned to the right hand, and proceeded along a corridor, upwards of fifty yards in length, out of which opened a number of lofty rooms. Before the door of one of these Nikola paused.

"This is the apartment I have set aside for your own particular use, my dear young lady," he said; and with that he threw open the door, and showed us a large room, carpeted, curtained, and furnished in a fashion I was far from expecting to find in so sombre a building.

"Should there be anything wanting," he said, "you will honour me by mentioning it, when I will do all that lies in my power to supply it."

Her face was very pale, and her lips trembled a little as she faltered a question as to where her great-grandfather was to be domiciled.

"I have come to the conclusion that, for the future, it would be better," said Nikola, speaking very slowly and distinctly, as if in anticipation of future trouble, "that you should entrust him to my care. Ingleby and I, between us, will make ourselves responsible for his safety, and you may rest assured we will see that no harm comes to him. You must endeavour to amuse yourself as best you can, consoling yourself with the knowledge that we are doing all that science can do for him."

As he said this he smiled a little sarcastically, as if her reading of the word science would be likely to differ considerably from his.

"But surely you do not mean that I am to give him up to you entirely?" she cried, this time in real terror. "You cannot be so cruel as to mean that. Oh, Dr. Nikola, I implore you not to take him altogether from me. I cannot bear it."

"My dear young lady," said Nikola, a little more sternly than he had yet spoken, "in this matter you must be guided by me. I can brook no interference of any description. Surely you should know me well enough by this time to be aware of that."

"But he is all I have to live for—all I have to love," the girl faltered. "Can you not make allowance for that?"

Her voice was piteous in its pleading, and when I heard Nikola's chilling tones as he answered her, I could have found it in my heart to strike him. To have interfered at all, however, would have done no sort of good; so, hard as it seemed, I was perforce compelled to hold my tongue.

"If you love your great-grandfather," he said, "you will offer no opposition to my scheme. Have I not already assured you that I will return him to you a different man? But we are wasting time, and these stone corridors are too cold and draughty for him. If you will be guided by me, you will rest a little after your exertions. There is an old woman below who shall come to you, and do her best to make herself useful to you." Seeing that to protest further would be useless, the girl turned and went into the room, trying to stifle the sobs that would not be kept back. The sight was one which would have grieved a harder heart than mine, and it hurt me the more because I knew that I was powerless to help her.

All this time the four sailors, who had carried the litter up from the beach, had been silent spectators of the scene. Now they took up their burden once more and followed Nikola, along the corridor, up some more steps, down still another passage, until I lost all count of the way that we had come. The greater portion of the castle had been allowed to fall into disrepair. Heavy masses of cobwebs stretched from wall to wall, a large proportion of the doors were worm-eaten, and in some instances had even fallen in altogether, revealing desolate apartments, in which the wind from the sea whistled, and the noise of the waves echoed with blood-curdling effect. Reaching the end of the second corridor, Nikola paused before a heavy curtain which was drawn closely from wall to wall, and ordered the men to set down their burden. They obeyed; and, on being told to do so, took their departure with as much speed as they could put into the operation. If I know anything of the human face, they were not a little relieved at receiving permission to clear out of a place that had every right to be considered the abode of a certain Old Gentleman whom it scarcely becomes me to mention.

****

When the sound of their footsteps had died away, Nikola drew back the curtain and displayed a plain but very strong wooden door. From the fact that the workmanship was almost new I surmised that my host had placed it there himself, but for what purpose I could only conjecture. Taking a key from his pocket, he slipped it into the patent lock, turned the handle, and the door swung open.

"Take up your end of the litter," he said, "and help me to carry it inside."

I did as I was ordered; and, bearing the old man between us, we passed into that portion of the castle which, as I soon discovered, he had fitted up in readiness for the great experiment.

Having passed the door, we found ourselves in a comparatively lofty room, or perhaps I had better say hall, the walls of which were covered almost entirely with anatomical specimens. From what I could see of them I should say that many of them were quite unique, while all were extremely valuable. Where and by what means he had collected them I was never able to discover, although Nikola, on one or two occasions, threw out hints. There they were, however, and I promised myself that during my stay in the place I would use them for perfecting my own knowledge on the subject.

At the end of this hall, and looking over the sea, was a large window, while in either wall were several doors, all of which, like that in the corridor, were heavily curtained. The carpet was of cork and quite noiseless; the lights were electric, the batteries and dynamos being in a room below. The heating arrangements were excellent, while the ventilation was of the most modern and improved description. I noticed that Nikola smiled a little contemptuously at my astonishment.

"You were unprepared for this surprise," he said. "Well, let me give you a little piece of advice, and that is, never be astonished at anything you may see or hear while you are with me. The commonplace and I, I can assure you once and for all, do not live together. I have homes in all parts of the world; I am in England today, engaged upon one piece of work, and in six months' time I may be in India, Japan, Peru, Kamtschatka, or if you like it better, shall we say playing tricks with niggers in Cape Coast Castle? But see, we are keeping our old friend waiting. I will find out if all the preparations I have ordered are complete; if so, we will convey him at once to the chamber set apart for him."

With that he touched a bell, and almost before he had removed his finger from the button, a curtain at the farther end was drawn aside, and the same Chinese servant—the deaf-and-dumb individual, I mean, who had brought the letter to me at my lodgings in London the previous week—entered the room. Seeing his master, he bent himself nearly double, and when he had resumed his upright posture as curious a conversation commenced as ever I have known. I use the word "conversation" for the simple reason that I do not know how else to describe it. As a matter of fact it was not a conversation at all, for the reason that not a word was spoken on either side; their lips moved, but not a sound came from them. And yet they seemed quite able to understand one another. If, however, it was a strange performance, it had at least the merit of being an extremely successful one.

"He tells me that everything is prepared," Nikola remarked, as the man crossed the room and drew back another curtain from a doorway on our left. "This is the room; but before we carry him into it I think we had better have a little light upon the subject."

To press the electric switch was the work of a moment, and as soon as this had been done we once more took up our burden and carried it into the inner room. Prepared as I had been by the outer hall for something extraordinary, I was perhaps not so much surprised at the apartment in which I now found myself as I should otherwise have been. And yet it was sufficiently remarkable to fill any one with wonder.

It was upwards of twenty feet in length by possibly eighteen in width. The walls and the ceilings were as black as charcoal, and, when the electric light was extinguished, not a ray of anything would be visible. In the centre was a strange contrivance which I could see was intended to serve as a bed, and for some other purpose, which at the moment was not quite apparent to me. In the farther corners were a couple of queer-looking pieces of machinery, one of which reminded me somewhat of an unusually large electric battery; the other I could not understand at all. A machine twice the size of those usually employed for manufacturing ozone stood opposite the door; thermometers of every sort and description were arranged at intervals along the walls; while on one side was an ingenious apparatus for heating the room, and on the other a similar one for cooling it. At the head and foot of the bed were two brass pillars, the construction and arrangements of which reminded me of electric terminals on an exaggerated scale.

We placed the old gentleman on the bed. The litter was thereupon removed by the servant, and Nikola and I stood facing each other across the form of the man who was to prove, or disprove, the feasibility of the discovery my extraordinary employer claimed to have made.

"For twenty-four hours," said Nikola, "he must have absolute peace and quiet. Nothing must disturb him. Nor must he taste food."

"But is he capable, do you think," I asked, "of going without nourishment for so long a time?"

"Perfectly! On the draught I am about to administer to him, he could do without it, were such a thing necessary, for a much longer period. Indeed, it would not hurt him if he were to eat nothing for a month."

He left the room for a moment, and when he returned he carried in his hand a tiny phial of the same description, though much smaller, as those which had been stolen from me on board the steamer. It contained a thick, red mixture, which, when he removed the stopper, threw off a highly pungent odour. He opened the mouth of the patient and poured upwards of a teaspoonful into it. As before, I expected to see some immediate result, but my curiosity was not gratified. Deftly arranging the bed-coverings, Nikola inspected the thermometers, tested the hot and cold air apparatus, and then turned to me.

"He will require little or no supervision for some hours to come," he said, "so we may safely leave him. To while away the time, if you care about it, I will show you something of my abode. I think I can promise you both instruction and amusement."

CHAPTER 6

Life in the Castle

Leaving the room in which we had placed Don Miguel de Moreno, as described in the previous chapter, we returned to the hall, the same in which was contained the magnificent collection of anatomical specimens already mentioned. Tired as I was,—for it must be remembered that I had had but little sleep during the first night I had spent on board the Dona Mercedes, and none at all on that through which we had just passed, while I had had a great deal of excitement, and my fair share of hard work,—I would not have lost the opportunity of exploring Nikola's quarters in this grim old castle for any consideration whatsoever. Nikola himself, though one would scarcely have thought it from his appearance, must have possessed a constitution of iron, for he seemed as fresh as when I had first seen him at Kelleran's house in London. There was a vitality about him, a briskness, and, if I may so express it, an enjoyment of labour for its own sake, that I do not remember ever to have found in another man. As I was soon to discover, my description of him was not very wide of the mark. He would do the work of half a dozen men, and at the end be ready, and not only ready but eager, for more. In addition to this, I noticed another peculiarity about him. Unlike most people who are fond of work, he possessed an infinite fund of patience; could wait for an issue, whatever it might be, to develop itself naturally, and, unlike so many experimentalists, betrayed no desire to hurry it by the employment of extraneous means. In thus putting forward my reading of the most complex character that has ever come under my notice, I do so with an absolute freedom from bias. Indeed, I might almost say, that I do so in a great measure against my own inclinations, as will be apparent to you when you have finished my story.

"As I informed you in London," said this strange individual, after he had closed the door of the patient's room behind him, had drawn the heavy curtain, and switched off the electric light, "I purchased this famous castle expressly for the experiment we are about to try. The owner, so my business people informed me, was amazed that I should want it at all; but then, you see, he did not understand its value. If I had searched the world, I could not have discovered a better. While we are near enough to civilisation to be able to obtain anything we may require in the way of drugs or incidental apparatus, we have no prying neighbours; such household stores as we require the yacht brings us direct from Newcastle; an old man and woman, who take care of the place when I am absent, have their quarters in the keep; my Chinese servant cooks for me personally, and attends to the wants, which are not many, of the other people under my care."

"Other people under your care?" I echoed. "I had no idea there was any one in the house save yourself and your servants."

"It is scarcely likely you would have any idea of it," he observed, "seeing that no one knows of it save Ah-Win, who, for reasons you have seen, is unable to talk about them, and myself, who would be even less likely to do so. Would you care to see them?"

I replied that I would very much like to do so, and he was about to lead me across the hall towards the door, through which the Chinese servant had entered some little time before, when a curious circumstance happened. With a bound that was not unlike the spring of a tiger, an enormous cat, black as the Pit of Tophet, jumped from the room, and, approaching his master, rubbed himself backwards and forwards against his legs. Seeing my astonishment, Nikola condescended to explain.

"You are going to say, I can tell, that you have never seen such a cat as Apollyon. I don't suppose you have. If he could talk, he would be able to tell some strange stories; would you not, old man? He has been my almost constant companion for many years, and more than once he has been the means of saving my life."

Replacing Apollyon, whom he had picked up, on the floor, he conducted me towards the entrance of another corridor which led in the direction of the keep. Half-way down it was a rough iron gate, which was securely padlocked.

Nikola undid it, and when we were on the other side carefully relocked it after him.

"Though you might not think so," he said, "these precautions are necessary. Some of my patients are extremely valuable, and I have not the least desire that they should escape from my keeping and fall over the battlements into the sea below. Follow me."

I accompanied him towards yet another door, which he also unlocked. The scene which met my gaze when he threw it open, to employ a hackneyed phrase, beggars description. The room was about the same size as that occupied by the Dona Consuelo, but it was not its proportions that amazed me, but its occupants. Accustomed as I had necessarily been, by virtue of my profession, to what are commonly called horrors, I found that I was not proof against what I had before me now. It was sufficient to make my blood run cold. Anything more gruesome could scarcely have been discovered or even imagined. Try to picture for yourself the inmates of a dozen freak museums, and the worst of the monstrosities of which you have ever read or heard, and you will only have some dim notion of the folk whom Nikola so ironically called his patients. Some were like men, but not men as we know them; some were like monkeys, but of a kind I had never seen before, and which I sincerely hope I may never see again; there were things, dull, flabby, faceless things—but there, I can go no farther. To attempt to describe them to you in detail is a work of which my pen is quite incapable.

"A happy family," said Nikola, advancing into the room, "and without exception devoted to their nurse, Ah-Win, yonder, who, as you are aware, in a measure shares their afflictions with them. Some day, if you care about it, I should be only too pleased to give you a lecture, with demonstrations, such as you would get in no medical school in the world."

Though I have attempted to set down his offer word for word, I have but the vaguest recollection of it; for, long before he had finished speaking, I had staggered, sick and faint with horror, into the corridor outside. Not for the wealth of England would I have remained there a minute longer. To see those loathsome creatures fawning round Nikola, clutching at his legs and stroking his clothes, was too much for me, and I verily believe an hour in that room would have had the effect of making me an idiot like themselves. A few moments later Nikola joined me in the passage.

"You are very easily affected, my dear Ingleby," he said, with one of his peculiar smiles. "I should have thought your hospital experience would have endowed you with stronger nerves. My poor people in yonder—"

"Don't, don't," I cried, holding up my hand in entreaty. "Don't speak to me of them. Don't let me think of them. If I do, I believe I shall go mad. My God! are you human, that you can live with such things about you?"

"I believe I am," he answered with the utmost coolness. "But why make such a fuss? Do like I do, and regard them from a scientific standpoint only. The poor things have come into this world handicapped by misfortune; I endeavour as far as possible to ameliorate their conditions, and in return they enable me to perfect my knowledge of the human frame as no other living man can ever hope to do. Of course, I know there are people who look askance at me for keeping them; but that does not trouble me. At one time they lived with me in Port Said, which, when you come to think of it, is a fit and proper place for such a hospital. Circumstances, however, combined to induce me to leave. Eventually we came here. Some time, if you care to hear it, I will tell you the story of their voyage home. It would interest you."

I protested, however, that I desired to hear no more about them; I had both seen and heard too much already. That being so, Nikola led me along the passage and through the iron gate, which he locked behind him as before, and so conducted me to the hall whence we had first set out. Once there, he went to a corner cabinet, and from it produced a decanter. Pouring me out a stiff glass of brandy, he bade me drink it.

"You look as if you want it," he said. And Heaven knows he was right.

"And now," he said, when I had finished it, "if you will take my advice, you will lie down for an hour or two. For the convenience of our work, I have arranged that you shall occupy a room near me. This is it. Should I want you, I will ring a bell."

The room to which he alluded adjoined his own, and was situated at the far end of the hall, the door, like those of the others I have described, being concealed behind a curtain. Never was permission to retire more willingly accepted, and within five minutes of leaving him I was in bed and asleep.

It must have been between ten and eleven o'clock in the forenoon when I retired; and the afternoon was well advanced before I woke again. Heavily as I slept, however, it had not been restful slumber. All things considered, I had much better have been waking.

Over and over again I saw the Dona Consuelo standing before me, just as she had done before Nikola that day; there was this difference, however—instead of asking to be allowed to remain with her great-grandfather, her prayer was that I should save both him and her from Nikola. While she pleaded to me, the faces of the terrible creatures I had seen in that room down the passage peered at us from all sorts of hiding-places. It was night, an hour or so before dawn. I had acceded to the Dona's request, and was flying from the castle, carrying her in my arms.

At last, after I appeared to have been running for an eternity, we reached the shore, where I hoped to find a boat awaiting us. But not a sign of one was to be seen. While I waited day broke, and I placed my burden on the sand, only to spring back from it with a cry of horror. It was not the Dona Consuelo I had been carrying, but one of those loathsome creatures I had seen in that terrible room. A fit of rage came over me, and I was about to wreak my vengeance on the unhappy idiot, when I woke. I looked about me at the somewhat sparsely furnished room, and some seconds elapsed before I realised where I was. Then the memory of our arrival at the castle, and of all that had happened since, returned to me. I shuddered, and had it not been for that poor girl, so lonely and friendless, I could have found it in my heart to wish myself back in London once more. Having dressed myself, I went out into the hall. Nikola was not there. I waited for some time, but as he did not put in an appearance I left the room and made my way down the corridor in the direction of the Dona Consuelo's sitting-room. Not able to get any answer when I knocked, I continued my walk, ascended another flight of stairs, and eventually found myself upon the battlements. A better place for observing the construction of the castle, and of obtaining a view of the surrounding country, could not have been desired. On one side I could look away across the moorland towards a distant range of hills, and on the other along the cliffs and across the wide expanse of sea. In the tiny bay to my right the yacht which had brought us from Newcastle lay at anchor; and had it not been for that and a column of grey smoke rising from a chimney, I might have believed myself to be living in a world of my own. For some time I stood watching the panorama spread out before me. I was still looking at it when a soft footfall sounded on the stones behind me. I turned to find Dona Consuelo approaching me. She was dressed entirely in black, and wore a lace mantilla over her shoulders.

"Thank Heaven, I have found you, Dr. Ingleby," she cried, as she hastened towards me. "I had begun to think myself deserted by everybody."

"Why should you do that?" I asked. "You know that could never be."

"I am certain of nothing now," she answered. "You cannot imagine what I have been through today."

"I am indeed sorry to hear you have been unhappy," I continued. "Is there any way in which I can be of service to you?"

"There are many ways, but I fear you would not employ them," she replied. "I am hungering to be with my great-grandfather again. Can you tell me why Dr. Nikola takes him away from me?"

"I fancied that he had told you," I answered; "but if it be any consolation to you, let me give you my assurance that he is tenderly cared for. His comfort is secured in every way; and from what Dr. Nikola has said to me, and from what I have seen myself, I feel convinced he will be able to do what he has promised and make your great-grandfather a hale and hearty man once more."

"It is all very well for him to say that," she said, "but why am I not permitted to be with him? If he needs nursing, who would be likely to wait upon him so devotedly as the woman who loves him? Surely Dr. Nikola cannot imagine his secret would be unsafe with me if he reveals it to you, a rival in his own profession?"

"It is not that at all," I answered. "I do not fancy Nikola has given a moment's consideration to the safety of his secret." Then, seeing the loophole of escape she presented to me, I added: "From what you know of him, I should have thought you would have understood that he has no great liking for your sex. To put it bluntly, Nikola is a woman-hater of the most determined order, and I fancy he would find it impossible to carry out his plans if you were in attendance upon the Don."

"Ah well! I suppose I must be content with your assurance," she said with a sigh.

"For the present, I am very much afraid so," I replied.

At this moment the old woman whom Nikola had appointed to wait upon us made her appearance, and informed the Dona that her dinner awaited her. About my own meals she knew nothing, so I concluded from this that I was to take them with Nikola in our own portion of the castle. Such proved to be the case; for when we reached the Dona Consuelo's apartments on the floor below, we met Nikola awaiting us in the corridor.

"I have been looking for you, Ingleby," he said, with a note of command in his voice. "You are quite ready for dinner, I have no doubt; and if you will accompany me, I think we shall find it waiting for us."

As may be supposed, I would rather have partaken of it with Dona Consuelo; but as it was not to be, I bade her good morning, and was about to follow Nikola along the corridor, when he stopped, and, turning to the girl, said:

"I can see from your face that you have been worrying about your grandfather. I assure you, you have not the least cause to do so; and I think Ingleby here, if he has not done so already, will bear me out in what I say. The old gentleman is doing excellently, and almost before you know he has been taken away from you, you will have him back again."

"I thank you for your news," she replied; but there was very little friendliness in her voice. "I would rather, however, see him and convince myself of the fact." Then, bowing to us, she retired into her own apartments, while we made our way to the hall in search of our meal.

"Tomorrow morning," said Nikola, as we drew our chairs up to the table, "we must commence work in earnest. After that for some weeks to come I am afraid you will see but little of your fair friend down yonder. You seem to be on excellent terms with one another."

As he said this he shot a keen glance at me, as though he were desirous of discovering what was passing in my mind. I was quite prepared for him, however, and answered in such an unconcerned way that I nattered(?) myself, should he have got it into his head that there was anything more than mere friendship in our intimacy, he would be immediately disabused of the notion.

As he had predicted, the following morning saw the commencement of that gigantic struggle with the forces of Nature, upon the result of which Nikola had pinned so much faith and which was destined, so he affirmed, to revolutionise the world. The most exhaustive preparations had been made, the duration of our watches in the sick-room were duly apportioned, and a minute outline of the treatment proposed was propounded to me.

On entering the dark room in which the old Don lay, I discovered that the two bronze pedestals, the use of which had puzzled me so much on my first visit, had been moved near the bed, one been placed at its head and the other at its foot. These, as Nikola pointed out to me, were the terminals of an electric conductor for producing a constant current, which was to play without intermission a few feet above the patient's head. A peculiar and penetrating smell filled the room, which I had no difficulty in recognising as ozone, though Nikola's reason for using it in such a case was not at first apparent to me. The old Don himself lay just as we had left him the previous morning. His hands were by his sides; his eyes, as usual, were open, but saw nothing. It was not until I examined him closely that a slight respiratory movement was observable.

"When I am not here," said Nikola, "it must be your business to see that this electric current is kept continually playing above him. It must not be permitted for an instant to abate one unit of its strength." Then, pointing to an instrument fixed at the further wall, he continued: "Here is a volt meter, with the maximum and minimum points plainly marked upon it Your record must also include temperature, which you will take on these dry and wet thermometers once every quarter of an hour. The currents of hot and cold air you can regulate by means of these handles. The temperature of the patient himself must be noted once in every hour, and should on no account be permitted to get higher or lower than it is at the present moment."

Taking a clinical thermometer from his pocket, he applied it, and, when he had noted the result, handed it to me.

"If it rises two points above that before the same hour three days hence, he will die—no skill can save him. If it drops, well, in eighty per cent, of cases, the result will be the same."

"And suppose I detect a tendency to rise?"

"In that case you must communicate instantly with me. Here is an electric button which will put you in touch with my room. I hope, however, that you will have no necessity to use it." Then, placing his hand upon my shoulder, he looked me full in the face. "Ingleby," he said, "you see how much trust I am placing in you. I tell you frankly, you have a great responsibility upon your shoulders. I am not going to beat about the bush with you. In this case there is no such thing as certainty. I have made the attempt three times before, and on each occasion my man has died simply through a moment's inattention on the part of my assistant. If the love of our science and a proper appreciation of the compliment I have paid you in asking you to share with me the honour of this great discovery do not weigh with you, think of the girl with whom you talked upon the battlements yesterday. You tried to make me believe that she was nothing to you. Some day, however, she may be. Remember what her grandfather's death would mean to her."

"You need have no fear," I replied. "I assure you, you can trust me implicitly."

"I do trust you," he answered. "Now let us get to work."

So saying, he crossed the room and opened a square box, heavily clamped with iron, from which he took two china pots of ointment. Then, disrobing the old man, we anointed him with the most scrupulous care from head to foot. This we did three times, after which the second curious apparatus I had seen standing in the corner was wheeled up to the bedside. That it was an electrical instrument of some sort was plain, but what its specific use was I could not even conjecture. Nikola, however, very soon enlightened me upon the matter. Taking a number of large velvet pads, each of which was moulded to fit a definite portion of the human body, he placed them in position, attached the wires that connected them with the machine, and when all was ready turned on the current. At first no effect was observable.

In about a minute and a half, however, if my memory serves me, the usual deathly pallor of the skin gave place to a faint blush, which presently increased until the skin exhibited a healthy glow; little by little the temporal veins, until then so prominent, gradually disappeared. In half an hour, during which the current had been slowly and very gradually increased, another dressing of both ointments was applied.

"Take this glass and examine his skin," said Nikola, whose eyes were gleaming with excitement, as he handed me a powerful magnifying glass. When I bent over the patient and did as he directed, it was indeed a wonderful thing that I beheld. An hour before the skin had been soft and hung in loose folds upon the bones, while the pressure of a finger upon it would not leave it for upwards of a minute. Now it had in a measure regained its youthful elasticity, and upon my softly pinching it between my fingers I found that it recovered its colour almost immediately.

"It is wonderful," I whispered. "Had I not seen it myself, I would never have believed it."

When it had been applied for an hour, the electric current was turned off and the pads removed.

"Now watch what happens very closely," said Nikola, "for, I assure you, the effect is curious."

Scarcely able to breathe by reason of my excitement, I watched, and as I did so I saw the flush of apparent health gradually decrease, the skin become white and loose once more, while the superficial veins rose into prominence upon the temples. I glanced at Nikola, thinking that some mistake must have occurred and that he would show signs of disappointment. This, however, he did not do.

"You surely did not imagine," he said, when I had questioned him upon the subject, "that the effect I produced would be permanent on the first application? No! we may hope to achieve a more lasting result in a fortnight's time, but not till then.

"Meanwhile, the effect must be produced in the same fashion every six hours, both day and night. Now give me those rugs; we must cover him carefully. In his present state the least draught would be fatal. Record the state of the volt meter, read your thermometers, and see that your ventilating apparatus is working properly. As I said just now, should you need me, remember the bell. One ring, when you have recorded your results, will inform me that all is progressing satisfactorily, while three will immediately bring me to your assistance. Do you understand?"

When I had assured him that I did, he left me. I accordingly switched

260

off three of the electric lights, and sat myself down in a chair in semi-darkness, the centre of light being the patient on the bed. There was no fear of my feeling dull, for I had a great deal to think about. Taken altogether, the situation in which I found myself was as extraordinary as the most inveterate seeker after excitement could desire. Not a sound was to be heard. The stillness was that of the tomb, and yet I smiled to myself as I thought that, if Nikola's experiment achieved the result he expected of it, the simile was not an appropriate one, for it was not the silence of the tomb but of perpetual life itself. I looked at the figure on the bed before me, and tried to picture what the mystery he was unravelling would mean to mankind. It was a solemn thought. Should the experiment prove successful, how would it affect the world? Would it prove a blessing or a curse? But the thoughts it conjured up were too vast, the issues too great, and to attempt to solve them was only to lose oneself in the fields of wildest conjecture.

For four hours I remained on duty, noting all that occurred; reading my thermometers, regulating the hot and cold air apparatus, and at intervals signalling to Nikola that everything was progressing satisfactorily. When he relieved me, I retired to rest and slept like a top, too tired even to dream.

Of what happened during the fortnight following I have little to tell. Nikola and I watched by the bedside in turn, took our exercise upon the battlements, ate and slept with the regularity of automata. The life on one side was monotonous in the extreme; on the other it was filled with an unholy excitement that was the greater inasmuch as it had to be so carefully suppressed. To say that I was deeply interested in the work upon which I was engaged would be a by no means strong enough expression. The fire of enthusiasm, to which I have before alluded, was raging once more in my heart, and yet there had been little enough so far in the experiment to excite it. With that regularity which characterised the whole of our operations, we carried on the work I have described. Every sixth hour saw the skin tighten and become elastic, the hue of the flesh change from white to pink, the veins recede, and the hollows fill, only to return to their original state as soon as the electric current was withdrawn. Towards the end of the fortnight, however, there were not wanting signs to show that the effect was gradually becoming more lasting. In place of doing so at once, the change to the original condition did not occur until some eight or ten minutes after the pads had been removed. And here I must remark that there was one other point in the case which struck me as peculiar. When I had first seen the old man, his finger-nails were of that pale yellow tint so often observable in the very old, now they were a delicate shade of pink; while his hair was, I felt convinced, a darker shade than it had been before. As Nikola was careful to point out, we had arrived at the most critical stage of the experiment. A mistake at this juncture, would not only undo all the work we had accomplished, but, what was more serious still, might very possibly cost us the life of the patient himself.

The night I am about to describe was at the end of the fourteenth day after our arrival at the castle. Nikola had been on watch from four o'clock in the afternoon until eight, when I relieved him.

"Do not let your eyes wander from him for a minute," he said, as I took my place beside the bed. "From certain symptoms I have noticed during the last few hours, I am convinced the crisis is close at hand. Should a rise in the temperature occur, summon me instantly. I shall be in the laboratory ready at a moment's notice to prepare the elixir upon which the success we hope to achieve depends."

"But you are worn out," I said, as I noticed the haggard expression upon his face. "Why don't you take some rest?"

"Rest!" he cried scornfully. "Is it likely that I could rest with such a discovery just coming within my grasp? No; you need not fear for me; I shall not break down. I have a constitution of iron."

Having once more warned me to advise him of any change that might occur, he left me; and when I had examined my instruments, attended to the electrical apparatus, and taken the patient's temperature, I sat down to the vigil to which I had by this time become accustomed. Hour by hour I followed the customary routine. My watch was early at an end. In twenty minutes it would be time for Nikola to relieve me. Leaning over the old man, I convinced myself that no change had taken place in his condition; his temperature was exactly what it had been throughout the preceding fortnight. I carefully wiped the clinical thermometer, and replaced it in its case. As I did so, I was startled by hearing a wild shriek in the hall outside. It was a woman's voice, and the accent was one of deadly terror. I should have recognised the voice anywhere: it was the Dona Consuelo's. What could have happened? Once more it rang out, and almost before I knew what I was doing I had rung the bell for Nikola, and had rushed from the room into the hall outside. No one was to be seen there. I ran in the direction of the corridor which led towards the Dona's own quarters, but she was not there! I returned and followed that leading towards that terrible room behind the iron gate. The passage was in semi-darkness, but there was still sufficient light for me to see a body lying upon the floor. As I thought, it was the Dona Consuelo, and she had fainted. Picking her up in my arms, I carried her to the hall, where the meal of which I was to partake at the end of my watch was already prepared. To bathe her forehead was the work of a moment. She revived almost immediately.

"What is the matter?" she asked faintly. "What has happened?" But before I could reply, the recollection of what she had seen returned to her. A look of abject terror came into her face.

"Save me, save me, Dr. Ingleby!" she cried, clinging to my arm like a frightened child. "If I see them again, I shall go mad. It will kill me. You don't know how frightened I have been."

* * * * * * * *

I thought I was in a position to understand exactly.

"Hush!" I answered. "Try to think of something else. You are quite safe with me. Nothing shall harm you here."

She covered her face with her hands, and her slender frame trembled under the violence of her emotion. Five minutes had elapsed before she was sufficiently recovered to tell me everything. For some days, as I soon discovered, she had been left almost entirely alone, and having nothing to occupy her mind, had been brooding over her enforced separation from her aged relative. The more she thought of him the more became her craving to see him, in order to convince herself that no harm had befallen him. A semi-hysterical condition must have ensued, for she rose from her bed, dressed herself, and, taking a candle in her hand, started in the hope of finding him. By some stroke of ill-fortune she must have discovered a passage leading to Ah-Win's portion of the castle, and at last found herself standing before the open door of that demon-haunted room.

"What does it all mean?" she cried piteously "What is this place, and why are these dreadful things here?"

I was about to reply, when the curtain at the end of the hall, covering the door of the laboratory, was drawn aside, and to my horrified amazement Nikola, who I imagined had taken my place in the patient's room, stood before us. As I saw him and realised the significance of the position, a cold sweat broke out upon my forehead. What construction would he be likely to place upon my presence there? For a few seconds he stood watching us, then an expression that I can only describe as being one of terror spread over his face.

"What does this mean?" he cried hoarsely. "What have you done?" Then running to the door of the Don's room, he drew back the curtain and entered. Leaving the Dona where she was, I followed with such fear in my heart as I had never known before. I found Nikola fumbling with the case of the clinical thermometer, and trembling like a leaf as he did so. Thrusting it into the old man's mouth, he hung over him and waited as if his whole life depended on the result. Withdrawing it again and holding it up to the light, he gazed at it.

"Too late!" he cried, and I scarcely recognised his voice, so changed was it. "His temperature has dropped a point! Ingleby, this is your doing. For all you know to the contrary, you may have killed him."

CHAPTER 7

Love Reigns

In the preceding chapter I made you acquainted with the calamity which befell our patient, and of the serious position in which I found myself placed with Nikola in consequence. While knowing in my own heart that I was quite innocent of any intentional neglect of duty, I had yet to remember that had I remained on watch, instead of leaving the room to ascertain what had befallen the Dona Consuelo, it would in all probability never have happened. On the other hand, I had signalled Nikola and called him to my assistance before abandoning my charge. How it was he had not answered my summons was more than I could understand. As it transpired afterwards, however, and as is usual in such things, the explanation was a very simple one. In the last chapter I said that when he left me to go to the laboratory, he was quite exhausted; he had eaten nothing for many hours, and as a natural result the fumes of the herbs he was distilling had overpowered him and he had fallen in a dead faint upon the floor.

As long as I live I shall retain the recollection of the next fourteen hours. During the whole of that time Nikola and I fought death inch by inch for the body of the old Don. From midnight until the following afternoon, neither of us crossed the threshold of the sick-chamber; and during the whole of that time, save to give me brief directions, Nikola spoke no word to me at all. It was only when the mercury in the clinical thermometer was once more established on its accustomed mark that he addressed me. Rearranging the bed-covering and wiping his clammy forehead with his pocket-handkerchief, he turned to me.

"I think he will do now," he said, "provided he does not lose ground within the next half-hour, we may take it for granted that he is out of danger."

This was the opportunity for which I was waiting: I accordingly seized it.

"I am afraid, Dr. Nikola," I said, mustering courage as I progressed, "that you consider me to blame for what has happened." He looked sharply at me, and then said coldly:

"I fail to see how I could very well think otherwise. I left you in charge, and you deserted your post."

"But I assure you," I continued, "that you are misjudging me. I could not help myself. I heard the girl scream, and ran to her assistance. At the same time I took care to ring the bell for you before I left the room."

"You should not have left it at all until I had joined you," he answered, still in the same icy tone. "As a matter of fact, I did not hear your summons; I had fainted. And one other question, What was the girl doing in this portion of the castle?"

"She was hysterical," I answered, "and was searching for her great-grandfather. She did not know, herself, how she got here; but, as ill-luck would have it, she saw your terrible people, and was frightened nearly to death in consequence.

"For common humanity's sake I could not leave her as she was. Having rung for you, I naturally thought you were with the Don, and that I was free to render her what assistance I could."

"Your argument is certainly plausible; but supposing the man had died during your absence? How would you have felt then?"

"I should have regretted it all my life," I answered. "But surely you must admit that would have been better than that a young girl should have been driven mad by fear."

"You do not seem to understand," Nikola replied, "that I would willingly sacrifice a thousand girls to accomplish the great object I have in view. No! no! Ingleby, you have been found wanting in your duty; you have checked the progress of the experiment, and if that old man had died"—here he took a step towards me, and his face suddenly became livid with passion—"as I live at this moment you would never have seen the light of day again. I swear I would have killed you with as little compunction as I would have destroyed a dog who had bitten me."

So menacing was his attitude, and so fiendish the expression on his face, that I instinctively recoiled a step from him, and yet I don't think my worst enemy could accuse me of being a coward. Was the man a lunatic? I asked myself; had the magnitude of his discovery turned his head? If so, I must be careful in my dealings with him.

"I am afraid I do not understand you, Dr. Nikola," I said, trying to appear calmer than I felt. "You talk in an exaggerated fashion, and one which I cannot permit. I confess to being in a certain measure to blame for what has happened; but if you feel that you can no longer repose the trust in me that you once felt, I would rather resign my post with you, and leave your house at once."

For a moment I thought I had detected a sign of fear in his face. Then his manner changed completely.

"My dear Ingleby," he said, patting me on the shoulder and speaking in quite a different tone, "we are wrangling like a pair of schoolboys. If I hurt your feelings just now, I hope you will forgive me and ascribe it to my anxiety. For the last two days, as you are aware, I have been overwrought. When I stated that I considered you to blame, I said more than I meant; for, of course, I know that you had no intention of injuring our patient, or of doing anything to prejudice the end we have in view. It was a combination of unfortunate circumstances, the ill-effects of which by good luck we have been able to remedy. Let us forget all about it."

"With all my heart," I said, with a momentary friendliness I had never felt for him before, and held out my hand to him. He took it, when to my surprise I found that his hand was as cold as ice. In this fashion the cloud between us appeared to have been blown away; but though it was no longer visible to the naked eye, it still existed, for I was unable to dispel from my mind the recollection of the threat he had used to me. If he were not in earnest now, he had at least been so then; and, for my own part, I put more faith in his threats than in his protestations of friendship.

"Come, come, this will never do," said Nikola, after the few moments' silence which had followed after our reconciliation. "It is nearly three o'clock. You had better go to your room and rest for a couple of hours, after which you can relieve me."

Seeing his haggard and weary face, I offered to remain on duty while he went to lie down, but to this he would not consent. It was plain he was still brooding over what had happened, and that he did not intend to trust me any further than he was absolutely obliged. Accordingly, I did not press him; but, as soon as I had noted the various temperatures, and had done what I could to help him, I left him to his vigil and went to my own apartment. I had had nineteen hours in the sick-room, and in consequence was completely worn out. During that time I had heard nothing of the Dona Consuelo. But when I laid my head upon my pillow and closed my eyes, her terrified face, as I had seen it the previous night, rose before me. Even then I could feel the thrill which had run through me as I took that lovely body in my arms. What place was this terrible castle,

267

I asked myself, for such a woman? How dreary was the life she was compelled to lead in it; without companions, and cut off from the one person who only a week before had been all her world to her. This suggested another and a sweeter thought to me. Was there only one person she loved? I remembered how she had clung to me in the hall, and how she had appealed to me to save her. The mere thought that there might be something more than simple liking in her attitude was sufficient to set my heart beating like a sledge-hammer. Was it possible I could be falling in love? I, who had thought myself done with that sort of thing for ever? I smiled at the idea. A nice sort of position I was in to contemplate such a thing. And yet I was so lonely in the world that it soothed me to think there might be some one to whom I was a little more than the average man, and that that some one was a beautiful and noble woman. With these thoughts in my brain I fell asleep. A moment later, so it seemed, the electric bell above my head brought me wide awake again. One glance at my watch was sufficient, however, to show me that I had been asleep two hours. I dressed as quickly as possible and returned to the Don's room, when, much to my relief, Nikola informed me that there had been no relapse, and that all was progressing as satisfactorily as he could wish. Bidding me exercise the greatest vigilance, he left me and staggered from the room.

"A little more of this sort of thing, my friend," I said to myself, as I watched him pass out of the door—"only a little more, and you will be unfit for anything."

But I had yet to learn the strength of Nikola's constitution. He was like a steel bow: he might often be bent, but never broken.

It was not until the following morning that I saw Dona Consuelo again. We met upon the battlements as usual.

"Dr. Ingleby," she said, after we had been standing together some time, "I feel there is something I should say to you. I want to tell you how sorry I am for what occurred the other night. But for my folly in wandering about the castle as I did, I should not have seen"—she paused for a moment, and a shudder swept over her at the recollection. "I should not have seen what I did, and you would not have got into trouble with Dr. Nikola."

"But how did you know that I did get into trouble with Nikola?" I asked.

"Because Dr. Nikola spoke to me about it," she replied.

On hearing this, I pricked up my ears. Had Nikola taken her to task for what she had done?

In all probability he had blamed her. I tried to catch her on this point, but she would tell me nothing.

"You will accept my apology, won't you?" she asked; "it has made me so unhappy."

"You must not apologise to me at all," I answered; "I assure you none is needed. I would have given anything to have prevented your seeing—well, what you did, and still more to have prevented Nikola from speaking to you. He had no right to do so." Then, drawing a little closer to her, I took her hand: "Dona Consuelo," I said, "I am very much afraid your life here is a very unhappy one."

"I was happier in Spain," she answered. "But I do not want you to think that I am grumbling; you have given me your promise that no ill shall befall my great-grandfather, and for this reason I have no fear. If he is well, what right have I to complain of anything that may happen to myself? Some day perhaps Dr. Nikola will allow us to go back to Spain, and then I shall forget all about this terrible castle."

I wondered if the hope she entertained would ever be realised. But I was not going to permit her to suppose that I entertained any doubt at all about it. I felt I should like to have said more, but prudence restrained me. She looked so beautiful that the temptation was almost more than I could withstand. Whether she knew anything of what was in my mind, I cannot say; but somehow I fancied she must have done so, for, though I have no desire to appear conceited, I could not help thinking, when we bade each other goodbye, there was a look of sorrow in her face. Once more a fortnight went by. A month had now elapsed since our arrival at the castle, and, as I could plainly see, Nikola's experiment was at length achieving a definite result. The changes effected by the use of the electric batteries and the constant anointing which I have already described having ceased within a short time of the removal of the means by which they were occasioned, were now almost permanent, and were becoming more so every day. The patient's flesh was firmer and his skin was more elastic, while his usual pallor had given place to what might almost be described as a healthy tint. So far success had crowned Nikola's endeavours; but whether the final result would be what he desired was more than I could say. After the little contretemps which followed my mistake, already described, Nikola and I had agreed fairly well together. I was aware, however, that he was suspicious of my intimacy with the old Don's great-granddaughter; and from the way in which he glanced at the patient and the various instruments whenever he relieved me in the sick-room, I could tell that he was always anxious to satisfy himself that I had not done anything to prejudice the work he had in hand. It may easily be supposed therefore, that our partnership was far from being as pleasant as it had promised in London to be. To live in an atmosphere of continual suspicion is unpleasant at any time, but it becomes doubly so when another's happiness depends in a very large measure upon it. Of course, the reason was apparent to me; but there must have been something more in Nikola's mind than I could fathom, for I think I can assert most truthfully that never for a moment did I allow an effort to be wanting on my part to show how much I had his interest at heart. There was yet another thing which puzzled me. It was this: what was to happen when the required result had been achieved, and the old Don was transformed into a young man again? And more important still, what would become of his great-granddaughter? The whole thing seemed so absurd—so unnatural—if you like it better—that I could see no proper conclusion to it. Still, there was time to talk of that later on. The old Don was already, I am prepared to admit, in a certain sense, younger; that is to say, he did not present that appearance of great age which had been noticeable on board the Dona Mercedes; at the same time, he was still very far from being a young man.

One day I found sufficient courage to speak on this point to Nikola.

"That is one of the most remarkable points in my argument," he answered. "If he were to change his state so quickly, I should despair of success. As it is, I am more than hopeful, I am sanguine. Tomorrow, if he continues to progress so favourably, we shall enter upon the third stage of the experiment. Granted that is successful, I shall be within measurable distance of the greatest medical discovery of this or any other century."

Knowing it was useless attempting to question him further, I was compelled to possess my soul in patience until the time should arrive for him to enlighten me. The following morning, as soon as I had finished my period of duty in the Don's chamber, I informed Nikola of my intention of going for a short stroll. The time, he had decided, was not ripe yet for the third phase; and as I knew that I should be kept closely employed as soon as it was, I was anxious to obtain as much exercise as possible while I had the opportunity. Accordingly, I placed my hat upon my head and descended to the courtyard. Strangely enough it was the first time I had set foot in it since our arrival at the castle. It was an exquisite morning for walking, and the sky was blue overhead, a brisk breeze was blowing, and when I had crossed the drawbridge and looked down into the little bay where the waves rolled in and broke with a noise like thunder upon the beach, I felt happier than I had done for some considerable time past. I watched the white gulls wheeling above my head, and as I did so the recollection of the time when I had last seen them rose before my mind's eye. It was the day that I had come so near speaking words of love to Dona Consuelo upon the battlements. I remembered the look I had seen on her sweet face, and as I did so I realised how much she was to me. With a light step and a feeling of elation in my heart, I made my way down the path towards the beach. Not a soul was to be seen, for I remembered having heard Nikola say that the yacht had gone south for stores. Reaching the water's edge, I stood and looked back at the castle. It was a sombre enough place in all conscience, and yet there was something about it now which affected me in a manner I can scarce describe. I looked at it for a few moments, and then, turning my back upon it, I set off along the beach at a brisk pace, whistling gaily as I went. Eventually I reached the further side of the bay, opposite that on which the castle was situated. Here the sand gave place to large rocks, which in their turn terminated in a tall headland. The view from these rocks was grand in the extreme. Night and day the rollers of the North Sea broke upon them, throwing showers of spray high into the air. Clambering up, I struggled for fifty yards or so, and finally seating myself upon a rock somewhat larger than the rest, prepared to enjoy the view. A surprise was in store for me. Looking back upon the way I had come, I caught sight of a figure walking towards me on the sands. Needless to say, it was the Dona Consuelo. Whether she was aware of my presence upon the rocks, I cannot say; I only know that as soon as I saw her I rose from where I was sitting and hastened to meet her. How beautiful she looked, and how her face lighted up as I came closer, are things which I must leave to the imagination of my reader.

"You are further abroad than usual today, are you not?" I said, as we shook hands.

"Might I not say the same of you?" she answered with a smile. "The morning was so beautiful that I could not remain in that terrible old building. Every corner seems to suggest unhappy memories to me."

"Do you really think all the memories connected with it will be unpleasant?" I inquired.

She looked up at me in a little startled way, and blushed divinely as she did so.

* * * * * * * *

271

"Could you expect me to regard the time I have spent in it with any sort of pleasure?" she inquired, fencing with my meaning, and giving me a Roland for an Oliver. "Only think what I have suffered in it!"

By this time we were strolling back together towards the rocks I have already described. The beach at this point narrowed considerably, and for some reason or another we walked a little nearer the cliff than I had done. Suddenly my companion stopped, and, pointing to the sand, said:

"You had a companion this morning?"

"I? I had no companion," I answered. "What makes you think so?"

"Look here," she said, and as she spoke she pointed to some footmarks on the sand before us.

"As you went up the beach you walked near the water's edge, and as you came to meet me you passed midway between your former tracks and the cliff. If you did not have a companion, whose footprints are these? They must have been made this morning, for, as you are aware, when the tide is full, it comes right up to the cliffs, and would be certain to wash out anything that existed before."

I stooped and examined the tracks carefully before I answered. They were evidently those of a man, and from the fact that the sand was hard the outline could be plainly distinguished. The foot that was responsible for them was a large one, and must have been clad in an exceedingly clumsy boot.

"I don't know what to think of it," I said. "One thing, however, is quite certain: I had no companion this morning. What about the old man and his wife at the castle?"

"I happen to know that they have both been hard at work all the morning," she answered. "Besides, what object could they have in following you? The beach leads nowhere, and from here to yonder point there is no place where you can reach the land above."

I shook my head. The problem was too much for me. At the same time I must own it disquieted me strangely. Who was this mysterious person who had dogged my footsteps? and what could have been his object in following me? For a moment I inclined to the belief that it might have been Dr. Nikola, who was anxious to discover how I spent my leisure. But on second thoughts the absurdity of the idea became apparent to me. But if it were not Nikola, who could it have been?

On reaching the rocks we seated ourselves, and fell to criticising the picture spread out before our gaze. There was something in my companion's manner this morning which, analyse it as I would, I could not understand. She was by turns light-hearted and sad; the two expressions chased each other across her face like clouds across an April sky. At last she returned to the topic which I knew must come sooner or later—that of her great-grandfather's condition.

* * * * * * * *

"I seem cut off from him for ever," she said with infinite sadness. "I hear nothing of him from week's end to week's end, and I see nothing of him. He is gone completely out of my life."

"But only for the time being," I answered. "Dr. Nikola has assured you that he will restore him to health and strength. Think what that will mean, and how happy you will be together then."

"I know it is very wrong of me to say so," she continued; "but I cannot keep it back, Dr. Ingleby—I distrust Dr. Nikola. He is deceiving me; of that I feel sure."

Knowing what I did, I could not contradict her; but I saw my opportunity, and acted upon it.

"But if you do not trust Dr. Nikola," I said, "am I to suppose that you do not trust me?"

She was silent, and I noticed that she turned her face away from me, as if she were anxious to study the castle and the cliff. What was more, I noticed that her hand trembled a little as it rested on the rock beside me.

Once more I put the question, and as I did so, I leant a little towards her.

"I do trust you," she answered, but so softly that I could scarcely hear it.

"Consuelo," I said, in a voice but little louder than that in which she had addressed me, "you cannot think what happiness it is to me to hear you say that. As I have tried to show you, there is nothing I would not do to prove how anxious I am to be worthy of your trust. We have known each other but little longer than a month. In that time, however, I have learnt to know you as well as any man could know a woman. I have learnt more than that, Consuelo; I have learnt to love you better than life itself."

"No, no," she answered, "you must not say that. I cannot hear you."

"But it must be said," I answered. "My love will not be denied. You do love me, Consuelo; I can see it in your face. Don't you think that I watched and longed for it?"

Instead of turning her face to me, she turned it still further from me.

I took her little hand in mine.

"What is your answer, Consuelo?" I asked. "Be brave and tell me, darling."

"If I were brave," she said, "I should tell you that what you ask must never be. That it is hopeless—impossible. That it would be madness for us to think of such a thing. But I am not brave. I am so lonely in the world, and have lost so much that I cannot lose you also."

"Then you love me!" I cried, in such triumph as I had never felt for anything else in my life before. "Thank God, thank God for that!"

"Yes, I love you," she answered; and the great waves breaking on the rocks seemed to echo the happiness we both were feeling.

Over the next half-hour I must draw a veil. By the end of that time it was necessary for me to think of returning to the castle. Nikola's watch would be up in an hour, and I knew it would not do for me to keep him waiting. I said as much to Consuelo, and we immediately rose and set out on our return. As I walked beside her, I would not have changed position with any living man, so happy was I. My peace of mind, however, was destined to be but short-lived. We had crossed the greater number of the rocks, and were approaching the sand once more, when I received a shock which I shall not forget as long as I can remember anything. Clambering over the sharp and slippery rocks was by no means an easy business. It was, however, delightful to hold my sweetheart's hand in the pretence of assisting her. Occasionally it became necessary for us to make considerable detours, and once I bade her remain where she was until I had climbed a somewhat bigger rock than usual in order to find out whether we could proceed that way. I had reached the top, and was about to extend my hand to her assistance, when something caused me to look behind me. Judge of my surprise and consternation at finding, in the hollow below me, a man crouching on the sand, watching me.

It was the Chinaman I had seen on board the *Dona Mercedes*, the man who had thrown the knife which had so nearly terminated Nikola's existence.

How I managed to retain my presence of mind at that trying moment, I find it difficult now to understand. I only know this, that I realised in a flash the fact that it would be madness to pretend to have seen him. Accordingly, I stood for a moment looking out to sea, and then with a laugh that must have sounded far from natural, I rejoined Consuelo on the rock below and chose another path towards the sands.

"What is the matter?" she inquired when we had proceeded a short distance. "Your face is quite pale."

"I did not feel very well for a moment," I answered, making use of the first excuse that occurred to me.

"I am afraid you are not telling me the truth," she answered. "I feel convinced something has frightened you. Can you not trust me?"

Under the circumstances I thought it would be better for me to make a clean breast of it.

"I will trust you," I answered. "The fact of the matter is, I have discovered an explanation for the footsteps you pointed out to me upon the beach. We are being followed. When I jumped on the top of that rock, I found a man lying on the other side of it."

"A man? Who could he have been, and why should he be spying upon us? Did you recognise him?"

"Perfectly; I should have known him anywhere."

"Then who was he?"

"The Chinaman we saw on board the steamer. The man who stole the drugs Nikola entrusted to my care."

"Do you mean the man who entered my cabin and bent over to look at me?" she cried in alarm.

I nodded, and threw a quick glance back over my shoulder to discover whether we were still being followed. I could see nothing, however, of the man; a circumstance which by no means allayed my anxiety.

"What do you think we had better do?" inquired Consuelo.

"Hasten home as fast as we can go, and tell Nikola," I answered. "It is imperative he should know at once."

We accordingly continued our walk at increased speed, every now and then throwing apprehensive glances behind us. It is possible some of my readers may regard it as an exhibition of cowardice on my part to have sought refuge in flight; but when all the circumstances connected with it are taken into consideration, I am sure every fair-minded person will acquit me of this charge. Had I been alone, it is possible I might have turned and risked an encounter with the man; but Consuelo being with me rendered such a course impossible. For the first time since we had known it, the grim old castle, perched up on the cliffs, seemed a desirable place, and it was with a feeling of profound relief that I led my sweetheart across the drawbridge, and was able to tell myself that, for the time being at least, she was safe. On reaching the hall, I found that I had still twenty minutes to spare. I had no desire, however, for further leisure. What I wanted was to see Nikola at once, in order to tell him my unpalatable news.

On entering the room, I found him engaged in taking the old man's temperature. He looked up at me as if he were surprised to see me return so soon, but said nothing until he had finished the work upon which he was engaged.

"I can see from your face that you have had a fright, and that you have something to say to me concerning it," he began, when he had returned the thermometer to its case. "Our friend Quong Ma has turned up again, I suppose?"

"How did you know it?" I asked: for I had no idea that he was aware of the man's appearance in the neighbourhood.

"I guessed it," he answered, with one of his peculiar smiles. "You are the possessor of a most expressive countenance. Consider for a moment, and you will understand how it is I am able to arrive at a conclusion so quickly. In the first place, you have been for a walk with the young lady whom you love and who loves you in return."

"Perhaps you saw me," I replied sharply, feeling myself blushing to the roots of my hair.

"I have not left this room," he answered. "There is a long black hair on your collar, which would not have been there if you had spent your liberty by yourself. The same thing tells me that you love her, and she loves you. As for the other matter, the caretaker and his wife have been busily employed in the castle all the morning, while Ah-Win never leaves his own portion of the premises. There is only one person outside the walls who could have put that expression into your face, and that person is Quong Ma. Am I right?"

"Quite right," I replied. "He followed me along the sands, and hid himself among the rocks. In recrossing them from the point, I, as nearly as possible, jumped on him."

"I am very glad you did not quite do so," he answered. "Had you experienced that misfortune, you would not have been here to tell the tale. But enough of him for the present. Take your place here and watch our patient. In an hour's time his temperature should have risen two points. When it has done so, give him ten drops of this fluid in twenty drops of distilled water. A profuse perspiration should result, which will herald the return of consciousness and the new life. In twenty-four hours he should not only be conscious, but on his way to the commencement of his second youth; in forty-eight the improvement should be firmly established; while in a week we should have him on his legs, a living, moving, thinking man, and of my own creation. Watch him, therefore, and whatever happens do not leave this room. Meanwhile, I will have the drawbridge raised, and if Quong Ma can leap the chasm, and make his way into the castle, well, all I can say is, he is a cleverer man than I take him to be."

With that, Nikola left me, and I sat down to watch beside the aged Don. Apart from my duty towards him, I had plenty to think about, and over and over again I found myself recalling the incidents of the morning. Consuelo loved me, and happen what might I would prove myself worthy of her love. At the end of the hour, as Nikola had predicted, the patient's temperature had risen two points. I accordingly measured out the stipulated quantity of the medicine he had placed in readiness for me, added the necessary quantity of water, and poured it into the old man's mouth. Then I sat myself down to wait. Slowly the hands of the clock upon the wall went round, and sixty minutes later, just as Nikola had prophesied, small beads of perspiration made their appearance upon his forehead. It was an exciting moment, and one for which we had been eagerly waiting. I immediately rang the bell for Nikola, and upon his arrival informed him of the fact.

"At last, at last," he whispered. "It is certain now that I have made no mistake. From this moment forward his progress should be assured. In a week you will be rewarded by a sight such as the eye of man has never yet seen. Be faithful to me, Ingleby, and I pledge my word your future with the woman you love is assured."

For the remainder of that day, and, indeed, until eleven o'clock on the morning following, there was but little change in the old Don's condition. The casual observer would have seen but little difference from the day on which I had first taken charge of him on board the steamer. To Nikola and myself, however, who had spent so much time with him, and who had noted every change, there was a difference so vast that it seemed almost incomprehensible.

My watch next morning was from four o'clock until eight. At eight I breakfasted, and afterwards repaired to the battlements above in the hope of meeting Consuelo. Since Nikola had ordered the drawbridge to be raised, we had been compelled to make this our meeting-place, and, as it happened, Consuelo was first at the rendezvous.

"You have good news for me!" she cried, after I had kissed her. "I can see it in your face. What is it? Does it concern my great-grandfather?"

"It does," I answered. "It concerns him inasmuch as I am able to tell you that what Nikola promised you should happen has in reality come to pass. Everything has been satisfactory beyond our wildest hopes."

"And do you mean that all need of anxiety is over?" she cried.

"I do not mean that exactly," I answered. "But I think it very possible we shall soon be able to say so. Nikola is certainly the most wonderful man upon this earth."

What she said in reply it would be vanity on my part to recall, and would be only another instance of the folly of lovers' talk. Let it suffice that for upwards of an hour our converse was of the sweetest description. Hand in hand we sat upon the battlements, looking out across the sunlit sea, and building our castles in the air. We were interrupted by Ah-Win, who suddenly made his appearance before us and beckoned me to follow him.

Bidding Consuelo goodbye, I followed the fellow to the hall, where he pointed to the old Don's room and left me. I found Nikola in a state of the wildest excitement.

****

"I sent for you because the crisis is close at hand," he whispered. "At any moment now I may know my fate. Little by little I have built up this worn-out frame, strengthening, renewing, revivifying, and now the object of my ambition is almost achieved. A thousand years ago the secret was guessed by a certain secret sect in Asia. After working a hundred years or more upon it they at length perfected it But by the law of their order only one man was permitted to derive any benefit from it. I obtained their secret—how it does not matter, added to it what I thought it lacked, and here is the result."

As he spoke a visible tremor ran over the form on the bed before us. The excitement was well-nigh unbearable. For the first time in more than thirty days, movement was to be detected, the eyelids flickered, the mouth twitched, and little by little the eyes opened. Nikola immediately stooped over him, and concentrated all his attention upon the pupils. Then, placing his fingertips so close that they almost touched the lashes, he drew them away again in long transverse passes.

"Do you know me?" he asked, in a voice that shook with emotion. Almost instantly the man replied:

"I know you."

"Do you suffer any pain?"

"I do not."

"Sleep then, rest and gain strength, and in two days from this hour wake again a strong man."

Once more he placed his hands before the patient's eyes, and as he drew them away the lids closed. Nikola bent over him and listened, and when he rose he nodded reassuringly to me.

"It is all right," he said. "His respiration is as even and unbroken as that of a sleeping child."

As usual, my watch that night was from eight o'clock until midnight. From the fact that Don Miguel continued to sleep as quietly as at the moment when Nikola had hypnotised him, it was neither as difficult nor as anxious as before. Nor was I altogether discontented with my lot. I was in love, and was loved in my turn; I was engaged in deeply interesting employment, which, should the experiment terminate successfully, would in all probability ensure my being able to start for a second time in my profession, and with an added knowledge that would bring me to the top of the tree at once. The room in which I sat was warm and comfortable; outside, however, a violent storm was raging. The rain and wind beat against the window in the hall with wildest fury. Now, ever since I had watched by the Don's bedside, I had made it my habit to carefully lock the door as soon as Nikola had left the room. On this particular occasion I had not departed from my custom. The hands of the clock on the wall stood at ten minutes past eleven, and I was reflecting that I should not be sorry when my watch was over, and I at liberty to retire to bed, when to my astonishment I saw the handle of the door slowly turn. At first I almost believed that my imagination was playing me a trick; but when the handle revolved and was afterwards turned again, I was satisfied that this was not the case. Who was the person on the other side? It would not be Ah-Win, for the reason that he had been particularly instructed on no account ever to touch the door; Consuelo would not venture into that portion of the castle again on any consideration whatsoever; while Nikola himself, being aware that I always kept it locked, would have knocked before attempting to enter. Whoever it was must have been satisfied that the task was a hopeless one. At any rate he desisted, and I heard no more of him. A few moments later the ventilator required my attention, and I was too busy to bestow any more thought upon the matter. Indeed, it was not until Nikola knocked upon the door and relieved me that it entered my mind again. It became apparent immediately that he attached more importance to the incident than I was inclined to do.

"It's very strange," he said, "but it accounts for one thing which I must confess has puzzled me."

"What is that?" I inquired.

"I will show you," he answered, and led the way to the hall. At the farther end, near the window, he paused and pointed to a mark upon the floor. Not being able to see it very distinctly, I went down upon my hands and knees.

"Do you know what it is?" asked Nikola.

"I do," I answered. "It is the print of a naked foot."

"Yes," said Nikola, "and that foot was wet. It was more than that." Here he took a magnifying glass from his pocket, and also went down upon his hands and knees. "The chimney leading from Ah-Win's room," he said, "is almost exactly above our heads. In consequence, as you may have noticed, the battlements at that point are invariably covered with smuts. The naked foot which made this mark brought some of these particles with it, which tells us that there was only one way in which the owner could have come, and that was down a rope and through the window. Let us examine the window."

We did so, but, so far as I could see, there was nothing there to reward us. The rain was pelting down, and the wind blew as I had never heard it do before.

"The man, whoever he was, was certainly not deficient in pluck," said Nikola. "I shouldn't have called to lower myself over the battlements on a night like this."

"Are you sure that he did so lower himself?" I inquired.

"I am quite sure," Nikola answered. "How else could he have come? The old Don is safe for half an hour at least; get your revolver, I will get mine, and we will go upstairs in search of the intruder."

I did as he directed, but with no great willingness. As you may suppose, I was quite convinced as to the identity of the mysterious visitor; and knowing his proficiency in the art of knife-throwing, I had not the smallest desire to become better acquainted with him. However, I was not going to allow Nikola to think I was afraid; so, putting the best face I could upon it, I did as he directed, and having assured myself that my weapon was loaded in every chamber, followed him along the corridor, up the stone staircase, and so out on to the battlements above. Of all the storms in my experience, I think that particular one was certainly the worst. The rain beat in our faces, and so great was the strength of the wind that the very castle itself seemed to shake and tremble before it. Revolver in hand, expecting every moment to be confronted by the man of whom we were in search, I followed Nikola in the direction of the engine-room chimney. I knew very well for what he was looking. He thought he would find a rope there, but in this he was disappointed. Nor were we able to discover any traces of human beings. We searched the whole length of the battlements in vain, and at last were perforce compelled to give up the hunt as hopeless. Returning to the stairway once more, we were about to descend, when I saw Nikola stoop and pick something up. Whatever it was, he said nothing to me until we had reached the light of the corridor below. Then he held it up for me to see. It was a grey felt hat, the same that I had seen upon the Chinaman's head that morning.

"Mark my words," said Nikola, "we shall have trouble with Quong Ma before very long."

Chapter 8

The Result of the Experiment

When we had returned to the corridor below the battlements, after our search for the man who had lowered himself down to the window of the hall, Nikola brought with him the soft felt hat I had observed upon the head of that villainous Chinaman, Quong Ma, that morning. Though neither of us was altogether surprised at finding that he was the man we suspected of being in the castle, we were none the more pleased at having our suspicions confirmed. The thing which puzzled us most, however, was how he had obtained admission, seeing that he had not been in sight when I had entered the castle that morning, that I had informed Nikola of my meeting with him within five minutes of my arrival, and that the drawbridge had been raised, if not at once, certainly within a quarter of an hour of my making my report. And yet it was plain, since he had been upon the battlements, that he was in the castle, and that his being there boded no good was as apparent as his presence.

"I always knew they had original ideas," said Nikola, "but I had no idea they were as clever as this. We shall have to be very careful what we do for the future; for from what I know of them, they would stick at nothing. Tomorrow morning we must search the castle from dungeon to turret."

"And if we find them?"

"In that case," said Nikola, "I fancy I know a way of dealing with them. Dona Consuelo locks her door at night, I suppose?"

I informed him that I had advised her to do so.

"It would be better that we should make certain," he answered, and, proceeding to the door in question, he softly turned the handle. It was securely fastened from the inside.

"It seems all right," said Nikola. "Now we will return to our own quarters, and make everything secure there."

We did as suggested, and when everything was made fast, securely locked the door in the corridor behind us. Reaching the hall once more, we made a careful survey of the various rooms, including not only the apartments leading out of it, but also the passage leading to Ah-Win's quarters. No sign, however, of the man we wanted was to be seen there. Returning to the hall, we assured ourselves that our patient was still sleeping quietly, and then I bade Nikola good-night, and prepared to go to my room.

"I should advise you to lock your door," he said, as we parted. "You cannot take too many precautions when Quong Ma and his companion are about. Should I require your assistance during the night, I will ring for you."

I promised to answer his call immediately, and was about to turn away, when it occurred to me to ask him a question to which he had promised me an answer upwards of a month before.

"On the night that we left Newcastle," I said, "you were kind enough to say that when a fitting opportunity occurred you would tell me what has induced these men to follow you as they are doing."

"There is no reason why you should not hear," Nikola replied. "To tell it in full, however, would be too long a story, but I will briefly summarise it for you. In order to obtain the information necessary for carrying out the experiment upon which we are now engaged, I penetrated, as I think I have already informed you, into a certain monastery situated in the least known portion of Tibet. My companion and I carried our lives in our hands if ever men have done so in the history of the world. The better to carry out my scheme, I might explain, I impersonated a high official who had lately been elected one of the rulers of the order. At a most unfortunate moment the fraud was discovered, and my companion and I were ordered to be hurled from the roof of the monastery into the precipice below. We managed to escape, however, but not before I had secured the precious secret for which I had risked so much. The monks traced us on our journey back to civilisation, and two of the order, who have had special experience in this sort of work, were detailed to follow us, in the hope that they might not only regain possession of a book which contained the secret, but at the same time revenge the insult which had been offered to them."

"And you still have that book?"

"Would you care to see it?" asked Nikola.

I replied that I should like to immensely, whereupon he retired to his own apartment, to presently return bringing with him a small packet, which he placed upon the table. Untying the string which bound it, and removing a sheet of thin leather, he exposed to my gaze a small book, possibly eight inches long by four wide. The materials in which it was bound were almost dropping apart with age; the backs and corners, however, were clamped with rusty iron. The interior was filled with writing in the Sanskrit character, a great deal of which had faded and was barely decipherable. I took it tenderly in my hands.

"And it is to regain possession of this book that these men are following you?" I asked.

"To do that," he answered, "and to punish me for the trick I played them. They have not, however, accomplished their task yet; nor shall they do so if I can help it. Let me once get hold of Quong Ma, and he'll do no more mischief for some time to come."

As Nikola said this, his great cat, which for the past few moments had been sitting upon his knees, suddenly stood up, and, placing its forepaws upon the table, scratched at the cloth. Nikola was watching my face, and what he saw there must have considerably amused him.

"You are thinking that Apollyon and I are not unlike. When we get out our claws, we are dangerous. It would be well for our Chinese friend if he understood as much. Now you had better be off to bed, and I to my watch."

When Nikola relieved me at eight o'clock the morning following, it was plain that there was something important toward.

"Get your breakfast as soon as you can," he said, "and when you have done we will search the castle. You heard nothing suspicious during your watch, I suppose?"

"Nothing," I replied. "Everything has gone on just as usual."

As soon as I had finished my breakfast, Ah-Win was summoned, and together we set off on our errand. Beginning with the battlements, we took the castle corridor by corridor, floor by floor, examining every corner and staircase in which it would be possible for a human being to hide himself. Having exhausted the inhabited portion of the building, we searched the rooms into which no one had penetrated from year's end to year's end. These we also drew blank. Then descending another flight of stairs, we reached the basement, explored the great kitchens, once so busy, and now tenanted only by rats and beetles, and examined the various domestic offices, including the buttery and armoury, still without success. If Quong Ma was in the castle, it looked as if he must certainly possess the power of rendering himself invisible at will. At last we reached the keep, where the old couple who, as Nikola had said, officiated as caretakers during his absence, had their quarters. At the moment of our arrival the woman was bitterly upbraiding her husband for some misdeed.

"I tell 'ee," she was saying, slapping the table with her hand to emphasise her words, "that when I went to bed last night they vittals was in yonder cupboard. What I want 'ee to say is where they be now? Don't 'ee say 'ee never saw them, or that it was the cat as stole 'em, for 'ee may talk till 'ee be black in the face and I'll not believe 'ee. Cats don't turn handles and undo latches, and mutton don't walk out of the front door on its own leg. If 'ee be a man, 'ee'll tell the truth an' shame the devil."

I must leave you to picture for yourself the vehemence with which all this was said. The words poured from her mouth in a torrent, and every sentence was punctuated with slaps upon the table. So engaged were they in their quarrel that some moments elapsed before they perceived Nikola and myself standing in the doorway. When they did, the tumult ceased as if by magic.

"You seem to be enjoying yourselves," said Nikola drily; "perhaps you will be kind enough to tell me what it is all about."

He had no sooner finished than the irate old lady recommenced.

"It's just this way, my lord," she said, though why she should have bestowed a title upon Nikola I could not understand. "Last night I was troubled with the rheumatism mortal bad, and went to bed early. My old man there, beggin' your pardon for the liberty I'm takin', was a-sittin' by the fire smokin' his pipe, such bein' his custom of an evening. He had had his supper, and as I se'd with my own eyes when he'd a finished there was the end of a leg of mutton in yon cupboard. When I comes this mornin' to take it out for breakfast, it's gone, and with it the bread as I baked with my own hands but yesterday. And he stands there, savin' your presence, my lord, and wants I for to believe as how he's not touched it, and the latch of the cupboard down, as you can see for yourselves, honourable gentlemen both, with your own eyes. I've been married these three-and-forty years, and I don't know as how you will believe it, my lord—"

Seeing that she was getting up steam once more, Nikola held up his hand to her to be silent.

"What you tell me is very interesting," he said, fixing his dark eyes upon her; "but let me understand you properly. You say you went to bed leaving your husband smoking his pipe in this room. Before retiring you convinced yourself that the food which is now not forthcoming was in the cupboard. Is that so?"

"Yes, my lord, and honourable gentlemen both."

Then, addressing her husband, Nikola continued:

"I suppose you went to sleep over your pipe?" The question had to be repeated, and his wife had to admonish him with, "Speak up to his lordship like a man," before he could answer. Even then his reply was scarcely satisfactory; he thought he might have fallen asleep, but he was not at all sure upon the point. He admitted he was in the habit of doing so; and, as far as Nikola was concerned, this settled the matter.

"Quong Ma," he said, turning to me. "Now I understand where he gets his food from." Then, turning to the woman, he said, "Your husband is a heavy sleeper, I suppose?"

"Why, bless you, sir," she replied, "he sleeps that heavy you can't wake him. And, as for snoring, why, the rattling of that old bridge out yonder, when they're a-drawin' of it up, ain't to be compared with him, as the sayin' is. I did hear of a man, when I lived down Sunderland, as did snore so that, when he woke up, the folks next door sent in to ask him to go on again, the stillness bein' that lonesome that they couldn't bear it."

Nikola peremptorily bade the old woman be silent, and ordered her for the future to see that her door was locked at dusk every evening. Then, addressing her husband, he inquired if the latter was conversant with the subterranean passages of the castle, and when he had replied in the affirmative, bade him light a lantern, and show us all he could. The man did so, and having conducted us across the courtyard, entered a long, low chamber, which might once have been used as a bakehouse. In this was a large wooden door, secured with many bolts, but now falling into considerable disrepair. These bolts he drew one by one with an air of importance that was indescribably comic.

"I don't quite understand how these bolts come to be fastened if the man is down below," said Nikola, addressing me. I shook my head, whereupon he bade the old man inform him whether there were any other entrances to the vaults in question.

"Lor', sir," the man replied, "the castle be fair mazed with them. If 'ee likes, I can take 'ee into most any room in the place from down below."

"I should have thought of that," said Nikola, more to himself than to me. "I am sorry I didn't question our friend here before. Quong Ma has evidently mastered the situation, and is playing a game of hide-and-seek. However, we'll examine the dungeons first, and the passages afterwards. So lead the way, my friend."

The old man going ahead carrying the lantern, Nikola following, and Ah-Win and myself bringing up the rear, we made our way down the clammy stone staircase into the subterranean portion of the castle.

It was an experience that would have been worth anything to a novelist seeking colour for a historical tale; but knowing what I did about the man we were after, I cannot say that I appreciated the incident so much. In addition to my nervousness, my head was aching, while hot and cold perspirations alternately contributed to my general discomfort. What was the matter with me I could not think. As it was, I was the only member of the party, I believe, who felt any symptoms of fright. The old man with the lantern knew nothing of his danger. Ah-Win was an Asiatic and a fatalist, and in his master's presence appeared not to care whom or what he faced; while, as for Nikola himself, I believe most implicitly that cold-blooded individual would have faced certain death as coolly and contentedly as he would have tossed off a glass of wine. Lower and lower we descended, glancing into dungeons into which no light of day had ever penetrated, and stooping to make our way along passages in which the moisture from the roof fell drip, drip, drip, upon our heads. Search as we would, however, we could discover no trace of that villainous Celestial.

"We be close down alongside the sea now, your lordship," said the old man, "and when I tells 'ee that, I tells 'ee summat as not many folks as has bided in this 'ere castle ever knowed."

"Most admirable of men," said Nikola, "you are telling me exactly what I want to know. Do you mean that it's possible for us to reach the sea from where we are now standing without crossing the drawbridge?"

"That is exactly what I do mean, my lord," he answered. "And if your lordship and the honourable gentleman will come wi' I, I'll let 'ee see for your own selves."

Forthwith the old fellow, holding his lantern aloft, turned down a narrow passage, leading to the right, and a few minutes later brought us up to some steps, at the bottom of which the light of day could be plainly seen. To reach the bottom of the steps was the work of a moment, and once there a curious scene was revealed to us. The doorway opened into the chasm which I have described earlier, and was situated almost directly beneath the drawbridge and the keep. Kneeling down, Nikola and I looked over the edge and could plainly see a number of iron steps let into the rock one above the other. At the bottom—for it was now full tide—the sea washed and dashed with terrific force. Rising to his feet again, Nikola addressed the old man.

"Is it possible at low tide," he said, "to reach the sands from here?"

"Lor' bless you, yes, sir," the man replied. "When the tide is down, 'ee can get along from rock to rock without as much as wetting shoe leather."

"That accounts for everything," said Nikola with considerable satisfaction. "I understand exactly how Quong Ma got into the castle now; he must have laughed to himself when he saw that we had raised the drawbridge in the hope of keeping him out. However, forewarned is forearmed, and this place shall be bricked up this morning. You, my old friend, had better see to it, and be sure that you make a good job of it'"

The man promised to do so, and seeing that there was nothing further to be gained by remaining where we were, Nikola bade him conduct us back again to our own portion of the building by a secret passage if possible. The man assured us that he could do so, and was as good as his word. We climbed, crawled, and scrambled our way up the narrow steps and along a rabbit warren of a small passage behind our guide. At last he stopped.

"Would your lordship be kind enough to say where 'ee think 'ee are now?" he added.

"I have not the least notion," said Nikola.

"Nor I," I added.

"Well, sir, I will show 'ee," said the man, and after a little hunting he found and pressed something in the wall. There was a grating noise, a sound as of rusty hinges being slowly unfolded and then a portion of the wall swung outward and we found ourselves standing at the top of the great staircase within a few yards of Consuelo's apartments.

"This is uncanny, to say the least of it," remarked Nikola. "Pray do any of these interesting passages open into the young lady's room opposite, or into the smaller hall occupied by this gentleman and myself?"

"Not now, my lord," the man replied. "Time was when they did, but the old lord didn't take kindly to 'em, and they was bricked up as much as five year ago."

"I am glad to hear it," said Nikola; and you may imagine that I echoed the sentiment. Nikola thereupon thanked the old man and dismissed him, at the same time reiterating his order that the opening in the chasm below the drawbridge should be made secure.

The excitement of the search for Quong Ma and the damp of the passages had been too much for me, and by the time we reached the hall I could scarcely stand.

"Good heavens, Ingleby," said Nikola, as I dropped into a chair, "you're looking awfully ill. What is the matter?"

"I can't exactly say," I answered. "I fear I must have caught a chill on the battlements last night."

"And yet you accompanied me down to those damp passages this morning. Was that wise?"

"I was not going to let you go alone," I replied.

He glanced sharply at me, as if he would read my thoughts.

"Well, well, I'll tell you what you must do: you must be off to bed at once. There can be no doubt about that."

I tried to protest: I explained my desire to see the end of the experiment; but Nikola was adamant. To bed I must go, willy-nilly; and to bed I accordingly went, but not in my own room off the hall. An apartment farther down the corridor, next door to that occupied by Consuelo, was arranged for me; and when I was safely between the blankets, Nikola prescribed for me, and my sweetheart was duly installed as nurse. My indisposition must have been more severe than I had supposed, for before nightfall I was in a high state of fever, and by midnight was delirious.

I remember nothing further until I opened my eyes and found Consuelo sitting by my side.

"What does this mean?" I inquired, surprised to find her there.

"It means that you have been very ill," she answered, "and that I am your nurse, and am not going to permit you to talk very much."

To do this was a feat of which I was incapable, but I was not going to be silent until I had learnt something of what had happened.

"How long have I been ill?" I inquired.

"More than a week," she answered; and then added, "You naughty boy, you little know what a fright you have given me. But you must not talk any more, or Dr. Nikola will be angry."

She poured out some medicine for me, bade me drink it, and then reseated herself beside me. In five minutes I was wrapped in a heavy slumber, from which I did not wake for several hours. When I did, I found Dr. Nikola installed as nurse; Consuelo had disappeared.

"Well, Ingleby," said Nikola cheerily, as he felt my pulse, "you have had a sharp bout of it, but I am glad to see we have managed to pull you through. How do you feel in yourself?"

"Much better," I answered, "though still a bit shaky."

"I don't wonder at it," he said. "Do you feel hungry?"

"I feel as if I could eat anything," I answered.

"Well, that's a good sign. I'll see that something is sent you. In the meanwhile keep as quiet as possible. When I leave you, I'll send your sweetheart to you; she has been a devoted nurse, and between ourselves I rather fancy you owe your life to her."

"God bless her!" I answered fervently. "But you call her my sweetheart. What do you mean by that?"

"My dear fellow, I know everything. One night the young lady in

288

question was rather concerned about you, and in her agitation she allowed the cat to slip out of the bag. You young people seem to have managed the matter pretty well in the short time you have known each other. Now keep quiet for a few moments while I see if I can find her."

He was making for the door, when I stopped him.

"You have not told me how the Don is," I said. "How does the experiment progress?"

His face clouded over.

"It has proved successful," he answered, but with a sudden sternness that surprised me. It was for all the world as if he were trying to convince me that what he said was correct, although in his own heart he knew it was not so. When he spoke again, it was very slowly.

"Yes, Ingleby," he said, as if he were weighing every word before he uttered it, "the experiment has proved a success. I have made the Don a young man, but—well, to tell the truth, I have made a mistake in my calculations—a mistake that I cannot explain and that I can in no way account for."

"And the result?"

"Don't ask me," he said, "for I am afraid I do not know myself. By the time you are on your feet again, I shall hope to have come nearer an understanding of the situation. Then I shall be able to tell you more of what I hope and fear. At present I scarcely like to think of it myself."

To my surprise, as I watched him, I saw great beads of perspiration start out upon his forehead, and, for the first time since I had known him, I saw a look of terror in Dr. Nikola's face. I tried to question him further upon the subject, but he bade me wait until I was stronger, and, presently repeating that he would find Consuelo, he left me. When my sweetheart entered the room, looking more beautiful than I had ever seen her, I forgot, for the time being, about Nikola.

"You are looking much better," she said, as she came toward me and put down upon the table the tray she carried in her hand. "Here is some beef-tea which I have made for you myself. If you don't drink it all up, I shall let the old woman in the kitchen make it for you in the future and bring it to you herself."

"You had better not," I answered. "In that case, I should refuse to touch a drop of it, and should die of slow starvation in consequence."

With a gentleness that was infinitely becoming to her, she lifted my head and held the cup while I drank. If I took longer over it than I should have done at any other time, the fact must, of course, be attributed to my weakness.

"Dr. Nikola says he is very pleased with the progress you have made," she said, when she had replaced the cup upon the table. "But you are to be kept very quiet for some days, and to sleep as much as possible."

"And when am I to get up?" I asked.

"Get up!" she cried in mock horror. "You must not even think of such a thing for a week at least."

"A week!" I replied. "Do you think I've to stay here for a week?"

"So Dr. Nikola says."

The remainder of our conversation is too sacred to be set down in cold-drawn type. Let it suffice that, when I fell asleep again, it was with her hand in mine. I was more in love even than I had been before.

As Consuelo had predicted, more than a week had elapsed before I was permitted to leave my room. Even then I was not allowed to return to my duties at once, but spent the greater portion of my time with Consuelo on the battlements gaining strength with every breath of sea air that I inhaled.

Nikola I saw but little of. He examined me every morning, and on one or two occasions honoured us with his company for a brief period on the castle roof. At the best of times, however, he was not a good companion. He was invariably absorbed in his own thoughts, spoke but little, and struck me as being anxious to say goodbye almost as soon as he arrived. Since then I have learned the true reason of it all, and I have been able to see that complex character in a new light. It never struck me how lonely the man's life must be. During the whole time that I was associated with him I never once heard him speak of kith or kin. Friends he appeared to have none, while his acquaintances numbered only such men as were necessary to the particular work he happened to be engaged in at the moment of their meeting. His very attainments, his peculiar knowledge of the world, of its under and mystic side, were sufficient to make him hold aloof from his fellow-men. In all matters of comfort a rigid ascetic, the good things of life had no temptation for him. To sum it all up, of this I feel certain, so certain indeed that at times it becomes almost a pain, that Nikola, with all his sternness, his self-denial, his genius and his failings, hungered for one thing, and that was to be loved. Why should I say this, considering that the only evidence I have to offer tends to lead one's thoughts in a contrary direction? I do not know, but as I remarked just now, I feel convinced that my hypothesis is a correct one, as I am that I love Consuelo. But to return to my story. It was not until nearly a fortnight had elapsed, since my return to consciousness, that I was permitted to take up my duties again. When

I did, I returned to my old quarters leading out of the hall, and I think Nikola was pleased to once more have my co-operation,—at any rate, he led me to suppose that he was.

"When you think you are up to the mark, I shall be pleased to show you the Don," he said, "and to hear your opinion of him."

I expressed myself as being quite equal to seeing him at once.

"Very good," he answered, "but I warn you to be prepared for a great and somewhat unpleasant change in the man."

So saying, he led me across the hall towards the room in which I had, before my illness, spent so many hours. Inserting the key in the lock, he turned it and we entered. I had expected to find it exactly as I had last seen it. A surprise, however, was in store for me. The bedplace in the centre was gone, as were both the electrical appliances. The clock and thermometers had been removed, the only things that still remained being the electric lights which were suspended from the ceiling and the enclosed fixtures for regulating the supply of hot and cold air. In point of fact, it was as bare a room as well could be imagined.

"Don Miguel," said Nikola, "I have brought an old friend to see you."

I looked about the room, but for a moment could see nothing of the old man in question. Then my eye lighted on what looked like a heap of clothes huddled up on a mattress in the corner. On hearing Nikola's voice, a face looked up at me—a face so terrible, so demoniacal I might say, that I involuntarily shrank from it. What there was about it that caused me such revulsion, I cannot say. It was the countenance of a young man, if you can imagine a man endowed with perpetual youth, and with that youth the cunning, the cruelty, and the vice of countless centuries.

"Steady, my friend," I heard Nikola say, and as he did so he placed his hand upon my arm. "Remember, Ingleby, this is nothing more than an experiment."

Then addressing the crouching figure, he bade him stand up. With a snarl like that of a dog, or rather of a wild beast, who is compelled to do a thing very much against his will, the man obeyed. I was able then to take better stock of him. Accustomed as I was to the old Don's face, I found it difficult to realise that the healthy, vigorous man standing before me was he, and yet I had only to look at him carefully to have all doubt upon the subject removed. He was the same and yet not the same. At any rate, he was an illustration of the marvellous, nay, the almost unbelievable, success of Nikola's experiment.

"You remember the Don as he was, and you can see to what I have

291

been able to bring him," said Nikola sadly, and for one moment without a trace of triumph. This, however, was soon forthcoming.

"Out of an old man tottering on the brink of the grave, I have manufactured a young and vigorous creature such as you now see before you. I have made him, I have transformed him, I have subjected Nature to science, I have revolutionised the world, abolished death, and upset the teachings, and the essential idea, of all religions. I have proved that old age can be prevented, and the grave defied. And—and—I have failed."

Under the intensity of his emotion his voice broke, and something very like a sob burst from him. Never since I had known Nikola had I seen him as he was then. To all appearances he was well-nigh broken-hearted.

"If you have done all this," I asked, "how can you say that you have failed?"

"Are you so blind that you cannot see?" he answered. "Examine the man for yourself, and you will find that he is a human being in animal life only. I have given him back his youth, his strength, his enjoyment in living, but I cannot give him back his mind. In his body I have triumphed; in his brain I have completely failed."

"But cannot this be set right?" I inquired. "Is the case quite hopeless?"

"Nothing is hopeless," he answered; "but it will take years, centuries perhaps, of work to find the secret. I thought, when I built up the body, I should be building up the brain as well. It was not so. In proportion as his body renewed its youth, his brain shrunk. Let me give you an illustration."

He went forward towards the man, who was now once more crouching upon the floor, watching us over his right shoulder, as if he were afraid we were going to do him harm.

"Well, Miguel," said Nikola, patting him upon the head, and speaking to him in the same tone he would have used to a favourite monkey, "how is it with you today?"

The man, however, took no notice, but bending down played with the lace of Nikola's shoe, now and again looking swiftly up into his face, as if he dreaded a blow, and as swiftly looking away again.

"This should prove to you what I mean," said Nikola, addressing me. "In his present condition he is less than a man, and yet where would you find a finer frame? His heart, his lungs, his constitution, all are perfect."

While he had been speaking, he had turned his back upon the

beast upon the floor, and as he uttered the last words he moved towards me. He had not taken a step, however, before the Don was half on his feet. From childish idiocy his expression had changed until it was a fiendish malignity that surpasses all description in words.

In another moment he would have thrown himself on Nikola. As it was, he glared at him until he turned, when in an instant the wild expression had gone, and he was crouching upon the floor once more, picking at his fingers and smiling to himself.

"You can see for yourself what he is," said Nikola: "an imbecile; but for one ray of hope I should despair of him."

"There is, then, a ray of hope," I said eagerly, clutching like a drowning man at the straw he held out. "Thank God for that!"

"There is a ray," he answered, "but it is a very little one. I will give you an example."

Turning to the wretched creature on the floor, he extended his hand towards him, and, gradually lifting it, bade him rise. The effect was instantaneous. The man rose little by little until he stood upright Once more pointing his hand directly at him, Nikola moved towards him, until the points of his fingers were scarcely an inch from the other's eyes. Then, slowly raising his fingers, he made an upward and a downward pass.

The eyes closed, and yet the man still remained rigid against the wall. Turning to me, Nikola said:

"You can see for yourself that he is absolutely under my influence and control."

I approached and made a careful examination. There could be no doubt about his condition: it was one of hypnotic coma; and, on raising one of the eyelids, I found the ball turned upwards and wandering in its orbit.

"You are satisfied?" inquired Nikola.

"Perfectly," I answered.

"In that case let us proceed."

"To whom am I speaking?" asked Nikola, addressing the man before him.

"To Miguel de Moreno," was the answer, given in a perfectly clear and strong voice, and without apparent hesitation. "Do you know where you are?"

"I am with Dr. Nikola."

"Before you came to me, with whom and where did you live?"

"I lived with my great-granddaughter in Cadiz." "Have you any recollection of coming to England?"

293

"I remember it perfectly." "Now lie down upon that mattress, and sleep without waking until eight o'clock tomorrow morning."

The man did as he was ordered without hesitation. Nikola covered him with the blankets, and as soon as we had made sure of his safety, we left the room, carefully locking the door after us.

"You can have no idea, Ingleby, what a disappointment this has been to me. Three times before I have tried and failed, but this time I made sure I had success within my grasp. I have progressed farther now than I have ever done before, it is true; but it is the brain that has beaten me. As long as I live I will persevere, and the perfect man, who shall retain his youth through all ages, shall eventually walk the earth. Now good-night."

He held out his hand to me, and as I shook it Apollyon came up, and rubbed himself against my leg, as if to show that he too appreciated my sympathy. I was about to retire to my room, when it struck me that I had heard nothing of our friend Quong Ma since we had searched the subterranean portion of the castle for him. I asked Nikola if he had anything to tell me concerning him.

"Nothing," he answered, "save that last night I felt certain that I saw a man cross the courtyard. It was just before midnight, the moon was about the building, and I am ready to stake anything that I am not deceived."

"But who could it have been?"

"That's exactly what I want to know," he answered. "You were safe in bed and asleep. It was not the caretaker, for I tried his door and found it locked, and from the sound that greeted me I had good proof it was not he."

"But might it not have been Ah-Win?" I asked.

"I thought so, and before going in search of the figure I hastened to his room, only to find him also asleep."

"In that case it must have been Quong Ma. But how does the fellow live? and why does he not strike?"

"Because he has not yet found his opportunity. When he does, you may be sure he will avail himself of it. Now once more good-night You need not trouble about our patient; I shall take a look at him about midnight."

"Good-night," I said, and went to my room, the door of which I carefully locked. My last waking thoughts were of Consuelo, and my speculations as to what her feelings would be when she realised the terrible change that had taken place in her great-grandfather were sufficient to give me a nightmare. Over and over again I was afflicted with the most horrible dreams; and when I was roused by a loud thumping on my door, and Nikola's voice calling for admittance, it seemed so much part and parcel of the horror my brain had just pictured for me, that for the moment I took no notice of it. It sounded again; so, springing from my bed, I ran to the door, and opened it.

"What is the matter?" I asked, when he was standing before me. His usual pale face was now ghastly in its whiteness.

"Good heavens, man!" he cried, "you have no notion of what has happened. Dress yourself immediately and come with me!" He sat upon my bed while I huddled my clothes on; then, when I was ready, he seized me by the wrist, and half-dragged me, half-led me into the hall. Once there, he pointed to the figure of a man stretched out before his door. It was Ah-Win; and his throat was cut from ear to ear!

The sight was so sudden, and so totally unexpected, that it was almost too much for me. Recovering my presence of mind, however, I knelt down and examined him.

"Look at his hands!" said Nikola. "They are cut to the bone by some sharp-bladed instrument. The murderer must have come here in search of me. Ah-Win must have met him, tried to prevent him reaching the door, was unable to warn us, and so have met his fate."

We were both too much overcome to continue the discussion. Quong Ma had struck at last!

CHAPTER 9

War and Peace

At the conclusion of the preceding chapter, I described to you the terrible discovery we had made of the death of Ah-Win. That he had met his fate in an endeavour to prevent Quong Ma from reaching his master's room seemed quite in accordance with the evidence before us. Small wonder was it, therefore, that Nikola was affected. But even in his grief he proved himself unlike the average man. Another man would have bewailed his loss, or at least have expressed some sorrow at his servant's unhappy lot. Nikola, however, did neither, and yet his grief was plain to the eye as if he had wept copious tears. Having satisfied himself that the poor fellow really was dead, he bade me help him carry the body down the passage to an empty room which adjoined his former quarters.

We laid it upon a bed there, and Nikola followed me into the passage, carefully locking the door behind him. When we were back in the hall once more, Nikola spoke.

"This has gone far enough," he said. "Come what may, we must find Quong Ma. The fellow must be in the castle at this minute."

"Shall we organise a search for him?" I said. "The man must be captured at any hazard; we are risking valuable lives by allowing him to remain at large."

Though I used the plural, I must confess I was thinking more of my darling than of anybody else. How did I know that, when Quong Ma found it impossible for him to get hold of Nikola, he would not revenge himself upon Consuelo?

"That we must find him goes without saying," Nikola replied. "I doubt very much, however, if it would be prudent for you to take part in the search. In the first place, you are still as weak as a baby; and in the second, the damp of the subterranean passages might very easily bring on a return of the fever."

"You surely do not imagine that I should permit you to go alone," I said.

Nikola gave a short laugh.

"I do not want to appear boastful," he said, "but I am very much afraid you do not know me yet, my dear Ingleby. However, I will confess that if you really do desire it, and feel equal to the exertion, I shall be very glad of your company."

"When do you propose to start?"

"At once," he answered. "I shall not know a minute's peace until I have revenged Ah-Win."

"And supposing we catch the fellow, what do you propose to do with him? It is a long way from here to the nearest police station."

"I don't fancy somehow I shall trouble the police," he said. "But we will talk of what we will do with him when we have got him. Now, if you are ready, come along."

Thereupon, for the second time we searched the castle for Quong Ma. As before, we first visited the battlements and the rooms on the next floor, the basement offices followed, and still being unsuccessful, we unbolted the door leading to the dungeons and entered the subterranean portion of the building. Cool as I endeavoured to appear, I am prepared to confess that, when the icy wind came up to greet us from those dark and dreary passages, I was far from feeling comfortable. I don't set up to be a braver man than my fellows, but it seemed to me to require more pluck to enter those dismal regions than to take part in a forlorn hope. With our revolvers in our hands, and Nikola holding the lantern above his head, we explored passage after passage and dungeon after dungeon. Rats scuttled away from beneath our feet, bats flew in the darkness above our heads; but, as before, not a sign of Quong Ma.

"I cannot understand it," said Nikola at last, and his voice echoed along the rocky passages. "We have explored every room in the castle and every dungeon underneath it, and not a trace of the man can we discover. We have bricked up the opening into the chasm, and lifted the drawbridge that connects us with the outside world, and yet we cannot catch him. He must be here somewhere."

"Exactly; but where?"

"If I knew, do you think I should be standing here?" Nikola replied sharply. "But let us try back again. I want to explore that secret passage the old man showed us the other day. I remember now that there was something that struck me as being rather peculiar about it."

We accordingly retraced our steps, found the passage in question, and ascended it. Reaching the point where, on the previous occasion, we had turned off to find the trap-door, opening at the head on the great staircase, we found, as Nikola had supposed, a second and smaller turning half hidden in shadow and which bore away to the right, that is to say in the direction of the keep. Fortunately, it was now level going, but so narrow was the passage that it was still impossible to walk two abreast.

"Hark! what was that?" Nikola suddenly cried, stopping and holding the lantern above his head.

We stopped and listened, and sure enough a shuffling noise came from the passage in front. A moment later the same sound we had heard when the old caretaker had opened the secret door reached us.

"If I am not mistaken, we have found his lair at last," my companion shouted and ran forward.

But certain as we felt that it was Quong Ma we had heard, we were too late to convince ourselves of the fact. The secret door stood open; the man, however, was not to be seen in the passage outside.

"Where are we?" I asked, for I was not familiar with the corridor in which we found ourselves.

"Between the keep and Ah-Win's quarters," Nikola replied. "Now I understand how that fiend has found his way into the hall. But let me think for a moment: there is the gate between us and the hall, and I have the key in my pocket. There is no other exit in either direction, so it seems to me that we have got our man at last. Is your revolver ready?"

"Quite ready," I replied.

"Come along, then. But remember this: if he attacks you, show him no mercy. He'll show you none. Remember Ah-Win."

With that we made our way along the corridor in the direction of the room where Nikola's—well, where the murdered man had been quartered.

Nikola unlocked the door and looked in, while I remained in the passage outside. I really believe I was more afraid of what I should see in there than of Quong Ma himself.

"He is not there," said Nikola when he rejoined me, and then went to the gate and tested it. "And he can't get out here. We've missed him somewhere, and must look back again."

We accordingly retraced our steps, examining room by room and preparing ourselves every time lest, when we turned the handle, Quong Ma should jump out upon us. But in every case we were disappointed.

"I was surprised just now," said Nikola, after we had left the last apartment and stood in the corridor once more, "but I am doubly so now. What on earth can have become of the fellow? He seems to vanish into thin air every time we get near him. There must be another secret passage hereabout of which we are ignorant. Before we return, however, I want to make quite certain of one thing; let us continue that passage by which we ascended from the dungeons just now."

We did so, Nikola once more going ahead with the lantern.

"Just as I thought," he cried. "Look here!"

He stopped, and stood with his back to the wall. At this point the passage came to an abrupt termination, and on the floor before us was an old blanket, a quantity of straw, about a loaf and a half of bread, and an earthenware pipkin containing a quart or so of water. Under the blanket was a half-used packet of candles, and from the grease that bespattered everything it was easily seen how he had obtained his illumination.

"We have found our bird's nest at last," said Nikola, "but I am afraid we have driven him away from it for good and all. But we will have him yet, or my name's not Nikola. Now let us go back to the hall; we can do no good by staying here."

We returned, but not before we had taken possession of the things we had found, and had carefully marked the position of the secret door, in case we should want to use it again.

"After breakfast we will have another try," said Nikola. "In the meantime we had better take a little rest. You look as if you stood in need of it."

It would have been better for me had I abandoned any thought of such a thing, for with Ah-Win lying dead only a few yards away and Quong Ma still at large, the drowsy god was difficult, if not impossible, to woo. Every danger that it would be possible for a man to imagine, I pictured for Consuelo; and when at last I did fall asleep, the dreams that harassed me were of the most horrible description. Right glad was I when morning broke and it became necessary to attend to the duties of the day.

"If I were you, I should say nothing to your sweetheart either of her great-grandfather's condition or of the tragedy of last night," said Nikola. I agreed with him, although I knew that it could not be very long before the former would become known to Consuelo.

"But surely she will hear about Ah-Win before very long?" I said. "Will it not be necessary for you to communicate with the county police, and for an inquest to be held?"

"Ingleby," replied Nikola, "ask me no questions I have no desire to draw you into the matter. It is sufficient for you to know that Ah-Win is dead,"—he paused for a minute, and then added, significantly—"and buried!"

Try how I would, I could not contain my surprise. How, when, and by whom had the poor Chinaman been buried? Had Nikola carried it out himself? It seemed impossible, and yet, knowing as I did the indomitable energy and working powers of the man, I felt it might very well be true. I would have questioned him further, but I could see that he was not in the humour to permit it. For this reason I held my peace, though I knew full well at the time that by so doing I was giving my consent to what was undoubtedly an illegal act.

From what I have said, I fancy it will be readily agreed that the past two or three days had been as full of incident as the greatest craver after excitement could desire. I had recovered from a serious illness, had witnessed the result of one of the most extraordinary experiments the world had seen, Ah-Win had been murdered, we had discovered Quong Ma's hiding-place in the castle, and had had a most exciting chase after him. Now Ah-Win had been buried secretly by Nikola, and if what had been done was discovered by the authorities, there is no saying in what sort of trouble we might not find ourselves. As soon as we had seen the Don, who was still wrapped in the same hypnotic slumber, and had breakfasted, we organised another search, only to meet with the same result. Later, I spent an hour with Consuelo upon the battlements. I was careful, however, to tell her nothing of the death of Ah-Win, nor of the reappearance of the detestable Chinaman in the castle. It would have served no good purpose, and would only have frightened her needlessly. When she reiterated her desire to see her great-grandfather, I found myself, if possible, at a still greater disadvantage. On returning to Nikola in the hall, I placed the matter before him. To my surprise, he did not receive it in the same spirit as I had expected he would do. I had anticipated a direct refusal, but he gave me nothing of the kind.

"Why should she not see him?" he said. "Provided she give me proper notice, I fancy I can arrange that he shall behave in every way as she would wish him to do."

"When, then, may the interview take place?"

"Let us say at midday. Will that suit you? But before we arrange anything definitely, let us examine him ourselves, and see how he is likely to conduct himself."

We accordingly made our way to the patient's room. I had noticed by the hall clock that it wanted only three minutes of the hour at which

Nikola had ordered the Don to wake. On approaching his bedplace, we found him still sleeping peacefully, in exactly the same position as when we had seen him last. With his eyes closed and one strong arm thrown out upon the floor, he looked a magnificent specimen of a man. If only Dr. Nikola could perfect the brain, here was a being seemingly capable of anything. But would he be able to do so? That was the question. Watch in hand, Nikola knelt down beside the bed, and for some time not a sound broke the stillness of the room. Punctually, however, as the long hand of the clock pointed to the hour, the Don gave a long sigh. I jumped to the conclusion that he was about to wake in obedience to Nikola's command; but, to our surprise, he did not do so.

"Strange," I heard Nikola mutter to himself, and, stooping over the patient, he lifted the eyelids and carefully examined the pupils.

Five minutes went by, and still he did not wake.

"Don Miguel," said Nikola at last, "I command you to wake. You cannot disobey me,"

A slight movement was visible, but still the sleeper did not comply with the order given him. It was not until a quarter of an hour had elapsed that consciousness returned to him. With the opening of his eyes the animal look which I had noticed on the previous day came back to him. Instead of rising to his feet as he was ordered, he crouched and cowered in the corner, pulling at his bedclothes, and watching us the while, as if he would do us a mischief on the slightest provocation. Dangerous as the man had appeared the day before, it struck me that he was even more so today.

* * * * * * * *

"It is very plain that we shall have to keep an eye on you, my friend," said Nikola. "I am not quite certain that you are going to be docile much longer. Let me feel your pulse."

He stooped, and was about to take hold of the other's wrist, when the man sprang forward, and, seizing the Doctor with both hands, laid hold of his arm with his teeth, just below the elbow. Fortunately, Nikola was wearing a thick velvet coat, otherwise the injury might have been a severe one. Seeing what had happened, I threw myself upon the man, and, tearing him off, forced him down upon his bed. He struggled in my grasp, snapping at me and foaming at the mouth like a mad dog; but I had him too secure, and did not let go my hold until Nikola had fixed his arms behind him.

"Good heavens, Nikola!" I cried, scarcely able to contain my emotion, "this is too terrible! What on earth are we to do with him?"

"I do not quite see what we can do," Nikola replied, wiping the perspiration from his forehead as he spoke. "However, I must try my hand on him once more. If you can manage to keep him still, and I can get him under my influence, we ought to be able to keep him quiet while we have time to think."

I did as requested, while Nikola made slow mesmeric passes before the man's eyes. It was fully ten minutes, however, before he succeeded; but as soon as he did, the patient's heartrending struggles ceased, and he lay down upon his bed, sleeping quietly.

"I began to be afraid I was losing my influence over him," said Nikola, as he rose to his feet.

"One thing is quite certain," I answered, "and that is, Consuelo must not see him while he is in this state. It would frighten her to death."

"And she would never forgive me," said Nikola; and I thought I detected a note of sadness in his voice. "Are you going to leave him as he is?" I inquired.

"For the present," Nikola answered. "I must make up something that will have a soothing effect upon him. You need have no fear; he will be quite safe where he is."

The words were scarcely out of his mouth before a movement on the bed caused us both to look round. Little as we had anticipated such a thing, Nikola's influence was slowly but surely working off, and the man was returning to his old state again. Even now, I never like to think of what happened during the next ten minutes.

Before we could reach him, the Don was on his feet and had rushed upon me, Nikola ran to my assistance, and, strong men as we both were, I assure you that at first we could not cope with him. The struggle was a terrific one. He fought like the madman he certainly was, and with an animal ferocity that rendered him doubly difficult to deal with. When, at last, we did manage to force him back on to his bed and make him secure, we were both completely exhausted; we could only lean against the wall and pant: conversation was out of the question.

"This will never do," said Nikola, when he had sufficiently recovered to speak; "if this sort of thing goes on, he will murder some one."

"But how are you going to prevent it?" I asked. "It is plain that your influence has lost its effect."

"There is nothing for it but to administer an opiate," he answered. "Do you think you can manage to hold him while I procure one?"

I fancied I could; at any rate, I expressed myself as very willing to try. Nikola immediately hurried away. He informed me afterwards that he was not gone more than a minute, but had I been asked I should have put the time down as at least a quarter of an hour. To describe to you my feelings during that wait would be impossible; the loathing, the horror, and the abject personal fear of the man writhing below me seemed to fill my whole being.

"I don't think we shall have very much more trouble with him for an hour or two to come," said Nikola, when the drug had taken effect, and we were on our feet once more.

"But we cannot go on administering drugs for ever," I answered; "what do you propose to do later on?"

"That is what we've got to find out," he replied. "In the meantime we must keep him up like this, and take it in turns to watch him. You had better go out now and get a breath of fresh air. If you see your sweetheart, pacify her with the best excuse you can think of."

"Are you quite sure you are safe with him alone?" I asked.

"I must risk it," he replied. But as I moved towards the door, he stopped me.

"Ingleby," he said, speaking slowly and sadly, "I don't know whether you will believe me or not when I say how deeply I regret what has happened in this case. I would have given anything, my own life even, that things should not have fallen out in this way. And what is more, I do not say this for my own sake."

"You are thinking of Consuelo," I said.

"I am," he answered. "It is for her sake I feel the regret. As a rule, I am not given to sentiment, but somehow this seems altogether different. But there, go away and tell her what you think best."

I left him and went in search of Consuelo. She was in her usual place in the tower above her room. And when she saw me she ran to greet me with outstretched hands. Something—it might have been my pale face—frightened her.

"My darling," I said, "you are not ill, are you? What makes you look so alarmed?"

"I have been frightened," she answered; "more frightened than I can tell you."

For a moment I thought she must have heard about her great-grandfather, but such was not the case.

"I have only been up here a few moments," she answered. "The caretaker's wife was in my room when I left. The door was open, and, as I climbed the turret stairs, I thought I heard her call me. Turning round, I was about to descend again, when I saw, standing at the foot of the stairs, a man. He was looking up at me. For a moment I could scarcely believe my eyes. Who do you think it was?"

303

Though I could easily guess, I managed to force myself to utter the word "Who?"

"He was the man you saw behind the rock, the same I saw bending over me in my cabin on board the Dona Mercedes, that terrible Chinaman with half an ear."

I feared that she might see from my face that I knew more than I cared to tell; but, as good fortune had it, she failed to notice it.

* * * * * * * *

"Surely you must have been mistaken," I answered. "What could the man be doing in the castle?"

"I do not know," she answered. "But I am as certain I saw him as I am of anything. He was standing at the foot of the stairs, watching me. Then he began to move in my direction; but before he could reach the bottom step, I heard a door open along the corridor. This must have frightened him, for he fled round the corner, and I saw no more of him."

"It must have been my opening the door that saved you," I said. "Thank God I came when I did!"

"But what does it mean?" she asked. "Why did that man come on board the boat, and why has he followed us here?"

"I think the reason is to be found in the fact that he is Dr. Nikola's enemy," I replied. "They had a private quarrel in China some years ago, and ever since then this man has been following him about the world, endeavouring to do him harm. The case is a serious one, darling, and as you love me you must run no risks. Be on your guard night and day. See that your door is locked at night, and never venture from your room after dusk, unless I am with you. It makes my blood run cold when I think of your running such risks as you did this morning."

"But what about you?" she said, looking up at me with her beautiful, frightened eyes. "Oh, why cannot we take my grandfather and go away, and never see this dreadful place again?"

"We must wait patiently," I answered; "the Don is not fit to travel just yet."

She gave a little sigh, and next moment it was time for me to leave her.

For the next two or three days following, Nikola and I took it in turns to act as sentry over the Don. If it was not difficult work, it was the reverse of pleasant; for as soon as the effect of each successive opiate wore off, his evil nature invariably reasserted itself. Sometimes he would sit for an hour or more watching me, as if he intended springing upon me the instant I was off my guard. At others he would crouch in a corner, tearing into atoms everything within his reach. More than once he was really violent, and it became necessary for me to signal to Nikola for assistance. The horror of those days I shall never forget. When I say that, not once but several times, I have left that room dripping with perspiration, the pure sweat of terror, my feelings may be partially imagined. It was not madness we had to contend with; it was worse than that. It was the fighting of a lost soul against the effect of man's prying into what should have been the realms of the unknowable.

"This sort of thing cannot last much longer," said Nikola, when our patient was lying drugged and helpless upon his mattress on the third night after the death of Ah-Win. And I knew he was right. Outraged nature would avenge herself.

When Nikola had bade me good-night, I examined the Don to make sure that he was not shamming sleep in order to try and get the better of me directly I was alone. Finding him to be quite helpless, I seated myself in my chair and prepared to spend my watch in as comfortable a fashion as possible under the circumstances. During the day I had passed a considerable portion of my time with my sweetheart in the open air, and, in consequence, I found myself growing exceedingly sleepy. Knowing it would never do to allow slumber to get the better of me in that room, I rose from my chair and began to pace the floor. This had the effect of temporarily rousing me, and, when I reseated myself, I thought I had dispelled the attack. It soon returned, however, and this time it would not be denied. I rubbed my eyes, I pinched myself, I got up and walked about. It was no good, however, I returned to my chair, my eyelids closed, and, almost without knowing it, I dozed off. When I woke again, it was with a start. I rubbed my eyes and looked about me. Heavens! what mischief had I done? The Don was not in his corner, the key was gone from the hook upon which it usually hung, and, worse than all, the door stood open!

For a moment I was so overwhelmed with horror that I could do nothing. But only for a moment. Then I knew that I must act, and at once. I rang the bell for Nikola, and, having done so, dashed into the hall. Almost simultaneously Nikola made his appearance, coming from his room.

"What is the matter?" he cried. "Why do you ring for me?"

"The Don has escaped!" I almost shouted. "Like the fool I am, I fell asleep, and during that time he must have recovered his wits, stolen the key, and escaped from the room. Oh, what have I done? If she should see him as he is, it will kill her!"

For a moment it looked as if Nikola would have swept me off the face of the earth, but the look scarcely came into his eyes before it was gone again.

"We must find him," he cried, "before he can do any mischief, and, what is more, we must not separate, for he would be more than a match for us single-handed."

Accordingly we left the hall and proceeded towards the Dona Consuelo's apartments. I thanked Heaven when I found that the door was locked. Calling to her, in answer to her cry of "Who is there?" I told her that I only desired to assure myself of her safety, and after that we passed on up the turret stairs and along the battlements, but no sign of the Don could we discover there. Returning to the corridor again, we descended to the great entrance hall and searched the courtyard and basement.

The moon shone clear, and the courtyard was as light as day. Had there been any one there, we must certainly have seen him. Suddenly there rang out the most unearthly scream it has ever been my ill-luck to hear. It came from the direction of the chapel, which lay between the keep and what had once been the banqueting hall. From where we stood the interior of the latter was quite visible to us. On either side it had tall windows, so that the light shone directly through. The scream had scarcely died away before we distinctly saw a short figure dash into the room, and out again upon the other side. An instant later and a taller figure followed, and also disappeared. Again and again the scream rang out, while Nikola stood rooted to the spot, unable to move hand or foot.

"I see it all!" cried Nikola. "That was Quong Ma and the other was the Don. They'll kill each other if they meet."

I thought of Consuelo, and of the terror she would feel should she hear that dreadful noise.

* * * * * * * *

"They must not meet!" I cried. "It is too terrible. At any cost we must prevent it Where do you think they are now?"

As if to let us know, another scream rang out. This time it came from our own quarters.

"Come on!" cried Nikola, and dashed into the building. As you may suppose, I followed close upon his heels. In this order we flew up the stairs and along the first gallery, intending, if possible, to reach the small hall by the staircase near the kitchen in which Ah-Win had worked, and thus cut them off. As we crossed the threshold however, a wild hubbub came from the passage ahead, and told us that we were too late. I knew what it meant, and, if I had not been by that time quite bankrupt of emotions, I should certainly have been doubly terrified now.

Leaving the kitchen, we dashed along the passage, only to find that the room usually occupied by Nikola's unfortunates was empty. With the exception of one solitary specimen, who by reason of his infirmity was unable to fly, they had all vanished. Leaving him to his own desires, we passed the iron gate, now thrown open, and a moment later had entered the hall itself. Once more the cry sounded, this time coming from a spot somewhat nearer Consuelo's apartment. On hearing it, my heart seemed to stand still. What if she should imagine that I was in danger and should open her door? The same thought must have been in Nikola's mind, for I heard him say to himself—"Anything but that."

Side by side we raced for her door, only to find it was still shut and locked.

Almost at the same instant a scream, louder than any we had yet heard, sounded from the battlements above.

"At last!" I cried, and led the way up the stone stairs. I can only say that of all the horrid scenes I have ever witnessed, that I saw before me then was the very worst. In the centre of the open space between the parapets, fighting like wild beasts, were the two men of whom we were in search. Their arms were twined about each other, and, as they swayed to and fro, the sound of their heavy breathing could be distinctly heard. Having reached the top of the stairs, we paused irresolute. What was to be done? To have attempted to separate them would only have been to draw their anger upon ourselves, and to have made the fight a general one. The moon shone down upon us, revealing the smooth sea on one side and the many turrets of the castle on the other. From fighting in the centre of the open space, they gradually came nearer the parapet of the wall. Quong Ma must then have realised how near he stood to death, for he redoubled his energy.

"They will be over!" shouted Nikola, and started to run towards them. He had scarcely spoken before they reached the edge. For a moment, locked in each other's arms, they paused upon the brink; then, with a wild shriek from Quong Ma, they lost their balance and disappeared. I clapped my hands to my eyes to shut out the fearful sight. When I took them away again, all was over, and both Nikola and I knew that Quong Ma and Don Miguel de Moreno were dead.

I suppose I must have fainted, for when I returned to my senses once more, I found myself seated on the top of the stairs, and Consuelo's arms about me.

There remains but little more to tell.

At the time of that dreadful scene upon the battlements it was full tide; and though Nikola and I searched every nook and cranny along the coast-line for many miles, the bodies of the two men could not be found. In all probability they had drifted out to sea. The same day I summoned up my courage, and prepared to tell my sweetheart everything; but when I sought her out, and was about to commence my confession, she stopped me.

"Say nothing to me about it, dear," she began. "I cannot bear it yet. Dr. Nikola has told me everything. He exonerates you completely."

"But what of ourselves?" I asked. "Consuelo, you and I are alone together in the world; will you give me the right to care for your future happiness? My darling, will you be my wife?"

"When and where you please," she answered, holding out her hands to me and looking up at me with her beautiful, trusting eyes. I told her of my straitened means, and how hard the struggle would be at first.

"No matter," she answered bravely, "we will fight the world together. I am used to poverty, and with you beside me I shall know no fear."

A hour later I had an interview with Nikola in the hall.

"Ingleby," he said, "this is the end of our intercourse. I have tried my experiment, and though I have succeeded in many particulars, I have failed in the main essential. How much I regret what has happened, I must leave you to imagine; but it is too late—what is done cannot be undone. I have given orders that the yacht shall be prepared. She will convey you to Newcastle, whence you can proceed in any direction you may desire. One thing is certain: Dona Consuelo must leave this place, and, as you are to be her husband, it is only fit and proper that you should go with her. I have only one wish to offer you: it is that you may be as happy as these past weeks have been sad."

He held out his hand to me, and I took it.

"We shall meet no more," he said. "Go away and forget that you ever met Dr. Nikola. Goodbye."

"Goodbye," I answered. Without another word he turned and left the room.

Shortly before midday we boarded the yacht. Steam was up when we arrived, and within a few minutes we were steaming out of the little bay. Consuelo and I stood together at the taffrail, and looked up at the grim old castle on the cliff above our heads. Standing on the battlements we could distinctly see a solitary figure, who waved his hands to us. Then the little vessel passed round the headland, and that was the last we saw of Dr. Nikola.

Book #3
Finale

Farewell, Nikola

Chapter 1

We were in Venice; Venice the silent and mysterious; the one European city of which I never tire. My wife had not enjoyed good health for some months past, and for this reason we had been wintering in Southern Italy. After that we had come slowly north, spending a month in Florence, and a fortnight in Rome en route, until we found ourselves in Venice, occupying a suite of apartments at Galaghetti's famous hotel overlooking the Grand Canal. Our party was a small one; it consisted of my wife, her friend Gertrude Trevor, and myself, Richard Hatteras, once of the South Sea Islands, but now of the New Forest, Hampshire, England. It may account for our fondness of Venice when I say that four years previous we had spent the greater part of our honeymoon there. Whatever the cause may have been, however, there could be no sort of doubt that the grand old city, with its palaces and churches, its associations stretching back to long-forgotten centuries, and its silent waterways, possessed a great fascination for us. We were never tired of exploring it, finding something to interest us in even the most out-of-the-way corners. In Miss Trevor we possessed a charming companion, a vital necessity, as you will admit, when people travel together. She was an uncommon girl in more ways than one; a girl, so it seems to me, England alone is able to produce. She could not be described as a pretty girl, but then the word "pretty" is one that sometimes comes perilously near carrying contempt with it; one does not speak of Venus de Medici as pretty, nor would one describe the Apollo Belvedere as very nice-looking. That Miss Trevor was exceedingly handsome would, I fancy, be generally admitted. At any rate she would command attention wherever she might go, and that is an advantage which few of us possess. Should a more detailed description of her be necessary, I might add that she was tall and dark, with black hair and large luminous eyes that haunted one, and were suggestive of a southern ancestor. She was the daughter, and indeed the only child, of the well-known Dean of Bedminster, and this was the first time she had visited Italy, or that she had been abroad. The wonders of the Art Country were all new to her, and in consequence our wanderings were one long succession of delight. Every day added some new pleasure to her experiences, while each night saw a life-desire gratified.

In my humble opinion, to understand Italy properly one should not presume to visit her until after the first blush of youth has departed, and then only when one has prepared oneself to properly appreciate her many beauties. Venice, above all others, is a city that must be taken seriously. To come at a proper spirit of the place one must be in a reverent mood. Cheap jokes and Cockney laughter are as unsuited to the place, where Falieri yielded his life, as a downcast face would be in Nice at carnival time. On the afternoon of the particular day from which I date my story, we had been to the Island of Murano to pay a visit to the famous glass factories of which it is the home. By the time we reached Venice once more it was nearly sunset. Having something like an hour to spare we made our way, at my wife's suggestion, to the Florian cafe on the piazza of Saint Mark in order to watch the people. As usual the place was crowded, and at first glance it looked as if we should be unable to find sufficient vacant chairs. Fortune favoured us, however, and when we had seated ourselves and I had ordered coffee, we gave ourselves up to the enjoyment of what is perhaps one of the most amusing scenes in Venice. To a thoughtful mind the Great Square must at all times be an object of absorbing interest. I have seen it at every hour, and under almost every aspect: at break of day, when one has it to oneself and is able to enjoy its beauty undisturbed; at midday, when the importunate shopkeepers endeavour to seduce one into entering their doors (by tales of the marvels therein); at sunset, when the cafes are crowded, the band plays, and all is merriment; and last, but not least, at midnight, when the moon is sailing above Saint Mark's, the square is full of strange shadows, and the only sound to be heard is the cry of a gull on the lagoon, or the *"Sa Premi"* of some belated gondolier.

"This is the moment to which I have looked forward all my life," said Miss Trevor, as she sat back in her chair and watched the animated crowd before her. "Look at that pretty little boy with the pigeons knocking around him. What a picture he would make if one only had a camera."

"If you care to have a photo of him one can easily be obtained," I remarked. "Any one of these enterprising photographers would be only to pleased to take one for you for a few *centissimi*. I regret to say that many of our countrymen have a weakness for being taken in that way."

"Fancy Septimus Brown, of Tooting," my wife remarked, "a typical English paterfamilias, with a green veil, blue spectacles, and white umbrella, daring to ask the sun to record his image with the pigeons of St. Mark's clustering above his venerable head. Can't you picture the pride of that worthy gentleman's family when they produce the album on Sunday afternoons and show it to their friends? 'This is pa,' the eldest girl will probably remark, 'when he was travelling in Venice' (as if Venice were a country in which one must be perpetually moving on), 'and that's how the pigeons came down to be fed. Isn't it splendid of him?' Papa, who has never ventured beyond Brighton beach before, will be a person of importance from that moment."

"You forget one circumstance, however," Miss Trevor replied, who enjoyed an argument, and for this reason contradicted my wife on principle, "that in allowing himself to be taken at all, Brown of Tooting has advanced a step."

For the moment he dared to throw off his insularity, as the picture at which you are laughing is indisputable testimony. Do you think he would dare to be photographed in a similar fashion in his own market-place, standing outside his shop-door with his assistants watching him from behind the counter? I am quite sure he would not!"

"A very excellent argument," I answered. "Unfortunately, however, it carries its own refutation. The mere fact that Brown takes the photograph home to show to his friends goes a long way towards proving that he is still as insular as when he set out. If he did not consider himself of sufficient importance to shut out a portion of Saint Mark's with his voluminous personality, he would not have employed the photographer at all, in which case we are no further advanced than before."

These little sparring-matches were a source of great amusement to us. The Cockney tourist was Miss Trevor's *bete noir*. And upon this failing my wife and I loved to twit her. On the whole I rather fancy she liked being teased by us.

We had finished our coffee and were still idly watching the people about us when I noticed that my wife had turned a little pale. I was about to remark upon it, when she uttered an exclamation as if something had startled her.

"Good gracious! Dick," she cried, "surely it is not possible. It must be a mistake."

"What is it cannot be possible?" I inquired, "What do you think you see?"

I glanced in the direction she indicated, but could recognise no one with whom I was acquainted. An English clergyman and his daughter were sitting near the entrance to the cafe, and some officers in uniform were on the other side of them again, but still my wife was looking in the same direction and with an equally startled face. I placed my hand upon her arm. It was a long time since I had seen her so agitated. "Come, darling," I said, "tell me what it is that troubles you."

"Look," she answered, "can you see the table to the right of that at which those officers are seated?" I was about to reply in the affirmative, but the shock I received deprived me of speech. The person to whom my wife had referred had risen from his chair, and was in the act of walking towards us. I looked at him, looked away, and then looked again. No! there was no room for doubt; the likeness was unmistakable. I should have known him anywhere. He was Doctor Nikola; the man who had played such an important part in our life's drama. Five years had elapsed since I had last seen him, but in that time he was scarcely changed at all. It was the same tall, thin figure; the same sallow, clean-shaven face; the same piercing black eyes. As he drew nearer I noticed that his hair was a little more grey, that he looked slightly older; otherwise he was unchanged. But why was he coming to us? Surely he did not mean to speak to us? After the manner in which he had treated us in bygone days I scarcely knew how to receive him. He, on his side, however, was quite self-possessed. Raising his hat with that easy grace that always distinguished him, he advanced and held out his hand to my wife.

"My dear Lady Hatteras," he began in his most conciliatory tone, "I felt sure you would recognise me. Observing that you had not forgotten me, I took the liberty of coming to pay my respects to you."

Then before my wife could reply he had turned to me and was holding out his hand. For a moment I had half determined not to take it, but when his glittering eyes looked into mine I changed my mind and shook hands with him more cordially than I should ever have thought it possible for me to do. Having thus broken the ice, and as we had to all intents and purposes permitted him to derive the impression that we were prepared to forgive the past, nothing remained for us but to introduce him to Miss Trevor. From the moment that he had approached us she had been watching him covertly, and that he had produced a decided impression upon her was easily seen. For the first time since we had known her she, usually so staid and unimpressionable, was nervous and ill at ease. The introduction effected she drew back a little, and pretended to be absorbed in watching a party of our fellow-countrymen who had taken their places at a table a short distance from us. For my part I do not mind confessing that I was by no means comfortable. I remembered my bitter hatred of Nikola in days gone by. I recalled that terrible house in Port Said, and thought of the night on the island when I had rescued my wife from his clutches. In my estimation then he had been a villain of the deepest dye, and yet here he was sitting beside me as calm and collected, and apparently as interested in the resume of our travels in Italy that my wife was giving him, as if we had been bosom friends throughout our lives. In any one else it would have been a piece of marvellous effrontery; in Nikola's case, however, it did not strike one in the same light. As I have so often remarked, he seemed incapable of acting like any other human being. His extraordinary personality lent a glamour to his simplest actions, and demanded for them an attention they would scarcely have received had he been less endowed.

"Have you been long in Venice?" my wife inquired when she had completed the record of our doings, feeling that she must say something.

"I seldom remain anywhere for very long," he answered, with one of his curious smiles. "I come and go like a will-o'-the-wisp; I am here today and gone tomorrow."

It may have been an unfortunate remark, but I could not help uttering it.

"For instance, you are in London today," I said, "in Port Said next week, and in the South Sea Islands a couple of months later."

He was not in the least disconcerted.

"Ah! I see you have not forgotten our South Sea adventure," he replied cheerfully. "How long ago it seems, does it not? To me it is like a chapter out of another life." Then, turning to Miss Trevor, who of course had heard the story of our dealings with him sufficiently often to be weary of it, he added, "I hope you are not altogether disposed to think ill of me. Perhaps some day you will be able to persuade Lady Hatteras to forgive me, that is to say if she has not already done so. Yet I do not know why I should plead for pardon, seeing that I am far from being in a repentant mood. As a matter of fact I am very much afraid that should the necessity arise, I should be compelled to act as I did then."

"Then let us pray most fervently that the necessity may never arise," I answered. "I for one do not entertain a very pleasant recollection of that time."

I spoke so seriously that my wife looked sharply up at me. Fearing, I suppose, that I might commit myself, she added quickly:

"I trust it may not. For I can assure you, Doctor Nikola, that my inclinations lie much nearer Bond Street than the South Sea Islands."

All this time Miss Trevor said nothing, but I could tell from the expression upon her face that Nikola interested her more than she would have been willing to admit.

"Is it permissible to ask where you are staying?" he inquired, breaking the silence and speaking as if it were a point upon which he was most anxious to be assured.

"At Galaghetti's," I answered. "While in Venice we always make it our home."

"Ah! the good Galaghetti," said Nikola softly. "It is a long time since I last had the pleasure of seeing him. I fancy, however, he would remember me. I was able to do him a slight service some time ago, and I have always understood that he possesses a retentive memory."

Then, doubtless feeling that he had stayed long enough, he rose and prepared to take leave of us.

"Perhaps, Lady Hatteras, you will permit me to do myself the honour of calling upon you?" he said.

"We shall be very pleased to see you," my wife replied, though with no real cordiality.

He then bowed to Miss Trevor, and shook hands with myself.

"Goodbye, Hatteras," he continued. "I shall hope soon to see you again. I expect we have lots of news for each other, and doubtless you will be interested to learn the history and subsequent adventures of that peculiar little stick which caused you so much anxiety, and myself so much trouble, five years ago. My address is the Palace Revecce, in the Rio del Consiglio, where, needless to say, I shall be delighted to see you if you care to pay me a visit."

I thanked him for his invitation, and promised that I would call upon him.

Then with a bow he took his departure, leaving behind him a sensation of something missing, something that could not be replaced. To sit down and continue the conversation where he had broken into it was out of the question. We accordingly rose, and after I had discharged the bill, strolled across the piazza towards the lagoon. Observing that Miss Trevor was still very silent, I inquired the cause.

"If you really want me to tell you, I can only account for it by saying that your friend, Dr. Nikola, has occasioned it," she answered, "I don't know why it should be so, but that man has made a curious impression upon me."

"He seems to affect every one in a different manner," I said, and for some reason made no further comment upon her speech.

When we had called a gondola, and were on our way back to our hotel, she referred to the subject again.

"I think I ought to tell you that it is not the first time I have seen Doctor Nikola," she said. "You may remember that yesterday, while Phyllis was lying down, I went out to do some shopping. I cannot describe exactly which direction I took, save that I went towards the Rialto. It is sufficient that in the end I reached a chemist's shop. It was only a small place, and very dark, so dark indeed that I did not see that it contained another customer until I was really inside. Then I noticed a tall man busily engaged in conversation with the shopkeeper. He was declaiming against some drugs he had purchased there on the previous day, and demanding that for the future they should be of better quality, otherwise he would be compelled to take his patronage elsewhere. In the middle of this harangue he turned round, and I was permitted an opportunity of seeing his face. He was none other than your friend, Doctor Nikola."

"But, my dear Gertrude," said Phyllis, "with all due respect to your narrative, I do not see that the mere fact of your having met Doctor Nikola in a chemist's shop yesterday, and your having been introduced to him today, should have caused you so much concern."

"I do not know why it should," she answered, "but it is a fact, nevertheless. Ever since I saw him yesterday, his face, with its terrible eyes, has haunted me. I dreamt of it last night. All day long I have had it before me, and now, as if to add to the strangeness of the coincidence, he proves to be the man of whom you have so often told me—your demoniacal, fascinating Nikola. You must admit that it is very strange."

"A coincidence, a mere coincidence, that is all," I replied. "Nikola possesses an extraordinary face, and it must have impressed itself more deeply upon you than the average countenance is happy enough to do."

Whether my explanation satisfied her or not she said no more upon the subject. But that our strange meeting with Nikola had had an extraordinary effect upon her was plainly observable. As a rule she was as bright and merry a companion as one could wish to have; on this particular evening, however, she was not herself at all. It was the more annoying for the reason that I was anxious that she should shine on this occasion, as I was expecting an old friend, who was going to spend a few days with us in Venice. That friend was none other than the Duke of Glenbarth, who previous to his succession to the Dukedom had been known as the Marquis of Beckenham, and who, as the readers of the history of my adventures with Doctor Nikola may remember, figured as a very important factor in that strange affair. Ever since the day when I had the good fortune to render him a signal service in the bay of a certain south-coast watering-place, and from the time that he had accepted my invitation to join him in Venice, I had looked forward to his coming with the greatest possible eagerness. As it happened it was well-nigh seven o'clock by the time we reached our hotel. Without pausing in the hall further than to examine the letter-rack, we ascended to our rooms on the floor above. My wife and Miss Trevor had gone to their apartments, and I was about to follow their example as soon as I had obtained something from the sitting-room.

"A nice sort of host, a very nice host," said a laughing voice as I entered. "He invites me to stay with him, and is not at home to bid me welcome. My dear old Dick, how are you?"

"My dear fellow," I cried, hastening forward to greet him, "I must beg your pardon ten thousand times. I had not the least idea that you would be here so early. We have been sitting on the piazza, and did not hurry home."

"You needn't apologise," he answered. "For once an Italian train was before its time. And now tell me about yourself. How is your wife, how are you, and what sort of holiday are you having?"

I answered his questions to the best of my ability, keeping back my most important item as a surprise for him.

"And now," I said, "it is time to dress for dinner. But before you do so, I have some important news for you. Who do you think is in Venice?"

Needless to say he mentioned every one but the right person.

"You had better give it up, you will never guess," I said. "Who is the most unlikely person you would expect to see in Venice at the present moment?"

"Old Macpherson, my solicitor," he replied promptly. "The rascal would no more think of crossing the Channel than he would contemplate standing on his head in the middle of the Strand. It must be Macpherson."

"Nonsense," I cried. "I don't know Macpherson in the first place, and I doubt if he would interest me in the second. No! no! this man is neither a Scotchman nor a lawyer. He is an individual bearing the name of Nikola."

I had quite expected to surprise him, but I scarcely looked for such an outbreak of astonishment.

"What?" he cried, in amazement. "You must be joking. You don't mean to say you have seen Nikola again?"

"I not only mean that I have seen him," I replied, "but I will go further than that, and say that he was sitting on the piazza, with us not more than half an hour ago. What do you think his appearance in Venice means?"

"I don't know what to think," he replied, with an expression of almost comic bewilderment upon his face. "It seems impossible, and yet you don't look as if you were joking."

"I tell you the news in all sober earnestness," I answered, dropping my bantering tone. "It is a fact that Nikola is in Venice, and, what is more, that he has given me his address. He has invited me to call upon him, and if you like we will go together. What do you say?"

"I shall have to take time to think about it," Glenbarth replied seriously. "I don't suppose for a moment he has any intention of abducting me again; nevertheless, I am not going to give him the opportunity. By Jove, how that fellow's face comes back to me. It haunts me!"

"Miss Trevor has been complaining of the same thing," I said.

"Miss Trevor?" the Duke repeated. "And pray who may Miss Trevor be?"

"A friend of my wife's," I answered. "She has been travelling with us for the last few months. I think you will like her. And now come along with me and I'll show you your room. I suppose your man has discovered it by this time?"

"Stevens would find it if this hotel were constructed on the same principle as the maze at Hampton Court," he answered. "He has the virtue of persistence, and when he wants to find a thing he secures the person who would be the most likely to tell him, and sticks to him until his desire has been gratified."

It turned out as he had predicted, and three-quarters of an hour later our quartet sat down to dinner. My wife and Glenbarth, by virtue of an old friendship, agreed remarkably well, while Miss Trevor, now somewhat recovered from her Nikola indisposition, was more like her old self. It was a beautiful night, and after dinner it was proposed, seconded, and carried unanimously, that we should charter a gondola and go for a row upon the canal. On our homeward voyage the gondolier, by some strange chance, turned into the Rio del Consiglio.

"Perhaps you can tell me which is the Palace Revecce?" I said to the man.

He pointed to a building we were in the act of approaching.

"There it is, signor," he said. "At one time it was a very great palace, but now—" here he shrugged his shoulders to enable us to understand that its glory had departed from it. Not another word was said upon the subject, but I noticed that all our faces turned in the direction of the building. With the exception of one solitary window it was in total darkness. As I looked at the latter I wondered whether Nikola were in the room, and if so, what he was doing? Was he poring over some of his curious books, trying some new experiment in chemistry, or putting to the test some theory such as I had found him at work upon in that curious house in Port Said? A few minutes later we had left the Rio del Consiglio behind us, had turned to the right, and were making our way back by another watery thoroughfare towards the Grand Canal.

"Thanks to your proposition we have had a delightful evening," Miss Trevor said, as we paused to say good night at the foot of the staircase a quarter of an hour or so later. "I have enjoyed myself immensely."

"You should not tell him that, dear," said my wife. "You know how conceited he is already. He will take all the credit, and be unbearable for days afterwards." Then turning to me she added, "You are going to smoke, I suppose?"

"I had thought of doing so," I replied; and then added with mock humility, "if you do not wish it of course I will not do so. I was only going to keep Glenbarth company."

They laughed and bade us good night, and when we had seen them depart in the direction of their rooms we lit our cigars and passed into the balcony outside.

At this hour of the night the Grand Canal looked very still and beautiful, and we both felt in the humour for confidences.

"Do you know, Hatteras," said Glenbarth, after a few moments' pause that followed our arrival in the open air, "that Nikola's turning up in Venice at this particular juncture savours to me a little of the uncanny. What his mission may be, of course I cannot tell, but that it is some diabolical thing or another I haven't a doubt."

"One thing is quite certain," I answered, "he would hardly be here without an object, and, after our dealings with him in the past, I am prepared to admit that I don't trust him any more than you do."

"And now that he has asked you to call upon him, what are you going to do?"

I paused before I replied. The question involved greater responsibilities than were at first glance apparent. Knowing Nikola so well, I had not the least desire or intention to be drawn into any of the plots or machinations he was so fond of working against other people. I must confess, nevertheless, that I could not help feeling a large amount of curiosity as to the subsequent history of that little stick, to obtain which he had spent so much money, and had risked so many lives.

"Yes, I think I shall call upon him," I said reflectively, as if I had not quite made up my mind. "Surely to see him once more could do no harm? Good heavens! what an extraordinary fellow he is! Fancy you or I being afraid of any other man as we are afraid of him, for mind you, I know that you stand quite as much in awe of him as I do. Why, do you know when my eyes fell upon him this afternoon, I felt a return of the old dread his presence used to cause in me five years ago! The effect he had upon Miss Trevor was also very singular, when you come to, think of it."

"By the way, Hatteras, talking of Miss Trevor, what an awfully nice girl she is. I don't know when I have ever met a nicer. Who is she?"

"She is the daughter of the Dean of Bedminster," I answered; "a splendid old fellow."

"I like his daughter," the Duke remarked. "Yes, I must say that I like her very much."

I was glad to hear this, for I had my own little dreams, and my wife, who, by the way, is a born matchmaker, had long ago come to a similar conclusion.

"She is a very nice girl," I replied, "and what is more, she is as good as she is nice." Then I continued: "He will be indeed a lucky man who wins Gertrude Trevor for his wife. And now, since our cigars are finished, what do you say to bed? It is growing late, and I expect you are tired after your journey."

"I am quite ready," he answered. "I shall sleep like a top. I only hope and pray that I shall not dream of Nikola."

Chapter 2

Whether it was our excursion upon the canal that was responsible for it, I cannot say; the fact, however, remains, that next morning every member of our party was late for breakfast. My wife and I were the first to put in an appearance, Glenbarth followed shortly after, and Miss Trevor was last of all. It struck me that the girl looked a little pale as she approached the window to bid me good morning, and as she prided herself upon her punctuality, I jestingly reproved her for her late rising.

"I am afraid your gondola excursion proved too much for you," I said, in a bantering tone, "or perhaps you dreamt of Doctor Nikola."

I expected her to declare in her usual vehement fashion that she would not waste her time dreaming of any man, but to my combined astonishment and horror her eyes filled with tears, until she was compelled to turn her head away in order to hide them from me. It was all so unexpected that I did not know what to think. As may be supposed, I had not the slightest intention of giving her pain, nor could I quite see how I managed to do so. It was plain, however, that my thoughtless speech had been the means of upsetting her, and I was heartily sorry for my indiscretion. Fortunately my wife had not overheard what had passed between us "Is he teasing you again, Gertrude?" she said, as she slipped her arm through her friend's. "Take my advice and have nothing to do with him. Treat him with contempt. Besides, the coffee is getting cold, and that is a very much more important matter. Let us sit down to breakfast."

Nothing could have been more opportune. We took our places at the table, and by the time the servant had handed the first dishes Miss Trevor had recovered herself sufficiently to be able to look me in the face, and to join in the conversation without the likelihood of a catastrophe. Still there could be no doubt that she was far from being in a happy frame of mind. I said as much to my wife afterwards, when we were alone together.

"She told me she had had a very bad night," the little woman replied. "Our meeting with Doctor Nikola yesterday on the piazza upset her for some reason or another. She said that she had dreamt of nothing else. As you know, she is very highly strung, and when you think of the descriptions we have given her of him, it is scarcely to be wondered at that she should attach an exaggerated importance to our unexpected meeting with him. That is the real explanation of the mystery. One thing, however, is quite certain; in her present state of mind she must see no more of him than can be helped. It might upset her altogether. Oh, why did he come here to spoil our holiday?"

"I cannot see that he has spoilt it, my dear," I returned, putting my arm round her waist and leading her to the window. "The girl will very soon recover from her fit of depression, and afterwards will be as merry as a marriage-bell. By the way, I don't know why I should think of it just now, but talking of marriage-bells reminds me that Glenbarth told me last night that he thought Gertrude one of the nicest girls he had ever met."

"I am delighted to hear it," my wife answered. "And still more delighted to think that he has such good sense. Do you know, I have set my heart upon that coming to something. No! you needn't shake your head. For very many reasons it would be a most desirable match."

"For my own part I believe it was for no other reason that you bothered me into inviting him to join our party here. You are a matchmaker. I challenge you to refute the accusation."

"I shall not attempt to do so," she retorted with considerable hauteur. "It is always a waste of time to argue with you. At any rate you must agree with me that Gertrude would make an ideal duchess."

"So you have travelled as far as that, have you?" I inquired. "I must say that you jump to conclusions very quickly. Because Glenbarth happens to have said in confidence to me (a confidence I am willing to admit I have shamefully abused) that he considers Gertrude Trevor a very charming girl, it does not follow that he has the very slightest intention of asking her to be his wife. Why should he?"

"Lords," she answered, as if that ought to clinch the argument. "Fancy a man posing as one of our hereditary legislators who doesn't know how to seize such a golden opportunity. As a good churchwoman I pray for the nobility every Sunday morning; and if not knowing where to look for the best wife in the world may be taken as a weakness and it undoubtedly is, then all I can say is, that they require all the praying for they can get!"

"But I should like to know, how is he going to marry the best wife in the world?" I asked.

"By asking her," she retorted. "He doesn't surely suppose she is going to ask him?"

"If he values his life he'd better not do that!" I said savagely. "He will have to answer for it to me if he does!"

"Ah," she answered, her lips curling. "I thought as much. You are jealous of him. You don't want him to ask her because you fancy that if he does your reign will be over. A nice admission for a married man, I must say!"

"I presume you mean because I refuse to allow him to flirt with my wife?"

"I mean nothing of the kind, and you know it. How dare you say, Dick, that I flirt with the Duke?"

"Because you have confessed it," I answered with a grin of triumph, for I had got her cornered at last. "Did you not say, only a moment ago, that if he did not know where to find the best wife in the world he was unfit to sit in the House of Lords? Did you not say that he ought to be ashamed of himself if he did not ask her to be his wife? Answer that, my lady."

"I admit that I did say it; but you know very well that I referred to Gertrude Trevor!"

"Gertrude Trevor is not yet a wife. The best wife in the world is beside me now; and since you are already proved to be in the wrong you must perforce pay the penalty."

She was in the act of doing so when Gertrude entered the room.

"Oh, dear," she began, hesitating in pretended consternation, "is there never to be an end of it?"

"An end of what?" demanded my wife with some little asperity, for she does not like her little endearments to be witnessed by other people.

"Of this billing and cooing," the other replied. "You two insane creatures have been married more than four years, and yet a third person can never enter the room without finding you love-making. I declare it upsets all one's theories of marriage. One of my most cherished ideas was that this sort of thing ceased with the honeymoon, and that the couple invariably lead a cat-and-dog life for the remainder of their existence."

"So they do," my wife answered unblushingly "And what can you expect when one is a great silly creature who will not learn to jump away and be looking innocently out of the window when he hears the handle turned? Never marry, Gertrude. Mark my words: you will repent it if you do!"

"Well, for ingratitude and cool impudence, that surpasses everything!" I said in astonishment. "Why, you audacious creature, not more than five minutes ago you were inviting me to co-operate in the noble task of finding a husband for Miss Trevor!"

"Richard, how can you stand there and say such things?" she ejaculated. "Gertrude, my dear, I insist that you come away at once. I don't know what he will say next."

Miss Trevor laughed.

"I like to hear you two squabbling," she said. "Please go on, it amuses me!"

"Yes, I will certainly go on," I returned. "Perhaps you heard her declare that she fears what I may say next. Of course she does. Allow me to tell you, Lady Hatteras, that you are a coward. If the truth were known, it would be found that you are trembling in your shoes at this moment. For two centimes, paid down, I would turn King's evidence, and reveal the whole plot."

"You had better not, sir," she replied, shaking a warning finger at me. "In that case the letters from home shall be withheld from you, and you will not know how your son and heir is progressing."

"I capitulate," I answered. "Threatened by such awful punishment I dare say no more. Miss Gertrude, will you not intercede for me?"

"I think that you scarcely deserve it," she retorted. "Even now you are keeping something back from me."

"Never mind, my dear, we'll let him off this time with a caution," said my wife, "provided he promises not to offend again. And now, let us settle what we are going to do today."

When this important matter had been arranged it was reported to us that the ladies were to spend the morning shopping, leaving the Duke and myself free to follow our own inclinations. Accordingly, when we had seen them safely on their way to the Merceria, we held a smoking council to arrange how we should pass the hours until lunch-time. As we discovered afterwards, we both had a certain thought in our minds, which for some reason we scarcely liked to broach to each other. It was settled, however, just as we desired, but in a fashion we least expected.

We were seated in the balcony outside our room, watching the animated traffic on the Grand Canal below, when a servant came in search of us and handed me a note. One glance at the characteristic writing was sufficient to show me that it was from Doctor Nikola. I opened it with an eagerness that I did not attempt to conceal, and read as follows:

Dear Hatteras,

If you have nothing more important on hand this morning, can you spare the time to come and see me? As I understand the Duke of Glenbarth is with you, will you not bring him also? It will be very pleasant to have a chat upon bygone days, and, what is more, I fancy this old house will interest you."

Yours very truly,

Nikola."

"What do you say?" I inquired, when I had finished reading, "shall we go?"

"Let us do so by all means," the Duke replied. "It will be very interesting to meet Nikola once more. There is one thing, however, that puzzles me: how did he become aware of my arrival in Venice? You say he was with you on the piazza, last night, so that he could not have been at the railway station, as I haven't been outside since I came, except for the row after dinner, I confess it puzzles me."

"You should know by this time that it is useless to wonder how Nikola acquires his knowledge," I replied. "For my own part I should like to discover his reason for being in Venice. I am very curious on that point."

Glenbarth shook his head solemnly.

"IF Nikola does not want us to know," he argued, "we shall leave his house as wise as we entered it. If he does let us know, I shall begin to grow suspicious, for in that case it is a thousand pounds to this half-smoked cigar that we shall be called upon to render him assistance. However, if you are prepared to run the risk I will do so also."

"In that case," I said, rising from my chair and tossing what remained of my cigar into the water below, "let us get ready and be off. We may change our minds."

Ten minutes later we had chartered a gondola and were on our way to the Palace Revecce.

As a general rule when one sets out to pay a morning call one is not the victim of any particular nervousness; on this occasion; however, both Glenbarth and I, as we confessed to each other afterwards, were distinctly conscious of being in a condition which would be described by persons of mature years as an unpleasant state of expectancy, but which by school boys is denominated "funk." The Duke, I noticed, fidgeted with his cigar, allowed it to go out, and then sat with it in his mouth unlighted. There was a far-away look on his handsome face that told me that he was recalling some of the events connected with the time when he had been in Nikola's company. This proved to be the case, for as we turned from the Grand Canal into the street in which the palace is situated, he said:

"By the way, Hatteras, I wonder what became of Baxter, Prendergast, and those other fellows?"

"Nikola may be able to tell us," I answered. Then I added after a short pause, "By Jove, what strange times those were."

"Not half so strange to my thinking as our finding Nikola in Venice," Glenbarth replied. "That is the coincidence that astonishes me. But see, here we are."

As he spoke the gondola drew up at the steps of the Palace Revecce, and we prepared to step ashore. As we did so I noticed that the armorial bearings of the family still decorated the posts on either side of the door, but by the light of day the palace did not look nearly so imposing as it had done by moonlight the night before. One thing about it was certainly peculiar. When we ordered the gondolier to wait for us he shook his head. Not for anything would he remain there longer than was necessary to set us down. I accordingly paid him off, and when we had ascended the steps we entered the building. On pushing open the door we found ourselves standing in a handsome courtyard, in the centre of which was a well, its coping elegantly carved with a design of fruit and flowers. A broad stone staircase at the further end led up to the floor above, but this, as was the case with everything else, showed unmistakable signs of having been allowed to fall to decay. As no concierge was to be seen, and there was no one in sight of whom we might make inquiries, we scarcely knew how to proceed. Indeed, we were just wondering whether we should take our chance and explore the lower regions in search of Nikola, when he appeared at the head of the staircase and greeted us.

"Good morning," he said, "pray come up. I must apologise for not having been downstairs to receive you."

By the time he had finished speaking he had reached us, and was shaking hands with Glenbarth with the heartiness of an old friend.

"Let me offer you a hearty welcome to Venice," he said to Glenbarth after he had shaken hands with myself. Then looking at him once more, he added, "If you will permit me to say so, you have changed a great deal since we last saw each other."

"And you, scarcely at all," Glenbarth replied.

"It is strange that I should not have done so," Nikola answered, I thought a little sadly, "for I think I may say without any fear of boasting that, since we parted at Pipa Lannu, I have passed through sufficient to change a dozen men. But we will not talk of that here. Let us come up to my room, which is the only place in this great house that is in the least degree comfortable."

So saying he led the way up the stairs, and then along a corridor, which had once been beautifully frescoed, but which was now sadly given over to damp and decay. At last, reaching a room in the front of the building, he threw open the door and invited us to enter. And here I might digress for a moment to remark, that of all the men I have ever met, Nikola possessed the faculty of being able to make himself comfortable wherever he might be, in the greatest degree. He would have been at home anywhere. As a matter of fact, this particular apartment was furnished in a style that caused me considerable surprise. The room itself was large and lofty, while the walls were beautifully frescoed the work of one Andrea Bunopelli, of whom I shall have more to say anon. The furniture was simple, but extremely good; a massive oak writing-table stood beside one wall, another covered with books and papers was opposite it, several easy-chairs were placed here and there, another table in the centre of the room supported various chemical paraphernalia, while books of all sorts and descriptions, in all languages and bindings, were to be discovered in every direction.

"After what you have seen of the rest of the house, this strikes you as being more homelike, does it not?" Nikola inquired, as he noticed the look of astonishment upon our faces. "It is a queer old place, and the more I see of it the stranger it becomes. Some time ago, and quite by chance, I became acquainted with its history; I do not mean the political history of the respective families that have occupied it; you can find that in any guide-book. I mean the real, inner history of the house itself, embracing not a few of the deeds which have taken place inside its walls. I wonder if you would be interested if I were to tell you that in this very room, in the year fifteen hundred and eleven, one of the most repellent and cold-blooded murders of the Middle Ages took place. Perhaps now that you have the scene before you you would like to hear the story. You would? In that case pray sit down. Let me offer you this chair, Duke," he continued, and as he spoke he wheeled forward a handsomely carved chair from beside his writing-table. "Here, Hatteras, is one for you. I myself will take up my position here, so that I may be better able to retain your attention for my narrative."

So saying he stood between us on the strip of polished floor which showed between two heavy oriental rugs.

"For some reasons," he began, "I regret that the story I have to tell should run upon such familiar lines. I fancy, however, that the denouement will prove sufficiently original to merit your attention. The year fifteen hundred and nine, the same which found the French victorious at Agnadello, and the Venetian Republic at the commencement of that decline from which it has never recovered, saw this house in its glory. The owner, the illustrious Francesco del Revecce, was a sailor, and had the honour of commanding one of the many fleets of the Republic. He was an ambitious man, a good fighter, and as such twice defeated the fleet of the League of Camberi."

"It was after the last of these victories that he married the beautiful daughter of the Duke of Levano, one of the most bitter enemies of the Council of Ten. The husband being rich, famous, and still young enough to be admired for his personal attractions; the bride one of the wealthiest, as well as one of the most beautiful women in the Republic, it appeared as if all must be well with them for the remainder of their lives. A series of dazzling fetes, to which all the noblest and most distinguished of the city were invited, celebrated their nuptials and their possession of this house. Yet with it all the woman was perhaps the most unhappy individual in the universe. Unknown to her husband and her father she had long since given her love elsewhere; she was passionately attached to young Andrea Bunopelli, the man by whom the frescoes of this room were painted. Finding that Fate demanded her renunciation of Bunopelli, and her marriage to Revecce, she resolved to see no more of the man to whom she had given her heart. Love, however, proved stronger than her sense of duty, and while her husband, by order of the Senate, had put to sea once more in order to drive back the French, who were threatening the Adriatic, Bunopelli put into operation the scheme that was ultimately to prove their mutual undoing. Unfortunately for Revecce he was not successful in his venture, and by and by news reached Venice that his fleet had been destroyed, and that he himself had been taken prisoner. 'Now,' said the astute Bunopelli, 'is the time to act.' He accordingly took pens, paper, and his ink-horn, and in this very room concocted a letter which purported to bear the signature of the commander of the French forces, into whose hands the Venetian admiral had fallen and then was. Its meaning was plain enough. It proved that for a large sum of money Revecce had agreed to surrender the Venetian fleet, and, in order to secure his own safety, in case the Republic should lay hands on him afterwards, it was to be supposed that he himself had only been taken prisoner after a desperate resistance, as had really been the case. The letter was written, and that night the painter himself dropped it into the lion's mouth. Revecce might return now as soon as he pleased. His

329

fate was prepared for him. Meanwhile the guilty pair spent the time as happily as was possible under the circumstances, knowing full well, that should the man against whom they had plotted return to Venice, it would only be to find himself arrested, and with the certainty, on the evidence of the incriminating letter, of being immediately condemned to death. Weeks and months went by. At last Revecce, worn almost to a skeleton by reason of his long imprisonment, did manage to escape. In the guise of a common fisherman he returned to Venice; reached his own house, where a faithful servant recognised him and admitted him to the palace. From the latter's lips he learnt all that had transpired during his absence, and was informed of the villainous plot that had been prepared against him. His wrath knew no bounds; but with it all he was prudent. He was aware that if his presence in the city were discovered, nothing could save him from arrest. He accordingly hid himself in his own house and watched the course of events. What he saw was sufficient to confirm his worst suspicion. His wife was unfaithful to him, and her paramour was the man to whom he had been so kind a friend, and so generous a benefactor. Then when the time was ripe, assisted only by his servant, the same who had admitted him to his house, he descended upon the unhappy couple. Under threats of instant death he extorted from them a written confession of their treachery. After having made them secure, he departed for the council-chamber and demanded to be heard. He was the victim of a conspiracy, he declared, and to prove that what he said was true he produced the confession he had that day obtained. He had many powerful friends, and by their influence an immediate pardon was granted him, while permission was also given him to deal with his enemies as he might consider most desirable. He accordingly returned to this house with a scheme he was prepared to put into instant execution. It is not a pretty story, but it certainly lends an interest to this room. The painter he imprisoned here."

So saying Nikola stooped and drew back one of the rugs to which I have already referred. The square outline of a trap-door showed itself in the floor. He pressed a spring in the wall behind him, and the lid shot back, swung round, and disappeared, showing the black abyss below. A smell of damp vaults came up to us. Then, when he had closed the trap-door again, Nikola drew the carpet back to its old position.

"The wretched man died slowly of starvation in that hole, and the woman, living in this room above, was compelled to listen to his agony without being permitted the means of saving him. Can you imagine the scene? The dying wretch below, doing his best to die like a man in order not to distress the woman he loved, and the outraged husband calmly pursuing his studies, regardless of both."

He looked from one to the other of us and his eyes burnt like living coals.

"It was brutish, it was hellish," cried Glenbarth, upon whom either the story, or Nikola's manner of narrating it, had produced an extraordinary effect. "Why did the woman allow it to continue? Was she mad that she did not summon assistance? Surely the authorities of a State which prided itself upon its enlightenment, even in those dark ages, would not have tolerated such a thing?"

"You must bear in mind the fact that the Republic had given the husband permission to avenge his wrongs," said Nikola very quietly. "Besides, the woman could not cry out for the reason that her tongue had been torn out at the roots. When both were dead their bodies were tied together and thrown into the canal, and the same day Revecce set sail again, to ultimately perish in a storm off the coast of Sicily. Now you know one of the many stories connected with this old room. There are others in which that trap-door has played an equally important part. I fear, however, none of them can boast so dramatic a setting as that I have just narrated to you."

"How, knowing all this, you can live in the house passes my comprehension," gasped Glenbarth, "I don't think I am a coward, but I tell you candidly that I would not spend a night here, after what you have told me, for anything the world could give me."

"But surely you don't suppose that what happened in this room upwards of several hundred years ago could have any effect upon a living being today?" said Nikola, with what I could not help thinking was a double meaning. "Let me tell you, that far from being unpleasant it has decided advantages. As a matter of fact, it gives me the opportunity of being free to do what I like. That is my greatest safeguard. I can go away for five years, if I please, and leave the most valuable of my things lying about, and come back to the discovery that nothing is missing. I am not pestered by tourists who ask to see the frescoes, for the simple reason that the guides take very good care not to tell them the legend of the house, lest they may be called upon to take them over it. Many of the gondoliers will not stop here after nightfall, and the few who are brave enough to do so, invariably cross themselves before reaching, and after leaving it."

"I do not wonder at it," I said. "Taken altogether it is the most dismal dwelling I have ever set foot in. Do you mean to tell me that you live alone in it?"

"Not entirely," he replied. "I have companions: an old man who comes in once a day to attend to my simple wants, and my ever-faithful friend—"

"Apollyon," I cried, forestalling what he was about to say.

"Exactly, Apollyon. I am glad to see that you remember him."

He uttered a low whistle, and a moment later the great beast that I remembered so well stalked solemnly into the room, and began to rub himself against the leg of his master's chair.

"Poor old fellow," continued Nikola, picking him up and gently stroking him, "he is growing very feeble. Perhaps it is not to be wondered at, for he is already far past the average age of the feline race. He has been in many strange places, and has seen many queer things since last we met, but never anything much stranger than he has witnessed in this room."

"What do you mean?" I inquired. "What has the cat seen in this room that is so strange?"

"Objects that we are not yet permitted to see," Nikola answered gravely. "When all is quiet at night, and I am working at that table, he lies curled up in yonder chair. For a time he will sleep contentedly, then I see him lift his head and watch something, or somebody, I cannot say which, moving about in the room. At first I came to the conclusion that it must be a bat, or some night bird, but that theory exploded. Bats do not remain at the same exact distance from the floor, nor do they stand stationary behind a man's chair for any length of time. The hour will come, however, when it will be possible for us to see these things; I am on the track even now."

Had I not known Nikola, and if I had not remembered some very curious experiments he had performed for my special benefit two years before, I should have inclined to the belief that he was boasting. I knew him too well, however, to deem it possible that he would waste his time in such an idle fashion.

"Do you mean to say," I asked, "that you really think that in time it will be possible for us to see things which at present we have no notion of? That we shall be able to look into the world we have always been taught to consider Unknowable?"

"I do mean it," he replied. "And though you may scarcely believe it, it was for the sake of the information necessary to that end that I pestered Mr. Wetherall, in Sydney, imprisoned you in Port Said, and carried the lady, who is now your wife, away to the island in the South Seas."

"This is most interesting," I said, while Glenbarth drew his chair a little closer.

"Pray tell us some of your adventures since we last saw you," he put in. "You may imagine how eager we are to hear."

Thereupon Nikola furnished us with a detailed description of all that he had been through since that momentous day when he had obtained possession of the stick that had been bequeathed to Mr. Wetherall, by China Pete. He told us how, armed with this talisman, he had set out for China, where he engaged a man named Bruce, who must have been as plucky as Nikola himself, and together they started off in search of an almost unknown monastery in Tibet. He described with a wealth of exciting detail the perilous adventures they had passed through, and how near they had been to losing their lives in attempting to obtain possession of a certain curious book in which were set forth the most wonderful secrets relating to the laws of Life and Death. He told us of their hairbreadth escapes on the journey back to civilisation, and showed how they were followed to England by a mysterious Chinaman, whose undoubted mission was to avenge the robbery, and to obtain possession of the book. At this moment he paused, and I found the opportunity of asking him whether he had the book in his possession now.

"Would you care to see it?" he inquired. "If so, I will show it to you."

On our answering in the affirmative he crossed to his writing-table, unlocked a drawer, and took from it a small, curiously-bound book, the pages of which were yellow with age, and the writing so faded that it was almost impossible to decipher it.

"And now that you have plotted and planned, and suffered so much to obtain possession of this book, what use has it been to you?" I inquired, with almost a feeling of awe, for it seemed impossible that a man could have endured so much for so trifling a return.

"In dabbling with such matters," Nikola returned, "one of the first lessons one learns is not to expect immediate results. There is the collected wisdom of untold ages in that little volume, and when I have mastered the secret it contains, I shall, like the eaters of forbidden fruit, possess a knowledge of all things, Good and Evil."

Replacing the book in the drawer he continued his narrative, told us of his great attempt to probe the secret of existence, and explained to us his endeavour to put new life into a body already worn out by age.

"I was unsuccessful in what I set out to accomplish," he said; "but I advanced so far that I was able to restore the man his youth again. What I failed to do was to give him the power of thought or will. It was the brain that was too much for me—that vital part of man without which he is nothing. When I have mastered that secret I shall try again, and then, perhaps, I shall succeed. But there is much to be accomplished first. Only I know how much!"

I looked at him in amazement. Was he jesting, or did he really suppose that it was possible for him, or any other son of man, to restore youth, and by so doing to prolong life perpetually? Yet he spoke with all his usual earnestness, and seemed as convinced of the truth of what he said as if he were narrating some well-known fact. I did not know what to think. At last, seeing the bewilderment on our faces, I suppose, he smiled, and rising from his chair reminded us that if we had been bored we had only ourselves to thank for it. He accordingly changed the conversation by inquiring whether we had made any arrangements for that evening. I replied that so far as I knew we had not, whereupon he came forward with a proposition.

"In that case," said he, "if you will allow me to act as your guide to Venice, I think I could show you a side of the city you have never seen before. I know her as thoroughly as any man living, and I think I may safely promise that your party will spend an interesting couple of hours. What have you to say to my proposal?"

"I am quite sure we shall be delighted," I replied, though not without certain misgivings. "But I think I had better not decide until I have seen my wife. If she has made no other arrangements, at what hour shall we start?"

"At what time do you dine?" he inquired.

"At seven o'clock," I replied. "Perhaps we might be able to persuade you to give us the pleasure of your company?"

"I thank you," he answered. "I fear I must decline, however. I am hermit-like in my habits so far as meals are concerned. If you will allow me I will call for you, shall we say at half-past eight? The moon will have risen by that time, and we should spend a most enjoyable evening."

"At half-past eight," I said, "unless you hear to the contrary," and then rose from my chair. Glenbarth followed my example, and we accordingly bade Nikola goodbye. Despite our protest, he insisted on accompanying us down the great staircase to the courtyard below, his terrible cat following close upon his heels. Hailing a gondola, we bade the man take us back to our hotel. For some minutes after we had said goodbye to Nikola we sat in silence as the boat skimmed over the placid water.

"Well, what is your opinion of Nikola now?" I said, as we turned from the Rio del Consiglio into the Grand Canal once more. "Has he grown any more commonplace, think you, since you last saw him?"

"On the contrary, he is stranger than ever," Glenbarth replied. "I have never met any other man who resembled him in the slightest degree. What a ghastly story that was! His dramatic telling of it made it appear so real that towards the end of it I was almost convinced that I could hear the groans of the poor wretch in the pit below, and see the woman wringing her hands and moaning in the room in which we were sitting. Why he should have told it to us is what I cannot understand, neither can I make out what his reasons can be for living in that house."

"Nikola's actions are like himself, entirely inexplicable," he answered. "But that he has some motive beyond the desire he expressed for peace and quiet, I have not the shadow of a doubt."

"And now with regard to tonight," said the Duke, I am afraid a little pettishly. "I was surprised when you accepted his offer. Do you think Lady Hatteras and Miss Trevor will care about such an excursion?"

"That is a question I cannot answer at present," I replied. "We must leave it to them to decide. For my own part, I can scarcely imagine anything more interesting."

When I reached Galaghetti's we informed my wife and Miss Trevor of Nikola's offer, half expecting that the latter, from the manner in which she had behaved at the mere mention of his name that morning, would decline to accompany us, and, therefore, that the excursion would fall through. To my surprise, however, she did nothing of the kind. She fell in with the idea at once, and, so far as we could see, without reluctance of any kind.

There was nothing for it, therefore, under these circumstances, but for me to fall back upon the old commonplace, and declare that women are difficult creatures to understand.

Chapter 3

In the previous chapter I recorded the surprise I felt at Miss Trevor's acceptance of Doctor Nikola's invitation to a gondola excursion. Almost as suddenly as she had shown her fear of him, she had recovered her tranquillity, and the result, as I have stated, was complete perplexity on my part. With a united desire to reserve our energies for the evening, we did not arrange a long excursion for that afternoon, but contented ourselves with a visit to the church of SS. Giovanni e Paolo. Miss Trevor was quite recovered by this time, and in very good spirits. She and Glenbarth were on the most friendly terms, consequently my wife was a most happy woman.

"Isn't it nice to see them together?" she whispered, as we crossed the hall and went down the steps to our gondola. "They are suited to each other almost as—well, if I really wanted to pay you a compliment, which you don't deserve, I should say as we are! Do you notice how prettily she gives him her hand so that he can help her into the boat?"

"I do," I answered grimly. "And it only shows the wickedness of the girl. She is as capable of getting into the boat without assistance as he is."

"And yet you yourself help her every time you get the chance," my wife retorted. "I have observed you take the greatest care that she should not fall, even when the step has been one of only a few inches, and I have been left to get down by myself. Perhaps you cannot recall that day at Capri?"

"I have the happiest recollections of it," I replied. "I helped her quite half a dozen times."

"And yet you grudge that poor boy the opportunities that you yourself were once eager to enjoy. You cannot deny it."

"I am not going to attempt to deny it," I returned. "I do grudge him his chances. And why shouldn't I? Has she not the second prettiest hands, and the second neatest ankle, in all Europe?"

My wife looked up at me with a suspicion of a smile hovering around her mouth. When she does that her dimples are charming.

"And the neatest?" she inquired, as if she had not guessed. Women can do that sort of thing with excellent effect.

"Lady Hatteras, may I help you into the gondola?" I said politely, and for some reason, best known to herself, the reply appeared to satisfy her.

Of one thing there could be no sort of doubt. Miss Trevor had taken a decided liking to Glenbarth, and the young fellow's delight in her company was more than equal to it. By my wife's orders I left them together as much as possible during the afternoon, that is to say as far as was consistent with the duties of an observant chaperon. For instance, while we were in the right aisle of the church, examining the mauso-leum of the Doge, Pietro Mocenningo, and the statues of Lombardi, they were in the choir proper, before the famous tomb of Andrea Ven-dramin, considered by many to be the finest of its kind in Venice. As we entered the choir, they departed into the left transept. I fancy, however, Glenbarth must have been a little chagrined when she, playing her hand according to the recognised rules, suggested that they should turn back in search of us. Back they came accordingly, to be received by my wife with a speech that still further revealed to me the duplicity of women.

"You are two naughty children," she said, with fairly simulated wrath. "Where on earth have you been? We have been looking for you everywhere!"

"You are so slow," put in Miss Trevor, and then she added, without a quaver in her voice or a blush upon her cheek, "We dawdled about in order to let you catch us up."

I thought it was time for me to interfere.

"Perhaps I should remind you young people that at the present moment you are in a church," I said. "Would it not be as well, do you think, for you to preserve those pretty little prevarications until you are in the gondola? You will be able to quarrel in greater comfort there. It will also give Phyllis time to collect her thoughts, and to pre-pare a new indictment."

My wife treated me to a look that would have annihilated another man. After that I washed my hands of them and turned to the copy of Tit-ian's Martyrdom of Saint Peter, which Victor Emmanuel had presented to the church in place of the original, which had been destroyed. Later on we made our way, by a long series of tortuous thoroughfares, to the piazza of Saint Mark, where we intended to sit in front of Florian's cafe and watch the people until it was time for us to return and dress for dinner.

As I have already said, Miss Trevor had all the afternoon been in the best of spirits. Nothing could have been happier than her demeanour when we left the church, yet when we reached the piazza everything was changed. Apparently she was not really unhappy, nor did she look about her in the frightened way that had struck me so unpleasantly on the previous evening. It was only her manner that was strange. At first she was silent, then, as if she were afraid we might notice it, she set herself to talk as if she were doing it for mere talking's sake. Then, without any apparent reason, she became as silent as a mouse once more. Remembering what had happened that morning before breakfast, I did not question her, nor did I attempt to rally her upon the subject. To have done either would have been to have risked a recurrence of the catastrophe we had so narrowly escaped earlier in the day. I accordingly left her alone, and my wife, in the hope of distracting her attention, entered upon an amusing argument with Glenbarth upon the evils attendant upon excessive smoking, which was the young man's one, and, so far as I knew, only failing. Unable to combat her assertions he appealed to me for protection.

"Take my part, there's a good fellow," he said pathetically. "I am not strong enough to stand against Lady Hatteras alone."

"No," I returned; "you must fight your own battles. When I see a chance of having a little peace I like to grasp it. I am going to take Miss Trevor to Maya's shop on the other side of the piazza, in search of new photographs. We will leave you to quarrel in comfort here."

So saying Miss Trevor and I left them and made our way to the famous shop, where I purchased for her a number of photographs, of which she had expressed her admiration a few days before. After that we rejoined my wife and Glenbarth and returned to our hotel for dinner.

Nikola, as you may remember, had arranged to call for us with his gondola at half-past eight, and ten minutes before that time I suggested that the ladies should prepare themselves for the excursion. I bade them wrap up well for I knew by experience that it is seldom warm upon the water at night. When they had left us the Duke and I strolled into the balcony.

"I hope to goodness Nikola won't frighten Miss Trevor this evening," said my companion, after we had been there a few moments. (I noticed that he spoke with an anxiety that was by no means usual with him.) "She is awfully sensitive, you know, and when he likes he can curdle the very marrow in your bones. I shouldn't have liked her to have heard that story he told us this morning. I suppose there is no fear of his repeating it tonight?"

"I should not think so," I returned. "Nikola has more tact in his little finger than you or I have in our whole bodies. He would be scarcely likely to make such a mistake. No, I rather fancy that tonight we shall see a new side of his character. For my own part I am prepared to confess that I am looking forward to the excursion with a good deal of pleasure."

"I am glad to hear it," Glenbarth replied, as I thought with a savour of sarcasm in his voice. "I only hope you won't have reason to regret it."

This little speech set me thinking. Was it possible that Glenbarth was jealous of Nikola? Surely he could not be foolish enough for that. That Miss Trevor had made an impression upon him was apparent, but it was full early for him to grow jealous, and particularly of such a man.

While I was thinking of this the ladies entered the room, and at the same moment we heard Nikola's gondola draw up at the steps. I thought Miss Trevor looked a little pale, but though still very quiet she was more cheerful than she had been before dinner.

"Our guide has arrived," I remarked, as I closed the windows behind us. "We had better go down to the hall. Miss Trevor, if you will accompany me, the Duke will bring Phyllis. We must not keep Nikola waiting."

We accordingly left our apartments and proceeded downstairs.

"I trust you are looking forward to your excursion, Miss Trevor?" I said as we descended the stairs. "If I am not mistaken you will see Venice tonight under circumstances such as you could never have dreamed of before."

"I do not doubt it," she answered simply. "It will be a night to remember."

Little did she guess how true her prophecy was destined to be. It was indeed a night that every member of the party would remember all his, or her, life long. When we had reached the hall, Nikola had just entered it, and was in the act of sending up a servant to announce his arrival. He shook hands with my wife, with Miss Trevor, afterwards with Glenbarth and myself. His hand was, as usual, as cold as ice and his face was deathly pale. His tall, lithe figure was concealed by his voluminous coat, but what was lost in one direction was compensated for by the mystery that it imparted to his personality. For same reason I thought of Mephistopheles as I looked at him, and in many ways the illustration does not seem an altogether inapt one.

"Permit me to express the gratification I feel that you have consented to allow me to be your guide this evening, Lady Hatteras," he said as he conducted my wife towards the boat. "While it is an impertinence on my part to imagine that I can add to your enjoyment of

Venice, I fancy it is, nevertheless, in my power to show you a side of the city with which you are not as yet acquainted. The night being so beautiful, and believing that you would wish to see all you can, I have brought a gondola without a cabin. I trust I did not do wrong."

"I am sure it will be delightful," my wife answered. "It would have been unendurable on such a beautiful evening to be cooped up in a close cabin. Besides, we should have seen nothing."

By this time we were on the steps, at the foot of which the gondola in question, a large one of its class, was lying. As soon as we had boarded her the gondolier bent to his oar the boat shot out into the stream, and the excursion, which, as I have said, we were each of us to remember all our lives, had commenced. If I shut my eyes now I can recall the whole scene: the still moonlit waters of the canal, the houses on one side of which were brilliantly illuminated by the moon, the other being entirely in the shadow. Where we were in mid stream a boat decorated with lanterns passed us. It contained a merry party, whose progress was enlivened by the strains of the invariable *Finiculi Finicula*. The words and the tune ring in my memory even now. Years before we had grown heartily sick of the song; now, however, it possessed a charm that was quite its own.

"How pretty it is," remarked my wife and Miss Trevor almost simultaneously. And the former added, "I could never have believed that it possessed such a wealth of tenderness."

"Might it not be the association that is responsible?" put in Nikola gravely. "You have probably heard that song at some time when you have been so happy that all the world has seemed the same. Hearing it tonight has unconsciously recalled that association, and *Finiculi Finicula*, once so despised, immediately becomes a melody that touches your heart strings and so wins for itself a place in your regard that it can never altogether lose."

We had crossed the canal by this time; the gondola with the singers proceeding towards the Rialto bridge. The echo of the music still lingered in our ears, and seemed the sweeter by reason of the distance that separated us from it. Turning to the gondolier, who in the moonlight presented a picturesque figure in the stern of the boat, Nikola said something in Italian. The boat's head was immediately turned in the direction of a side-street, and a moment later we entered it. It is not my intention, nor would it be possible for me, to attempt to furnish you with a definite description of the route we followed. In the daytime I flatter myself that I have a knowledge of the Venice of a tourist; if you were to give me a pencil and paper I believe I would be able to draw a rough outline of the city, and to place St. Mark's Cathedral, Galaghetti's Hotel, the Rialto bridge, the Arsenal, and certainly the railway station, in something like their proper positions. But at night, when I have left the Grand Canal, the city becomes a sealed book to me. On this particular evening, every street when once we had left the fashionable quarter behind us, seemed alike. There was the same darkness, the same silence, and the same reflection of the lights in the water. Occasionally we happened upon places where business was still being transacted, and where the noise of voices smote the air with a vehemence that was like sacrilege. A few moments would then elapse, and then we were plunged into a silence that was almost unearthly. All this time Nikola kept us continually interested. Here was a house with a history as old as Venice itself; there the home of a famous painter; yonder the birthplace of a poet or a soldier, who had fought his way to fame by pen or by sword. On one side of the street was the first dwelling of one who had been a plebeian and had died a Doge; while on the other side was that of a man who had given his life to save his friend. Nor were Nikola's illustrations confined to the past alone. Men whose names were household words to us had preceded us, and had seen Venice as we were seeing it now. Of each he could tell us something we had never heard before. It was the perfect mastery of his subject, like that of a man who plays upon an instrument of which he has made a lifelong study, that astonished us. He could rouse in our hearts such emotions as he pleased; could induce us to pity at one moment, and to loathing at the next; could make us see the city with his eyes, and in a measure to love it with his own love. That Nikola did entertain a deep affection for it was as certain as his knowledge of its history.

"I think I may say now," he said, when we had been absent from the hotel for upwards of an hour, "that I have furnished you with a superficial idea of the city. Let me attempt after this to show you something of its inner life. That it will repay you I think you will admit when you have seen it."

Once more he gave the gondolier an order. Without a word the man entered a narrow street on the right, then turned to the left, after which to the right again. What were we going to see next? That it would be something interesting I had not the least doubt. Presently, the gondolier made an indescribable movement with his oar, the first signal that he was about to stop. With two strokes he brought the boat alongside the steps, and Nikola, who was the first to spring out, assisted the ladies to alight. We were now in a portion of Venice with which I was entirely unacquainted. The houses were old and lofty though sadly fallen to decay. Where shops existed business was still being carried on, but the majority of the owners of the houses in the neighbourhood appeared to be early birds, for no lights were visible in their dwellings. Once or twice men approached us and stared insolently at the ladies of our party. One of these, more impertinent than his companions, placed his hand upon Miss Trevor's arm. In a second, without any apparent effort, Nikola had laid him upon his back.

"Do not be afraid, Miss Trevor," he said; "the fellow has only forgotten himself for a moment."

So saying he approached the man, who scrambled to his feet, and addressed him in a low voice.

"No, no, your Excellency," the rascal whined; "for the pity of the blessed saints. Had I known it was you I would not have dared."

Nikola said something in a whisper to him; what it was I have not the least idea, but its effect was certainly excellent, for the man slunk away without another word.

After this little incident we continued our walk without further opposition, took several turnings, and at last found ourselves standing before a low doorway. That it was closely barred on the inside was evident from the sounds that followed when, in response to Nikola's knocks, some one commenced to open it. Presently an old man looked out. At first he seemed surprised to see us, but when his eyes fell upon Nikola all was changed. With a low bow he invited him, in Russian, to enter.

Crossing the threshold we found ourselves in a church of the smallest possible description. By the dim light a priest could be seen officiating at the high altar, and there were possibly a dozen worshippers present. There was an air of secrecy about it all, the light, the voices, and the precautions taken to prevent a stranger entering, that appealed to my curiosity. As we turned to leave the building the little man who had admitted us crept up to Nikola's side and said something in a low voice to him. Nikola replied, and at the same time patted the man affectionately upon the shoulder. Then with the same obsequious respect the latter opened the door once more, and permitted us to pass out, quickly barring it behind us afterwards however.

"You have seen many churches during your stay in Venice, Lady Hatteras," Nikola remarked, as we made our way back towards the gondola, "I doubt very much, however, whether you have ever entered a stranger place of worship than that."

"I know that I have not," my wife replied. "Pray who were the people we saw there? And why was so much secrecy observed?"

"Because nearly all the poor souls you saw there are either suspected or wanted by the Russian Government. They are fugitives from injustice, if I may so express it, and it is for that reason that they are compelled to worship, as well as live, in hiding."

"But who are they?"

"Nihilists," Nikola answered. "A poor, hot-headed lot of people, who, seeing their country drifting in a wrong direction, have taken it into their heads to try and remedy matters by drastic measures. Finding their efforts hopeless, their properties confiscated, and they themselves in danger of death, or exile, which is worse, they have fled from Russia. Some of them, the richest, manage to get to England, some come to Venice, but knowing that the Italian police will turn them out *sans ceremonie* if they discover them, they are compelled to remain in hiding until they are in a position to proceed elsewhere."

"And you help them?" asked Miss Trevor in a strange voice, as if his answer were a foregone conclusion.

"What makes you think that?" Nikola inquired.

"Because the doorkeeper knew you, and you spoke so kindly to him."

"The poor fellow has a son," Nikola replied; "a hot-headed young rascal who has got into trouble in Moscow. If he is caught he will without doubt go to Siberia for the rest of his life. But he will not be caught."

Once more Miss Trevor spoke as if with authority and in the same hushed voice.

"You have saved him?"

"He has been saved," Nikola replied. "He left for America this morning. The old fellow was merely expressing to me the gratification he felt at having got him out of such a difficulty. Now, here is our gondola. Let us get into it. We still have much to see, and time is not standing still with us."

Once more we took our places, and once more the gondola proceeded on its way. To furnish you with a complete resume of all we saw would take too long, and would occupy too great a space. Let it suffice that we visited places, the mere existence of which I had never heard of before.

One thing impressed me throughout. Wherever we went Nikola was known, and not only known, but feared and respected. His face was a key that opened every lock, and in his company the ladies were as safe, in the roughest parts of Venice, as if they had been surrounded by a troop of soldiery. When we had seen all that he was able to show us it was nearly midnight, and time for us to be getting back to our hotel.

"I trust I have not tired you?" he said, as the ladies took their places in the gondola for the last time.

"Not in the least," both answered at once, and I fancy my wife spoke not only for herself but also for Miss Trevor when she continued, "we have spent a most delightful evening."

"You must not praise the performance until the epilogue is spoken," Nikola answered. "I have still one more item on my programme."

As he said this the gondola drew up at some steps, where a solitary figure was standing, apparently waiting for us. He wore a cloak and carried a somewhat bulky object in his hand. As soon as the boat came alongside Nikola sprang out and approached him. To our surprise he helped him into the gondola and placed him in the stern.

"Tonight, Luigi," he said, "you must sing your best for the honour of the city."

The young man replied in an undertone, and then the gondola passed down a by-street and a moment later we were back in the Grand Canal. There was not a breath of air, and the moon shone full and clear upon the placid water. Never had Venice appeared more beautiful. Away to the right was the piazza, with the Cathedral of Saint Mark; on our left were the shadows of the islands. The silence of Venice, and there is no silence in the world like it, lay upon everything. The only sound to be heard was the dripping of the water from the gondolier's oar as it rose and fell in rhythmic motion. Then the musician drew his fingers across the strings of his guitar, and after a little prelude commenced to sing. The song he had chosen was the *Salve D'amora* from Faust, surely one of the most delightful melodies that has ever occurred to the brain of a musician. Before he had sung a dozen bars we were entranced. Though not a strong tenor, his voice was one of the most perfect I have ever heard. It was of the purest quality, so rich and sweet that the greatest connoisseur could not tire of it. The beauty of the evening, the silence of the lagoon, and the perfectness of the surroundings, helped it to appeal to us as no music had ever done before. It was significant proof of the effect produced upon us, that when he ceased not one of us spoke for some moments. Our hearts were too full for words. By the time we had recovered ourselves the gondola had drawn up at the steps of the hotel, and we had disembarked. The Duke and I desired to reward the musician; Nikola, however, begged us to do nothing of the kind.

"He sings tonight to please me," he said. "It would hurt him beyond words were you to offer him any other reward." After that there was nothing more to be said, except to thank him in the best Italian we could muster for the treat he had given us.

344

"Why on earth does he not try his fortune upon the stage?" asked my wife, when we had disembarked from the gondola and had assembled on the steps. "With such a voice he might achieve a European reputation."

"Alas," answered Nikola, "he will never do that. Did you notice his infirmity?"

Phyllis replied that she had not observed anything extraordinary about him.

"The poor fellow is blind," Nikola answered very quietly. "He is a singing-bird shut up always in the dark. And now, good night. I have trespassed too long upon your time already."

He bowed low to the ladies, shook hands with the Duke and myself, and then, before we had time to thank him for the delightful evening he had given us, was in his gondola once more and out in midstream. We watched him until he had disappeared in the direction of the Rio del Consiglio, after we entered the hotel and made our way to our own sitting-room.

"I cannot say when I have enjoyed myself so much," said my wife, as we stood talking together before bidding each other good night.

"It has been delightful," said Glenbarth, whose little attack of jealousy seemed to have quite left him. "Have you enjoyed it, Hatteras?"

I said something in reply, I cannot remember what, but I recollect that, as I did so, I glanced at Miss Trevor's face. It was still very pale, but her eyes shone with extraordinary brilliance.

"I hope you have had a pleasant evening," I said to her a few moments later, when we were alone together.

"Yes, I think I can say that I have," she answered, with a far-away look upon her face. "The music was exquisite. The thought of it haunts me still."

Then, having bade me good night, she went off with my wife, leaving me to attempt to understand why she had replied as she had done.

"And what do you think of it, my friend?" I inquired of Glenbarth, when we had taken our cigars out into the balcony.

"I am extremely glad we went," he returned quickly. "There can be no doubt that you were right when you said that it would show us Nikola's character in a new light. Did you notice with what respect he was treated by everybody we met, and how anxious they were not to run the risk of offending him?"

"Of course I noticed it, and you may be sure I drew my own conclusions from it," I replied.

"And those conclusions were?"

"That Nikola's character is even more inexplicable than before."

After that we smoked in silence for some time. At last I rose and tossed what remained of my cigar over the rails into the dark waters below.

"It is getting late," I said. "Don't you think we had better bid each other good night?"

"Perhaps we had, and yet I don't feel a bit tired."

"Are you quite sure that you have had a pleasant day?"

"Quite sure," he said, with a laugh. "The only thing I regret is having heard that wretched story this morning. Do you recall the gusto with which Nikola related it?" I replied in the affirmative, and asked him his reason for referring to it now.

"Because I could not help thinking of it this evening, when his voice was so pleasant and his manner so kind. When I picture him going back to that house tonight, to that dreadful room, to sleep alone in that great building, it fairly makes me shudder. Good night, old fellow, you have treated me royally today; I could scarcely have had more sensations compressed into my waking hours if I'd been a king."

Chapter 4

After our excursion through Venice with Nikola by night, an interval of a week elapsed before we saw anything of him. During that time matters, so far as our party was concerned, progressed with the smoothness of a well-regulated clock. In my own mind I had not the shadow of a doubt that Glenbarth was head over ears in love with Gertrude Trevor. He followed her about wherever she went; seemed never to tire of paying her attention, and whenever we were alone together, endeavoured to inveigle me into a discussion of her merits. That she had faults nothing would convince him.

Whether she reciprocated his good-feeling was a matter on which, to my mind, there existed a considerable amount of doubt. Women are proverbially more secretive in these affairs than men, and if Miss Trevor entertained a warmer feeling than friendship for the young Duke, she certainly managed to conceal it admirably. More than once, I believe, my wife endeavoured to sound her upon the subject. She had to confess herself beaten, however. Miss Trevor liked the Duke of Glenbarth very much; she was quite agreed that he had not an atom of conceit in his constitution; he gave himself no airs: moreover, she was prepared to meet my wife halfway, and to say that she thought it a pity he did not marry.

No, she had never heard that there was an American millionaire girl, extremely beautiful, and accomplished beyond the average, who was pining to throw her millions and herself at his feet!

"And then," added my wife, in a tone that seemed to suggest that she considered it my fault that the matter had not been brought to a successful conclusion long since, "what do you think she said? 'Why on earth doesn't he marry this American? So many men of title do nowadays.' What do you think of that? I can tell you, Dick, I could have shaken her!"

"My dear little woman," I said in reply, "will nothing convince you that you are playing with fire? If you are not very careful you will burn your fingers. Gertrude is almost as clever as you are. She sees that you are trying to pump her, and very naturally declines to be pumped. You would feel as she does were you in her position."

"I do not know why you should say I am trying to pump her," she answered with considerable dignity. "I consider it a very uncalled-for expression."

"Well, my dear," I answered, "if you are going to attempt to improve your position by splitting straws, then I must stop."

The episode I have just described had taken place after we had retired for the night, and at a time when I am far from being at my best. My wife, on the other hand, as I have repeatedly noticed, is invariably wide awake at that hour. Moreover she has an established belief that it would be an impossibility for her to obtain any rest until she has cleared up all matters of mystery that may have attracted her attention during the day. I generally fall asleep before she is halfway through, and for this reason I am told that I lack interest in what most nearly concerns our welfare.

"One would at least imagine that you could remain awake to discuss events of so much importance to us and to those about us," I have known her say. "I have observed that you can talk about horses, hunting, and shooting, with your bachelor friends until two or three o'clock in the morning without falling asleep, but when your wife is anxious to ask your opinion about something that does not concern your amusements, then you must needs go to sleep."

"My dear," I replied, "when all is said and done we are but human. You know as well as I do, that if a man were to come to me when I had settled down for the night, and were to tell me that he knew where to lay his hand upon the finest horse in England, and where he could put me on to ten coveys of partridges within a couple of hundred yards of my own front door, that he could even tell me the winner of the Derby, I should answer him as I am now answering you."

"And your reply would be?"

I am afraid the pains I had been at to illustrate my own argument must have proved too much for me, for I was informed in the morning that I had talked a vast amount of nonsense about seeing Nikola concerning a new pigeon-trap, and had then resigned myself to the arms of Morpheus. If there should be any husbands whose experience have ran on similar lines, I should be glad to hear from them. But to return to my story.

One evening, exactly a week after Glenbarth's arrival in Venice, I was dressing for dinner when a letter was brought to me. Much to my surprise I found it was from Nikola, and in it he inquired whether it would be possible for me to spare the time to come and see him that evening. It appeared that he was anxious to discuss a certain important matter with me. I noticed, however, that he did not mention what that matter was. In a postscript he asked me, as a favour to himself, to come alone.

Having read the letter I stood for a few moments with it in my hand, wondering what I should do. I was not altogether anxious to go out that evening; on the other hand I had a strange craving to see Nikola once more. The suggestion that he desired to consult me upon, a matter of importance flattered my vanity, particularly as it was of such a nature that he did not desire the presence of a third person. "Yes," I thought, "after all, I will go." Accordingly I wrote a note to him saying that, if the hour would suit him, I hoped to be with him at half-past nine o'clock. Then I continued my dressing and presently went down to dinner.

During the progress of the meal I mentioned the fact that I had received the letter in question, and asked my friends if they would excuse me if I went round in the course of the evening to find out what it was that Nikola had to say to me. Perhaps by virtue of my early training, perhaps by natural instinct, I am a keen observer of trifles. On this occasion I noticed that from the moment I mentioned the fact of my having received a letter from Nikola, Miss Trevor ate scarcely any more dinner. Upon my mentioning his name she had looked at me with a startled expression upon her face. She said nothing, however, but I observed that her left hand, which she had a trick of keeping below the table as much as possible, was for some moments busily engaged in picking pieces from the roll beside her plate. For some reason she had suddenly grown nervous again, but why she should have done so passes my comprehension. When the ladies had retired, and we were sitting together over our wine, Glenbarth returned to the subject of my visit that evening.

"By Jove, my dear fellow," he said, "I don't envy you your excursion to that house. Don't you feel a bit nervous about it yourself?" I shook my head.

"Why should I?" I asked. "If the truth must be told I am a good deal more afraid of Nikola than I am of his house. I don't fancy on the present occasion, however, I have any reason to dread either."

"Well," said the Duke with a laugh, "if you are not home by break-fast-time tomorrow morning I shall bring the police round, and look down that trap-door. You'll take a revolver with you of course?"

"I shall do nothing of the kind," I replied. "'I am quite able to take care of myself without having recourse to fire-arms.'"

Nevertheless, when I went up to my room to change my coat, prior to leaving the house, I took a small revolver from my dressing-case and weighed it in my hand. "Shall I take it or shall I not?" was the question I asked myself. Eventually I shook my head and replaced it in its hiding-place. Then, switching off the electric light, I made for the door, only to return, re-open the dressing-case, and take out the revolver. Without further argument I slipped it into the pocket of my coat and then left the room.

A quarter of an hour later my gondolier had turned into the Rio del Consiglio, and was approaching the Palace Revecce. The house was in deep shadow, and looked very dark and lonesome. The gondolier seemed to be of the same opinion, for he was anxious to set me down, to collect his fare, and to get away again as soon as possible. Standing in the porch I rang the great bell which Nikola had pointed out to me, and which we had not observed on the morning of our first visit. It clanged and echoed somewhere in the rearmost portion of the house, intensifying the loneliness of the situation, and adding a new element of mystery to that abominable dwelling. In spite of my boast to Glenbarth I was not altogether at my ease It was one thing to pretend that I had no objection to the place when I was seated in a well-lighted room, with a glass of port at my hand, and a stalwart friend opposite; it was quite another, however, to be standing in the dark at that ancient portal, with the black water of the canal at my feet and the anticipation of that sombre room ahead. Then I heard the sound of footsteps crossing the courtyard, and a moment later Nikola himself stood before me and invited me to enter. A solitary lamp had been placed upon the coping of the wall, and its fitful light illuminated the courtyard, throwing long shadows across the pavement and making it look even drearier and more unwholesome than when I had last seen it. After we had shaken hands we made our way in silence up the great staircase, our steps echoing along the stone corridors with startling reverberations. How thankful I was at last to reach the warm, well-lit room, despite the story Nikola had told us about it, I must leave you to imagine.

"Please sit down," said Nikola, pushing a chair forward for my occupation. "It is exceedingly kind of you to have complied with my request. I trust Lady Hatteras and Miss Trevor are well?"

"Thank you, they are both well," I replied. "They both begged to be remembered to you."

Nikola bowed his thanks, and then, when he had placed a box of excellent cigars at my elbow, prepared and lighted a cigarette for himself. All this time I was occupying myself wondering why he had asked me to come to him that evening, and what the upshot of the interview was to be. Knowing him as I did, I was aware that his actions were never motiveless. Everything he did was to be accounted for by some very good reason. After he had tendered his thanks to me for coming to see him, he was silent for some minutes, for so long indeed that I began to wonder whether he had forgotten my presence. In order to attract his attention I commented upon the fact that we had not seen him for more than a week.

"I have been away," he answered, with what was plainly an attempt to pull himself together. "Business of a most important nature called me to the South of Italy, to Naples in fact, and I only returned this morning." Once more he was silent. Then leaning towards me and speaking with even greater impressiveness than he had yet done, he continued:

"Hatteras, I am going to ask you a question, and then, with your permission, I should like to tell you a story."

Not knowing what else to do I simply bowed I was more than ever convinced that Nikola was going to make use of me.

"Have you ever wondered," he began, still looking me straight in the face, and speaking with great earnestness, "what it was first made me the man I am?"

I replied to the effect that I had often wondered, but naturally had never been able to come to a satisfactory conclusion.

"Some day you shall know the history of my life," he answered, "but not just yet. There is much to be done before then. And now I am going to give you the story I promised you. You will see why I have told it to you when I have finished."

He rose from his chair and began to pace the room. I had never seen Nikola so agitated before. When he turned and faced me again his eyes shone like diamonds, while his body quivered with suppressed excitement.

"Hatteras," he went on, when he had somewhat, mastered his emotion, "I doubt very much if ever in this world's history there has been a man who has suffered more than I have done. As I said just now, the whole story I cannot tell you at present. Some day it will come in its proper place and you will know everything. In the meantime—"

He paused for a few moments and then continued abruptly:

"The story concerns a woman, a native of this city; the last of an impoverished but ancient family. She married a man many years her

351

senior, whom she did not love. When they had been married just over four years her husband died, leaving her with one child to fight the battles of the world alone. The boy was nearly three years old, a sturdy, clever little urchin, who, up to that time, had never known the meaning of the word trouble. Then there came to Venice a man, a Spaniard, as handsome as a serpent, and as cruel. After a while he made the woman believe that he loved her. She returned his affection, and in due time they were married. A month later he was appointed Governor of one of the Spanish Islands off the American coast—a post he had long been eager to obtain. When he departed to take up his position it was arranged that, as soon as all was prepared, the woman and her child should follow him. They did so, and at length reached the island and took up their abode, not at the palace, as the woman had expected, but in the native city. For the Governor feared, or pretended to fear, that, as his marriage had not been made public at first, it might compromise his position. The woman, however, who loved him, was content, for her one thought was to promote his happiness. At first the man made believe to be overjoyed at having her with him once again, then, little by little, he showed that he was tired of her. Another woman had attracted his fancy, and he had transferred his affections to her. The other heard of it. Her southern blood was roused; for though she had been poor, she was, as I have said, the descendant of one of the oldest Venetian families. As his wife she endeavoured to defend herself, then came the crushing blow, delivered with all the brutality of a savage nature.

"'You are not my wife,' he said. 'I had already a wife living when I married you.'

"She left him without another word and went away to hide her shame. Six months later the fever took her and she died. Thus the boy was left, at five years old, without a friend or protector in the world. Happily, however, a humble couple took compassion on him, and, after a time, determined to bring him up as their own. The old man was a great scholar, and had devoted all his life to the exhaustive study of the occult sciences. To educate the boy, when he grew old enough to understand, was his one delight. He was never weary of teaching him, nor did the boy ever tire of learning. It was a mutual labour of love. Seven years later saw both the lad's benefactors at rest in the little churchyard beneath the palms, and the boy himself homeless once more. But he was not destined to remain so for very long; the priest, who had buried his adopted parents, spoke to the Governor, little dreaming what he was doing, of the boy's pitiable condition. It was as if the devil had prompted him, for the Spaniard was anxious to find a playfellow for his son, a lad two years the other's junior. It struck him that the waif would fill the position admirably. He was accordingly deported to the palace to enter upon the most miserable period of his life. His likeness to his mother was unmistakable, and when he noticed it, the Governor, who had learned the secret, hated him for it, as only those hate who are conscious of their wrongdoing. From that moment his cruelty knew no bounds. The boy was powerless to defend himself. All that he could do was to loathe his oppressor with all the intensity of his fiery nature, and to pray that the day might come when he should be able to repay. To his own son the Governor was passionately attached. In his eyes the latter could do no wrong. For any of his misdeeds it was the stranger who bore the punishment. On the least excuse he was stripped and beaten like a slave. The Governor's son, knowing his power, and the other's inordinate sensitiveness, derived his chief pleasure in inventing new cruelties for him. To describe all that followed would be impossible. When nothing else would rouse him, it was easy to bring him to an ungovernable pitch of fury by insulting his mother's name, with whose history the servants had, by this time, made their master's son acquainted. Once, driven into a paroxysm of fury by the other's insults, the lad picked up a knife and rushed at his tormentor with the intention of stabbing him. His attempt, however, failed, and the boy, foaming at the mouth, was carried before the Governor. I will spare you a description of the punishment that was meted out for his offence. Let it suffice that there are times even now, when the mere thought of it is sufficient to bring—but there—why should I continue in this strain? All that I am telling you happened many years ago, but the memory remains clear and distinct, while the desire for vengeance is as keen as if it had happened but yesterday. What is more, the end is coming, as surely as the lad once hoped and prophesied it would."

Nikola paused for a moment and sank into his chair. I had never seen him so affected. His face was deathly pale, while his eyes blazed like living coals.

"What became of the boy at last?" I inquired, knowing all the while that he had been speaking of himself.

"He escaped from the island, and went out into the world. The Governor is dead; he has gone to meet the woman, or women, he has so cruelly wronged. His son has climbed the ladder of Fame, but he has never lost, as his record shows, the cruel heart he possessed as a boy. Do you remember the story of the Revolution in the Republic of Equinata?"

I shook my head.

"The Republics of South America indulge so constantly in their little amusements that it is difficult for an outsider to remember every particular one," I answered.

"Well, let me tell you about it. When the Republic of Equinata suffered from its first Revolution, this man was its President. But for his tyranny and injustice it would not have taken place. He it was who, finding that the rebellion was spreading, captured a certain town, and bade the eldest son of each of the influential families wait upon him at his headquarters on the morning following its capitulation. His excuse was that he desired them as hostages for their parents' good behaviour. As it was, however, to wreak his vengeance on the city, which had opposed him, instead of siding with him, he placed them against a wall and shot them down by the half-dozen. But he was not destined to succeed. Gradually he was driven back upon his Capital, his troops deserting day by day. Then, one night he boarded a ship that was waiting for him in the harbour, and from that moment Equinata saw him no more. It was not until some days afterwards that it was discovered that he had dispatched vast sums of money, which he had misappropriated, out of the country, ahead of him. Where he is now hiding I am the only man who knows. I have tracked him to his lair, and I am waiting—waiting—waiting—for the moment to arrive when the innocent blood that has so long cried to Heaven will be avenged. Let him look to himself when that day arrives. For as there is a God above us, he will be punished as man was never punished before."

The expression upon his face as he said this was little short of devilish; the ghastly pallor of his skin, the dark, glittering eyes, and his jet-black hair made up a picture that will never fade from my memory.

"God help his enemy if they should meet," I said to myself. Then his mood suddenly changed, and he was once more the quiet, suave Nikola to whom I had become accustomed. Every sign of passion had vanished from his face. A transformation more complete could scarcely have been imagined.

"My dear fellow," he said, without a trade of emotion in his voice, "you must really forgive me for having bored you with my long story. I cannot think what made me do so, unless it is that I have been brooding over it all day, and felt the need of a confidant. You will make an allowance for me, will you not?"

"Most willingly," I answered. "If the story you have told me concerns yourself, you have my most heartfelt sympathy. You have suffered indeed."

He stopped for a moment in his restless walk up and down the room, and eyed me carefully as if he were trying to read my thoughts.

"Suffered?" he said at last, and then paused. "Yes, I have suffered—but others have suffered more. But do not let us talk of it. I was foolish to have touched upon it, for I know by experience the effect it produces upon me."

As he spoke he crossed to the window, which he threw open. It was a glorious night, and the sound of women's voices singing reached us from the Grand Canal. On the other side of the watery highway the houses looked strangely mysterious in the weird light. At that moment I felt more drawn towards Nikola than I had ever done before. The man's loneliness, his sufferings, had a note of singular pathos for me. I forgot the injuries he had done me, and before I knew what I was doing, I had placed my hand upon his shoulder.

"Nikola," I said, "if I were to try I could not make you understand how truly sorry I am for you. The life you lead is so unlike that of any other man. You see only the worst side of human nature. Why not leave this terrible gloom? Give up these experiments upon which you are always engaged, and live only in the pure air of the commonplace everyday world. Your very surroundings—this house, for instance—are not like those of other men. Believe me, there are other things worth living for besides the science which binds you in its chains. If you could learn to love a good woman—"

"My dear Hatteras," he put in, more softly than I had ever heard him speak, "woman's love is not for me. As you say, I am lonely in the world, God knows how lonely, yet lonely I must be content to remain." Then leaning his hands upon the window-sill, he looked out upon the silent night, and I heard him mutter to himself, "Yes, lonely to the end." After that he closed the window abruptly, and turning to me asked how long we contemplated remaining in Venice.

"I cannot say yet," I answered, "the change is doing my wife so much good that I am anxious to prolong our stay. At first we thought of going to the South of France, but that idea has been abandoned, and we may be here another month."

"A month," he said to himself, as if he were reflecting upon something; then he added somewhat inconsequently, "You should be able to see a great deal of Venice in a month."

"And how long will you be here?" I asked.

He shook his head.

"It is impossible to say," he answered. "I never know my own mind for two days together. I may be here another week, or I may be here

355

a year. Somehow, I have a conviction, I cannot say why, that this will prove to be my last visit to Venice. I should be sorry never to see it again, yet what must be, must. Destiny will have its way, whatever we may say or do to the contrary."

At that moment there was the sound of a bell clanging in the courtyard below. At such an hour it had an awe-inspiring sound, and I know that I shuddered as I heard it.

"Who can it be?" said Nikola, turning towards the door. "This is somewhat late for calling hours. Will you excuse me if I go down and find out the meaning of it?"

"Do so, by all means," I answered. "I think I must be going also. It is getting late."

"No, no," he said, "stay a little longer. If it is as I suspect, I fancy I shall be able to show you something that may interest you. Endeavour to make yourself comfortable until I return. I shall not be away many minutes."

So saying, he left me, closing the door behind him. When I was alone, I lit a cigar and strolled to the window, which I opened. My worst enemy could not call me a coward, but I must confess that I derived no pleasure from being in that room alone. The memory of what lay under that oriental rug was vividly impressed upon my memory. In my mind I could smell the vaults below, and it would have required only a very small stretch of the imagination to have fancied I could hear the groans of the dying man proceeding from it. Then a feeling of curiosity came over me to see who Nikola's visitor was. By leaning well out of the window, I could look down on the great door below. At the foot of the steps a gondola was drawn up, but I was unable to see whether there was any one in it or not. Who was Nikola's mysterious caller, and what made him come at such an hour? Knowing the superstitious horror in which the house was held by the populace of Venice, I felt that whoever he was, he must have an imperative reason for his visit. I was still turning the subject over in my mind, when the door opened and Nikola entered, followed by two men. One was tall and swarthy, wore a short black beard, and had a crafty expression upon his face. The other was about middle height, very broad, and was the possessor of a bullet-head covered with close-cropped hair. Both were of the lower class, and their nationality was unmistakable. Turning to me Nikola said in English:

"It is as I expected. Now, if you care to study character, here is your opportunity. The taller man is a Police Agent, the other the chief of a notorious Secret Society. I should first explain that within the last two or three days I have been helping a young Italian of rather advanced

356

views, not to put too fine a point upon it, to leave the country for America. This dog has dared to try to upset my plans. Immediately I heard of it I sent word to him, by means of our friend, here, that he was to present himself here before twelve o'clock tonight without fail. From his action it would appear that he is more frightened of me than he is of the Secret Society. That is as it should be; for I intend to teach him a little lesson which will prevent him from interfering with my plans in the future. You were talking of my science just now, and advising me to abandon it. Could the life you offer me give me the power I possess now? Could the respectability of Clapham recompense me for the knowledge with which the East can furnish me?"

Then turning to the Police Agent he addressed him in Italian, speaking so fast that it was impossible for me to follow him. From what little I could make out, however, I gathered that he was rating him for daring to interfere with his concerns. When, at the end of three or four minutes, he paused and spoke more slowly, this was the gist of his speech:

"You know me and the power I control. You are aware that those who thwart me, or who interfere with me and my concerns, do so at their own risk. Since no harm has come of it, thanks to certain good friends, I will forgive on this occasion, but let it happen again and this is what your end will be."

As he spoke he took from his pocket a small glass bottle with a gold top, not unlike a vinaigrette, and emptied some of the white powder it contained into the palm of his hand. Turning down the lamp he dropped this into the chimney. A green flame shot up for a moment, which was succeeded by a cloud of perfumed smoke that filled the room so completely that for a moment it was impossible for us to see each other. Presently a picture shaped itself in the cloud and held my attention spellbound. Little by little it developed until I was able to make out a room, or rather I should say a vault, in which upwards of a dozen men were seated at a long table. They were all masked, and without exception were clad in long monkish robes with cowls of black cloth. Presently a sign was made by the man at the head of the table, an individual with a venerable grey beard, and two more black figures entered, who led a man between them. Their prisoner was none other than the Police Agent whom Nikola had warned. He looked thinner, however, and was evidently much frightened by his position. Once more the man at the head of the table raised his hand, and there entered at the other side an old man with white hair and a long beard of the same colour. Unlike the others he wore no cowl, nor was he masked. From his gestures I could see that he was addressing those seated at the table, and, as he pointed to the prisoner, a look of undying hatred spread over his face. Then the man at the head of the table rose, and though I could hear nothing of what he said, I gathered that he was addressing his brethren concerning the case. When he had finished, and each of the assembly had voted by holding up his hand, he turned to the prisoner. As he did so the scene vanished instantly and another took its place.

It was a small room that I looked upon now, furnished only with a bed, a table, and a chair. At the door was a man who had figured as a prisoner in the previous picture, but now sadly changed. He seemed to have shrunk to half his former size, his face was pinched by starvation, his eyes were sunken, but there was an even greater look of terror in them than had been there before. Opening the door of the room he listened, and then shut and locked it again. It was as if he were afraid to go out, and yet knew that if he remained where he was, he must perish of starvation. Gradually the room began to grow dark, and the terrified wretch paced restlessly up and down, listening at the door every now and then. Once more the picture vanished as its companion had done, and a third took its place. This proved to be a narrow street scene by moonlight. On either side the houses towered up towards the sky, and since there was no one about, it was plain that the night was far advanced. Presently, creeping along in the shadow, on the left-hand side, searching among the refuse and garbage of the street for food, came the man I had seen afraid to leave his attic. Times out of number he looked swiftly behind him, as if he thought it possible that he might be followed. He was but little more than halfway up the street, and was stooping to pick up something, when two dark figures emerged from a passage on the left, and swiftly approached him. Before he had time to defend himself, they were upon him, and a moment later he was lying stretched out upon his back in the middle of the street, a dead man. The moon shone down full and clear upon his face, the memory of which makes me shudder even now. Then the picture faded away and the loom was light once more. Instinctively I looked at the Police Agent. His usually swarthy face was deathly pale, and from the great beads of perspiration that stood upon his forehead, I gathered that he had seen the picture too.

"Now," said Nikola, addressing him, "you have seen what is in store for you if you persist in pitting yourself against me. You recognised that grey-haired man, who had appealed to the Council against you. Then, rest assured of this! So surely as you continue your present conduct, so surely will the doom I have just revealed to you overtake you. Now go, and remember what I have said."

Turning to the smaller man, Nikola placed his hand in a kindly fashion upon his shoulder.

"You have done well, Tomasso," he said, "and I am pleased with you. Drop our friend here at the usual place, and see that some one keeps an eye on him. I don't think, however, he will dare to offend again."

On hearing this, the two men left the room and descended to the courtyard together, and I could easily imagine with what delight one of them would leave the house. When they had gone, Nikola, who was standing at the window, turned to me, saying:

"What do you think of my conjuring?"

I knew not what answer to make that would satisfy him. The whole thing seemed so impossible that, had it not been for the pungent odour that still lingered in the room, I could have believed I had fallen asleep and dreamed it all.

"You can give me no explanation, then?" said Nikola, with one of his inscrutable smiles. "And yet, having accumulated this power, this knowledge, call it what you will, you would still bid me give up Science. Come, my friend, you have seen something of what I can do; would you be brave enough to try, with my help, to look into what is called The Great Unknown, and see what the future has in store for you? I fancy it could be done. Are you to be tempted to see your own end?"

"No, no," I cried, "I will have nothing to do with such an unholy thing. Good heavens, man! From that moment life would be unendurable!"

"You think so, do you?" he said slowly, still keeping his eyes fixed on me. "And yet I have tried it myself."

"My God, Nikola!" I answered in amazement, for I knew him well enough to feel sure that he was not talking idly. "You don't mean to tell me that that you know what your own end is going to be?"

"Exactly," he answered. "I have seen it all. It is not pleasant; but I think I may say without vanity that it will be an end worthy of myself."

"But now that you know it, can you not avert it?"

"Nothing can be averted," he answered solemnly. "As I said before these men entered, what must be, must. What does Schiller say? *'Noch niemand entfloh dem verhangten Geschick.'*"

"And you were brave enough to look?"

"Does it require so much bravery, do you think? Believe me, there are things which require more."

"What do you mean?"

"Ah! I cannot tell you now," he answered, shaking his head. "Some day you will know."

Then there was a silence for a few seconds, during which we both stood looking down at the moonlit water below. At last, having consulted my watch and seeing how late it was, I told him that it was time for me to bid him good night.

"I am very grateful to you for coming Hatteras," he said. "It has cheered me up. It does me good to see you. Through you I get a whiff of that other life of which you spoke a while back. I want to make you like me, and I fancy I am succeeding."

Then we left the room together, and went down the stairs to the courtyard below. Side by side we stood upon the steps waiting for a gondola to put in an appearance. It was some time before one came in sight, but when it did so I hailed it, and then shook Nikola by the hand and bade him good night.

"Good night," he answered. "Pray remember me kindly to Lady Hatteras and to—Miss Trevor."

The little pause before Miss Trevor's name caused me to look at him in some surprise. He noticed it and spoke at once.

"You may think it strange of me to say so," he said, "but I cannot help feeling interested in that young lady. Impossible though it may seem, I have a well-founded conviction that in some way her star is destined to cross mine, and before very long. I have only seen her twice in my life in the flesh; but many years ago her presence on the earth was revealed to me, and I was warned that some day we should meet. What that meeting will mean to me it is impossible to say, but in its own good time Fate will doubtless tell me. And now, once more, good night."

"Good night," I answered mechanically, for I was too much surprised by his words to think what I was saying. Then I entered the gondola and bade the man take me back to my hotel.

"Surely Nikola has taken leave of his senses," I said to myself as I was rowed along. "Gertrude Trevor was the very last person in the world that I should have expected Nikola to make such a statement about."

At this point, however, I remembered how curiously she had been affected by their first meeting, and my mind began to be troubled concerning her.

"Let us hope and pray that Nikola doesn't take it into his head to imagine himself in love with her," I continued to myself. "If he were to do so I scarcely know what the consequences would be."

Then, with a touch of the absurd, I wondered what her father, the eminently-respected dean, would say to having Nikola for a son-in-law. By the time I had reached this point in my reverie the gondola had drawn up at the steps of the hotel.

My wife and Miss Trevor had gone to bed, but Glenbarth was sitting up for me.

"Well, you have paid him a long visit, in all conscience," he said a little reproachfully. Then he added, with what was intended to be a touch of sarcasm, "I hope you have spent a pleasant evening?"

"I am not quite so certain about that," I replied.

"Indeed. Then what have you discovered?"

"One thing of importance," I answered; "that Nikola grows more and more inscrutable every day."

Chapter 5

The more I thought upon my strange visit to the Palace Revecce that evening, the more puzzled I was by it. It had so many sides, and each so complex, that I scarcely knew which presented the most curious feature. What Nikola's real reason had been for inviting me to call upon him, and why he should have told me the story, which I felt quite certain was that of his own life, was more than I could understand. Moreover, why, having told it me, he should have so suddenly requested me to think no more about it, only added to my bewilderment. The incident of the two men, and the extraordinary conjuring trick, for conjuring trick it certainly was in the real meaning of the word, he had shown us, did not help to elucidate matters. If the truth must be told it rather added to the mystery than detracted from it. To sum it all up, I found, when I endeavoured to fit the pieces of the puzzle together, remembering also his strange remark concerning Miss Trevor, that I was as far from coming to any conclusion as I had been at the beginning.

"You can have no idea how nervous I have been on your account tonight," said my wife, when I reached her room. "After dinner the Duke gave us a description of Doctor Nikola's room, and told us its history. When I thought of your being there alone with him, I must confess I felt almost inclined to send a message to you imploring you to come home."

"That would have been a great mistake, my dear," I answered. "You would have offended Nikola, and we don't want to do that. I am sorry the Duke told you that terrible story. He should not have frightened you with it. What did Gertrude Trevor think of it?"

"She did not say anything about it," my wife replied. "But I could see that she was as frightened as I was. I am quite sure you would not get either of us to go there, however pressing Doctor Nikola's invitation might be. Now tell me what he wanted to see you about."

"He felt lonely and wanted some society," I answered, having resolved that on no account would I tell her all the truth concerning my visit to the Palace Revecce. "He also wanted me to witness something connected with a scheme he has originated for enabling people to get out of the country unobserved by the police. Before I left he gave me a good example of the power he possessed."

I then described to her the arrival of the two men and the lesson Nikola had read to the Police Agent. The portion dealing with the conjuring trick I omitted. No good could have accrued from frightening her, and I knew that the sort of description I should be able to give of it would not be sufficiently impressive to enable her to see it in the light I desired. In any other way it would have struck her as ridiculous.

"The man grows more and more extraordinary every day," she said. "And not the least extraordinary thing about him is the way he affects other people. For my own part I must confess that, while I fear him, I like him; the Duke is frankly afraid of him; you are interested and repelled in turn; while Gertrude, I fancy, regards him as a sort of supernatural being, who may turn one into a horse or a dog at a moment's notice; while Senor Galaghetti, with whom I had a short conversation today concerning him, was so enthusiastic in his praises that for once words failed him. He had never met any one so wonderful, he declared. He would lay down his life for him. It would appear that, on one occasion, when Nikola was staying at the hotel, he cured Galaghetti's eldest child of diphtheria. The child was at the last gasp and the doctors had given her up, when Nikola made his appearance upon the scene. What he did, or how he did it, Galaghetti did not tell me, but it must have been something decidedly irregular, for the other doctors were aghast and left the house in a body. The child, however, rallied from that moment, and, as Galaghetti proudly informed me, 'is now de artiste of great repute upon de pianoforte in Paris.' I have never heard of her, but it would appear that Galaghetti not only attributes her life, but also her musical success, to the fact that Nikola was staying in the hotel at the time when the child was taken ill. The Duke was with me when Galaghetti told me this, and, when he heard it, he turned away with an exclamation that sounded very like 'humbug!' I do hope that Doctor Nikola and the Duke won't quarrel?" As she put this in the form of a question, I felt inclined to reply with the expression the Duke had used. I did not do so, however, but contented myself with assuring her that she need have no fears upon that score. A surprise, however, was in store for me.

"What have they to quarrel about?" I asked. "They have nothing in common."

"That only proves how blind you are to what goes on around you," my wife replied. "Have you not noticed that they both admire Gertrude Trevor?"

Falling so pat upon my own thoughts, this gave me food for serious reflection.

"How do you know that Nikola admires her?" I asked, a little sharply, I fear, for when one has uncomfortable suspicions one is not always best pleased to find that another shares them. A double suspicion might be described as almost amounting to a certainty.

"I am confident of it," she replied. "Did you not notice his manner towards her on the night of our excursion? It was most marked."

"My dear girl," I said irritably, "if you are going to begin this sort of thing, you don't know where you will find yourself in the end. Nikola has been a wanderer all his life. He has met people of every nationality, of every rank and description. It is scarcely probable, charming though I am prepared to admit she is, that he would be attracted by our friend. Besides, I had it from his own lips this morning that he will never marry."

"You may be just as certain as you please," she answered. "Nevertheless, I adhere to my opinion."

Knowing what was in my own mind, and feeling that if the argument continued I might let something slip that I should regret, I withdrew from the field, and, having questioned her concerning certain news she had received from England that day, bade her good night.

Next morning we paid a visit to the Palace of the Doges, and spent a pleasant and instructive couple of hours in the various rooms. Whatever Nikola's feelings may have been, there was by this time not the least doubt that the Duke admired Miss Trevor. Though the lad had known her for so short a time he was already head over ears in love. I think Gertrude was aware of the fact, and I feel sure that she liked him, but whether the time was not yet ripe, or her feminine instinct warned her to play her fish for a while before attempting to land him, I cannot say; at any rate, she more than once availed herself of an opportunity and moved away from him to take her place at my side. As you may suppose, Glenbarth was not rendered any the happier by these manoeuvres; indeed, by the time we left the Palace, he was as miserable a human being as could have been found in all Venice. Before lunch, however, she relented a little towards him, and when we sat down to the meal in question our friend had in some measure recovered his former spirits. Not so my wife, however; though I did not guess it, I was in for a wigging.

"How could you treat the poor fellow so badly?" she said indignantly, when we were alone together afterwards. "If you are not very careful you'll spoil everything."

"Spoil what?" I inquired, as if I did not understand to what she alluded. "You have lately developed a habit of speaking in riddles."

"Fiddle-de-dee!" she answered scornfully, "you know very well to what I allude. I think your conduct at the Palace this morning was disgraceful. You, a married man and a father, to try and spoil the pleasure of that poor young man."

"But she began it," I answered in self-defence. "Did you not see that she preferred my company to his?"

"Of course, that was only make-believe," my wife replied. "You are as well aware of that as I am."

"I know nothing of the kind," I returned. "If the girl does not know her own mind, then it is safer that she should pretend, as she did today."

"She was not pretending. You know that Gertrude Trevor is as honest as the day."

"Then you admit that she was only 'playing her fish'?" I said.

"If you are going to be vulgar I shall leave you," she retorted; "I don't know what you mean by 'playing her fish.' Gertrude only came to you because she did not want her liking for the Duke to appear too conspicuous."

"It's the, same thing in the end," I answered. "Believe me, it is! You describe it as not making her conduct appear, too conspicuous, while I call it 'playing her fish.' I have the best possible recollection of a young lady who used to play quoits with me on the deck of the *Orotava* a good many years ago. One day—we were approaching Naples at the time—she played game after game with the doctor, and snubbed me unmercifully."

"You know very well that I didn't mean it," she answered with a stamp of her foot. "You know I had to act as I did."

"I don't mind admitting that," I replied. "Nevertheless, you were playing your fish. That night after dinner you forgave me and—"

She slipped her arm through mine and gave it a hug. I could afford to be generous.

"Those were dear old days, were they not? I, for one, am not going to quarrel about them. Now let us go and find the others."

We discovered them in the balcony, listening to some musicians in

365

a gondola below. Miss Trevor plainly hailed our coming with delight; the Duke, however, was by no means so well pleased. He did his best, however, to conceal his chagrin. Going to the edge of the balcony I looked down at the boat. The musicians were four in number, two men and two girls, and, at the moment of our putting in an appearance, one of them was singing the *Ave Maria* from the *Cavalleria Rusticana*, in a manner that I had seldom heard it sung before. She was a handsome girl, and knew the value of her good looks. Beside her stood a man with a guitar, and I gave a start as I looked at him. Did my eyes deceive me, or was this the man who had accompanied the Police Agent to Nikola's residence on the previous evening? I looked again and felt sure that I could not be mistaken. He possessed the same bullet-head with the close-cropped hair, the same clean-shaven face, and the same peculiarly square shoulders. No! I felt sure that he was the man. But if so, what was he doing here under our windows? One thing was quite apparent; if he recognised me, he did not give me evidence of the fact. He played and looked up at us without the slightest sign of recognition. To all intents and purposes he was the picture of indifference. While they were performing I recalled the scene of the previous night, and wondered what had become of the police officer, and what the man below me had thought of the curious trick Nikola had performed? It was only when they had finished their entertainment and, having received our reward, were about to move away, that I received any information to the effect that the man had recognised me.

"Illustrious *Senora, Senorita*, and *Senors*, I thank you," he said, politely lifting his hat as he spoke. "Our performance has been successful, and the obstacle which threatened it at one time has been removed."

The gondola then passed on, and I turned to the Duke as if for an explanation.

"At first the hall-porter was not inclined to let them sing here," the Duke remarked, "but Miss Trevor wanted to hear them, so I sent word down that I wished them to remain."

In spite of the explanation I understood to what the man had referred, but for the life of me I could not arrive at his reason for visiting our hotel that day. I argued that it might have been all a matter of chance, but I soon put that idea aside as absurd. The coincidence was too remarkable.

At lunch my wife announced that she had heard that morning that Lady Beltringham, the wife of our neighbour in the Forest, was in Venice, and staying at a certain hotel further along the Grand Canal.

"Gertrude and I are going to call upon her this afternoon," she said, "so that you two gentlemen must amuse yourselves as best you can without us."

"That is very easily done," I answered; "the Duke is going to have his hair cut, and I am going to witness the atrocity. You may expect to see him return not unlike that man with the guitar in the boat this morning."

"By the way," said Glenbarth, "that reminds me that I was going to point but a curious thing to you concerning that man. Did you notice, Miss Trevor, that when we were alone together in the balcony he did not once touch his instrument, but directly Hatteras and Lady Hatteras arrived, he jumped up and began to play?"

This confirmed my suspicions. I had quite come to the conclusion by this time that the man had only made his appearance before the hotel in order to be certain of my address. Yet, I had to ask myself, if he were in Nikola's employ, why should he have been anxious to do so?

An hour later the ladies departed on their polite errand, and the Duke and I were left together. He was not what I should call a good companion. He was in an irritable mood, and nothing I could do or say seemed to comfort him. I knew very well what was the matter, and when we had exhausted English politics, the rise and fall of Venice, Ruskin, and the advantages of foreign travel, I mentioned incidentally the name of Miss Trevor. The frown vanished from his face, and he answered like a coherent mortal.

"Look here, Hatteras," he said, with a fine burst of confidence, "you and I have been friends for a good many years, and I think we know each other about as well as two men can do."

"That is so," I answered, wondering what he was driving at; "we have been through some strange adventures together, and should certainly know each other. I hope that you are riot going to propose that we should depart on some harum-scarum expedition like that you wanted me to join you in last year, to the Pamirs, was it not? If so, I can tell you once and for all that my lady won't hear of it."

"Confound the Pamirs!" he replied angrily. "Is it likely that I should think of going there just now? You misunderstand my meaning entirely. What I want is a sympathetic friend, who can enter into my troubles, and if possible help me out of them."

For the life of me I could not forbear from teasing him for a little longer.

"My dear old fellow," I said, "you know that I will do anything I possibly can to help you. Take my advice and get rid of the man at once. As I told you in my letter to you before I left England, it is only misplaced kindness to keep him on. You know very well that he has been unfaithful to you for some years past. Then why allow him to continue his wrong-doing? The smash will come sooner or later."

"What do you mean?" he asked.

"Well, I suppose your trouble is connected with the agent you were telling me of yesterday. The man who, it was discovered, had been cooking the accounts, selling your game, pocketing the proceeds, and generally feathering his own nest at your expense."

An ominous frown gathered upon my friend's forehead.

"Upon my word," he said, "I really believe you are taking leave of your senses. Do you think I am bothering myself at such a time about that wretched Mitchell? Let him sell every beast upon the farms, every head of game, and, in point of fact, let him swindle me as much as he likes, and I wouldn't give a second thought to him."

"I am very sorry," I answered penitently, rolling the leaf of my cigar. "Then it was the yacht you were thinking about? You have had what I consider a very good offer for her. Let her go! You are rich enough to be able to build another, and the work will amuse you. You want employment of some sort."

"I am not thinking of the yacht either," he growled. "You know that as well as I do."

"How should I know it?" I answered. "I am not able to tell what is in your mind. I do not happen to be like Nikola."

"You are singularly obtuse today," he asserted, throwing what remained of his cigar into the canal and taking another from his case.

"Look here," I said, "you're pitching into me because I can't appreciate your position. Now how am I likely to be able to do so, considering that you've told me nothing about it? Before we left London you informed me that the place you had purchased in Warwickshire was going to prove your chief worry in life. I said, 'sell it again.' Then you found that your agent in Yorkshire was not what he might be. I advised you to get rid of him. You would not do so because of his family. Then you confessed in a most lugubrious fashion that your yacht was practically becoming unseaworthy by reason of her age. I suggested that you should sell her to Deeside, who likes her, or part with her for a junk. You vowed you would not do so because she was a favourite. Now you are unhappy, and I naturally suppose that it must be one of those things which is causing you uneasiness. You scoff at the idea. What, therefore, am I to believe? Upon my word, my friend, if I did not remember that you have always declared your abhorrence of the sex, I should begin to think you must be in love."

He looked at me out of the corner of his eye. I pretended not to notice it, however, and still rolled the leaf of my cigar.

"Would it be such a very mad thing if I did fall in love?" he asked at last. "My father did so before me, and I believe my grandfather did also. You, yourself, committed the same indiscretion."

"And you have seen the miserable result?"

"I have observed one of the happiest couples in the world," he replied. "But, joking apart, Hatteras, I want to talk the matter over with you seriously. I don't mind telling you at once, as between friend and friend, that I want to marry Miss Trevor."

I endeavoured to look surprised, but I fear the attempt was a failure.

"May I remind you," I said, "that you have known her barely a week? I don't want to discourage you, but is not your affection of rather quick growth?"

"It is but it does not mean that I am any the less sincere. I tell you candidly, Dick, I have never seen such a girl in my life. She would make any man happy."

"Very likely, but would any man make her happy?"

His face fell, and he shifted uneasily in his chair.

"Confound you," he said, "you put everything in a new light. Why should I not be able to make her happy? There are lots of women who would give their lives to be a duchess!"

"I admit that," I answered. "I don't fancy, however, your rank will make much difference to Miss Trevor. When a woman is a lady, and in love, she doesn't mind very much whether the object of her affections is a duke or a chimneysweep. Don't make the mistake of believing that a dukedom counts for everything where the heart is concerned. We outsiders should have no chance at all if that were the case."

"But, Hatteras," he said, "I didn't mean that. I'm not such a cad as to imagine that Miss Trevor would marry me simply because I happen to have a handle to my name. I want to put the matter plainly before you. I have told you that I love her, do you think there is any chance of her taking a liking to me?"

"Now that you have told me what is in your mind," I answered, "I can safely state my opinion. Mind you, I know nothing about the young lady's ideas, but if I were a young woman, and an exceedingly presentable young man—you may thank me for the compliment afterwards—were to lay his heart at my feet, especially when that heart is served up in strawberry leaves and five-pound notes, I fancy I should be inclined to think twice before I discouraged his advances. Whether Miss Trevor will do so, is quite another matter."

"Then you are not able to give me any encouragement?"

"I wish you God-speed upon your enterprise," I said, "if that is any satisfaction to you. I cannot do more."

As I said it I held out my hand, which he took and shook.

"God bless you, old man," he said, "you don't know what all this means to me. I've suffered agonies these last two days. I believe I should go mad if it continued. Yesterday she was kindness itself. Today she will scarcely speak to me. I believe Lady Hatteras takes my side?"

I was not to be caught napping.

"You must remember that Lady Hatteras herself is an impressionable young woman," I answered. "She likes you and believes in you, and because she does she thinks her friend ought to do so also. Now look here, your Grace—"

"You needn't put on any side of that kind," he answered reproachfully.

"I believe I am talking to the Duke of Glenbarth," I returned.

"You are talking to your old friend, the man who went round the world with you, if that's what you mean," he answered. "What is it you have to say?"

"I want you to plainly understand that Miss Trevor is my guest. I want you also to try to realise, however difficult it may be, that you have only known her a very short time. She is a particularly nice girl, as you yourself have admitted. It would be scarcely fair, therefore, if I were to permit you to give her the impression that you were in love with her until you have really made up your mind. Think it well over. Take another week, or shall we say a fortnight? A month would be better still."

He groaned in despair.

"You might as well say a year while you are about it. What is the use of my waiting even a week when I know your mind already?"

"Because you must give your affection time to set. Take a week. If at the end of that time you are still as much in earnest as you are now, well, the matter will be worth thinking about. You can then speak to the young lady or not, as you please. On the other hand, should your opinion have changed, then I have been your only confidant, and no harm has been done. If she accepts you, I can honestly say that no one will be more delighted than myself. If not, you must look elsewhere, and then she must marry the man she likes better. Do you agree?"

"As I can't help myself I suppose I must," he answered. "But my position during the next week is not likely to be a very cheerful one."

"I don't at all see why," I replied. "Lots of others have been compelled to do their courting under harder auspices. Myself, for instance.

Here you are staying in the same house as the object of your affections. You meet her almost every hour of the day; you have innumerable opportunities of paying your court to her, and yet with all these advantages you abuse your lot."

"I know I am an ungrateful beast," he said. "But, by Jove, Dick, when one is as much in love as I am, and with the most adorable woman in the world, and matters don't seem to go right, one ought to be excused if one feels inclined to quarrel with somebody."

"Quarrel away with all your heart," I answered. "And now I am going down with you to the hairdresser. After that we'll go to the piazza."

"I suppose I must," he said, rising from his chair with a fine air of resignation. "Though what fun you can discover in that crowd I cannot for the life of me imagine."

I did not remind him that on the previous afternoon he had declared it to be the most amusing sight in Europe. That would have been an unfair advantage to have taken, particularly as I had punished him enough already. We accordingly procured our hats and sticks, and having secured a gondola, set off. It was a lovely afternoon, and the Grand Canal was crowded. As we passed the entrance to the Rio del Consiglio, I stole a glance at the Palace Revecce. No gondola was at the door, so whether Nikola was at home or aboard I could not say. When Glenbarth had been operated upon we proceeded to the piazza of Saint Mark, which we reached somewhat before the usual afternoon promenade. The band had not commenced to play, and the idlers were few in number. Having engaged two chairs at one of the tables, we sat down and ordered coffee. The duke was plainly ill at ease. He fretted and fidgeted continually. His eyes scarcely wandered from the steps of the lagoon, and every gondola that drew up received his scrutinising attention. When at last two ladies disembarked and made their way across the stones towards Florian's cafe, where we were seated, I thought he would have made an exhibition of himself.

Lady Beltringham, it would appear, had arrived, but was so fatigued by her long journey that she was unable to receive visitors.

"We returned almost immediately to the hotel," said my wife reproachfully. "We thought you would have waited for us there."

Glenbarth looked at me as if nothing I could ever do would make up for the enormity of my offence. He then described to Miss Trevor some wonderful photographs he had discovered that morning in a certain shop on the other side of the piazza. She questioned him concerning them, and I suggested that they should go and overhaul them. This they did, and when they had departed my wife produced some letters for me she had taken from the rack at the hotel. I looked at the writing upon the envelope of the first, but for a moment could not recall where I had seen it before. Then I opened it and withdrew the contents. "Why, it's from George Anstruther," I exclaimed when I had examined the signature. "He is in Algiers."

"But what is the letter about?" my wife said. "You have not heard from him for so long."

"I'll read it," I said, and began as follows:

"My dear Hatteras,

"Here I am in the most charming place on the whole Mediterranean, and I ought to know, for I've seen and loathed all the others. My villa overlooks the sea, and my yacht rides at anchor in the bay. There are many nice people here, and not the least pleasant is my very good friend, Don Jose de Martinos, who is leaving today for his first visit to Venice, via Nice, and I understand from him that he is to stay at your hotel. He is a delightful creature; has seen much of the world, and if you will admit him to the circle of your acquaintance, I don't think you will regret it. I need not bore either myself or you by repeating the hackneyed phrase to the effect that any civility you show him will be considered a kindness to myself, etc., etc. Remember me most kindly to Lady Hatteras and,

"Believe me to be, Ever sincerely yours,

"George Anstruther."

My wife uttered a little cry of vexation. "Pleasant though he may prove, I cannot help saying that I am sorry Don Jose Martinos is coming," she said. "Our little party of four was so happily arranged, and who knows but that a fifth may upset its peace altogether?"

"But he is Anstruther's friend," I said in expostulation. "One must be civil to one's friends' friends."

"I do not at all see why," she answered. "Because we like Mr. Anstruther it does not follow that we shall like his friend."

At that moment the young couple were to be observed crossing the piazza in our direction. Glenbarth carried a parcel under his arm.

"I don't think there is much doubt about that affair," said my wife, approvingly.

"Don't be too sure," I answered. "There is many a slip 'twixt the cup and the lip, and there is another old saying to the effect that those who live longest see most."

One is sometimes oracular even in jest.

Chapter 6

On the following day, having sent my servant to inquire, I was informed that the Don Jose de Martinos had arrived at the hotel, and had engaged rooms on the floor above our own. Accordingly, after luncheon I ascended to the rooms in question, and asked whether he would receive me. I had scarcely waited more than a minute before he made his appearance. He paused on the threshold to give an order to his man, and while he did so, I was permitted an opportunity of taking stock of him. He was a tall, muscular man of between thirty-five and forty years of age. His appearance did not betray so much of his Spanish origin as I had expected. Indeed, it would have been difficult to have given him a nationality. I noticed that his beard, which he wore closely clipped, was not innocent of the touch of Time. His face was a powerful one, but at first glance I was not altogether prepossessed in its favour. His hands and feet were small, the former particularly so for a man of his size and build. Moreover, he was faultlessly dressed, and carried himself with the air of a man of the world and of good breeding.

"Sir Richard Hatteras," he said, as he crossed the room to greet me, "this is kind of you indeed. My friend, Anstruther, informed me that you were in Venice, and was good enough to take upon himself the responsibility of introducing me to you."

His voice was strong and musical, and he pronounced every word (he spoke excellent English) as if it had a value of its own. I inquired after Anstruther's health, which for some time past had been precarious, and it was with satisfaction that I learnt of the improvement that had taken place in it.

"You would scarcely know him now," said Martinos. "He looks quite strong again. But permit me to offer you a cigar. We Spaniards say that we cannot talk unless we smoke; you English that you cannot smoke if you talk."

As he said this he handed me a box of cigars.

"I fancy you will like them," he said. "The tobacco was grown upon my own estate in Cuba; for that reason I can guarantee their purity."

The weed I selected was excellent, in fact one of the best cigars I had ever smoked. While he was lighting his I stole another glance at him. Decidedly he was a handsome man, but—here was the stumbling-block—there was something, I cannot say what, about him that I did not altogether like. It was not a crafty face, far from it. The eyes were well placed; the mouth from what one could see of it under his black moustache, was well moulded, with white, even teeth; the nose was slightly aquiline; and the chin large, firm, and square. Nevertheless, there was something about it that did not suit my fancy. Once I told myself it was a cruel face, yet the singularly winning smile that followed a remark of mine a moment later went some way towards disabusing my mind upon that point.

"Lady Hatteras, I understood from Senor Anstruther, is with you," he said, after we had talked of other things.

"She is downstairs at this moment," I answered. "We are a party of four—Miss Trevor (the daughter of the Dean of Bedminster), the Duke of Glenbarth, my wife, and myself. I hope you will permit me the pleasure of introducing you to them at an early date."

"I shall be most happy," he replied. "I am particularly fond of Venice, but, when all is said and done, one must have companions to enjoy it thoroughly."

I had been given to understand that this was his first visit to the Queen of the Adriatic, but I did not comment upon the fact.

"One is inclined to believe that Adam would have enjoyed the Garden of Eden if it had not been for Eve," I remarked, with a smile.

"Poor Adam," he answered, "I have always thought him a much-abused man. Unlike ourselves, he was without experience; he had a companion forced upon him who worked his ruin, and his loss on the transaction was not only physical but financial."

"How long do you contemplate remaining in Venice?" I asked, after the little pause that followed his last speech.

"I scarcely know," he answered. "My movements are most erratic. I am that most unfortunate of God's creatures, a wanderer on the face of the earth. I have no relations and few friends. I roam about as the fancy takes me, remain in a place as long as it pleases me, and then, like the Arab in the poem, silently take up my tent and move on as soon as the city I happen to be in at the time has lost its charm. I possess a *pied-d-terre* of four rooms in Cairo, I have lived amongst the Khabyles in the desert, and with the Armenians in the mountains. To sum it up, I have the instincts of the Wandering Jew, and fortunately the means of gratifying them."

What it was I cannot say, but there was something in his speech that grated upon my feelings. Whether what he had said were true or not, I am not in a position to affirm, but the impression I received was that he was talking for effect, and every one will know what that means.

"As you are such a globe-trotter," I said, "I suppose there is scarcely a portion of the world that you have not visited?"

"I have perhaps had more than my share of travelling," he answered. "I think I can safely say that, with the exception of South America, I have visited every portion of the known globe."

"You have never been in South America, then?" I asked in some surprise.

"Never," he replied, and immediately changed the conversation by inquiring whether I had met certain of Anstruther's friends who were supposed to be on their way to Venice. A few minutes later, after having given him an invitation to dinner on the next evening, I bade him goodbye and left him. On my return my wife was eager to question me concerning him, but as things stood I did not feel capable of giving her a detailed reply. There are some acquaintances who, one feels, will prove friends from the outset; there are others who fill one from the first with a vague distrust. Not that I altogether distrusted Martinos, I had not seen enough of him to do that; at the same time, however, I could not conscientiously say, as I have already observed, that I was altogether prepossessed in his favour.

The following morning he accepted my invitation for that evening, and punctually at half-past seven he made his appearance in the drawing-room. I introduced him to my wife, and also to Miss Trevor when she joined us.

"My husband tells me that you are a great traveller," said Phyllis, after they had seated themselves. "He says you know the world as we know London."

"Your husband does me too much honour," he answered modestly. "From what I have heard of you, you must know the world almost as well as I do. My friend, Anstruther, has told me a romantic story about you. Something connected with a South Sea island, and a mysterious personage named—"

He paused for a moment as if to remember the name.

"Nikola," I said; "you do not happen to have met him, I suppose?"

"To my knowledge, never," he answered. "It is a strange surname."

At that moment Glenbarth entered the room, and I introduced the two men to each other. For some reason of my own I was quite prepared to find that the Duke would not take a fancy to our new acquaintance, nor was I destined to be disappointed. Before dinner was half over I could see that he had a great difficulty in being civil to the stranger. Had Martinos not been our guest, I doubt very much whether he would have been able to control himself. And yet the Spaniard laid himself out in every way to please. His attentions were paid chiefly to my wife; I do not believe that he addressed Miss Trevor more than a dozen times throughout the meal. Notwithstanding this fact, Glenbarth regarded him with evident animosity, insomuch that Miss Trevor more than once looked at him with an expression of positive alarm upon her face. She had not seen him in this humour before, and though she may have had her suspicions as to the reason of it, it was plain that she was far from approving of his line of action. When the ladies withdrew, and the wine was being circulated, I endeavoured to draw the two men into greater harmony with each other. The attempt, however, was unsuccessful. More than once Glenbarth said things which bordered on rudeness, until I began to feel angry with him. On one occasion, happening to look up suddenly from the cigar which I was cutting, I detected a look upon the Spaniard's face that startled me. It however showed me one thing, and that was the fact that despite his genial behaviour, Martinos had not been blind to the young man's treatment of himself, and also that, should a time ever arrive when he would have a chance of doing Glenbarth a mischief, he would not be forgetful of the debt he owed him. Matters were not much better when we adjourned to the drawing-room. Glenbarth, according to custom, seated himself beside Miss Trevor, and studiously ignored the Spaniard. I was more sorry for this than I could say. It was the behaviour of a school boy, not that of a man of the world; and the worst part of it was, that it was doing Glenbarth no sort of good in the eyes of the person with whom he wished to stand best. The truth was the poor lad was far from being himself. He was suffering from an acute attack of a disease which has not yet received the proper attention of science—the disease of first love. So overwhelmed was he by his passion that he could not bear any stranger even to look upon the object of his adoration. Later in the evening matters reached their climax, when my wife asked the Don to sing.

"I feel sure that you do sing," she said in that artless way which women often affect.

"I try sometimes to amuse my friends," said he, and begging us to excuse him, he retired to his own rooms to presently return with a large Spanish guitar. Having taken a seat near the window, and when he had swept his fingers over the strings in a few preliminary chords, he commenced to sing. He was the possessor of a rich baritone, which he used with excellent effect. My wife was delighted, and asked him to sing again. Miss Trevor also expressed her delight, and seconded my wife's proposal. This was altogether too much for Glenbarth. Muttering something about a severe headache, he hurriedly left the room. My wife and I exchanged glances, but Martinos and Miss Trevor did not appear to notice his absence. This time he sang a Spanish fishing song, but I did not pay much attention to it. A little later the Don, having thanked us for our hospitality, took his departure, and when Miss Trevor had said " good night "to us, and had retired to her own room, my wife and I were left alone together.

"What could have made the Duke behave like that?" she said.

"He is madly in love, my dear, and also madly jealous," I answered. "I hope and trust, however, that he is not going to repeat this performance."

"If he does he will imperil any chance he has of winning Gertrude's love," she replied. "He will also place us in a decidedly awkward position."

"Let this be a lesson to you, my dear, never to play with fire again," I replied. "You bring two inflammable people together, and wonder that there should be an explosion."

"Well, I'm really very angry with him. I don't know what the Don Jose must have thought."

"Probably he thought nothing about it," I replied. "You mustn't be too angry with Glenbarth, however. Leave him to me, and I'll talk to him. Tomorrow, I promise you, he'll be sorry for himself. If I know anything of women, Gertrude will make him wish he had acted differently."

"I don't think she will bother about the matter. She has too much sense."

"Very well; we shall see." I then bade her go to bed, promising myself to sit up for Glenbarth, who, I discovered, had gone out. It was nearly midnight when he returned. I noticed that every trace of ill-humour had vanished from his face, and that he was quite himself once more.

"My dear Dick," he said, "I don't know how to apologise for my ridiculous and rude behaviour of tonight. I am more ashamed of myself than I can say. I behaved like a child."

Because he happened to be in a repentant mood I was not going to let him off the chastising I felt that I ought to give him.

"A nice sort of young fellow you are, upon my word," I said, putting down the paper I had been reading as I spoke. "I've a very good mind to tell you exactly what I think of you."

"It would be only wasting your time," he returned. "For you can't think half as badly of me as I do of myself. I can't imagine what made me do it."

"Can't you?" I said. "Well, I can, and as you are pretty certain to catch it in one particular quarter tomorrow; on mature reflection, that I can afford to forgive you. The man had done you no harm; he not only did not interfere with you, but he was not trespassing upon your—"

"Don't speak of him," said the young fellow, flaring up at once. "If I think of him I shall get angry again. I can't bear the look of the beggar."

"Steady, my young friend, steady," I returned. "You mustn't call other people's friends by that name."

"He is not your friend," said Glenbarth excitedly. "You've never seen him until tonight, and you've known me ever since I was about so high."

"I began to imagine you only 'so high' this evening," I said. "It's a good thing for you that the wife has gone to bed, or I fancy you would have heard something that would have made your ears tingle. After the foolish manner of women, she has come to the conclusion that she would like you to marry Miss Trevor."

"God bless her!" he said fervently. "I knew that she was my friend."

"In that case you would probably have enjoyed a friend's privilege, had you been here tonight before she retired, and have received a dressing-down that is usually reserved for her husband. I live in hopes that you may get it tomorrow."

"Bosh!" he answered. "And now, if you have forgiven me, I think I will go to bed. I've had enough of myself for one day."

With that we shook hands, and bade each other "good night." At his bedroom door he stopped me.

"Do you think she will forgive me?" he asked as humbly as would a boy who had been caught stealing sugar-plums.

"My wife," I answered. "Yes, I think it is very probable that she will."

"No, no; how dense you are; I mean—" Here he nodded his head in the direction of the room occupied by Miss Trevor.

"You'll have to find out that for yourself," I replied, and then went on to my dressing-room.

"That will give your Grace something to think about all night," I said, as I took off my coat.

As it turned out, I was destined to be fairly accurate in the prophecy I had made concerning Miss Trevor's treatment of Glenbarth on the morrow. At breakfast she did not altogether ignore him, but when I say that she devoted the larger share of her attention to myself, those of my readers who are married, and have probably had the same experience, will understand. My wife, on the other hand, was affability itself, and from her behaviour towards him appeared to be quite willing to forgive and forget the unfortunate episode of the previous evening. I chuckled to myself, but said nothing. He was not at the end of his punishment yet.

All that day we saw nothing of Martinos. Whether he remained at home or went abroad we could not say. On returning to the hotel to lunch, however, we discovered a basket of roses in the drawing-room, with the Don's card tied to the handle.

"Oh, what lovely flowers!" cried my wife in an ecstasy. "Look, Gertrude, are they not beautiful?"

Miss Trevor cordially admired them; and in order, I suppose, that Glenbarth's punishment might be the more complete, begged for a bud to wear herself. One was given her, while I watched Glenbarth's face over the top of the letter I was reading at the moment. My heart was touched by his miserable face, and when he and my wife had left the room to prepare for lunch, I determined to put in a good word for him.

"Miss Gertrude," I said, "as an old friend, I have a favour to ask of you. Do you think you can grant it?"

"You must first tell me what it is," she said, with a smile upon her face. "I know from experience that you are not to be trusted."

"A nice sort of character for a family man," I protested. "Lady Hatteras has been telling tales, I can see."

"Your wife would never tell a tale of any one, particularly of you," she asserted. "But what would you ask of me?"

"Only a plea for human happiness," I said with mock gravity. "I have seen absolute despair written indelibly on a certain human countenance today, and the sight has troubled me ever since. Are you aware that there is a poor young man in this hotel, whose face opens like a daisy to the sun when you smile upon him, and closes in the darkness of your neglect?"

"How absurd you are!"

"Why am I absurd?"

"Because you talk in this fashion."

"Will you smile upon him again? He has suffered a great deal these last two days."

"Really you are too ridiculous. I don't know what you mean."

"That is not the truth, Miss Trevor, and you know it."

"But what have I done wrong?"

"That business with the rose just now, for instance, was cruel, to say the least of it."

"Really, Sir Richard, you do say such foolish things. If I want a rose to wear, surely I may have one. But I must not stay talking to you, it's five-and-twenty minutes past one. I must go and get ready for lunch"

I held open the door for her, and as she passed I said:

"You will do what I ask? Just to please me?"

"I don't know what you mean, but I will think it over," she replied, and then departed to her room.

She must have done as she promised, for the rose was absent from her dress when she sat down to lunch. Glenbarth noticed it, and from that moment his drooping spirits revived.

That afternoon my wife and I went down to meet the P. and O. mail-boat, in order to discover some friends who were on their way to Egypt. As neither the Duke of Glenbarth nor Miss Trevor was acquainted with them, they were excused from attendance. When we joined them it was plain that all traces of trouble had been removed, and in consequence the Duke was basking in the seventh heaven of happiness. Had I asked the young man at that moment for half his estates I believe he would willingly have given them to me. He would have done so even more willingly had he known that it was to my agency that he owed the wondrous change in his affairs. For some reason of her own Miss Trevor was also in the best of spirits. My wife was happy because her turtledoves were happy, and I beamed upon them all with the complacency of the God out of the machine.

All this time I had been wondering as to the reason why we had not heard or seen anything of Nikola. Why I should have expected to do so I cannot say, but after the events of three evenings ago, I had entertained a vague hope that I should have seen him, or that he would have communicated with me in some form or another. We were to see him, however, before very long.

We had arranged to visit the Academy on our return from the mail-boat, where my wife was anxious to renew her acquaintance with the Titians. For my own part, I am prepared to admit that my knowledge of the pictures is not sufficiently cultivated to enable me to derive any pleasure from the constant perusal of these Masters. Phyllis and Miss Trevor, however, managed to discover a source of considerable satisfaction in them. When we left the gallery, we made our way, according to custom, in the direction of the piazza of Saint Mark. We had not advanced very far upon our walk, however, before I chanced to turn round, to discover, striding after us, no less a person than our new acquaintance, Don Jose Martinos. He bowed to the ladies, shook hands with myself, and nodded to the Duke.

"If you are proceeding in the direction of the piazza, will you permit me to accompany you?" he asked, and that permission having been given by my wife, we continued our walk. What Glenbarth thought of it I do not know, but as he had Miss Trevor to himself, I do not see that he had anything to complain of. On reaching Florian's cafe, we took our customary seats, the Don placing himself next to my wife, and laying himself out to be agreeable. Once he addressed Glenbarth, and I was astonished to see the conciliatory manner that the other adopted towards him.

"Now that he sees that he has nothing to fear, perhaps he will not be so jealous," I said to myself, and indeed it appeared as if this were likely to be the case. I was more relieved by this discovery than I could say. As we should probably be some time in Venice, and the Don had arrived with the same intention, and we were to be located in the same hotel, it was of the utmost importance to our mutual comfort that there should be no friction between the two men. But enough of this subject for the present. There are other matters to be considered. In the first place, I must put on record a curious circumstance. In the light of after events it bears a strange significance, and he would be a courageous man who would dare to say that he could explain it.

It must be borne in mind, in order that the importance of what I am now about to describe may be plainly understood, that Miss Trevor was seated facing me, that is to say, with her back towards the Cathedral of St. Mark. She was in the best of spirits, and at the moment was engaged in an animated discussion with my wife on the effect of Ancient Art upon her *bete noir*, the Cockney tourist. Suddenly, without any apparent reason, her face grew deathly pale, and she came to a sudden stop in the middle of a sentence. Fortunately no one noticed it but my wife and myself, and as she was herself again in a moment, we neither of us called attention to it. A moment later I glanced across the square, and to my amazement saw no less a person than Doctor Nikola approaching us. Was it possible that Miss Trevor, in some extraordinary manner, had become aware of his proximity to her, or was it only one of those strange coincidences that are so difficult to explain away? I did not know what to think then, nor, as a matter of fact, do I now.

Reaching our party, Nikola raised his hat to the ladies.

"I fear, Lady Hatteras," he said, "that I must have incurred your displeasure for keeping your husband so long away from you the other night. If so, I hope you will forgive me."

"I will endeavour to do so," said my wife with a smile, "but you must be very careful how you offend again."

Then, turning to Miss Trevor, he said, "I hope you will grant me your gracious intercession, Miss Trevor?"

"I will do my best for you," she answered, with a seriousness that made my wife and me look at her.

Then Nikola shook hands with Glenbarth, and glanced at the Don.

"Permit me to introduce you to Don Jose de Martinos, Doctor Nikola," I said; "he has lately arrived from Algiers."

The two men bowed gravely to each other.

"You are fond of travelling, I presume, Senor," said Nikola, fixing his eyes upon the Don.

"I have seen a considerable portion of the world," the other answered. "I have seen the Midnight Sun at Cape North and the drift ice off the Horn."

"And have not found it all barren," Nikola remarked gravely

From that moment the conversation flowed smoothly. Miss Trevor had quite recovered herself, and I could see that the Don was intensely interested in Nikola. And indeed on this particular occasion the latter exerted himself to the utmost to please. I will admit, however, that something not unlike a shudder passed over me as I contrasted his present affability with his manner when he had threatened the unfortunate Police Agent a few nights before. Now he was a suave, pleasant-mannered man of the world, then he figured almost as an avenging angel; now he discussed modern literature, then I had heard him threaten a human being with the direst penalties that it was possible for a man to inflict. When it was time for us to return to our hotel, Nikola rose and bade us goodbye.

"I hope you will permit me the pleasure of seeing more of you while you are in Venice," said Nikola, addressing the Don. "If you are an admirer of the old palaces of this wonderful city, and our friends will accompany you, I shall be delighted to show you my own poor abode. It possesses points of interest that many of the other palaces lack, and, though it has fallen somewhat to decay, I fancy you will admit that the fact does not altogether detract from its interest."

"I shall hasten to avail myself of the opportunity you are kind enough to offer me," the other replied, after which they bowed ceremoniously to each other and parted.

"Your friend is an extraordinary man," said the Don as we walked towards the steps. "I have never met a more interesting person. Does he altogether reside in Venice?"

"Oh, dear, no," I replied. "If one were asked to say where Nikola had his abode, it would be almost necessary to say 'in the world.' I myself met him first in London, afterwards in Egypt, then in Australia, and later on in the South Sea Islands. Now we are together again in Venice. I have good reason for knowing that he is also familiar with China and Tibet. He himself confesses to a knowledge of Africa and Central America."

"To Central America?" said the Don quickly. "Pray what part of Central America does he know?"

"That I am unable to say," I replied. "I have never questioned him upon the subject."

From that moment the Don almost exclusively addressed himself to my wife, and did not refer to Nikola again. We parted in the hall of the hotel. Next morning we saw him for a few moments at the post-office, but at no other time during the day. On the following day he accompanied us on an excursion to Chioggia, and dined with us afterwards. Though I knew that Glenbarth still disliked him, his hostility was so veiled as to be scarcely noticeable. Towards the end of the evening a note was brought to me. One glance at the handwriting upon the envelope was sufficient to show me that it was from Nikola. It ran as follows:

My dear Hatteras,
Remembering your friend Don Martinos' desire to see my poor palace, I have written to ask him if he will dine with me tomorrow evening at eight o'clock. If I can persuade you and the Duke of Glenbarth to give me the pleasure of your society, I need scarcely say that you will be adding to my delight.—
Sincerely yours,
Nikola

"You have not, of course, received your letter yet," I said, addressing the Don. "What do you say to the invitation?"

"I shall accept it only too willingly," he answered without delay. "Provided, of course, you will go too."

"Have you any objection, Duke?" I asked, addressing Glenbarth.

I could see that he was not very anxious to go, but under the circumstances he could not very well refuse.

"I shall be very happy," he answered.

And for once in his life he deliberately said what he knew to be untrue.

Chapter 7

"You surely are not going to dine with Doctor Nikola in that strange house?" said my wife, when we were alone together that night. "After what the Duke has told us, I wonder that you can be so foolish."

"My dear girl," I answered, "I don't see the force of your argument. I shan't be the first who has eaten a meal in the house in question, and I don't suppose I shall be the last. What do you think will happen to me? Do you think that we have returned to the times of the Borgias, and that Nikola will poison us? No, I am looking forward to a very enjoyable and instructive evening."

"While we are sitting at home, wondering if the table is disappearing bodily into the vaults and taking you with it, or whether Nikola is charging the side-dishes with some of his abominable chemistry, by which you will be put to sleep for three months, or otherwise experimenting upon you in the interests of what he calls Science, I don't think it is at all kind of you to go."

"Dear girl," I answered, "are you not a little unreasonable? Knowing that De Martinos has but lately arrived in Venice, also that he is a friend of ours—for did he not meet him when in our company?—it is only natural that Nikola should desire to show him some courtesy. In spite of its decay, the Palace Revecce is an exceedingly beautiful building, and when he heard that Martinos would like to visit it, he invited him to dinner. What could be more natural? This is the twentieth century!"

"I am sure I don't mind what century it is," she replied. "Still I adhere to what I said just now. I am sorry you are going."

"In that case I am sorry also," I answered, "but as the matter stands I fail to see how I can get out of it. I could not let the Duke and Martinos go alone, so what can I do?"

"I suppose you will have to go," she replied ruefully. "I have a presentiment, however, that trouble will result from it."

With that the subject was dropped, and it was not until the following morning, when I was smoking with Glenbarth after breakfast, that it cropped up again.

"Look here, Dick," said my companion then. "What about this dinner at Nikola's house tonight? You seemed to be very keen on going last night; are you of the same mind this morning?"

"Why not?" I answered. "My wife does not like the notion, but I am looking forward to seeing Nikola play the host. The last time I dined with him, you must remember, was in Port Said, and then the banquet could scarcely be described as a pleasant one. What is more, I am anxious to see what effect Nikola and his house will produce upon our friend the Don."

"I wish he'd get rid of him altogether," my companion replied. "I dislike the fellow more and more every time I see him."

"Why should you? He does you no harm!"

"It's not that," said Glenbarth. "My dislike to him is instinctive; just as one shudders when one looks into the face of a snake, or as one is repelled by a toad or a rat. In spite of his present apparent respectability, I should not be at all surprised to hear that at some period of his career he had committed murders innumerable."

"Nonsense, nonsense," I replied, "you must not imagine such things as that. You were jealous when you first saw him, because you thought he was going to come between you and Miss Trevor. You have never been able to overcome the feeling, and this continued dislike is the result. You must fight against it. Doubtless, when you have seen more of him, you will like him better."

"I shall never like him better than I do now," he answered, with conviction. "As they say in the plays, 'my gorge rises at him'! If you saw him in the light I do, you would not let Lady Hatteras—"

"My dear fellow," I began, rising from my chair and interrupting him, "this is theatrical and very ridiculous, and I assume the right of an old friend to tell you so. If you prefer not to go tonight, I'll make some excuse for you, but don't, for goodness' sake, go and make things unpleasant for us all while you're there."

"I have no desire to do so," he replied stiffly. "What is more, I am not going to let you go alone. Write your letter and accept for us both. Bother Nikola and Martinos as well, I wish they were both on the other wide of the world." I thereupon wrote a note to Nikola accepting, on Glenbarth's behalf and my own, his invitation to dinner for that evening. Then I dismissed the matter from my mind for the time being. An hour or so later my wife came to me with a serious face.

"I am afraid, Dick, that there is something the matter with Gertrude," she said. "She has gone to her room to lie down, complaining of a very bad headache and a numbness in all her limbs. I have done what I can for her, but if she does not get better by lunch-time, I think I shall send for a doctor."

As, by lunch-time, she was no better, the services of an English doctor were called in. His report to my wife was certainly a puzzling one. He declared he could discover nothing the matter with the girl, nor anything to account for the mysterious symptoms.

"Is she usually of an excitable disposition?" he inquired, when we discussed the matter together in the drawing-room.

"Not in the least," I replied. "I should say she is what might be called a very evenly-dispositioned woman."

He asked one or two other questions and then took leave of us, promising to call again next day.

"I cannot understand it at all," said my wife when he had gone; "Gertrude seemed so well last night. Now she lies upon her bed and complains of this continued pain in her head and the numbness in all her limbs. Her hands and feet are as cold as ice, and her face is as white as a sheet of note-paper."

During the afternoon Miss Trevor determined to get up, only to be compelled to return to bed again. Her headache had left her, but the strange numbness still remained. She seemed incapable, so my wife informed me, of using her limbs. The effect upon the Duke may be better imagined than described. His face was the picture of desolation, and his anxiety was all the greater inasmuch as he was precluded from giving vent to it in speech. I am afraid that, at this period of his life, the young gentleman's temper was by no means as placid as we were accustomed to consider it. He was given to flaring up without the slightest warning, and to looking upon himself and his own little world in a light that was very far removed from cheerful. Realising that we could do no good at home, I took him out in the afternoon, and was given to understand that I was quite without heart, because, when we had been an hour abroad, I refused to return to the hotel.

"I wonder if there is anything that Miss Trevor would like," he said, as we crossed the piazza of Saint Mark. "It could be sent up to her, you know, in your name."

"You might send her some flowers," I answered. "You could then send them from yourself."

"By Jove, that's the very thing. You do have some good ideas sometimes."

"Thank you," I said quietly. "Approbation from Sir Hubert Stanley is praise indeed."

"Bother your silly quotations!" he retorted. "Let's get back to that flower-shop."

We did so, and thereupon that reckless youth spent upon flowers what would have kept me in cigars for a month. Having paid for them and given orders that they should be sent to the Hotel Galaghetti at once, we left the shop. When we stood outside, I had to answer all sorts of questions as to whether I thought she would like them, whether it would not have been better to have chosen more of one sort than another, and whether the scent would not be too strong for a sick-room. After that he felt doubtful whether the shopkeeper would send them in time, and felt half inclined to return in order to impress this fact upon the man. Let it be counted to me for righteousness that I bore with him patiently, remembering my own feelings at a similar stage in my career. When we reached the hotel on our return, we discovered that the patient was somewhat better. She had had a short sleep, and it had refreshed her. My wife was going to sit with her during the evening, and knowing this, I felt that we might go out with clear consciences.

At a quarter to seven we retired to our rooms to dress, and at a quarter past the hour were ready to start. When we reached the hall we found the Don awaiting us there. He was dressed with the greatest care, and presented a not unhandsome figure. He shook hands cordially with me and bowed to Glenbarth, who had made no sign of offering him his hand. Previous to setting out, I had extorted from that young man his promise that he would behave with courtesy towards the other during the evening.

"You can't expect me to treat the fellow as a friend," he had said in reply, "but I will give you my word that I'll be civil to him—if that's what you want."

And with this assurance I was perforce compelled to be content.

Having taken our places in the gondola which was waiting for us, we set off.

"I had the pleasure of seeing Doctor Nikola this morning," said Martinos, as we turned into the Rio del Consiglio. "He did me the honour of calling upon me."

I gave a start of surprise on hearing this.

"Indeed," I replied. "And at what hour was that?"

"Exactly at eleven o'clock," the Don answered. "I remember the time because I was in the act of going out, and we encountered each other in the hall."

Now it is a singular thing, a coincidence, if you like, but it was almost on the stroke of eleven that Miss Trevor had been seized with her mysterious illness. At a quarter past the hour she felt so poorly as to be compelled to retire to her room. Of course, there could be no connection between the two affairs, but it was certainly a coincidence of a nature calculated to afford me ample food for reflection. A few moments later the gondola drew up at the steps of the Palace Revecce. Almost at the same instant the door opened and we entered the house. The courtyard had been lighted in preparation for our coming, and, following the man who had admitted us, we ascended the stone staircase to the corridor above. Though not so dismal as when I had last seen it, lighted only by Nikola's lantern, it was still sufficiently awesome to create a decided impression upon the Don.

"You were certainly not wrong when you described it as a lonely building," he said, as we passed along the corridor to Nikola's room.

As he said this the door opened, and Nikola stood before us. He shook hands with the Duke first, afterwards with the Don, and then with myself.

"Let me offer you a hearty welcome," he began. "Pray enter."

We followed him into the room I have already described, and the door was closed behind us. It was in this apartment that I had expected we should dine, but I discovered that this was not to be the case. The tables were still littered with papers, books, and scientific apparatus, just as when I had last seen it. Glenbarth seated himself in a chair by the window, but I noticed that his eyes wandered continually to the oriental rug upon the floor by the fireplace. He was doubtless thinking of the vaults below, and, as I could easily imagine, wishing himself anywhere else than where he was. The black cat, Apollyon, which was curled up in an arm-chair, regarded us for a few seconds with attentive eyes, as if to make sure of our identities, and then returned to his slumbers. The windows were open, I remember, and the moon was just rising above the house tops opposite. I had just gone to the casement, and was looking down upon the still waters below, when the tapestry of the wall on the right hand was drawn aside by the man who had admitted us to the house, who informed Nikola in Italian that dinner was upon the table.

"In that case let us go in to it," said our host. "Perhaps your Grace will be kind enough to lead the way."

Glenbarth did as he was requested, and we followed him, to find ourselves in a large, handsome apartment, which had once been richly frescoed, but was now, like the rest of the palace, sadly fallen to decay.

In the centre of the room was a small oval table, well illuminated by a silver lamp, which diffused a soft light upon the board, the remainder of the room being in heavy shadow. The decorations, the napery, and the glass and silver, were, as I could see at one glance, unique. Three men-servants awaited our coming, though where they hailed from and how Nikola had induced them to enter the palace, I could not understand. Nikola, as our host, occupied one end of the table; Glenbarth, being the principal guest of the evening, was given the chair on his left; the Don took that on the right, while I faced him at the further end. How, or by whom, the dinner was cooked was another mystery. Nikola had told us on the occasion of our first visit that he possessed no servants, and that such cooking as he required was done for him by an old man who came in once every day. Yet the dinner he gave us on this particular occasion was worthy of the finest chef in Europe. It was perfect in every particular. Though Nikola scarcely touched anything, he did the honours of his table royally, and with a grace that was quite in keeping with the situation. Had my wife and Miss Trevor been present, they might, for all the terrors they had anticipated for us, very well have imagined themselves in the dining-room of some old English country mansion, waited upon by the family butler, and taken in to dinner by the Bishop and the Rural Dean. The Nikola I had seen when I had last visited the house was as distant from our present host as if he had never existed. When I looked at him, I could scarcely believe that he had ever been anything else but the most delightful man of my acquaintance.

"As a great traveller, Don Jose," he said, addressing the guest on his right hand, "you have of course dined in a great number of countries, and I expect under a variety of startling circumstances. Now tell me, what is your most pleasant recollection of a meal?"

"That which I managed to obtain after the fall of Valparaiso," said Martinos. "We had been without food for two days, that is to say, without a decent meal, when I chanced upon a house where breakfast had been abandoned without being touched. I can see it now. Ye gods! it was delightful. And not the less so because the old rascal we were after had managed to make his escape."

"You were in opposition to Balmaceda, then?" said Nikola quietly.

Martinos paused for a moment before he answered.

"Yes, against Balmaceda," he replied. "I wonder whether the old villain really died, and if so, what became of his money."

"That is a question one would like to have settled concerning a good many people," Glenbarth put in.

"There was that man up in the Central States, the Republic of—ah! what was its name?—Equinata," said Nikola. "I don't know whether you remember the story."

"Do you mean the fellow who shot those unfortunate young men?" I asked. "The man you were telling me of the other night."

"The same," Nikola replied. "Well, he managed to fly his country, taking with him something like two million dollars. From that moment he has never been heard of, and as a matter of fact I do not suppose he ever will be. After all, luck has a great deal to do with things in this world."

"Permit me to pour out a libation to the God of Chance," said Martinos. "He has served me well."

"I think we can all subscribe to that," said Nikola. "You, Sir Richard, would not be the happy man you are had it not been for a stroke of good fortune which shipwrecked you on one island in the Pacific instead of another. You, my dear Duke, would certainly have been drowned in Bournemouth Bay had not our friend Hatteras chanced to be an early riser, and to have taken a certain cruise before breakfast; while you, Don Martinos, would in all probability not be my guest tonight had not—"

The Spaniard looked sharply at him as if he feared what he was about to hear.

"Had not what happened?" he asked.

"Had President Balmaceda won his day," was the quiet reply. "He did not do so, however, and so we four sit here tonight. Certainly, a libation to the God of Chance."

At last the dinner came to an end, and the servants withdrew, having placed the wine upon the table. The conversation drifted from one subject to another until it reached the history of the palace in which we were then the guests.

For the Spaniard's information Nikola related it in detail. He did not lay any particular emphasis upon it, however, as he had done upon the story he had told the Duke and myself concerning the room in which he had received us. He merely narrated it in a matter-of-fact way, as if it were one in which he was only remotely interested. Yet I could not help thinking that he fixed his eyes more keenly than usual on the Spaniard, sat sipping his wine and listening with an expression of polite attention upon his sallow face. When the wine had been circulated for the last time, Nikola suggested that we should leave the dining-room and return to his own sitting-room.

"I do not feel at home in this room," he said by way of explanation;

"for that reason I never use it. I usually partake of such food as I need in the next, and allow the rest of the house to fall undisturbed into that decay which you see about you."

With that we rose from the table and returned to the room in which he had received us. A box of cigars was produced and handed round; Nikola made coffee with his own hands at a table in the corner, and then I waited the further developments that I knew would come. Presently Nikola began to speak of the history of Venice. As I had already had good reason to know, he had made a perfect study of it, particularly of the part played in it by the Revecce family. He dealt with particular emphasis upon the betrayal through the Lion's Mouth, and then, with an apology to Glenbarth and myself for boring us with it again, referred to the tragedy of the vaults below the room in which we were then seated. Once more he drew back the carpet and the murderous trap-door opened. A cold draught, suggestive of unspeakable horrors, came up to us.

"And there the starving wretch died with the moans of the woman he loved sounding in his ears from the room above," said Nikola. "Does it not seem that you can hear them now? For my part, I think they will echo through all eternity."

If he had been an actor what a wonderful tragedian he would have made! As he stood before us pointing down into the abyss he held us spell-bound. As for Martinos, all the accumulated superstition of the centuries seemed to be concentrated in him, and he watched Nikola's face as if he were fascinated beyond the power of movement.

"Come," Nikola began at last, closing the trap-door and placing the rug upon it as he spoke, "you have heard the history of the house. You shall now do more than that! You shall see it!"

Fixing his eyes upon us, he made two or three passes in the air with his long white hands. Meanwhile, it seemed to me as if he were looking into my brain. I tried to avert my eyes, but without success. They were chained to his face, and I could not remove them. Then an overwhelming feeling of drowsiness took possession of me, and I must have lost consciousness, for I have no recollection of anything until I found myself in a place I thought for a moment I had never seen before. And yet after a time I recognised it. It was a bright day in the early spring, the fresh breeze coming over the islands from the open sea was rippling the water of the lagoons. I looked at my surroundings. I was in Venice, and yet it was not the Venice with which I was familiar. I was standing with Nikola upon the steps of a house, the building of which was well-nigh completed. It was a magnificent edifice, and

I could easily understand the pride of the owner as he stood in his gondola and surveyed it from the stretch of open water opposite. He was a tall and handsome man, and wore a doublet and hose, shoes with large bows, and a cloak trimmed with fur. There was also a chain of gold suspended round his neck. Beside him was a man whom I rightly guessed to be the architect, for presently the taller man placed his hand upon his shoulder and praised him for the work he had done, vowing that it was admirable. Then, at a signal, the gondolier gave a stroke of his oar and the little vessel shot across to the steps, where they landed close to where I was standing. I stepped back in order that they might pass, but they took no sort of notice of my presence. Passing on, they entered the house.

"They do not see us," said Nikola, who was beside me. "Let us enter and hear what the famous Admiral Francesco del Revecce thinks of his property."

We accordingly did so, to find ourselves in a magnificent courtyard. In the centre of this courtyard was a well, upon which a carver in stone was putting the finishing touches to a design of leaves and fruit. From here led a staircase, and this we ascended. In the different rooms artists were to be observed at work upon the walls, depicting sea-fights, episodes in the history of the Republic, and of the famous master of the house. Before each the owner paused, bestowing approval, giving advice, or suggesting such alteration or improvement as he considered needful. In his company we visited, the kitchens, the pantler's offices, and penetrated even to the dungeons below the water-level. Then we once more ascended to the courtyard, and stood at the great doors while the owner took his departure in his barge, pleased beyond measure with his new abode. Then the scene changed.

Once more I stood before the house with Nikola. It was night, but it was not dark, for great cressets flared on either side of the door, and a hundred torches helped to illuminate the scene. All the great world of Venice was making its way to the Palace Revecce that night. The first of the series of gorgeous fetes given to celebrate the nuptials of Francesco del Revecce, the most famous sailor of the Republic, who had twice defeated the French fleet, and who had that day married the daughter of the Duke of Levano, was in progress. The bridegroom was still comparatively young, he was also rich and powerful; the bride was one of the greatest heiresses of Venice, besides being one of its fairest daughters. Their new home was as beautiful as money and the taste of the period could make it. Small wonder was it, therefore, that the world hastened to pay court to them.

"Let us once more enter and look about us," said Nikola.

"One moment," I answered, drawing him back a step as he was in the act of coming into collision with a beautiful girl who had just disembarked from her gondola upon the arm of a grey-haired man.

"You need have no fear," he replied. "You forget that we are Spirits in a Spirit World, and that they are not conscious of our presence."

And indeed this appeared to be the case, for no one recognised us, and more than once I saw people approach Nikola, and, scarcely believable though it may seem, walk through him without being the least aware of the fact.

On this occasion the great courtyard was brilliantly illuminated. Scores of beautiful figures were ascending the stairs continually, while strains of music sounded from the rooms above.

"Let us ascend," said Nikola, "and see the pageant there."

It was indeed a sumptuous entertainment, and when we entered the great reception-rooms, no fairer scene could have been witnessed in Venice. I looked upon the bridegroom and his bride, and recognised the former as being the man I had seen praising the architect on the skill he had displayed in the building of the palace. He was more bravely attired now, however, than on that occasion, and did the honours of his house with the ease and assurance of one accustomed to uphold the dignity of his name and position in the world. His bride was a beautiful girl, with a pale, sweet face, and eyes that haunted one long after they had looked at them. She was doing her best to appear happy before her guests, but in my own heart I knew that such was not the case. Knowing what was before her, I realised something of the misery that was weighing so heavily upon her heart. Surrounding her were the proudest citizens of the proudest Republic of all time. There was not one who did not do her honour, and among the women who were her guests that night, how many were there who envied her good fortune? Then the scene once more changed.

This time the room was that with which I was best acquainted, the same in which Nikola had taken up his abode. The frescoes upon the walls and ceilings were barely dry, and Revecce was at sea again, opposing his old enemy the French, who once more threatened an attack upon the city. It was towards evening, and the red glow of the sunset shone upon a woman's face, as she stood beside the table at which a man was writing. I at once recognised her as Revecce's bride. The man himself was young and handsome, and when he looked up at the woman and smiled, the love-light shone in her eyes, as it had not done when she had looked upon Revecce. There was no need for Nikola to tell me that he was Andrea Bunopelli, the artist to whose skill the room owed its paintings.

"Art thou sure 'twill be safe, love?" asked the woman in a low voice, as she placed her hand upon his shoulder. "Remember 'tis death to bring a false accusation against a citizen of the Republic, and 'twill be worse when 'tis against the great Revecce."

"I have borne that in mind," the man answered. "But there is nought to fear, dear love. The writing will not be suspected, and I will drop it in the Lion's Mouth myself—and then?"

Her only answer was to bend over him and kiss him. He scattered the sand upon the letter he had written, and when it was dry, folded it up and placed it in his bosom. Then he kissed the woman once more and prepared to leave the room. The whole scene was so real that I could have sworn that he saw me as I stood watching him.

"Do not linger," she said in farewell. "I shall know no peace till you return."

Drawing aside the curtain, he disappeared, and then once more the scene changed.

A cold wind blew across the lagoon, and there was a suspicion of coming thunder in the air. A haggard, ragged tatterdemalion was standing on the steps of a small door of the palace. Presently it was opened to him by an ancient servant, who asked his business, and would have driven him away. When he had whispered something to him, however, the other realised that it was his master, whom he thought to be a prisoner in the hands of the French. Then, amazed beyond measure, the man admitted him. Having before me the discovery he was about to make, I looked at him with pity, and when he stumbled and almost fell, I hastened forward to pick him up, but only clasped air. At last, when his servant had told him everything, he followed him to a distant portion of the palace, where he was destined to remain hidden for some days, taking advantage of the many secret passages the palace contained, and by so doing confirming his suspicions. His wife was unfaithful to him, and the man who had wrought his dishonour was the man to whom he had been so kind and generous a benefactor. I seemed to crouch by his side time after time in the narrow passage behind the arras, watching through a secret opening the love-making going on within. I could see the figure beside me quiver with rage and hate, until I thought he would burst in upon them, and then the old servant would lead him away, his finger upon his lips. How many times I stood with him there I cannot say, it is sufficient that at last

394

he could bear the pain no longer, and, throwing open the secret door, entered the room and confronted the man and woman. As I write, I can recall the trembling figures of the guilty pair, and the woman's shriek rings in my ears even now. I can see Bunopelli rising from the table, at which he had been seated, with the death-look in his face. Within an hour the confession of the crime they had perpetrated against Revecce had been written and signed, and they were separated and made secure until the time for punishment should arrive. Then, for the first time since he had arrived in Venice, he ordered his barge and set off for the Council Chamber to look his accusers in the face and to demand the right to punish those who had betrayed him.

When he returned his face was grim and set, and there was a look in his eyes that had not been there before. He ascended to the room in which there was a trap-door in the floor, and presently the wretched couple were brought before him. In vain Bunopelli pleaded for mercy for the woman. There was no mercy to be obtained there. I would have pleaded for them too, but I was powerless to make myself heard. I saw the great beads of perspiration that stood upon the man's brow, the look of agonising entreaty in the woman's face, and the relentless decision on her husband's countenance Nothing could save them now. The man was torn, crying to the last for mercy for her, from the woman's side, the trap-door gave a click, and he disappeared. Then they laid hands upon the woman, and I saw them force open her mouth—but I cannot set down the rest. My tongue clove to the roof of my mouth, and though I rushed forward in the hope of preventing their horrible task, my efforts were as useless as before. Then, with the pitiless smile still upon the husband's face, and the moans ascending from the vault below, and the woman with. . . The scene changed.

When I saw it again a stream of bright sunshine was flooding the room. It was still the same apartment, and yet in a sense not the same. The frescoes were faded upon the walls, there was a vast difference in the shape and make of the furniture, and in certain other things, but it was nevertheless the room in which Francesco del Revecce had taken his terrible revenge. A tall and beautiful woman, some thirty years of age, was standing beside the window holding a letter in her hand. She had finished the perusal of it and was lingering with it in her hand looking lovingly upon the signature. At last she raised it to her lips and kissed it passionately. Then, crossing to a cradle at the further end of the room, she knelt beside it and looked down at the child it contained. She had bent her head in prayer, and was still praying, when with a start I awoke to find myself sitting beside Glenbarth and the

Don in the room in which we had been smoking after dinner. Nikola was standing before the fireplace, and there was a look like that of death upon his face. It was not until afterwards that the Spaniard and Glenbarth informed me that they had witnessed exactly what I had seen. Both, however, were at a loss to understand the meaning of the last picture, and, having my own thoughts in my mind, I was not to be tempted into explaining it to them. That it was Nikola's own mother, and that this house was her property, and the same in which the infamous governor of the Spanish Colony had made his love known to her, I could now see. And if anything were wanting to confirm my suspicions, Nikola's face, when my senses returned to me, was sufficient to do so.

"Let me get out of this house," cried the Duke thickly. "I cannot breathe while I am in it. Take me away, Hatteras; for God's sake take me away!"

I had already risen to my feet and had hastened to his side.

"I think it would be better that we should be going, Doctor Nikola," I said, turning to our host.

The Spaniard, on his side, did not utter a word. He was so dazed as to be beyond the power of speech. But Nikola did not seem to comprehend what I said. Never before had I seen such a look upon his face. His complexion was always white; now, however, it was scarcely human. For my own part I knew what was passing in his mind, but I could give no utterance to it.

"Come," I said to my companions, "let us return to our hotel."

They rose and began to move mechanically towards the door. The Duke had scarcely reached it, however, before Nikola, with what I could see was a violent effort, recovered his self-possession.

"You must forgive me," he said in almost his usual voice. "I had for the moment forgotten my duties as host. I fear you have had but a poor evening."

When we had donned our hats and cloaks, we accompanied him downstairs through the house, which was now as silent as the grave, to the great doors upon the steps. Having hailed a gondola, we entered it, after wishing Nikola "good night." He shook hands with Glenbarth and myself, but I noticed that he did not offer to do so with the Don. Then we shot out into the middle of the canal and had presently turned the corner and were making our way towards the hotel. I am perfectly certain that during the journey not one of us spoke. The events of the evening had proved too much for us, and conversation was impossible. We bade Martinos "good night" in the hall, and then the Duke and I ascended to our own apartments. Spirits had been placed upon the table, and I noticed that the Duke helped himself to almost twice his usual quantity. He looked as if he needed it.

"My God, Dick," he said, "did you see what happened in that room? Did you see that woman kneeling with the—"

He put down his glass hurriedly and walked to the window. I could sympathise with him, for had I not seen the same thing myself?

"It's certain, Dick," he said, when he returned a few moments later, "that, were I to see much more of Nikola in that house, I should go mad. But why did he let me see it? Why? Why? For Heaven's sake answer me."

How could I tell him the thought that was in my own mind? How could I reveal to him the awful fear that was slowly but surely taking possession of me? Why had Nikola invited the Don to his house? Why had he shown him the picture of that terrible crime? Like Glenbarth, I could only ask the same question—Why? Why? Why?

Chapter 8

Before Glenbarth and I parted on the terrible evening described in the previous chapter, we had made a contract with each other to say nothing about what we had seen to the ladies. For this reason, when my wife endeavoured to interrogate me concerning our entertainment, I furnished her with an elaborate description of the dinner itself; spoke of the marvellous cooking, and I hope gave her a fairly accurate account of the menu, or rather so much of it as I could remember.

"I suppose I must confess to defeat, then," she said, when I had exhausted my powers of narration. "I had a settled conviction that something out of the common would have occurred. You seem simply to have had a good dinner, to have smoked some excellent cigars, and the rest to have been bounded merely by the commonplace. For once I fear Doctor Nikola has not acted up to his reputation."

If she had known the truth, I wonder what she would have said! Long after she had bade me "good night" I lay awake ruminating on the different events of the evening. The memory of what I had seen in that awful room was still as fresh with me as if I were still watching it. And yet, I asked myself, why should I worry so much about it? Nikola had willed that his audience should see certain things. We had done so. It was no more concerned with the supernatural than I was myself. Any man who had the power could have impressed us in the same way. But though I told myself all this, I must confess that I was by no means convinced. I knew in my heart that the whole thing had been too real to be merely a matter of make-believe. No human brain could have invented the ghastly horrors of that room in such complete detail. Even to think of it now, is to bring the scene almost too vividly before me; and when I lie awake at night I seem to hear the shrieks of the wretched woman, and the moans of the man perishing in the vaults below.

On my retiring to rest my wife had informed me that she fancied Miss Trevor had been slightly better that evening. She had slept peacefully for upwards of an hour, and seemed much refreshed by it.

"Her maid is going to spend the night in her room," said Phyllis; "I have told her that, if she sees any change in Gertrude's condition, she is to let me know at once. I do hope that she may be herself again tomorrow."

This, however, was unhappily not destined to be the case; for a little before three o'clock there was a tapping upon our bedroom door. Guessing who it would be, my wife went to it, and, having opened it a little, was informed that Miss Trevor was worse.

"I must go to her at once," said Phyllis, and, having clothed herself warmly, for the night was cold, she departed to our guest's room.

"I am really afraid that there is something very serious the matter with her," she said, when she returned after about a quarter of an hour's absence. "She is in a high state of fever, and is inclined to be delirious. Don't you think we had better send for the doctor?"

"I will have a messenger dispatched to him at once if you think it necessary," I returned. "Poor girl, I wonder what on earth it can be?"

"Perhaps the doctor will be able to tell us now," said my wife. "The symptoms are more fully developed, and he should surely be able to make his diagnosis. But I must not stay here talking. I must go back to her."

When she had departed, I dressed myself and went down to the hall in search of the night watchman. He undertook to find a messenger to go and fetch the doctor, and, when I had seen him dispatched on his errand, I returned to the drawing-room, switched on the electric light, and tried to interest myself in a book until the medico should arrive. I was not very successful, however, for interesting though I was given to understand the book was, I found my thoughts continually leaving it and returning to the house in the Rio del Consiglio. I wondered what Nikola was doing at that moment, and fancied I could picture him still at work, late though the hour was. At last, tiring of the book and wanting something else to occupy my thoughts, I went to the window and drew back the shutters. It was a beautiful morning, and the myriad stars overhead were reflected in the black waters of the canal like the lamps of a large town. Not a sound was to be heard; it might have been a city of the dead, so still was it. As I stood looking across the water, I thought of the city's past history, of her ancient grandeur, of her wondrous art, and of the great men who had been her children. There was a tremendous lesson to be learnt from her fall if one could only master it. I was interrupted in my reverie by the entrance of the doctor, whom I had told the night watchman to conduct to my presence immediately upon his arrival.

"I am sorry to bring you out at this time of the night, doctor," I said; "but the fact is, Miss Trevor is much worse. My wife spent the greater part of the evening with her, and informed me on my return from a dinner that she was better. Three-quarters of an hour ago, however, her maid, who had been sleeping in her room, came to us with the news that a change for the worse had set in. This being the case, I thought it better to send for you at once."

"You did quite right, my dear sir, quite right," the medico replied. "There is nothing like promptness in these matters. Perhaps I had better see her without further delay."

With that I conducted him to the door of Miss Trevor's room. He knocked upon it, was admitted by my wife, and then disappeared from my gaze. Something like half an hour elapsed before he returned to me in the drawing-room. When he did so his face looked grave and troubled. "What do you think of her condition now, doctor?" I asked.

"She is certainly in a state of high fever," he answered. "Her pulse is very high, and she is inclined to be delirious. At the same time I am bound to confess to you that I am at a loss to understand the reason of it. The case puzzled me considerably yesterday, but I am even more puzzled by it now. There are various symptoms that I can neither account for nor explain. One thing, however, is quite certain—the young lady must have a trained nurse, and, with your permission, I will see that one comes in after breakfast. Lady Hatteras is not strong enough for the task."

"I am quite with you there," I answered. "And I am vastly obliged to you for putting your foot down. At the same time, will you tell me whether you deem it necessary for me to summon her father from England?"

"So far as I can see at present, I do not think there is any immediate need," he replied. "Should I see any reason for so doing, I would at once tell you. I have given a prescription to Lady Hatteras, and furnished her with the name of a reliable chemist. I shall return between nine and ten o'clock and shall hope to have better news for you then."

"I sincerely trust you may," I said. "As you may suppose, her illness has been a great shock to us."

I then escorted him downstairs and afterwards returned to my bedroom. The news which he had given me of Miss Trevor's condition was most distressing, and made me feel more anxious than I cared to admit. At seven o'clock I saw my wife for a few minutes, but, as before, she had no good news to give me.

"She is quite delirious now," she said, "and talks continually of some great trouble which she fears is going to befall her; implores me to help her to escape from it, but will not say definitely what it is. It goes to my heart to hear her, and to know that I cannot comfort her."

"You must be careful what you are doing," I replied. "The doctor has promised to bring a trained nurse with him after breakfast, who will relieve you of the responsibility. I inquired whether he thought we had better send for her father, and it is in a way encouraging to know that, so far, he does not think there is any necessity for such an extreme step. In the meantime, however, I think I will write to the Dean and tell him how matters stand. It will prepare him, but I am afraid it will give the poor old gentleman a sad fright."

"It could not give him a greater fright than it has done us," said Phyllis. "I do not know why I should do so, but I cannot help thinking that I am to blame in some way."

"What nonsense, my dear girl," I replied. "I am sure you have nothing whatsoever to reproach yourself with. Far from it. You must not worry yourself about it, or we shall be having you upon our hands before long. You must remember that you are yourself far from strong."

"I am quite myself again now," she answered. "It is only on account of your anxiety that I treat myself as an invalid." Then she added, "I wonder what the Duke will say when he hears the news?"

"He was very nearly off his head yesterday," I answered. "He will be neither to hold nor to bind today."

She was silent for a few moments, then she said thoughtfully:

"Do you know, Dick, it may seem strange to you, but I do not mind saying that I attribute all this trouble to Nikola."

"Good gracious," I cried, in well-simulated amazement, "why on earth to Nikola?"

"Because, as was the case five years ago, it has been all trouble since we met him. You remember how he affected Gertrude at the outset. She was far from being herself on the night of our tour through the city, and now in her delirium she talks continually of his dreadful house, and from what she says, and the way she behaves, I cannot help feeling inclined to believe that she imagines herself to be seeing some of the dreadful events which have occurred or are occurring in it."

"God help her," I said to myself. And then I continued aloud to my wife, "Doubtless Nikola's extraordinary personality has affected her in some measure, as it does other people, but you are surely not going to jump to the conclusion that because she has spoken to him he is necessarily responsible for her illness? That would be the wildest flight of fancy."

"And yet, do you know," she continued, "I have made a curious discovery."

"What is that?" I asked, not without some asperity, for, having so much on my mind, I was not in the humour for fresh discoveries.

She paused for a moment before she replied. Doubtless she expected that I would receive it with scepticism, if not with laughter; and Phyllis, ever since I have known her, has a distinct fear of ridicule.

"You may laugh at me if you please," she said, "yet the coincidence is too extraordinary to be left unnoticed. Do you happen to be aware, Dick, that Doctor Nikola called at this hotel at exactly eleven o'clock?"

I almost betrayed myself in my surprise. This was the last question I expected her to put to me.

"Yes," I answered, with an endeavour to appear calm, "I do happen to be aware of that fact. He merely paid a visit of courtesy to the Don, prior to the other's accepting his hospitality. I see nothing remarkable in that. I did the same myself, if you remember."

"Of course, I know that," she replied, "but there is more to come. Are you also aware that it was at the very moment of his arrival in the house that Gertrude was taken ill? What do you think of that?"

She put this question to me with an air of triumph, as if it were one that no argument on my part could refute. At any rate, I did not attempt the task.

"I think nothing of it," I replied. "You may remember that you once fell down in a dead faint within a few minutes of the vicar's arrival at our house at home. Would you therefore have me suppose that it was on account of his arrival that you were taken ill? Why should you attribute Miss Trevor's illness to Nikola's courtesy to our friend the Don?"

"I beg that you will not call him our friend," said Phyllis with considerable dignity. "I do not like the man."

I did not tell her that the Duke was equally outspoken concerning our companion. I could see that they would put their heads together, and that trouble would be the inevitable result. Like a wise husband, I held my peace, knowing that whatever I might say would not better the situation.

Half an hour later it was my unhappy lot to have to inform Glenbarth of Miss Trevor's condition.

"I told you yesterday that it was a matter not to be trifled with," he said, as if I were personally responsible for her grave condition. "The doctor evidently doesn't understand the case, and what you ought to do, if you have any regard for her life, is to send a telegram at once to London ordering competent advice."

"The Dean of Bedminster has a salary of eight hundred pounds per annum," I answered quietly. "Such a man as you would want me to send for would require a fee of some hundreds of guineas to make such a journey."

"And you would allow her to die for the sake of a few paltry pounds?" he cried. "Good heavens, Dick, I never thought you were a money-grabber."

"I am glad you did not," I answered. "It is of her father I am thinking. Besides, I do not know that the doctor here is as ignorant as you say. He has a most complicated and unusual case to deal with, and I honour him for admitting the fact that he does not understand it. Many men in his profession would have thrown dust in our eyes, and have pretended to a perfect knowledge of the case."

The young man did not see it in the same light as I did, and was plainly of the opinion that we were not doing what we might for the woman he loved. My wife, however, took him in hand after breakfast, and talked quietly but firmly to him.

She succeeded where I had failed, and when I returned from an excursion to the chemist's, where I had the prescriptions made up, I found him in a tolerably reasonable frame of mind.

At a quarter to ten the doctor put in an appearance once more, and, after a careful inspection of his patient, informed me that it was his opinion that a consultant should be called in. This was done, and to our dismay the result came no nearer elucidating the mystery than before. The case was such a one as had never entered into the experience of either man. To all intents and purposes there was nothing that would in any way account for the patient's condition. The fever had left her, and she complained of no pain, while her mind, save for occasional relapses, was clear enough. They were certain it was not a case of paralysis, yet she was incapable of moving, or of doing anything to help herself. The duration of her illness was not sufficient to justify her extreme weakness, nor to account for the presence of certain other symptoms. There was nothing for it, therefore, but for us to possess our souls in patience and to wait the turn of events. When the doctors had departed, I went in search of Glenbarth, and gave him their report. The poor fellow was far from being consoled by it. He had hoped to receive good news, and their inability to give a satisfactory decision only confirmed his belief in their incompetency. Had I permitted him to do so, he would have telegraphed at once for the best medical advice in Europe, and would have expended half his own princely revenues in an attempt to make her herself once more. It was

403

difficult to convince him that he had not the right to heap liabilities on the old gentleman's shoulder, which, in honour bound, he would feel he must repay.

I will not bore my readers with the abusive arguments against society, and social etiquette, with which he favoured me in reply to my speech. The poor fellow was beside himself with anxiety, and it was difficult to make him understand that, because he had not placed a narrow band of gold upon a certain pretty finger, he was debarred from saving the life of the owner of that selfsame finger. Towards nightfall it was certain that Miss Trevor's condition was gradually going from bad to worse. With the closing of the day the delirium had returned, and the fever had also come with it. We spent a wretchedly anxious night, and in the morning, at the conclusion of his first visit, the doctor informed me that, in his opinion, it would be advisable that I should telegraph to the young lady's father. This was an extreme step, and, needless to say, it caused me great alarm. It was all so sudden that it was scarcely possible to realise the extent of the calamity. Only two days before Miss Trevor had been as well as any of us, and certainly in stronger health than my wife. Now she was lying, if not at death's door, at least at no great distance from that grim portal. Immediately this sad intelligence was made known to me I hastened to the telegraph-office, and dispatched a message to the Dean, asking him to come to us with all possible speed. Before luncheon I received a reply to the effect that he had already started. Then we sat ourselves down to wait and to watch, hoping almost against hope that this beautiful, happy young life might be spared to us. All this time we had seen nothing of the Don or of Nikola. The former, however, had heard of Miss Trevor's illness, and sent polite messages as to her condition. I did not tell Glenbarth of this, for the young man had sufficient to think of just then without my adding to his worries.

I must pass on now to describe to you the arrival of the Dean of Bedminster in Venice. Feeling that he would be anxious to question me concerning his daughter's condition, I made a point of going to meet him alone. Needless to say, he was much agitated on seeing me, and implored me to give him the latest bulletin.

"God's will be done," he said quietly, when he had heard all I had to tell him. "I did not receive your letter," he remarked, as we made our way from the station in the direction of Galaghetti's hotel, "so that you will understand that I know nothing of the nature of poor Gertrude's illness. What does the doctor say is the matter with her?"

I then informed him how the case stood, and of the uncertainty felt by the two members of the medical profession I had called in. "Surely that is very singular, is it not?" he asked, when I had finished. "There are not many diseases left that they are unable to diagnose."

"In this case, however, I fear they are at a loss to assign a name to it," I said. "However, you will be able very soon to see her for yourself, and to draw your own conclusions."

The meeting between the worthy old gentleman and his daughter was on his side affecting in the extreme. She did not recognise him, nor did she know my wife. When he joined me in the drawing-room a quarter of an hour or so later his grief was pitiful to witness. While we were talking Glenbarth entered, and I introduced them to each other. The Dean knew nothing of the latter's infatuation for his daughter, but I fancy, after a time, he must have guessed that there was something in the wind from the other's extraordinary sympathy with him in his trial. As it happened, the old gentleman had not arrived any too soon. That afternoon Miss Trevor was decidedly worse, and the medical men expressed their gravest fears for her safety. All that day and the next we waited in suspense, but there was no material change. Nature was fighting her battle stubbornly inch by inch. The girl did not seem any worse, nor was there any visible improvement. On the doctor's advice a third physician was called in, but with no greater success than before. Then on one never-to-be-forgotten afternoon the first doctor took me on one side and informed me that in his opinion, and those of his colleagues, it would not be wise to cherish any further hopes. The patient was undeniably weaker, and was growing more so every hour. With a heart surcharged with sorrow I went to the Dean's room and broke the news to him. The poor old man heard me out in silence, and then walked to the window and looked down upon the Grand Canal. After a while he turned, and coming back to me once more, laid his hand upon my arm.

"If it is the Lord's will that I lose her, what can I do but submit?" he said. "When shall I be allowed to see her?"

"I will make inquiries," I answered, and hastened away in search of the doctor. As I passed along the passage I met Galaghetti. The little man had been deeply grieved to hear the sad intelligence, and hastened in search of me at once.

"M'lord," said he, for do what I would I could never cure him of the habit, "believe me, it is not so hopeless, though they say so, if you will but listen to me. There is Doctor Nikola, your friend! He could cure her if you went to him. Did he not cure my child?"

I gave a start of surprise. I will confess that the idea had occurred to

405

me, but I had never given the probability of putting it into execution a thought. Why should it not be done? Galaghetti had reminded me how Nikola had cured his child when she lay at the point of death, and the other doctors of Venice had given her up. He was so enthusiastic in his praise of the doctor that I felt almost inclined to risk it. When I reached the drawing-room Glenbarth hastened towards me.

"What news?" he inquired, his anxiety showing itself plainly upon his face.

I shook my head.

"For God's sake don't trifle with me," he cried. "You can have no idea what I am suffering."

Feeling that it would be better if I told him everything, I made a clean breast of it. He heard me out before he spoke.

"She must not die," he said, with the fierceness of despair. "If there is any power on earth that can be evoked, it shall be brought to bear. Can you not think of anything? Try! Remember that every second is of importance."

"Would it be safe to try Nikola?" I inquired, looking him steadfastly in the face. "Galaghetti is wild for me to do so."

In spite of his dislike to Nikola, Glenbarth jumped at the suggestion as a drowning man clutches at a straw.

"Let us find him at once!" he cried, seizing me by the arm. "If any one can save her he is the man. Let us go to him without a moment's delay."

"No, no," I answered, "that will never do. Even in a case of such gravity the proprieties must be observed. I must consult the doctors before calling in another."

I regret very much to say that here the Duke made use of some language that was neither parliamentary nor courteous to those amiable gentlemen. I sought them out and placed the matter before them. To the idea of calling in a fourth consultant they had not the least objection, though they were all of the opinion that it could do no good. When, however, I mentioned the fact that that consultant's name was Nikola, I could plainly see that a storm was rising.

"Gentlemen," I said, "you must forgive me if I speak plainly and to the point. You have given us to understand that your patient's case is hopeless. Now I have had considerable experience of Doctor Nikola's skill, and I feel that we should not be justified in withholding him from our counsel, if he will consent to be called in. I have no desire to act contrary to medical etiquette, but we must remember that the patient's life comes before aught else."

One doctor looked at the other, and all shook their heads.

"I fear," said the tallest of them, who invariably acted as spokesman, "that if the services of the gentleman in question are called in, it will be necessary for my colleagues and myself to abandon our interest in the case. I do not of course know how far your knowledge extends, but I hope you will allow me to say, sir, that the most curious stories are circulated both as to the behaviour and the attainments of this Doctor Nikola."

Though I knew it to be true, his words nettled me. And yet I had such a deep-rooted belief in Nikola that, although they were determined to give up the case, I felt we should still be equally, if not more, powerful without them.

"I sincerely hope, gentlemen," I said, "that you will not do as you propose. Nevertheless, I feel that I should not be myself acting rightly if I were to allow your professional prejudices to stand in the way of my friend's recovery."

"In that case I fear there is nothing left to us but to most reluctantly withdraw," said one of the men.

"You are determined?"

"Quite determined," they replied together. Then the tallest added, "We much regret it, but our decision is irrevocable."

Ten minutes later they had left the hotel in a huff, and I found myself seated upon the horns of a serious dilemma. What would my position be if Nikola's presence should exercise a bad effect upon the patient, or if he should decline to render us assistance? In that case I should have offended the best doctors in Venice, and should in all probability have killed her. It was a nice position to be placed in. One thing, however, was as certain as anything could be, and that was the fact that there was no time to lose. My wife was seriously alarmed when I informed her of my decision, but both Glenbarth and I felt that we were acting for the best, and the Dean sided with us.

"Since you deem it necessary, go in search of Doctor Nikola at once," said my wife, when the latter had left us. "Implore him to come without delay; in another hour it may be too late." Then in a heart-broken whisper she added, "She is growing weaker every moment. Oh, Dick, Heaven grant that we are not acting wrongly, and that he may be able to save her."

"I feel convinced that we are doing right," I answered. "And now I will go in search of Nikola, and if possible bring him back with me."

"God grant you may be successful in your search," said Glenbarth, wringing my hand. "If Nikola saves her I will do anything he may ask, and shall be grateful to him all the days of my life."

Then I set off upon my errand.

Chapter 9

With a heart as heavy as lead I made my way downstairs, and having chartered a gondola, bade the man take me to the Palace Revecce with all possible haste. Old Galaghetti, who stood upon the steps, nodded vehement approval, and rubbed his hands with delight as he thought of the triumph his great doctor must inevitably achieve. As I left the hotel I looked back at it with a feeling of genuine sorrow. Only a few days before our party had all been so happy together, and now one was stricken down with a mysterious malady that, so far as I could see, was likely to end in her death. Whether the gondolier had been admonished by Galaghetti to make haste, and was anxious to do so in sympathy with my trouble, I cannot say; the fact, however, remains that we accomplished the distance that separated the hotel from the palace in what could have been little more than half the time usually taken. My star was still in the ascendant when we reached the palace, for when I disembarked at the steps, the old man who did menial service for Nikola had just opened it and looked out. I inquired whether his master was at home, and, if so, whether I could see him? He evidently realised that my Italian was of the most rudimentary description, for it was necessary for me to repeat my question three or four times before he could comprehend my meaning. When at last he did so, he pointed up the stairs to signify that Nikola was at home, and also that, if I desired to see him, I had better go in search of him. I immediately did so, and hastened up the stairs to the room I have already described, of which I entertained such ghastly recollections. I knocked upon the door, and a well-known voice bade me in English to "come in." I was in too great a haste to fulfil my mission to observe at the time the significance these words contained. It was not until afterwards that I remembered the fact that, as we approached the palace, I had looked up at Nikola's window and had seen no sign of him there. As I had not rung the bell, but had been admitted by the old man-servant, how could he have become aware of my presence? But, as I say, I thought of all that afterwards. For the moment the only desire I had was to inform Nikola of my errand.

Upon my entering the room I found Nikola standing before a table on which were glasses, test-tubes, and various chemical paraphernalia. He was engaged in pouring some dark-coloured liquid into a graduating glass, and when he spoke it was without looking round at me.

"I am very glad to see you, my dear Hatteras," he said. "It is kind of you to take pity on my loneliness. If you don't mind sitting down for a few moments, and lighting a cigar—you'll find the box on the table—I shall have finished this, and then we can talk."

"But I am afraid I can't wait," I answered. "I have come on the most important business. There is not a moment to lose."

"In that case I am to suppose that Miss Trevor is worse," he said, putting down the bottle from which he had been pouring, and afterwards replacing the glass stopper with the same hand. "I was afraid it might be so."

"How do you know that she is ill?" I asked, not a little surprised to hear that he was aware of our trouble.

"I manage to know a good many things," he replied. "I was aware that she was ill, and have been wondering how long it would be before I was called in. The other doctors don't like my interference, I suppose?"

"They certainly do not," I answered. "But they have done no good for her."

"And you think I may be able to help you?" he inquired, looking at me over the graduating glass with his strange, dark eyes.

"I certainly do," I replied.

"I am your debtor for the compliment."

"And you will come?"

"You really wish it?"

"I believe it is the only thing that will save her life," I answered. "But you must come quickly, or it will be too late. She was sinking when I left the hotel."

With a hand that never shook he poured the contents of the glass into a small phial, and then placed the latter in his pocket.

"I am at your disposal now," he answered. "We will set off as soon as you like. As you say, we must lose no time."

"But will it not be necessary for you to take some drugs with you?" I asked.

409

"I am taking this one," he replied, placing his hat upon his head as he spoke.

I remembered that he had been making his prescription up as I entered the room. Had he then intended calling to see her, even supposing I had not come to ask his assistance? I had no chance of putting the question to him, however.

"Have you a gondola below?" he asked, as we went down the stairs.

I replied in the affirmative; and when we gained the hall door we descended the steps and took our places in it. On reaching the hotel I conducted him to the drawing-room, where we found the Dean and Glenbarth eagerly awaiting our coming. I presented the former to Nikola, and then went off to inform my wife of his arrival. She accompanied me back to the drawing-room, and when she entered the room, Nikola crossed it to receive her. Though she looked at him in a frightened way I thought his manner soon put her at her ease.

"Perhaps you will be kind enough to take me to my patient," he said, when they had greeted each other. "As the case is so serious, I had better lose no time in seeing her."

He followed my wife from the room, and then we sat down to await his verdict, with what anxiety you may imagine.

Of all that transpired during his stay with Miss Trevor I can only speak from hearsay. My wife, however, was unfortunately too agitated to remember everything that occurred. She informed me that on entering the room he advanced very quietly towards the bed, and for a few moments stood looking down at the frail burden it supported. Then he felt her pulse, lifted the lids of her eyes, and for a space during which a man might have counted fifty slowly, laid his hand upon her forehead. Then, turning to the nurse, who had of course heard of the withdrawal of the other doctors, he bade her bring him a wine-glass full of iced water. She disappeared, and while she was absent Nikola sat by the bedside holding the sick girl's hand, and never for a moment taking his eyes from her face. Presently the woman returned, bringing the water as directed. He took it from her, and going to the window poured from a phial, which he had taken from his pocket, some twenty drops of the dark liquid it contained. Then with a spoon he gave her nearly half of the contents of the glass. This done he once more seated himself beside the bed, and waited patiently for the result. Several times within the next half-hour he bent over the recumbent figure, and was evidently surprised at not seeing some change which he expected would take place. At the end of that time he gave her another spoonful of the liquid, and once more sat down to watch. When an hour had passed he permitted a sigh of satisfaction to escape him, then, turning to my wife, whose anxiety was plainly expressed upon her face, he said:

"I think, Lady Hatteras, that you may tell them that she will not die. There is still much to be done, but I pledge my word that she will live."

The reaction was too much for my wife; she felt as if she were choking, then she turned giddy, and at last was possessed with a frantic desire to cry. Softly leaving the room, she came in search of us. The moment that she opened the door of the drawing-room, and I looked upon her face, I knew that there was good news for us.

"What does he say about her?" cried the Duke, forgetting the Dean's presence, while the latter rose and drew a step nearer, without speaking a word.

"There is good news," she said, fumbling with her handkerchief in a suspicious manner. "Doctor Nikola says she will live."

"Thank God!" we all said in one breath. And Glenbarth murmured something more that I did not catch.

So implicit was our belief in Nikola that, as you have doubtless observed, we accepted his verdict without a second thought. I kissed my wife, and then shook hands solemnly with the Dean. The Duke had meanwhile vanished, presumably to his own apartment, where he could meditate on certain matters undisturbed. After that, Phyllis left us and returned to the sickroom, where she found Nikola still seated beside the bed, just as she had left him. So far as she could judge, Miss Trevor did not appear to be any different, though perhaps she did not breathe as heavily as she had hitherto done; Nikola, however, appeared to be will satisfied. He nodded approvingly to Phyllis as she entered, and then returned to the contemplation of his patient once more. In this fashion hour after hour went by. Once during each my wife would come to me with reassuring bulletins. "Miss Trevor was, if anything, a little better, she did not seem so restless as before."

"The fever seems to be abating;" and then, towards nine o'clock that night, "at last Gertrude was sleeping peacefully." It was not, however, until nearly midnight that Nikola himself made his appearance.

"The worst is over," he said, approaching the Dean; "your daughter is now asleep, and will only require watching for the next two hours. At the end of that time I shall return, and shall hope to find a decided improvement in her condition."

"I can never thank you enough, my dear sir," said the worthy old clergyman, shaking the other by the hand while the tears ran down his wrinkled cheeks. "But for your wonderful skill there can be no sort of doubt that she would be lost to us now. She is my only child, my ewe lamb, and may Heaven bless you for your goodness to me."

I thought that Nikola looked at him very curiously as he said this. It was the first time I had seen Nikola brought into the society of a dignitary of the English Church, and I was anxious to see how the pair comported themselves under the circumstances. A couple more diametrically opposite could be scarcely imagined. They were as oil and water, and could scarcely be expected to assimilate.

"Sir, I should have been less than human if I had not done everything possible to save that beautiful young life," said Nikola, with what was to me the suggestion of a double meaning in his speech. "And now you must permit me to bid you goodbye for the present. In two hours I shall return again."

Thinking he might prefer to remain near his patient, I pressed him to stay at the hotel, offering to do all that lay in my power to make him comfortable. But he would not hear of such a thing.

"As you should be aware by this time, I never rest away from my own house," he answered, in a tone that settled the matter once and for all. "If anything should occur in the meantime, send for me and I will come at once. I do not apprehend any change, however."

When he had gone I went in search of the Duke and found him in his own room.

"Dick," he said, "look at me and tell me if you can see any difference. I feel as though I had passed through years of suffering. Another week would have made an old man of me. How is she now?"

"Progressing famously," I answered. "You need not look so sceptical, for this must surely be the case, since Nikola has gone home to take some rest and will not return for two hours."

He wrung my hand on hearing this.

"How little I dreamt," he said, "when we were confined in that wretched room in Port Said, and when he played that trick upon me in Sydney, that some day he was destined to do me the greatest service any man has ever done me in my life. Didn't I tell you that those other medicos did not know what they were doing, and that Nikola is the greatest doctor in the world?"

I admitted that he had given me the first assurance, but I was not quite so certain about the latter. Then, realising how he must be feeling, I proposed that we should row down the canal for a breath of fresh sea air. At first the Duke was for refusing the invitation, eventually however he assented, and when we had induced the Dean to accompany us we set off. When we reached the hotel once more it was to discover that Nikola had returned, and that he had again taken up his watch in the sickroom. He remained there all night, passing hour after hour at the bedside, without, so my wife asserted, moving, save to give the medicine, and without apparently feeling the least fatigue.

It was not until between seven and eight o'clock next morning that I caught a glimpse of him. He was in the dining-room then, partaking of a small cup of black coffee, into which he had poured some curious decoction of his own. For my part I have never yet been able to discover how Nikola managed to keep body and soul together on his frugal fare.

"How is the patient this morning?" I asked, when we had greeted each other.

"Out of danger," he replied, slowly stirring his coffee as he spoke. "She will continue to progress now. I hope you are satisfied that I have done all I can in her interests?"

"I am more than satisfied," I answered. "I am deeply grateful. As her father said yesterday, if it had not been for you, Nikola, she must inevitably have succumbed. She will have cause to bless your name for the remainder of her existence."

He looked at me very curiously as I said this.

"Do you think she will do that?" he asked, with unusual emphasis. "Do you think it will please her to remember that she owes her life to me?"

"I am sure she will always be deeply grateful," I replied somewhat ambiguously. "I fancy you know that yourself."

"And your wife? What does she say?"

"She thinks you are certainly the greatest of all doctors," I answered, with a laugh. "I feel that I ought to be jealous, but strangely enough I'm not."

"And yet I have done nothing so very wonderful," he continued, almost as if he were talking to himself. "But that those other blind worms are content to go digging in their mud, when they should be seeking the light in another direction, they could do as much as I have done. By the way, have you seen our friend, Don Martinos, since you dined together at my house?"

I replied to the effect that I had not done so, but reported that the Don had sent repeated messages of sympathy to us during Miss Trevor's illness. I then inquired whether Nikola had seen him?

"I saw him yesterday morning," he replied. "We devoted upwards of four hours to exploring the city together."

I could not help wondering how the Don had enjoyed the excursion, but I did not say anything on this score to my companion.

That night Nikola was again in attendance upon his patient. Next day she was decidedly better; she recognised her father and my wife, and every hour was becoming more and more like her former self.

"Was she surprised when she regained consciousness to find Nikola at her bedside?"

I inquired of Phyllis when the great news was reported to me.

"Strangely enough she was not," Phyllis replied. "I fully expected, remembering my previous suspicions, that it would have a bad effect upon her, but it did nothing of the kind. It was just as if she had expected to find him there."

"And what were his first words to her?"

"'I hope you are feeling better, Miss Trevor,' he said, and she replied, 'Much better,' that was all. It was as commonplace as could be."

Next day Nikola only looked in twice, the day after once, and at the end of the week informed me that she stood in no further need of his attention.

"How shall we ever be able to reward you, Nikola?" I asked, for about the hundredth time, as we stood together in the corridor outside the sickroom.

"I have no desire to be rewarded," he answered. "It is enough for me to see Miss Trevor restored to health. Endeavour, if you can, to recall a certain conversation we had together respecting the lady in question on the evening that I narrated to you the story concerning the boy who was so badly treated by the Spanish Governor. Did I not tell you then that our destinies were inextricably woven together? I informed you that it had been revealed to me many years ago that we should meet; should you feel surprised, therefore, if I told you that I had also been warned of this illness?"

Once more I found myself staring at him in amazement.

"You are surprised? Believe me, however astonishing it may seem, it is quite true. I knew that Miss Trevor would come into my life; I knew also that it would be my lot also to save her from death. What is more, I know that in the end the one thing, which has seemed to me most desirable in life, will be taken from me by her hands."

"I am afraid I cannot follow you," I said.

"Perhaps not, but you will be able to some day," he answered. "That moment has not yet arrived. In the meantime watch and wait, for before we know it it will be upon us."

Then, with a look that was destined to haunt me for many a long day, he bade me farewell, and left the hotel.

414

Chapter 10

To the joy of every one, by the Thursday following Miss Trevor was sufficiently recovered to be able to leave her room. It was a happy day for every one concerned, particularly for the Duke, who came nearer presenting the appearance of an amiable lunatic on that occasion than I had ever seen him before. Why my wife should have encouraged him in his extravagance I cannot say, but the fact remains that she allowed him to go out with her that morning with the professed idea of purchasing a few flowers to decorate the drawing-room for the invalid's reception. So great was their extravagance that the room more resembled a hot-house, or a flower-show, than a civilised apartment. I pointed this out to my wife with a gentle remonstrance, and was informed that, being a mere husband, I knew nothing at all about the matter. I trust that I preserved my balance and lived up to my reputation for sanity in the midst of this general excitement, though I am prepared to confess that I was scarcely myself when the triumphal procession, consisting of my wife and the Dean, set off to the invalid's apartment to escort her in. When she appeared it was like a ghost of her former self, and a poor wan ghost too. Her father, of course, she had already seen, but neither I nor Glenbarth had of course had the honour of meeting her since she was taken ill. She received him very graciously, and was kind enough to thank me for the little I had done for her. We seated her between us in a comfortable chair, placed a footstool under her feet, and then, in order that she should not have too much excitement, and that she might rest quietly, the Dean, the Duke, and myself were sent about our business for an hour. When we returned, a basket of exquisite roses stood on the table, and on examining it the card of Don Jose de Martinos was found to be attached to it.

It is some proof of the anxiety that Glenbarth felt not to do anything that might worry her when I say that he read the card and noted the giver without betraying the least trace of annoyance. It is true that he afterwards furnished me with his opinion of the giver for presuming to send them, but the casual observer would have declared, had he been present to observe the manner in which he behaved when he had first seen the gift, that he had taken no interest in the matter at all.

Next day Miss Trevor was permitted to get up a little earlier and on the day following a little earlier still. In the meantime more flowers had arrived from the Don, while he himself had twice made personal inquiries as to the progress she was making. It was not until the third day of her convalescence that Nikola called to see his patient. I was sitting alone with her at the time, my wife and our other two guests having gone shopping in the Merceria. I was idly cutting a copy of a Tauchnitz publication that I had procured for her on the previous day.

The weather was steadily growing warmer, and, for this reason, the windows were open and a flood of brilliant sunshine was streaming into the room. From the canal outside there came the sounds of rippling laughter, then an unmistakably American voice called out, "Say, girls, what do you think of Venice now you're here?"

Then another voice replied, "Plenty of water about, but they don't seem to wash their buildings much." Miss Trevor was about to speak, in fact she had opened her lips to do so, when a strange expression appeared upon her face. She closed her eyes for a moment, and I began to fear that she was ill. When she opened them again I was struck by a strange fact; the eyes were certainly there, but there was no sort of life in them. They were like those of a sleepwalker who, while his eyes are open, sees nothing of things about him. A moment later there was a knock at the door, and Doctor Nikola, escorted by a servant, entered the room. Wishing us "good morning," he crossed the room and shook hands with Miss Trevor, afterwards with myself.

"You are certainly looking better," he said, addressing his patient, and placing his finger and thumb upon her wrist as he spoke.

"I am much better," she answered, but for some reason without her usual animation.

"In that case I think this is the last visit I shall pay you in my professional capacity," he said. "You have been an excellent patient, and in the interests of what our friend Sir Richard here calls Science, permit me to offer you my grateful thanks."

"It is I who should thank you," she answered, as if she were repeating some lessons she had learnt by heart.

416

"I trust then, on the principle that one seldom or never acts as one should, that you will not do it," he replied, with a smile. "I am amply rewarded by observing that the flush of health is returning to your cheeks."

He then inquired after my wife's health, bade me be careful of her for the reason that, since I had behaved so outrageously towards them, no other doctors in Venice would attend her, should she be taken ill, and then rose to bid us adieu.

"This is a very short visit," I said. "Cannot we persuade you to give us a little more of your society?"

"I fear not," he answered. "I am developing quite a practice in Venice, and my time is no longer my own."

"You have other patients?" I asked, in some surprise, for I did not think he would condescend to such a thing.

"I have your friend, Don Martinos, now upon my hands," he said. "The good Galaghetti is so abominably grateful for what I did for his child, that he will insist on trying to draw me into experimenting upon other people."

"Would it be indiscreet to ask what is the matter with the Don?" I said. "He does not look like a man who would be likely to be an invalid."

"I do not think there is very much wrong with him," Nikola replied vaguely. "At any rate it is not anything that cannot be very easily put right."

When he left the room I accompanied him down the corridor as far as the hall.

"The fact of the matter is," he began, when we were alone together, "our friend the Don has been running the machinery of life a little too fast of late. I am told that he lost no less a sum than fifty thousand pounds in English money last week, and certainly his nerves are not what they once were."

"He is a gambler, then?" I said.

"An inveterate gambler, I should say," Nikola answered. "And when a Spaniard takes to that sort of amusement, he generally does it most thoroughly."

Whatever the Don's illness may have been, it certainly had made its mark upon his appearance. I chanced to meet him that afternoon on the Rialto bridge, and was thunderstruck at the change. The man's face was white, and his eyes had dark rings under them, that to my thinking spoke for an enfeebled heart. When he stopped to speak to me, I noticed that his hands trembled as though he were afflicted with St. Vitus's dance.

417

"I hope Miss Trevor is better," he said, after I had commented upon the fact that I had not seen him of late.

"Much better," I answered. "In fact, she may now be said to be convalescent. I was sorry to hear from Doctor Nikola, however, that you yourself are not quite the thing."

"Nerves, only nerves," he answered, with what was almost a frightened look in his eyes. "Doctor Nikola will set me right in no time, I am sure of that. I have had a run of beastly luck lately, and it has upset me more than I can say."

I knew to what he referred, but I did not betray my knowledge. After that he bade me farewell, and continued his walk. That evening another exquisite basket of flowers arrived for Miss Trevor. There was no card attached to it, but as the Duke denied all knowledge of it, I felt certain as to whence it came. On the day following, for the first time since her illness, Miss Trevor was able to leave the house and to go for a short airing upon the canal. We were rejoiced to take her, and made arrangements for her comfort, but there was one young man who was more attentive than the rest of all the party put together. Would Miss Trevor like another cushion? Was she quite sure that she was comfortable? Would she have preferred a gondola to a *barca*? I said nothing but I wondered what the Dean thought, for he is an observant old gentleman. As for the young lady herself, she accepted the other's attentions with the most charmed good-humour, and thus all went merry as marriage-bells. On the day following she went out again, and on the afternoon of the next day felt so much stronger as to express a desire to walk for a short time on the piazza of St. Mark. We accordingly landed at the well-known steps, and strolled slowly towards the cathedral. It was a lovely afternoon, the air being soft and warm, with a gentle breeze blowing in from the sea.

It is needless for me to say that Glenbarth was in the seventh heaven of delight, and was already beginning to drop sundry little confidences into my ear. Her illness had ruined the opportunity he had hoped to have had, but he was going to make up for it now. Indeed it looked very much as if she had at last made up her mind concerning him, but, having had one experience of the sex, I was not going to assure myself that all was satisfactory until a definite announcement was made by the lady herself. As it turned out it was just as well that I did so, for that afternoon, not altogether unexpectedly I must confess, was destined to prove the truth of the old saying that the course of true love never runs smooth. Miss Trevor, with the Duke on one side and my wife on the other, was slowly passing across the great square, when a man suddenly appeared before us from one of the shops on our right. This individual was none other than the Don Jose de Martinos, who raised his hat politely to the ladies and expressed his delight at seeing Miss Trevor abroad once more. As usual, he was faultlessly dressed, and on the whole looked somewhat better in health than he had done when I had last seen him. By some means, I scarcely know how it was done, he managed to slip in between my wife and Miss Trevor, and in this order we made our way towards our usual resting place, Florian's cafe. Never, since we had known him, had the Don exerted himself so much to please. The Duke, however, did not seem satisfied. His high spirits had entirely left him, and, in consequence, he was now as quiet as he had been talkative before. It was plain to all of us that the Don admired Miss Trevor, and that he wanted her to become aware of the fact. Next morning he made an excuse and joined our party again. At this the Duke's anger knew no bounds.

Personally I must confess that I was sorry for the young fellow. It was very hard upon him, just as he was progressing so favourably, that another should appear upon the scene and distract the lady's attention. Yet there was only one way of ending it, if only he could summon up sufficient courage to do it. I fear, however, that he was either too uncertain as to the result, or that he dreaded his fate, should she consign him to the outer darkness, too much to put it into execution. For this reason he had to submit to sharing her smiles with the Spaniard, which, if only he could have understood it, was an excellent thing for his patience, and a salutary trial for his character.

Meanwhile, my wife looked on in despair.

"I thought it was all settled," she said pathetically, on one occasion, "and now they are as far off as ever. Why on earth does that troublesome man come between them?"

"Because he has quite as much right to be there as the other," I answered. "If the Duke wants her, let him ask her, but that's just what he won't do. The whole matter should have been settled by now."

"It's all very well for you to say that," she returned. "The poor boy would have done it before Gertrude was taken ill, but that you opposed him."

"And a very proper proceeding too," I answered. "Miss Trevor was under my charge, and I was certainly not going to let any young man, doubtless very desirable, but who had only known her two days, propose to her, get sent about his business, render it impossible for your party to continue together, and by so doing take all the pleasure out of our holiday."

"So it was only of yourself you were thinking?" she returned, with that wonderful inconsistency that is such a marked trait in her character. "Why do you urge him now to do it?"

"Because Miss Gertrude is no longer under my charge," I answered. "Her father is here, and is able to look after her." Then an idea occurred to me, and I acted upon it at once. "When you come to think of it, my dear," I said, as if I had been carefully considering the question, "why should the Don not make Gertrude as good a husband as Glenbarth? He is rich, doubtless comes of a very good family, and would certainly make a very presentable figure in society."

She stared at me aghast.

"Well," she said in astonishment, "I must say that I think you are a loyal friend. You know the Duke has set his heart on marrying her, and yet you are championing the cause of his rival. I should never have thought it of you, Dick."

I hastened to assure her that I was not in earnest, but for a moment I almost fancy she thought I was.

"If you are on the Duke's side I wonder that you encourage Don Martinos to continue his visits," she went on, after the other matter had been satisfactorily settled. "I cannot tell you how much I dislike him. I feel that I would rather see Gertrude married to a crossing-sweeper than to that man. How she can even tolerate him, I do not know. I find it very difficult to do so."

"Poor Don," I said, "he does not appear to have made a very good impression. In common justice I must admit that, so far as I am concerned, he has been invariably extremely civil."

"Because he wants your interest. You are the head of the house."

"It is a pretty fiction—let it pass however."

She pretended not to notice my gibe.

"He is gambling away every halfpenny he possesses."

I regarded her with unfeigned astonishment. How could she have become aware of this fact? I put the question to her.

"Some one connected with the hotel told my maid, Phillipa," she answered "They say he never returns to the hotel until between two and three in the morning."

"He is not married," I retorted.

She vouchsafed no remark to this speech, but, bidding me keep my eyes open, and beware lest there should be trouble between the two men, left me to my own thoughts.

The warning she had given me was not a futile one, for it needed only half an eye to see that Glenbarth and Martinos were desperately jealous of one another. They eyed each other when they met as if, at any moment, they were prepared to fly at each other's throats. Once the Duke's behaviour was such as to warrant my speaking to him upon the subject when we were alone together.

"My dear fellow," I said, "I must ask you to keep yourself in hand. I don't like having to talk to you, but I have to remember that there are ladies in the case."

"Then why on earth doesn't Martinos keep out of my way?" he asked angrily. "You pitch into me for getting riled, but you don't see how villainously rude he is to me. He contradicts me as often as he can, and, for the rest of the time, treats me as if I were a child."

"In return you treat him as if he were an outsider, and had no right to look at, much less to speak to, Miss Trevor. Nevertheless he is our friend—or if he is not our friend, he has at least been introduced to us by a friend. Now I have no desire that you should quarrel at all, but if you must do so, let it be when you are alone together, and also when you are out of the hotel."

I had no idea how literally my words were to be taken.

That night, according to a custom he had of late adopted, Martinos put in an appearance after dinner, and brought his guitar with him. As he bade us "good evening" I looked at the Duke's face. It was pale and set as if he had at last come to an understanding with himself. Presently my wife and I sang a duet together, in a fashion, that pointed very plainly to the fact that our thoughts were elsewhere. Miss Trevor thanked us in a tone that showed me that she also had given but small attention to our performance. Then Gertrude sang a song of Tosti's very prettily, and was rewarded with enthusiastic applause. After this the Don was called upon to perform. He took up his guitar, and having tuned it, struck a few chords and began to sing. Though I look back upon that moment now with real pain, I must confess that I do not think I have ever heard him sing better; the merry laughter of the song suited his voice to perfection. It was plainly a comic ditty with some absurd imitations of the farmyard at the end of each verse. When he had finished, my wife politely asked him to give us a translation of the words. Fate willed that she should ask, I suppose, and also that he should answer it.

"It is a story of a foolish young man who loved a fair maid," he replied, speaking with the utmost deliberation. "Unfortunately, however, he was afraid to tell her of his love. He pined to be with her, yet, whenever he was desirous of declaring his passion his courage failed him at the last moment, and he was compelled to talk of the most commonplace things, such as the animals upon his father's farm. At last she, tiring of such a laggard, sent him away in disgust to learn how to woo In the meantime she married a man who was better acquainted with his business."

Whether the song was exactly as he described it, I am not in a position to say; the fact, however, remains that at least four of our party saw the insinuation and bitterly resented it. I saw the Duke's face flush and then go pale. I thought for a moment that he was going to say something, but he contented himself by picking up a book from the table at his side, and glancing carelessly at it. I could guess, by the way his hands gripped it, something of the storm that was raging in his breast. My wife, meanwhile, had turned the conversation into another channel by asking the Dean what he had thought of a certain old church he had visited that morning. This gave a little relief, but not very much. Ten minutes later the Don rose and bade us "good night." With a sneer on his face, he even extended his good wish to the Duke, who bowed, but did not reply. When he had gone, my wife gave the signal for a general dispersal, and Glenbarth and I were presently left in the drawing-room alone. I half expected an immediate outburst, but to my surprise he said nothing on the subject. I had no intention of referring to it unless he did, and so the matter remained for a time in abeyance. After a conversation on general topics, lasting perhaps a quarter of an hour, we wished each other "good night," and retired to our respective rooms. When I entered my wife's room later, I was prepared for the discussion which I knew was inevitable.

"What do you think of your friend now?" she asked, with a touch of sarcasm thrown into the word "friend." "You of course heard how he insulted the Duke?"

"I noticed that he did a very foolish thing, not only for his own interests with us, but also for several other reasons. You may rely upon it that if ever he had any chance with Gertrude—"

"He never had the remotest chance, I can promise you that," my wife interrupted.

"I say if ever he had a chance with Gertrude, he has lost it now. Surely that should satisfy you."

"It does not satisfy me that he should be rude to our guest at any time, but I am particularly averse to his insulting him in our presence."

"You need not worry yourself," I said. "In all probability you will see no more of him. I shall convey a hint to him upon the subject. It will not be pleasant, for Anstruther's sake."

"Mr. Anstruther should have known better than to have sent him to us," she replied. "There is one thing I am devoutly thankful for, and that is that the Duke took it so beautifully. He might have been angry, and have made a scene. Indeed I should not have blamed him, had he done so."

I did not ask her, for reasons of my own, whether she was sure that his Grace of Glenbarth was not angry. I must confess that I was rendered more uneasy by the quiet way he had taken it, than if he had burst into an explosion. Concealed fires are invariably more dangerous than open ones.

Next morning after breakfast, while we were smoking together in the balcony, a note was brought to Glenbarth. He took it, opened it, and when he had read the contents, thrust it hastily into his pocket.

"No answer," he said, as he lit a cigar, and I thought his hand trembled a little as he put the match to it.

His face was certainly paler than usual, and there was a far-away look in his eyes that showed me that it was not the canal or the houses opposite that he was looking upon.

"There is something behind all this, and I must find out what it is," I said to myself. "Surely he can't be going to make a fool of himself."

I knew, however, that my chance of getting anything satisfactory out of him lay in saying nothing about the matter just then. I must play my game in another fashion.

"What do you say if we run down to Rome next week?" I asked, after a little pause. "My wife and Miss Trevor seem to think they would enjoy it. There are lots of people we know there just now."

"I shall be very pleased," he answered, but with a visible effort.

At any other time he would have jumped eagerly at the suggestion. Decidedly there was something wrong! At luncheon he was preoccupied, so much so, that I could see Miss Trevor wondered what was the matter. Had she known the terrible suspicion that was growing in my own mind, I wonder what she would have said, and also how she would have acted?

That afternoon the ladies resolved to remain at home, and the Dean decided to stay with them. In consequence, the Duke and I went out together. He was still as quiet as he had been in the morning, but as yet I had not been able to screw up my courage to such a pitch as to be able to put the question to him. Once, however, I asked the reason for his quietness, and received the evasive reply "that he was not feeling quite up to the mark that day."

This time I came a little nearer to the point.

"You are not worrying about that wretched fellow's rudeness, I hope?" I said, looking him fairly and squarely in the face.

"Not in the least," he answered. "Why should I be?"

"Well, because I know you are hot-tempered," I returned, rather puzzled to find an explanation for him.

"Oh, I'll have it out with him at some time or another, I have no doubt," he continued, and then changed the subject by referring to some letters he had had from home that day.

When later we returned to the hotel for afternoon tea, we found the two ladies eagerly awaiting our coming. From the moment that he entered the room, Miss Trevor was graciousness itself to the young man. She smiled upon him, and encouraged him, until he scarcely knew whether he was standing upon his head or his heels. I fancy she was anxious to compensate him for the Don's rudeness to him.

That evening we all complained of feeling tired, and accordingly went to bed early. I was the latest of the party, and my own man had not left my dressing-room more than a minute before he returned with the information that the Duke's valet would be glad if he could have a few words with me.

"Send him in," I said, and forthwith the man made his appearance.

"What is it, Henry?" I inquired. "Is your master not well?"

"I don't know what's wrong with his Grace, sir," the man replied. "I'm very much frightened about him, and I thought I would come to you at once."

"Why, what is the matter? He seemed well enough when I bade him good night, half an hour or so ago."

"It isn't that, sir. He's well enough in his body," said the man. "There's something else behind it all. I know, sir, you won't mind my coming to you. I didn't know what else to do."

"You had better tell me everything, then I shall know how to act. What do you think is the reason of it?"

"Well, sir, it's like this," Henry went on. "His Grace has been very quiet all day. He wrote a lot of letters this morning and put them in his despatch box. 'I'll tell you what to do with them later, Henry,' he said when he had finished. Well, I didn't think very much of that, but when tonight he asked me what I had made up my mind to do with myself if ever I should leave his service, and told me that he had put it down in his will that I was to have five hundred pounds if he should die before I left him, I began to think there was something the matter. Well, sir, I took his things tonight, and was in the act of leaving the room, when he called me back. 'I'm going out early for a swim in the sea tomorrow morning,' he said, 'but I shan't say anything to Sir Richard Hatteras about it, because I happen to know that he thinks the currents about

424

here are dangerous. Well, one never knows what may turn up,' he goes on to say 'and if, by any chance, Henry—though I hope such a thing will not happen—I should be caught, and should not return, I want you to give this letter to Sir Richard. But remember this, you are on no account to touch it until mid-day. Do you understand?'

"I told him that I did, but I was so frightened, sir, by what he said, that I made up my mind to come and see you at once."

This was disturbing intelligence indeed. From what he said there could be no doubt that the Don and Glenbarth contemplated fighting a duel. In that case what was to be done? To attempt to reason with the Duke in his present humour would be absurd, besides, his honour was at stake, and, though I am totally against duels, that counts for something.

"I am glad you told me this, Henry," I said, "for now I shall know how to act. Don't worry about your master's safety. Leave him to me. He is safe in my hands. He shall have his swim tomorrow morning, but I shall take very good care that he is watched. You may go to bed with an easy heart, and don't think about that letter. It will not be needed, for he will come to no harm."

The man thanked me civilly and withdrew, considerably relieved in his mind by his interview with me. Then I sat myself down to think the matter out. What was I to do? Doubtless the Don was an experienced duellist, while Glenbarth, though a very fair shot with a rifle or fowling-piece, would have no chance against him with the pistol or the sword. It was by no means an enviable position for a man to be placed in, and I fully realised my responsibility in the matter. I felt that I needed help, but to whom should I apply for it? The Dean would be worse than useless; while to go to the Don and ask him to sacrifice his honour to our friendship for Glenbarth would be to run the risk of being shown the door. Then I thought of Nikola, and made up my mind to go to him at once. Since the Duke had spoken of leaving the hotel early in the morning, there could be no doubt as to the hour of the meeting. In that case there was no time to be lost. I thereupon went to explain matters to my wife.

"I had a suspicion that this would happen," she said, when she had heard me out. "Oh, Dick! you must stop it without fail. I should never forgive myself if anything were to happen to him while he is our guest. Go to Dr. Nikola at once and tell him everything, and implore him to help us as he has helped us before."

Thus encouraged, I left her, and went back to my dressing-room to complete my attire. This done I descended to the hall to endeavour to obtain a gondola. Good fortune favoured me, for the American party who had but lately arrived at the hotel, had just returned from the theatre. I engaged the man who had brought them, and told him to take me to the Palace Revecce with all possible speed.

"It's a late hour, Senor," he replied, "and I'd rather go anywhere than to that house in the Rio de Consiglio."

"You will be well paid for your trouble and also for your fear," I replied as I got into the boat.

Next moment we were on our way. A light was burning in Nikola's room as we drew up at the palace steps. I bade the gondolier wait for me, and to ensure his doing so, refused to pay him until my return. Then I rang the bell and was rewarded in a few minutes by hearing Nikola's footsteps on the flag-stones of the courtyard. When the door opened he was vastly surprised at seeing me; he soon recovered his equilibrium, however. It took more than a small surprise to upset Nikola. He invited me to enter.

"I hope there is nothing wrong," he said politely, "Otherwise how am I to account for this late call?"

"Something is very wrong indeed," I said. "I have come to consult you, and to ask for your assistance."

By this time he had reached his own room—that horrible room I remembered so well.

"The fact of the matter is," I said, seating myself in the chair he offered me as I spoke, "the Duke of Glenbarth and Don de Martinos have arranged to fight a duel soon after daybreak."

"To fight a duel?" Nikola repeated. "So it has come to this has it? Well, what do you want me to do?"

"Surely it is needless for me to say," I replied "I want you to help me to stop it. You like the Duke, I know. Surely you will not allow that brave young life to be sacrificed by that Spaniard?"

"From the way you speak it would appear that you do not care for that Martinos?" Nikola replied.

"I frankly confess that I do not," I replied. "He was introduced to me by a personal friend, but none of my party care very much for him. And now this new affair only adds to our dislike. He insulted the Duke most unwarrantably in my drawing-room last night, and this duel is the result."

"Always the same, always the same," Nikola muttered to himself. "But the end is coming, and his evil deeds will bear their own fruit." Then turning to me, he said aloud—"Since you wish it, I will help you. Don Jose is a magnificent shot, and he would place a bullet in the Duke's anatomy wherever he might choose to receive it. The issue would never for one moment be in doubt."

"But how do you know the Don is such a good shot?" I inquired with considerable surprise, for until the moment that I had introduced them to each other I had no idea that they had ever met.

"I know more about him than you think," he answered, fixing his glittering eyes upon me. "But now to business. If they fight at day-break there is not much time to be lost."

He went to his writing-table at the other side of the room and wrote a few lines on a sheet of note-paper. Placing it in an envelope he inquired whether I had told my gondolier to wait. Upon my answering in the affirmative, he left me and went downstairs.

"What have you done?" I inquired when he returned.

"I have sent word to an agent I sometimes employ," he said. "He will keep his eyes open. Now you had better get back to your hotel and to bed. Sleep secure on my promise that the two men shall not fight. When you are called, take the gondola you will find awaiting you outside the hotel, and I will meet you at a certain place. Now let me wish you a good night."

He conducted me to the hall below and saw me into the gondola. Then saying something to the gondolier that I didn't catch, he bade me adieu, and I returned to the hotel. Punctually at five o'clock I was awakened by a tapping at my bedroom door. I dressed, donned a cloak, for the morning was cold, and descended to the hall. The night watchman informed me that a gondola was awaiting me at the steps, and conducted me to it. Without a word I got in, and the little craft shot out into the canal. We entered a narrow street on the other side, took two or three turnings to right and left, and at last came to a standstill at some steps that I had never noticed before. A tall figure, wrapped in a black cloak, was awaiting us there. It was Nikola! Entering the gondola he took his place at my side. Then once more we set off.

At the same moment, so Nikola informed me, Glenbarth was leaving the hotel.

427

Chapter 11

When I had picked up Nikola we continued our voyage. Dawn was just breaking, and Venice appeared very strange and uncanny in the weird morning light. A cold wind was blowing in from the sea, and when I experienced its sharpness, I could not help feeling thankful that I had the foresight to bring my cloak.

"How do you know where the meeting is to take place?" I asked, after we had been travelling a few minutes.

"Because, when I am unable to find things out for myself, I have agents who can do it for me," he replied. "What would appear difficult, in reality is very simple. To reach the place in question it would be necessary for them to employ gondolas, and for the reason that, as you are aware, there are not many plying in the streets of Venice at such an early hour, it would be incumbent upon them to bespeak them beforehand. A few inquiries among the gondoliers elicited the information I wanted. That point satisfactorily settled, the rest was easy."

"And you think we shall be there in time to prevent the meeting?" I asked.

"We shall be at the rendezvous before they are," he answered. "And I have promised you they shall not fight."

Comforted by this reassuring news, I settled myself down to watch the tortuous thoroughfares through which we were passing. Presently we passed the church of St. Maria del Formosa, and later the Ducal Palace, thence out into the commencement of the Grand Canal itself. It was then that Nikola urged the gondoliers, for we had two, to greater speed. Under their powerful strokes the light little craft sped over the smooth bay, passed the island of St. Georgio Maggiore, and then turned almost due south. Then I thought of Glenbarth, and wondered what his feelings were at that moment. At last I began to have an inkling of our destination. We were proceeding in the direction of the Lido, and it was upon the sandy beach that separates the lagoons and Venice from the open sea that the duel was to be fought. Presently we landed, and Nikola said something to the gondoliers, who turned their craft and moved slowly away. After walking along the sands for some distance, we hid ourselves at a place where it was possible to see the strip of beach, while we ourselves remained hidden.

"They will not be here before another ten minutes," said Nikola, consulting his watch; "we had a good start of them."

Seating ourselves we awaited their arrival, and while we did so, Nikola talked of the value set upon human life by the inhabitants of different countries. No one was more competent to speak on such a subject than he, for he had seen it in every clime and in every phase. He spoke with a bitterness and a greater scorn for the petty vanities and aims of men than I had ever noticed in him before. Suddenly he stopped, and looking towards the left said:

"If I am not mistaken, the Duke of Glenbarth has arrived."

I looked in the direction indicated, and was able to descry the tall figure of the Duke coming along the sands. A little later two other persons made their appearance and followed him. One was undoubtedly the Don, but who was the third? As they drew closer, I discovered that he was unknown to me; not so to Nikola, however.

"Balmaceda," he said to himself, and there was an ugly sneer upon his face.

The Duke bowed ceremoniously to the two men, and the stranger, having returned his salute, knelt upon the sand, and commenced to open a box he had brought with him. From it he produced a pair of pistols which he loaded with ostentatious care. This work finished, he took them by their barrels and gave Glenbarth his choice. The Spaniard, I noticed, was dressed entirely in black, not showing a particle of white; the Duke was attired very much as usual. When each had taken a pistol, the stranger measured the distance upon the sands and allotted them their respective positions. By this time I was in such a fever of excitement that Nikola laid his hand upon my arm to restrain me.

"Wait," he whispered. "Have I not pledged you my word that your friend shall not be hurt? Do not interrupt them yet. I have my suspicions, and am anxious to confirm them."

I accordingly waited, but though it was only for a few seconds it seemed to me an eternity.

The two men were in position, and the stranger, I gathered, was giving them their final instructions. They were to stand with their faces turned from each other, and at the word of command were to wheel round and fire. In a flash I saw what Nikola had in his mind. The stranger was favouring the Don, for while Glenbarth would have faithfully carried out his portion of the contract, the Spaniard did not turn at all, a fact which his opponent was scarcely likely to become aware of, seeing that he would in all probability have a bullet in his heart before he would have had time to realise the trick that had been played upon him. The stranger had raised his hand above his head, and was about to give the signal, when Nikola sprang from beside me, and in a loud voice called to them to "stop." I rose to my feet at the same instant, and followed him across the sands to where the men stood.

"Put down your pistols, gentlemen," said Nikola in a voice that rang like a trumpet-call. "I forbid the duel. Your Grace, the challenge comes from you, I beg that you will apologise to Don Martinos for having sent it."

"I shall do nothing of the kind," the Duke returned.

On learning this Nikola took him on one side and talked earnestly with him for a few minutes. Then, still with his hand upon the other's arm, he led him back to where we were standing.

"I express my regret for having challenged you," said Glenbarth, but with no good grace.

"I thank you, your Grace," said Nikola. Then turning to the Don, he went on—"And now, Don Martinos, I hope you will apologise to the Duke for the insults that occasioned the challenge."

With an oath the Spaniard vowed that he was the last man to do anything of the kind. He had never apologised to any man in his life, and he was not going to do so now, with more to the same effect. Then Nikola fixed his glittering eyes upon him. His voice, however, when he spoke, was as conciliatory as ever.

"To oblige me you will do it," he said, and then drawing a little closer to him he murmured something that we could not hear. The effect upon the Don was magical His face turned a leaden hue, and for a moment I thought he would have fallen, but he recovered his self-possession with an effort, and muttered the apology Nikola had demanded of him.

"I thank you gentlemen," said Nikola. "Now, with your permission we will return to the city." Here he wheeled round upon the stranger, and continued:—"This is not the first of these little affairs in which you have played a part. You have been warned before, profit by it, for the time may come when it will be too late. Remember Pietro Sallomi."

I do not know who Pietro Sallomi may have been, but I know that the mere mention of his name was sufficient to take all the swagger out of the stranger. He fell to pieces like a house of cards.

"Now gentlemen, let us be moving," said Nikola, and taking the Don with him he set off quickly in the direction of the spot where we had disembarked from the gondola. I followed with the Duke.

"My dear boy," I said, as we walked along, "why on earth did you do it? Is your life of so little value to yourself or to your friends, that you try to throw it away in this reckless fashion?"

"I am the most miserable brute on the face of the earth," he replied. "I think it would have been far better for me had I been shot back there."

"Look here, Glenbarth," I said with some anger, "if you talk nonsense in this manner, I shall begin to think that you are not accountable for your actions. What on earth have you to be so unhappy about?"

"You know very well," he answered gloomily.

"You are making yourself miserable because Miss Trevor will not marry you," I said "You have not asked her, how therefore can you tell?"

"But she seems to prefer Don Martinos," he went on.

"Fiddlesticks!" I answered. "I'm quite certain she hasn't thought of him in that way. Now, I am going to talk plainly to you I have made up my mind that we leave today for Rome. We shall spend a fortnight there, and you should have a fair opportunity of putting the question to Miss Trevor. If you can't do it in that time, well, all I can say is, that you are not the man I took you for. You must remember one thing, however: I'll have no more of this nonsense. It's all very well for a Spanish braggart to go swaggering about the world, endeavouring to put bullets into inoffensive people, but it's not the thing for an English gentleman."

"I'm sorry, Dick. Try to forgive me. You won't tell Lady Hatteras, will you?"

"She knows it already," I answered. "I don't fancy you would get much sympathy from her. Try for a moment to picture what their feelings would have been—mine may be left out of the question—if you had been lying dead on the beach yonder. Think of your relations at home. What would they have said and thought? And for what?"

"Because he insulted me," Glenbarth replied. "Was I to put up with that?"

"You should have treated him with the contempt he merited. But there, do not let us discuss the matter any further. All's well that ends well: and I don't think we shall see much more of the Don."

When we reached the gondolas Nikola took me aside.

"You had better return to the city with the Duke in one," he said; "I will take the Don back in another."

"And what about the other fellow?" I inquired.

"Let him swim if he likes," said Nikola, with a shrug of his shoulders "By the way, I suppose you saw what took place back yonder?"

I nodded.

"Then say nothing about it," he replied. "Such matters are best kept to one's self."

It was a very sober-minded and reflective young man that sat down to breakfast with us that morning. My wife, seeing how matters stood, laid herself out to be especially kind to him. So affable indeed was she, that Miss Trevor regarded her with considerable surprise. During the meal the journey to Rome was discussed, and it was decided that I should telegraph for our old rooms, and that we should leave Venice at half-past two. This arrangement was duly carried out, and nightfall saw us well advanced on our journey to the capital. The journey is so well known that I need not attempt to describe it here. Only one incident struck me as remarkable about it. No sooner had we crossed the railway bridge that unites Venice with the mainland, than Miss Trevor's lethargy, if I may describe it, suddenly left her. She seemed to be her old self instantly. It was as though she had at last thrown off the load under which she had so long been staggering. She laughed and joked with my wife, teased her father, and was even inclined to be flippant with the head of the family. After the events of the morning the effects upon the Duke was just what we all wanted.

In due course we reached Rome, and installed ourselves at our old quarters in the Piazza Barberini. From that moment the time we had allowed ourselves sped by on lightning wings. We seemed scarcely to have got there before it was time to go back to Venice. It was unfortunately necessary for the Dean to return to England, at the end of our stay in Rome, and though it was considerably out of his way, he proposed journeying thither by way of Venice. The change had certainly done his daughter good. She was quite her old self once more, and the listless, preoccupied air that had taken such a hold upon her in Venice had entirely disappeared.

"Make the most of the Eternal City," my wife announced at dinner on the eve of our departure, "for tomorrow morning you will look your last upon it. The dragon who has us in his power has issued his decree, and, like the laws of the Medes and Persians, it changeth not."

"A dragon?" I answered. "You should say the family scapegoat! I protest to you, my dear Dean, that it is most unfair. If it is some disagreeable duty to be performed, then it is by my order; if it is something that will bestow happiness upon another, then it is my lady that gets the credit."

"A very proper arrangement," said my wife, "as I am sure the Dean will agree with me."

"I agree with you in everything," replied the polite old gentleman. "Could I do otherwise?"

"I appeal to the Duke, then. Is it your Grace's opinion that a husband should of necessity take upon himself the properties of a dragon?"

Even that wretched young man would not stand by an old friend.

"I am not going to be drawn into an argument with you," he said. "If Lady Hatteras calls you a dragon, then a dragon you must remain until the end of the chapter, so far as I am concerned."

"Phyllis is always right," answered Miss Trevor unblushingly.

"I give in," I said in mock despair. "If you are all against me, I am undone."

It was a beautiful moonlight night when we rose from dinner, and it was arranged that our last evening in Rome should be spent in a visit to the Coliseum. A carriage was immediately ordered, and when the ladies had wrapped themselves up warmly we set off. To those unfortunate individuals who have not had an opportunity of visiting that ancient structure, I can only justify my incompetency by saying that it would be well nigh impossible to furnish a description that would give them an adequate idea of the feeling of awe it inspires in one. By moonlight it presents a picture that for solemn grandeur is, to my thinking, without its equal in the world. Pompeii by moonlight suggests reflections. The great square of St. Mark's in Venice seen by the same mellow light is a sight never to be forgotten; but in my humble opinion the Coliseum eclipses them all. We entered it and stood in the great ring looking up at the tiers of seats, and recalling its past. The Dean was profoundly impressed, and spoke of the men who had given up their lives in martyrdom within those great walls.

"How many of the crowd gathered here to witness the agony of the tortured Christians," he said, "believed that the very religion which they so heartily despised was destined to sway the world, and to see the mighty Coliseum and the mightier power that built it, a ruin? It is a wonderful thought."

After the Dean's speech we crossed to a spot where a better view was obtainable. It was only then that we discovered that the Duke and Miss Trevor were not of our party. When, however, it was time to return they emerged from the shadow and followed us out. Both were unusually silent, and my wife, putting two and two together in her own fashion, came to the conclusion that they had quarrelled. When, later on, the Duke and I were alone together, and the ladies and the Dean had retired to their respective rooms, I was about to take him to task when he stopped me.

"Dick, old man," he said with a solemnity that could not have been greater had he been telling me of some great tragedy, "I want you to give me your congratulations. Miss Trevor has consented to become my wife."

I was so surprised that I scarcely knew what to do or say.

"Good gracious, man!—then why are you so downcast?" I replied. "I had made up my mind that she had refused you I—"

"I am far from being downcast," he said as solemnly as before. "I am the happiest man in the world. Can't you understand how I feel? Somehow—now that it is over, and I have won her—it seems so great a thing that it almost overwhelms me. You don't know, Dick, how proud I am that she should have taken me!"

"And so you ought to be," I said enthusiastically. "You'll have a splendid wife, and I know you'll make a good husband."

"I don't deserve it, Dick," he continued in humiliating self-abasement. "She is too good for me, much too good."

"I remember that I said the same thing myself," I replied. "Come to me in five years' time and let me hear what you have to say then."

"Confound you," he answered; "why do you talk like that?"

"Because it's the way of the world, my lad," I answered. "But there, you'll learn all for yourself soon enough. Now let me order a whisky-and-potash for you, and then off you go to bed."

"A whisky-and-potash?" he cried, with horror depicted on his face. "Do you think I'm going to drink whisky on the night that she has accepted me? You must be mad."

"Well, have your own way," I answered. "For my own part, I have no such scruples. I have been married too long."

I rang the bell, and, when my refreshment was brought to me, drank it slowly, as became a philosopher.

It would appear that Miss Trevor had already told my wife, for I was destined to listen to a considerable amount of information concerning it before I was allowed to close my eyes that night.

"I always said that they were suited to each other," she observed. "She will make an ideal duchess, and I think he may consider himself a very lucky fellow. What did he say about it?"

"He admitted that he was not nearly good enough for her."

"That was nice of him. And what did you say?"

"I told him to come to me in five years' time and let me hear what he had to say then," I answered with a yawn.

I had an idea that I should get into trouble over that remark, and I was not mistaken. I was told that it was an unfeeling thing to have said, that it was not the sort of idea to put into a young man's head at such a time, and that if every one had such a good wife as some other people she could name, they would have reason to thank their good fortune.

"If I am not mistaken, you told me you were not good enough for me when I accepted you," she retorted. "What do you say now?"

"Exactly what I said then," I answered diplomatically. "I am not good enough for you. You should have married the Dean."

"Don't be absurd. The Dean is a dear old thing, but is old enough to be my father."

"He will be Glenbarth's father-in-law directly," I said with a chuckle, "and then that young man will have to drink his claret and listen to his sermons. In consideration of that I will forgive him all his sins against me."

Then I fell asleep, to dream that I was a rival of St. George chasing a dragon over the seats of the Coliseum; to find, when I had run him to earth, that he had assumed human shape, and was no other than my old friend the Dean of Bedminster.

Next morning the young couple's behaviour at breakfast was circumspection itself. The worthy old Dean ate his breakfast unconscious of the shell that was to be dropped into his camp an hour later, while my wife purred approval over the teapot. Meanwhile I wondered what Nikola would have to say when he heard of the engagement. After the meal was over we left the Duke and Dean together. Somehow, I don't think Glenbarth was exactly at his ease, but when he reappeared half an hour later and shook me by the hand, he vowed that the old gentleman was the biggest trump in the world, and that I was the next. From this I gathered that the matter had been satisfactorily settled, and that, so far as parental consent was concerned, Miss Gertrude Trevor was likely to become the Duchess of Glenbarth without any unnecessary delay. Though there was not much time to spare before our train started, there was still sufficient for the lovers to make a journey to the Piazza di Trevi, where a magnificent diamond ring was purchased to celebrate the engagement. A bracelet that would have made any woman's mouth water was also dedicated to the same purpose. A memorial bracelet on the Etruscan model was next purchased for my wife, and was handed to her later on by her grateful friends.

"You did so much for us," said the Duke simply, when Miss Trevor made the presentation.

My lady thereupon kissed Miss Trevor and thanked the Duke, while I looked on in amazement.

"Come, now," I said, "I call that scarcely fair. Is the poor dragon to receive nothing? I was under the impression that I had done more than any one to bring about this happy result."

"You shall have our gratitude," Miss Trevor replied. "That would be so nice, wouldn't it?"

"We'll see what the Duke says in five years," I answered, and with this Parthian shot I left them.

Next morning we reached Venice. The journey had been a very pleasant one, but I must say that I was not sorry when it was over. The picture of two young lovers, gazing with devotion into each other's eyes hour after hour, is apt to pall upon one. We had left Mestre behind us, and were approaching the bridge I have described before as connecting Venice with the mainland, when I noticed that Gertrude Trevor had suddenly become silent and preoccupied. She had a headache, she declared to my wife, but thought it would soon pass off. On reaching the railway-station we chartered a *barca* to take us to our hotel. When we reached it, Galaghetti was on the steps to receive us. His honest face beamed with satisfaction, and the compliments he paid my wife when she set foot upon the steps, were such as to cover her with confusion. I directed my party to go upstairs, and then drew the old man on one side.

"Don Jose de Martinos?" I asked, knowing that it was sufficient merely to mention his name.

"He is gone, my lord," Galaghetti replied. "Since he was a friend of yours, I am sorry I could keep him no longer. Perhaps your lordship does not know that he has gambled all his money away, and that he has not even enough left to discharge his indebtedness to me."

"I certainly did not know it," I replied. "And I am sorry to hear it. Where is he now?"

"I could not say," Galaghetti replied. "But doubtless I could find out if your lordship desires to know."

"You need not do that," I answered. "I merely asked out of curiosity. Don Martinos was no friend of mine."

Then, bidding him good day, I made my way upstairs, turning over in my mind what I had heard. I was not at all surprised to hear that the Don had come to grief, though I had not expected that the catastrophe would happen in so short a time. It was satisfactory to know, however, that in all probability he would never trouble us again.

That afternoon, according to custom, we spent an hour at Florian's cafe. The Duke and Gertrude strolled up and down, while my wife drew my attention to their happiness. I had on several occasions sang Glenbarth's praises to the Dean, and as a result the old gentleman was charmed with his future son-in-law, and seemed to think that the summit of his ambition had been achieved. During our sojourn on the piazza. I kept my eyes open, for I was in hopes of seeing Nikola, but I saw nothing of him. If I was not successful in that way, however, I was more so in another. I had found a budget of letters awaiting me on my return from Rome, and as two of them necessitated my sending telegrams to England, I allowed the rest of the party to return to the hotel by boat, while I made my way to the telegraph-office. Having sent them off, I walked on to the Rio del Barcaroli, engaged a gondola there, and was about to step into it, when I became aware of a man watching me. He proved to be none other than the Spaniard, Don Martinos, but so great was the change in him that for a moment I scarcely recognised him. Though only a fortnight had elapsed since I had last seen him, he had shrunk to what was only a shadow of his former self. His face was of a pasty, fishy whiteness, and his eyes had a light in them that I had not seen there before. For the moment I thought he had been drinking, and that his unnatural appearance was the result. Remembering his murderous intention on the morning of the frustrated duel, I felt inclined not to speak to him. My pity, however, got the better of me, and I bade him good day. He did not return my salutation, however, but looked at me as if I were some one he had seen before, but could not remember where. I then addressed him by name.

In reply he beckoned to me to follow him out of earshot of the gondolier.

"I cannot remember your name," he said, gripping me by the arm, "but I know that I have met you before. I cannot remember anything now because—because—" Here he paused and put his hand to his forehead as if he were in pain. I endeavoured to make him understand who I was, but without success. He shook his head and looked at me, talking for a moment in Italian, then in Spanish, with interludes of English. A more pitiable condition for a man to get into could scarcely be imagined. At last I tried him with a question I thought might have some effect upon him.

"Have you met Doctor Nikola lately?" I inquired.

The effect it produced upon him was instantaneous. He shrunk from me as if he had been struck, and, leaning against the wall of the house behind him, trembled like an aspen leaf. For a man usually so self-assertive—one might almost say so aggressive—here was a terrible change. I was more than ever at a loss to account for it. He was the last man I should have thought would have been taken in such a way.

"Don't tell him; you must not tell him, promise me that you will not do so," he whispered in English. "He would punish me if he knew, and—and—" Here he fell to whimpering like a child who feared chastisement. It was not a pretty exhibition, and I was more shocked by it than I can say. At this juncture I remembered the fact that he was without means, and as my heart had been touched by his pathetic condition, I was anxious to render him such assistance as was in my power. For this reason I endeavoured to press a loan upon him, telling him that he could repay me when things brightened.

"No, no," he answered, with a flash of his old spirit; then he added in a whisper, "He would know of it!"

"Who would know if it?" I asked.

"Doctor Nikola," he answered. Then laying his hand upon my arm again, and placing his mouth close to my ear as if he were anxious to make sure that no one else should hear, he went on, "I would rather die of starvation in the streets than fall into his hands. Look at me," he continued, after a moment's pause. "Look what I am! I tell you he has got me, body and soul. I cannot escape from him. I have no will but his, and he is killing me inch by inch. I have tried to escape, but it is impossible. If I were on the other side of the world and he wanted me I should be obliged to come." Then with another change as swift as thought he began to defy Nikola, vowing that he would go away, and that nothing should ever induce him to see him again. But a moment later he was back in his old condition once more.

"Farewell, Senor," he whispered. "I must be going. There is no time to lose. He is awaiting me."

"But you have not told me where you are living now?"

"Cannot you guess?" he answered, still in the same curious voice. "My home is the Palace Revecce in the Rio del Consiglio."

Here was surprise indeed! The Don had gone to live with Nikola. Was it kindness that had induced the latter to take him in? If not, what were his reasons for so doing?

Chapter 12

As may be supposed, my meeting with the Don afforded me abundant food for reflection. Was it true, as he had said, that in his hour of distress, Nikola had afforded him an asylum? and if so, why was the latter doing so? I knew Nikola too well by this time to doubt that he had some good and sufficient reason for his action. Lurking at the back of my mind was a hideous suspicion that, although I tried my hardest not to think of it, would not allow itself to be banished altogether. I could not but remember the story Nikola had told me on that eventful evening concerning his early, life, and the chance remark he had let fall one day that he knew more about the man, Don Martinos, than I supposed, only tended to confirm it. If that were so, and he still cherished, as I had not the least doubt he did—for Nikola was one who never forgave or forgot—the same undying hatred and desire for vengeance against his old enemy, the son of his mother's betrayer, then there was—but here I was compelled to stop. I could not go on. The death-like face of the man I had just left rose before my mind's eye like an accusing angel, whereupon I made a resolution that I would think no more of him nor would I say anything to any member of our party concerning my meeting with him that afternoon. It is superfluous to remark that the latter resolve was more easily kept than the former.

The first dinner in Venice after our return was far from being a success. Miss Gertrude's headache, instead of leaving her, had become so bad that she was compelled to go forthwith to bed, leaving Glenbarth in despair, and the rest of our party as low-spirited as possible. Next morning she declared she was a little better, though she complained of having passed a wretched night.

"I had such horrible dreams," she told my wife, "that when I woke up I scarcely dared close my eyes again."

"I cannot remember quite what she said she dreamt," said Phyllis when she told me the story; "but I know that it had something to do with Doctor Nikola and his dreadful house, and that it frightened her terribly."

The girl certainly looked pale and haggard, and not a bit like the happy creature who had stepped into the train at Rome.

"Heaven grant that there is not more trouble ahead," I said to myself, as I smoked my pipe and thought over the matter. "I am beginning to wish we had not come to Venice at all. In that case we should not have seen Nikola or the Don, Miss Trevor would not have been in this state, and I should not have been haunted day and night with this horrible suspicion of foul play."

It was no use, however, talking of what might or might not have happened. It was sufficient that the things I have narrated had come to pass, and I must endeavour to derive what satisfaction I could from the reflection that I had done all that was possible under the circumstances.

On the day following our return to Venice, the Dean of Bedminster set off for England. I fancy he was sorry to go, and of one thing I am quite sure, and that was that we regretted losing him. It was arranged that, as soon as we returned to England, we should pay him a visit at Bedminster, and that the Duke should accompany us. Transparently honest though he was in all things, I fancy the old gentleman had a touch of vanity in his composition, and I could quite understand that he would be anxious to show off his future son-in-law before the society of his quiet cathedral town.

On the night following his departure, I had the most terrible dream I have had in my life. Though some time has elapsed since then, I can still recall the fright it gave me. My wife declares that she could see the effect of it upon my face for more than a day afterwards. But this, I think, is going a little too far. I am willing, however, to admit that it made a very great impression upon me at the time—the more so for the reason that it touched my thought, and I was quite at a loss to understand it. It was night, I remember, and I had just entered the Palace Revecce. I must have been invisible, for, though I stood in the room with Nikola, he did not appear to be aware of my presence. As usual he was at work upon some of his chemical experiments. Then I looked at his face and saw that it wore an expression that I had never seen there before. I can describe it best by saying that it was one of absolute cruelty, unrelieved by even the smallest gleam of pity. And yet it was not cruelty in the accepted meaning of the word, so much as an overwhelming desire to punish and avenge. I am quite aware, on reading over what I have just written, that my inability to convey the

440

exact impression renders my meaning obscure. Yet I can do no more. It was a look beyond the power of my pen to describe. Presently he put down the glass he held in his hand, and looked up with his head a little on one side, as if he were listening for some sound in the adjoining room. There was a shuffling footstep in the corridor outside, and then the door opened and there entered a figure so awful that I shrank back from it appalled. It was Don Martinos, and yet it was not the Don. The face and the height were perhaps the same, but the man himself was—oh, so different. On seeing Nikola he shambled forward, rather than walked, and dropped in a heap at his feet, clutching at his knees, and making a feeble whining noise, not unlike that of an animal in pain.

"Get up," said Nikola sternly, and as he said it he pointed to a couch on the further side of the room.

The man went and stretched himself out upon it as if in obedience to some unspoken command. Nikola followed him, and having exposed the other's chest, took from the table what looked like a hypodermic syringe, filled it from one of the graduated glasses upon the table, and injected the contents beneath the prostrate man's skin. An immediate and violent fit of trembling was the result, followed by awful contortions of the face; then suddenly he stiffened himself out and lay like one dead. Taking his watch from his pocket Nikola made a careful note of the time. So vivid was my dream that I can even remember hearing the ticking of the watch. Minute after minute went by, until at last the Don opened his eyes.

Then I realised that the man was no longer a human being, but an animal. He uttered horrible noises in his throat, that were not unlike the short, sharp bark of a wolf, and when Nikola bade him move he crawled upon the floor like a dog. After that he retreated to a corner, where he crouched and glowered upon his master, as if he were prepared at any moment to spring upon him and drag him down. As one throws a bone to a dog so did Nikola toss him food. He devoured it ravenously, as would a starving cur. There was foam at the corners of his mouth, and the light of madness in his eyes. Nikola returned to the table and began to pour some liquid into a glass. So busily occupied was he, that he did not see the thing, I cannot call it a man, in the corner, get on his feet. He had taken up a small tube and was stirring the contents of the glass with it, when the other was less than a couple of feet from him. I tried to warn him of his danger, only to find that I could not utter a word. Then the object sprang upon him and clawed at his throat. He turned, and, a moment later, the madman

441

was lying, whining feebly, upon the floor, and Nikola was wiping the blood from a scratch on the left-hand side of his throat. At that moment I awoke to find myself sitting up in bed, with the perspiration streaming down my face.

"I have had such an awful dream!" I said, in answer to my wife's startled inquiry as to what was the matter. "I don't know that I have ever been so frightened before."

"You are trembling now," said my wife. "Try not to think of it, dear. Remember it was only a dream."

That it was something more than a mere dream I felt certain. It was so complete and dovetailed so exactly with my horrible suspicions that I could not altogether consign it to the realms of fancy. Fearing a repetition if I attempted to go to sleep again, I switched on the electric light and endeavoured to interest myself in a book, but it was of no use. The face of the poor brute I had seen crouching in the corner haunted me continually, and would not be dispelled. Never in my life before had I been so thankful to see the dawn. At breakfast my wife commented upon my dream. Miss Trevor, however, said nothing. She became quieter and more distracted every day. Towards the evening Glenbarth spoke to me concerning her.

"I don't know what to make of it all," he said anxiously. "She assures me that she is perfectly well and happy, but seeing the condition she is in, I can scarcely believe that. It is as much as I can do to get a word out of her. If I didn't know that she loves me I should begin to imagine that she regretted having promised to be my wife."

"I don't think you need be afraid of that," I answered. "One has only to look at her face to see how deeply attached she is to you. The truth of the whole matter is, my dear fellow, I have come to the conclusion that we have had enough of Venice. Nikola is at the bottom of our troubles, and the sooner we see the last of him the better it will be for all parties concerned."

"Hear, hear, to that," he answered, fervently. "Deeply grateful though I am to him for what he did when Gertrude was ill, I can honestly say that I never want to see him again."

At luncheon that day I accordingly broached the subject of our return to England. It was received by my wife and the Duke with unfeigned satisfaction, and by Miss Trevor with what appeared to be approval. It struck me, however, that she did not seem so anxious to leave as I expected she would be. This somewhat puzzled me, but I was not destined to remain very long in ignorance of the reason.

That afternoon I happened to be left alone with her for some little

442

time. We talked for a while on a variety of topics, but I could see all the time that there was something she was desirous of saying to me, though she could not quite make up her mind how to commence. At last she rose, and crossing the room took a chair by my side.

"Sir Richard, I am going to ask a favour of you," she said, with a far-away look in her eyes.

"Let me assure you that it is granted before you ask it," I replied. "Will you tell me what it is?"

"It may appear strange to you," she said, "but I have a conviction, absurd, superstitious, or whatever you may term it, that some great misfortune will befall me if I leave Venice just yet. I am not my own mistress, and must stay. I want you to arrange it."

This was a nice sort of shell to have dropped into one's camp, particularly at such a time and under such circumstances, and I scarcely knew what reply to make.

"But what possible misfortune could befall you?" I asked.

"I cannot say," she replied. "I am only certain that I must remain for a little while longer. You can have no idea what I have suffered lately. Bear with me, Sir Richard." Here she lifted a face of piteous entreaty to me, which I was powerless to resist, adding, "I implore you not to be angry with me."

"Is it likely that I should be angry with you, Gertrude?" I replied. "Why should I be? If you really desire to remain for a little longer there is nothing to prevent it. But you must not allow yourself to become ill again. Believe me it is only your imagination that is playing tricks with you."

"Ah! you do not know everything," she answered. "Every night I have such terrible dreams that I have come to dread going to bed."

I thought of my own dream on the previous night, and could well understand how she felt. After her last remark she was silent for some moments. That there was something still to come, I could see, but what it was I had no more idea than a child. At last she spoke.

"Sir Richard," she said, "would you mind very much if I were to ask you a most important question? I scarcely like to do so, but I know that you are my friend, and that you will give me good advice."

"I will endeavour to do so," I replied. "What is the question you wish to ask me?"

"It is about my engagement," she replied. "You know how good and unselfish the Duke is and how truly he believes in me. I could not bear to bring trouble upon him, but in love there should be no secrets—nothing should be hidden one from the other. Yet I feel that I am hiding so much—can you understand what I mean?"

"In a great measure," I answered, "but I should like to do so thoroughly. Gertrude, if I may hazard a guess, I should say that you have been dreaming about Doctor Nikola again?"

"Yes," she answered after a moment's hesitation. "Absurd though it may be, I can think of no one else. He weighs upon my spirits like lead, and yet I know that I should be grateful to him for all he did for me when I was so ill. But for him I should not be alive now."

"I am afraid that you have been allowing the thought of your recent danger to lie too heavily upon your mind," I continued. "Remember that this is the twentieth century, and that there are no such things as you think Nikola would have you believe."

"When I know that there are?" she asked, looking at me reproachfully. "Ah, Sir Richard," she continued, "if you knew all that I do you would pity me. But no one will ever know, and I cannot tell them. But one thing is quite certain. I must stay in Venice for the present—happen what may. Something tells me so, day and night. And when I think of the Duke my heart well-nigh breaks for fear I should bring trouble upon him."

I did my best to comfort her; promised that if she really desired to remain in Venice I would arrange it for her, and by so doing committed myself to a policy that I very well knew, when I came to consider it later, was not expedient, and very far from being judicious. Regarded seriously in a sober commonplace light, the whole affair seems too absurd, and yet at the time nothing could possibly have been more real or earnest. When she had heard me out, she thanked me very prettily for the interest I had taken, and then with a little sigh, that went to my heart, left the room. Later in the afternoon I broke the news to my wife, and told her of the promise I had given Gertrude.

"But what does it all mean, Dick?" she asked, looking at me with startled eyes. "What is it she fears will happen if she goes away from Venice?"

"That is what I cannot get her to say," I replied. "Indeed I am not altogether certain that she knows herself. It's a most perplexing business, and I wish to goodness I had never had anything to do with it. The better plan, I think, would be to humour her, keep her as cheerful as we can, and when the proper time arrives, get her away from Venice and home to England as quickly as we can."

My wife agreed with me on this point, and our course of action was thereupon settled.

Later in the afternoon I made a resolution. My own suspicions concerning the wretched Martinos were growing so intolerable that

I could bear them no longer. The memory of the dream I had had on the previous night was never absent from my thoughts, and I felt that unless I could set matters right once and for all, and convince myself that they were not as I suspected with Anstruther's friend, I should be unable to close my eyes when next I went to bed. For this reason I determined to set off to the Palace Revecce at once, and to have an interview with Nikola in the hope of being able to extort some information from him.

"Perhaps after all," I argued, "I am worrying myself unnecessarily. There may be no connection between Martinos and that South American."

I determined, however, to set the matter at rest that afternoon. Accordingly at four o'clock I made an excuse and departed for the Rio del Consiglio.

It was a dark, cloudy afternoon, and the house as I approached it, looked drearier, if such a thing were possible, than I had ever seen it. I disembarked from my gondola at the steps, and having bade the man wait for me, which he did on the other side of the street, I rang the bell. The same old servant whom I remembered having seen on a previous occasion answered it, and informed me that his master was not at home, but that he expected him every minute. I determined to wait for him and ascended the stairs to his room. The windows were open, and from where I stood I could watch the gondolier placidly eating his bread and onions on the other side of the street. So far as I could see there was no change in the room itself. The centre table as usual was littered with papers and books, that near the window was covered with chemical apparatus, while the old black cat was fast asleep upon the couch on the other side. The oriental rug, described in another place, covered the ominous trap-door so that no portion of it could be seen. I was still standing at the window looking down upon the canal below, when the door at the further end softly opened and a face looked in at me. Good heavens! I can even now feel the horror which swept over me. It was the countenance of Don Martinos, but so changed, even from what it had been when I had seen him in the Rio del Barcaroli, that I scarcely recognised it. It was like the face of an animal and of a madman, if such could be combined. He looked at me and then withdrew, closing the door behind him, only to reopen it a few moments later. Having apparently made sure that I was alone, he crept in, and, crossing the room, approached me. For a moment I was at a loss how to act. I was not afraid that the poor wretch might do me any mischief, but my whole being shrank from him with a physical revulsion beyond all description in words. I can understand now something of the dislike my wife and the Duke declared they entertained for him. On tip-toe, with his finger to his lips, as if to enjoin silence, he crept towards me, muttering something in Spanish that I could not understand; then in English he continued: "Hush, Senor, cannot you see them?" He pointed his hand in various directions as if he could see the figures of men and women moving about the apartment. Once he bowed low as if to some imaginary dignitary, drawing back at the same time, as if to permit him to pass. Then turning to me he continued, "Do you know who that is? No! Then I will tell you. Senor, that is the most noble Admiral Revecce, the owner of this house."

Then for a short time he stood silent, picking feebly at his fingers and regarding me ever and anon from the corner of his eye. Suddenly there was a sharp quick step in the corridor outside, the handle of the door turned, and Nikola entered the room. As his glance fell upon the wretched being at my side a look not unlike that I had seen in my dream flashed into his countenance. It was gone again, however, as suddenly as it had come, and he was advancing to greet me with all his old politeness. It was then that the folly of my errand was borne in upon me. Even if my suspicions were correct what could I do, and what chance could I hope to have of being able to induce Nikola to confide in me? Meanwhile, he had pointed to the door, and Martinos, trembling in every limb, was slinking towards it like a whipped hound. At that moment I made a discovery that I confess came near to depriving me of my presence of mind altogether. You can judge of its value for yourself when I say, that extending to the lobe of Nikola's left ear half-way down and across his throat was a newly-made scar, just such an one, in fact, as would be made by a hand with sharp fingernails clutching at it. Could my dream have been true, after all?

"I cannot tell you how delighted I am to see you, my dear Sir Richard," said Nikola as he seated himself. "I understood that you had returned to Venice."

Having outgrown the desire to learn how Nikola had become aware of anything, I merely agreed that we had returned, and then took the chair he offered me.

When all the circumstances are taken into consideration, I really think that that moment was certainly the most embarrassing of my life. Nikola's eyes were fixed steadily upon mine, and I could see in them what was almost an expression of malicious amusement. As usual he was making capital out of my awkwardness, and as I knew that I could do no good, I felt that there was nothing for it but for me to

446

submit. Then the miserable Spaniard's face rose before my mind's eye, and I felt that I could not abandon him without an effort, to what I knew would be his fate. Nikola brought me up to the mark even quicker than I expected.

"It is very plain," he said, with a satirical smile playing round his thin lips, "that you have come with the intention of saying something important to me. What is it?"

At this I rose from my chair and went across the room to where he was sitting. Placing my hand upon his shoulder I looked down into his face, took courage, and began.

"Doctor Nikola," I said, "you and I have known each other for many years now. We have seen some strange things together, one of us perhaps less willingly than the other. But I venture to think, however, that we have never stood on stranger or more dangerous ground than we do tonight."

"I am afraid I am scarcely able to follow your meaning," he replied.

I knew that this was not the case, but I was equally convinced that to argue the question with him would be worse than useless.

"Do you remember the night on which you told me that story concerning the woman who lived in this house, who was betrayed by the Spaniard, and who died on that Spanish island?" I asked.

He rose hurriedly from his chair and went to the window. I heard him catch his breath, and knew that I had moved him at last.

"What of it?" he inquired, turning on me sharply as he spoke.

"Only that I have come to see you concerning the denouement of that story," I answered. "I have come because I cannot possibly stay away. You have no idea how deeply I have been thinking over this matter. Do you think I cannot see through it and read between the lines? You told it to me because in some inscrutable fashion of your own you had become aware that Don Martinos would bring a letter of introduction to me from my friend Anstruther. Remember it was I who introduced him to you! Do you think that I did not notice the expression that came into your face whenever you looked at him? Later my suspicions were aroused. The Don was a Spaniard, he was rich, and he had made the mistake of admitting that while he had been in Chile he had never been in Equinata. You persuaded me to bring him to this house, and here you obtained your first influence over him."

"My dear Hatteras," said Nikola, "you are presupposing a great deal. And you get beyond my depth. Don't you think it would be wiser if you were to stick to plain facts?"

"My suppositions are stronger than my facts," I answered. "You laid yourself out to meet him, and your influence over him became greater every day. It could be seen in his face. He was fascinated, and could not escape. Then he began to gamble, and found his money slipping through his fingers like water through a sieve."

"You have come to the conclusion, then, that I am responsible for that also?"

"I do not say that it was your doing exactly," I said, gathering courage from the calmness of his manner and the attention he was giving me. "But it fits in too well with the whole scheme to free you entirely from responsibility. Then look at the change that began to come over the man himself. His faculties were leaving him one by one, being wiped, out, just as a schoolboy wipes his lesson from a slate. If he had been an old man I should have said that it was the commencement of his second childhood; but he is still a comparatively young man."

"You forget that while he had been gambling he had also been drinking heavily. May not debauchery tell its own tale?"

"It is not debauchery that has brought about this terrible change. Who knows that better than yourself? After the duel, which you providentially prevented, we went to Rome for a fortnight. On the afternoon of our return I met him near the telegraph-office. At first glance I scarcely recognised him, so terrible was the change in his appearance. If ever a poor wretch was on the verge of idiocy he was that one. Moreover, he informed me that he was living with you. Why should the fact that he was so doing produce such a result? I cannot say! I dare not try to understand it! But, for pity's sake, Nikola, by all you hold dear I implore you to solve the riddle. Last night I had a dream!"

"You are perhaps a believer in dreams?" he remarked very quietly, as if the question scarcely interested him.

"This dream was of a description such as I have never had in my life before," I answered, disregarding the sneer, and then told it to him, increasing rather than lessening the abominable details. He heard me out without moving a muscle of his face, and it was only when I had reached the climax and paused that he spoke.

"This is a strange rigmarole you tell me," he said. "Fortunately you confess that it was only a dream."

"Doctor Nikola," I cried, "it was more than a dream. To prove it let me ask you how you received that long scratch that shows upon your neck and throat?"

I pointed my finger at it, but Nikola returned my gaze still without a flicker of his eyelids.

"What if I do admit it?" he began. "What if your dream were correct? What difference would it make?"

I looked at him in amazement. To tell the truth I was more astonished by his admission of the correctness of my suspicions than I should have been had he denied them altogether. As it was, I was too much overcome to be able to answer him for a few moments.

"Come," he said, "answer my question. What if I do admit the truth of all you say?"

"You confess then that the whole business has been one long scheme to entrap this wretched man, and to get him into your power?"

"'Tis," he answered, still keeping his eyes fixed upon me. "You see I am candid! Go on!"

My brain began to reel under the strain placed upon it. Since he had owned to it, what was I to do? What could I say?

"Sir Richard Hatteras," said Nikola, approaching a little nearer to me, resting one hand upon the table and speaking very impressively, "I wonder if it has struck you that you are a brave man to come to me today and to say this to me? In the whole circle of the men I know I may declare with truth that I am not aware of one other who would do so much. What is this man to you that you should befriend him? He would have robbed you or your dearest friend without a second thought, as he would rob you of your wife if the idea occurred to him. He is without bowels of compassion; the blood of thousands stains his hands and cries aloud for vengeance. He is a fugitive from justice, a thief, a liar, and a traitor to the country he swore to govern as an honest man. On a certain little island on the other side of the world there is a lonely churchyard, and in that churchyard a still lonelier grave. In it lies the body of a woman—my mother. In this very room that woman was betrayed by his father. So in this room also shall that betrayal be avenged. I have waited all my life; the opportunity has been long in coming. Now, however, it has arrived, and I am decreed by Fate to be the instrument of Vengeance!"

I am a tall man, but as he said this Nikola seemed to tower over me, his face set hard as a rock, his eyes blazing like living coals, and his voice trembling under the influence of his passion. Little by little I was growing to think as he did, and to look upon Martinos as he saw him.

"But this cannot go—it cannot go on," I repeated, in a last feeble protest against the horror of the thing. "Surely you could not find it in your heart to treat a fellow-creature so?"

"He is no fellow-creature of yours or mine," Nikola retorted sternly, as if he were rebuking a childish mistake. "Would you call the man who shot down those innocent young men of Equinata, before their mother's eyes, a fellow-creature? Is it possible that the son of the man who so cruelly wronged and betrayed the trusting woman he first saw in this room, who led her across the seas to desert her, and to send her to her grave, could be called a man? I will give you one more instance of his barbarity."

So saying, he threw off the black velvet coat he was wearing, and drawing up his right shirt-sleeve, bade me examine his arm. I saw that from the shoulder to the elbow it was covered with the scars of old wounds, strange white marks, in pairs, and each about half an inch long.

"Those scars," he went on, "were made by his orders, and with hot pincers, when I was a boy. And as his negro servants made them he laughed and taunted me with my mother's shame. No! No! This is no man—rather a dangerous animal, that were best out of the way. It has been told me that you and I shall only meet twice more. Let those meetings lead you to think better of me. The time is not far distant when I must leave the world! When that hour arrives there is a lonely monastery in a range of eastern mountains, upon which no Englishman has ever set his foot. Of that monastery I shall become an inmate. No one outside its walls shall ever look upon my face again. There I shall work out my destiny, and, if I have sinned, be sure I shall receive my punishment at those hands that alone can bestow it. Now leave me!"

God help me for the coward I am, but the fact remains that I left him without another word.

Chapter 13

If I were offered my heart's desire in return for so doing, I could not tell you how I got home after my interview with Nikola at the Palace Revecce. I was unconscious of everything save that I had gone to Nikola's house in the hope of being able to save the life of a man whom I had the best reasons for hating, and that at the last moment I had turned coward and fled the field. No humiliation could have been more complete. Nikola had won a victory, and I knew it, and despaired of retrieving it. On reaching the hotel I was about to disembark from my gondola, when a voice hailed me from another craft, proceeding in the direction I had come.

"Dick Hatteras, as I'm a sinner!" it cried. "Don't you know me, Dick?"

I turned to see a face I well remembered smiling at me from the gondola. I immediately bade my own man put me out into the stream, which he did, and presently the two gondolas lay side by side. The man who had hailed me was none other than George Beckworth, a Queensland sugar-planter with whom I had been on terms of the most intimate friendship in bygone days. And as there was a lady seated beside him, I derived the impression that he had married since I had last seen him.

"This is indeed a surprise," he said, as we shook hands. "By the way let me introduce you to my wife, Dick." He said this with all the pride of a newly-married man. "My dear, this is my old friend, Dick Hatteras, of whom I have so often spoken to you. What are you doing in Venice, Dick?"

"I have my wife and some friends travelling with me," I answered. "We are staying at Galaghetti's hotel yonder. Cannot you and your wife dine with us tonight?"

"Impossible, I am afraid," he answered. "We sail tonight in the P. and O. boat. Won't you come and dine with us?"

"That is equally impossible," I replied. "We have friends with us. But I should like to see something more of you before you go, and if you will allow me I will run down after dinner for a chat about old times."

"I shall be delighted," he answered. "Be sure that you do not forget it."

Having assured him that I would not permit it to escape my memory, I bade him "goodbye," and then returned to my hotel. A more fortunate meeting could scarcely have occurred, for now I was furnished with an excellent excuse for leaving my party, and for being alone for a time. Once more I felt that I was a coward for not daring to face my fellow-men. Under the circumstances, however, I knew that it was impossible. I could no more have spent the evening listening to Glenbarth's happy laughter than I could have jumped the Grand Canal. For the time being the society of my fellow-creatures was absolutely distasteful to me. On ascending to my rooms I discovered my wife and the Duke in the drawing-room, and was informed by the latter that Miss Trevor had again been compelled to retire to her room with a severe headache.

"In that case I am afraid you will only be a small party for dinner," I said. "I am going to ask you to excuse me. You have often heard me speak, my dear, of George Beckworth, the Queensland sugar-planter, with whom I used to be on such friendly terms in the old days?"

My wife admitted that she remembered hearing me speak of the gentleman in question.

"Well, he is in Venice," I replied, "and he sails tonight by the P. and O. boat for Colombo. As it is the last time I shall be likely to see him for many years, I feel sure you will not mind my accepting his invitation?"

"Of course not, if the Duke will excuse you," she said, and, when the question was put to him, Glenbarth willingly consented to do so.

I accordingly went to my room to make my toilet. Then, having bade my wife "goodbye," I chartered a gondola and ordered the man to row me to the piazza, of Saint Mark. Thence I set off for a walk through the city, caring little in which way I went. It was growing dark by this time, and I knew there was little chance of my being recognised, or of my recognising any one else. All the time, however, my memory was haunted by the recollection of that room at the Palace Revecce, and of what was in all probability going on in it. My gorge rose at the idea—all my manhood revolted from it. A loathing of Nikola, such as I had never known before, was succeeded by a deathly chill, as I realised how impotent I was to avert the catastrophe. What could I do? To have attempted to stay him in his course would have been worse than useless, while to have appealed to the authorities would only have had the effect of putting myself in direct opposition to him, and who knew what would happen then? I looked at it from another point of view. Why should I be so anxious to interfere on the wretched Spaniard's behalf? I had seen his murderous intention on the morning of the frustrated duel; I had heard from Nikola of the assassination of those unfortunate lads in Equinata; moreover, I was well aware that he was a thief, and also a traitor to his country. Why should he not be punished as he deserved, and why should not Nikola be his executioner?

I endeavoured to convince myself that this was only fit and proper retribution, but this argument was no more successful than the last had been.

Arguing in this way I walked on and on, turning to right or left, just as the fancy took me. Presently I found myself in a portion of the town into which I had never hitherto penetrated. At the moment of which I am about to write, I was standing in a narrow lane, paved with large stones, having high dismal houses on either side. Suddenly an old man turned the corner and approached me. As he passed, I saw his face, and recognised an individual to whom Nikola had spoken in the little church on that memorable evening when he had taken us on a tour of inspection through the city. He was visibly agitated, and was moreover in hot haste. For some reason that I cannot explain, nor, I suppose, shall I ever be able to do so, an intense desire to follow him took possession of me. It must have been more than a desire, for I felt that I must go with him whether I wished to or not. I accordingly dived into the house after him, and followed him along the passage and up the rickety flight of stairs that ascended from it. Having attained one floor we continued our ascent; the sounds of voices reached us from the different rooms, but we saw no one. On the second landing the old man paused before a door, opened it very softly, and entered. I followed him, and looked about me. It was a pathetic scene that met my eyes. The room was a poor one and scantily furnished. A rough table and a narrow bed were its only furniture. On the latter a young man was lying, and kneeling on the floor beside him, holding the thin hands in his own, was no less a person than Doctor Nikola himself. I saw that he was aware of my presence, but he took no more notice of me than if I had not existed.

"You called me too late, my poor Antonio," he said, addressing the old man I had followed. "Nothing can save him now. He was dying when I arrived."

On hearing this the old man fell on his knees beside the bed and burst into a flood of weeping. Nikola placed his hand with a kindly gesture upon the other's shoulder and at the moment that he did so the man upon the bed expired.

"Do not grieve for him, my friend," said Nikola. "Believe me, it was hopeless from the first. He is better as it is."

Then, with all the gentleness of a woman, he proceeded to comfort the old man, whose only son lay dead upon the bed. I knew no more of the story than what I had seen, nor have I heard more of it since, but I had been permitted to see another side of his character, and one which, in the light of existing circumstances, was not to be denied. He had scarcely finished his kindly offices before there was a heavy step outside, and a black-browed priest entered the room. He looked from Nikola to myself, and then' at the dead man upon the bed.

"Farewell, my good Antonio," said Nikola. "Have no fear. Remember that your future is my care."

Then, having said something in an undertone to the priest, he placed his hand upon my arm and led me from the room. When we had left them he murmured in a voice not unlike that in which he had addressed the old man, "Hatteras, this is another lesson. Is it so difficult to learn?"

I do not pretend that I made any answer. We passed down the stairs together, and, when we reached the street, stood for a moment at the house-door.

"You will not be able to understand me," he said; "nevertheless, I tell you that the end is brought nearer by that one scene. It will not be long before it comes now. All things considered I do not know that I shall regret it."

Then, without another word, he strode away into the darkness, leaving me to place what construction I pleased upon his last speech. For some moments I stood where he had left me, pondering over his words, and then set off in the direction I had come. As may be imagined, I felt even less inclined than before for the happy, jovial party I knew I should find on board the steamer, but I had given my promise, and could not get out of it.

When I reached the piazza of Saint Mark once more, I went to the steps and hailed a gondola, telling the man to take me to the P. and O. vessel then lying at anchor in the harbour. He did so, and I made my way up the accommodation-ladder to the deck above, to find that the passengers in the first saloon had just finished their dinner, and were making their appearance on the promenade deck. I inquired of the steward for Mr. Beckworth, and discovered him in the act of lighting a cigar at the smoking-room door.

He greeted me effusively, and begged me to remain where I was while he went in search of his wife. When she arrived, I found her to be a pretty little woman, with big brown eyes, and a sympathetic manner. She was good enough to say that she had heard such a lot concerning me from her husband, and had always looked forward to making my acquaintance, I accepted a cigar from Beckworth's case, and we then adjourned to the smoking-room for a long talk together. When we had comfortably installed ourselves, my friend's flow of conversation commenced, and I was made aware of all the principal events that had occurred in Queensland since my departure, was favoured with his opinion of England, which he had never before visited, and was furnished with the details as to how he had met his wife, and of the happy event with which their courtship had been concluded.

"Altogether," he said, "taking one thing with another, I don't know that you'd be able to find a much happier fellow in the world than I am at this moment."

I said I was glad to hear it, and as I did so contrasted his breezy, happy-go-lucky manner with those of certain other people I had been brought into contact with that day. My interview with him must have done me good, for I stayed on, and the hour was consequently late when I left the ship. Indeed, it wanted only a few minutes of eleven o'clock as I went down the accommodation-ladder to the gondola, which I had ordered to come for me at ten.

"Galaghetti's hotel," I said to the man, "and as quickly as you can."

When I bade my friends "goodbye," and left the ship, I felt comparatively cheerful, but no sooner had the silence of Venice closed in upon me again than all my old despondency returned to me. A foreboding of coming misfortune settled upon me, and do what I would I could not shake it off.

When I reached the hotel I found that my party had retired to rest. My wife was sleeping quietly, and not feeling inclined for bed, and dreading lest if I did go I might be assailed by more dreams of a similar description to that I had had on the previous night, I resolved to go back to the drawing-room and read there for a time. This plan I carried into execution, and taking up a new book in which I was very much interested, seated myself in an easy-chair and determined to peruse it. I found some difficulty, however, in concentrating my attention upon it. My thoughts continually reverted to my interview that afternoon with Nikola, and also to the scene I had witnessed in the poorer quarter after dark. I suppose eventually I must have fallen asleep, for I remember nothing else until I awoke and found myself sitting up listening to a light step in the corridor outside. I looked at my watch to discover that the time was exactly a quarter to one. In that case, as we monopolised the whole of the corridor, who could it be? In order to find out I went to the door, and softly opened it. A dim light was always left in the passage throughout the night, and by it I was able to see a tall and graceful figure, which I instantly recognised, making for the secondary stairs at the end. Now these stairs, so I had been given to understand, led to another portion of the hotel into which I had never penetrated. Why, therefore, Miss Trevor was using them at such an hour, and, above all, dressed for going out, I could not for the life of me determine. I could see that, if I was anxious to find out, I must be quick; so, turning swiftly into the room again, I picked up my hat and set off in pursuit. As the sequel will prove it was, perhaps, as well that I did so.

By the time I had reached the top of the stairs she was at the bottom, and was speeding along another passage to the right. At the end of this was a door, the fastenings of which she undid with the ease and assurance that bewildered me. So certain was she of her whereabouts, and so easily did she manipulate the heavy door, that I felt inclined to believe that she must have used that passage many times before. At last she opened it and passed out into the darkness, drawing it to after her. I paused to watch her; now I hastened on even faster than before, fearing that, if I were not careful, I might lose her outside. Having passed the door I found myself in a narrow lane, bounded on either side by high walls, and some fifty or sixty yards in extent. The lane, in its turn, opened into a small square, out of which led two or three other narrow streets. She turned to the left and passed down one of these; I followed close upon her heels. Of all the strange experiences to which our stay in Venice had given rise, this was certainly one of the most remarkable. That Gertrude Trevor, the honest English girl, the daughter of a dignitary of the church and a prospective bishop, should leave her hotel in the middle of the night in order to wander about streets with which she was most imperfectly acquainted, was a mystery I found difficult to solve. When she had crossed a bridge, which spanned a small canal, she once more turned to the left, passed along the footway before a dilapidated palace, and then entered a narrow passage on the right. The buildings hereabouts were all large, and, as a natural consequence, the streets were so dark that I had some difficulty in keeping her in sight. As a matter of fact she had stopped, and I was almost upon her before I became aware of it. Even then she did not seem to realise my presence. She was standing before a small door, which she was endeavouring to push open. At last she succeeded, and without hesitation began to descend some steps inside.

Once more I took up the chase, though where we were, and what we were going to do there. I had not the least idea. The small yard in which we found ourselves was stone-paved, and for this reason I wondered that she did not hear my footsteps. It is certain, however, that she did not, for she made for a door I could just discern on the opposite side to that by which we had entered, without turning her head. It was at this point that I began to wish I had brought a revolver or some weapon with me. When she was about to open the door I have just mentioned, I called her softly by name, and implored her to wait for me, but still she took no notice. Could she be a somnambulist? I asked myself. But if this were so, why had she chosen this particular house? Having passed the door we stood in a second and larger courtyard, and it was then that the whole mystery became apparent to me. The house to which I had followed her was the Palace Revecce, and she was on her way to Nikola! But for what reason? Was this a trick of Nikola's, or had her terrible dreams taken such a hold upon her that she was not responsible for her actions? Either alternative was bad enough. Pausing for a moment in the courtyard beside the well, she turned quickly to her right hand and began to ascend the stairs towards that awful room, which, so far as I knew, she had never visited before. When she reached it I scarcely knew how to act. Should I enter behind her and accuse Nikola of having enticed her there, or should I wait outside and overhear what transpired between them? At last I made up my mind to adopt the latter course, and when she had entered I accordingly remained outside and waited for her. Through the half-open door I could see Nikola, stooping over what looked like a microscope at a side-table. He looked up as Miss Trevor entered, and uttered a cry of surprise. As I heard this a sigh of relief escaped me, for his action proved to me that her visit had not been anticipated.

"Miss Trevor!" he said, moving forward to greet her, "what does this mean? How did you get here?"

"I have come to you," she faltered, "because I could not remain away. I have come to you that I may beg of you that wretched man's life. Doctor Nikola, I implore you to spare him!"

"My dear young lady," said Nikola, with a softness in his voice which reminded me of that I had heard in the death chamber a few hours before, "you cannot understand what you are doing. You must let me take you back to your friends. You should not be here at this hour of the night."

"But I was bound to come—don't I tell you I could not remain away? Spare him! Oh! for God's sake, spare him!"

"You do not know what you are asking. You are not yourself to-night."

"I only know that I am thinking of you," she answered. "You must not do it! You are so great, so powerful, that you can afford to forgive. Take my life rather than harm him. I will yield it gladly to save you from this sin."

"To—save—me," I heard him mutter to himself. "She would save me!"

"God would never forgive," she continued, still in the same dreamy voice.

He moved away from her, and from where I stood I could see how agitated he was. For some moments she knelt, looking up at him, with arms outstretched in supplication; then he said something to her in a low voice, which I could not catch. Her answer, however, was plain to me.

"Yes, I have known it always in my dreams," she said.

"And knowing that, you would still wish me to pardon him?"

"In the name of God I would urge you to do so," she answered. "The safety of your soul depends upon it."

Once more Nikola turned away and paced the room.

"Are you aware that Sir Richard Hatteras was here on the same errand this afternoon?" he asked.

"I know it," she replied, though how she could have done so I could not conceive, nor have I been able to do so since.

"And does he know that you have come to me now asking me to forgive?"

"He knows it," she answered, as before. "He followed me here."

As she had never looked behind her, how had she known this also? Then Nikola approached the door and threw it open.

"Come in, Hatteras," he said. "Your presence is discovered."

"For heaven's sake, Nikola, tell me what this means," I cried, seeing that the girl did not turn towards me. "Is she asleep, or have you brought your diabolical influence upon her?"

"She is not asleep, and yet she is not conscious of her actions," he answered. "There is something in this that passes our philosophy. Had I any idea that she contemplated such a thing, I would have used every effort to prevent it. Miss Trevor, believe me, you must go home with Sir Richard," he continued, tenderly raising the girl to her feet as he spoke.

"I cannot go until you have sworn to forgive," was her reply.

"I must have time to think," he answered. "In the morning you will know everything. Trust me until then, and remember always that while Nikola lives he will be grateful."

Then he assisted me to conduct her downstairs, and across the two courtyards, to the little postern door through which we had entered the palace.

"Have no fear of her," he said, addressing me. "She will go home as she came. And in the morning she will remember nothing of what has transpired."

Then taking her hand in his he raised it to his lips, and a moment later had bade me farewell, and had vanished into the palace once more.

As I tracked her from the hotel, so I followed her back to it again. I was none the less anxious, however. If only Nikola would abandon his purpose, and release his enemy, her action and my anxiety would not be in vain. But would he do so, and in the event of his doing this, would his prophecy that Miss Trevor would, in the morning, remember nothing of what had transpired, prove true?

Turning, twisting as before, we proceeded on our way. My chief fear was that the door through which we had made our exit would be found to be shut on our return. Happily, however, this did not prove to be the case. I saw Miss Trevor enter, and then swiftly followed her. She hastened down the passage, ascended the stairs, passed along the corridor, and made her way to her own room. As soon as I had made certain that she was safely there, I went on to my own dressing-room, and on entering my wife's apartment had the good fortune to find her still asleep. I was still more thankful in the morning when I discovered that she had not missed me, and being satisfied on this point, I decided to say nothing whatsoever concerning our adventure.

Miss Trevor was the last to put in an appearance at breakfast, and, as you may suppose, I scanned her face with some anxiety. She looked pale and worn, but it was evident from her manner when she greeted me, that she had not the least idea what she had done during the night. Nikola's promise had proved to be true, and for that reason I was more determined than ever to keep my information to myself. Events could not have turned out more fortunately for all parties concerned.

Shortly after breakfast a letter was handed to me, and, glancing at the writing, I saw that it was from Nikola. I was alone at the time of receiving it, a fact for which I was grateful. I will leave you to imagine with what impatience I opened it. It was short, and merely contained a request that I would call at the Palace Revecce before noon that day, if I could spare the hour. I decided to do so, and I reached the palace twenty minutes or so before the appointed time. The old servitor, who by this time had become familiar with my face, opened the door and permitted me to enter. I inquired if Doctor Nikola were at home and to my surprise was informed that he was not.

"Perhaps your Excellency would like to see the other Senor?" the old man asked, pointing up the stairs.

I was about to decline this invitation with all possible haste, when a voice I recognised as that of the Don's greeted me from the gallery above.

"Won't you come upstairs, Sir Richard?" it said. "I have a letter for you from my friend, Doctor Nikola!"

I could scarcely believe the evidence of my eyes and ears, and when I reached the room of which I had such terrible recollections, my surprise was intensified rather than lessened. Martinos had undergone a complete metamorphosis. In outward appearance he was no longer the same person, who only the day before had filled me with such terrible repulsion. If such a thing could be believed, he was more like his old self—as I had first seen him.

"Where is Doctor Nikola?" I inquired, when I had looked round the room and noticed the absence of the chemical paraphernalia, the multitude of books, and the general change in it.

"He went away early this morning," the Don replied. "He left a letter for you, and requested me to give it you as soon as you should call. I have much pleasure in doing so now."

I took it and placed it almost mechanically in my pocket.

"Are you aware when he will return?" I asked.

"He will never do so," Martinos replied. "I heard the old man below wailing this morning, because he had lost the best master he had ever had."

"And you?"

"I am ruined, as you know," he said, without any reference to his illness, "but the good doctor has been good enough to place twenty thousand *lira* to my credit, and I shall go elsewhere and attempt to double it."

He must have been much better, for he smiled in the old deceitful way as he said this. Remembering what I knew of him, I turned from the man in disgust, and bidding him good day, left the room which

I hoped never to see again as long as I might live. In the courtyard I encountered the old caretaker once more.

"So the Senor Nikola has gone away never to return?" I said.

"That is so, Senor," said the old man with a heavy sigh. "He has left me a rich man, but I do not like to think that I shall never see him again."

Sitting down on the edge of the well, I took from my pocket the letter the Don had handed me.

> Farewell, friend Hatteras. By the time you receive this I shall have left Venice, never more to set foot in it. We shall not meet again. I go to the Fate which claims me, and of which I told you. Think of me sometimes, and, if it be possible, with kindness,
> *Nikola*

I rose and moved towards the door, placing a gold piece in the old man's hand as I passed him. Then, with a last look at the courtyard, I went down the steps and took my place in the gondola, with a feeling of sadness in my heart for the sad destiny of the most wonderful man I had ever known.

Chapter 14

Next day, much to Galaghetti's sorrow, we suddenly brought our stay in Venice to a conclusion, and set off for Paris. The Queen of the Adriatic had lost her charm for us, and for once in our lives we were not sorry to say goodbye to her. The train left the station, crossed the bridge to the mainland, and was presently speeding on her way across Europe. Ever since the morning Miss Trevor's spirits had been steadily improving. She seemed to have become her old self in a few hours, and Glenbarth's delight was beautiful to witness. He had been through a good deal, poor fellow, and deserved some recompense for it. We had been upwards of an hour upon our way, when my wife made a curious remark.

"Good gracious!" she said, "in our hurry to get away we have quite forgotten to say goodbye to Doctor Nikola!"

I saw Miss Trevor give a little shudder.

"Do you know," she said, "I had such a curious dream about him last night. I dreamt that I saw him standing in the courtyard of a great building on a mountain-side. He was dressed in a strange sort of yellow gown, not unlike that worn by the Buddhist priests, and was worn almost to a shadow and looked very old. He approached me, and taking my hands, said something that, in the commonplace light of day, doesn't seem to have much sense in it. But I know it affected me very much at the time."

"What was it?" I asked, trying to keep my voice steady.

"It is this," she answered—"'Remember that I have forgiven; it is for you to forget.' What could he have meant?"

"Since it is only a dream, it is impossible to say," observed my wife, and thus saved me the danger of attempting a solution.

To bring my long narrative to a conclusion, I might say that the Duke and Miss Trevor were married last May. They spent their honeymoon yachting to the West Indies. Some one proposed that they should visit Venice; indeed, the Earl of Sellingbourne, who had lately purchased the Palace Revecce, and had furnished it,—placed it at their disposal. From what I have been told I gather that he was somewhat ill-pleased because his offer was not accepted.

When the wind howls round the house at night and the world seems very lonely, I sometimes try to picture a monastery on a mountain-side, and then, in my fancy, I see a yellow-robed, mysterious figure, whose dark, searching eyes look into mine with a light that is no longer of this world. To him I cry:

"Farewell, Nikola!"

LEONAUR

ALSO FROM LEONAUR

AVAILABLE IN SOFTCOVER OR HARDCOVER WITH DUST JACKET

CHARLIE CHAN VOLUME 1: THE HOUSE WITHOUT A KEY & THE CHINESE PARROT *by Earl Derr Biggers*—Two Complete Novels Featuring the Legendary Chinese-Hawaiian Detective.

CHARLIE CHAN VOLUME 2: BEHIND THAT CURTAIN & THE BLACK CAMEL *by Earl Derr Biggers*—Two Complete Novels Featuring the Legendary Chinese-Hawaiian Detective.

CHARLIE CHAN VOLUME 3: CHARLIE CHAN CARRIES ON & KEEPER OF THE KEYS *by Earl Derr Biggers*—Two Complete Novels Featuring the Legendary Chinese-Hawaiian Detective.

THE PHILO VANCE MURDER CASES: 1—THE BENSON MURDER CASE & THE 'CANARY' MURDER CASE *by S. S. Van Dine*—Two complete cases featuring the great fictional detective.

THE PHILO VANCE MURDER CASES: 2—THE GREENE MURDER CASE & THE BISHOP MURDER CASE *by S. S. Van Dine*—Two complete cases featuring the great fictional detective.

THE PHILO VANCE MURDER CASES: 3—THE SCARAB MURDER CASE & THE KENNEL MURDER CASE *by S. S. Van Dine*—Two complete cases featuring the great fictional detective.

THE PHILO VANCE MURDER CASES: 4—THE DRAGON MURDER CASE & THE CASINO MURDER CASE *by S. S. Van Dine*—Two complete cases featuring the great fictional detective.

THE PHILO VANCE MURDER CASES: 5—THE GARDEN MURDER CASE & THE KIDNAP MURDER CASE *by S. S. Van Dine*—Two complete cases featuring the great fictional detective.

THE PHILO VANCE MURDER CASES: 6—THE GRACIE ALLEN MURDER CASE & THE WINTER MURDER CASE *by S. S. Van Dine*—Two complete cases featuring the great fictional detective.

THE COMPLETE RAFFLES: 1—THE AMATEUR CRACKSMAN & THE BLACK MASK *by E. W. Hornung*—The classic tales of the gentleman thief.

THE COMPLETE RAFFLES: 2—A THIEF IN THE NIGHT & MR JUSTICE RAFFLES *by E. W. Hornung*—The classic tales of the gentleman thief..

LEONAUR

ALSO FROM LEONAUR
AVAILABLE IN SOFTCOVER OR HARDCOVER WITH DUST JACKET

TROS OF SAMOTHRACE 1: WOLVES OF THE TIBER *by Talbot Mundy*—When his ship is taken and his crew slaughtered Tros of Samothrace is captured by Imperial Rome.

TROS OF SAMOTHRACE 2: DRAGONS OF THE NORTH *by Talbot Mundy*—Tros of Samothrace burns for vengeance and has declared himself the implacable enemy of Rome.

TROS OF SAMOTHRACE 3: SERPENT OF THE WAVES *by Talbot Mundy*—Tros, his allies and the forces of Rome have drawn apart to prepare for the conflict to come.

TROS OF SAMOTHRACE 4: CITY OF THE EAGLES *by Talbot Mundy*—As Tros of Samothrace continues in his attempts to confound Caesar's plans for the invasion of Britain, he journeys to the Eternal City to seek the aid of its great leaders—and Caesar's opponents—Cato, Pompey and the Vestal Virgins themselves!

TROS OF SAMOTHRACE 5: CLEOPATRA *by Talbot Mundy*—Cleopatra—Queen of Egypt—is a formidable character ever ready to play the game of intrigue, betrayal and shifting loyalties to suit her own objectives. Blood will surely be spilt and once again Tros finds himself inexorably caught up in monumental events that threaten his life and those he loves.

TROS OF SAMOTHRACE 6: THE PURPLE PIRATE *by Talbot Mundy*—The epic saga of the ancient world—Tros of Samothrace—draws to a conclusion in this sixth—and final—volume. Julius Caesar has been assassinated and Queen Cleopatra of Egypt finds herself in a perilous position and desperate for allies to secure her power.

THE ILLUSTRATED & COMPLETE BRIGADIER GERARD *by Sir Arthur Conan Doyle*—These are the adventures of Conan Doyle's incomparable French hero-the finest swordsman in the Light Cavalry-Etienne Gerard. Arranged for the first time in historical chronological order, his many enthusiasts can now properly appreciate his colourful career as he fights, loves and blunders his way through the Napoleonic epoch-from his earliest adventure as a young blade determined to reach his lady love despite the unwelcome attention of her fathers bull-through many campaigns and special missions-to the bloody field of Waterloo, the downfall of his beloved Emperor and beyond. This is the complete collection of these classic stories. What makes this edition exceptional is the inclusion of nearly 140 illustrations-mostly by the famed military artist William Barnes Wollen-which accurately portray the spirit of the stories and the uniforms and scenes of the events they portray.

ALSO FROM LEONAUR

AVAILABLE IN SOFTCOVER OR HARDCOVER WITH DUST JACKET

GARRETT P. SERVISS' SCIENCE FICTION by *Garrett P. Serviss*—Three Interplanetary Adventures including the unauthorised sequel to H. G. Wells' *War of the Worlds--Edison's Conquest of Mars, A Columbus of Space, The Moon Metal.*

JUNK DAY by *Arthur Sellings*—". . . . his finest novel was his last, *Junk Day,* a post-holocaust tale set in the ruins of his native London and peopled with engrossing character types . . . . perhaps grimmer than his previous work but pointedly more energetic." *The Encyclopedia of Science Fiction.*

KIPLING'S SCIENCE FICTION by *Rudyard Kipling*—Science Fiction & Fantasy stories by a Master Storyteller including 'As East As A,B,C' 'With The Night Mail'.

THE COLLECTED SCIENCE FICTION AND FANTASY OF STANLEY G. WEINBAUM: THE BLACK HEART by *Stanley G. Weinbaum*—Classic Strange Tales Including: the Complete Novel The Dark Other, Plus Proteus Island and Others Stories included in this Volume The Dark Other (novel) Proteus Island The Adaptive Ultimate Pymalion's Spectacles.

THE COLLECTED SCIENCE FICTION AND FANTASY OF STANLEY G. WEINBAUM: STRANGE GENIUS by *Stanley G. Weinbaum*—Classic Tales of the Human Mind at Work Including the Complete Novel The New Adam, the 'van Manderpootz' Stories and Others Stories included in this Volume The New Adam (novel) The Brink of Infinity The Circle of Zero Graph The Worlds of If The Ideal The Point of View.

THE COLLECTED SCIENCE FICTION AND FANTASY OF STANLEY G. WEINBAUM OTHER EARTHS by *Stanley G. Weinbaum*—Classic Futuristic Tales Including: Dawn of Flame & its Sequel The Black Flame, plus The Revolution of 1960 & Others.

THE COLLECTED SCIENCE FICTION AND FANTASY OF STANLEY G. WEINBAUM INTERPLANETARY ODYSSEYS by *Stanley G. Weinbaum*—Classic Tales of Interplanetary Adventure Including: A Martian Odyssey, its Sequel Valley of Dreams, the Complete 'Ham' Hammond Stories and Others Stories included in this Volume Mars A Martian Odyssey Valley of Dreams Venus Parasite Planet The Lotus Eaters Uranus The Planet of Doubt Titan Flight on Titan Pluto The Red Peri Io The Mad Moon Europa Redemption Cairn Ganymede Tidal Moon.

SUPERNATURAL BUCHAN by *John Buchan*—Stories of Ancient Spirits, Uncanny Places & Strange Creatures.

CPSIA information can be obtained at www.ICGtesting.com
Printed in the USA
LVOW07s2008061215

465601LV00001B/38/P